PENGUIN BOOKS

GUYS AND DOLLS

Damon Runyon was born in Kansas in 1884 and grew up in Pueblo, Colorado. As a teenager he wrote articles for the local newspapers and in 1898, at the age of fourteen, enlisted in the Spanish-American War. He returned to work on various newspapers and became a sportswriter for the New York *American* in 1911. During the First World War he was a war correspondent for the Hearst newspaper chain and after the war continued to work as a Hearst columnist. He died in 1946.

DAMON RUNYON

GUYS

&

DOLLS

THE STORIES OF

DAMON RUNYON

INTRODUCTION BY WILLIAM KENNEDY

PENGUIN BOOKS

PENGUIN BOOKS
Published by the Penguin Group
Penguin Books USA Inc.,
375 Hudson Street, New York, New York 10014, U.S.A.
Penguin Books Ltd, 27 Wrights Lane,
London W8 5TZ, England
Penguin Books Australia Ltd, Ringwood,
Victoria, Australia
Penguin Books Canada Ltd, 10 Alcorn Avenue,
Toronto, Ontario, Canada M4V 3B2
Penguin Books (N.Z.) Ltd, 182–190 Wairau Road,
Auckland 10, New Zealand

Penguin Books Ltd, Registered Offices:
Harmondsworth, Middlesex, England

This collection first published in Penguin Books 1992

10

The stories in this collection first appeared
in *Collier's, Cosmopolitan, Liberty,*
and *The Saturday Evening Post.*

Pages 412–413 constitute an extension of this copyright page.
Frontis photo from UPI/Bettman Archives.

LIBRARY OF CONGRESS CATALOGING IN PUBLICATION DATA
Runyon, Damon, 1884–1946.
    Guys and dolls/ Damon Runyon.
        p.   cm.
    ISBN 0 14 01.7659 4
    1. Broadway (New York, N.Y.)—Fiction.   I. Title.
PS3535.U52A6   1992b
813'.52—dc20   92-27639

Printed in the United States of America
Set in Old Style No. 7
Designed by Brian Mulligan

ACKNOWLEDGMENTS

This book is dedicated to the memory of the late Damon Runyon and his son, Damon Runyon, Jr. We wish to give special thanks to the following, whose cooperation by way of research, permissions, interviews, and unswerving perseverance made this book possible: Mary Runyon McCann, daughter of Damon Runyon; her guardian, David P. Faulkner, Esq.; his law associate, R. Edward Tepe, of Cincinnati; Raoul Lionel Felder, Esq., distinguished New York City attorney and former executor of the estate of Damon Runyon, Jr.; Damon Runyon III and his sister D'Ann McKibben, the children of Damon Runyon, Jr.; and lastly, but very nicely, Al Silverman, the publisher and editor-in-chief of Viking Books, who put it all together.

Our gratitude extends to certain Runyon fans, themselves modern Runyonesque characters, for their loyalty and for just being who they are: Sheldon Abend, who played Long John in Columbia's 1988 feature *The Bloodhounds of Broadway* and was characterized as Big Shelly, played by Tommy Longo (an inside joke of the director); Robert E. Ossanna of Minneapolis and New York; Pete V. of Corona, New York; Robbie Margolis of New York; Bert Sugar, noted sportswriter and publisher of *Boxing*; Con ("The Scamp") Erico, who, when it counted, stood up higher than when he rode as a jockey in New York; Elliott S. Blair, Esq., of New York; Tommy F. Saullo, Jr., of England and New York; Jack Behen; G. M. Martin; Paul Miller of Putnam County, New York; "George Just" of Florida and New York; Stewart Wallach of Los Angeles; Shelly Finkel, who managed four world boxing champions, including Evander Holyfield; Joe Glitz,

Joe D., and Nicky C. of The Bronx; Dr. Elliot J. Rayfield, brilliant M.D. and scientist, of New York City; Nick ("Ali Baba") the Greek of London and New York; Charlie ("Ha-ha") Celeste of Boston; Philip ("The Rabbit") Cassese of Putnam County, New York; Jake ("The Raging Bull") LaMotta, former middleweight champion of the world; Tommy ("The Gun") Davey of New York; Steve ("Mister Las Vegas") Wynn; Jerry Weintraub, a.k.a. Bugsy, of New York and Los Angeles; Nicky Blair, gracious owner of Nicky Blair's restaurant in Los Angeles; Tony Conforte; Danny Aiello; Joe Pesci; Richie; Rodney Dangerfield of New York and Los Angeles; Carmine DeNoia, a.k.a. Wassell, whose father, Jardine, had a legendary appetite and was in fact the role model for a character created by Damon Runyon; and of course the chairman of the board, Frank Sinatra.

The dolls are Jane Morgan, the renowned singer and b.w. of Jerry Weintraub; Nancy Skates Bretzfield of Los Angeles and New York; Annie Simpson; Barbara Adams; Karen Foy; Cathy Travis of Putnam County, New York; Jackie Behen; Sharon Groves of Tyler, Texas; Erin Kummer; Shannon D. Grimes of Los Angeles; Angela Lisa Cordova of Denver; Joan Loretta Hubi of New York; and Zsuzsa Molnar of New York.

We wish to pay special tribute to the entire cast of the current Tony Award-winning Broadway production of *Guys and Dolls* and to two of Damon Runyon's greatet fans, the late Abe Margolis, Prince of the High Rollers and a prince of a man himself, and the late Rocky Graziano, former middleweight champion of the world, who was spotted by Damon Runyon in an undercard fight and tagged as a future contender for the crown.

—S.A.

CONTENTS

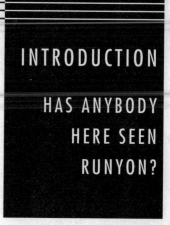

There's really only one question to ask about Damon Runyon: Is he, or isn't he, back in town? We all know he's back on Broadway, ever since the spring of 1992, when the remarkable revival of *Guys and Dolls* opened. But there is also something else going on. I have been approached twice in the past month about writing a movie about his private life, something in which I have a minus-twenty-seven-percent interest; and now here comes Al Silverman (Viking out of Penguin) saying he has snatched up the rights to 125 of Runyon's short stories that have been lying doggo for a number of years and is looking for somebody to handicap two and a half dozen of them and see if there is enough left in the old guy to justify a wager that he can still wow them not only on Broadway but also in Albany.

When I was eleven years old I thought Runyon was the funniest man alive. He was a great newspaperman, which is how I first came to know his name; and then I discovered his short stories and found he could make me laugh three times in one sentence. That was maybe 1939. Now it is 1992 and I laugh four, maybe five times in a paragraph, like this one about a character named Feet Samuels:

"He is a big heavy guy with several chins and very funny feet, which is why he is called Feet. These feet are extra large feet, even for a big guy, and Dave the Dude says Feet wears violin cases for shoes. Of course this is not true, because Feet cannot get either of his feet in a violin case, unless it is a case for a very large violin, such as a cello."

Feet Samuels is a relatively peaceful citizen, but Big Jule (usually pronounced Julie), who made a comeback by being the crapshooting villain of *Guys and Dolls*, is something else. He came on the scene long ago in the Runyon story *The Hottest Guy in the World*. Big Jule is considered hot because he is wanted for robbery or safecracking in such locations as Pittsburgh, Minneapolis, Kansas City, Toledo, Spokane, San Francisco, and Canton, Ohio, and there is, as Runyon puts it, "also something about a shooting match in Chicago, but of course this does not count so much as only one party is fatally injured."

But the tally makes Big Jule very hot indeed, about as hot as John Gotti, the Mafia chieftain who in early April of '92 was convicted in Brooklyn of racketeering, which included five murders, a murder conspiracy, extortion, and such things.

Mr. Gotti, visited in the courtroom by movie stars, his wardrobe written about as a fashion trend, was, at the moment of trial, a celebrity of serious note, although having been sentenced after trial to life in prison, the note stands some chance of being muffled. But there are always appeals to higher courts, and John Gotti may make a comeback like Big Jule. What is certain is that if Damon Runyon had been alive in '92 he would have covered the Gotti trial and probably would have been a sometime dinner companion of Mr. Gotti also, as he was with Al Capone before Mr. Capone's trial for tax evasion; such was Runyon's fascination with gangsters and his need to know what made them what they were.

In his younger years Mr. Gotti served prison terms for attempted burglary and attempted manslaughter. But thereafter he avoided conviction on assault and racketeering charges in widely publicized trials. Incriminating tape recordings were used in his 1992 trial, but Mr. Gotti's lawyers argued that these were not evidence of criminality, much as Big Jule says of himself in *Guys and Dolls*: "I used to be bad when I was a kid but ever since then I have gone straight as I can prove by my record—33 arrests and no convictions."

Many of Runyon's characters are viewed at times as romanticized gangsters, defanged and cuddly, when they are really deadly citizens; and this sugarcoating of evil is said to be responsible for the popularity of his tales.

Some consider this to be a knock on Runyon, but such a knock isn't worth anybody's time. Crime and criminals in any form are a given in literature, movies, and theater, and this fact antedates Runyon by centuries: in John Gay's *The Beggar's Opera* of 1728, for instance, from which the Brecht-Weill *Threepenny Opera* of 1928 derives, and where that engaging scoundrel Macheath, or Mack the Knife, was born. It was Jonathan Swift who suggested that a Newgate prison pastoral "might make an odd pretty sort of thing," which it did in Mr. Gay's hands, and it has continued to do so on Broadway and also in Hollywood, where sixteen (at least) of Runyon's short stories have been turned into movies, some terrific, some dreadful. God must have loved gangster movies, he made so many of them.

Criticism of Runyon that is more to the point of argument here was reported in a biography, *A Gentleman of Broadway*, by Edwin P. Hoyt, published in 1964. Mr. Hoyt wrote that in the early 1960s, 150 academics, mostly literature teachers, decided that Damon Runyon, in the biographer's dismissive synthesis, "stood and stands nowhere."

This was the man, two of whose short-story collections in the late 1920s and early 1930s had sold more than a million copies each in paperback; who was translated into French, Dutch, Italian, Indonesian, and British. Lord Beaverbrook published him at length in the *London Evening Standard*, and the *Standard*'s literary critic called Runyon (according to Clark Kinnaird's preface in the Modern Library treasury) a genius as authentic as Laurence Sterne or James M. Barrie, saying Runyon had "invented a humanity as new and startling as Lewis Carroll did."

(In his story *The Lily of St. Pierre*, Runyon makes balanced mention of a Lewis Carroll work: "Lily talks English very good," says the speaker, Jack O'Hearts, while he is recuperating from pneumonia in Lily's house, "and she is always bringing me things . . . and sometimes she reads to me out of a book which is called *Alice in Wonderland*, and which is nothing but a pack of lies, but very interesting in spots.")

Runyon being embraced by the British prompted John Lardner to conclude that "very plainly . . . after a long, slow pull, by way of Poe, Whitman, James, Twain, Cather and Hemingway, our culture finally hit the jackpot with Runyon."

But Runyon died in 1946, his reputation faded, and at the time when he was standing "nowhere," only two of his books and the Modern Library treasury were in print (it's now out of print), and the man did seem to be going the way of yesterday's newspaper.

Today eleven, perhaps twelve of his collections of stories and journalism are in print, which is pleasant news for Runyon fanatics, of which there are several. Also, three more biographies have appeared: *The World of Damon Runyon*, by Tom Clark (1978); *The Men Who Invented Broadway: Damon Runyon, Walter Winchell and Their World* (1981), by John Mosedale; and *Damon Runyon* (1991), by Jimmy Breslin. These and the Hoyt book complement each other, filling in gaps in the life and the work and the age, and so we have a detailed overview of the maestro in his own time.

Jimmy Breslin, whom some regard as the Runyon of his own era (but far more politically sophisticated), is the revisionist, bringing us into the Runyon private life, and finding the famous writer much more wanting as a human being than we previously thought. Mr. Breslin also offers this evaluation of the man's achievement as a writer:

"Damon Runyon," he writes, "invented the Broadway of *Guys and Dolls* and the Roaring Twenties, neither of which existed, but whose names and phrases became part of theater history and the American language. . . . He made gangsters so enjoyable that they could walk off a page and across a movie screen. . . . He stressed fine, upstanding, dishonest people who fell in love, often to the sound of gunfire that sounded harmless. . . . Many of his people and their actions in real life were frightening to temporal authorities, but what does this have to do with the most important work on earth, placing merriment into the hearts of people?"

This Runyon merriment was, and is, chiefly an achievement of language—the language of gamblers, hoodlums, chorus girls, and cops, that he acquired by listening, then used in his stories, and is therefore credited with inventing. It is a nonesuch argot, and he uses it like no other writer who came before or after him. In the best of his short stories there is a comic fluency in this invented tongue, an originality of syntax, a fluidity of word and event that is a relentless delight.

In a story called *Broadway Incident* he tells of the suffering love of Ambrose Hammer, a Broadway drama critic, for a beautiful doll named Hilda Hiffenbrower, whose husband, Herbert, will not give her a divorce. Runyon writes:

"Well I happen to know Hilda better than Ambrose does. To tell the truth I know her when her name is Mame something and she is dealing them off her arm in a little eating gaff on Seventh Avenue, which is before she goes in show business and changes her name to Hilda, and I also know that the real reason Herbert will not give her this divorce is because she wants eight gallons of his heart's blood and both legs in the divorce settlement, but as Herbert has a good business head he is by no means agreeable to these terms, though I hear he is willing to compromise on one leg to get rid of Hilda."

This is a bit of serious character building through language; but Runyon's asides are often what ring the gong, for instance in that St. Pierre story again: "The first time I see St. Pierre I will not give you eight cents for the whole layout, although of course it is very useful to parties in our line of business [smuggling whiskey]. It does not look like much, and it belongs to France, and nearly all the citizens speak French, because most of them are French, and it seems it is the custom of the French people to speak French no matter where they are, even away off up yonder among the fish."

Far more serious writers than Runyon have fallen on their faces and other parts because they lacked what he had: a love and mastery of his language, a playful use of its idiosyncrasies. His plots, on the other hand, were usually convoluted exercises in simply irony—O. Henry reversals, frequently predictable, sometimes zany, with resolutions, often sticky with treacle—and will not stand up in court.

And yet he salvaged these stories, more often than not, with his rhythmic street idioms, his indefatigable wit, and his peculiar acceptance of the paralegal rules of this world that he chronicled. If he'd been a moralist among the grifters, goons, and golddiggers, he'd have remained an outsider, without the privileged insights that have made his work so singular.

The Runyon method was to be the nameless narrator, the detached observer, the reticent sponge, taking it all in, but not even asking questions; for, as he pointed out, when you start asking questions, people are liable to think that you are perhaps looking for answers. He knows everybody and has formed cogent opinions on them all. As to Judge Goldfobber in the story *Breach of Promise*, the narrator points out that he is only a lawyer, not a judge, "and he is 100 to 1 in my line against ever being a judge, but he is called Judge because it pleases him, and everybody always wishes to please [him because he] is a wonderful hand for keeping citizens from getting into the sneezer, and better than Houdini when it comes to getting them out of the sneezer after they are in."

The chance of any writer's work surviving his own death for very long is always a longshot. I used to quote Runyon as saying "All life is nine-to-five against." But Peter Maas, the writer, countered my numbers and said that the true quote was as follows: "All life is six-to-five against, just enough to keep you interested." It turns out that Peter is somewhat correct. The quote comes out of the story *A Nice Price*, in which Sam the Gonoph hears that the odds on a boat race between Harvard and Yale is one-to-three, Yale, and Sam the Gonoph, who is handy at making odds, says, "Nothing between human beings is one-to-three. In fact I long ago come to the conclusion that all life is six-to-five against."

And so, confronting the question of whether Damon Runyon is back in town, we must consider the catalytic effect of the *Guys and Dolls* revival, and then all these old Runyon films turning up regularly on cable TV—like *Lady for a Day* and its remake, *Pocketful of Miracles*, both of which I always watch all over again. And I think of how I was convulsed many years ago by the movie made from the Runyon–Howard Lindsay play, *A Slight Case of Murder*; and I think of the vibrant journalism Runyon wrote—*Trials and Other Tribulations*, for instance, which was the book he was preparing for publication when he died.

And I think, most of all, of the short stories in this book, which I have just been rereading for the past week as a way of challenging my most significant values, such as, can I still read these things? And half a century after I discovered them I am delighted to report that I find myself tickled silly by them still, all of them, and want to pass them on to my grandchildren. I already passed them on to my children.

Like a second-story man who can't stand heights, I don't want to get too lofty about all this; and, what is more, I have predicted comebacks in the past for John O'Hara and William Saroyan and I am still waiting for their trains; and I know the thinning ranks of modern readers will be put off by Runyon's antique argot, and by the prehistoric hipness (hepness in those days) of his world; and yet I am willing to take a little of that six-to-five that Damon Runyon is back, not quite settled in yet, a little unsteady on his pins after the journey, but definitely here: our literary equivalent of his contemporaries, the Marx Brothers (does anybody ever knock them because of their plots?), which is to say that his work has not turned into dusty dingbats but has proven to be enduringly comic, thoroughly original, and that he ranks as one of the funniest dead men ever to use the English language. Six-to-five, a nice price. Bet me.

—William Kennedy

GUYS

&

DOLLS

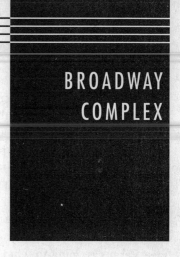

BROADWAY COMPLEX

I t is along toward four o'clock one morning, and I am sitting in Mindy's restaurant on Broadway with Ambrose Hammer, the newspaper scribe, enjoying a sturgeon sandwich, which is wonderful brain food, and listening to Ambrose tell me what is wrong with the world, and I am somewhat discouraged by what he tells me, for Ambrose is such a guy as is always very pessimistic about everything.

He is especially very pessimistic about the show business, as Ambrose is what is called a dramatic critic, and he has to go around nearly every night and look at the new plays that people are always putting in the theaters, and I judge from what Ambrose says that this is a very great hardship, and that he seldom gets much pleasure out of life.

Furthermore, I judge from what Ambrose tells me that there is no little danger in being a dramatic critic, because it seems that only a short time before this he goes to a play that is called Never-Never, and Ambrose says it is a very bad play, indeed, and he so states in his newspaper, and in fact Ambrose states in his newspaper that the play smells in nine different keys, and that so does the acting of the leading man, a guy by the name of Fergus Appleton.

Well, the next day Ambrose runs into this Fergus Appleton in front of the Hotel Astor, and what does Fergus Appleton do but haul off and belt Ambrose over the noggin with a cane, and ruin a nice new fall derby for Ambrose, and when Ambrose puts in an expense account to his newspaper for this kady they refuse to pay it, so Ambrose is out four bobs.

And anyway, Ambrose says, the theatergoing public never appreciates what a dramatic critic does for it, because it seems that even though he tips the public off that Never-Never is strictly a turkey, it is a great success, and, moreover, Fergus Appleton is now going around with a doll who is nobody but Miss Florentine Fayette, the daughter of old Hannibal Fayette.

And anybody will tell you that old Hannibal Fayette is very, very, very rich, and has a piece of many different propositions, including the newspaper that Ambrose Hammer works for, although of course at the time Ambrose speaks of Fergus Appleton's acting, he has no idea Fergus is going to wind up going around with Miss Florentine Fayette.

So Ambrose says the chances are his newspaper will give him the heave-o as soon as Fergus Appleton gets the opportunity to drop the zing in on him, but Ambrose says he does not care a cuss as he is writing a play himself that will show the theater-going public what a real play is.

Well, Ambrose is writing this play ever since I know him, which is a matter of several years, and he tells me about it so often that I can play any part in it myself with a little practice, and he is just getting around to going over his first act with me again when in comes a guy by the name of Cecil Earl, who is what is called a master of ceremonies at the Golden Slipper nightclub.

Personally, I never see Cecil Earl but once or twice before in my life, and he always strikes me as a very quiet and modest young guy, for a master of ceremonies, and I am greatly surprised at the way he comes in, as he is acting very bold and aggressive toward one and all, and is speaking out loud in a harsh, disagreeable tone of voice, and in general is acting like a guy who is looking for trouble, which is certainly no way for a master of ceremonies to act.

But of course if a guy is looking for trouble on Broadway along towards four o'clock in the morning, anybody will tell you that the right address is nowhere else but Mindy's, because at such an hour many citizens are gathered there, and are commencing to get a little cross wondering where they are going to make a scratch for the morrow's operations, such as playing the horses.

It is a sure thing that any citizen who makes his scratch before four o'clock in the morning is at home getting his rest, so he will arise fully refreshed for whatever the day may bring forth, and also to avoid the bite he is apt to encounter in Mindy's from citizens who do not make a scratch.

However, the citizens who are present the morning I am speaking of do not pay much attention to Cecil Earl when he comes in, as he is nothing but a tall, skinny young guy, with slick black hair, such as you are apt to see anywhere along Broadway at any time, especially standing in front of theatrical booking offices. In fact, to look at Cecil you will bet he is maybe a saxophone player, as there is something about him that makes you think of a saxophone player right away and, to tell the truth, Cecil can tootle a pretty fair sax, at that, if the play happens to come up.

Well, Cecil sits down at a table where several influential citizens are sitting, including Nathan Detroit, who runs the crap game, and Big Nig, the crap shooter, and Regret, the horse player, and Upstate Red, who is one of the best faro bank players in the world whenever he can find a faro bank and something to play it with, and these citizens are discussing some very serious matters, when out of a clear sky Cecil ups and speaks to them as follows:

"Listen," Cecil says, "if youse guys do not stop making so much noise, I may cool you all off."

Well, naturally, this is most repulsive language to use to such influential citizens, and furthermore it is very illiterate to say youse, so without changing the subject Nathan Detroit reaches out and picks up an order for ham and eggs, Southern style, that Charley, the waiter, just puts in front of Upstate Red, and taps Cecil on the onion with same.

It is unfortunate for Cecil that Nathan Detroit does not remove the ham and eggs, Southern style, from the platter before tapping Cecil with the order, because it is a very hard platter, and Cecil is knocked as stiff as a plank, and maybe stiffer, and it becomes necessary to summon old Doctor Moggs to bring him back to life.

Well, of course none of us know that Cecil is at the moment Jack Legs Diamond, or Mad Dog Coll, or some other very tough gorill, and in fact this does not come out until Ambrose Hammer later starts in investigating the strange actions of Cecil Earl, and then Nathan Detroit apologizes to Cecil, and also to the chef in Mindy's for treating an order of ham and eggs, Southern style, so disrespectfully.

It comes out that Cecil is subject to spells of being somebody else besides Cecil Earl, and Ambrose Hammer gives us a very long explanation of this situation, only Ambrose finally becomes so scientific that nobody can keep cases on him. But we gather in a general way from what Ambrose says that Cecil Earl is very susceptible to suggestion from anything he reads, or is told.

In fact, Ambrose says he is the most susceptible guy of this kind he ever meets up with in his life, and it seems that when he is going to Harvard College, which is before he starts in being a dramatic critic, Ambrose makes quite a study of these matters.

Personally, I always claim that Cecil Earl is a little screwy, or if he is not screwy that he will do very well as a pinch-hitter until a screwy guy comes to bat, but Ambrose Hammer says no. Ambrose says it is true that Cecil may be bobbing a trifle, but that he is by no means entirely off his nut. Ambrose says that Cecil only has delusions of grandeur, and complexes, and I do not know what all else, but Ambrose says it is 9 to 10 and take your pick whether Cecil is a genius or a daffydill.

Ambrose says that Cecil is like an actor playing a different part every now and then, only Cecil tries to live every part he plays, and Ambrose claims that if we have actors with as much sense as Cecil in playing parts, the show business will be a lot better off. But of course Ambrose cares very little for actors since Fergus Appleton ruins his kady.

Well, the next time I see Cecil he comes in Mindy's again, and this time it seems he is Jack Dempsey, and while ordinarily nobody will mind him being Jack Dempsey, or even Gene Tunney, although he is not the type for Gene Tunney, Cecil takes to throwing left hooks at citizens' chins, so finally Sam the Singer gets up and lets a right hand go inside a left hook, and once more Cecil folds up like an old accordion.

When I speak of this to Ambrose Hammer, he says that being Jack Dempsey is entirely a false complex for Cecil, brought on mainly by Cecil taking a few belts at the Golden Slipper liquor during the evening. In fact, Ambrose says this particular complex does not count. But I notice that after this Cecil is never anybody very brash when he is around Mindy's.

Sometimes he is somebody else besides Cecil Earl for as long as a week at a stretch, and in fact once he is Napoleon for two whole weeks, but Ambrose Hammer says this is nothing. Ambrose says he personally knows guys who are Napoleon all their lives. But of course Ambrose means that these guys are only Napoleons in their own minds. He says that the only difference between Cecil and them is that Cecil's complex breaks out on him in public, while the other guys are Napoleons only in their own bedrooms.

Personally, I think such guys are entitled to be locked up in spots with high walls around and about, but Ambrose seems to make nothing much of it, and anyway this Cecil Earl is as harmless as a bag of marshmallows, no matter who he is being.

One thing I must say for Cecil Earl, he is nearly always an interesting guy to talk to, because he nearly always has a different personality, and in fact the only time he is uninteresting is when he is being nobody but Cecil Earl. Then he is a very quiet guy with a sad face and he is so bashful and retiring that you will scarcely believe he is the same guy who goes around all one week being Mussolini in his own mind.

Now I wish to say that Cecil Earl does not often go around making any public display of these spells of his, except when the character calls for a display, such as the time he is George Bernard Shaw, and in fact unless you know him personally you may sometimes figure him just a guy sitting back in a corner somewhere with nothing whatever on his mind, and you will never even suspect that you are in the presence of J. Pierpont Morgan studying out a way to make us all rich.

It gets so that nobody resents Cecil being anything he pleases, except once when he is Senator Huey Long, and once when he is Hitler, and makes the mistake of wandering down on the lower East Side and saying so. In fact, it gets so everybody along Broadway puts in with him and helps him be whoever he is, as much as possible, although I always claim he has a bad influence on some citizens, for instance Regret, the horse player.

It seems that Regret catches a complex off of Cecil Earl one day, and for twenty-four hours he is Pittsburgh Phil, the racetrack plunger, and goes overboard with every bookie down at Belmont Park and has to hide out for some time before he can get himself straightened out.

Now Cecil Earl is a good master of ceremonies in a nightclub, if you care for masters of ceremonies, a master of ceremonies in a nightclub being a guy who is supposed to make cute cracks, and to introduce any celebrities who happen to be sitting around the joint, such as actors and prominent merchants, so the other customers can give them a big hand, and this is by no means an easy job, as sometimes a master of ceremonies may overlook a celebrity, and the celebrity becomes terribly insulted.

But it seems that Cecil Earl is smart enough to introduce all the people in the Golden Slipper every night and call for a big hand for them, no matter who they are, so nobody can get insulted, although one night he introduces a new headwaiter, thinking he is nothing but a customer, and the headwaiter is somewhat insulted, at that, and threatens to quit, because he claims being introduced in a nightclub is no boost for him.

Anyway, Cecil gets a nice piece of money for being master of ceremonies at the Golden Slipper, and when he is working there his complexes do not seem to bother him very much, and he is never anybody more serious than Harry Richman or Mort Downey. And it is at the Golden Slipper that he meets this guy, Fergus Appleton, and Miss Florentine Fayette.

Now Miss Florentine Fayette is a tall, slim, black-haired doll, and so beautiful she is practically untrue, but she has a kisser that never seems to relax, and furthermore she never seems much interested in anything whatever. In fact, if Miss Florentine Fayette's papa does not have so many cucumbers, I will say she is slightly dumb, but for all I know it may be against the law to say a doll whose papa has all these cucumbers is dumb. So I will only say that she does not strike me as right bright.

She is a great hand for going around nightclubs and sitting there practically unconscious for hours at a time, and always this Fergus Appleton is with her, and before long it gets around that Fergus Appleton wishes to make Miss Florentine Fayette his ever-loving wife, and everybody admits that it will be a very nice score, indeed, for an actor.

Personally, I see nothing wrong with this situation because, to tell you the truth, I will just naturally love to make Miss Florentine Fayette my own ever-loving wife if her papa's cucumbers go with it, but of course Ambrose Hammer does not approve of the idea of her becoming Fergus Appleton's wife, because Ambrose can see how it may work out to his disadvantage.

This Fergus Appleton is a fine-looking guy of maybe forty, with iron-gray hair that makes him appear very romantic, and he is always well dressed in spats and one thing and another, and he smokes cigarettes in a holder nearly a foot long, and wears a watch on one wrist and a slave bracelet on the other, and a big ring on each hand, and sometimes a monocle in one eye, although Ambrose Hammer claims that this is strictly the old ackamarackuss.

There is no doubt that Fergus Appleton is a very chesty guy, and likes to pose around in public places, but I see maybe a million guys like him in my time on Broadway, and not all of them are actors, so I do not hate him for his posing, or for his slave bracelet, or the monocle either, although naturally I consider him out of line in busting my friend Ambrose Hammer's new derby, and I promise Ambrose that the first time Fergus Appleton shows up in a new derby, or even an old one, I will see that somebody busts it, if I have to do it myself.

The only thing wrong I see about Fergus Appleton is that he is a smart-alecky guy, and when he first finds out about Cecil Earl's complexes he starts working on them to amuse the guys and dolls who hang out around the Golden Slipper with him and Miss Florentine Fayette.

Moreover, it seems that somehow Cecil Earl is very susceptible, indeed, to Fergus Appleton's suggestions, and for a while Fergus Appleton makes quite a sucker of Cecil Earl.

Then all of a sudden Fergus Appleton stops making a sucker of Cecil, and the next thing anybody knows Fergus Appleton is becoming quite pally with Cecil, and I see them around Mindy's, and other late spots after the Golden Slipper closes, and sometimes Miss Florentine Fayette is with them, although Cecil Earl is such a guy as does not care much for the society of dolls, and in fact is very much embarrassed when they are around, which is most surprising conduct for a master of ceremonies in a nightclub, as such characters are usually pretty fresh with dolls.

But of course even the freshest master of ceremonies is apt to be a little bashful when such a doll as Miss Florentine Fayette is around, on account of her papa having so many cucumbers, and when she is present Cecil Earl seldom opens his trap, but just sits looking at her and letting Fergus Appleton do all the gabbing, which suits Fergus Appleton fine, as he does not mind hearing himself gab, and in fact loves it.

Sometimes I run into just Cecil Earl and Fergus Appleton, and generally they have their heads close together, and are talking low and serious, like two business guys with a large deal coming up between them.

Furthermore I can see that Cecil Earl is looking very mysterious and solemn himself, so I figure that maybe they are doping out a new play together and that Cecil is acting one of the parts, and whatever it is they are doing I consider it quite big-hearted of Fergus Appleton to take such a friendly interest in Cecil.

But somehow Ambrose Hammer does not like it. In fact, Ambrose Hammer speaks of the matter at some length to me, and says to me like this:

"It is unnatural," he says. "It is unnatural for a guy like Fergus Appleton, who is such a guy as never has a thought in the world for anybody but himself, to be playing the warm for a guy like Cecil Earl. There is something wrong in this business, and," Ambrose says, "I am going to find out what it is."

Well, personally I do not see where it is any of Ambrose Hammer's put-in even if there is something wrong, but Ambrose is always poking his beezer into other people's business, and he starts watching Cecil and Fergus Appleton with great interest whenever he happens to run into them.

Finally it comes an early Sunday morning, and Ambrose Hammer and I are in Mindy's as usual, when in comes Cecil Earl all alone, with a book under one arm. He sits down at a table in a corner booth all by himself and orders a western sandwich and starts in to read his book, and nothing will do Ambrose Hammer but for us to go over and talk to Cecil.

When he sees us coming, he closes his book, and drops it in his lap and gives us a very weak hello. It is the first time we see him alone in quite a spell, and finally, Ambrose Hammer asks where is Fergus Appleton, although Ambrose really does not care where he is, unless it happens to turn out that he is in a pesthouse suffering from smallpox.

Cecil says Fergus Appleton has to go over to Philadelphia on business over the weekend, and then Ambrose asks Cecil where Miss Florentine Fayette is, and Cecil says he does not know but supposes she is home.

"Well," Ambrose Hammer says, "Miss Florentine Fayette is certainly a beautiful doll, even if she does look a little bit colder than I like them, but," he says, "what she sees in such a pish-tush as Fergus Appleton I do not know."

Now at this Cecil Earl busts right out crying, and naturally Ambrose Hammer and I are greatly astonished at such an exhibition, because we do not see any occasion for tears, and personally I am figuring on taking it on the Dan O'Leary away from there before somebody gets to thinking we do Cecil some great wrong, when Cecil speaks as follows:

"I love her," Cecil says. "I love her with all my heart and soul. But she belongs to my best friend. For two cents I will take this dagger that Fergus gives me and end it all, because life is not worth living without Miss Florentine Fayette."

And with this Cecil Earl outs with a big long stabber, which is a spectacle that is most disquieting to me as I know such articles are against the law in this man's town. So I make Cecil put it right back in his pocket and while I am doing this Ambrose Hammer reaches down beside Cecil and grabs the book Cecil is reading, and while Cecil is still sobbing Ambrose looks this volume over.

It turns out to be a book called The Hundred-Percent-Perfect Crime, but what interests Ambrose Hammer more than anything else is a lead-pencil drawing on one of the blank pages in the front part of the book. Afterwards Ambrose sketches this drawing out for me as near as he can remember it on the back of one of Mindy's menu cards, and it looks to me like the drawing of the ground floor of a small house, with a line on one side on which is written the word Menahan, and Ambrose says he figures this means a street.

But in the meantime Ambrose tries to soothe Cecil Earl and to get him to stop crying, and when Cecil finally does dry up he sees Ambrose has his book, and he makes a grab for it and creates quite a scene until he gets it back.

Personally, I cannot make head or tail of the sketch that Ambrose draws for me, and I cannot see that there is anything to it anyway, but Ambrose seems to regard it as of some importance.

Well, I do not see Ambrose Hammer for several days, but I am hearing strange stories of him being seen with Cecil Earl in the afternoons when Fergus Appleton is playing matinees in Never-Never, and early in the evenings when Fergus Appleton is doing his night performances, and I also hear that Ambrose always seems to be talking very earnestly to Cecil Earl, and sometimes throwing his arms about in a most excited manner.

Then one morning Ambrose Hammer looks me up again in Mindy's, and he is smiling a very large smile, as if he is greatly pleased with something, which is quite surprising as Ambrose Hammer is seldom pleased with anything. Finally he says to me like this:

"Well," Ambrose says, "I learn the meaning of the drawing in Cecil Earl's book. It is the plan of a house on Menahan street, away over in Brooklyn. And the way I learn this is very, very clever, indeed," Ambrose says. "I stake a chambermaid to let me into Fergus Appleton's joint in the Dazzy apartments, and what do I find there just as I expect but a letter from a certain number on this street?"

"Why," I say to Ambrose Hammer, "I am greatly horrified by your statement. You are nothing but a burglar, and if Fergus Appleton finds this out he will turn you over to the officers of the law, and you will lose your job and everything else."

"No," Ambrose says, "I will not lose my job, because old Hannibal Fayette is around the office yesterday raising an awful row about his daughter wishing to marry an actor, and saying he will give he does not know what if anybody can bust this romance up. The chances are," Ambrose says, "he will make me editor in chief of the paper, and then I will can a lot of guys I do not like. Fergus Appleton is to meet Cecil Earl here this morning, and in the meantime I will relate the story to you."

But before Ambrose can tell me the story, in comes Fergus Appleton, and Miss Florentine Fayette is with him, and they sit down at a table not far from us, and Fergus Appleton looks around and sees Ambrose and gives him a terrible scowl. Furthermore, he says something to Miss Florentine Fayette, and she looks at Ambrose, too, but she does not scowl or anything else, but only looks very dead-pan.

Fergus Appleton is in evening clothes and has on his monocle, and Miss Florentine Fayette is wearing such a gown that anybody can see how beautiful she is, no matter if her face does not have much expression. They are sitting there without much conversation passing between them, when all of a sudden in walks Cecil Earl, full of speed and much excited.

He comes in with such a rush that he almost flattens Regret, the horse player, who is on his way out, and Regret is about to call him a dirty name when he sees a spectacle that will always be remembered in Mindy's, for Cecil Earl walks right over to Miss Florentine Fayette as she is sitting there beside Fergus Appleton, and without saying as much as boo to Fergus Appleton, Cecil grabs Miss Florentine Fayette up in his arms with surprising strength and gives her a big sizzling kiss, and says to her like this:

"Florentine," he says, "I love you."

Then he squeezes her to his bosom so tight that it looks as if he is about to squeeze her right out through the top of her gown like squeezing toothpaste out of a tube, and says to her again, as follows:

"I love you. Oh, how I love you."

Well, at first Fergus Appleton is so astonished at this proposition that he can scarcely stir, and the chances are he cannot believe his eyes. Furthermore, many other citizens who are present partaking of their Bismarck herring, and one thing and another, are also astonished, and they are commencing to think that maybe Cecil Earl is having a complex about being King Kong, when Fergus Appleton finally gets to his feet and speaks in a loud tone of voice as follows:

"Why," Fergus Appleton says, "you are nothing but a scurvy fellow, and unless you unhand my fiancée, the chances are I will annihilate you."

Naturally, Fergus Appleton is somewhat excited, and in fact he is so excited that he drops his monocle to the floor, and it breaks into several pieces. At first he seems to have some idea of dropping a big right hand on Cecil Earl somewhere, but Cecil is pretty well covered by Miss Florentine Fayette, so Fergus Appleton can see that if he lets a right hand go he is bound to strike Miss Florentine Fayette right where she lives.

So he only grabs hold of Miss Florentine Fayette, and tries to pull her loose from Cecil Earl, and Cecil Earl not only holds her tighter, but Miss Florentine Fayette seems to be doing some holding to Cecil herself, so Fergus Appleton cannot peel her off, although he gets one stocking and a piece of elastic strap from somewhere. Then one and all are greatly surprised to hear Miss Florentine Fayette speak to Fergus Appleton like this:

"Go away, you old porous plaster," Miss Florentine Fayette says. "I love only my Cecil. Hold me tighter, Cecil, you great big bear," Miss Florentine Fayette says, although of course Cecil looks about as much like a bear as Ambrose Hammer looks like a porcupine.

Well, of course there is great commotion in Mindy's, because Cecil Earl is putting on a love scene such as makes many citizens very homesick, and Fergus Appleton does not seem to know what to do, when Ambrose Hammer gets to him and whispers a few words in his ear, and all of a sudden Fergus Appleton turns and walks out of Mindy's and disappears, and furthermore nobody ever sees him in these parts again.

By and by Mindy himself comes up and tells Cecil Earl and Miss Florentine Fayette that the chef is complaining because he cannot seem to make ice in his refrigerator while they are in the joint, and will they please go away. So Cecil Earl and Miss Florentine Fayette go, and then Ambrose Hammer comes back to me and finishes his story.

"Well," Ambrose says, "I go over to the certain number on Menahan Street, and what do I find there but a crippled-up, middle-aged doll who is nobody but Fergus Appleton's ever-loving wife, and furthermore she is such for over twenty years. She tells me that Fergus is the meanest guy that ever breathes the breath of life, and that he is persecuting her for a long time in every way he can think of because she will not give him a divorce.

"And," Ambrose says, "the reason she will not give him a divorce is because he knocks her downstairs a long time ago, and makes her a cripple for life, and leaves her to the care of her own people. But of course I do not tell her," Ambrose says, "that she narrowly escapes being murdered through him, for the meaning of the floor plan of the house in Cecil's book, and the meaning of the book itself, and of the dagger, is that Fergus Appleton is working on Cecil Earl until he has him believing that he can be the supermurderer of the age."

"Why," I say to Ambrose Hammer, "I am greatly shocked by these revelations. Why, Fergus Appleton is nothing but a fellow."

"Well," Ambrose says, "he is pretty cute, at that. He has Cecil thinking that it will be a wonderful thing to be the guy who commits the hundred-percent-perfect crime, and furthermore Fergus promises to make Cecil rich after he marries Miss Florentine Fayette."

"But," I say, "what I do not understand is what makes Cecil become such a violent lover all of a sudden."

"Why," Ambrose Hammer says, "when Cecil lets it out that he loves Miss Florentine Fayette, it gives me a nice clue to the whole situation. I take Cecil in hand and give him a little coaching and, furthermore, I make him a present of a book myself. He finds it more interesting than anything Fergus Appleton gives him. In fact," Ambrose says, "I recommend it to you. When Cecil comes in here this morning, he is not Cecil Earl, the potential Perfect Murderer. He is nobody but the world's champion heavy lover, old Don Juan."

Well, Ambrose does not get to be editor in chief of his newspaper. In fact, he just misses getting the outdoors, because Cecil Earl and Miss Florentine Fayette elope, and get married, and go out to Hollywood on a honeymoon, and never return, and old Hannibal Fayette claims it is just as bad for his daughter to marry a movie actor as a guy on the stage, even though Cecil turns out to be the greatest drawing card on the screen because he can heat up love scenes so good.

But I always say that Cecil Earl is quite an ingrate, because he refuses a part in Ambrose Hammer's play when Ambrose finally gets it written, and makes his biggest hit in a screen version of Never-Never.

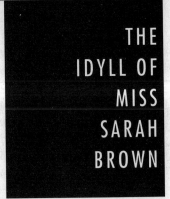

THE
IDYLL OF
MISS
SARAH
BROWN

O f all the high players this country ever sees, there is no doubt but that the guy they call The Sky is the highest. In fact, the reason he is called The Sky is because he goes so high when it comes to betting on any proposition whatever. He will bet all he has, and nobody can bet any more than this.

His right name is Obadiah Masterson, and he is originally out of a little town in southern Colorado where he learns to shoot craps, and play cards, and one thing and another, and where his old man is a very well-known citizen, and something of a sport himself. In fact, The Sky tells me that when he finally cleans up all the loose scratch around his home town and decides he needs more room, his old man has a little private talk with him and says to him like this:

"Son," the old guy says, "you are now going out into the wide, wide world to make your own way, and it is a very good thing to do, as there are no more opportunities for you in this burg. I am only sorry," he says, "that I am not able to bankroll you to a very large start, but," he says, "not having any potatoes to give you, I am now going to stake you to some very valuable advice, which I personally collect in my years of experience around and about, and I hope and trust you will always bear this advice in mind.

"Son," the old guy says, "no matter how far you travel, or how smart you get, always remember this: Some day, somewhere," he says, "a guy is going to come to you and show you a nice brand-new deck of cards on which the seal is never broken, and this guy is going to offer to bet you that the jack of spades will jump out of this deck and squirt cider in your ear. But, son," the old guy says, "do not bet him, for as sure as you do you are going to get an ear full of cider."

Well, The Sky remembers what his old man says, and he is always very cautious about betting on such propositions as the jack of spades jumping out of a sealed deck of cards and squirting cider in his ear, and so he makes few mistakes as he goes along. In fact, the only real mistake The Sky makes is when he hits St. Louis after leaving his old home town, and loses all his potatoes betting a guy St. Louis is the biggest town in the world.

Now of course this is before The Sky ever sees any bigger towns, and he is never much of a hand for reading up on matters such as this. In fact, the only reading The Sky ever does as he goes along through life is in these Gideon Bibles such as he finds in the hotel rooms where he lives, for The Sky never lives anywhere else but in hotel rooms for years.

He tells me that he reads many items of great interest in these Gideon Bibles, and furthermore The Sky says that several times these Gideon Bibles keep him from getting out of line, such as the time he finds himself pretty much frozen-in over in Cincinnati, what with owing everybody in town except maybe the mayor from playing games of chance of one kind and another.

Well, The Sky says he sees no way of meeting these obligations and he is figuring the only thing he can do is to take a run-out powder, when he happens to read in one of these Gideon Bibles where it says like this:

"Better is it," the Gideon Bible says, "that thou shouldest not vow, than that thou shouldest vow and not pay."

Well, The Sky says he can see that there is no doubt whatever but that this means a guy shall not welsh, so he remains in Cincinnati until he manages to wiggle himself out of the situation, and from that day to this, The Sky never thinks of welshing.

He is maybe thirty years old, and is a tall guy with a round kisser, and big blue eyes, and he always looks as innocent as a little baby. But The Sky is by no means as innocent as he looks. In fact, The Sky is smarter than three Philadelphia lawyers, which makes him very smart, indeed, and he is well established as a high player in New Orleans, and Chicago, and Los Angeles, and wherever else there is any action in the way of card-playing, or crap-shooting, or horse-racing, or betting on the baseball games, for The Sky is always moving around the country following the action.

But while The Sky will bet on anything whatever, he is more of a short-card player and a crap-shooter than anything else, and furthermore he is a great hand for propositions, such as are always coming up among citizens who follow games of chance for a living. Many citizens prefer betting on propositions to anything you can think of, because they figure a proposition gives them a chance to out-smart somebody, and in fact I know citizens who will sit up all night making up propositions to offer other citizens the next day.

A proposition may be only a problem in cards, such as what is the price against a guy getting aces back-to-back, or how often a pair of deuces will win a hand in stud, and then again it may be some very daffy proposition, indeed, although the daffier any proposition seems to be, the more some citizens like it. And no one ever sees The Sky when he does not have some proposition of his own.

The first time he ever shows up around this town, he goes to a baseball game at the Polo Grounds with several prominent citizens, and while he is at the ball game, he buys himself a sack of Harry Stevens's peanuts, which he dumps in a side pocket of his coat. He is eating these peanuts all through the game, and after the game is over and he is walking across the field with the citizens, he says to them like this:

"What price," The Sky says, "I cannot throw a peanut from second base to the home plate?"

Well, everybody knows that a peanut is too light for anybody to throw it this far, so Big Nig, the crap shooter, who always likes to have a little the best of it running for him, speaks as follows:

"You can have 3 to 1 from me, stranger," Big Nig says.

"Two C's against six," The Sky says, and then he stands on second base, and takes a peanut out of his pocket, and not only whips it to the home plate, but on into the lap of a fat guy who is still sitting in the grandstand putting the zing on Bill Terry for not taking Walker out of the box when Walker is getting a pasting from the other club.

Well, naturally, this is a most astonishing throw, indeed, but afterwards it comes out that The Sky throws a peanut loaded with lead, and of course it is not one of Harry Stevens's peanuts, either, as Harry is not selling peanuts full of lead at a dime a bag, with the price of lead what it is.

It is only a few nights after this that The Sky states another most unusual proposition to a group of citizens sitting in Mindy's restaurant when he offers to bet a C note that he can go down into Mindy's cellar and catch a live rat with his bare hands and everybody is greatly astonished when Mindy himself steps up and takes the bet, for ordinarily Mindy will not bet you a nickel he is alive.

But it seems that Mindy knows that The Sky plants a tame rat in the cellar, and this rat knows The Sky and loves him dearly, and will let him catch it any time he wishes, and it also seems that Mindy knows that one of his dishwashers happens upon this rat, and not knowing it is tame, knocks it flatter than a pancake. So when The Sky goes down into the cellar and starts trying to catch a rat with his bare hands he is greatly surprised how inhospitable the rat turns out to be, because it is one of Mindy's personal rats, and Mindy is around afterwards saying he will lay plenty of 7 to 5 against even Strangler Lewis being able to catch one of his rats with his bare hands, or with boxing gloves on.

I am only telling you all this to show you what a smart guy The Sky is, and I am only sorry I do not have time to tell you about many other very remarkable propositions that he thinks up outside of his regular business.

It is well-known to one and all that he is very honest in every respect, and that he hates and despises cheaters at cards, or dice, and furthermore The Sky never wishes to play with any the best of it himself, or anyway not much. He will never take the inside of any situation, as many gamblers love to do, such as owning a gambling house, and having the percentage run for him instead of against him, for always The Sky is strictly a player, because he says he will never care to settle down in one spot long enough to become the owner of anything.

In fact, in all the years The Sky is drifting around the country, nobody ever knows him to own anything except maybe a bank roll, and when he comes to Broadway the last time, which is the time I am now speaking of, he has a hundred G's in cash money, and an extra suit of clothes, and this is all he has in the world. He never owns such a thing as a house, or an automobile, or a piece of jewelry.

He never owns a watch, because The Sky says time means nothing to him.

Of course some guys will figure a hundred G's comes under the head of owning something, but as far as The Sky is concerned, money is nothing but just something for him to play with and the dollars may as well be doughnuts as far as value goes with him. The only time The Sky ever thinks of money as money is when he is broke, and the only way he can tell he is broke is when he reaches into his pocket and finds nothing there but his fingers.

Then it is necessary for The Sky to go out and dig up some fresh scratch somewhere, and when it comes to digging up scratch, The Sky is practically supernatural. He can get more potatoes on the strength of a telegram to some place or other than John D. Rockefeller can get on collateral, for everybody knows The Sky's word is as good as wheat in the bin.

Now one Sunday evening The Sky is walking along Broadway, and at the corner of Forty-ninth Street he comes upon a little bunch of mission workers who are holding a religious meeting, such as mission workers love to do of a Sunday evening, the idea being that they may round up a few sinners here and there, although personally I always claim the mission workers come out too early to catch any sinners on this part of Broadway. At such an hour the sinners are still in bed resting up from their sinning of the night before, so they will be in good shape for more sinning a little later on.

There are only four of these mission workers, and two of them are old guys, and one is an old doll, while the other is a young doll who is tootling on a cornet. And after a couple of ganders at this young doll, The Sky is a goner, for this is one of the most beautiful young dolls anybody ever sees on Broadway, and especially as a mission worker. Her name is Miss Sarah Brown.

She is tall, and thin, and has a first-class shape, and her hair is a light brown, going on blond, and her eyes are like I do not know what, except that they are one-hundred-percent eyes in every respect. Furthermore, she is not a bad cornet player, if you like cornet players, although at this spot on Broadway she has to play against a scat band in a chop-suey joint near by, and this is tough competition, although at that many citizens believe Miss Sarah Brown will win by a large score if she only gets a little more support from one of the old guys with her who has a big bass drum, but does not pound it hearty enough.

Well, The Sky stands there listening to Miss Sarah Brown tootling on the cornet for quite a spell, and then he hears her make a speech in which she puts the blast on sin very good, and boosts religion quite some, and says if there are any souls around that need saving the owners of same may step forward at once. But no one steps forward, so The Sky comes over to Mindy's restaurant where many citizens are congregated, and starts telling us about Miss Sarah Brown. But of course we already know about Miss Sarah Brown, because she is so beautiful, and so good.

Furthermore, everybody feels somewhat sorry for Miss Sarah Brown, for while she is always tootling the cornet, and making speeches, and looking to save any souls that need saving, she never seems to find any souls to save, or at least her bunch of mission workers never gets any bigger. In fact, it gets smaller, as she starts out with a guy who plays a very fair sort of trombone, but this guy takes it on the lam one night with the trombone, which one and all consider a dirty trick.

Now from this time on, The Sky does not take any interest in anything but Miss Sarah Brown, and any night she is out on the corner with the other mission workers, you will see The Sky standing around looking at her, and naturally after a few weeks of this, Miss Sarah Brown must know The Sky is looking at her, or she is dumber than seems possible. And nobody ever figures Miss Sarah Brown dumb, as she is always on her toes, and seems plenty able to take care of herself, even on Broadway.

Sometimes after the street meeting is over, The Sky follows the mission workers to their headquarters in an old storeroom around in Forty-eighth Street where they generally hold an indoor session, and I hear The Sky drops many a large coarse note in the collection box while looking at Miss Sarah Brown, and there is no doubt these notes come in handy around the mission, as I hear business is by no means so good there.

It is called the Save-a-Soul Mission, and it is run mainly by Miss Sarah Brown's grandfather, an old guy with whiskers, by the name of Arvide Abernathy, but Miss Sarah Brown seems to do most of the work, including tootling the cornet, and visiting the poor people around and about, and all this and that, and many citizens claim it is a great shame that such a beautiful doll is wasting her time being good.

How The Sky ever becomes acquainted with Miss Sarah Brown is a very great mystery, but the next thing anybody knows, he is saying hello to her, and she is smiling at him out of her one-hundred-percent eyes, and one evening when I happen to be with The Sky we run into her walking along Forty-ninth Street, and The Sky hauls off and stops her, and says it is a nice evening, which it is, at that. Then The Sky says to Miss Sarah Brown like this:

"Well," The Sky says, "how is the mission dodge going these days? Are you saving any souls?" he says.

Well, it seems from what Miss Sarah Brown says the soul-saving is very slow, indeed, these days.

"In fact," Miss Sarah Brown says, "I worry greatly about how few souls we seem to save. Sometimes I wonder if we are lacking in grace."

She goes on up the street, and The Sky stands looking after her, and he says to me like this:

"I wish I can think of some way to help this little doll," he says, "especially," he says, "in saving a few souls to build up her mob at the mission. I must speak to her again, and see if I can figure something out."

But The Sky does not get to speak to Miss Sarah Brown again, because somebody weighs in the sacks on him by telling her he is nothing but a professional gambler, and that he is a very undesirable character, and that his only interest in hanging around the mission is because she is a good-looking doll. So all of a sudden Miss Sarah Brown plays a plenty of chill for The Sky. Furthermore, she sends him word that she does not care to accept any more of his potatoes in the collection box, because his potatoes are nothing but ill-gotten gains.

Well, naturally, this hurts The Sky's feelings no little, so he quits standing around looking at Miss Sarah Brown, and going to the mission, and takes to mingling again with the citizens in Mindy's, and showing some interest in the affairs of the community, especially the crap games.

Of course the crap games that are going on at this time are nothing much, because practically everybody in the world is broke, but there is a head-and-head game run by Nathan Detroit over a garage in Fifty-second Street where there is occasionally some action, and who shows up at this crap game early one evening but The Sky, although it seems he shows up there more to find company than anything else.

In fact, he only stands around watching the play, and talking with other guys who are also standing around and watching, and many of these guys are very high shots during the gold rush, although most of them are now as clean as a jaybird, and maybe cleaner. One of these guys is a guy by the name of Brandy Bottle Bates, who is known from coast to coast as a high player when he has anything to play with, and who is called Brandy Bottle Bates because it seems that years ago he is a great hand for belting a brandy bottle around.

This Brandy Bottle Bates is a big, black-looking guy, with a large beezer, and a head shaped like a pear, and he is considered a very immoral and wicked character, but he is a pretty slick gambler, and a fast man with a dollar when he is in the money.

Well, finally The Sky asks Brandy Bottle why he is not playing and Brandy laughs, and states as follows:

"Why," he says, "in the first place I have no potatoes, and in the second place I doubt if it will do me much good if I do have any potatoes the way I am going the past year. Why," Brandy Bottle says, "I cannot win a bet to save my soul."

Now this crack seems to give The Sky an idea, as he stands looking at Brandy Bottle very strangely, and while he is looking, Big Nig, the crap shooter, picks up the dice and hits three times hand-running, bing, bing, bing. Then Big Nig comes out on a six and Brandy Bottle Bates speaks as follows:

"You see how my luck is," he says. "Here is Big Nig hotter than a stove, and here I am without a bob to follow him with, especially," Brandy says, "when he is looking for nothing but a six. Why," he says, "Nig can make sixes all night when he is hot. If he does not make this six, the way he is, I will be willing to turn square and quit gambling forever."

"Well, Brandy," The Sky says, "I will make you a proposition. I will lay you a G note Big Nig does not get his six. I will lay you a G note against nothing but your soul," he says. "I mean if Big Nig does not get his six, you are to turn square and join Miss Sarah Brown's mission for six months."

"Bet!" Brandy Bottle Bates says right away, meaning the proposition is on, although the chances are he does not quite understand the proposition. All Brandy understands is The Sky wishes to wager that Big Nig does not make his six, and Brandy Bottle Bates will be willing to bet his soul a couple of times over on Big Nig making his six, and figure he is getting the best of it, at that, as Brandy has great confidence in Nig.

Well, sure enough, Big Nig makes the six, so The Sky weeds Brandy Bottle Bates a G note, although everybody around is saying The Sky makes a terrible over-lay of the natural price in giving Brandy Bottle a G against his soul. Furthermore, everybody around figures the chances are The Sky only wishes to give Brandy an opportunity to get in action, and nobody figures The Sky is on the level about trying to win Brandy Bottle Bates's soul, especially as The Sky does not seem to wish to go any further after paying the bet.

He only stands there looking on and seeming somewhat depressed as Brandy Bottle goes into action on his own account with the G note, fading other guys around the table with cash money. But Brandy Bottle Bates seems to figure what is in The Sky's mind pretty well, because Brandy Bottle is a crafty old guy.

It finally comes his turn to handle the dice, and he hits a couple of times, and then he comes out on a four, and anybody will tell you that a four is a very tough point to make, even with a lead pencil. Then Brandy Bottle turns to The Sky and speaks to him as follows:

"Well, Sky," he says, "I will take the odds off you on this one. I know you do not want my dough," he says. "I know you only want my soul for Miss Sarah Brown, and," he says, "without wishing to be fresh about it, I know why you want it for her. I am young once myself," Brandy Bottle says. "And you know if I lose to you, I will be over there in Forty-eighth Street in an hour pounding on the door, for Brandy always settles.

"But, Sky," he says, "now I am in the money, and my price goes up. Will you lay me ten G's against my soul I do not make this four?"

"Bet!" The Sky says, and right away Brandy Bottle hits with a four.

Well, when word goes around that The Sky is up at Nathan Detroit's crap game trying to win Brandy Bottle Bates's soul for Miss Sarah Brown, the excitement is practically intense. Somebody telephones Mindy's, where a large number of citizens are sitting around arguing about this and that, and telling one another how much they

will bet in support of their arguments, if only they have something
to bet, and Mindy himself is almost killed in the rush for the door.

One of the first guys out of Mindy's and up to the crap game is
Regret, the horse player, and as he comes in Brandy Bottle is looking
for a nine, and The Sky is laying him twelve G's against his soul that
he does not make this nine, for it seems Brandy Bottle's soul keeps
getting more and more expensive.

Well, Regret wishes to bet his soul against a G that Brandy Bottle
get his nine, and is greatly insulted when The Sky cannot figure his
price any better than a double saw, but finally Regret accepts this
price, and Brandy Bottle hits again.

Now many other citizens request a little action from The Sky,
and if there is one thing The Sky cannot deny a citizen it is action,
so he says he will lay them according to how he figures their word
to join Miss Sarah Brown's mission if Brandy Bottle misses out, but
about this time The Sky finds he has no more potatoes on him, being
now around thirty-five G's loser, and he wishes to give markers.

But Brandy Bottle says that while ordinarily he will be pleased
to extend The Sky this accommodation, he does not care to accept
markers against his soul, so then The Sky has to leave the joint and
go over to his hotel two or three blocks away, and get the night clerk
to open his damper so The Sky can get the rest of his bank roll. In
the meantime the crap game continues at Nathan Detroit's among
the small operators, while the other citizens stand around and say
that while they hear of many a daffy proposition in their time, this
is the daffiest that ever comes to their attention, although Big Nig
claims he hears of a daffier one, but cannot think what it is.

Big Nig claims that all gamblers are daffy anyway, and in fact
he says if they are not daffy they will not be gamblers, and while he
is arguing this matter back comes The Sky with fresh scratch, and
Brandy Bottle Bates takes up where he leaves off, although Brandy
says he is accepting the worst of it, as the dice have a chance to
cool off.

Now the upshot of the whole business is that Brandy Bottle hits
thirteen licks in a row, and the last lick he makes is on a ten, and it
is for twenty G's against his soul, with about a dozen other citizens
getting anywhere from one to five C's against their souls, and complaining bitterly of the price.

And as Brandy Bottle makes his ten, I happen to look at The

Sky and I see him watching Brandy with a very peculiar expression on his face, and furthermore I see The Sky's right hand creeping inside his coat where I know he always packs a Betsy in a shoulder holster, so I can see something is wrong somewhere.

But before I can figure out what it is, there is quite a fuss at the door, and loud talking, and a doll's voice, and all of a sudden in bobs nobody else but Miss Sarah Brown. It is plain to be seen that she is all steamed up about something.

She marches right up to the crap table where Brandy Bottle Bates and The Sky and the other citizens are standing, and one and all are feeling sorry for Dobber, the doorman, thinking of what Nathan Detroit is bound to say to him for letting her in. The dice are still lying on the table showing Brandy Bottle Bates's last throw, which cleans The Sky and gives many citizens the first means they enjoy in several months.

Well, Miss Sarah Brown looks at The Sky, and The Sky looks at Miss Sarah Brown, and Miss Sarah Brown looks at the citizens around and about, and one and all are somewhat dumbfounded, and nobody seems to be able to think of much to say, although The Sky finally speaks up as follows:

"Good evening," The Sky says. "It is a nice evening," he says. "I am trying to win a few souls for you around here, but," he says, "I seem to be about half out of luck."

"Well," Miss Sarah Brown says, looking at The Sky most severely out of her hundred-percent eyes, "you are taking too much upon yourself. I can win any souls I need myself. You better be thinking of your own soul. By the way," she says, "are you risking your own soul, or just your money?"

Well, of course up to this time The Sky is not risking anything but his potatoes, so he only shakes his head to Miss Sarah Brown's question, and looks somewhat disorganized.

"I know something about gambling," Miss Sarah Brown says, "especially about crap games. I ought to," she says. "It ruins my poor papa and my brother Joe. If you wish to gamble for souls, Mister Sky, gamble for your own soul."

Now Miss Sarah Brown opens a small black leather pocketbook she is carrying in one hand, and pulls out a two-dollar bill, and it is such a two-dollar bill as seems to have seen much service in its time, and holding up this deuce, Miss Sarah Brown speaks as follows:

"I will gamble with you, Mister Sky," she says. "I will gamble with you," she says, "on the same terms you gamble with these parties here. This two dollars against your soul, Mister Sky. It is all I have, but," she says, "it is more than your soul is worth."

Well, of course anybody can see that Miss Sarah Brown is doing this because she is very angry, and wishes to make The Sky look small, but right away The Sky's duke comes from inside his coat, and he picks up the dice and hands them to her and speaks as follows:

"Roll them," The Sky says, and Miss Sarah Brown snatches the dice out of his hand and gives them a quick sling on the table in such a way that anybody can see she is not a professional crap shooter, and not even an amateur crap shooter, for all amateur crap shooters first breathe on the dice, and rattle them good, and make remarks to them, such as "Come on, baby!"

In fact, there is some criticism of Miss Sarah Brown afterwards on account of her haste, as many citizens are eager to string with her to hit, while others are just as anxious to bet she misses, and she does not give them a chance to get down.

Well, Scranton Slim is the stick guy, and he takes a gander at the dice as they hit up against the side of the table and bounce back, and then Slim hollers, "Winner, winner, winner," as stick guys love to do, and what is showing on the dice as big as life, but a six and a five, which makes eleven, no matter how you figure, so The Sky's soul belongs to Miss Sarah Brown.

She turns at once and pushes through the citizens around the table without even waiting to pick up the deuce she lays down when she grabs the dice. Afterwards a most obnoxious character by the name of Red Nose Regan tries to claim the deuce as a sleeper and gets the heave-o from Nathan Detroit, who becomes very indignant about this, stating that Red Nose is trying to give his joint a wrong rap.

Naturally, The Sky follows Miss Brown, and Dobber, the doorman, tells me that as they are waiting for him to unlock the door and let them out, Miss Sarah Brown turns on The Sky and speaks to him as follows:

"You are a fool," Miss Sarah Brown says.

Well, at this Dobber figures The Sky is bound to let one go, as this seems to be most insulting language, but instead of letting one go, The Sky only smiles at Miss Sarah Brown and says to her like this:

"Why," The Sky says, "Paul says 'If any man among you seemeth to be wise in this world, let him become a fool, that he may be wise.' I love you, Miss Sarah Brown," The Sky says.

Well, now, Dobber has a pretty fair sort of memory, and he says that Miss Sarah Brown tells The Sky that since he seems to know so much about the Bible, maybe he remembers the second verse of the Song of Solomon, but the chances are Dobber muffs the number of the verse, because I look the matter up in one of these Gideon Bibles, and the verse seems a little too much for Miss Sarah Brown, although of course you never can tell.

Anyway, this is about all there is to the story, except that Brandy Bottle Bates slides out during the confusion so quietly even Dobber scarcely remembers letting him out, and he takes most of The Sky's potatoes with him, but he soon gets batted in against the faro bank out in Chicago, and the last anybody hears of him he gets religion all over again, and is preaching out in San Jose, so The Sky always claims he beats Brandy for his soul, at that.

I see The Sky the other night at Forty-ninth Street and Broadway, and he is with quite a raft of mission workers, including Mrs. Sky, for it seems that the soul-saving business picks up wonderfully, and The Sky is giving a big bass drum such a first-class whacking that the scat band in the chop-suey joint can scarcely be heard. Furthermore, The Sky is hollering between whacks, and I never see a guy look happier, especially when Mrs. Sky smiles at him out of her hundred-percent eyes. But I do not linger long, because The Sky gets a gander at me, and right away he begins hollering:

"I see before me a sinner of the deepest dye," he hollers. "Oh, sinner, repent before it is too late. Join with us, sinner," he hollers, "and let us save your soul."

Naturally, this crack about me being a sinner embarrasses me no little, as it is by no means true, and it is a good thing for The Sky there is no copper in me, or I will go to Mrs. Sky, who is always bragging about how she wins The Sky's soul by outplaying him at his own game, and tell her the truth.

And the truth is that the dice with which she wins The Sky's soul, and which are the same dice with which Brandy Bottle Bates wins all his potatoes, are strictly phony, and that she gets into Nathan Detroit's just in time to keep The Sky from killing old Brandy Bottle.

DELEGATES AT LARGE

When it comes on summer, and the nights get nice and warm, I love to sit on the steps in front of the bank at Forty-eighth Street and Seventh Avenue, where a guy can keep himself cool. Many other citizens are fond of sitting on the bank steps with me, and usually we sit with our coats off, speaking of this and that.

Sometimes you can see very prominent citizens sitting with me on the bank steps, including such as Regret, the horse player, and old Sorrowful, the bookie, and Doc Daro and Professor D. and Johnny Oakley and The Greek, and often strangers in the city, seeing us sitting there and looking so cool, stop and take off their coats and sit down with us, although personally if I am a stranger in the city I will be a little careful who I sit down with no matter how hot I am.

Well, one night I am sitting on the bank steps with Big Nig, the crap shooter, and a guy by the name of Skyrocket, who is nobody much, when all of a sudden I notice three guys standing on the sidewalk taking a very good long gander at me, and who are these guys but certain characters from Brooklyn by the name of Harry the Horse, and Spanish John and Little Isadore, and they are very hard characters indeed.

In fact, these characters are so hard that I am glad that none of the depositors of the bank can see them standing there, as such a scene is just naturally bound to make any depositor nervous. In fact, it makes me more nervous than somewhat, and I am by no means a depositor. But of course I do not let on to Harry the Horse and

Spanish John and Little Isadore that I am nervous, because they may get the idea that I am nervous about them and take offense.

Well finally I say hello to them, and they all say hello right back, and I can see that they are not inclined to take offense at me, but then they start looking at Big Nig and Skyrocket in such a way that I can see they are taking offense at Big Nig's face and at Skyrocket's too, and personally I do not blame them, at that, as these are faces such as may give offense to anybody.

Furthermore, Big Nig and Skyrocket can see that these Brooklyn characters are taking offense at their faces and in practically no time Big Nig and Skyrocket are walking briskly up Forty-eighth Street.

Then Harry the Horse and Spanish John and Little Isadore take off their coats and sit there with me quite a while, with nobody saying much of anything, and I am wondering what these characters are doing in this neighborhood, because they know they are by no means welcome along Broadway or anywhere else in town for that matter, when finally Harry the Horse speaks as follows:

"Well," Harry says, "we are going out West tomorrow. Yes," he says, "we are going away out to Chicago, but," he says, "do not ask us to call on anybody in Chicago for you, as we will be very busy while we are there."

Now it happens I do not know anybody in Chicago for them to call on, and if I do know anybody there I will just as soon think of sending them a bottle of prussic acid as to ask Harry the Horse and Spanish John and Little Isadore to call on them, but naturally I do not mention such an idea out loud. And although I am dying to know why they are going to Chicago, of course I do not ask them, as such a question is bound to be regarded as inquisitive by these characters.

So I only say I hope and trust that they will have a very pleasant journey to Chicago and that they will return safe and sound, although I am secretly hoping they never return at all, because if there are any citizens this town can spare it is Harry the Horse and Spanish John and Little Isadore, and especially Harry the Horse.

In fact, the chances are that Brooklyn, where Harry resides, will be glad to pay him a bonus to move away from there, because he is always carrying on in such a way as to give Brooklyn a bad name, while Spanish John and Little Isadore are no boost to the borough, either. But Spanish John and Little Isadore only do what Harry tells

them, and what Harry tells them is generally something that causes
somebody plenty of bother.

There is no doubt that Harry the Horse has a wild streak in him
and he is very mischievous, and is always putting Spanish John and
Little Isadore up to such tricks as robbing their fellow citizens of
Brooklyn and maybe taking shots at them, and sometimes Harry the
Horse personally takes a shot or two himself. Naturally, this practice
is most distasteful to the citizens of Brooklyn, who are very fond of
peace and quiet.

Well, anyway, Harry the Horse and Spanish John and Little
Isadore sit on the bank steps with me quite a while. Finally however,
they get up and put on their coats and shake hands with me and say
they hope to see me when they get back from Chicago, and then they
go away, and I do not hear of them again for several weeks.

Now one hot night I am again sitting on the steps with a number of
prominent citizens, when who comes along but Little Isadore, and
he motions me to follow him up the street. It is the first time I ever
see Little Isadore without either Harry the Horse or Spanish John
and when I join him, naturally I ask him about the others, and Little
Isadore speaks to me as follows:

"Harry is in a hospital in Chicago," Little Isadore says. "Spanish
John is out there waiting for him to get well. I come back home,"
Little Isadore says, "to raise some scratch to pay Harry's hospital
fees.

"He is all bunged up. It comes of mixing in politics with a doll,"
he says. "Maybe you will like to hear the story."

Naturally I say I will be greatly pleased to hear it, so we walk
around to Mindy's restaurant, and Little Isadore orders up a sirloin
steak smothered in onions, and while he is eating this steak he begins
to talk.

Well (Little Isadore says), we go to Chicago all right the day after
we last see you, and we go to Chicago by special invitation of some

very prominent parties out there. I will mention no names, but these parties are very prominent indeed, especially in beer, and they invite us out there to take care of a guy by the name of Donkey O'Neill, as it seems this Donkey O'Neill is also in beer in opposition to the prominent parties I speak of.

Naturally, these parties will not tolerate opposition, and there is nothing for them to do but to see that Donkey O'Neill is taken care of. But of course they do not wish him to be taken care of by local talent, as this is a very old-fashioned way of transacting such matters, and nowadays when anybody is to be taken care of in any town it is customary to invite outsiders in, as they are not apt to leave any familiar traces such as local talent is bound to do.

So the prominent parties in Chicago get in touch with Angie the Ox, in Brooklyn, and Angie speaks so highly of Harry the Horse and Spanish John and me that we get the invitation, which anybody will tell you is a great honor. Furthermore, six G's and all expenses go with the invitation, and this is by no means alfalfa.

We go to Chicago by the Twentieth Century train, and it is a nice trip generally, except that while we are in the club car playing pinocle Harry the Horse gets to looking at a doll with more interest than somewhat. Now, it is by no means like Harry the Horse to look at a doll. In fact, in all the years I am associated with Harry the Horse, socially and in business, he never before looks at a doll more than once, or maybe twice, because he claims that all dolls are more or less daffy.

But I will say that the doll in the club car is worth looking at, and anybody can see that she has plenty of class, although personally I like them with legs that are not quite so spindly. She is by no means a real young doll, being maybe twenty-five or twenty-six, and anybody can see that she knows what time it is.

Furthermore, she is very stylish, and even if Harry the Horse is a guy who gives dolls a tumble this is about the last doll you will figure him to tumble, because she looks as if she may be such a doll as will holler for the gendarmes if anybody as much as says boo to her.

But Harry the Horse does not seem to be able to keep his eyes off her, and by and by he quits our pinochle game and takes a chair next to her and lets on he is reading a magazine. The next thing anybody knows, Harry is talking to the doll very friendly, which is a most astonishing sight to Spanish John and me, although Harry can talk first rate when he feels like it, and furthermore he is by no means as bad looking as the photos of him the cops send around make him out.

Well, the conversation between Harry the Horse and the doll is also most astonishing to Spanish John and me, because we hear her say to him like this:

"Yes," she says, "I am going to Chicago. I am going to attend the convention," she says. "I am a member of the New York Delegation. Some great questions are to be decided in Chicago," she says. "I love politics, and I think it will be a good thing if all women take an interest in politics. Do you not think so?"

Well, Harry the Horse may not be the smartest guy in the country, but he is smart enough to say yes every now and then to the doll, because if a guy keeps yessing a doll long enough, she is bound to figure him a bright guy, and worth looking into.

By and by the doll mentions that her name is Miss Maribel Marlo and that she lives on Park Avenue in the winter and at Southampton in the summer, so it does not take a mind-reader to figure that she must have plenty of potatoes.

Finally she takes to asking Harry the Horse questions, and as Harry is about as good an off-hand liar as there is in the United States, his answers are very satisfactory indeed, although personally I figure he is stretching it a little bit when he tells her that we are also going to the convention in Chicago.

Well, Miss Maribel Marlo seems pleased to learn this news from Harry the Horse, and she says to him as follows: "Of course you are delegates?" she says.

"Yes," Harry says, "such is indeed the case."

"Why," Miss Maribel Marlo says, "we will all be in the convention together. How nice!" she says. "What district are you from?"

Well, naturally Harry does not wish to speak of Brooklyn, because it is never a good policy for a guy to mention his address when he is away from home, so he says we are from no district in particular, which does not sound to me like the right answer, but it seems to suit Miss Maribel Marlo.

"Oh," she says, "I understand. You are delegates at large."

Well, I am glad Harry the Horse lets it go at this and turns the conversation back to Miss Maribel Marlo, and anybody can see that Miss Maribel Marlo is such a doll as does not mind having the conversation about herself, although it makes me very nervous when I hear Harry the Horse speak to her as follows: "Lady," Harry says, "does anybody tell you how beautiful you are?"

Naturally, I expect to see Harry the Horse given plenty of wind at once for this crack, but it seems it proves interesting to Miss Maribel Marlo, and she is still listening to Harry when Spanish John and me go to bed.

Afterwards I learn Miss Maribel Marlo listens to Harry the Horse until midnight, which is most surprising because Harry is a guy whose grammar is by no means perfect, but it seems that no doll minds a guy's grammar as long as he is speaking well of her. And Harry the Horse tells me that he does not fail to give Miss Maribel Marlo plenty the best of it in all his remarks. Furthermore, Harry says, she is deserving of everything he says, which shows that Harry is impressed by Miss Maribel Marlo more than somewhat.

The next morning when our train pulls into Chicago we see her on the platform, but she is so surrounded by other dolls, and also by several guys who wear swell clothes and little mustaches, that she does not see us, and Harry the Horse is very thoughtful all the rest of the day.

Well, Chicago is a very large and busy city, with many citizens walking around and about, and among these citizens are many parties wearing large badges, and it seems that these parties are from different parts of the country and are delegates to the national convention that is going on in Chicago at this time.

Furthermore, it seems that this convention is a political proposition, and the idea is to nominate a candidate for President, and also a candidate for Vice-President, if they can get anybody to take it. It is this convention that Miss Maribel Marlo is talking about on the train.

But of course Harry the Horse and Spanish John and me have no interest in a matter of this kind, because our business is to look up these prominent parties who invite us to Chicago, and find out just what is what. But Harry the Horse does not seem anxious to get down to business at once, and is wandering around looking as if he is slug-nutty, and I hear he goes over to the Blackstone on Michigan Boulevard where Miss Maribel Marlo is stopping, to see if he can get a peek at her.

Naturally, I am somewhat disgusted with Harry the Horse, and so is Spanish John to think that he becomes interested in a doll when we have important business to attend to, so I am very glad when a representative of the prominent parties who invite us to Chicago calls on us at our hotel to explain just what our hosts expect of us. This representative is a guy by the name of Snooksy, and he is very apologetic because he says it looks as if we may be delayed in town a few days.

"This Donkey O'Neill has plenty of political strength," Snooksy says. "In fact," he says, "he is a delegate to the big convention, and," he says, "we figure it may not be a good idea to take care of him when he is in such a prominent spot. It may cause gossip," Snooksy says. "The idea is to wait until after the convention, and in the meantime I will entertain you gentlemen the best I know how."

Well, this seems fair enough, and the news cheers up Harry the Horse, as he figures the delay will give him more chance to see Miss Maribel Marlo, although he admits to me that he cannot get near her at the Blackstone, what with her having so many friends around.

I ask Harry the Horse why he does not walk right in and send his name up to her, but it seems he cannot remember the name he gives her on the train, and anyway, he does not wish her to find out that it is all the phonus bolonus about us being delegates to the convention.

Harry says there is no doubt in his mind that he must be in love with Miss Maribel Marlo, and he will not listen to my idea that maybe it is the change in climate that does not agree with him.

Well, I wish to say that this Snooksy is a splendid entertainer in every respect, and he takes us around and about the city of Chicago, and wherever we go he introduces us to many prominent characters, although I noticed that Snooksy never introduces us by the same names twice, and before the evening is over I am from four different cities, including San Francisco, Dallas, Texas, Shreveport, Louisiana, and Oskaloosa, Iowa.

But nobody ever asks any questions, as it seems the citizens of Chicago are very polite in this respect, so we all enjoy ourselves thoroughly, especially Spanish John, who claims the beer in Chicago is almost as good as the kind Angie the Ox sells in Brooklyn.

Well, for a couple of days and nights we are entertained by Snooksy, and even Harry the Horse cheers up, and I commence to think he forgets Miss Maribel Marlo, until early one A.M. we are in a joint where there is plenty of beer and other entertainment, including blondes, when a bunch of guys wearing badges happen in.

Anybody can see from the badges that these guys are delegates such as are walking around and about all over town, and, furthermore, that some of them are delegates from New Jersey, which is a spot well known to Harry the Horse and Spanish John and me, although one guy seems to be from Massachusetts and another from Texas. But they are all full of fun and beer, and one thing and another, and they take a table next to us, and the first thing anybody knows we are very neighborly together.

Well, by and by I notice Harry the Horse examining the badge one of the New Jersey guys is wearing, and I also hear Harry asking questions about it, and it seems from what the guy says that anybody wearing such a badge and carrying a certain card can walk in and out of the convention, and no questions asked. Then I hear Harry the Horse speak to the guy as follows:

"Well," Harry says, "I am never in a convention in my life. I only wish I have such a badge," he says, "so I can see how a convention works."

"Why," the guy says, speaking out loud so the others hear him, "this is a terrible state of affairs. Here is a guy who is never in a convention," he says. "Why," he says, "you will have my seat at the morning session while I will be catching up on some sleep, although," the guy says, "the chances are you will find it all very tiresome."

With this the guy unpins the badge on his chest and pins it on Harry the Horse, and furthermore he takes a card out of his pocket and gives it to Harry, and then he calls for more beer, while the other boys commence asking Snooksy and Spanish John and me if we will care to see the convention, too.

Personally, I do not care a whoop about seeing any convention, but the guys are so cordial about the matter that I do not have the heart to say no, so pretty soon there I am wearing a New Jersey badge, while Spanish John has a Massachusetts badge and Snooksy the badge belonging to the guy from Texas.

Also, we have cards saying we are delegates, and are full of instructions how to act and what to answer in case anybody starts asking questions. And now you know how it comes that Snooksy and Harry the Horse and Spanish John and me are sitting in the convention next day, although Spanish John and Snooksy are not doing much sitting, but are wandering around, and afterwards I hear there is some complaint from delegates about losing their leathers containing their return tickets and funds.

Now of course I never have any idea of going to the convention when the guys pin the badges on us, and I have no idea Harry the Horse will even think of such a thing, but nothing will do him but we must go, and he will not listen to my argument that the other delegates from New Jersey will see that we are strictly counterfeit. So there we are, and as it turns out there is great confusion in the convention when we get in, and nobody pays any attention to anybody else, which is a break for us.

In fact, Harry the Horse and me become quite pally with some of the guys around us, especially as Harry remembers before we start for the convention about a case of good beer that Snooksy sends us, and figuring we may need a refreshing dram while sitting in the convention, he slips several of these bottles into his pockets and wraps up several more, and this beer goes very nice indeed when Harry starts passing it about.

Personally I am greatly disappointed in the convention, because it is nothing but a lot of guys and dolls in a large hall, with signs stuck up here and there on sticks, with the names of different states on the signs. A guy up on a big platform is hammering on a table and yelling very loud, and everybody else seems to be yelling, and it strikes me as most undignified, especially as some of the guys start marching up and down the aisles carrying on quite some.

Several of the signs with the names of states on them are being lugged up and down the aisles, and every now and then a new sign bobs up in the procession, and then the racket gets worse than ever. I am about to mention to Harry the Horse that we will be better off in some more quiet spot when I notice him looking toward a sign that says New York on it, and who is sitting in a chair alongside this sign but Miss Maribel Marlo, looking very beautiful indeed.

Well, I know enough to know that this sign means that the New York delegates are somewhere around close, and I am wondering if any of my friends from my old hometown are present among them, because by this time I am getting more homesick than somewhat.

Then all of a sudden some of the New York bunch joins the marchers, and a tall, skinny guy reaches for the New York sign with the idea of carrying it on the march.

At this, Miss Maribel Marlo stands up on her chair and grabs hold of the sign, and the skinny guy starts to pull and haul with her, trying to get the sign away from her. Personally, I will not give you two cents for a roomful of such signs, but afterward somebody explains to me that the marching up and down the aisles, and the hollering, is a demonstration in favor of some proposition before the convention, such as a candidate, or something else, and in this case it turns out to be something else.

It seems that a state sign in such a procession means that the delegates from this state like the proposition, but it also seems that sometimes the delegates from a state are all split up, and some are by no means in favor of the proposition, and they do not like to see their sign lugged around and about, as it gives a wrong impression.

Well, it all sounds like a lot of foolishness to me and most unbecoming of grown guys and dolls, but there the skinny guy is, tugging one way at the New York sign, and there Miss Maribel Marlo is, tugging the other way and showing a strength that is most surprising. In fact, she is even money in my book to outtug the skinny guy, when Harry the Horse arrives on the spot and lets go with a neat left hook which connects with the skinny guy's chin.

He drops to the floor all spraddled out, leaving Miss Maribel Marlo still standing on the chair with the sign, and anybody can see that she is greatly pleased with Harry the Horse's hook, as she gives him a large smile and speaks as follows:

"Oh," she says, "thank you so much! I am glad to see you are on our side."

Well, just then a short chunky guy makes a reach for the sign, and Harry the Horse lets go another hook, but this one lands on the guy's noggin and only staggers him. Now the marching seems to stop, and one and all commence surging toward Harry the Horse.

Nearly everybody present, including many dolls, seems to be trying to get a pop at Harry, and he is letting punches fly right and left, and doing very well with them indeed. In fact, he has quite a number of guys down when a guy who seems to be about seven feet high and very thick through the chest, comes pushing his way through the crowd.

The big guy is wearing an Illinois badge, and as he pushes through the crowd he speaks as follows: "Let me attend to this matter," he says. Then when he finally gets close enough to Harry, he hauls off and hits the back of Harry's neck and knocks him into the chair on which Miss Maribel Marlo is standing. Personally I consider the blow a rabbit punch, which is very illegal, but anybody can see that the big guy is such a guy as is not apt to pay any attention to the rules.

The chair on which Miss Maribel Marlo is standing goes down as Harry the Horse hits it, and Miss Maribel Marlo goes with it, still holding on to the sign, and as she gets down she lets out a loud scream. She is up at once, however, and she does not seem to be hurt, but she is very indignant, because she realizes the public must see what kind of underwear she has on when she goes down.

She is holding the sign in both hands as she arises, and at the same time Harry the Horse also comes up, but very weak and staggering, and it is nothing but instinct that causes Harry to reach for his hip pocket, because generally Harry has the old equalizer in his pocket.

But when we arrive in town one of the first things Snooksy tells us is that we must not go around rodded up except when he tells us, as it seems that being rodded up is against the law in Chicago, especially for strangers, so instead of the old equalizer what does Harry find in his hip pocket but a bottle of good beer.

And when Harry finds this bottle of good beer in his hip pocket, he also remembers about another bottle of good beer in the side pocket of his coat, so he outs with both these bottles of good beer, holding one in each hand by the nozzle, and starts waving them around to get a good windup on them before dropping them on some nearby noggins.

Well, personally I always consider this action most unfortunate, as it seems the bottles of good beer give Miss Maribel Marlo a wrong impression of Harry the Horse, especially as one of the bottles suddenly pops open with a bang, what with the good beer getting all churned up from the waving around, and the foam flies every which way, some of it flying over Miss Maribel Marlo, who speaks to Harry the Horse as follows:

"Oh," she says, "so you are one of the enemy, too, are you?"

And with this, Miss Maribel Marlo hauls off and whacks Harry over the noggin with the New York sign, busting the sign staff in two pieces, and knocking Harry out into the aisle, where the big guy with the Illinois badge walks across Harry's chest, with Colorado, Indiana, New Mexico, California and Georgia following him one after the other.

Personally, I consider Miss Maribel Marlo's action very unladylike, especially as it causes a great waste of good beer, but when I visit Harry the Horse in hospital the next day he does not seem as mad at her as he is sorrowful, because Harry says he learns she makes a mistake, and he says anybody is apt to make a mistake.

But, Harry says, it ends all his ideas of romance because he can see that such mistakes are bad for a guy's health, especially as this one mistake gives him five broken ribs, a broken collarbone, a cauliflower ear and internal injuries. Harry says his future will be devoted entirely to getting even with the big guy with the Illinois badge, although, he says, he will not take this matter up until after we dispose of the business for which we are invited to Chicago.

But Snooksy, who is present at this discussion, does not seem to think there will be any business for us. In fact, Snooksy states that our hosts are disappointed in the outcome of our visit.

"You see," Snooksy says, "the big guy who assaults Harry is nobody but Donkey O'Neill himself, in person, and," Snooksy says, "the chances are, if he ever sees Harry again he will break his legs as well as his ribs. So," Snooksy says, "my people think the best thing you can do is to go home as soon as you are able, although," he says, "they are greatly obliged to you, at that."

Now (Little Isadore says) you know the story of our trip to Chicago, and what happens out there.

"But," I says to Little Isadore, "what is this convention of which you speak, a Republican or a Democratic convention?"

"Well," Little Isadore says, "I never think to ask, and anyway, this is not worrying me one way or the other. What is worrying me," he says, "and what is also worrying Harry the Horse and Spanish John, is that Angie the Ox may hear the false rumor that is being circulated in Chicago that we try to break up a demonstration in the convention, in favor of beer because of Harry the Horse's love for Miss Maribel Marlo. You see," Little Isadore says, "it seems that Miss Maribel Marlo is one of the most notorious Drys in this country."

A PIECE OF PIE

O n Boylston Street, in the city of Boston, Mass., there is a joint where you can get as nice a broiled lobster as anybody ever slaps a lip over, and who is in there one evening partaking of this tidbit but a character by the name of Horse Thief and me.

This Horse Thief is called Horsey for short, and he is not called by this name because he ever steals a horse but because it is the consensus of public opinion from coast to coast that he may steal one if the opportunity presents.

Personally, I consider Horsey a very fine character, because any time he is holding anything he is willing to share his good fortune with one and all, and at this time in Boston he is holding plenty. It is the time we make the race meeting at Suffolk Down, and Horsey gets to going very good, indeed, and in fact he is now a character of means, and is my host against the broiled lobster.

Well, at a table next to us are four or five characters who all seem to be well-dressed, and stout-set, and red-faced, and prosperous-looking, and who all speak with the true Boston accent, which consists of many ah's and very few r's. Characters such as these are familiar to anybody who is ever in Boston very much, and they are bound to be politicians, retired cops, or contractors, because Boston is really quite infested with characters of this nature.

I am paying no attention to them, because they are drinking local ale, and talking loud, and long ago I learn that when a Boston

40

character is engaged in aleing himself up, it is a good idea to let him alone, because the best you can get out of him is maybe a boff on the beezer. But Horsey is in there on the old Ear-ie, and very much interested in their conversation, and finally I listen myself just to hear what is attracting his attention, when one of the characters speaks as follows:

"Well," he says, "I am willing to bet ten thousand dollars that he can outeat anybody in the United States any time."

Now at this, Horsey gets right up and steps over to the table and bows and smiles in a friendly way on one and all, and says:

"Gentlemen," he says, "pardon the intrusion, and excuse me for billing in, but," he says, "do I understand you are speaking of a great eater who resides in your fair city?"

Well, these Boston characters all gaze at Horsey in such a hostile manner that I am expecting any one of them to get up and request him to let them miss him, but he keeps on bowing and smiling, and they can see that he is a gentleman, and finally one of them says:

"Yes," he says, "we are speaking of a character by the name of Joel Duffle. He is without doubt the greatest eater alive. He just wins a unique wager. He bets a character from Bangor, Me., that he can eat a whole window display of oysters in this very restaurant, and he not only eats all the oysters but he then wishes to wager that he can also eat the shells, but," he says, "it seems that the character from Bangor, Me., unfortunately taps out on the first proposition and has nothing with which to bet on the second."

"Very interesting," Horsey says. "Very interesting, if true, but," he says, "unless my ears deceive me, I hear one of you state that he is willing to wager ten thousand dollars on this eater of yours against anybody in the United States."

"Your ears are perfect," another of the Boston characters says. "I state it, although," he says, "I admit it is a sort of figure of speech. But I state it all right," he says, "and never let it be said that a Conway ever pigs it on a betting proposition."

"Well," Horsey says, "I do not have a tenner on me at the moment, but," he says, "I have here a thousand dollars to put up as a forfeit that I can produce a character who will outeat your party for ten thousand, and as much more as you care to put up."

And with this, Horsey outs with a bundle of coarse notes and tosses it on the table, and right away one of the Boston characters, whose name turns out to be Carroll, slaps his hand on the money and says:

"Bet."

Well, now this is prompt action to be sure, and if there is one thing I admire more than anything else, it is action, and I can see that these are characters of true sporting instincts and I commence wondering where I can raise a few dibs to take a piece of Horsey's proposition, because of course I know that he has nobody in mind to do the eating for his side but Nicely-Nicely Jones.

And knowing Nicely-Nicely Jones, I am prepared to wager all the money I can possibly raise that he can outeat anything that walks on two legs. In fact, I will take a chance on Nicely-Nicely against anything on four legs, except maybe an elephant, and at that he may give the elephant a photo finish.

I do not say that Nicely-Nicely is the greatest eater in all history, but what I do say is he belongs up there as a contender. In fact, Professor D, who is a professor in a college out West before he turns to playing the horses for a livelihood, and who makes a study of history in his time, says he will not be surprised but what Nicely-Nicely figures one-two.

Professor D says we must always remember that Nicely-Nicely eats under the handicaps of modern civilization, which require that an eater use a knife and fork, or anyway a knife, while in the old days eating with the hands was a popular custom and much faster. Professor D says he has no doubt that under the old rules Nicely-Nicely will hang up a record that will endure through the ages, but of course maybe Professor D overlays Nicely-Nicely somewhat.

Well, now that the match is agreed upon, naturally Horsey and the Boston characters begin discussing where it is to take place, and one of the Boston characters suggests a neutral ground, such as New London, Conn., or Providence, R.I., but Horsey holds out for New York, and it seems that Boston characters are always ready to visit New York, so he does not meet with any great opposition on this point.

They all agree on a date four weeks later so as to give the principals plenty of time to get ready, although Horsey and I know that this is really unnecessary as far as Nicely-Nicely is concerned, because one thing about him is he is always in condition to eat.

This Nicely-Nicely Jones is a character who is maybe five feet eight inches tall, and about five feet nine inches wide, and when he is in good shape he will weigh upward of two hundred and eighty-three pounds. He is a horse player by trade, and eating is really just a hobby, but he is undoubtedly a wonderful eater even when he is not hungry.

Well, as soon as Horsey and I return to New York, we hasten to Mindy's restaurant on Broadway and relate the bet Horsey makes in Boston, and right away so many citizens, including Mindy himself, wish to take a piece of the proposition that it is oversubscribed by a large sum in no time.

Then Mindy remarks that he does not see Nicely-Nicely Jones for a month of Sundays, and then everybody present remembers that they do not see Nicely-Nicely around lately, either, and this leads to a discussion of where Nicely-Nicely can be, although up to this moment if nobody sees Nicely-Nicely but once in the next ten years it will be considered sufficient.

Well, Willie the Worrier, who is a bookmaker by trade, is among those present, and he remembers that the last time he looks for Nicely-Nicely hoping to collect a marker of some years' standing, Nicely-Nicely is living at the Rest Hotel in West Forty-ninth Street, and nothing will do Horsey but I must go with him over to the Rest to make inquiry for Nicely-Nicely, and there we learn that he leaves a forwarding address away up on Morningside Heights in care of somebody by the name of Slocum.

So Horsey calls a short, and away we go to this address, which turns out to be a five-story walk-up apartment, and a card downstairs shows that Slocum lives on the top floor. It takes Horsey and me ten minutes to walk up the five flights as we are by no means accustomed to exercise of this nature, and when we finally reach a door marked Slocum, we are plumb tuckered out, and have to sit down on the top step and rest a while.

Then I ring the bell at this door marked Slocum, and who appears but a tall young Judy with black hair who is without doubt beautiful, but who is so skinny we have to look twice to see her, and when I ask her if she can give me any information about a party named Nicely-Nicely Jones, she says to me like this:

"I guess you mean Quentin," she says. "Yes," she says, "Quentin is here. Come in, gentlemen."

So we step into an apartment, and as we do so a thin, sickly looking character gets up out of a chair by the window, and in a weak voice says good evening. It is a good evening, at that, so Horsey and I say good evening right back at him, very polite, and then we stand there waiting for Nicely-Nicely to appear, when the beautiful skinny young Judy says:

"Well," she says, "this is Mr. Quentin Jones."

Then Horsey and I take another swivel at the thin character, and we can see that it is nobody but Nicely-Nicely, at that, but the way he changes since we last observe him is practically shocking to us both, because he is undoubtedly all shrunk up. In fact, he looks as if he is about half what he is in his prime, and his face is pale and thin, and his eyes are away back in his head, and while we both shake hands with him it is some time before either of us is able to speak. Then Horsey finally says:

"Nicely," he says, "can we have a few words with you in private on a very important proposition?"

Well, at this, and before Nicely-Nicely can answer aye, yes or no, the beautiful skinny young Judy goes out of the room and slams a door behind her, and Nicely-Nicely says:

"My fiancée, Miss Hilda Slocum," he says. "She is a wonderful character. We are to be married as soon as I lose twenty pounds more. It will take a couple of weeks longer," he says.

"My goodness gracious, Nicely," Horsey says. "What do you mean lose twenty pounds more? You are practically emaciated now. Are you just out of a sickbed, or what?"

"Why," Nicely-Nicely says, "certainly I am not out of a sickbed. I am never healthier in my life. I am on a diet. I lose eighty-three pounds in two months, and am now down to two hundred. I feel great," he says. "It is all because of my fiancée, Miss Hilda Slocum. She rescues me from gluttony and obesity, or anyway," Nicely-Nicely says, "this is what Miss Hilda Slocum calls it. My, I feel good. I love Miss Hilda Slocum very much," Nicely-Nicely says. "It is a case of love at first sight on both sides the day we meet in the subway. I am wedged in one of the turnstile gates, and she kindly pushes on me from behind until I wiggle through. I can see she has a kind heart, so I date her up for a movie that night and propose to her while the newsreel is on. But," Nicely-Nicely says, "Hilda tells me at once that she will never marry a fat slob. She says I must put myself in her hands and she will reduce me by scientific methods and then she will become my ever-loving wife, but not before.

"So," Nicely-Nicely says, "I come to live here with Miss Hilda Slocum and her mother, so she can supervise my diet. Her mother is thinner than Hilda. And I surely feel great," Nicely-Nicely says. "Look," he says.

And with this, he pulls out the waistband of his pants, and shows enough spare space to hide War Admiral in, but the effort seems to be a strain on him, and he has to sit down in his chair again.

"My goodness gracious," Horsey says. "What do you eat, Nicely?"

"Well," Nicely-Nicely says, "I eat anything that does not contain starch, but," he says, "of course everything worth eating contains starch, so I really do not eat much of anything whatever. My fiancée, Miss Hilda Slocum, arranges my diet. She is an expert dietician and runs a widely known department in a diet magazine by the name of *Let's Keep House.*"

Then Horsey tells Nicely-Nicely of how he is matched to eat against this Joel Duffle, of Boston, for a nice side bet, and how he has a forfeit of a thousand dollars already posted for appearance, and how many of Nicely-Nicely's admirers along Broadway are looking to win themselves out of all their troubles by betting on him, and at first Nicely-Nicely listens with great interest, and his eyes are shining like six bits, but then he becomes very sad, and says:

"It is no use, gentlemen," he says. "My fiancée, Miss Hilda Slocum, will never hear of me going off my diet even for a little while. Only yesterday I try to talk her into letting me have a little pumpernickel instead of toasted whole wheat bread, and she says if I even think of such a thing again, she will break our engagement. Horsey," he says, "do you ever eat toasted whole wheat bread for a month hand running? Toasted?" he says.

"No," Horsey says. "What I eat is nice, white French bread, and corn muffins, and hot biscuits with gravy on them."

"Stop," Nicely-Nicely says. "You are eating yourself into an early grave, and, furthermore," he says, "you are breaking my heart. But," he says, "the more I think of my following depending on me in this emergency, the sadder it makes me feel to think I am unable to oblige them. However," he says, "let us call Miss Hilda Slocum in on an outside chance and see what her reactions to your proposition are."

So we call Miss Hilda Slocum in, and Horsey explains our predicament in putting so much faith in Nicely-Nicely only to find him dieting, and Miss Hilda Slocum's reactions are to order Horsey and me out of the joint with instructions never to darken her door again, and when we are a block away we can still hear her voice speaking very firmly to Nicely-Nicely.

Well, personally, I figure this ends the matter, for I can see that Miss Hilda Slocum is a most determined character, indeed, and the chances are it does end it, at that, if Horsey does not happen to get a wonderful break.

He is at Belmont Park one afternoon, and he has a real good thing in a jump race, and when a brisk young character in a hard straw hat and eyeglasses comes along and asks him what he likes, Horsey mentions this good thing, figuring he will move himself in for a few dibs if the good thing connects.

Well, it connects all right, and the brisk young character is very grateful to Horsey for his information, and is giving him plenty of much-obliges, and nothing else, and Horsey is about to mention that they do not accept much-obliges at his hotel, when the brisk young character mentions that he is nobody but Mr. McBurgle and that he is the editor of the *Let's Keep House* magazine, and for Horsey to drop in and see him any time he is around his way.

Naturally, Horsey remembers what Nicely-Nicely says about Miss Hilda Slocum working for this *Let's Keep House* magazine, and he relates the story of the eating contest to Mr. McBurgle and asks him if he will kindly use his influence with Miss Hilda Slocum to get her to release Nicely-Nicely from his diet long enough for the contest. Then Horsey gives Mr. McBurgle a tip on another winner, and Mr. McBurgle must use plenty of influence on Miss Hilda Slocum at once, as the next day she calls Horsey up at his hotel before he is out of bed, and speaks to him as follows:

"Of course," Miss Hilda Slocum says, "I will never change my attitude about Quentin, but," she says, "I can appreciate that he feels very bad about you gentlemen relying on him and having to disappoint you. He feels that he lets you down, which is by no means true, but it weighs upon his mind. It is interfering with his diet.

"Now," Miss Hilda Slocum says, "I do not approve of your contest, because," she says, "it is placing a premium on gluttony, but I have a friend by the name of Miss Violette Shumberger who may answer your purpose. She is my dearest friend from childhood, but it is only because I love her dearly that this friendship endures. She is extremely fond of eating," Miss Hilda Slocum says. "In spite of my pleadings, and my warnings, and my own example, she persists in food. It is disgusting to me but I finally learn that it is no use arguing with her.

"She remains my dearest friend," Miss Hilda Slocum says, "though she continues her practice of eating, and I am informed that she is phenomenal in this respect. In fact," she says, "Nicely-Nicely tells me to say to you that if Miss Violette Shumberger can perform the eating exploits I relate to him from hearsay she is a lily. Good-bye," Miss Hilda Slocum says. "You cannot have Nicely-Nicely."

Well, nobody cares much about this idea of a stand-in for Nicely-Nicely in such a situation, and especially a Judy that no one ever hears of before, and many citizens are in favor of pulling out of the contest altogether. But Horsey has his thousand-dollar forfeit to think of, and as no one can suggest anyone else, he finally arranges a personal meet with the Judy suggested by Miss Hilda Slocum.

He comes into Mindy's one evening with a female character who is so fat it is necessary to push three tables together to give her room for her lap, and it seems that this character is Miss Violette Shumberger. She weighs maybe two hundred and fifty pounds, but she is by no means an old Judy, and by no means bad-looking. She has a face the size of a town clock and enough chins for a fire escape, but she has a nice smile and pretty teeth, and a laugh that is so hearty it knocks the whipped cream off an order of strawberry shortcake on a table fifty feet away and arouses the indignation of a customer by the name of Goldstein who is about to consume same.

Well, Horsey's idea in bringing her into Mindy's is to get some kind of line on her eating form, and she is clocked by many experts when she starts putting on the hot meat, and it is agreed by one and all that she is by no means a selling-plater. In fact, by the time she gets through, even Mindy admits she has plenty of class, and the upshot of it all is Miss Violette Shumberger is chosen to eat against Joel Duffle.

Maybe you hear something of this great eating contest that comes off in New York one night in the early summer of 1937. Of course eating contests are by no means anything new, and in fact they are quite an old-fashioned pastime in some sections of this country, such as the South and East, but this is the first big public contest of the kind in years, and it creates no little comment along Broadway.

In fact, there is some mention of it in the blats, and it is not a frivolous proposition in any respect, and more dough is wagered on it than any other eating contest in history, with Joel Duffle a 6 to 5 favorite over Miss Violette Shumberger all the way through.

This Joel Duffle comes to New York several days before the contest with the character by the name of Conway, and requests a meet with Miss Violette Shumberger to agree on the final details and who shows up with Miss Violette Shumberger as her coach and adviser but Nicely-Nicely Jones. He is even thinner and more peaked-looking than when Horsey and I see him last, but he says he feels great, and that he is within six pounds of his marriage to Miss Hilda Slocum.

Well, it seems that his presence is really due to Miss Hilda Slocum herself, because she says that after getting her dearest friend Miss Violette Shumberger into this jackpot, it is only fair to do all she can to help her win it, and the only way she can think of is to let Nicely-Nicely give Violette the benefit of his experience and advice.

But afterward we learn that what really happens is that this editor, Mr. McBurgle, gets greatly interested in the contest, and when he discovers that in spite of his influence, Miss Hilda Slocum declines to permit Nicely-Nicely to personally compete, but puts in a pinch eater, he is quite indignant and insists on her letting Nicely-Nicely school Violette.

Furthermore we afterward learn that when Nicely-Nicely returns to the apartment on Morningside Heights after giving Violette a lesson, Miss Hilda Slocum always smells his breath to see if he indulges in any food during his absence.

Well, this Joel Duffle is a tall character with stooped shoulders, and a sad expression, and he does not look as if he can eat his way out of a tea shop, but as soon as he commences to discuss the details of the contest, anybody can see that he knows what time it is in situations such as this. In fact, Nicely-Nicely says he can tell at once from the way Joel Duffle talks that he is a dangerous opponent, and he says while Miss Violette Shumberger impresses him as an improving eater, he is only sorry she does not have more seasoning.

This Joel Duffle suggests that the contest consist of twelve courses of strictly American food, each side to be allowed to pick six dishes, doing the picking in rotation, and specifying the weight and quantity of the course selected to any amount the contestant making the pick desires, and each course is to be divided for eating exactly in half, and after Miss Violette Shumberger and Nicely-Nicely whisper together awhile, they say the terms are quite satisfactory.

Then Horsey tosses a coin for the first pick, and Joel Duffle says heads, and it is heads, and he chooses, as the first course, two quarts of ripe olives, twelve bunches of celery, and four pounds of shelled nuts, all this to be split fifty-fifty between them. Miss Violette Shumberger names twelve dozen cherry-stone clams as the second course, and Joel Duffle says two gallons of Philadelphia pepper-pot soup as the third.

Well, Miss Violette Shumberger and Nicely-Nicely whisper together again, and Violette puts in two five-pound striped bass, the heads and tails not to count in the eating, and Joel Duffle names a twenty-two-pound roast turkey. Each vegetable is rated as one course, and Miss Violette Shumberger asks for twelve pounds of mashed potatoes with brown gravy. Joel Duffle says two dozen ears of corn on the cob, and Violette replies with two quarts of lima beans. Joel Duffle calls for twelve bunches of asparagus cooked in butter, and Violette mentions ten pounds of stewed new peas.

This gets them down to the salad, and it is Joel Duffle's play, so he says six pounds of mixed green salad with vinegar and oil dressing, and now Miss Violette Shumberger has the final selection, which is the dessert. She says it is a pumpkin pie, two feet across, and not less than three inches deep.

It is agreed that they must eat with knife, fork or spoon, but speed is not to count, and there is to be no time limit, except they cannot pause more than two consecutive minutes at any stage, except in case of hiccoughs. They can drink anything, and as much as they please, but liquids are not to count in the scoring. The decision is to be strictly on the amount of food consumed, and the judges are to take account of anything left on the plates after a course, but not of loose chewings on bosom or vest up to an ounce. The losing side is to pay for the food, and in case of a tie they are to eat it off immediately on ham and eggs only.

Well, the scene of this contest is the second-floor dining room of Mindy's restaurant, which is closed to the general public for the occasion, and only parties immediately concerned in the contest are admitted. The contestants are seated on either side of a big table in the center of the room, and each contestant has three waiters.

No talking and no rooting from the spectators is permitted, but of course in any eating contest the principals may speak to each other if they wish, though smart eaters never wish to do this, as talking only wastes energy, and about all they ever say to each other is please pass the mustard.

About fifty characters from Boston are present to witness the contest, and the same number of citizens of New York are admitted, and among them is this editor, Mr. McBurgle, and he is around asking Horsey if he thinks Miss Violette Shumberger is as good a thing as the jumper at the race track.

Nicely-Nicely arrives on the scene quite early, and his appearance is really most distressing to his old friends and admirers, as by this time he is shy so much weight that he is a pitiful scene, to be sure, but he tells Horsey and me that he thinks Miss Violette Shumberger has a good chance.

"Of course," he says, "she is green. She does not know how to pace herself in competition. But," he says, "she has a wonderful style. I love to watch her eat. She likes the same things I do in the days when I am eating. She is a wonderful character, too. Do you ever notice her smile?" Nicely-Nicely says.

"But," he says, "she is the dearest friend of my fiancée, Miss Hilda Slocum, so let us not speak of this. I try to get Hilda to come to see the contest, but she says it is repulsive. Well, anyway," Nicely-Nicely says, "I manage to borrow a few dibs, and am wagering on Miss Violette Shumberger. By the way," he says, "if you happen to think of it, notice her smile."

Well, Nicely-Nicely takes a chair about ten feet behind Miss Violette Shumberger, which is as close as the judges will allow him, and he is warned by them that no coaching from the corners will be permitted, but of course Nicely-Nicely knows this rule as well as they do, and furthermore by this time his exertions seem to have left him without any more energy.

There are three judges, and they are all from neutral territory. One of these judges is a party from Baltimore, Md., by the name of Packard, who runs a restaurant, and another is a party from Providence, R.I., by the name of Croppers, who is a sausage manufacturer. The third judge is an old Judy by the name of Mrs. Rhubarb, who comes from Philadelphia, and once keeps an actors' boarding-house, and is considered an excellent judge of eaters.

Well, Mindy is the official starter, and at 8:30 P.M. sharp, when there is still much betting among the spectators, he outs with his watch, and says like this:

"Are you ready, Boston? Are you ready, New York?"

Miss Violette Shumberger and Joel Duffle both nod their heads, and Mindy says commence, and the contest is on, with Joel Duffle getting the jump at once on the celery and olives and nuts.

It is apparent that this Joel Duffle is one of these rough-and-tumble eaters that you can hear quite a distance off, especially on clams and soups. He is also an eyebrow eater, an eater whose eyebrows go up as high as the part in his hair as he eats, and this type of eater is undoubtedly very efficient.

In fact, the way Joel Duffle goes through the groceries down to the turkey causes the Broadway spectators some uneasiness, and they are whispering to each other that they only wish the old Nicely-Nicely is in there. But personally, I like the way Miss Violette Shumberger eats without undue excitement, and with great zest. She cannot keep close to Joel Duffle in the matter of speed in the early stages of the contest, as she seems to enjoy chewing her food, but I observe that as it goes along she pulls up on him, and I figure this is not because she is stepping up her pace, but because he is slowing down.

When the turkey finally comes on, and is split in two halves right down the middle, Miss Violette Shumberger looks greatly disappointed, and she speaks for the first time as follows:

"Why," she says, "where is the stuffing?"

Well, it seems that nobody mentions any stuffing for the turkey to the chef, so he does not make any stuffing, and Miss Violette Shumberger's disappointment is so plain to be seen that the confidence of the Boston characters is somewhat shaken. They can see that a Judy who can pack away as much fodder as Miss Violette Shumberger has to date, and then beef for stuffing, is really quite an eater.

In fact, Joel Duffle looks quite startled when he observes Miss Violette Shumberger's disappointment, and he gazes at her with great respect as she disposes of her share of the turkey, and the mashed potatoes, and one thing and another in such a manner that she moves up on the pumpkin pie on dead even terms with him. In fact, there is little to choose between them at this point, although the judge from

Baltimore is calling the attention of the other judges to a turkey leg that he claims Miss Violette Shumberger does not clean as neatly as Joel Duffle does his, but the other judges dismiss this as a technicality.

Then the waiters bring on the pumpkin pie, and it is without doubt quite a large pie, and in fact it is about the size of a manhole cover, and I can see that Joel Duffle is observing this pie with a strange expression on his face, although to tell the truth I do not care for the expression on Miss Violette Shumberger's face, either.

Well, the pie is cut in two dead center, and one half is placed before Miss Violette Shumberger and the other half before Joel Duffle, and he does not take more than two bites before I see him loosen his waistband and take a big swig of water, and thinks I to myself, he is now down to a slow walk, and the pie will decide the whole heat, and I am only wishing I am able to wager a little more dough on Miss Violette Shumberger. But about this moment, and before she as much as touches her pie, all of a sudden Violette turns her head and motions to Nicely-Nicely to approach her, and as he approaches, she whispers in his ear.

Now at this, the Boston character by the name of Conway jumps up and claims a foul and several other Boston characters join him in this claim, and so does Joel Duffle, although afterwards even the Boston characters admit that Joel Duffle is no gentleman to make such a claim against a lady.

Well, there is some confusion over this, and the judges hold a conference, and they rule that there is certainly no foul in the actual eating that they can see, because Miss Violette Shumberger does not touch her pie so far.

But they say that whether it is a foul otherwise all depends on whether Miss Violette Shumberger is requesting advice on the contest from Nicely-Nicely and the judge from Providence, R.I., wishes to know if Nicely-Nicely will kindly relate what passes between him and Violette so they may make a decision.

"Why," Nicely-Nicely says, "all she asks me is can I get her another piece of pie when she finishes the one in front of her."

Now at this, Joel Duffle throws down his knife, and pushes back his plate with all but two bites of his pie left on it, and says to the Boston characters like this:

"Gentlemen," he says, "I am licked. I cannot eat another mouthful. You must admit I put up a game battle, but," he says, "it is useless for me to go on against this Judy who is asking for more pie before she even starts on what is before her. I am almost dying as it is, and I do not wish to destroy myself in a hopeless effort. Gentlemen," he says, "she is not human."

Well, of course this amounts to throwing in the old napkin and Nicely-Nicely stands up on his chair, and says:

"Three cheers for Miss Violette Shumberger!"

Then Nicely-Nicely gives the first cheer in person, but the effort overtaxes his strength, and he falls off the chair in a faint just as Joel Duffle collapses under the table, and the doctors at the Clinic Hospital are greatly baffled to receive, from the same address at the same time, one patient who is suffering from undernourishment, and another patient who is unconscious from overeating.

Well, in the meantime, after the excitement subsides, and wagers are settled, we take Miss Violette Shumberger to the main floor in Mindy's for a midnight snack, and when she speaks of her wonderful triumph, she is disposed to give much credit to Nicely-Nicely Jones.

"You see," Violette says, "what I really whisper to him is that I am a goner. I whisper to him that I cannot possibly take one bite of the pie if my life depends on it, and if he has any bets down to try and hedge them off as quickly as possible.

"I fear," she says, "that Nicely-Nicely will be greatly disappointed in my showing, but I have a confession to make to him when he gets out of the hospital. I forget about the contest," Violette says, "and eat my regular dinner of pig's knuckles and sauerkraut an hour before the contest starts and," she says, "I have no doubt this tends to affect my form somewhat. So," she says, "I owe everything to Nicely-Nicely's quick thinking."

It is several weeks after the great eating contest that I run into Miss Hilda Slocum on Broadway and it seems to me that she looks much better nourished than the last time I see her, and when I mention this she says:

"Yes," she says, "I cease dieting. I learn my lesson," she says. "I learn that male characters do not appreciate anybody who tries to ward off surplus tissue. What male characters wish is substance. Why," she says, "only a week ago my editor, Mr. McBurgle, tells me he will love to take me dancing if only I get something on me for him to take hold of. I am very fond of dancing," she says.

"But," I say, "what of Nicely-Nicely Jones? I do not see him around lately."

"Why," Miss Hilda Slocum says, "do you not hear what this cad does? Why, as soon as he is strong enough to leave the hospital, he elopes with my dearest friend, Miss Violette Shumberger, leaving me a note saying something about two souls with but a single thought. They are down in Florida running a barbecue stand, and," she says, "the chances are, eating like seven mules."

"Miss Slocum," I say, "can I interest you in a portion of Mindy's chicken fricassee?"

"With dumplings?" Miss Hilda Slocum says. "Yes," she says, "you can. Afterwards I have a date to go dancing with Mr. McBurgle. I am crazy about dancing," she says.

LONELY
HEART

I t seems that one spring day, a character by the name of Nicely-Nicely Jones arrives in a ward in a hospital in the City of Newark, N.J., with such a severe case of pneumonia that the attending physician, who is a horse player at heart, and very absentminded, writes 100, 40 and 10 on the chart over Nicely-Nicely's bed.

It comes out afterward that what the physician means is that it is 100 to 1 in his line that Nicely-Nicely does not recover at all, 40 to 1 that he will not last a week, and 10 to 1 that if he does get well he will never be the same again.

Well, Nicely-Nicely is greatly discouraged when he sees this price against him, because he is personally a chalk eater when it comes to price, a chalk eater being a character who always plays the short-priced favorites, and he can see that such a long shot as he is has very little chance to win. In fact, he is so discouraged that he does not even feel like taking a little of the price against him to show.

Afterward there is some criticism of Nicely-Nicely among the citizens around Mindy's restaurant on Broadway, because he does not advise them of this marker, as these citizens are always willing to bet that what Nicely-Nicely dies of will be overfeeding and never anything small like pneumonia, for Nicely-Nicely is known far and wide as a character who dearly loves to commit eating.

But Nicely-Nicely is so discouraged that he does not as much as send them word that he is sick, let alone anything about the price. He just pulls the covers up over his head and lies there waiting for the finish and thinking to himself what a tough thing it is to pass away of pneumonia, and especially in Newark, N.J., and nobody along Broadway knows of his predicament until Nicely-Nicely appears in person some months later and relates this story to me.

So now I will tell you about Nicely-Nicely Jones, who is called Nicely-Nicely because any time anybody asks him how he is feeling, or how things are going with him, he always says nicely, nicely, in a very pleasant tone of voice, although generally this is by no means the gospel truth, especially about how he is going.

He is a character of maybe forty-odd, and he is short, and fat, and very good-natured, and what he does for a livelihood is the best he can, which is an occupation that is greatly overcrowded at all times along Broadway.

Mostly, Nicely-Nicely follows the races, playing them whenever he has anything to play them with, but anyway following them, and the reason he finds himself in Newark, N.J., in the first place is because of a business proposition in connection with the races. He hears of a barber in Newark, N.J., who likes to make a wager on a sure thing now and then, and Nicely-Nicely goes over there to tell him about a sure thing that is coming up at Pimlico the very next Tuesday.

Nicely-Nicely figures that the barber will make a wager on this sure thing and cut him in on the profits, but it seems that somebody else gets to the barber the week before with a sure thing that is coming up a Monday, and the barber bets on this sure thing, and the sure thing blows, and now the barber will have to shave half of Newark, N.J., to catch even.

Nicely-Nicely always claims that the frost he meets when he approaches the barber with his sure thing gives him a cold that results in the pneumonia I am speaking of, and furthermore that his nervous system is so disorganized by the barber chasing him nine blocks with a razor in his hand that he has no vitality left to resist the germs.

But at that it seems that he has enough vitality left to beat the pneumonia by so far the attending physician is somewhat embarrassed, although afterward he claims that he makes a mistake in chalking up the 100, 40 and 10 on Nicely-Nicely's chart. The attending physician claims he really means the character in the bed next to Nicely-Nicely, who passes away of lockjaw the second day after Nicely-Nicely arrives.

Well, while he is convalescing in the hospital of this pneumonia, Nicely-Nicely has a chance to do plenty of thinking, and what he thinks about most is the uselessness of the life he leads all these years, and how he has nothing to show for same except some high-class knowledge of race horses, which at this time is practically a drug on the market.

There are many other patients in the same ward with Nicely-Nicely, and he sees their ever-loving wives, and daughters, and maybe their sweet-peas visiting them, and hears their cheerful chatter, and he gets to thinking that here he is without chick or child, and no home to go to, and it just about breaks his heart.

He gets to thinking of how he will relish a soft, gentle, loving hand on his brow at this time, and finally he makes a pass at one of the nurses, figuring she may comfort his lonely hours, but what she lays on his brow is a beautiful straight right cross, and furthermore she hollers watch, murder, police, and Nicely-Nicely has to pretend he has a relapse and is in a delirium to avoid being mistreated by the interns.

As Nicely-Nicely begins getting some of his strength back, he takes to thinking, too, of such matters as food, and when Nicely-Nicely thinks of food it is generally very nourishing food, such as a nice double sirloin, smothered with chops, and thinking of these matters, and of hamburgers, and wiener schnitzel and goulash with noodles, and lamb stew, adds to his depression, especially when they bring him the light diet provided for invalids by the hospital.

He takes to reading to keep himself from thinking of his favorite dishes, and of his solitary life, and one day in a bundle of old magazines and newspapers that they give him to read, he comes upon a bladder that is called the *Matrimonial Tribune*, which seems to be all about marriage, and in this *Matrimonial Tribune* Nicely-Nicely observes an advertisement that reads as follows:

LONELY HEART

Widow of middle age, no children, cheerful companion, neat, excellent cook, owner of nice farm in Central New Jersey, wishes to meet home-loving gentleman of not more than fifty who need not necessarily be possessed of means but who will appreciate warm, tender companionship and pleasant home. Object, matrimony. Address Lonely Heart, this paper.

Well, Nicely-Nicely feels romance stirring in his bosom as he reads these lines, because he is never married, and has no idea that marriage is as described in this advertisement. So what does he do but write a letter to Lonely Heart in care of the *Matrimonial Tribune* stating that he is looking for a warm, tender companionship, and a pleasant home, and an excellent cook, especially an excellent cook, all his life, and the next thing he knows he is gazing into what at first seems to be an old-fashioned round cheese, but which he finally makes out as the face of a large Judy seated at his bedside.

She is anywhere between forty and fifty-five years of age, and she is as big and rawboned as a first baseman, but she is by no means a crow. In fact, she is rather nice-looking, except that she has a pair of eyes as pale as hens' eggs, and these eyes never change expression.

She asks Nicely-Nicely as many questions as an assistant district attorney, and especially if he has any money, and does he have any relatives, and Nicely-Nicely is able to state truthfully that he is all out of both, although she does not seem to mind. She wishes to know about his personal habits, and Nicely-Nicely says they are all good, but of course he does not mention his habit of tapping out any time a 4-to-5 shot comes along, which is as bad a habit as anybody can have, and finally she says she is well satisfied with him and will be pleased to marry him when he is able to walk.

She has a short, sharp voice that reminds Nicely-Nicely of a tough starter talking to the jockeys at the post, and she never seems to smile, and, take her all around, the chances are she is not such a character as Nicely-Nicely will choose as his ever-loving wife if he has the pick of a herd, but he figures that she is not bad for an offhand draw.

So Nicely-Nicely and the Widow Crumb are married, and they go to live on her farm in Central New Jersey, and it is a very nice little farm, to be sure, if you care for farms, but it is ten miles from the nearest town, and in a very lonesome country, and furthermore there are no neighbors handy, and the Widow Crumb does not have a telephone or even a radio in her house.

In fact, about all she has on this farm are a couple of cows, and a horse, and a very old joskin with a chin whisker and rheumatism and a mean look, whose name seems to be Harley something, and who also seems to be the Widow Crumb's hired hand. Nicely-Nicely can see at once that Harley has no use for him, but afterward he learns that Harley has no use for anybody much, not even himself.

Well, it comes on suppertime the first night. Nicely-Nicely is there and he is delighted to observe that the Widow Crumb is making quite an uproar in the kitchen with the pots and pans, and this uproar is music to Nicely-Nicely's ears as by now he is in the mood to put on the hot meat very good, and he is wondering if the Widow Crumb is as excellent a cook as she lets on in her advertisement.

It turns out that she is even better. It turns out that she is as fine a cook as ever straddles a skillet, and the supper she spreads for Nicely-Nicely is too good for a king. There is round steak hammered flat and fried in a pan, with thick cream gravy, and hot biscuits, and corn on the cob, and turnip greens, and cottage-fried potatoes, and lettuce with hot bacon grease poured over it, and apple-pie, and coffee, and I do not know what all else, and Nicely-Nicely almost founders himself, because it is the first time since he leaves the hospital that he gets a chance to move into real food.

Harley, the old joskin, eats with them, and Nicely-Nicely notices that there is a fourth place set at the table, and he figures that maybe another hired hand is going to show up, but nobody appears to fill the vacant chair, and at first Nicely-Nicely is glad of it, as it gives him more room in which to eat.

But then Nicely-Nicely notices that the Widow Crumb loads the plate at the vacant place with even more food than she does any of the others, and all through the meal Nicely-Nicely keeps expecting someone to come in and knock off these victuals. Nobody ever appears, however, and when they are through eating, the Widow Crumb clears up the extra place the same as the others, and scrapes the food off the plate into a garbage pail.

Well, of course, Nicely-Nicely is somewhat perplexed by this proceeding, but he does not ask any questions, because where he comes from only suckers go around asking questions. The next morning at breakfast, and again at dinner, and in fact at every meal put on the table the extra place is fixed, and the Widow Crumb goes through the same performance of serving the food to this place, and afterward throwing it away, and while Nicely-Nicely commences thinking it is a great waste of excellent food, he keeps his trap closed.

Now being the Widow Crumb's husband is by no means a bad dodge, as she is anything but a gabby Judy, and will go all day long without saying more than a few words, and as Nicely-Nicely is a character who likes to chat this gives him a chance to do all the talking, although she never seems to be listening to him much. She seldom asks him to do any work, except now and then to help the old joskin around the barn, so Nicely-Nicely commences to figure this is about as soft a drop-in as anybody can wish.

The only drawback is that sometimes the Widow Crumb likes to sit on Nicely-Nicely's lap of an evening, and as he does not have much lap to begin with, and it is getting less every day under her feeding, this is quite a handicap, but he can see that it comes of her affectionate nature, and he bears up the best he can.

One evening after they are married several months, the Widow Crumb is sitting on what is left of Nicely-Nicely's lap, and she puts her arms around his neck, and speaks to him as follows:

"Nicely," she says, "do you love me?"

"Love you?" Nicely-Nicely says. "Why, I love you like anything. Maybe more. You are a wonderful cook. How can I help loving you?" he says.

"Well," the Widow Crumb says, "do you ever stop to consider that if anything happens to you, I will be left here lone and lorn, because you do not have any means with which to provide for me after you are gone?"

"What do you mean after I am gone?" Nicely-Nicely says. "I am not going anywhere."

"Life is always a very uncertain proposition," the Widow Crumb says. "Who can say when something is apt to happen to you and take you away from me, leaving me without a cent of life insurance?"

Naturally, Nicely-Nicely has to admit to himself that what she says is very true, and of course he never gives the matter a thought before, because he figures from the way the Widow Crumb feeds him that she must have some scratch of her own stashed away somewhere, although this is the first time the subject of money is ever mentioned between them since they are married.

"Why," Nicely-Nicely says, "you are quite right, and I will get my life insured as soon as I get enough strength to go out and raise a few dibs. Yes, indeed," Nicely-Nicely says, "I will take care of this situation promptly."

Well, the Widow Crumb says there is no sense in waiting on a matter as important as this, and that she will provide the money for the payment of the premiums herself, and for Nicely-Nicely to forget about going out to raise anything, as she cannot bear to have him out of her sight for any length of time, and then she gets to telling Nicely-Nicely what she is going to give him for breakfast, and he forgets about the insurance business.

But the next thing Nicely-Nicely knows, a thin character with a nose like a herring comes out from town, and there is another character with him who has whiskers that smell of corn whiskey, but who seems to be a doctor, and in practically no time at all Nicely-Nicely's life is insured for five thousand dollars, with double indemnity if he gets used up by accident, and Nicely-Nicely is greatly pleased by this arrangement because he sees that he is now worth something for the first time in his career, although everybody on Broadway claims it is a terrible overlay by the insurance company when they hear the story.

Well, several months more go by, and Nicely-Nicely finds life on the farm very pleasant and peaceful as there is nothing much for him to do but eat and sleep, and he often finds himself wondering how he ever endures his old life, following the races and associating with the low characters of the turf.

He gets along first class with the Widow Crumb and never has a cross word with her, and he even makes friends with the old joskin, Harley, by helping him with his work, although Nicely-Nicely is really not fitted by nature for much work, and what he likes best at the farm is the eating and sleeping, especially the eating.

For a while he finds it difficult to get as much sleep as he requires, because the Widow Crumb is a great hand for staying up late reading books in their bedroom by kerosene lamp, and at the same time eating molasses candy which she personally manufactures, and sometimes she does both in bed, and the molasses candy bothers Nicely-Nicely no little until he becomes accustomed to it.

Once he tries reading one of her books to put himself to sleep after she dozes off ahead of him, but he discovers that it is all about nothing but spiritualism, and about parties in this life getting in touch with characters in the next world, and Nicely-Nicely has no interest whatever in matters of this nature, although he personally knows a character by the name of Spooks McGurk who claims to be a spiritualist, and who makes a nice thing of it in connection with tips on the races, until a race-track fuzz catches up with him.

Nicely-Nicely never discusses the books with the Widow Crumb, because in the first place he figures it is none of his business, and in the second place, the more she reads the better chance he has of getting to sleep before she starts snoring, because it seems that as a snorer the Widow Crumb is really all-America material, although of course Nicely-Nicely is too much of a gentleman to make an issue of this.

She gives him three meals every day, and every meal is better than the last, and finally Nicely-Nicely is as fat as a goose, and can scarcely wobble. But he notices that the Widow Crumb never once fails to set the fourth place that nobody ever fills, and furthermore he suddenly commences to notice that she always puts the best cuts of meat, and the best of everything else on the plate at this place, even though she throws it all away afterward.

Well, this situation preys on Nicely-Nicely's mind, as he cannot bear to see all this good fodder going to waste, so one morning he gets hold of old Harley and puts the siphon on him, because by this time Harley talks freely with Nicely-Nicely, although Nicely-Nicely can see that Harley is somewhat simple in spots and his conversation seldom makes much sense.

Anyway, he asks Harley what the Widow Crumb's idea is about the extra place at the table, and Harley says like this: "Why," he says, "the place is for Jake."

"Jake who?" Nicely-Nicely says.

"I do not recall his other name," Harley says. "He is her third or fourth husband, I do not remember which. Jake is the only one the Widow Crumb ever loves, although she does not discover this until after Jake departs. So," Harley says, "in memory of Jake she always sets his place at the table, and gives him the best she has. She misses Jake and wishes to feel that he is still with her."

"What happens to Jake?" Nicely-Nicely says.

"Arsenic," Harley says. "Jake departs ten years ago."

Well, of course all this is news to Nicely-Nicely, and he becomes very thoughtful to be sure, because in all the time he is married to her the Widow Crumb does not crack to him about her other husbands, and in fact Nicely-Nicely has no idea there is ever more than one.

"What happens to the others?" he says. "Do they depart the same as Jake?"

"Yes," Harley says, "they all depart. One by one. I remember

Number Two well. In fact, you remind me of him. Carbon monoxide," Harley says. "A charcoal stove in his room. It is most ingenious. The coroner says Number Three commits suicide by hanging himself with a rope in the barn loft. Number Three is small and weak, and it is no trouble whatever to handle him.

"Then comes Jake," Harley says, "unless Jake is Number Three and the hanging item is Number Four. I do not remember exactly. But the Widow Crumb never employs arsenic or other matters of this nature again. It is too slow. Jake lingers for hours. Besides," Harley says, "she realizes it may leave traces if anybody happens to get nosy.

"Jake is a fine-looking character," Harley says. "But a ne'er-dowell. He is a plumber from Salt Lake City, Utah, and has a hearty laugh. He is always telling funny stories. He is a great eater, even better than you, and he loves beans the way the Widow Crumb cooks them, with bacon and tomatoes. He suffers no little from the arsenic. He gets it in his beans. Number Five comes upon a black widow spider in his bed. He is no good. I mean Number Five."

Well, by this time, Nicely-Nicely is very thoughtful to be sure, because what Harley says is commencing to sound somewhat disquieting.

"Number Six steps on a plank in the doorway of the house that drops a two-hundred-pound keystone on his head," Harley says. "The Widow Crumb personally figures this out herself. She is very bright. It is like a figure-4 trap, and has to be very accurate. An inch one way or the other, and the stone misses Number Six. I remember he has a big wen on the back of his neck. He is a carpenter from Keokuk, Iowa," Harley says.

"Why," Nicely-Nicely says, "do you mean to say that the Widow Crumb purposely arranges to use up husbands in the manner you describe?"

"Oh, sure," Harley says. "Why do you suppose she marries them? It is a good living to her because of the insurance," he says, "although," he says, "to show you how bright she is, she does not insure Number Five for a dime, so people can never say she is making a business of the matter. He is a total loss to her, but it quiets talk. I am wondering," Harley says, "what she will think up for you."

Well, Nicely-Nicely now commences to wonder about this, too, and he hopes and trusts that whatever she thinks up it will not be a black widow spider, because if there is one thing Nicely-Nicely despises, it is insects. Furthermore, he does not approve of hanging, or of dropping weights on people.

After giving the matter much thought, he steps into the house and mentions to the Widow Crumb that he will like to pay a little visit to town, figuring that if he can get to town, she will never see him again for heel dust.

But he finds that the Widow Crumb is by no means in favor of the idea of him visiting the town. In fact, she says it will bring great sorrow to her if he absents himself from her side more than two minutes, and moreover, she points out that it is coming on winter, and that the roads are bad, and she cannot spare the horse for such a trip just now.

Well, Nicely-Nicely says he is a fair sort of walker and, in fact, he mentions that he once walks from Saratoga Springs to Albany to avoid a bookmaker who claims there is a slight difference between them, but the Widow Crumb says she will not hear of him trying to walk to town because it may develop varicose veins in his legs.

In fact, Nicely-Nicely can see that the subject of his leaving the farm is very distasteful to her in every respect, and the chances are he will feel quite flattered by her concern for him if he does not happen to go into the house again a little later this same afternoon, and find her cleaning a double-barreled shotgun.

She says she is thinking of going rabbit hunting, and wishes him to keep her company, saying it may take his mind off the idea of a visit to town; but she goes out of the room for a minute, and Nicely-Nicely picks up one of the shotgun shells she lays out on a table, and notices that it is loaded with buckshot.

So he tells her he guesses he will not go, as he is not feeling so good, and in fact he is not feeling so good, at that, because it seems that Nicely-Nicely is a rabbit hunter from infancy, and he never before hears of anyone hunting these creatures with buckshot. Then the Widow Crumb says all right, she will postpone her hunting until he feels better, but Nicely-Nicely cannot help noticing that she loads the shotgun and stands it in a corner where it is good and handy.

Well, Nicely-Nicely now sits down and gives this general situation some serious consideration, because he is now convinced that the Widow Crumb is unworthy of his companionship as a husband. In fact, Nicely-Nicely makes up his mind to take steps at his earliest convenience to sue her for divorce on the grounds of incompatibility, but in the meantime he has to think up a means of getting away from her, and while he is thinking of this phase of the problem, she calls him to supper.

It is now coming on dark, and she has the lamps lit and the table set when Nicely-Nicely goes into the dining room, and a fire is going in the base burner, and usually this is a pleasant and comforting scene to Nicely-Nicely, but tonight he does not seem to find it as attractive as usual.

As he sits down at the table he notices that Harley is not present at the moment, though his place at the table is laid, and as a rule Harley is Johnny-at-the-rat-hole when it comes time to scoff, and moreover he is a pretty good doer at that. The fourth place that nobody ever occupies is also laid as usual, and now that he knows who this place is for, Nicely-Nicely notes that it is more neatly laid than his own, and that none of the china at this place is chipped, and that the bread and butter, and the salt and pepper, and the vinegar cruet and the bottle of Worcestershire sauce are handier to it than to any other place, and naturally his feelings are deeply wounded.

Then the Widow Crumb comes out of the kitchen with two plates loaded with spareribs and sauerkraut, and she puts one plate in front of Nicely-Nicely, and the other at Jake's place, and she says to Nicely-Nicely like this:

"Nicely," she says, "Harley is working late down at the barn, and when you get through with your supper, you can go down and call him. But," she says, "go ahead and eat first."

Then she returns to the kitchen, which is right next to the dining room with a swinging door in between, and Nicely-Nicely now observes that the very choicest spareribs are on Jake's plate, and also the most kraut, and this is really more than Nicely-Nicely can bear, for if there is one thing he adores it is spareribs, so he gets to feeling very moody to be sure about this discrimination, and he turns to Jake's place, and in a very sarcastic tone of voice he speaks out loud as follows:

"Well," he says, "it is pretty soft for you, you big lob, living on the fat of the land around here."

Now of course what Nicely-Nicely is speaking is what he is thinking, and he does not realize that he is speaking out loud until the

Widow Crumb pops into the dining room carrying a bowl of salad, and looking all around and about.

"Nicely," she says, "do I hear you talking to someone?"

Well, at first Nicely-Nicely is about to deny it, but then he takes another look at the choice spareribs on Jake's plate, and he figures that he may as well let her know that he is on to her playing Jake for a favorite over him, and maybe cure her of it, for by this time Nicely-Nicely is so vexed about the spareribs that he almost forgets about leaving the farm, and is thinking of his future meals, so he says to the Widow Crumb like this:

"Why, sure," he says. "I am talking to Jake."

"Jake?" she says. "What Jake?"

And with this she starts looking all around and about again, and Nicely-Nicely can see that she is very pale, and that her hands are shaking so that she can scarcely hold the bowl of salad, and there is no doubt but what she is agitated no little, and quite some.

"What Jake?" the Widow Crumb says again.

Nicely-Nicely points to the empty chair, and says:

"Why, Jake here," he says. "You know Jake. Nice fellow, Jake."

Then Nicely-Nicely goes on talking to the empty chair as follows:

"I notice you are not eating much tonight, Jake," Nicely-Nicely says. "What is the matter, Jake? The food cannot disagree with you, because it is all picked out and cooked to suit you, Jake. The best is none too good for you around here, Jake," he says.

Then he lets on that he is listening to something Jake is saying in reply, and Nicely-Nicely says is that so, and I am surprised, and what do you think of that, and tut-tut, and my-my, just as if Jake is talking a blue streak to him, although, of course, Jake is by no means present.

Now Nicely-Nicely is really only being sarcastic in this conversation for the Widow Crumb's benefit, and naturally he does not figure that she will take it seriously, because he knows she can see Jake is not there, but Nicely-Nicely happens to look at her while he is talking, and he observes that she is still standing with the bowl of salad in her hands, and looking at the empty chair with a most unusual expression on her face, and in fact, it is such an unusual expression that it makes Nicely-Nicely feel somewhat uneasy, and he readies himself up to dodge the salad bowl at any minute.

He commences to remember the loaded shotgun in the corner,

and what Harley gives him to understand about the Widow Crumb's attitude towards Jake, and Nicely-Nicely is sorry he ever brings Jake's name up, but it seems that Nicely-Nicely now finds that he cannot stop talking to save his life with the Widow Crumb standing there with the unusual expression on her face, and then he remembers the books she reads in her bed at night, and he goes on as follows:

"Maybe the pains in your stomach are just indigestion, Jake," he says. "I have stomach trouble in my youth myself. You are suffering terribly, eh, Jake? Well, maybe a little of the old bicarb will help you, Jake. Oh," Nicely-Nicely says, "there he goes."

And with this he jumps up and runs to Jake's chair and lets on that he is helping a character up from the floor, and as he stoops over and pretends to be lifting this character, Nicely-Nicely grunts no little, as if the character is very heavy, and the grunts are really on the level with Nicely-Nicely as he is now full of spareribs, because he never really stops eating while he is talking, and stooping is not easy for him.

At these actions the Widow Crumb lets out a scream and drops the bowl of salad on the floor.

"I will help you to bed, Jake," he says. "Poor Jake. I know your stomach hurts, Jake. There now, Jake," he says, "take it easy. I know you are suffering horribly, but I will get something for you to ease the pain. Maybe it is the sauerkraut," Nicely-Nicely says.

Then when he seems to get Jake up on his legs, Nicely-Nicely pretends to be assisting him across the floor towards the bedroom and all the time he is talking in a comforting tone to Jake, although you must always remember that there really is no Jake.

Now, all of a sudden, Nicely-Nicely hears the Widow Crumb's voice, and it is nothing but a hoarse whisper that sounds very strange in the room, as she says like this:

"Yes," she says, "it is Jake. I see him. I see him as plain as day."

Well, at this Nicely-Nicely is personally somewhat startled, and he starts looking around and about himself, and it is a good thing for Jake that Nicely-Nicely is not really assisting Jake or Jake will find himself dropped on the floor, as the Widow Crumb says:

"Oh, Jake," she says, "I am so sorry. I am sorry for you in your suffering. I am sorry you ever leave me. I am sorry for everything. Please forgive me, Jake," she says. "I love you."

Then the Widow Crumb screams again and runs through the

swinging door into the kitchen and out the kitchen door and down the path that leads to the barn about two hundred yards away, and it is plain to be seen that she is very nervous. In fact, the last Nicely-Nicely sees of her before she disappears in the darkness down the path, she is throwing her hands up in the air, and letting out little screams, as follows: eee-eee-eee, and calling out old Harley's name.

Then Nicely-Nicely hears one extra loud scream, and after this there is much silence, and he figures that now is the time for him to take his departure, and he starts down the same path toward the barn, but figuring to cut off across the fields to the road that leads to the town when he observes a spark of light bobbing up and down on the path ahead of him, and presently he comes upon old Harley with a lantern in his hand.

Harley is down on his knees at what seems to be a big, round hole in the ground, and this hole is so wide it extends clear across the path, and Harley is poking his lantern down the hole, and when he sees Nicely-Nicely, he says:

"Oh," he says, "there you are. I guess there is some mistake here," he says. "The Widow Crumb tells me to wait in the barn until after supper and she will send you out after me, and," Harley says, "she also tells me to be sure and remove the cover of this old well as soon as it comes on dark. And," Harley says, "of course, I am expecting to find you in the well at this time, but who is in there but the Widow Crumb. I hear her screech as she drops in. I judge she must be hastening along the path and forgets about telling me to remove the cover of the well," Harley says. "It is most confusing," he says.

Then he pokes his lantern down the well again, and leans over and shouts as follows:

"Hello, down there," Harley shouts. "Hello, hello, hello."

But all that happens is an echo comes out of the well like this: Hello. And Nicely-Nicely observes that there is nothing to be seen down the well, but a great blackness.

"It is very deep, and dark, and cold down there," Harley says. "Deep, and dark, and cold, and half full of water. Oh, my poor baby," he says.

Then Harley busts out crying as if his heart will break, and in fact he is so shaken by his sobs that he almost drops the lantern down the well.

Naturally Nicely-Nicely is somewhat surprised to observe these tears because personally he is by no means greatly distressed by the Widow Crumb being down the well, especially when he thinks of how she tries to put him down the well first, and finally he asks Harley why he is so downcast, and Harley speaks as follows:

"I love her," Harley says. "I love her very, very, very much. I am her Number One husband, and while she divorces me thirty years ago when it comes out that I have a weak heart, and the insurance companies refuse to give me a policy, I love her just the same. And now," Harley says, "here she is down a well."

And with this he begins hollering into the hole some more, but the Widow Crumb never personally answers a human voice in this life again and when the story comes out, many citizens claim this is a right good thing, to be sure.

So Nicely-Nicely returns to Broadway, and he brings with him the sum of eleven hundred dollars, which is what he has left of the estate of his late ever-loving wife from the sale of the farm, and one thing and another, after generously declaring old Harley in for fifty percent of his bit when Harley states that the only ambition he has left in life is to rear a tombstone to the memory of the Widow Crumb, and Nicely-Nicely announces that he is through with betting on horses, and other frivolity, and will devote his money to providing himself with food and shelter, and maybe a few clothes.

Well, the chances are Nicely-Nicely will keep his vow, too, but what happens the second day of his return, but he observes in the entries for the third race at Jamaica a horse by the name of Apparition, at 10 to 1 in the morning line, and Nicely-Nicely considers this entry practically a message to him, so he goes for his entire bundle on Apparition.

And it is agreed by one and all along Broadway who knows Nicely-Nicely's story that nobody in his right mind can possibly ignore such a powerful hunch as this, even though it loses, and Nicely-Nicely is again around doing the best he can.

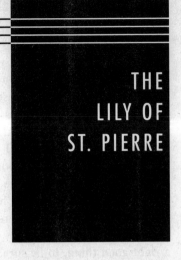

THE
LILY OF
ST. PIERRE

There are four of us sitting in Good Time Charley Bernstein's little joint in Forty-eighth Street one Tuesday morning about four o'clock, doing a bit of quartet singing, very low, so as not to disturb the copper on the beat outside, a very good guy by the name of Carrigan, who likes to get his rest at such an hour.

Good Time Charley's little joint is called the Crystal Room, although of course there is no crystal whatever in the room, but only twelve tables, and twelve hostesses, because Good Time Charley believes in his customers having plenty of social life.

So he has one hostess to a table, and if there are twelve different customers, which is very seldom, each customer has a hostess to talk with. And if there is only one customer, he has all twelve hostesses to gab with and buy drinks for, and no customer can ever go away claiming he is lonesome in Good Time Charley's.

Personally, I will not give you a nickel to talk with Good Time Charley's hostesses, one at a time or all together, because none of them are anything much to look at, and I figure they must all be pretty dumb or they will not be working as hostesses in Good Time Charley's little joint. I happen to speak of this to Good Time Charley, and he admits that I may be right, but he says it is very difficult to get any Peggy Joyces for twenty-five bobs per week.

Of course I never buy any drinks in Good Time Charley's for hostesses, or anybody else, and especially for myself, because I am a personal friend of Good Time Charley's, and he will not sell me

any drinks even if I wish to buy any, which is unlikely, as Good
Time Charley figures that anybody who buys drinks in his place is
apt to drink these drinks, and Charley does not care to see any of
his personal friends drinking drinks at his place. If one of his personal
friends wishes to buy a drink, Charley always sends him to Jack
Fogarty's little speak down the street, and in fact Charley will generally go with him.

So I only go to Good Time Charley's to talk with him, and to
sing in quartet with him. There are very seldom any customers in
Good Time Charley's until along about five o'clock in the morning
after all the other places are closed, and then it is sometimes a very
hot spot indeed, and it is no place to sing in quartet at such hours,
because everybody around always wishes to join in, and it ruins the
harmony. But just before five o'clock it is okay, as only the hostesses
are there, and of course none of them dast to join in our singing, or
Good Time Charley will run them plumb out of the joint.

If there is one thing I love to do more than anything else, it is to
sing in quartet. I sing baritone, and I wish to say I sing a very fine
baritone, at that. And what we are singing—this morning I am talking about—is a lot of songs such as "Little White Lies," and "The
Old Oaken Bucket," and "My Dad's Dinner Pail," and "Chloe," and
"Melancholy Baby," and I do not know what else, including "Home,
Sweet Home," although we do not go so good on this because nobody
remembers all the words, and half the time we are all just going ho-
hum-hum-ho-hum-hum, like guys nearly always do when they are
singing "Home, Sweet Home."

Also we sing "I Can't Give You Anything but Love, Baby," which
is a very fine song for quartet singing, especially when you have a
guy singing a nice bass, such as Good Time Charley, who can come
in on every line with a big bum-bum like this:

I can't give you anything but luh-huh-vuh,
Bay-hay-bee!
BUM-BUM!

I am the one who holds these last words, such as love, and baby,
and you can hear my fine baritone very far indeed, especially when
I give a little extra roll like bay-hay-ay-ay-BEE! Then when Good
Time Charley comes in with his old bum-bum, it is worth going a
long way to hear.

Well, naturally, we finally get around to torch songs, as guys who are singing in quartet are bound to do, especially at four o'clock in the morning, a torch song being a song which guys sing when they have the big burnt-up feeling inside themselves over a battle with their dolls.

When a guy has a battle with his doll, such as his sweetheart, or even his ever-loving wife, he certainly feels burnt up inside himself, and can scarcely think of anything much. In fact, I know guys who are carrying the torch to walk ten miles and never know they go an inch. It is surprising how much ground a guy can cover just walking around and about, wondering if his doll is out with some other guy, and everybody knows that at four o'clock in the morning the torch is hotter than at any other time of the day.

Good Time Charley, who is carrying a torch longer than anybody else on Broadway, which is nearly a year, or ever since his doll, Big Marge, gives him the wind for a rich Cuban, starts up a torch song by Tommy Lyman, which goes as follows, very, very slow, and sad:

> *Gee, but it's tough*
> *When the gang's gone home.*
> *Out on the corner*
> *You stand alone.*

Of course there is no spot in this song for Good Time Charley's bum-bum, but it gives me a great chance with my fine baritone, especially when I come to the line that says Gee, I wish I had my old gal back again.

I do not say I can make people bust out crying and give me money with this song like I see Tommy Lyman do in night clubs, but then Tommy is a professional singer, besides writing this song for himself, so naturally he figures to do a little better with it than me. But I wish to say it is nothing for me to make five or six of the hostesses in Good Time Charley's cry all over the joint when I hit this line about Gee, I wish I had my old gal back again, and making five or six hostesses out of twelve cry is a fair average anywhere, and especially Good Time Charley's hostesses.

Well, all of a sudden who comes popping into Good Time Charley's by way of the front door, looking here and there, and around and about, but Jack O'Hearts, and he no sooner pokes his snozzle into the joint than a guy by the name of Louie the Lug, who is singing a very fair tenor with us, jumps up and heads for the back door.

But just as he gets to the door, Jack O'Hearts outs with the old equalizer and goes whangity-whang-whang at Louie the Lug. As a general proposition, Jack O'Hearts is a fair kind of a shot, but all he does to Louie the Lug is to knock his right ear off. Then Louie gets the back door open and takes it on the lam through an areaway, but not before Jack O'Hearts gets one more crack at him, and it is this last crack which brings Louie down half an hour later on Broadway, where a copper finds him and sends him to the Polyclinic.

Personally, I do not see Louie's ear knocked off, because by the second shot I am out the front door, and on my way down Forty-eighth Street, but they tell me about it afterward.

I never know Jack O'Hearts is even mad at Louie, and I am wondering why he takes these shots at him, but I do not ask any questions, because when a guy goes around asking questions in this town people may get the idea he is such a guy as wishes to find things out.

Then the next night I run into Jack O'Hearts in Bobby's chophouse, putting on the hot meat, and he asks me to sit down and eat with him, so I sit down and order a hamburger steak, with plenty of onions, and while I am sitting there waiting for my hamburger, Jack O'Hearts says to me like this:

"I suppose," he says, "I owe you guys an apology for busting up your quartet when I toss those slugs at Louie the Lug?"

"Well," I say, "some considers it a dirty trick at that, Jack, but I figure you have a good reason, although I am wondering what it is."

"Louie the Lug is no good," Jack says.

Well, of course I know this much already, and so does everybody else in town for that matter, but I cannot figure what it has to do with Jack shooting off ears in this town for such a reason, or by and by there will be very few people left with ears.

"Let me tell you about Louie the Lug," Jack O'Hearts says. "You will see at once that my only mistake is I do not get my shots an inch to the left, I do not know what is the matter with me lately."

"Maybe you are letting go too quick," I say, very sympathetic, because I know how it annoys him to blow easy shots.

"Maybe," he says. "Anyway, the light in Charley's dump is no good. It is only an accident I get Louie with the last shot, and it is very sloppy work all around. But now I tell you about Louie the Lug."

It is back in 1924 [Jack O'Hearts says] that I go to St. Pierre for the first time to look after some business matters for John the Boss, rest his soul, who is at this time one of the largest operators in high-grade merchandise in the United States, especially when it comes to Scotch. Maybe you remember John the Boss, and the heat which develops around and about when he is scragged in Detroit? John the Boss is a very fine character, and it is a terrible blow to many citizens when he is scragged.

Now if you are never in St. Pierre, I wish to say you miss nothing much, because what is it but a little squirt of a burg sort of huddled up alongside some big rocks off Newfoundland, and very hard to get to, any way you go. Mostly you go there from Halifax by boat, though personally I go there in 1924 in John the Boss's schooner by the name of the *Maude*, in which we load a thousand cases of very nice merchandise for the Christmas trade.

The first time I see St. Pierre I will not give you eight cents for the whole layout, although of course it is very useful to parties in our line of business. It does not look like much, and it belongs to France, and nearly all the citizens speak French, because most of them are French, and it seems it is the custom of the French people to speak French no matter where they are, even away off up yonder among the fish.

Well, anyway, it is on this trip to St. Pierre in 1924 that I meet an old guy by the name of Doctor Armand Dorval, for what happens to me but I catch pneumonia, and it looks as if maybe I am a gone gosling, especially as there is no place in St. Pierre where a guy can have pneumonia with any comfort. But this Doctor Armand Dorval is a friend of John the Boss, and he takes me into his house and lets me be as sick there as I please, while he does his best to doctor me up.

Now this Doctor Armand Dorval is an old Frenchman with whiskers, and he has a little granddaughter by the name of Lily, who is maybe twelve years old at the time I am talking about, with her hair hanging down her back in two braids. It seems her papa, who is Doctor Armand's son, goes out one day looking for cod on the Grand Banks when Lily is nothing but a baby, and never comes back, and then her mama dies, so old Doc raises up Lily and is very fond of her indeed.

They live alone in the house where I am sick with this pneumonia, and it is a nice, quiet little house and very old-fashioned, with a good view of the fishing boats, if you care for fishing boats. In fact, it is the quietest place I am ever in in my life, and the only place I ever know any real peace. A big fat old doll who does not talk English comes in every day to look after things for Doctor Armand and Lily, because it seems Lily is not old enough to keep house as yet, although she makes quite a nurse for me.

Lily talks English very good, and she is always bringing me things, and sitting by my bed and chewing the rag with me about this and that, and sometimes she reads to me out of a book which is called *Alice in Wonderland*, and which is nothing but a pack of lies, but very interesting in spots. Furthermore, Lily has a big, blond, dumb-looking doll by the name of Yvonne, which she makes me hold while she is reading to me, and I am very glad indeed that the *Maude* goes on back to the United States and there is no danger of any of the guys walking in on me while I am holding this doll, or they will think I blow my topper.

Finally, when I am able to sit up around the house of an evening I play checkers with Lily, while old Doctor Armand Dorval sits back in a rocking chair, smoking a pipe and watching us, and sometimes I sing for her. I wish to say I sing a first-class tenor, and when I am in the war business in France with the Seventy-seventh Division I am always in great demand for singing a quartet. So I sing such songs to Lily as "There's a Long, Long Trail," and "Mademoiselle from Armentières," although of course when it comes to certain spots in this song I just go dum-dum-dee-dum and do not say the words right out.

By and by Lily gets to singing with me, and we sound very good together, especially when we sing the "Long, Long Trail," which Lily likes very much, and even old Doctor Armand joins in now and then, although his voice is very terrible. Anyway, Lily and me and Doctor Armand become very good pals indeed, and what is more I meet up with other citizens of St. Pierre and become friends with them, and they are by no means bad people to know, and it is certainly nice to be able to walk up and down without being afraid every other guy you meet is going to chuck a slug at you, or a copper put the old sleeve on you and say that they wish to see you at headquarters.

Finally I get rid of this pneumonia and take the boat to Halifax, and I am greatly surprised to find that Doctor Armand and Lily are very sorry to see me go, because never before in my life do I leave a place where anybody is sorry to see me go.

But Doctor Armand seems very sad and shakes me by the hand over and over again, and what does Lily do but bust out crying, and the first thing I know I am feeling sad myself and wishing that I am not going. So I promise Doctor Armand I will come back some day to see him, and then Lily hauls off and gives me a big kiss right in the smush and this astonishes me so much that it is half an hour afterward before I think to wipe it off.

Well, for the next few months I find myself pretty busy back in New York, what with one thing and another, and I do not have time to think much of Doctor Armand Dorval and Lily, and St. Pierre, but it comes along the summer of 1925, and I am all tired out from getting a slug in my chest in the run-in with Jerk Donovan's mob in Jersey, for I am now in beer and have no more truck with the boats.

But I get to thinking of St. Pierre and the quiet little house of Doctor Armand Dorval again, and how peaceful it is up there, and nothing will do but I must pop off to Halifax, and pretty soon I am in St. Pierre once more. I take a raft of things for Lily with me, such as dolls, and handkerchiefs, and perfume, and a phonograph, and also a set of razors for Doctor Armand, although afterward I am sorry I take these razors because I remember the old Doc does not shave and may take them as a hint I do not care for his whiskers. But as it turns out the Doc finds them very useful in operations, so the razors are a nice gift after all.

Well, I spend two peaceful weeks there again, walking up and down in the daytime and playing checkers and singing with Lily in the evening, and it is tough tearing myself away, especially as Doctor Armand Dorval looks very sad again and Lily busts out crying, louder than before. So nearly every year after this I can hardly wait until I can get to St. Pierre for a vacation, and Doctor Armand Dorval's house is like my home, only more peaceful.

Now in the summer of 1928 I am in Halifax on my way to St.

Pierre, when I run across Louie the Lug, and it seems Louie is a lammister out of Detroit on account of some job or other, and is broke, and does not know which way to turn. Personally, I always figure Louie a petty-larceny kind of guy, with no more moxie than a canary bird, but he always dresses well, and always has a fair line of guff, and some guys stand for him. Anyway, here he is in trouble, so what happens but I take him with me to St. Pierre, figuring he can lay dead there until things blow over.

Well, Lily and old Doctor Armand Dorval are certainly glad to see me, and I am just as glad to see them, especially Lily, for she is now maybe sixteen years old and as pretty a doll as ever steps in shoe leather, what with her long black hair, and her big black eyes, and a million dollars' worth of personality. Furthermore, by this time she swings a very mean skillet, indeed, and gets me up some very tasty fodder out of fish and one thing and another.

But somehow things are not like they used to be at St. Pierre with this guy Louie the Lug around, because he does not care for the place whatever, and goes roaming about very restless, and making cracks about the citizens, and especially the dolls, until one night I am compelled to tell him to keep his trap closed, although at that the dolls in St. Pierre, outside of Lily, are no such lookers as will get Ziegfeld heated up.

But even in the time when St. Pierre is headquarters for many citizens of the United States who are in the business of handling merchandise out of there, it is always sort of underhand that such citizens will never have any truck with the dolls at St. Pierre. This is partly because the dolls at St. Pierre never give the citizens of the United States a tumble, but more because we do not wish to get in any trouble around there, and if there is anything apt to cause trouble it is dolls.

Now I suppose if I have any brains I will see that Louie is playing the warm for Lily, but I never think of Lily as anything but a little doll with her hair in braids, and certainly not a doll such as a guy will start pitching to, especially a guy who calls himself one of the mob.

I notice Louie is always talking to Lily when he gets a chance, and sometimes he goes walking up and down with her, but I see nothing in this, because after all any guy is apt to get lonesome at St. Pierre and go walking up and down with anybody, even a little young doll. In fact, I never see Louie do anything that strikes me as out of line, except he tries to cut in on the singing between Lily and me, until I tell him one tenor at a time is enough in any singing combination. Personally, I consider Louie the Lug's tenor very flat, indeed.

Well, it comes time for me to go away, and I take Louie with me, because I do not wish him hanging around St. Pierre alone, especially as old Doctor Armand Dorval does not seem to care for him whatever, and while Lily seems as sad as ever to see me go I notice that for the first time she does not kiss me good-bye. But I figure this is fair enough, as she is now quite a young lady, and the chances are a little particular about who she kisses.

I leave Louie in Halifax and give him enough dough to go on to Denver, which is where he says he wishes to go, and I never see him again until the other night in Good Time Charley's. But almost a year later, when I happen to be in Montreal, I hear of him. I am standing in the lobby of the Mount Royal Hotel thinking of not much, when a guy by the name of Bob the Bookie, who is a hustler around the racetracks, gets to talking to me and mentions Louie's name. It brings back to me a memory of my last trip to St. Pierre, and I get to thinking that this is the longest stretch I ever go in several years without a visit there and of the different things that keep me from going.

I am not paying much attention to what Bob says, because he is putting the blast on Louie for running away from an ever-loving wife and a couple of kids in Cleveland several years before, which is something I do not know about Louie, at that. Then I hear Bob saying like this:

"He is an awful rat any way you take him. Why, when he hops out of here two weeks ago, he leaves a little doll he brings with him from St. Pierre dying in a hospital without a nickel to her name. It is a sin and a shame."

"Wait a minute, Bob," I say, waking up all of a sudden. "Do you say a doll from St. Pierre? What-for looking kind of a doll, Bob?" I say.

"Why," Bob says, "she is black-haired, and very young, and he calls her Lily, or some such. He is knocking around Canada with her for quite a spell. She strikes me as a TB, but Louie's dolls always look this way after he has them awhile. I judge," Bob says, "that Louie does not feed them any too good."

Well, it is Lily Dorval, all right, but never do I see such a change in anybody as there is in the poor little doll I find lying on a bed in a charity ward in a Montreal hospital. She does not look to weigh more than fifty pounds, and her black eyes are sunk away back in her head, and she is in tough shape generally. But she knows me right off the bat and tries to smile at me.

I am in the money very good at this time, and I have Lily moved into a private room, and get her all the nurses the law allows, and the best croakers in Montreal, and flowers, and one thing and another, but one of the medicos tells me it is even money she will not last three weeks, and 7 to 5 she does not go a month. Finally Lily tells me what happens, which is the same thing that happens to a million dolls before and will happen to a million dolls again. Louie never leaves Halifax, but cons her into coming over there to him, and she goes because she loves him, for this is the way dolls are, and personally I will never have them any other way.

"But," Lily whispers to me, "the bad, bad thing I do is to tell poor old Grandfather I am going to meet you, Jack O'Hearts, and marry you, because I know he does not like Louie and will never allow me to go to him. But he loves you, Jack O'Hearts, and he is so pleased in thinking you are to be his son. It is wrong to tell Grandfather this story, and wrong to use your name, and to keep writing him all this time making him think I am your wife, and with you, but I love Louie, and I wish Grandfather to be happy because he is very, very old. Do you understand, Jack O'Hearts?"

Now of course all this is very surprising news to me, indeed, and in fact I am quite flabbergasted, and as for understanding it, all I understand is she gets a rotten deal from Louie the Lug and that old Doctor Armand Dorval is going to be all busted up if he hears what really happens. And thinking about this nice old man, and thinking of how the only place I ever know peace and quiet is now ruined, I am very angry with Louie the Lug.

But this is something to be taken up later, so I dismiss him from my mind, and go out and get me a marriage license and a priest, and have this priest marry me to Lily Dorval just two days before she looks up at me for the last time, and smiles a little smile, and then closes her eyes for good and all. I wish to say, however, that up to this time I have no more idea of getting myself a wife than I have of jumping out the window, which is practically no idea at all.

I take her body back to St. Pierre myself in person, and we bury her in a little cemetery there, with a big fog around and about, and the siren moaning away very sad, and old Doctor Armand Dorval whispers to me like this:

"You will please to sing the song about the long trail, Jack O'Hearts."

So I stand there in the fog, the chances are looking like a big sap, and I sing as follows:

There's a long, long trail a-winding
Into the land of my dreams,
Where the nightingale is singing,
And the white moon beams.

But I can get no farther than this, for something comes up in my throat, and I sit down by the grave of Mrs. Jack O'Hearts, who was Lily Dorval, and for the first time I remember I bust out crying.

So [he says] this is why I say Louie the Lug is no good.

Well, I am sitting there thinking that Jack O'Hearts is right about Louie, at that, when in comes Jack's chauffeur, a guy by the name of Fingers, and he steps up to Jack and says, very low:

"Louie dies half an hour ago at the Polyclinic."

"What does he say before he goes?" Jack asks.

"Not a peep," Fingers says.

"Well," Jack O'Hearts says, "it is sloppy work, at that. I ought to get him the first crack. But maybe he had a chance to think a little of Lily Dorval."

Then he turns to me and says like this:

"You guys need not feel bad about losing your tenor, because," he says, "I will be glad to fill in for him at all times."

Personally I do not think Jack's tenor is as good as Louie the Lug's especially when it comes to hitting the very high notes in such songs as Sweet Adeline, because he does not hold them long enough to let Good Time Charley in with his bum-bum.

But of course this does not go if Jack O'Hearts hears it, as I am never sure he does not clip Louie the Lug just to get a place in our quartet, at that.

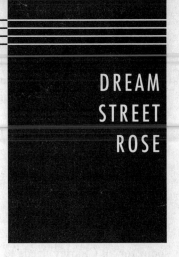

DREAM
STREET
ROSE

Of an early evening when there is nothing much doing any-where else, I go around to Good Time Charley's little speak in West Forty-seventh Street that he calls the Gingham Shop, and play a little klob with Charley, because business is quiet in the Gingham Shop at such an hour, and Charley gets very lonesome.

He once has a much livelier spot in Forty-eighth Street that he calls the Crystal Room, but one night a bunch of G-guys step into the joint and bust it wide open, besides confiscating all of Charley's stock of merchandise. It seems that these G-guys are members of a squad that comes on from Washington, and being strangers in the city they do not know that Good Time Charley's joint is not supposed to be busted up, so they go ahead and bust it, just the same as if it is any other joint.

Well, this action causes great indignation in many quarters, and a lot of citizens advise Charley to see somebody about it. But Charley says no. Charley says if this is the way the government is going to treat him after the way he walks himself bowlegged over in France with the Rainbow Division, making the Germans hard to catch, why, all right. But he is not going to holler copper about it, although Charley says he has his own opinion of Mr. Hoover, at that.

Personally, I greatly admire Charley for taking the disaster so calmly, especially as it catches him with very few potatoes. Charley is a great hand for playing the horses with any dough he makes out of the Crystal Room, and this particular season the guys who play the horses are being murdered by the bookies all over the country, and are in terrible distress.

So I know if Charley is not plumb broke that he has a terrible crack across his belly, and I am not surprised that I do not see him for a couple of weeks after the government guys knock off the Crystal Room. I hear rumors that he is at home reading the newspapers very carefully every day, especially the obituary notices, for it seems that Charley figures that some of the G-guys may be tempted to take a belt or two at the merchandise they confiscate, and Charley says if they do, he is even for life.

Finally I hear that Charley is seen buying a bolt of gingham in Bloomington's one day, so I know he will be in action again very soon, for all Charley needs to go into action is a bolt of gingham and a few bottles of Golden Wedding. In fact, I know Charley to go into action without the gingham, but as a rule he likes to drape a place of business with gingham to make it seem more homelike to his customers, and I wish to say that when it comes to draping gingham, Charley can make a sucker of Joseph Urban, or anybody else.

Well, when I arrive at the Gingham Shop this night I am talking about, which is around ten o'clock, I find Charley in a very indignant state of mind, because an old tomato by the name of Dream Street Rose comes in and tracks up his floor, just after Charley gets through mopping it up, for Charley does his mopping in person, not being able as yet to afford any help.

Rose is sitting at a table in a corner, paying no attention to Charley's remarks about wiping her feet on the Welcome mat at the door before she comes in, because Rose knows there is no Welcome mat at Charley's door, anyway, but I can see where Charley has a right to a few beefs, at that, as she leaves a trail of black hoofprints across the clean floor as if she is walking around in mud somewhere before she comes in, although I do not seem to remember that it is raining when I arrive.

Now this Dream Street Rose is an old doll of maybe fifty-odd, and is a very well-known character around and about, as she is wandering through the Forties for many a year, and especially through West Forty-seventh Street between Sixth and Seventh Avenues, and this block is called Dream Street. And the reason it is called Dream Street is because in this block are many characters of one kind and another who always seem to be dreaming of different matters.

In Dream Street there are many theatrical hotels, and rooming houses, and restaurants, and speaks, including Good Time Charley's Gingham Shop, and in the summer time the characters I mention sit on the stoops or lean against the railings along Dream Street, and the gab you hear sometimes sounds very dreamy indeed. In fact, it sometimes sounds very pipe-dreamy.

Many actors, male and female, and especially vaudeville actors, live in the hotels and rooming houses, and vaudeville actors, both male and female, are great hands for sitting around dreaming out loud about how they will practically assassinate the public in the Palace if ever they get a chance.

Furthermore, in Dream Street are always many hand-bookies and horse players, who sit on the church steps on the cool side of Dream Street in the summer and dream about big killings on the races, and there are also nearly always many fight managers, and sometimes fighters, hanging out in front of the restaurants, picking their teeth and dreaming about winning championships of the world, although up to this time no champion of the world has yet come out of Dream Street.

In this street you see burlesque dolls, and hoofers, and guys who write songs, and saxophone players, and newsboys, and newspaper scribes, and taxi drivers, and blind guys, and midgets, and blondes with Pomeranian pooches, or maybe French poodles, and guys with whiskers, and nightclub entertainers, and I do not know what all else. And all of these characters are interesting to look at, and some of them are very interesting to talk to, although if you listen to several I know long enough, you may get the idea that they are somewhat daffy, especially the horse players.

But personally I consider all horse players more or less daffy anyway. In fact, the way I look at it, if a guy is not daffy he will not be playing the horses.

Now this Dream Street Rose is a short, thick-set, square-looking old doll, with a square pan, and square shoulders, and she has heavy iron-gray hair that she wears in a square bob, and she stands very square on her feet. In fact, Rose is the squarest-looking doll I ever see, and she is as strong and lively as Jim Londos, the wrestler. In fact, Jim Londos will never be any better than 6 to 5 in my line over Dream Street Rose, if she is in any kind of shape.

Nobody in this town wishes any truck with Rose if she has a few shots of grog in her, and especially Good Time Charley's grog, for she can fight like the dickens when she is grogged up. In fact, Rose holds many a decision in this town, especially over coppers, because if there is one thing she hates and despises more than somewhat it is a copper, as coppers are always heaving her into the old can when they find her jerking citizens around and cutting up other didoes.

For many years Rose works in the different hotels along Dream Street as a chambermaid. She never works in any one hotel very long, because the minute she gets a few bobs together she likes to go out and enjoy a little recreation, such as visiting around the speaks, although she is about as welcome in most speaks as a G-guy with a search warrant. You see, nobody can ever tell when Rose may feel like taking the speak apart, and also the customers.

She never has any trouble getting a job back in any hotel she ever works in, for Rose is a wonderful hand for making up beds, although several times, when she is in a hurry to get off, I hear she makes up beds with guests still in them, which causes a few mild beefs to the management, but does not bother Rose. I speak of this matter only to show you that she is a very quaint character indeed, and full of zest.

Well, I sit down to play klob with Good Time Charley, but about this time several customers come into the Gingham Shop, so Charley has to go and take care of them, leaving me alone. And while I am sitting there alone I hear Dream Street Rose mumbling to herself over in the corner, but I pay no attention to her, although I wish to say I am by no means unfriendly with Rose.

In fact, I say hello to her at all times, and am always very courteous to her, as I do not wish to have her bawling me out in public, and maybe circulating rumors about me, as she is apt to do, if she feels I am snubbing her.

Finally I notice her motioning to me to come over to her table, and I go over at once and sit down, because I can see that Rose is well grogged up at this time, and I do not care to have her attracting my attention by chucking a cuspidor at me. She offers me a drink when I sit down, but of course I never drink anything that is sold in

Good Time Charley's, as a personal favor to Charley. He says he wishes to retain my friendship.

So I just sit there saying nothing much whatever, and Rose keeps on mumbling to herself, and I am not able to make much of her mumbling, until finally she looks at me and says to me like this:

"I am now going to tell you about my friend," Rose says.

"Well, Rose," I say, "personally I do not care to hear about your friend, although," I say, "I have no doubt that what you wish to tell me about this friend is very interesting. But I am here to play a little klob with Good Time Charley, and I do not have time to hear about your friend."

"Charley is busy selling his poison to the suckers," Rose says. "I am now going to tell you about my friend. It is quite a story," she says. "You will listen."

So I listen.

It is a matter of thirty-five years ago [Dream Street Rose says] and the spot is a town in Colorado by the name of Pueblo, where there are smelters and one thing and another. My friend is at this time maybe sixteen or seventeen years old, and a first-class looker in every respect. Her papa is dead, and her mama runs a boardinghouse for the guys who work in the smelters, and who are very hearty eaters. My friend deals them off the arm for the guys in her mama's boardinghouse to save her mama the expense of a waitress.

Now among the boarders in this boardinghouse are many guys who are always doing a little pitching to my friend, and trying to make dates with her to take her places, but my friend never gives them much of a tumble, because after she gets through dealing them off the arm all day her feet generally pain her too much to go anywhere on them except to the hay.

Finally, however, along comes a tall, skinny young guy from the East by the name of Frank something, who has things to say to my friend that are much more interesting than anything that has been said to her by a guy before, including such things as love and marriage, which are always very interesting subjects to any young doll.

This Frank is maybe twenty-five years old, and he comes from the East with the idea of making his fortune in the West, and while it is true that fortunes are being made in the West at this time, there is little chance that Frank is going to make any part of a fortune, as he does not care to work very hard. In fact, he does not care to work at all, being much more partial to playing a little poker, or shooting a few craps, or maybe hustling a sucker around Mike's pool room on Santa Fe Avenue, for Frank is an excellent pool player, especially when he is playing a sucker.

Now my friend is at this time a very innocent young doll, and a good doll in every respect, and her idea of love includes a nice little home, and children running here and there and around and about, and she never has a wrong thought in her life, and believes that everybody else in the world is like herself. And the chances are if this Frank does not happen along, my friend will marry a young guy in Pueblo by the name of Higginbottom, who is very fond of her indeed, and who is a decent young guy and afterward makes plenty of potatoes in the grocery dodge.

But my friend goes very daffy over Frank and cannot see anybody but him, and the upshot of it all is she runs away with him one day to Denver, being dumb enough to believe that he means it when he tells her that he loves her and is going to marry her. Why Frank ever bothers with such a doll as my friend in the first place is always a great mystery to one and all, and the only way anybody can explain it is that she is young and fresh, and he is a heel at heart.

"Well, Rose," I say, "I am now commencing to see the finish of this story about your friend, and," I say, "it is such a story as anybody can hear in a speak at any time in this town, except," I say, "maybe your story is longer than somewhat. So I will now thank you, and excuse myself, and play a little klob with Good Time Charley."

"You will listen," Dream Street Rose says, looking me slap-dab in the eye.

So I listen.

Moreover, I notice now that Good Time Charley is standing behind me, bending in an ear, as it seems that his customers take the wind after a couple of slams of Good Time Charley's merchandise, a couple of slams being about all that even a very hardy customer can stand at one session.

Of course [Rose goes on] the chances are Frank never intends marrying my friend at all, and she never knows until long afterward that the reason he leads her to the parson is that the young guy from Pueblo by the name of Higginbottom catches up with them at the old Windsor Hotel where they are stopping and privately pokes a six-pistol against Frank's ribs and promises faithfully to come back and blow a hole in Frank you can throw a watermelon through if Frank tries any finagling around with my friend.

Well, in practically no time whatever, love's young dream is over as far as my friend is concerned. This Frank turns out to be a most repulsive character indeed, especially if you are figuring him as an ever-loving husband. In fact, he is no good. He mistreats my friend in every way any guy ever thought of mistreating a doll, and besides the old established ways of mistreating a doll, Frank thinks up quite a number of new ways, being really quite ingenious in this respect.

Yes, this Frank is one hundred percent heel.

It is not so much that he gives her a thumping now and then, because, after all, a thumping wears off, and hurts heal up, even when they are such hurts as a broken nose and fractured ribs, and once an ankle cracked by a kick. It is what he does to her heart, and to her innocence. He is by no means a good husband, and does not know how to treat an ever-loving wife with any respect, especially as he winds up by taking my friend to San Francisco and hiring her out to a very loose character there by the name of Black Emanuel, who has a dance joint on the Barbary Coast, which, at the time I am talking about, is hotter than a stove. In this joint my friend has to dance with the customers, and get them to buy beer for her and one thing and another, and this occupation is most distasteful to my friend, as she never cares for beer.

It is there Frank leaves her for good after giving her an extra big thumping for a keepsake, and when my friend tries to leave Black Emanuel's to go looking for her ever-loving husband, she is somewhat surprised to hear Black Emanuel state that he pays Frank three C's for her to remain there and continue working. Furthermore, Black Emanuel resumes the thumpings where Frank leaves off, and by and by my friend is much bewildered and downhearted and does not care what happens to her.

Well, there is nothing much of interest in my friend's life for the next thirty-odd years, except that she finally gets so she does not mind the beer so much, and, in fact, takes quite a fondness for it, and also for light wines and Bourbon whiskey, and that she comes to realize that Frank does not love her after all, in spite of what he says. Furthermore, in later years, after she drifts around the country quite some, in and out of different joints, she realizes that the chances are she will never have a nice little home, with children running here and there, and she often thinks of what a disagreeable influence Frank has on her life.

In fact, this Frank is always on her mind more than somewhat. In fact, she thinks of him night and day, and says many a prayer that he will do well. She manages to keep track of him, which is not hard to do, at that, as Frank is in New York, and is becoming quite a guy in business, and is often in the newspapers. Maybe his success is due to my friend's prayers, but the chances are it is more because he connects up with some guy who has an invention for doing something very interesting in steel, and by grabbing an interest in this invention Frank gets a shove toward plenty of potatoes. Furthermore, he is married, and is raising up a family.

About ten or twelve years ago my friend comes to New York, and by this time she is getting a little faded around the edges. She is not so old, at that, but the air of the Western and Southern joints is bad on the complexion, and beer is no good for the figure. In fact, my friend is now quite a haybag, and she does not get any better-looking in the years she spends in New York as she is practically all out of the old sex appeal, and has to do a little heavy lifting to keep eating. But she never forgets to keep praying that Frank will continue to do well, and Frank certainly does this, as he is finally spoken of everywhere very respectfully as a millionaire and a high-class guy.

In all the years she is in New York my friend never runs into Frank, as Frank is by no means accustomed to visiting the spots where my friend hangs out, but my friend goes to a lot of bother to get acquainted with a doll who is a maid for some time in Frank's town house in East Seventy-fourth Street, and through this doll my friend keeps a pretty fair line on the way Frank lives. In fact, one day when Frank and his family are absent, my friend goes to Frank's house with her friend, just to see what it looks like, and after an hour there my friend has the joint pretty well cased.

So now my friend knows through her friend that on very hot nights such as tonight Frank's family is bound to be at their country place at Port Washington, but that Frank himself is spending the night at his town house, because he wishes to work on a lot of papers of some kind. My friend knows through her friend that all of Frank's servants are at Port Washington, too, except my friend's friend, who is in charge of the town house, and Frank's valet, a guy by the name of Sloggins.

Furthermore, my friend knows through her friend that both her friend and Sloggins have a date to go to a movie at 8:30 o'clock, to be gone a couple of hours, as it seems Frank is very big-hearted about giving his servants time off for such a purpose when he is at home alone; although one night he squawks no little when my friend is out with her friend drinking a little beer, and my friend's friend loses her door key and has to ring the bell to the servants' entrance, and rousts Frank out of a sound sleep.

Naturally, my friend's friend will be greatly astonished if she ever learns that it is with this key that my friend steps into Frank's house along about nine o'clock tonight. An electric light hangs over the servants' entrance, and my friend locates the button that controls this light just inside the door and turns it off, as my friend figures that maybe Frank and his family will not care to have any of their high-class neighbors, or anyone else, see an old doll who has no better hat than she is wearing, entering or leaving their house at such an hour.

It is an old-fashioned sort of house, four or five stories high, with the library on the third floor in the rear, looking out through French windows over a nice little garden, and my friend finds Frank in the library where she expects to find him, because she is smart enough to figure that a guy who is working on papers is not apt to be doing his work in the cellar.

But Frank is not working on anything when my friend moves in on him. He is dozing in a chair by the window, and, looking at him, after all these years, she finds something of a change, indeed. He is much heavier than he is thirty-five years back, and his hair is white, but he looks pretty well to my friend, at that, as she stands there for maybe five minutes watching him. Then he seems to realize somebody is in the room, as sleeping guys will do, for his regular breathing stops with a snort, and he opens his eyes, and looks into my friend's eyes, but without hardly stirring. And finally my friend speaks to Frank as follows:

"Well, Frank," she says, "do you know me?"

"Yes," he says, after a while, "I know you. At first I think maybe you are a ghost, as I once hear something about your being dead. But," he says, "I see now the report is a canard. You are too fat to be a ghost."

Well, of course, this is a most insulting crack, indeed, but my friend passes it off as she does not wish to get in any arguments with Frank at this time. She can see that he is upset more than somewhat and he keeps looking around the room as if he hopes he can see somebody else he can cut in on the conversation. In fact, he acts as if my friend is by no means a welcome visitor.

"Well, Frank," my friend says, very pleasant, "there you are, and here I am. I understand you are now a wealthy and prominent citizen of this town. I am glad to know this, Frank," she says. "You will be surprised to hear that for years and years I pray that you will do well for yourself and become a big guy in every respect, with a nice family, and everything else. I judge my prayers are answered," she says. "I see by the papers that you have two sons at Yale, and a daughter in Vassar, and that your ever-loving wife is getting to be very high mucky-mucky in society. Well, Frank," she says, "I am very glad. I pray something like all this will happen to you."

Now, at such a speech, Frank naturally figures that my friend is all right, at that, and the chances are he also figures that she still has a mighty soft spot in her heart for him, just as she has in the days when she deals them off the arm to keep him in gambling and drinking money. In fact, Frank brightens up somewhat, and he says to my friend like this:

"You pray for my success?" he says. "Why, this is very thoughtful of you, indeed. Well," he says, "I am sitting on top of the world. I have everything to live for."

"Yes," my friend says, "and this is exactly where I pray I will find you. On top of the world," she says, "and with everything to live for. It is where I am when you take my life. It is where I am when you kill me as surely as if you strangle me with your hands. I always pray you will not become a bum," my friend says, "because a bum has nothing to live for, anyway. I want to find you liking to live, so you will hate so much to die."

Naturally, this does not sound so good to Frank, and he begins all of a sudden to shake and shiver and to stutter somewhat.

"Why," he says, "what do you mean? Are you going to kill me?"

"Well," my friend says, "that remains to be seen. Personally," she says, "I will be much obliged if you will kill yourself, but it can be arranged one way or the other. However, I will explain the disadvantages of me killing you.

"The chances are," my friend says, "if I kill you I will be caught and a very great scandal will result, because," she says, "I have on my person the certificate of my marriage to you in Denver, and something tells me you never think to get a divorce. So," she says, "you are a bigamist."

"I can pay," Frank says. "I can pay plenty."

"Furthermore," my friend says, paying no attention to his remark, "I have a sworn statement from Black Emanuel about your transaction with him, for Black Emanuel gets religion before he dies from being shivved by Johnny Mizzoo, and he tries to round himself up by confessing all the sins he can think of, which are quite a lot. It is a very interesting statement," my friend says.

"Now then," she says, "if you knock yourself off you will leave an unsullied, respected name. If I kill you, all the years and effort you have devoted to building up your reputation will go for nothing. You are past sixty," my friend says, "and any way you figure it, you do not have so very far to go. If I kill you," she says, "you will go in horrible disgrace, and everybody around you will feel the disgrace, no matter how much dough you leave them. Your children will hang their heads in shame. Your ever-loving wife will not like it," my friend says.

"I wait on you a long time, Frank," my friend says. "A dozen times in the past twenty years I figure I may as well call on you and close up my case with you, but," she says, "then I always persuade myself to wait a little longer so you would rise higher and higher and life will be a bit sweeter to you. And there you are, Frank," she says, "and here I am."

Well, Frank sits there as if he is knocked plumb out, and he does not answer a word; so finally my friend outs with a large John Roscoe which she is packing in the bosom of her dress, and tosses it in his lap, and speaks as follows:

"Frank," she says, "do not think it will do you any good to pot me in the back when I turn around, because," she says, "you will be worse off than ever. I leave plenty of letters scattered around in case anything happens to me. And remember," she says, "if you do not do this job yourself, I will be back. Sooner or later, I will be back."

So [Dream Street Rose says] my friend goes out of the library and down the stairs, leaving Frank sprawled out in his chair, and when she reaches the first floor she hears what may be a shot in the upper part of the house, and then again maybe only a door slamming. My friend never knows for sure what it is, because a little later as she nears the servants' entrance she hears quite a commotion outside, and a guy cussing a blue streak, and a doll tee-heeing, and pretty soon my friend's friend, the maid, and Sloggins, the valet, come walking in.

Well, my friend just has time to scroonch herself back in a dark corner, and they go upstairs, the guy still cussing and the doll still giggling, and my friend cannot make out what it is all about except that they come home earlier than she figures. So my friend goes tippy-toe out of the servants' entrance, to grab a taxi not far from the house and get away from this neighborhood, and now you will soon hear of the suicide of a guy who is a millionaire, and it will be all even with my friend.

"Well, Rose," I say, "it is a nice long story, and full of romance and all this and that, and," I say, "of course I will never be ungentlemanly enough to call a lady a liar, but," I say, "if it is not a lie, it will do until a lie comes along."

"All right," Rose says. "Anyway, I tell you about my friend. Now," she says, "I am going where the liquor is better, which can be any other place in town, because," she says, "there is no chance of liquor anywhere being any worse."

So she goes out, making more tracks on Good Time Charley's floor, and Charley speaks most impolitely of her after she goes, and gets out his mop to clean the floor, for one thing about Charley, he is as neat as a pin, and maybe neater.

Well, along toward one o'clock I hear a newsboy in the street outside yelling something I cannot make out, because he is yelling as if he has a mouthful of mush, as newsboys are bound to do. But I am anxious to see what goes in the first race at Belmont, on account of having a first-class tip, so I poke my noggin outside Good Time Charley's and buy a paper, and across the front page, in large letters, it states that the wealthy Mr. Frank Billingsworth McQuiggan knocks himself off by putting a slug through his own noggin.

It says Mr. McQuiggan is found in a chair in his library as dead as a doornail with the pistol in his lap with which he knocks himself off, and the paper states that nobody can figure what causes Mr. McQuiggan to do such a thing to himself as he is in good health and has plenty of potatoes and is at the peak of his career. Then there is a lot about his history.

When Mr. McQuiggan is a young fellow returning from a visit to the Pacific Coast with about two hundred dollars in his pocket after paying his railroad fare, he meets in the train Jonas Calloway, famous inventor of the Calloway steel process. Calloway, also then young, is desperately in need of funds and he offers Mr. McQuiggan a third interest in his invention for what now seems the paltry sum of one hundred dollars. Mr. McQuiggan accepts the offer and thus paves the way to his own fortune.

I am telling all this to Good Time Charley while he is mopping away at the floor, and finally I come on a paragraph down near the finish which goes like this: "The body was discovered by Mr. McQuiggan's faithful valet, Thomas Sloggins, at eleven o'clock. Mr. McQuiggan was then apparently dead a couple of hours. Sloggins returned home shortly before ten o'clock with another servant after changing his mind about going to a movie. Instead of going to see his employer at once, as is his usual custom, Sloggins went to his own quarters and changed his clothes.

" 'The light over the servants' entrance was out when I returned home,' the valet said, 'and in the darkness I stumbled over some scaffolding and other material left near this entrance by workmen who are to regravel the roof of the house tomorrow, upsetting all over the entranceway a large bucket of tar, much of which got on my apparel when I fell, making a change necessary before going to see Mr. McQuiggan.' "

Well, Good Time Charley keeps on mopping harder than ever, though finally he stops a minute and speaks to me as follows:

"Listen," Charley says, "understand I do not say the guy does not deserve what he gets, and I am by no means hollering copper, but," Charley says, "if he knocks himself off, how does it come the rod is still in his lap where Dream Street Rose says her friend tosses it? Well, never mind," Charley says, "but can you think of something that will remove tar from a wood floor? It positively will not mop off."

One night a guy by the name of Bill Corum, who is one of these sport scribes, gives me a Chinee for a fight at Madison Square Garden, a Chinee being a ducket with holes punched in it like old-fashioned Chink money, to show that it is a free ducket, and the reason I am explaining to you how I get this ducket is because I do not wish anybody to think I am ever simple enough to pay out my own potatoes for a ducket to a fight, even if I have any potatoes.

Personally, I will not give you a bad two-bit piece to see a fight anywhere, because the way I look at it, half the time the guys who are supposed to do the fighting go in there and put on the old do-se-do, and I consider this a great fraud upon the public, and I do not believe in encouraging dishonesty.

But of course I never refuse a Chinee to such events, because the way I figure it, what can I lose except my time, and my time is not worth more than a bob a week the way things are. So on the night in question I am standing in the lobby of the Garden with many other citizens, and I am trying to find out if there is any skullduggery doing in connection with the fight, because any time there is any skullduggery doing I love to know it, as it is something worth knowing in case a guy wishes to get a small wager down.

Well, while I am standing there, somebody comes up behind me and hits me an awful belt on the back, knocking my wind plumb out of me, and making me very indignant indeed. As soon as I get a little of my wind back again, I turn around figuring to put a large blast on the guy who slaps me, but who is it but a guy by the name of Spider McCoy, who is known far and wide as a manager of fighters.

Well, of course I do not put the blast on Spider McCoy, because he is an old friend of mine, and furthermore, Spider McCoy is such a guy as is apt to let a left hook go at anybody who puts the blast on him, and I do not believe in getting in trouble, especially with good left-hookers.

So I say hello to Spider, and am willing to let it go at that, but Spider seems glad to see me, and says to me like this:

"Well, well, well, well, well!" Spider says.

"Well," I say to Spider McCoy, "how many wells does it take to make a river?"

"One, if it is big enough," Spider says, so I can see he knows the answer all right. "Listen," he says, "I just think up the greatest proposition I ever think of in my whole life, and who knows but what I can interest you in same."

"Well, Spider," I say, "I do not care to hear any propositions at this time, because it may be a long story, and I wish to step inside and see the impending battle. Anyway," I say, "if it is a proposition involving financial support, I wish to state that I do not have any resources whatever at this time."

"Never mind the battle inside," Spider says. "It is nothing but a tank job, anyway. And as for financial support," Spider says, "this does not require more than a pound note, tops, and I know you have a pound note because I know you put the bite on Overcoat Obie for this amount not an hour ago. Listen," Spider McCoy says, "I know where I can place my hands on the greatest heavyweight prospect in the world today, and all I need is the price of carfare to where he is."

Well, off and on, I know Spider McCoy twenty years, and in all this time I never know him when he is not looking for the greatest heavyweight prospect in the world. And as long as Spider knows I have the pound note, I know there is no use trying to play the duck for him, so I stand there wondering who the stool pigeon can be who informs him of my financial status.

"Listen," Spider says, "I just discover that I am all out of line in the way I am looking for heavyweight prospects in the past. I am always looking for nothing but plenty of size," he says. "Where I make my mistake is not looking for blood lines. Professor D just smartens me up," Spider says.

Well, when he mentions the name of Professor D, I commence taking a little interest, because it is well known to one and all that Professor D is one of the smartest old guys in the world. He is once a professor in a college out in Ohio, but quits this dodge to handicap the horses, and he is a first-rate handicapper, at that. But besides knowing how to handicap the horses, Professor D knows many other things, and is highly respected in all walks of life, especially on Broadway.

"Now then," Spider says, "Professor D calls my attention this afternoon to the fact that when a guy is looking for a racehorse, he does not take just any horse that comes along, but he finds out if the horse's papa is able to run in his day, and if the horse's mama can get out of her own way when she is young. Professor D shows me how a guy looks for speed in a horse's breeding away back to its great-great-great-greatgrandpa and grandmama," Spider McCoy says.

"Well," I say, "anybody knows this without asking Professor D. In fact," I say, "you even look up a horse's parents to see if they can mud before betting on a plug to win in heavy going."

"All right," Spider says, "I know all this myself, but I never think much about it before Professor D mentions it. Professor D says if a guy is looking for a hunting dog he does not pick a Pekingese pooch, but he gets a dog that is bred to hunt from away back yonder, and if he is after a game chicken he does not take a Plymouth Rock out of the backyard.

"So then," Spider says, "Professor D wishes to know if when I am looking for a fighter, if I do not look for one who comes of fighting stock. Professor D wishes to know," Spider says, "why I do not look for some guy who is bred to fight, and when I think this over, I can see the professor is right.

"And then all of a sudden," Spider says, "I get the largest idea I ever have in all my life. Do you remember a guy I have about twenty years back by the name of Shamus Mulrooney, the Fighting Harp?" Spider says. "A big, rough, tough heavyweight out of Newark?"

"Yes," I say, "I remember Shamus very well indeed. The last time I see him is the night Pounder Pat O'Shea almost murders him in the old Garden," I say. "I never see a guy with more ticker than Shamus, unless maybe it is Pat."

"Yes," Spider says, "Shamus has plenty of ticker. He is about through the night of the fight you speak of, otherwise Pat will never lay a glove on him. It is not long after this fight that Shamus packs in and goes back to bricklaying in Newark, and it is also about this same time," Spider says, "that he marries Pat O'Shea's sister, Bridget.

"Well, now," Spider says, "I remember they have a boy who must be around nineteen years old now, and if ever a guy is bred to fight it is a boy by Shamus Mulrooney out of Bridget O'Shea, because," Spider says, "Bridget herself can lick half the heavyweights I see around nowadays if she is half as good as she is the last time I see her. So now you have my wonderful idea. We will go to Newark and get this boy and make him heavyweight champion of the world."

"What you state is very interesting indeed, Spider," I say. "But," I say, "how do you know this boy is a heavyweight?"

"Why," Spider says, "how can he be anything else but a heavyweight, what with his papa as big as a house, and his mama weighing maybe a hundred and seventy pounds in her step-ins? Although of course," Spider says, "I never see Bridget weigh in in such manner.

"But," Spider says, "even if she does carry more weight than I will personally care to spot a doll, Bridget is by no means a pelican when she marries Shamus. In fact," he says, "she is pretty good-looking. I remember their wedding well, because it comes out that Bridget is in love with some other guy at the time, and this guy comes to see the nuptials, and Shamus runs him all the way from Newark to Elizabeth, figuring to break a couple of legs for the guy if he catches him. But," Spider says, "the guy is too speedy for Shamus, who never has much foot anyway."

Well, all that Spider says appeals to me as a very sound business proposition, so the upshot of it is I give him my pound note to finance his trip to Newark.

Then I do not see Spider McCoy again for a week, but one day he calls me up and tells me to hurry over to the Pioneer gymnasium to see the next heavyweight champion of the world, Thunderbolt Mulrooney.

I am personally somewhat disappointed when I see Thunderbolt Mulrooney, and especially when I find out his first name is Raymond and not Thunderbolt at all, because I am expecting to see a big, fierce guy with red hair and a chest like a barrel, such as Shamus Mulrooney has when he is in his prime. But who do I see but a tall, pale-looking young guy with blond hair and thin legs.

Furthermore, he has pale blue eyes, and a faraway look in them, and he speaks in a low voice, which is nothing like the voice of Shamus Mulrooney. But Spider seems satisfied with Thunderbolt, and when I tell him Thunderbolt does not look to me like the next heavyweight champion of the world, Spider says like this:

"Why," he says, "the guy is nothing but a baby, and you must give him time to fill out. He may grow to be bigger than his papa. But you know," Spider says, getting indignant as he thinks about it, "Bridget Mulrooney does not wish to let this guy be the next heavyweight champion of the world. In fact," Spider says, "she kicks up an awful row when I go to get him, and Shamus finally has to speak to her severely. Shamus says he does not know if I can ever make a fighter of this guy because Bridget coddles him until he is nothing but a mush-head, and Shamus says he is sick and tired of seeing the guy sitting around the house doing nothing but reading and playing the zither."

"Does he play the zither yet?" I ask Spider McCoy.

"No," Spider says, "I do not allow my fighters to play zithers. I figure it softens them up. This guy does not play anything at present. He seems to be in a daze most of the time, but of course everything is new to him. He is bound to come out okay, because," Spider says, "he is certainly bred right. I find out from Shamus that all the Mulrooneys are great fighters back in the old country," Spider says, "and furthermore he tells me Bridget's mother once licks four Newark cops who try to stop her from pasting her old man, so," Spider says, "this lad is just naturally steaming with fighting blood."

Well, I drop around to the Pioneer once or twice a week after this, and Spider McCoy is certainly working hard with Thunderbolt Mulrooney. Furthermore, the guy seems to be improving right along, and gets so he can box fairly well and punch the bag, and all this and that, but he always has that faraway look in his eyes, and personally I do not care for fighters with faraway looks.

Finally one day Spider calls me up and tells me he has Thunderbolt Mulrooney matched in a four-round preliminary bout at the St. Nick with a guy by the name of Bubbles Browning, who is fighting almost as far back as the first battle of Bull Run, so I can see Spider is being very careful in matching Thunderbolt. In fact I congratulate Spider on his carefulness.

"Well," Spider says, "I am taking this match just to give Thunderbolt the feel of the ring. I am taking Bubbles because he is an old friend of mine, and very deserving, and furthermore," Spider says, "he gives me his word he will not hit Thunderbolt very hard and will become unconscious the instant Thunderbolt hits him. You know," Spider says, "you must encourage a young heavyweight, and there is nothing that encourages one so much as knocking somebody unconscious."

Now of course it is nothing for Bubbles to promise not to hit anybody very hard because even when he is a young guy, Bubbles cannot punch his way out of a paper bag, but I am glad to learn that he also promises to become unconscious very soon, as naturally I am greatly interested in Thunderbolt's career, what with owning a piece of him, and having an investment of one pound in him already.

So the night of the fight, I am at the St. Nick very early, and many other citizens are there ahead of me, because by this time Spider McCoy gets plenty of publicity for Thunderbolt by telling the boxing scribes about his wonderful fighting bloodlines, and everybody wishes to see a guy who is bred for battle, like Thunderbolt.

I take a guest with me to the fight by the name of Harry the Horse, who comes from Brooklyn, and as I am anxious to help Spider McCoy all I can, as well as to protect my investment in Thunderbolt, I request Harry to call on Bubbles Browning in his dressing room and remind him of his promise about hitting Thunderbolt.

Harry the Horse does this for me, and furthermore he shows Bubbles a large revolver and tells Bubbles that he will be compelled to shoot his ears off if Bubbles forgets his promise, but Bubbles says all this is most unnecessary, as his eyesight is so bad he cannot see to hit anybody, anyway.

Well, I know a party who is a friend of the guy who is going to referee the preliminary bouts, and I am looking for this party to get him to tell the referee to disqualify Bubbles in case it looks as if he is forgetting his promise and is liable to hit Thunderbolt, but before I can locate the party, they are announcing the opening bout, and there is Thunderbolt in the ring looking very far away indeed, with Spider McCoy behind him.

It seems to me I never see a guy who is so pale all over as Thunderbolt Mulrooney, but Spider looks down at me and tips me a large wink, so I can see that everything is as right as rain, especially when Harry the Horse makes motions at Bubbles Browning like a guy firing a large revolver at somebody, and Bubbles smiles, and also winks.

Well, when the bell rings, Spider gives Thunderbolt a shove toward the center, and Thunderbolt comes out with his hands up, but looking more far away than somewhat, and something tells me that Thunderbolt by no means feels the killer instinct such as I love to see in fighters. In fact, something tells me that Thunderbolt is not feeling enthusiastic about this proposition in any way, shape, manner, or form.

Old Bubbles almost falls over his own feet coming out of his corner, and he starts bouncing around making passes at Thunderbolt, and waiting for Thunderbolt to hit him so he can become unconscious. Naturally, Bubbles does not wish to become unconscious without getting hit, as this may look suspicious to the public.

Well, instead of hitting Bubbles, what does Thunderbolt Mulrooney do but turn around and walk over to a neutral corner, and lean over the ropes with his face in his gloves, and bust out crying. Naturally, this is a most surprising incident to one and all, and especially to Bubbles Browning.

The referee walks over to Thunderbolt Mulrooney and tries to turn him around, but Thunderbolt keeps his face in his gloves and sobs so loud that the referee is deeply touched and starts sobbing with him. Between the sobs he asks Thunderbolt if he wishes to continue the fight, and Thunderbolt shakes his head, although as a matter of fact no fight whatever starts so far, so the referee declares Bubbles Browning the winner, which is a terrible surprise to Bubbles.

Then the referee puts his arm around Thunderbolt and leads him over to Spider McCoy, who is standing in his corner with a very strange expression on his face. Personally, I consider the entire spectacle so revolting that I go out into the air, and stand around awhile expecting to hear any minute that Spider McCoy is in the hands of the gendarmes on a charge of mayhem.

But it seems that nothing happens, and when Spider finally comes out of the St. Nick, he is only looking sorrowful because he just hears that the promoter declines to pay him the fifty bobs he is supposed to receive for Thunderbolt's services, the promoter claiming that Thunderbolt renders no service.

"Well," Spider says, "I fear this is not the next heavyweight champion of the world after all. There is nothing in Professor D's idea about bloodlines as far as fighters are concerned, although," he says, "it may work out all right with horses and dogs, and one thing and another. I am greatly disappointed," Spider says, "but then I am always being disappointed in heavyweights. There is nothing we can do but take this guy back home, because," Spider says, "the last thing I promise Bridget Mulrooney is that I will personally return him to her in case I am not able to make him heavyweight champion, as she is afraid he will get lost if he tries to find his way home alone."

So the next day, Spider McCoy and I take Thunderbolt Mulrooney over to Newark and to his home, which turns out to be a nice little house in a side street with a yard all round and about, and Spider and I are just as well pleased that old Shamus Mulrooney is absent when we arrive, because Spider says that Shamus is just such a guy as will be asking a lot of questions about the fifty bobbos that Thunderbolt does not get.

Well, when we reach the front door of the house, out comes a big, fine-looking doll with red cheeks, all excited, and she takes Thunderbolt in her arms and kisses him, so I know this is Bridget Mulrooney, and I can see she knows what happens, and in fact I afterward learn that Thunderbolt telephones her the night before.

After a while she pushes Thunderbolt into the house and stands at the door as if she is guarding it against us entering to get him again, which of course is very unnecessary. And all this time Thunderbolt is sobbing no little, although by and by the sobs die away, and from somewhere in the house comes the sound of music I seem to recognize as the music of a zither.

Well, Bridget Mulrooney never says a word to us as she stands in the door, and Spider McCoy keeps staring at her in a way that I consider very rude indeed. I am wondering if he is waiting for a receipt for Thunderbolt, but finally he speaks as follows:

"Bridget," Spider says, "I hope and trust that you will not consider me too fresh, but I wish to learn the name of the guy you are going around with just before you marry Shamus. I remember him well," Spider says, "but I cannot think of his name, and it bothers me not being able to think of names. He is a tall, skinny, stoop-shouldered guy," Spider says, "with a hollow chest and a soft voice, and he loves music."

Well, Bridget Mulrooney stands there in the doorway, staring back at Spider, and it seems to me that the red suddenly fades out of her cheeks, and just then we hear a lot of yelling, and around the corner of the house comes a bunch of five or six kids, who seem to be running from another kid.

This kid is not very big, and is maybe fifteen or sixteen years old, and he has red hair and many freckles, and he seems very mad at the other kids. In fact, when he catches up with them he starts belting away at them with his fists and before anybody can as much as say boo, he has three of them on the ground as flat as pancakes, while the others are yelling bloody murder.

Personally, I never see such wonderful punching by a kid, especially with his left hand, and Spider McCoy is also much impressed, and is watching the kid with great interest. Then Bridget Mulrooney runs out and grabs the freckle-faced kid with one hand and smacks him with the other hand and hauls him, squirming and kicking, over to Spider McCoy and says to Spider like this:

"Mr. McCoy," Bridget says, "this is my youngest son, Terence, and though he is not a heavyweight, and will never be a heavyweight, perhaps he will answer your purpose. Suppose you see his father about him sometime," she says, "and hoping you will learn to mind your own business, I wish you a very good day."

Then she takes the kid into the house under her arm and slams the door in our kissers, and there is nothing for us to do but walk away. And as we are walking away, all of a sudden Spider McCoy snaps his fingers as guys will do when they get an unexpected thought, and says like this:

"I remember the guy's name," he says. "It is Cedric Tilbury, and he is a floorwalker in Hamburgher's department store, and," Spider says, "how he can play the zither!"

I see in the papers the other day where Jimmy Johnston, the matchmaker at the Garden, matches Tearing Terry Mulrooney, the new sensation of the lightweight division, to fight for the championship, but it seems from what Spider McCoy tells me that my investment with him does not cover any fighters in his stable except maybe heavyweights.

And it also seems that Spider McCoy is not monkeying with heavyweights since he gets Tearing Terry.

LIITLE
MISS
MARKER

O ne evening along toward seven o'clock, many citizens are standing out on Broadway in front of Mindy's restaurant, speaking of one thing and another, and particularly about the tough luck they have playing the races in the afternoon, when who comes up the street with a little doll hanging on to his right thumb but a guy by the name of Sorrowful.

This guy is called Sorrowful because this is the way he always is about no matter what, and especially about the way things are with him when anybody tries to put the bite on him. In fact, if anybody who tries to put the bite on Sorrowful can listen to him for two minutes about how things are with him and not bust into tears, they must be very hard-hearted, indeed.

Regret, the horse player, is telling me that he once tries to put the bite on Sorrowful for a sawbuck, and by the time Sorrowful gets through explaining how things are with him, Regret feels so sorry for him that he goes out and puts the bite on somebody else for the saw and gives it to Sorrowful, although it is well known to one and all that Sorrowful has plenty of potatoes hid away somewhere.

He is a tall, skinny guy with a long, sad, mean-looking kisser, and a mournful voice. He is maybe sixty years old, give or take a couple of years, and for as long as I can remember he is running a handbook over in Forty-ninth Street next door to a chop-suey joint. In fact, Sorrowful is one of the largest handbook makers in this town.

Any time you see him he is generally by himself, because being by himself is not apt to cost him anything, and it is therefore a most surprising scene when he comes along Broadway with a little doll.

And there is much speculation among the citizens as to how this comes about, for no one ever hears of Sorrowful having any family, or relations of any kind, or even any friends.

The little doll is a very little doll indeed, the top of her noggin only coming up to Sorrowful's knee, although of course Sorrowful has very high knees, at that. Moreover, she is a very pretty little doll, with big blue eyes and fat pink cheeks, and a lot of yellow curls hanging down her back, and she has fat little legs and quite a large smile, although Sorrowful is lugging her along the street so fast that half the time her feet are dragging the sidewalk and she has a license to be bawling instead of smiling.

Sorrowful is looking sadder than somewhat, which makes his face practically heartrending, so he pulls up in front of Mindy's and motions us to follow him in. Anybody can see that he is worried about something very serious, and many citizens are figuring that maybe he suddenly discovers all his potatoes are counterfeit, because nobody can think of anything that will worry Sorrowful except money.

Anyway, four or five of us gather around the table where Sorrowful sits down with the little doll beside him, and he states a most surprising situation to us.

It seems that early in the afternoon a young guy who is playing the races with Sorrowful for several days pops into his place of business next door to the chop-suey joint, leading the little doll, and this guy wishes to know how much time he has before post in the first race at Empire.

Well, he only has about twenty-five minutes, and he seems very downhearted about this, because he explains to Sorrowful that he has a sure thing in this race, which he gets the night before off a guy who is a pal of a close friend of Jockey Workman's valet.

The young guy says he is figuring to bet himself about a deuce on this sure thing, but he does not have such a sum as a deuce on him when he goes to bed, so he plans to get up bright and early in the morning and hop down to a spot on Fourteenth Street where he knows a guy who will let him have the deuce.

But it seems he oversleeps, and here it is almost post time, and it is too late for him to get to Fourteenth Street and back before the race is run off, and it is all quite a sad story indeed, although of course it does not make much impression on Sorrowful, as he is already sadder than somewhat himself just from thinking that somebody may beat him for a bet during the day, even though the races do not start anywhere as yet.

Well, the young guy tells Sorrowful he is going to try to get to Fourteenth Street and back in time to bet on the sure thing, because he says it will be nothing short of a crime if he has to miss such a wonderful opportunity.

"But," he says to Sorrowful, "to make sure I do not miss, you take my marker for a deuce, and I will leave the kid here with you as security until I get back."

Now, ordinarily, asking Sorrowful to take a marker will be considered great foolishness, as it is well known to one and all that Sorrowful will not take a marker from Andrew Mellon. In fact, Sorrowful can almost break your heart telling you about the poorhouses that are full of bookmakers who take markers in their time.

But it happens that business is just opening up for the day, and Sorrowful is pretty busy, and besides the young guy is a steady customer for several days, and has an honest pan, and Sorrowful figures a guy is bound to take a little doll out of hock for a deuce. Furthermore, while Sorrowful does not know much about kids, he can see the little doll must be worth a deuce, at least, and maybe more.

So he nods his head, and the young guy puts the little doll on a chair and goes tearing out of the joint to get the dough, while Sorrowful marks down a deuce bet on Cold Cuts, which is the name of the sure thing. Then he forgets all about the proposition for a while, and all the time the little doll is sitting on the chair as quiet as a mouse, smiling at Sorrowful's customers, including the Chinks from the chop-suey joint who come in now and then to play the races.

Well, Cold Cuts blows, and in fact is not even fifth, and along late in the afternoon Sorrowful suddenly realizes that the young guy never shows up again, and that the little doll is still sitting in the chair, although she is now playing with a butcher knife which one of the Chinks from the chop-suey joint gives her to keep her amused.

Finally it comes on Sorrowful's closing time, and the little doll is still there, so he can think of nothing else to do in this situation, but to bring her around to Mindy's and get a little advice from different citizens, as he does not care to leave her in his place of business alone, as Sorrowful will not trust anybody in there alone, not even himself.

"Now," Sorrowful says, after giving us this long spiel, "what are we to do about this proposition?"

Well, of course, up to this minute none of the rest of us know we are being cut in on any proposition, and personally I do not care for any part of it, but Big Nig, the crap shooter, speaks up as follows:

"If this little doll is sitting in your joint all afternoon," Nig says, "the best thing to do right now is to throw a feed into her, as the chances are her stomach thinks her throat is cut."

Now this seems to be a fair sort of an idea, so Sorrowful orders up a couple of portions of ham hocks and sauerkraut, which is a very tasty dish in Mindy's at all times, and the little doll tears into it very enthusiastically, using both hands, although a fat old doll who is sitting at the next table speaks up and says this is terrible fodder to be tossing into a child at such an hour, and where is her mama?

"Well," Big Nig says to the old doll, "I hear of many people getting a bust in the snoot for not minding their own business in this town, but you give off an idea, at that. Listen," Big Nig says to the little doll, "where is your mama?"

But the little doll does not seem to know, or maybe she does not wish to make this information public, because she only shakes her head and smiles at Big Nig, as her mouth is too full of ham hocks and sauerkraut for her to talk.

"What is your name?" Big Nig asks, and she says something that Big Nig claims sounds like Marky, although personally I think she is trying to say Martha. Anyway it is from this that she gets the name we always call her afterward, which is Marky.

"It is a good monicker," Big Nig says. "It is short for marker, and she is certainly a marker unless Sorrowful is telling us a large lie. Why," Big Nig says, "this is a very cute little doll, at that, and pretty smart. How old are you, Marky?"

She only shakes her head again, so Regret, the horse player, who claims he can tell how old a horse is by its teeth, reaches over and sticks his finger in her mouth to get a peek at her crockery, but she seems to think Regret's finger is a hunk of ham hock and shuts down on it so hard Regret lets out an awful squawk. But he says that before she tries to cripple him for life he sees enough of her teeth to convince him she is maybe three, rising four, and this seems reasonable, at that. Anyway, she cannot be much older.

Well, about this time a guinea with a hand organ stops out in front of Mindy's and begins grinding out a tune while his ever-loving wife is passing a tambourine around among the citizens on the sidewalk and, on hearing this music, Marky slides off of her chair with her mouth still full of ham hock and sauerkraut, which she swallows so fast she almost chokes, and then she speaks as follows:

"Marky dance," she says.

Then she begins hopping and skipping around among the tables, holding her little short skirt up in her hands and showing a pair of white panties underneath. Pretty soon Mindy himself comes along and starts putting up a beef about making a dance hall of his joint, but a guy by the name of Sleep-out, who is watching Marky with much interest, offers to bounce a sugar bowl off of Mindy's sconce if he does not mind his own business.

So Mindy goes away, but he keeps muttering about the white panties being a most immodest spectacle, which of course is great nonsense, as many dolls older than Marky are known to do dances in Mindy's, especially on the late watch, when they stop by for a snack on their way home from the nightclubs and the speaks, and I hear some of them do not always wear white panties, either.

Personally, I like Marky's dancing very much, although of course she is no Pavlova, and finally she trips over her own feet and falls on her snoot. But she gets up smiling and climbs back on her chair and pretty soon she is sound asleep with her head against Sorrowful.

Well, now there is much discussion about what Sorrowful ought to do with her. Some claim he ought to take her to a police station, and others say the best thing to do is to put an ad in the Lost and Found columns of the morning bladders, the same as people do when they find Angora cats, and Pekes, and other animals which they do not wish to keep, but none of these ideas seems to appeal to Sorrowful.

Finally he says he will take her to his own home and let her sleep there while he is deciding what is to be done about her, so Sorrowful takes Marky in his arms and lugs her over to a fleabag in West Forty-ninth Street where he has a room for many years, and afterward a bellhop tells me Sorrowful sits up all night watching her while she is sleeping.

Now what happens but Sorrowful takes on a great fondness for the little doll, which is most surprising, as Sorrowful is never before fond of anybody or anything, and after he has her overnight he cannot bear the idea of giving her up.

Personally, I will just as soon have a three-year-old baby wolf around me as a little doll such as this, but Sorrowful thinks she is the greatest thing that ever happens. He has a few inquiries made around and about to see if he can find out who she belongs to, and he is tickled silly when nothing comes of these inquiries, although nobody else figures anything will come of them anyway, as it is by no means uncommon in this town for little kids to be left sitting in chairs, or on doorsteps, to be chucked into orphan asylums by whoever finds them.

Anyway, Sorrowful says he is going to keep Marky, and his attitude causes great surprise, as keeping Marky is bound to be an expense, and it does not seem reasonable that Sorrowful will go to any expense for anything. When it commences to look as if he means what he says, many citizens naturally figure there must be an angle, and soon there are a great many rumors on the subject.

Of course one of these rumors is that the chances are Marky is Sorrowful's own offspring which is tossed back on him by the wronged mama, but this rumor is started by a guy who does not know Sorrowful, and after he gets a gander at Sorrowful, the guy apologizes, saying he realizes that no wronged mama will be daffy enough to permit herself to be wronged by Sorrowful. Personally, I always say that if Sorrowful wishes to keep Marky it is his own business, and most of the citizens around Mindy's agree with me.

But the trouble is Sorrowful at once cuts everybody else in on the management of Marky, and the way he talks to the citizens around Mindy's about her, you will think we are all personally responsible for her. As most of the citizens around Mindy's are bachelors, or are wishing they are bachelors, it is most inconvenient to them to suddenly find themselves with a family.

Some of us try to explain to Sorrowful that if he is going to keep Marky it is up to him to handle all her play, but right away Sorrowful starts talking so sad about all his pals deserting him and Marky just when they need them most that it softens all hearts, although up to this time we are about as pally with Sorrowful as a burglar with a copper. Finally every night in Mindy's is meeting night for a committee to decide something or other about Marky.

The first thing we decide is that the fleabag where Sorrowful lives is no place for Marky, so Sorrowful hires a big apartment in one of the swellest joints on West Fifty-ninth Street, overlooking Central Park, and spends plenty of potatoes furnishing it, although up to this time Sorrowful never sets himself back more than about ten bobs per week for a place to live and considers it extravagance, at that. I hear it costs him five G's to fix up Marky's bedroom alone, not counting the solid gold toilet set that he buys for her.

Then he gets her an automobile and he has to hire a guy to drive it for her, and finally when we explain to Sorrowful that it does not look right for Marky to be living with nobody but him and a chauffeur, Sorrowful hires a French doll with bobbed hair and red cheeks by the name of Mam'selle Fifi as a nurse for Marky, and this seems to be quite a sensible move, as it insures Marky plenty of company.

In fact, up to the time that Sorrowful hires Mam'selle Fifi, many citizens are commencing to consider Marky something of a nuisance and are playing the duck for her and Sorrowful, but after Mam'selle Fifi comes along you can scarcely get in Sorrowful's joint on Fifty-ninth Street, or around his table in Mindy's when he brings Marky and Mam'selle Fifi to eat. But one night Sorrowful goes home early and catches Sleep-out guzzling Mam'selle Fifi, and Sorrowful makes Mam'selle Fifi take plenty of breeze, claiming she will set a bad example to Marky.

Then he gets an old tomato by the name of Mrs. Clancy to be Marky's nurse, and while there is no doubt Mrs. Clancy is a better nurse than Mam'selle Fifi and there is practically no danger of her setting Marky a bad example, the play at Sorrowful's joint is by no means as brisk as formerly.

You can see that from being closer than a dead heat with his potatoes, Sorrowful becomes as loose as ashes. He not only spends plenty on Marky, but he starts picking up checks in Mindy's and other spots, although up to this time picking up checks is something that is most repulsive to Sorrowful.

He gets so he will hold still for a bite, if the bite is not too savage and, what is more, a great change comes over his kisser. It is no longer so sad and mean looking, and in fact it is almost a pleasant sight at times, especially as Sorrowful gets so he smiles now and then, and has a big hello for one and all, and everybody says the Mayor ought to give Marky a medal for bringing about such a wonderful change.

Now Sorrowful is so fond of Marky that he wants her with him all the time, and by and by there is much criticism of him for having her around his handbook joint among the Chinks and the horse players, and especially the horse players, and for taking her around nightclubs and keeping her out at all hours, as some people do not consider this a proper bringing-up for a little doll.

We hold a meeting in Mindy's on this proposition one night, and we get Sorrowful to agree to keep Marky out of his joint, but we know Marky is so fond of nightclubs, especially where there is music, that it seems a sin and a shame to deprive her of this pleasure altogether, so we finally compromise by letting Sorrowful take her out one night a week to the Hot Box in Fifty-fourth Street, which is only a few blocks from where Marky lives, and Sorrowful can get her home fairly early. In fact, after this Sorrowful seldom keeps her out any later than 2 A.M.

The reason Marky likes nightclubs where there is music is because she can do her dance there, as Marky is practically daffy on the subject of dancing, especially by herself, even though she never seems to be able to get over winding up by falling on her snoot, which many citizens consider a very artistic finish, at that.

The Choo-Choo Boys' band in the Hot Box always play a special number for Marky in between the regular dances, and she gets plenty of applause, especially from the Broadway citizens who know her, although Henri, the manager of the Hot Box, once tells me he will just as soon Marky does not do her dancing there, because one night several of his best customers from Park Avenue, including two millionaires and two old dolls, who do not understand Marky's dancing, bust out laughing when she falls on her snoot, and Big Nig puts the slug on the guys, and is trying to put the slug on the old dolls, too, when he is finally headed off.

Now one cold, snowy night, many citizens are sitting around the tables in the Hot Box, speaking of one thing and another and having a few drams, when Sorrowful drops in on his way home, for Sorrowful has now become a guy who is around and about, and in and out. He does not have Marky with him, as it is not her night out and she is home with Mrs. Clancy.

A few minutes after Sorrowful arrives, a party by the name of Milk Ear Willie from the West Side comes in, this Milk Ear Willie being a party who is once a prizefighter and who has a milk ear, which is the reason he is called Milk Ear Willie, and who is known to carry a John Roscoe in his pants pocket. Furthermore, it is well known that he knocks off several guys in his time, so he is considered rather a suspicious character.

It seems that the reason he comes into the Hot Box is to shoot Sorrowful full of little holes, because he has a dispute with Sorrowful about a parlay on the races the day before, and the chances are Sorrowful will now be very dead if it does not happen that, just as Milk Ear outs with the old equalizer and starts taking dead aim at Sorrowful from a table across the room, who pops into the joint but Marky.

She is in a long nightgown that keeps getting tangled up in her bare feet as she runs across the dance floor and jumps into Sorrowful's arms, so if Milk Ear Willie lets go at this time he is apt to put a slug in Marky, and this is by no means Willie's intention. So Willie puts his rod back in his kick, but he is greatly disgusted and stops as he is going out and makes a large complaint to Henri about allowing children in a nightclub.

Well, Sorrowful does not learn until afterward how Marky saves his life, as he is too much horrified over her coming four or five blocks through the snow barefooted to think of anything else, and everybody present is also horrified and wondering how Marky finds her way there. But Marky does not seem to have any good explanation for her conduct, except that she wakes up and discovers Mrs. Clancy asleep and gets to feeling lonesome for Sorrowful.

About this time, the Choo-Choo Boys start playing Marky's tune, and she slips out of Sorrowful's arms and runs out on the dance floor.

"Marky dance," she says.

Then she lifts her nightgown in her hands and starts hopping and skipping about the floor until Sorrowful collects her in his arms again, and wraps her in an overcoat and takes her home.

Now what happens but the next day Marky is sick from being out in the snow barefooted and with nothing on but her nightgown, and by night she is very sick indeed, and it seems that she has pneumonia, so Sorrowful takes her to the Clinic hospital, and hires two nurses and two croakers, and wishes to hire more, only they tell him these will do for the present.

The next day Marky is no better, and the next night she is worse, and the management of the Clinic is very much upset because it has no place to put the baskets of fruit and candy and floral horseshoes and crates of dolls and toys that keep arriving every few minutes. Furthermore, the management by no means approves of the citizens who are tiptoeing along the hall on the floor where Marky has her room, especially such as Big Nig, and Sleep-out, and Wop Joey, and the Pale Face Kid and Guinea Mike and many other prominent characters, especially as these characters keep trying to date up the nurses.

Of course I can see the management's point of view, but I wish to say that no visitor to the Clinic ever brings more joy and cheer to the patients than Sleep-out, as he goes calling in all the private rooms and wards to say a pleasant word or two to the inmates, and I never take any stock in the rumor that he is looking around to see if there is anything worth picking up. In fact, an old doll from Rockville Center, who is suffering with yellow jaundice, puts up an awful holler when Sleep-out is heaved from her room, because she says he is right in the middle of a story about a traveling salesman and she wishes to learn what happens.

There are so many prominent characters in and around the Clinic that the morning bladders finally get the idea that some well-known mob guy must be in the hospital full of slugs, and by and by the reporters come buzzing around to see what is what. Naturally they find out that all this interest is in nothing but a little doll, and while you will naturally think that such a little doll as Marky can scarcely be worth the attention of the reporters, it seems they get more heated up over her when they hear the story than if she is Jack Diamond.

In fact, the next day all the bladders have large stories about Marky, and also about Sorrowful and about how all these prominent characters of Broadway are hanging around the Clinic on her account. Moreover, one story tells about Sleep-out entertaining the other patients in the hospital, and it makes Sleep-out sound like a very large-hearted guy.

It is maybe three o'clock on the morning of the fourth day Marky is in the hospital that Sorrowful comes into Mindy's looking very sad, indeed. He orders a sturgeon sandwich on pumpernickel, and then he explains that Marky seems to be getting worse by the minute and that he does not think his doctors are doing her any good, and at this Big Nig, the crap shooter, speaks up and states as follows:

"Well," Big Nig says, "if we are only able to get Doc Beerfeldt, the great pneumonia specialist, the chances are he will cure Marky like breaking sticks. But of course," Nig says, "it is impossible to get Doc Beerfeldt unless you are somebody like John D. Rockefeller, or maybe the President."

Naturally, everybody knows that what Big Nig says is very true, for Doc Beerfeldt is the biggest croaker in this town, but no ordinary guy can get close enough to Doc Beerfeldt to hand him a ripe peach, let alone get him to go out on a case. He is an old guy, and he does not practice much any more, and then only among a few very rich and influential people. Furthermore, he has plenty of potatoes himself, so money does not interest him whatever, and anyway it is great foolishness to be talking of getting Doc Beerfeldt out at such an hour as this.

"Who do we know who knows Doc Beerfeldt?" Sorrowful says. "Who can we call up who may have influence enough with him to get him to just look at Marky? I will pay any price," he says. "Think of somebody," he says.

Well, while we are all trying to think, who comes in but Milk Ear Willie, and he comes in to toss a few slugs at Sorrowful, but before Milk Ear can start blasting Sleep-out sees him and jumps up and takes him off to a corner table, and starts whispering in Milk Ear's good ear.

As Sleep-out talks to him Milk Ear looks at Sorrowful in great surprise, and finally he begins nodding his head, and by and by he gets up and goes out of the joint in a hurry, while Sleep-out comes back to our table and says like this:

"Well," Sleep-out says, "let us stroll over to the Clinic. I just send Milk Ear Willie up to Doc Beerfeldt's house on Park Avenue to get the old Doc and bring him to the hospital. But, Sorrowful," Sleep-out says, "if he gets him, you must pay Willie the parlay you dispute with him, whatever it is. The chances are," Sleep-out says, "Willie is right. I remember once you out-argue me on a parlay when I know I am right."

Personally, I consider Sleep-out's talk about sending Milk Ear Willie after Doc Beerfeldt just so much nonsense, and so does everybody else, but we figure maybe Sleep-out is trying to raise Sorrowful's hopes, and anyway he keeps Milk Ear from tossing these slugs at Sorrowful, which everybody considers very thoughtful of Sleep-out, at least, especially as Sorrowful is under too great a strain to be dodging slugs just now.

About a dozen of us walk over to the Clinic, and most of us stand around the lobby on the ground floor, although Sorrowful goes up to Marky's floor to wait outside her door. He is waiting there from the time she is first taken to the hospital, never leaving except to go over to Mindy's once in a while to get something to eat, and occasionally they open the door a little to let him get a peek at Marky.

Well, it is maybe six o'clock when we hear a taxi stop outside the hospital and pretty soon in comes Milk Ear Willie with another character from the West Side by the name of Fats Finstein, who is well known to one and all as a great friend of Willie's, and in between them they have a little old guy with a Vandyke beard, who does not seem to have on anything much but a silk dressing-gown and who seems somewhat agitated, especially as Milk Ear Willie and Fats Finstein keep prodding him from behind.

Now it comes out that this little old guy is nobody but Doc Beerfeldt, the great pneumonia specialist, and personally I never see a madder guy, although I wish to say I never blame him much for being mad when I learn how Milk Ear Willie and Fats Finstein boff his butler over the noggin when he answers their ring, and how they walk right into old Doc Beerfeldt's bedroom and haul him out of the hay at the point of their Roscoes and make him go with them.

In fact, I consider such treatment most discourteous to a prominent croaker, and if I am Doc Beerfeldt I will start hollering copper as soon as I hit the hospital, and for all I know maybe Doc Beerfeldt has just such an idea, but as Milk Ear Willie and Fats Finstein haul him into the lobby who comes downstairs but Sorrowful. And the minute Sorrowful sees Doc Beerfeldt he rushes up to him and says like this:

"Oh Doc," Sorrowful says, "do something for my little girl. She is dying, Doc," Sorrowful says. "Just a little bit of a girl, Doc. Her name is Marky. I am only a gambler, Doc, and I do not mean anything to you or to anybody else, but please save the little girl."

Well, old Doc Beerfeldt sticks out his Vandyke beard and looks at Sorrowful a minute, and he can see there are large tears in old Sorrowful's eyes, and for all I know maybe the Doc knows it has been many and many a year since there are tears in these eyes, at that. Then the Doc looks at Milk Ear Willie and Fats Finstein and the rest of us, and at the nurses and interns who are commencing to come running up from every which way. Finally, he speaks as follows:

"What is this?" he says. "A child? A little child? Why," he says, "I am under the impression that these gorillas are kidnaping me to attend to some other sick or wounded gorilla. A child? This is quite different. Why do you not say so in the first place? Where is the child?" Doc Beerfeldt says, "and," he says, "somebody get me some pants."

We all follow him upstairs to the door of Marky's room and we wait outside when he goes in, and we wait there for hours, because it seems that even old Doc Beerfeldt cannot think of anything to do in this situation no matter how he tries. And along toward ten-thirty in the morning he opens the door very quietly and motions Sorrowful to come in, and then he motions all the rest of us to follow, shaking his head very sad.

There are so many of us that we fill the room around a little high narrow bed on which Marky is lying like a flower against a white wall, her yellow curls spread out over her pillow. Old Sorrowful drops on his knees beside the bed and his shoulders heave quite some as he kneels there, and I hear Sleep-out sniffing as if he has a cold in his head. Marky seems to be asleep when we go in, but while we are standing around the bed looking down at her, she opens her eyes and seems to see us and, what is more, she seems to know us, because she smiles at each guy in turn and then tries to hold out one of her little hands to Sorrowful.

Now very faint, like from far away, comes a sound of music through a half-open window in the room, from a jazz band that is rehearsing in a hall just up the street from the hospital, and Marky hears this music because she holds her head in such a way that anybody can see she is listening, and then she smiles again at us and whispers very plain, as follows:

"Marky dance."

And she tries to reach down as if to pick up her skirt as she always does when she dances, but her hands fall across her breast as soft and white and light as snowflakes, and Marky never again dances in this world.

Well, old Doc Beerfeldt and the nurses make us go outside at once, and while we are standing there in the hall outside the door, saying nothing whatever, a young guy and two dolls, one of them old, and the other not so old, come along the hall much excited. The young guy seems to know Sorrowful, who is sitting down again in his chair just outside the door, because he rushes up to Sorrowful and says to him like this:

"Where is she?" he says. "Where is my darling child? You remember me?" he says. "I leave my little girl with you one day while I go on an errand, and while I am on this errand everything goes blank, and I wind up back in my home in Indianapolis with my mother and sister here, and recall nothing about where I leave my child, or anything else."

"The poor boy has amnesia," the old doll says. "The stories that he deliberately abandons his wife in Paris and his child in New York are untrue."

"Yes," the doll who is not old puts in. "If we do not see the stories in the newspapers about how you have the child in this hospital we may never learn where she is. But everything is all right now. Of course we never approve of Harold's marriage to a person of the stage, and we only recently learn of her death in Paris soon after their separation there and are very sorry. But everything is all right now. We will take full charge of the child."

Now while all this gab is going on, Sorrowful never glances at them. He is just sitting there looking at Marky's door. And now as he is looking at the door a very strange thing seems to happen to his kisser, for all of a sudden it becomes the sad, mean-looking kisser that it is in the days before he ever sees Marky, and furthermore it is never again anything else.

"We will be rich," the young guy says. "We just learn that my darling child will be sole heiress to her maternal grandpapa's fortune, and the old guy is only a hop ahead of the undertaker right now. I suppose," he says, "I owe you something?"

And then Sorrowful gets up off his chair, and looks at the young guy and at the two dolls, and speaks as follows:

"Yes," he says, "you owe me a two-dollar marker for the bet you blow on Cold Cuts, and," he says, "I will trouble you to send it to me at once, so I can wipe you off my books."

Now he walks down the hall and out of the hospital, never looking back again, and there is a very great silence behind him that is broken only by the sniffing of Sleep-out, and by some first-class sobbing from some of the rest of us, and I remember now that the guy who is doing the best job of sobbing of all is nobody but Milk Ear Willie.

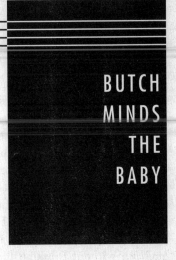

BUTCH
MINDS
THE
BABY

One evening along about seven o'clock I am sitting in Mindy's restaurant putting on the gefillte fish, which is a dish I am very fond of, when in come three parties from Brooklyn wearing caps as follows: Harry the Horse, Little Isadore and Spanish John.

Now these parties are not such parties as I will care to have much truck with, because I often hear rumors about them that are very discreditable, even if the rumors are not true. In fact, I hear that many citizens of Brooklyn will be very glad indeed to see Harry the Horse, Little Isadore and Spanish John move away from there, as they are always doing something that is considered a knock to the community, such as robbing people, or maybe shooting or stabbing them, and throwing pineapples, and carrying on generally.

I am really much surprised to see these parties on Broadway, as it is well known that the Broadway coppers just naturally love to shove such parties around, but there they are in Mindy's, and there I am, so of course I give them a very large hello, as I never wish to seem inhospitable, even to Brooklyn parties. Right away they come over to my table and sit down, and Little Isadore reaches out and spears himself a big hunk of my gefillte fish with his fingers, but I overlook this, as I am using the only knife on the table.

Then they all sit there looking at me without saying anything, and the way they look at me makes me very nervous indeed. Finally I figure that maybe they are a little embarrassed being in a high-class spot such as Mindy's, with legitimate people around and about, so I say to them, very polite:

"It is a nice night."

"What is nice about it?" asks Harry the Horse, who is a thin man with a sharp face and sharp eyes.

Well, now that it is put up to me in this way, I can see there is nothing so nice about the night, at that, so I try to think of something else jolly to say, while Little Isadore keeps spearing at my gefillte fish with his fingers, and Spanish John nabs one of my potatoes.

"Where does Big Butch live?" Harry the Horse asks.

"Big Butch?" I say, as if I never hear the name before in my life, because in this man's town it is never a good idea to answer any question without thinking it over, as some time you may give the right answer to the wrong guy, or the wrong answer to the right guy. "Where does Big Butch live?" I ask them again.

"Yes, where does he live?" Harry the Horse says, very impatient. "We wish you to take us to him."

"Now wait a minute, Harry," I say, and I am now more nervous than somewhat. "I am not sure I remember the exact house Big Butch lives in, and furthermore I am not sure Big Butch will care to have me bringing people to see him, especially three at a time, and especially from Brooklyn. You know Big Butch has a very bad disposition, and there is no telling what he may say to me if he does not like the idea of me taking you to him."

"Everything is very kosher," Harry the Horse says. "You need not be afraid of anything whatever. We have a business proposition for Big Butch. It means a nice score for him, so you take us to him at once, or the chances are I will have to put the arm on somebody around here."

Well, as the only one around there for him to put the arm on at this time seems to be me, I can see where it will be good policy for me to take these parties to Big Butch especially as the last of my gefillte fish is just going down Little Isadore's gullet, and Spanish John is finishing up my potatoes, and is donking a piece of rye bread in my coffee, so there is nothing more for me to eat.

So I lead them over into West Forty-ninth Street, near Tenth Avenue, where Big Butch lives on the ground floor of an old brownstone-front house, and who is sitting out on the stoop but Big Butch himself. In fact, everybody in the neighborhood is sitting out on the front stoops over there, including women and children, because sitting out on the front stoops is quite a custom in this section.

Big Butch is peeled down to his undershirt and pants, and he has no shoes on his feet, as Big Butch is a guy who loves his comfort. Furthermore, he is smoking a cigar, and laid out on the stoop beside him on a blanket is a little baby with not much clothes on. This baby seems to be asleep, and every now and then Big Butch fans it with a folded newspaper to shoo away the mosquitoes that wish to nibble on the baby. These mosquitoes come across the river from the Jersey side on hot nights and they seem to be very fond of babies.

"Hello, Butch," I say, as we stop in front of the stoop.

"Sh-h-h-h!" Butch says, pointing at the baby, and making more noise with his shush than an engine blowing off steam. Then he gets up and tiptoes down to the sidewalk where we are standing, and I am hoping that Butch feels all right, because when Butch does not feel so good he is apt to be very short with one and all. He is a guy of maybe six foot two and a couple of feet wide, and he has big hairy hands and a mean look.

In fact, Big Butch is known all over this man's town as a guy you must not monkey with in any respect, so it takes plenty of weight off me when I see that he seems to know the parties from Brooklyn, and nods at them very friendly, especially at Harry the Horse. And right away Harry states a most surprising proposition to Big Butch.

It seems that there is a big coal company which has an office in an old building down in West Eighteenth Street, and in this office is a safe, and in this safe is the company payroll of twenty thousand dollars cash money. Harry the Horse knows the money is there because a personal friend of his who is the paymaster for the company puts it there late this very afternoon.

It seems that the paymaster enters into a dicker with Harry the Horse and Little Isadore and Spanish John for them to slug him while he is carrying the payroll from the bank to the office in the afternoon, but something happens that they miss connections on the exact spot, so the paymaster has to carry the sugar on to the office without being slugged, and there it is now in two fat bundles.

Personally it seems to me as I listen to Harry's story that the paymaster must be a very dishonest character to be making deals to hold still while he is being slugged and the company's sugar taken away from him, but of course it is none of my business, so I take no part in the conversation.

Well, it seems that Harry the Horse and Little Isadore and Spanish John wish to get the money out of the safe, but none of them knows anything about opening safes, and while they are standing around over in Brooklyn talking over what is to be done in this emergency Harry suddenly remembers that Big Butch is once in the business of opening safes for a living.

In fact, I hear afterward that Big Butch is considered the best safe-opener east of the Mississippi River in his day, but the law finally takes to sending him to Sing Sing for opening these safes, and after he is in and out of Sing Sing three different times for opening safes Butch gets sick and tired of the place, especially as they pass what is called the Baumes Law in New York, which is a law that says if a guy is sent to Sing Sing four times hand running, he must stay there the rest of his life, without any argument about it.

So Big Butch gives up opening safes for a living, and goes into business in a small way, such as running beer, and handling a little Scotch now and then, and becomes an honest citizen. Furthermore, he marries one of the neighbors' children over on the West Side by the name of Mary Murphy, and I judge the baby on this stoop comes of this marriage between Big Butch and Mary because I can see that it is a very homely baby, indeed. Still, I never see many babies that I consider rose geraniums for looks, anyway.

Well, it finally comes out that the idea of Harry the Horse and Little Isadore and Spanish John is to get Big Butch to open the coal company's safe and take the payroll money out, and they are willing to give him fifty percent of the money for his bother, taking fifty percent for themselves for finding the plant, and paying all the over-head, such as the paymaster, out of their bit, which strikes me as a pretty fair sort of deal for Big Butch. But Butch only shakes his head.

"It is old-fashioned stuff," Butch says. "Nobody opens pete boxes for a living anymore. They make the boxes too good, and they are all wired up with alarms and are a lot of trouble generally. I am in a legitimate business now and going along. You boys know I cannot stand another fall, what with being away three times already, and in addition to this I must mind the baby. My old lady goes to Mrs. Clancy's wake tonight up in the Bronx, and the chances are she will be there all night, as she is very fond of wakes, so I must mind little John Ignatius Junior."

"Listen, Butch," Harry the Horse says, "this is a very soft pete. It is old-fashioned, and you can open it with a toothpick. There are no wires on it, because they never put more than a dime in it before in years. It just happens they have to put the twenty G's in it tonight because my pal the paymaster makes it a point not to get back from the jug with the scratch in time to pay off today, especially after he sees we miss out on him. It is the softest touch you will ever know, and where can a guy pick up ten G's like this?"

I can see that Big Butch is thinking the ten G's over very seriously, at that, because in these times nobody can afford to pass up ten G's, especially a guy in the beer business, which is very, very tough just now. But finally he shakes his head again and says like this:

"No," he says, "I must let it go, because I must mind the baby. My old lady is very, very particular about this, and I dast not leave little John Ignatius Junior for a minute. If Mary comes home and finds I am not minding the baby she will put the blast on me plenty. I like to turn a few honest bobs now and then as well as anybody, but," Butch says, "John Ignatius Junior comes first with me."

Then he turns away and goes back to the stoop as much as to say he is through arguing, and sits down beside John Ignatius Junior again just in time to keep a mosquito from carrying off one of John's legs. Anybody can see that Big Butch is very fond of this baby, though personally I will not give you a dime for a dozen babies, male and female.

Well, Harry the Horse and Little Isadore and Spanish John are very much disappointed, and stand around talking among themselves, and paying no attention to me, when all of a sudden Spanish John, who never has much to say up to this time, seems to have a bright idea. He talks to Harry and Isadore, and they get all pleasured up over what he has to say, and finally Harry goes to Big Butch.

"Sh-h-h-h!" Big Butch says, pointing to the baby as Harry opens his mouth.

"Listen, Butch," Harry says in a whisper, "we can take the baby with us, and you can mind it and work, too."

"Why," Big Butch whispers back, "this is quite an idea indeed. Let us go into the house and talk things over."

So he picks up the baby and leads us into his joint, and gets out some pretty fair beer, though it is needled a little, at that, and we sit around the kitchen chewing the fat in whispers. There is a crib in the kitchen, and Butch puts the baby in this crib, and it keeps on snoozing away first rate while we are talking. In fact, it is sleeping so sound that I am commencing to figure that Butch must give it some of the needled beer he is feeding us, because I am feeling a little dopey myself.

Finally Butch says that as long as he can take John Ignatius Junior with him he sees no reason why he shall not go and open the safe for them, only he says he must have five percent more to put in the baby's bank when he gets back, so as to round himself up with his ever-loving wife in case of a beef from her over keeping the baby out in the night air. Harry the Horse says he considers this extra five percent a little strong, but Spanish John, who seems to be a very square guy, says that after all it is only fair to cut the baby in if it is to be with them when making the score, and Little Isadore seems to think this is all right, too. So Harry the Horse gives in, and says five percent it is.

Well, as they do not wish to start out until after midnight, and as there is plenty of time, Big Butch gets out some more needled beer, and then he goes looking for the tools with which he opens safes, and which he says he does not see since the day John Ignatius Junior is born and he gets them out to build the crib.

Now this is a good time for me to bid one and all farewell, and what keeps me there is something I cannot tell you to this day, because personally I never before have any idea of taking part in a safe opening, especially with a baby, as I consider such actions very dishonorable. When I come to think over things afterward, the only thing I can figure is the needled beer, but I wish to say I am really very much surprised at myself when I find myself in a taxicab along about one o'clock in the morning with these Brooklyn parties and Big Butch and the baby.

Butch has John Ignatius Junior rolled up in a blanket, and John is still pounding his ear. Butch has a satchel of tools, and what looks to me like a big flat book, and just before we leave the house Butch hands me a package and tells me to be very careful with it. He gives Little Isadore a smaller package, which Isadore shoves into his pistol pocket, and when Isadore sits down in the taxi something goes wa-wa, like a sheep, and Big Butch becomes very indignant because it seems Isadore is sitting on John Ignatius Junior's doll, which says "Mama" when you squeeze it.

It seems Big Butch figures that John Ignatius Junior may wish something to play with in case he wakes up, and it is a good thing for Little Isadore that the mama doll is not squashed so it cannot say "Mama" any more, or the chances are Little Isadore will get a good bust in the snoot.

We let the taxicab go a block away from the spot we are headed for in West Eighteenth Street, between Seventh and Eighth Avenues, and walk the rest of the way two by two. I walk with Big Butch carrying my package, and Butch is lugging the baby and his satchel and the flat thing that looks like a book. It is so quiet down in West Eighteenth Street at such an hour that you can hear yourself think, and in fact I hear myself thinking very plain that I am a big sap to be on a job like this, especially with a baby, but I keep going just the same, which shows you what a very big sap I am, indeed.

There are very few people in West Eighteenth Street when we get there, and one of them is a fat guy who is leaning against a building almost in the center of the block, and who takes a walk for himself as soon as he sees us. It seems that this fat guy is the watchman at the coal company's office and is also a personal friend of Harry the Horse, which is why he takes the walk when he sees us coming.

It is agreed before we leave Big Butch's house that Harry the Horse and Spanish John are to stay outside the place as lookouts, while Big Butch is inside opening the safe, and that Little Isadore is to go with Butch. Nothing whatever is said by anybody about where I am to be at any time, and I can see that, no matter where I am, I will still be an outsider, but, as Butch gives me the package to carry, I figure he wishes me to remain with him.

It is no bother at all getting into the office of the coal company, which is on the ground floor, because it seems the watchman leaves the front door open, this watchman being a most obliging guy, indeed. In fact, he is so obliging that by and by he comes back and lets Harry the Horse and Spanish John tie him up good and tight, and stick a handkerchief in his mouth and chuck him in an areaway next to the office, so nobody will think he has anything to do with opening the safe in case anybody comes around asking.

The office looks out on the street, and the safe that Harry the Horse and Little Isadore and Spanish John wish Big Butch to open is standing up against the rear wall of the office facing the street windows. There is one little electric light burning very dim over the safe so that when anybody walks past the place outside, such as a watchman, they can look in through the window and see the safe at all times, unless they are blind. It is not a tall safe, and it is not a big safe, and I can see Big Butch grin when he sees it, so I figure this safe is not much of a safe, just as Harry the Horse claims.

Well, as soon as Big Butch and the baby and Little Isadore and me get into the office, Big Butch steps over to the safe and unfolds what I think is the big flat book, and what is it but a sort of screen painted on one side to look exactly like the front of a safe. Big Butch stands this screen up on the floor in front of the real safe, leaving plenty of space in between, the idea being that the screen will keep anyone passing in the street outside from seeing Butch while he is opening the safe, because when a man is opening a safe he needs all the privacy he can get.

Big Butch lays John Ignatius Junior down on the floor on the blanket behind the phony safe front and takes his tools out of the satchel and starts to work opening the safe, while Little Isadore and me get back in a corner where it is dark, because there is not room for all of us back of the screen. However, we can see what Big Butch is doing, and I wish to say while I never before see a professional safe-opener at work, and never wish to see another, this Butch handles himself like a real artist.

He starts drilling into the safe around the combination lock, working very fast and very quiet, when all of a sudden what happens but John Ignatius Junior sits up on the blanket and lets out a squall. Naturally this is most disquieting to me, and personally I am in favor of beaning John Ignatius Junior with something to make him keep still, because I am nervous enough as it is. But the squalling does not seem to bother Big Butch. He lays down his tools and picks up John Ignatius Junior and starts whispering, "There, there, there, my itty oddleums. Da-dad is here."

Well, this sounds very nonsensical to me in such a situation, and it makes no impression whatever on John Ignatius Junior. He keeps on squalling, and I judge he is squalling pretty loud because I see Harry the Horse and Spanish John both walk past the window and look in very anxious. Big Butch jiggles John Ignatius Junior up and down and keeps whispering baby talk to him, which sounds very undignified coming from a high-class safe-opener, and finally Butch whispers to me to hand him the package I am carrying.

He opens the package, and what is in it but a baby's nursing bottle full of milk. Moreover, there is a little tin stew pan, and Butch hands the pan to me and whispers to me to find a water tap somewhere in the joint and fill the pan with water. So I go stumbling around in the dark in a room behind the office and bark my shins several times before I find a tap and fill the pan. I take it back to Big Butch, and he squats there with the baby on one arm, and gets a tin of what is called canned heat out of the package, and lights this canned heat with his cigar lighter, and starts heating the pan of water with the nursing bottle in it.

Big Butch keeps sticking his finger in the pan of water while it is heating, and by and by he puts the rubber nipple of the nursing bottle in his mouth and takes a pull at it to see if the milk is warm enough, just like I see dolls who have babies do. Apparently the milk is okay, as Butch hands the bottle to John Ignatius Junior, who grabs hold of it with both hands, and starts sucking on the business end. Naturally he has to stop squalling, and Big Butch goes to work on the safe again, with John Ignatius Junior sitting on the blanket, pulling on the bottle and looking wiser than a treeful of owls.

It seems the safe is either a tougher job than anybody figures, or Big Butch's tools are not so good, what with being old and rusty and used for building baby cribs, because he breaks a couple of drills and works himself up into quite a sweat without getting anywhere. Butch afterward explains to me that he is one of the first guys in this country to open safes without explosives, but he says to do this work properly you have to know the safes so as to drill to the tumblers of the lock just right, and it seems that this particular safe is a new type to him, even if it is old, and he is out of practice.

Well, in the meantime, John Ignatius Junior finishes his bottle and starts mumbling again, and Big Butch gives him a tool to play with, and finally Butch needs this tool and tries to take it away from John Ignatius Junior, and the baby lets out such a squawk that Butch has to let him keep it until he can sneak it away from him, and this causes more delay.

Finally Big Butch gives up trying to drill the safe open, and he whispers to us that he will have to put a little shot in it to loosen up the lock, which is all right with us, because we are getting tired of hanging around and listening to John Ignatius Junior's glug-glugging. As far as I am personally concerned, I am wishing I am home in bed.

Well, Butch starts pawing through his satchel looking for something and it seems that what he is looking for is a little bottle of some kind of explosive with which to shake the lock on the safe up some, and at first he cannot find this bottle, but finally he discovers that John Ignatius Junior has it and is gnawing at the cork, and Butch has quite a battle making John Ignatius Junior give it up.

Anyway, he fixes the explosive in one of the holes he drills near the combination lock on the safe, and then he puts in a fuse, and just before he touches off the fuse Butch picks up John Ignatius Junior and hands him to Little Isadore, and tells us to go into the room behind the office. John Ignatius Junior does not seem to care for Little Isadore, and I do not blame him, at that, because he starts to squirm around quite some in Isadore's arms and lets out a squall, but all of a sudden he becomes very quiet indeed, and, while I am not able to prove it, something tells me that Little Isadore has his hand over John Ignatius Junior's mouth.

Well, Big Butch joins us right away in the back room, and sound comes out of John Ignatius Junior again as Butch takes him from Little Isadore, and I am thinking that it is a good thing for Isadore that the baby cannot tell Big Butch what Isadore does to him.

"I put in just a little bit of a shot," Big Butch says, "and it will not make any more noise than snapping your fingers."

But a second later there is a big whoom from the office, and the whole joint shakes, and John Ignatius laughs right out loud. The chances are he thinks it is the Fourth of July.

"I guess maybe I put in too big a charge," Big Butch says, and then he rushes into the office with Little Isadore and me after him, and John Ignatius Junior still laughing very heartily for a small baby. The door of the safe is swinging loose, and the whole joint looks somewhat wrecked, but Big Butch loses no time in getting his dukes into the safe and grabbing out two big bundles of cash money, which he sticks inside his shirt.

As we go into the street Harry the Horse and Spanish John come running up much excited, and Harry says to Big Butch like this:

"What are you trying to do," he says, "wake up the whole town?"

"Well," Butch says, "I guess maybe the charge is too strong, at that, but nobody seems to be coming, so you and Spanish John walk over to Eighth Avenue, and the rest of us will walk to Seventh, and if you go along quiet, like people minding their own business, it will be all right."

But I judge Little Isadore is tired of John Ignatius Junior's company by this time, because he says he will go with Harry the Horse and Spanish John, and this leaves Big Butch and John Ignatius Junior and me to go the other way. So we start moving, and all of a sudden two cops come tearing around the corner toward which Harry and Isadore and Spanish John are going. The chances are the cops hear the earthquake Big Butch lets off and are coming to investigate.

But the chances are, too, that if Harry the Horse and the other two keep on walking along very quietly like Butch tells them to, the coppers will pass them up entirely, because it is not likely that coppers will figure anybody to be opening safes with explosives in this neighborhood. But the minute Harry the Horse sees the coppers he loses his nut, and he outs with the old equalizer and starts blasting away, and what does Spanish John do but get his out, too, and open up.

The next thing anybody knows, the two coppers are down on the ground with slugs in them, but other coppers are coming from every which direction, blowing whistles and doing a little blasting themselves, and there is plenty of excitement, especially when the coppers who are not chasing Harry the Horse and Little Isadore and Spanish John start poking around the neighborhood and find Harry's pal, the watchman, all tied up nice and tight where Harry leaves him, and the watchman explains that some scoundrels blow open the safe he is watching.

All this time Big Butch and me are walking in the other direction toward Seventh Avenue, and Big Butch has John Ignatius in his arms, and John Ignatius is now squalling very loud indeed. The chances are he is still thinking of the big whoom back there which tickles him so and is wishing to hear some more whooms. Anyway, he is beating his own best record for squalling, and as we go walking along Big Butch says to me like this:

"I dast not run," he says, "because if any coppers see me running they will start popping at me and maybe hit John Ignatius Junior, and besides running will joggle the milk up in him and make him sick. My old lady always warns me never to joggle John Ignatius Junior when he is full of milk."

"Well, Butch," I say, "there is no milk in me, and I do not care if I am joggled up, so if you do not mind, I will start doing a piece of running at the next corner."

But just then around the corner of Seventh Avenue toward which we are headed comes two or three coppers with a big fat sergeant with them, and one of the coppers, who is half out of breath as if he has been doing plenty of sprinting, is explaining to the sergeant that somebody blows a safe down the street and shoots a couple of coppers in the getaway.

And there is Big Butch, with John Ignatius Junior in his arms and twenty G's in his shirt front and a tough record behind him, walking right up to them.

I am feeling very sorry, indeed, for Big Butch, and very sorry for myself, too, and I am saying to myself that if I get out of this I will never associate with anyone but ministers of the gospel as long as I live. I can remember thinking that I am getting a better break than Butch, at that, because I will not have to go to Sing Sing for the rest of my life, like him, and I also remember wondering what they will give John Ignatius Junior, who is still tearing off these squalls, with Big Butch saying, "There, there, there, Daddy's itty woogle-ums." Then I hear one of the coppers say to the fat sergeant:

"We better nail these guys. They may be in on this."

Well, I can see it is good-bye to Butch and John Ignatius Junior and me, as the fat sergeant steps up to Big Butch, but instead of putting the arm on Butch, the fat sergeant only points at John Ignatius Junior and asks very sympathetic:

"Teeth?"

"No," Big Butch says. "Not teeth. Colic. I just get the doctor here out of bed to do something for him, and we are going to a drug store to get some medicine."

Well, naturally I am very much surprised at this statement, because of course I am not a doctor, and if John Ignatius Junior has colic it serves him right, but I am only hoping they do not ask for my degree, when the fat sergeant says:

"Too bad. I know what it is. I got three of them at home. But," he says, "it acts more like it is teeth than colic."

Then as Big Butch and John Ignatius Junior and me go on about our business I hear the fat sergeant say to the copper, very sarcastic:

"Yes, of course a guy is out blowing safes with a baby in his arms! You will make a great detective, you will!"

I do not see Big Butch for several days after I learn that Harry the Horse and Little Isadore and Spanish John get back to Brooklyn all right, except they are a little nicked up here and there from the slugs the coppers toss at them, while the coppers they clip are not damaged so very much. Furthermore, the chances are I will not see Big Butch for several years, if it is left to me, but he comes looking for me one night, and he seems to be all pleasured up about something.

"Say," Big Butch says to me, "you know I never give a copper credit for knowing any too much about anything, but I wish to say that this fat sergeant we run into the other night is a very, very smart duck. He is right about it being teeth that is ailing John Ignatius Junior, for what happens yesterday but John cuts his first tooth."

THE
LEMON
DROP
KID

I am going to take you back a matter of four or five years ago to an August afternoon and the racetrack at Saratoga, which is a spot in New York state very pleasant to behold, and also to a young guy by the name of The Lemon Drop Kid, who is called The Lemon Drop Kid because he always has a little sack of lemon drops in the side pocket of his coat, and is always munching at same, a lemon drop being a breed of candy that is relished by many, although personally I prefer peppermints.

On this day I am talking about, The Lemon Drop Kid is looking about for business, and not doing so good for himself, at that, as The Lemon Drop Kid's business is telling the tale, and he is finding it very difficult indeed to discover citizens who are willing to listen to him tell the tale.

And of course if a guy whose business is telling the tale cannot find anybody to listen to him, he is greatly handicapped, for the tale such a guy tells is always about how he knows something is doing in a certain race, the idea of the tale being that it may cause the citizen who is listening to it to make a wager on this certain race, and if the race comes out the way the guy who is telling the tale says it will come out, naturally the citizen is bound to be very grateful to the guy, and maybe reward him liberally.

Furthermore, the citizen is bound to listen to more tales, and a guy whose business is telling the tale, such as The Lemon Drop Kid, always has tales to tell until the cows come home, and generally they are long tales, and sometimes they are very interesting and entertaining, according to who is telling them, and it is well known to one and all that nobody can tell the tale any better than The Lemon Drop Kid.

But old Cap Duhaine and his sleuths at the Saratoga track are greatly opposed to guys going around telling the tale, and claim that such guys are nothing but touts, and they are especially opposed to The Lemon Drop Kid, because they say he tells the tale so well that he weakens public confidence in horse racing. So they are casing The Lemon Drop Kid pretty close to see that he does not get some citizen's ear and start telling him the tale, and finally The Lemon Drop Kid is greatly disgusted and walks up the lawn toward the head of the stretch.

And while he is walking, he is eating lemon drops out of his pocket, and thinking about how much better off he will be if he puts in the last ten years of his life at some legitimate dodge, instead of hop-scotching from one end of the country to the other telling the tale, although just off-hand The Lemon Drop Kid cannot think of any legitimate dodge at which he will see as much of life as he sees around the racetracks since he gets out of the orphan asylum in Jersey City where he is raised.

At the time this story starts out, The Lemon Drop Kid is maybe twenty-four years old, and he is a quiet little guy with a low voice, which comes of keeping it confidential when he is telling the tale, and he is nearly always alone. In fact, The Lemon Drop Kid is never known to have a pal as long as he is around telling the tale, although he is by no means an unfriendly guy, and is always speaking to everybody, even when he is in the money.

But it is now a long time since The Lemon Drop Kid is in the money, or seems to have any chance of being in the money, and the landlady of the boardinghouse in Saratoga where he is residing is becoming quite hostile, and making derogatory cracks about him, and also about most of her other boarders, too, so The Lemon Drop Kid is unable to really enjoy his meals there, especially as they are very bad meals to start with.

Well, The Lemon Drop Kid goes off by himself up the lawn and stands there looking out across the track, munching a lemon drop from time to time, and thinking what a harsh old world it is, to be sure, and how much better off it will be if there are no sleuths whatever around and about.

It is a day when not many citizens are present at the track, and the only one near The Lemon Drop Kid seems to be an old guy in a wheelchair, with a steamer rug over his knees, and a big, sleepy-looking stove lid who appears to be in charge of the chair.

This old guy has a big white mouser, and big white bristly eyebrows, and he is a very fierce-looking old guy, indeed, and anybody can tell at once that he is nothing but a curmudgeon, and by no means worthy of attention. But he is a familiar spectacle at the racetrack at Saratoga, as he comes out nearly every day in a limousine the size of a hearse, and is rolled out of the limousine in his wheelchair on a little runway by the stove lid, and pushed up to this spot where he is sitting now, so he can view the sport of kings without being bothered by the crowds.

It is well known to one and all that his name is Rarus P. Griggsby, and that he has plenty of potatoes, which he makes in Wall Street, and that he is closer than the next second with his potatoes, and furthermore, it is also well known that he hates everybody in the world, including himself, so nobody goes anywhere near him if they can help it.

The Lemon Drop Kid does not realize he is standing so close to Rarus P. Griggsby, until he hears the old guy growling at the stove lid, and then The Lemon Drop Kid looks at Rarus P. Griggsby very sympathetic and speaks to him in his low voice as follows:

"Gout?" he says.

Now of course The Lemon Drop Kid knows who Rarus P. Griggsby is, and under ordinary circumstances The Lemon Drop Kid will not think of speaking to such a character, but afterward he explains that he is feeling so despondent that he addresses Rarus P. Griggsby just to show he does not care what happens. And under ordinary circumstances, the chances are Rarus P. Griggsby will start hollering for the gendarmes if a stranger has the gall to speak to him, but there is so much sympathy in The Lemon Drop Kid's voice and eyes, that Rarus P. Griggsby seems to be taken by surprise, and he answers like this:

"Arthritis," Rarus P. Griggsby says. "In my knees," he says. "I am not able to walk a step in three years."

"Why," The Lemon Drop Kid says, "I am greatly distressed to hear this. I know just how you feel, because I am troubled from infancy with this same disease."

Now of course this is strictly the old ackamarackus, as The Lemon Drop Kid cannot even spell arthritis, let alone have it, but he makes the above statement just by way of conversation, and furthermore he goes on to state as follows:

"In fact," The Lemon Drop Kid says, "I suffer so I can scarcely think, but one day I find a little remedy that fixes me up as right as rain, and I now have no trouble whatsoever."

And with this, he takes a lemon drop out of his pocket and pops it into his mouth, and then he hands one to Rarus P. Griggsby in a most hospitable manner, and the old guy holds the lemon drop between his thumb and forefinger and looks at it as if he expects it to explode right in his pan, while the stove lid gazes at The Lemon Drop Kid with a threatening expression.

"Well," Rarus P. Griggsby says, "personally I consider all cures fakes. I have a standing offer of five thousand dollars to anybody that can cure me of my pain, and nobody even comes close so far. Doctors are also fakes," he says. "I have seven of them, and they take out my tonsils, and all my teeth, and my appendix, and they keep me from eating anything I enjoy, and I only get worse. The waters here in Saratoga seem to help me some, but," he says, "they do not get me out of this wheelchair, and I am sick and tired of it all."

Then, as if he comes to a quick decision, he pops the lemon drop into his mouth, and begins munching it very slow, and after a while he says it tastes just like a lemon drop to him, and of course it is a lemon drop all along, but The Lemon Drop Kid says this taste is only to disguise the medicine in it.

Now, by and by, The Lemon Drop Kid commences telling Rarus P. Griggsby the tale, and afterward The Lemon Drop Kid says he has no idea Rarus P. Griggsby will listen to the tale, and that he only starts telling it to him in a spirit of good clean fun, just to see how he will take it, and he is greatly surprised to note that Rarus P. Griggsby is all attention.

Personally, I find nothing unusual in this situation, because I often see citizens around the racetracks as prominent as Rarus P. Griggsby, listening to the tale from guys who do not have as much as a seat in their pants, especially if the tale has any larceny in it, because it is only human nature to be deeply interested in larceny.

And the tale The Lemon Drop Kid tells Rarus P. Griggsby is that he is a brother of Sonny Saunders, the jock, and that Sonny tells him to be sure and be at the track this day to bet on a certain horse in the fifth race, because it is nothing but a boat race, and everything in it is as stiff as a plank, except this certain horse.

Now of course this is all a terrible lie, and The Lemon Drop Kid is taking a great liberty with Sonny Saunders's name, especially as Sonny does not have any brothers, anyway, and even if Sonny knows about a boat race the chances are he will never tell The Lemon Drop Kid, but then very few guys whose business is telling the tale ever stop to figure they may be committing perjury.

So The Lemon Drop Kid goes on to state that when he arrives at the track he has fifty bobs pinned to his wishbone to bet on this certain horse, but unfortunately he gets a tip on a real good thing in the very first race, and bets his fifty bobs right then and there, figuring to provide himself with a larger taw to bet on the certain horse in the fifth, but the real good thing receives practically a criminal ride from a jock who does not know one end of a horse from the other, and is beat a very dirty snoot, and there The Lemon Drop Kid is with the fifth race coming up, and an absolute cinch in it, the way his tale goes, but with no dough left to bet on it.

Well, personally I do not consider this tale as artistic as some The Lemon Drop Kid tells, and in fact The Lemon Drop Kid himself never rates it among his masterpieces, but old Rarus P. Griggsby listens to the tale quite intently without saying a word, and all the time he is munching the lemon drop and smacking his lips under his big white mouser, as if he greatly enjoys this delicacy, but when The Lemon Drop Kid concludes the tale, and is standing there gazing out across the track with a very sad expression on his face, Rarus P. Griggsby speaks as follows:

"I never bet on horse races," Rarus P. Griggsby says. "They are too uncertain. But this proposition you present sounds like finding money, and I love to find money. I will wager one hundred dollars on your assurance that this certain horse cannot miss."

And with this, he outs with a leather so old that The Lemon Drop Kid half expects a cockroach to leap out at him, and produces a C note which he hands to The Lemon Drop Kid, and as he does so, Rarus P. Griggsby inquires:

"What is the name of this certain horse?"

Well, of course this is a fair question, but it happens that The

Lemon Drop Kid is so busy all afternoon thinking of the injustice of the sleuths that he never even bothers to look up this particular race beforehand, and afterward he is quite generally criticized for slovenliness in this matter, for if a guy is around telling the tale about a race, he is entitled to pick out a horse that has at least some kind of a chance.

But of course The Lemon Drop Kid is not expecting the opportunity of telling the tale to arise, so the question finds him unprepared, as offhand he cannot think of the name of a horse in the race, as he never consults the scratches, and he does not wish to mention the name of some plug that may be scratched out, and lose the chance to make the C note. So as he seizes the C note from Rarus P. Griggsby and turns to dash for the bookmakers over in front of the grandstand, all The Lemon Drop Kid can think of to say at this moment is the following:

"Watch Number Two," he says.

And the reason he says No. 2, is he figures there is bound to be a No. 2 in the race, while he cannot be so sure about a No. 7 or a No. 9 until he looks them over, because you understand that all The Lemon Drop Kid states in telling the tale to Rarus P. Griggsby about knowing of something doing in this race is very false.

And of course The Lemon Drop Kid has no idea of betting the C note on anything whatever in the race. In the first place, he does not know of anything to bet on, and in the second place he needs the C note, but he is somewhat relieved when he inquires of the first bookie he comes to, and learns that No. 2 is an old walrus by the name of The Democrat, and anybody knows that The Democrat has no chance of winning even in a field of mud turtles.

So The Lemon Drop Kid puts the C note in his pants pocket, and walks around and about until the horses are going to the post, and you must not think there is anything dishonest in his not betting this money with a bookmaker, as The Lemon Drop Kid is only taking the bet himself, which is by no means unusual, and in fact it is so common that only guys like Cap Duhaine and his sleuths think much about it.

Finally The Lemon Drop Kid goes back to Rarus P. Griggsby, for it will be considered most ungenteel for a guy whose business is telling the tale to be absent when it comes time to explain why the tale does not stand up, and about this time the horses are turning for

home, and a few seconds later they go busting past the spot where
Rarus P. Griggsby is sitting in his wheelchair, and what is in front
to the wire by a Salt Lake City block but The Democrat with No. 2
on his blanket.

Well, old Rarus P. Griggsby starts yelling and waving his hands,
and making so much racket that he is soon the center of attention,
and when it comes out that he bets a C note on the winner, nobody
blames him for cutting up these didoes, for the horse is a twenty to
one shot, but all this time The Lemon Drop Kid only stands there
looking very, very sad and shaking his head, until finally Rarus P.
Griggsby notices his strange attitude.

"Why are you not cheering over our winning this nice bet?" he
says. "Of course I expect to declare you in," he says. "In fact I am
quite grateful to you."

"But," The Lemon Drop Kid says, "we do not win. Our horse
runs a jolly second."

"What do you mean, *second*?" Rarus P. Griggsby says. "Do you
not tell me to watch Number Two, and does not Number Two win?"

"Yes," The Lemon Drop Kid says, "what you state is quite true,
but what I mean when I say watch Number Two is that Number
Two is the only horse I am afraid of in the race, and it seems my
fear is well founded."

Now at this, old Rarus P. Griggsby sits looking at The Lemon
Drop Kid for as long as you can count up to ten, if you count slow,
and his mouser and eyebrows are all twitching at once, and anybody
can see that he is very much perturbed, and then all of a sudden
he lets out a yell and to the great amazement of one and all he
leaps right out of his wheelchair and makes a lunge at The Lemon
Drop Kid.

Well, there is no doubt that Rarus P. Griggsby has murder in his
heart, and nobody blames The Lemon Drop Kid when he turns and
starts running away at great speed, and in fact he has such speed
that finally his feet are throwing back little stones off the gravel paths
of the racetrack with such velocity that a couple of spectators who
get hit by these stones think they are shot.

For a few yards, old Rarus P. Griggsby is right at The Lemon
Drop Kid's heels, and furthermore Rarus P. Griggsby is yelling and
swearing in a most revolting manner. Then some of Cap Duhaine's
sleuths come running up and they take after The Lemon Drop Kid

too, and he has to have plenty of early foot to beat them to the racetrack gates, and while Rarus P. Griggsby does not figure much in the running after the first few jumps, The Lemon Drop Kid seems to remember hearing him cry out as follows:

"Stop, there! Please stop!" Rarus P. Griggsby cries. "I wish to see you."

But of course The Lemon Drop Kid is by no means a chump, and he does not even slacken up, let alone stop, until he is well beyond the gates, and the sleuths are turning back, and what is more, The Lemon Drop Kid takes the road leading out of Saratoga instead of going back to the city, because he figures that Saratoga may not be so congenial to him for a while.

In fact, The Lemon Drop Kid finds himself half-regretting that he ever tells the tale to Rarus P. Griggsby as The Lemon Drop Kid likes Saratoga in August, but of course such a thing as happens to him in calling a winner the way he does is just an unfortunate accident, and is not apt to happen again in a lifetime.

Well, The Lemon Drop Kid keeps on walking away from Saratoga for quite some time, and finally he is all tuckered out and wishes to take the load off his feet. So when he comes to a small town by the name of Kibbsville, he sits down on the porch of what seems to be a general store and gas station, and while he is sitting there thinking of how nice and quiet and restful this town seems to be, with pleasant shade trees, and white houses all around and about, he sees standing in the doorway of a very little white house across the street from the store, in a gingham dress, the most beautiful young doll that ever lives, and I know this is true, because The Lemon Drop Kid tells me so afterward.

This doll has brown hair hanging down her back, and her smile is so wonderful that when an old pappy guy with a goatee comes out of the store to sell a guy in a flivver some gas, The Lemon Drop Kid hauls off and asks him if he can use a clerk.

Well, it seems that the old guy can, at that, because it seems that a former clerk, a guy by the name of Pilloe, recently lays down and dies on the old guy from age and malnutrition, and so this is how The Lemon Drop Kid comes to be planted in Kibbsville, and clerking in Martin Potter's store for the next couple of years, at ten bobs per week.

And furthermore, this is how The Lemon Drop Kid meets up

with Miss Alicia Deering, who is nobody but the beautiful little doll that The Lemon Drop Kid sees standing in the doorway of the little house across the street.

She lives in this house with her papa, her mama being dead a long time, and her papa is really nothing but an old bum who dearly loves his applejack, and who is generally around with a good heat on. His first name is Jonas, and he is a housepainter by trade, but he seldom feels like doing any painting, as he claims he never really recovers from a terrible backache he gets when he is in the Spanish-American War with the First New York, so Miss Alicia Deering supports him by dealing them off her arm in the Commercial Hotel.

But although The Lemon Drop Kid now works for a very great old skinflint who even squawks about The Lemon Drop Kid's habit of filling his side pocket now and then with lemon drops out of a jar on the shelf in the store, The Lemon Drop Kid is very happy, for the truth of the matter is he loves Miss Alicia Deering, and it is the first time in his life he ever loves anybody, or anything. And furthermore, it is the first time in his life The Lemon Drop Kid is living quietly, and in peace, and not losing sleep trying to think of ways of cheating somebody.

In fact, The Lemon Drop Kid now looks back on his old life with great repugnance, for he can see that it is by no means the proper life for any guy, and sometimes he has half a mind to write to his former associates who may still be around telling the tale, and request them to mend their ways, only The Lemon Drop Kid does not wish these old associates to know where he is.

He never as much as peeks at a racing sheet nowadays, and he spends all his spare time with Miss Alicia Deering, which is not so much time, at that, as old Martin Potter does not care to see his employees loafing between the hours of 6 A.M. and 10 P.M., and neither does the Commercial Hotel. But one day in the spring, when the apple blossoms are blooming in these parts, and the air is chock-a-block with perfume, and the grass is getting nice and green, The Lemon Drop Kid speaks of his love to Miss Alicia Deering, stating that it is such a love that he can scarcely eat.

Well, Miss Alicia Deering states that she reciprocates this love one hundred percent, and then The Lemon Drop Kid suggests they get married up immediately, and she says she is in favor of the idea, only she can never think of leaving her papa, who has no one else in all this world but her, and while this is a little more extra weight than The Lemon Drop Kid figures on picking up, he says his love is so terrific he can even stand for her papa, too.

So they are married, and go to live in the little house across the street from Martin Potter's store with Miss Alicia Deering's papa.

When he marries Miss Alicia Deering, The Lemon Drop Kid has a bankroll of one hundred and eighteen dollars, including the C note he takes off of Rarus P. Griggsby, and eighteen bobs that he saves out of his salary from Martin Potter in a year, and three nights after the marriage, Miss Alicia Deering's papa sniffs out where The Lemon Drop Kid plants his roll and sneezes same. Then he goes on a big applejack toot, and spends all the dough.

But in spite of everything, including old man Deering, The Lemon Drop Kid and Miss Alicia Deering are very, very happy in the little house for about a year, especially when it seems that Miss Alicia Deering is going to have a baby, although this incident compels her to stop dealing them off the arm at the Commercial Hotel, and cuts down their resources.

Now one day, Miss Alicia Deering comes down with a great illness, and it is such an illness as causes old Doc Abernathy, the local croaker, to wag his head, and to state that it is beyond him, and that the only chance for her is to send her to a hospital in New York City where the experts can get a crack at her. But by this time, what with all his overhead, The Lemon Drop Kid is as clean as a jaybird, and he has no idea where he can get his dukes on any money in these parts, and it will cost a couple of C's, for low, to do what Doc Abernathy suggests.

Finally, The Lemon Drop Kid asks old Martin Potter if he can see his way clear to making him an advance on his salary, which still remains ten bobs per week, but Martin Potter laughs, and says he not only cannot see his way clear to doing such a thing, but that if conditions do not improve he is going to cut The Lemon Drop Kid off altogether. Furthermore, about this time the guy who owns the little house drops around and reminds The Lemon Drop Kid that he is now in arrears for two months' rent, amounting in all to twelve bobs, and if The Lemon Drop Kid is not able to meet this obligation shortly, he will have to vacate.

So one way and another The Lemon Drop Kid is in quite a quandary, and Miss Alicia Deering is getting worse by the minute, and finally The Lemon Drop Kid hoofs and hitchhikes a matter of maybe a hundred and fifty miles to New York City, with the idea of going out to Belmont Park, where the giddy-aps are now running, figuring he may be able to make some kind of a scratch around there, but he no sooner lights on Broadway than he runs into a guy he knows by the name of Short Boy, and this Short Boy pulls him into a doorway, and says to him like this:

"Listen, Lemon Drop," Short Boy says, "I do not know what it is you do to old Rarus P. Griggsby, and I do not wish to know, but it must be something terrible, indeed, as he has every elbow around the racetracks laying for you for the past couple of years. You know Rarus P. Griggsby has great weight around these tracks, and you must commit murder the way he is after you. Why," Short Boy says, "only last week over in Maryland, Whitey Jordan, the track copper, asks me if ever I hear of you, and I tell him I understand you are in Australia. Keep away from the tracks," Short Boy says, "or you will wind up in the clink."

So The Lemon Drop Kid hoofs and hitchhikes back to Kibbsville, as he does not wish to become involved in any trouble at this time, and the night he gets back home is the same night a masked guy with a big six pistol in his duke steps into the lobby of the Commercial Hotel and sticks up the night clerk and half a dozen citizens who are sitting around in the lobby, including old Jonas Deering, and robs the damper of over sixty bobs, and it is also the same night that Miss Alicia Deering's baby is born dead, and old Doc Abernathy afterward claims that it is all because the experts cannot get a crack at Miss Alicia Deering a matter of about twelve hours earlier.

And it is along in the morning after this night, around four bells, that Miss Alicia Deering finally opens her eyes, and sees The Lemon Drop Kid sitting beside her bed in the little house, crying very hard, and it is the first time The Lemon Drop Kid is leveling with his crying since the time one of the attendants in the orphans' asylum in Jersey City gives him a good belting years before.

Then Miss Alicia Deering motions to The Lemon Drop Kid to bend down so she can whisper to him, and what Miss Alicia Deering whispers, soft and low, is the following:

"Do not cry, Kid," she whispers. "Be a good boy after I am gone, Kid, and never forget I love you, and take good care of poor papa."

And then Miss Alicia Deering closes her eyes for good and all, and The Lemon Drop Kid sits there beside her, watching her face until some time later he hears a noise at the front door of the little house, and he opens the door to find old Sheriff Higginbotham waiting there, and after they stand looking at each other a while, the sheriff speaks as follows:

"Well, son," Sheriff Higginbotham says, "I am sorry, but I guess you will have to come along with me. We find the vinegar barrel spigot wrapped in tinfoil that you use for a gun in the backyard here where you throw it last night."

"All right," The Lemon Drop Kid says. "All right, Sheriff. But how do you come to think of me in the first place?"

"Well," Sheriff Higginbotham says, "I do not suppose you recall doing it, and the only guy in the hotel lobby that notices it is nobody but your papa-in-law, Jonas Deering, but," he says, "while you are holding your homemade pistol with one hand last night, you reach into the side pocket of your coat with the other hand and take out a lemon drop and pop it into your mouth."

I run into The Lemon Drop Kid out on the lawn at Hialeah in Miami last winter, and I am sorry to see that the twoer he does in Auburn leaves plenty of lines in his face, and a lot of gray in his hair.

But of course I do not refer to this, nor do I mention that he is the subject of considerable criticism from many citizens for turning over to Miss Alicia Deering's papa a purse of three C's that we raise to pay a mouthpiece for his defense.

Furthermore, I do not tell The Lemon Drop Kid that he is also criticized in some quarters for his action while in the sneezer at Auburn in sending the old guy the few bobs he is able to gather in by making and selling knickknacks of one kind and another to visitors, until finally Jonas Deering saves him any more bother by up and passing away of too much applejack.

The way I look at it, every guy knows his own business best, so I only duke The Lemon Drop Kid, and say I am glad to see him, and we are standing there carving up a few old scores, when all of a sudden there is a great commotion and out of the crowd around us on the lawn comes an old guy with a big white mouser, and bristly white eyebrows, and as he grabs The Lemon Drop Kid by the arm, I am somewhat surprised to see that it is nobody but old Rarus P. Griggsby, without his wheelchair, and to hear him speak as follows:

"Well, well, well, well, well!" Rarus P. Griggsby says to The

Lemon Drop Kid. "At last I find you," he says. "Where are you hiding all these years? Do you not know I have detectives looking for you high and low because I wish to pay you the reward I offer for anybody curing me of my arthritis? Yes," Rarus P. Griggsby says, "the medicine you give me at Saratoga which tastes like a lemon drop, works fine, although," he says, "my seven doctors all try to tell me it is nothing but their efforts finally getting in their work, while the city of Saratoga is attempting to cut in and claim credit for its waters.

"But," Rarus P. Griggsby says, "I know it is your medicine, and if it is not your medicine, it is your scalawagery that makes me so hot that I forget my arthritis, and never remember it since, so it is all one and the same thing. Anyway, you now have forty-nine hundred dollars coming from me, for of course I must hold out the hundred out of which you swindle me," he says.

Well, The Lemon Drop Kid stands looking at Rarus P. Griggsby and listening to him, and finally The Lemon Drop Kid begins to laugh in his low voice, ha-ha-ha-ha-ha, but somehow there does not seem to be any laughter in the laugh, and I cannot bear to hear it, so I move away leaving Rarus P. Griggsby and The Lemon Drop Kid there together.

I look back only once, and I see The Lemon Drop Kid stop laughing long enough to take a lemon drop out of the side pocket of his coat and pop it into his mouth, and then he goes on laughing, ha-ha-ha-ha-ha.

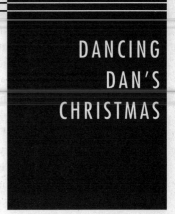

DANCING DAN'S CHRISTMAS

Now one time it comes on Christmas, and in fact it is the evening before Christmas, and I am in Good Time Charley Bernstein's little speakeasy in West Forty-seventh Street, wishing Charley a Merry Christmas and having a few hot Tom and Jerrys with him.

This hot Tom and Jerry is an old-time drink that is once used by one and all in this country to celebrate Christmas with, and in fact it is once so popular that many people think Christmas is invented only to furnish an excuse for hot Tom and Jerry, although of course this is by no means true.

But anybody will tell you that there is nothing that brings out the true holiday spirit like hot Tom and Jerry, and I hear that since Tom and Jerry goes out of style in the United States, the holiday spirit is never quite the same.

The reason hot Tom and Jerry goes out of style is because it is necessary to use rum and one thing and another in making Tom and Jerry, and naturally when rum becomes illegal in this country Tom and Jerry is also against the law, because rum is something that is very hard to get around town these days.

For a while some people try making hot Tom and Jerry without putting rum in it, but somehow it never has the same old holiday spirit, so nearly everybody finally gives up in disgust, and this is not surprising, as making Tom and Jerry is by no means child's play. In fact, it takes quite an expert to make good Tom and Jerry, and in the days when it is not illegal a good hot Tom and Jerry maker commands good wages and many friends.

Now of course Good Time Charley and I are not using rum in the Tom and Jerry we are making, as we do not wish to do anything illegal. What we are using is rye whiskey that Good Time Charley gets on a doctor's prescription from a drugstore, as we are personally drinking this hot Tom and Jerry and naturally we are not foolish enough to use any of Good Time Charley's own rye in it.

The prescription for the rye whiskey comes from old Doc Moggs, who prescribes it for Good Time Charley's rheumatism in case Charley happens to get any rheumatism, as Doc Moggs says there is nothing better for rheumatism than rye whiskey, especially if it is made up in a hot Tom and Jerry. In fact, old Doc Moggs comes around and has a few seidels of hot Tom and Jerry with us for his own rheumatism.

He comes around during the afternoon, for Good Time Charley and I start making this Tom and Jerry early in the day, so as to be sure to have enough to last us over Christmas, and it is now along toward six o'clock, and our holiday spirit is practically one hundred percent.

Well, as Good Time Charley and I are expressing our holiday sentiments to each other over our hot Tom and Jerry, and I am trying to think up the poem about the night before Christmas and all through the house, which I know will interest Charley no little, all of a sudden there is a big knock at the front door, and when Charley opens the door who comes in carrying a large package under one arm but a guy by the name of Dancing Dan.

This Dancing Dan is a good-looking young guy, who always seems well-dressed, and he is called by the name of Dancing Dan because he is a great hand for dancing around and about with dolls in nightclubs, and other spots where there is any dancing. In fact, Dan never seems to be doing anything else, although I hear rumors that when he is not dancing he is carrying on in a most illegal manner at one thing and another. But of course you can always hear rumors in this town about anybody, and personally I am rather fond of Dancing Dan as he always seems to be getting a great belt out of life.

Anybody in town will tell you that Dancing Dan is a guy with no Barnaby whatever in him, and in fact he has about as much gizzard as anybody around, although I wish to say I always question his judgment in dancing so much with Miss Muriel O'Neill, who works in the Half Moon nightclub. And the reason I question his judgment in this respect is because everybody knows that Miss Muriel O'Neill is a doll who is very well thought of by Heine Schmitz, and Heine Schmitz is not such a guy as will take kindly to anybody dancing more than once and a half with a doll that he thinks well of.

This Heine Schmitz is a very influential citizen of Harlem, where he has large interests in beer, and other business enterprises, and it is by no means violating any confidence to tell you that Heine Schmitz will just as soon blow your brains out as look at you. In fact, I hear sooner. Anyway, he is not a guy to monkey with and many citizens take the trouble to advise Dancing Dan that he is not only away out of line in dancing with Miss Muriel O'Neill, but that he is knocking his own price down to where he is no price at all.

But Dancing Dan only laughs ha-ha, and goes on dancing with Miss Muriel O'Neill any time he gets a chance, and Good Time Charley says he does not blame him, at that, as Miss Muriel O'Neill is so beautiful that he will be dancing with her himself no matter what, if he is five years younger and can get a Roscoe out as fast as in the days when he runs with Paddy the Link and other fast guys.

Well, anyway, as Dancing Dan comes in he weighs up the joint in one quick peek, and then he tosses the package he is carrying into a corner where it goes plunk, as if there is something very heavy in it, and then he steps up to the bar alongside of Charley and me and wishes to know what we are drinking.

Naturally we start boosting hot Tom and Jerry to Dancing Dan, and he says he will take a crack at it with us, and after one crack, Dancing Dan says he will have another crack, and Merry Christmas to us with it, and the first thing anybody knows it is a couple of hours later and we are still having cracks at the hot Tom and Jerry with Dancing Dan, and Dan says he never drinks anything so soothing in his life. In fact, Dancing Dan says he will recommend Tom and Jerry to everybody he knows, only he does not know anybody good enough for Tom and Jerry, except maybe Miss Muriel O'Neill, and she does not drink anything with drugstore rye in it.

Well, several times while we are drinking this Tom and Jerry, customers come to the door of Good Time Charley's little speakeasy and knock, but by now Charley is commencing to be afraid they will wish Tom and Jerry, too, and he does not feel we will have enough for ourselves, so he hangs out a sign which says "Closed on Account of Christmas," and the only one he will let in is a guy by the name of Ooky, who is nothing but an old rum-dum, and who is going around all week dressed like Santa Claus and carrying a sign advertising Moe Lewinsky's clothing joint around in Sixth Avenue.

This Ooky is still wearing his Santa Claus outfit when Charley lets him in, and the reason Charley permits such a character as Ooky in his joint is because Ooky does the porter work for Charley when he is not Santa Claus for Moe Lewinsky, such as sweeping out, and washing the glasses, and one thing and another.

Well, it is about nine-thirty when Ooky comes in, and his puppies are aching, and he is all petered out generally from walking up and down and here and there with his sign, for any time a guy is Santa Claus for Moe Lewinsky he must earn his dough. In fact, Ooky is so fatigued, and his puppies hurt him so much, that Dancing Dan and Good Time Charley and I all feel very sorry for him, and invite him to have a few mugs of hot Tom and Jerry with us, and wish him plenty of Merry Christmas.

But old Ooky is not accustomed to Tom and Jerry, and after about the fifth mug he folds up in a chair, and goes right to sleep on us. He is wearing a pretty good Santa Claus makeup, what with a nice red suit trimmed with white cotton, and a wig, and false nose, and long white whiskers, and a big sack stuffed with excelsior on his back, and if I do not know Santa Claus is not apt to be such a guy as will snore loud enough to rattle the windows, I will think Ooky is Santa Claus sure enough.

Well, we forget Ooky and let him sleep, and go on with our hot Tom and Jerry, and in the meantime we try to think up a few songs appropriate to Christmas, and Dancing Dan finally renders My Dad's Dinner Pail in a nice baritone and very loud, while I do first-rate with Will You Love Me in December As You Do in May? But personally I always think Good Time Charley Bernstein is a little out of line trying to sing a hymn in Jewish on such an occasion, and it causes words between us.

While we are singing many customers come to the door and knock, and then they read Charley's sign, and this seems to cause some unrest among them, and some of them stand outside saying it is a great outrage, until Charley sticks his noggin out the door and threatens to bust somebody's beezer if they do not go on about their business and stop disturbing peaceful citizens.

Naturally the customers go away, as they do not wish their beezers busted, and Dancing Dan and Charley and I continue drinking our hot Tom and Jerry, and with each Tom and Jerry we are wishing one another a very Merry Christmas, and sometimes a very Happy New Year, although of course this does not go for Good Time Charley as yet, because Charley has his New Year separate from Dancing Dan and me.

By and by we take to waking Ooky up in his Santa Claus outfit and offering him more hot Tom and Jerry, and wishing him Merry Christmas, but Ooky only gets sore and calls us names, so we can see he does not have the right holiday spirit in him, and let him alone until along about midnight when Dancing Dan wishes to see how he looks as Santa Claus.

So Good Time Charley and I help Dancing Dan pull off Ooky's outfit and put it on Dan, and this is easy as Ooky only has this Santa Claus outfit on over his ordinary clothes, and he does not even wake up when we are undressing him of the Santa Claus uniform.

Well, I wish to say I see many a Santa Claus in my time, but I never see a better-looking Santa Claus than Dancing Dan, especially after he gets the wig and white whiskers fixed just right, and we put a sofa pillow that Good Time Charley happens to have around the joint for the cat to sleep on down his pants to give Dancing Dan a nice fat stomach such as Santa Claus is bound to have.

In fact, after Dancing Dan looks at himself in a mirror awhile he is greatly pleased with his appearance, while Good Time Charley is practically hysterical, although personally I am commencing to resent Charley's interest in Santa Claus, and Christmas generally, as he by no means has any claim on these matters. But then I remember Charley furnishes the hot Tom and Jerry, so I am more tolerant toward him.

"Well," Charley finally says, "it is a great pity we do not know where there are some stockings hung up somewhere, because then," he says, "you can go around and stuff things in these stockings, as I always hear this is the main idea of a Santa Claus. But," Charley says, "I do not suppose anybody in this section has any stockings hung up, or if they have," he says, "the chances are they are so full of holes they will not hold anything. Anyway," Charley says, "even if there are any stockings hung up we do not have anything to stuff in them, although personally," he says, "I will gladly donate a few pints of Scotch."

Well, I am pointing out that we have no reindeer and that a Santa Claus is bound to look like a terrible sap if he goes around without any reindeer, but Charley's remarks seem to give Dancing Dan an idea, for all of a sudden he speaks as follows:

"Why," Dancing Dan says, "I know where a stocking is hung up. It is hung up at Miss Muriel O'Neill's flat over here in West Forty-ninth Street. This stocking is hung up by nobody but a party by the name of Gammer O'Neill, who is Miss Muriel O'Neill's grandmama," Dancing Dan says. "Gammer O'Neill is going on ninety-odd," he says, "and Miss Muriel O'Neill tells me she cannot hold out much longer, what with one thing and another, including being a little childish in spots.

"Now," Dancing Dan says, "I remember Miss Muriel O'Neill is telling me just the other night how Gammer O'Neill hangs up her stocking on Christmas Eve all her life, and," he says, "I judge from what Miss Muriel O'Neill says that the old doll always believes Santa Claus will come along some Christmas and fill the stocking full of beautiful gifts. "But," Dancing Dan says, "Miss Muriel O'Neill tells me Santa Claus never does this, although Miss Muriel O'Neill personally always takes a few gifts home and pops them into the stocking to make Gammer O'Neill feel better.

"But, of course," Dancing Dan says, "these gifts are nothing much because Miss Muriel O'Neill is very poor, and proud, and also good, and will not take a dime off of anybody, and I can lick the guy who says she will, although," Dancing Dan says, "between me, and Heine Schmitz, and a raft of other guys I can mention, Miss Muriel O'Neill can take plenty."

Well, I know that what Dancing Dan states about Miss Muriel O'Neill is quite true, and in fact it is a matter that is often discussed on Broadway, because Miss Muriel O'Neill cannot get more than twenty bobs per week working in the Half Moon, and it is well known to one and all that this is no kind of dough for a doll as beautiful as Miss Muriel O'Neill.

"Now," Dancing Dan goes on, "it seems that while Gammer O'Neill is very happy to get whatever she finds in her stocking on

Christmas morning, she does not understand why Santa Claus is not more liberal, and," he says, "Miss Muriel O'Neill is saying to me that she only wishes she can give Gammer O'Neill one real big Christmas before the old doll puts her checks back in the rack.

"So," Dancing Dan states, "here is a job for us. Miss Muriel O'Neill and her grandmama live all alone in this flat over in West Forty-ninth Street, and," he says, "at such an hour as this Miss Muriel O'Neill is bound to be working, and the chances are Gammer O'Neill is sound asleep, and we will just hop over there and Santa Claus will fill up her stocking with beautiful gifts."

Well, I say, I do not see where we are going to get any beautiful gifts at this time of night, what with all the stores being closed, unless we dash into an all-night drugstore and buy a few bottles of perfume and a bum toilet set as guys always do when they forget about their ever-loving wives until after store hours on Christmas Eve, but Dancing Dan says never mind about this, but let us have a few more Tom and Jerrys first.

So we have a few more Tom and Jerrys, and then Dancing Dan picks up the package he heaves into the corner, and dumps most of the excelsior out of Ooky's Santa Claus sack, and puts the bundle in, and Good Time Charley turns out all the lights but one, and leaves a bottle of Scotch on the table in front of Ooky for a Christmas gift, and away we go.

Personally, I regret very much leaving the hot Tom and Jerry, but then I am also very enthusiastic about going along to help Dancing Dan play Santa Claus, while Good Time Charley is practically over-joyed, as it is the first time in his life Charley is ever mixed up in so much holiday spirit. In fact, nothing will do Charley but that we stop in a couple of spots and have a few drinks to Santa Claus's health, and these visits are a big success, although everybody is much surprised to see Charley and me with Santa Claus, especially Charley, although nobody recognizes Dancing Dan.

But of course there are no hot Tom and Jerrys in these spots we visit, and we have to drink whatever is on hand, and personally I will always believe that the noggin I have on me afterward comes of mixing the drinks we get in these spots with my Tom and Jerry.

As we go up Broadway, headed for Forty-ninth Street, Charley and I see many citizens we know and give them a large hello, and wish them Merry Christmas, and some of these citizens shake hands with Santa Claus, not knowing he is nobody but Dancing Dan, although later I understand there is some gossip among these citizens because they claim a Santa Claus with such a breath on him as our Santa Claus has is a little out of line.

And once we are somewhat embarrassed when a lot of little kids going home with their parents from a late Christmas party somewhere gather about Santa Claus with shouts of childish glee, and some of them wish to climb up Santa Claus's legs. Naturally, Santa Claus gets a little peevish, and calls them a few names, and one of the parents comes up and wishes to know what is the idea of Santa Claus using such language, and Santa Claus takes a punch at the parent, all of which is no doubt most astonishing to the little kids who have an idea of Santa Claus as a very kindly old guy. But of course they do not know about Dancing Dan mixing the liquor we get in the spots we visit with his Tom and Jerry, or they will understand how even Santa Claus can lose his temper.

Well, finally we arrive in front of the place where Dancing Dan says Miss Muriel O'Neill and her grandmama live, and it is nothing but a tenement house not far back of Madison Square Garden, and furthermore it is a walk-up, and at this time there are no lights burning in the joint except a gas jet in the main hall, and by the light of this jet we look at the names on the letter-boxes, such as you always find in the hall of these joints, and we see that Miss Muriel O'Neill and her grandmama live on the fifth floor.

This is the top floor, and personally I do not like the idea of walking up five flights of stairs, and I am willing to let Dancing Dan and Good Time Charley go, but Dancing Dan insists we must all go, and finally I agree because Charley is commencing to argue that the right way for us to do is to get on the roof and let Santa Claus go down a chimney, and is making so much noise I am afraid he will wake somebody up.

So up the stairs we climb and finally we come to a door on the top floor that has a little card in a slot that says O'Neill, so we know we reach our destination. Dancing Dan first tries the knob, and right away the door opens, and we are in a little two- or three-room flat, with not much furniture in it, and what furniture there is very poor. One single gas jet is burning near a bed in a room just off the one the door opens into, and by this light we see a very old doll is sleeping on the bed, so we judge this is nobody but Gammer O'Neill.

On her face is a large smile, as if she is dreaming of something very pleasant. On a chair at the head of the bed is hung a long black stocking, and it seems to be such a stocking as is often patched and mended, so I can see what Miss Muriel O'Neill tells Dancing Dan about her grandmama hanging up her stocking is really true, although up to this time I have my doubts.

Well, I am willing to pack in after one gander at the old doll, especially as Good Time Charley is commencing to prowl around the flat to see if there is a chimney where Santa Claus can come down, and is knocking things over, but Dancing Dan stands looking down at Gammer O'Neill for a long time.

Finally he unslings the sack on his back, and takes out his package, and unties this package, and all of a sudden out pops a raft of big diamond bracelets, and diamond rings, and diamond brooches, and diamond necklaces, and I do not know what all else in the way of diamonds, and Dancing Dan and I begin stuffing these diamonds into the stocking and Good Time Charley pitches in and helps us.

There are enough diamonds to fill the stocking to the muzzle, and it is no small stocking, at that, and I judge that Gammer O'Neill has a pretty fair set of bunting sticks when she is young. In fact, there are so many diamonds that we have enough left over to make a nice little pile on the chair after we fill the stocking plumb up, leaving a nice diamond-studded vanity case sticking out the top where we figure it will hit Gammer O'Neill's eye when she wakes up.

And it is not until I get out in the fresh air again that all of a sudden I remember seeing large headlines in the afternoon papers about a five-hundred-G's stickup in the afternoon of one of the biggest diamond merchants in Maiden Lane while he is sitting in his office, and I also recall once hearing rumors that Dancing Dan is one of the best lone-hand git-'em-up guys in the world.

Naturally I commence to wonder if I am in the proper company when I am with Dancing Dan, even if he is Santa Claus. So I leave him on the next corner arguing with Good Time Charley about whether they ought to go and find some more presents somewhere, and look for other stockings to stuff, and I hasten on home, and go to bed.

The next day I find I have such a noggin that I do not care to stir around, and in fact I do not stir around much for a couple of weeks.

Then one night I drop around to Good Time Charley's little speakeasy, and ask Charley what is doing.

"Well," Charley says, "many things are doing, and personally," he says, "I am greatly surprised I do not see you at Gammer O'Neill's wake. You know Gammer O'Neill leaves this wicked old world a couple of days after Christmas," Good Time Charley says, "and," he says, "Miss Muriel O'Neill states that Doc Moggs claims it is at least a day after she is entitled to go, but she is sustained," Charley says, "by great happiness on finding her stocking filled with beautiful gifts on Christmas morning.

"According to Miss Muriel O'Neill," Charley says, "Gammer O'Neill dies practically convinced that there is a Santa Claus, although of course," he says, "Miss Muriel O'Neill does not tell her the real owner of the gifts, an all-right guy by the name of Shapiro, leaves the gifts with her after Miss Muriel O'Neill notifies him of the finding of same.

"It seems," Charley says, "this Shapiro is a tenderhearted guy, who is willing to help keep Gammer O'Neill with us a little longer when Doc Moggs says leaving the gifts with her will do it.

"So," Charley says, "everything is quite all right, as the coppers cannot figure anything except that maybe the rascal who takes the gifts from Shapiro gets conscience stricken, and leaves them the first place he can, and Miss Muriel O'Neill receives a ten-G's reward for finding the gifts and returning them. And," Charley says, "I hear Dancing Dan is in San Francisco and is figuring on reforming and becoming a dancing teacher, so he can marry Miss Muriel O'Neill, and of course," he says, "we all hope and trust she never learns any details of Dancing Dan's career."

Well, it is Christmas Eve a year later that I run into a guy by the name of Shotgun Sam, who is mobbed up with Heine Schmitz in Harlem, and who is a very, very obnoxious character indeed.

"Well, well, well," Shotgun says, "the last time I see you is another Christmas Eve like this, and you are coming out of Good Time Charley's joint, and," he says, "you certainly have your pots on."

"Well, Shotgun," I say, "I am sorry you get such a wrong impression of me, but the truth is," I say, "on the occasion you speak of, I am suffering from a dizzy feeling in my head."

"It is all right with me," Shotgun says. "I have a tip this guy Dancing Dan is in Good Time Charley's the night I see you, and

Mockie Morgan and Gunner Jack and me are casing the joint, be- cause," he says, "Heine Schmitz is all sored up at Dan over some doll, although of course," Shotgun says, "it is all right now, as Heine has another doll.

"Anyway," he says, "we never get to see Dancing Dan. We watch the joint from six-thirty in the evening until daylight Christmas morn- ing, and nobody goes in all night but old Ooky the Santa Claus guy in his Santa Claus makeup, and," Shotgun says, "nobody comes out except you and Good Time Charley and Ooky.

"Well," Shotgun says, "it is a great break for Dancing Dan he never goes in or comes out of Good Time Charley's, at that, because," he says, "we are waiting for him on the second-floor front of the building across the way with some nice little sawed-offs, and are under orders from Heine not to miss."

"Well, Shotgun," I say, "Merry Christmas."

"Well, all right," Shotgun says, "Merry Christmas."

BLOOD PRESSURE

I t is maybe eleven-thirty of a Wednesday night, and I am standing at the corner of Forty-eighth Street and Seventh Avenue, thinking about my blood pressure, which is a proposition I never before think much about.

In fact, I never hear of my blood pressure before this Wednesday afternoon when I go around to see Doc Brennan about my stomach, and he puts a gag on my arm and tells me that my blood pressure is higher than a cat's back, and the idea is for me to be careful about what I eat, and to avoid excitement, or I may pop off all of a sudden when I am least expecting it.

"A nervous man such as you with a blood pressure away up in the paint cards must live quietly," Doc Brennan says. "Ten bucks, please," he says.

Well, I am standing there thinking it is not going to be so tough to avoid excitement the way things are around this town right now, and wishing I have my ten bucks back to bet it on Sun Beau in the fourth race at Pimlico the next day, when all of a sudden I look up, and who is in front of me but Rusty Charley.

Now if I have any idea Rusty Charley is coming my way, you can go and bet all the coffee in Java I will be somewhere else at once, for Rusty Charley is not a guy I wish to have any truck with whatever. In fact, I wish no part of him. Furthermore, nobody else in this town wishes to have any part of Rusty Charley, for he is a hard guy indeed. In fact, there is no harder guy anywhere in the world. He is a big wide guy with two large hard hands and a great deal of very bad disposition, and he thinks nothing of knocking people down and stepping on their kissers if he feels like it.

In fact, this Rusty Charley is what is called a gorill, because he is known to often carry a gun in his pants pocket, and sometimes to shoot people down as dead as doornails with it if he does not like the way they wear their hats—and Rusty Charley is very critical of hats. The chances are Rusty Charley shoots many a guy in this man's town, and those he does not shoot he sticks with his shiv—which is a knife—and the only reason he is not in jail is because he just gets out of it, and the law does not have time to think up something to put him back in again for.

Anyway, the first thing I know about Rusty Charley being in my neighborhood is when I hear him saying: "Well, well, well, here we are!"

Then he grabs me by the collar, so it is no use of me thinking of taking it on the lam away from there, although I greatly wish to do so.

"Hello, Rusty," I say, very pleasant. "What is the score?"

"Everything is about even," Rusty says. "I am glad to see you, because I am looking for company. I am over in Philadelphia for three days on business."

"I hope and trust that you do all right for yourself in Philly, Rusty," I say; but his news makes me very nervous, because I am a great hand for reading the papers and I have a pretty good idea what Rusty's business in Philly is. It is only the day before that I see a little item from Philly in the papers about how Gloomy Gus Smallwood, who is a very large operator in the alcohol business there, is guzzled right at his front door.

Of course, I do not know that Rusty Charley is the party who guzzles Gloomy Gus Smallwood, but Rusty Charley is in Philly when Gus is guzzled, and I can put two and two together as well as anybody. It is the same thing as if there is a bank robbery in Cleveland, Ohio, and Rusty Charley is in Cleveland, Ohio, or near there. So I am very nervous, and I figure it is a sure thing my blood pressure is going up every second.

"How much dough do you have on you?" Rusty says. "I am plumb broke."

"I do not have more than a couple of bobs, Rusty," I say. "I pay a doctor ten bucks today to find out my blood pressure is very bad. But of course you are welcome to what I have."

"Well, a couple of bobs is no good to high-class guys like you and me," Rusty says. "Let us go to Nathan Detroit's crap game and win some money."

Now, of course, I do not wish to go to Nathan Detroit's crap game; and if I do wish to go there I do not wish to go with Rusty Charley, because a guy is sometimes judged by the company he keeps, especially around crap games, and Rusty Charley is apt to be considered bad company. Anyway, I do not have any dough to shoot craps with, and if I do have dough to shoot craps with, I will not shoot craps with it at all, but will bet it on Sun Beau, or maybe take it home and pay off some of the overhead around my joint, such as rent.

Furthermore, I remember what Doc Brennan tells me about avoiding excitement, and I know there is apt to be excitement around Nathan Detroit's crap game if Rusty Charley goes there, and maybe run my blood pressure up and cause me to pop off very unexpected. In fact, I already feel my blood jumping more than somewhat inside me, but naturally I am not going to give Rusty Charley any argument, so we go to Nathan Detroit's crap game.

This crap game is over a garage in Fifty-second Street this particular night, though sometimes it is over a restaurant in Forty-seventh Street, or in back of a cigar store in Forty-fourth Street. In fact, Nathan Detroit's crap game is apt to be anywhere, because it moves around every night, as there is no sense in a crap game staying in one spot until the coppers find out where it is.

So Nathan Detroit moves his crap game from spot to spot, and citizens wishing to do business with him have to ask where he is every night; and of course almost everybody on Broadway knows this, as Nathan Detroit has guys walking up and down, and around and about, telling the public his address, and giving out the password for the evening.

Well, Jack the Beefer is sitting in an automobile outside the garage in Fifty-second Street when Rusty Charley and I come along, and he says "Kansas City," very low, as we pass, this being the password for the evening; but we do not have to use any password whatever when we climb the stairs over the garage, because the minute Solid John, the doorman, peeks out through his peephole when we knock, and sees Rusty Charley with me, he opens up very quick indeed, and gives us a big castor-oil smile, for nobody in this town is keeping doors shut on Rusty Charley very long.

It is a very dirty room over the garage, and full of smoke, and the crap game is on an old pool table; and around the table, and packed in so close you cannot get a knitting needle between any two guys with a mawl, are all the high shots in town, for there is plenty of money around at this time, and many citizens are very prosperous. Furthermore, I wish to say there are some very tough guys around the table, too, including guys who will shoot you in the head, or maybe the stomach, and think nothing whatever about the matter.

In fact, when I see such guys as Harry the Horse, from Brooklyn, and Sleepout Sam Levinsky, and Lone Louie, from Harlem, I know this is a bad place for my blood pressure, for these are very tough guys indeed, and are known as such to one and all in this town.

But there they are wedged up against the table with Nick the Greek, Big Nig, Gray John, Okay Okun and many other high shots, and they all have big coarse G notes in their hands which they are tossing around back and forth as if these G notes are nothing but pieces of wastepaper.

On the outside of the mob at the table are a lot of small operators who are trying to cram their fists in between the high shots now and then to get down a bet, and there are also guys present who are called Shylocks, because they will lend you dough when you go broke at the table, on watches or rings, or maybe cuff links, at very good interest.

Well, as I say, there is no room at the table for as many as one more very thin guy when we walk into the joint, but Rusty Charley lets out a big hello as we enter, and the guys all look around, and the next minute there is space at the table big enough not only for Rusty Charley but for me, too. It really is quite magical the way there is suddenly room for us when there is no room whatever for anybody when we come in.

"Who is the gunner?" Rusty Charley asks, looking all around.

"Why, you are, Charley," Big Nig, the stick man in the game, says very quick, handing Charley a pair of dice, although afterward I hear that his pal is right in the middle of a roll trying to make nine when we step up to the table. Everybody is very quiet, just looking at Charley. Nobody pays any attention to me, because I am known to one and all as a guy who is just around, and nobody figures me in on any part of Charley, although Harry the Horse looks at me once in a way that I know is no good for my blood pressure, or for anybody else's blood pressure as far as this goes.

Well, Charley takes the dice and turns to a little guy in a derby hat who is standing next to him, scrooching back so Charley will not notice him, and Charley lifts the derby hat off the little guy's head, and rattles the dice in his hand and chucks them into the hat and goes "Hah!" like crap shooters always do when they are rolling the dice. Then Charley peeks into the hat and says "Ten," although he does not let anybody else look in the hat, not even me, so nobody knows if Charley throws a ten, or what.

But, of course, nobody around is going to up and doubt that Rusty Charley throws a ten, because Charley may figure it is the same thing as calling him a liar, and Charley is such a guy as is apt to hate being called a liar.

Now Nathan Detroit's crap game is what is called a head-and-head game, although some guys call it a fading game, because the guys bet against each other rather than against the bank, or house. It is just the same kind of game as when two guys get together and start shooting craps against each other, and Nathan Detroit does not have to bother with a regular crap table and layout such as they have in gambling houses. In fact, about all Nathan Detroit has to do with the game is to find a spot, furnish the dice and take his percentage, which is by no means bad.

In such a game as this there is no real action until a guy is out on a point, and then the guys around commence to bet he makes this point, or that he does not make this point, and the odds in any country in the world that a guy does not make a ten with a pair of dice before he rolls seven, is 2 to 1.

Well, when Charley says he rolls ten in the derby hat nobody opens their trap, and Charley looks all around the table, and all of a sudden he sees Jew Louie at one end, although Jew Louie seems to be trying to shrink himself up when Charley's eyes light on him.

"I will take the odds for five C's," Charley says, "and Louie, you get it"—meaning he is letting Louie bet him $1000 to $500 that he does not make his ten.

Now Jew Louie is a small operator at all times and more of a Shylock than he is a player, and the only reason he is up there against the table at all at this moment is because he moves up to lend Nick the Greek some dough; and ordinarily there is no more chance of Jew

Louie betting a thousand to five hundred on any proposition whatever than there is of him giving his dough to the Salvation Army, which is no chance at all. It is a sure thing he will never think of betting a thousand to five hundred a guy will not make ten with the dice, and when Rusty Charley tells Louie he has such a bet, Louie starts trembling all over.

The others around the table do not say a word, and so Charley rattles the dice again in his duke, blows on them, and chucks them into the derby hat and says "Hah!" But, of course, nobody can see in the derby hat except Charley, and he peeks in at the dice and says "Five." He rattles the dice once more and chucks them into the derby and says "Hah!" and then after peeking into the hat at the dice he says "Eight." I am commencing to sweat for fear he may heave a seven in the hat and blow his bet, and I know Charley has no five C's to pay off with, although, of course, I also know Charley has no idea of paying off, no matter what he heaves.

On the next chuck, Charley yells "Money!"—meaning he finally makes his ten, although nobody sees it but him; and he reaches out his hand to Jew Louie, and Jew Louie hands him a big fat G note, very, very slow. In all my life I never see a sadder-looking guy than Louie when he is parting with his dough. If Louie has any idea of asking Charley to let him see the dice in the hat to make sure about the ten, he does not speak about the matter, and as Charley does not seem to wish to show the ten around, nobody else says anything either, probably figuring Rusty Charley isn't a guy who is apt to let anybody question his word, especially over such a small matter as a ten.

"Well," Charley says, putting Louie's G note in his pocket, "I think this is enough for me tonight," and he hands the derby hat back to the little guy who owns it and motions me to come on, which I am glad to do, as the silence in the joint is making my stomach go up and down inside me, and I know this is bad for my blood pressure. Nobody as much as opens his face from the time we go in until we start out, and you will be surprised how nervous it makes you to be in a big crowd with everybody dead still, especially when you figure it a spot that is liable to get hot any minute. It is only just as we get to the door that anybody speaks, and who is it but Jew Louie, who pipes up and says to Rusty Charley like this:

"Charley," he says, "do you make it the hard way?"

Well, everybody laughs, and we go on out, but I never hear myself whether Charley makes his ten with a six and a four, or with two fives—which is the hard way to make a ten with the dice—although I often wonder about the matter afterward.

I am hoping that I can now get away from Rusty Charley and go on home, because I can see he is the last guy in the world to have around a blood pressure, and, furthermore, that people may get the wrong idea of me if I stick around with him, but when I suggest going to Charley, he seems to be hurt.

"Why," Charley says, "you are a fine guy to be talking of quitting a pal just as we are starting out. You will certainly stay with me because I like company, and we will go down to Ikey the Pig's and play stuss. Ikey is an old friend of mine, and I owe him a complimentary play."

Now, of course, I do not wish to go to Ikey the Pig's, because it is a place away downtown, and I do not wish to play stuss, because this is a game which I am never able to figure out myself, and, furthermore, I remember Doc Brennan says I ought to get a little sleep now and then; but I see no use in hurting Charley's feelings, especially as he is apt to do something drastic to me if I do not go.

So he calls a taxi, and we start downtown for Ikey the Pig's, and the jockey who is driving the short goes so fast that it makes my blood pressure go up a foot to a foot and a half from the way I feel inside, although Rusty Charley pays no attention to the speed. Finally I stick my head out of the window and ask the jockey to please take it a little easy, as I wish to get where I am going all in one piece, but the guy only keeps busting along.

We are at the corner of Nineteenth and Broadway when all of a sudden Rusty Charley yells at the jockey to pull up a minute, which the guy does. Then Charley steps out of the cab and says to the jockey like this:

"When a customer asks you to take it easy, why do you not be nice and take it easy? Now see what you get."

And Rusty Charley hauls off and clips the jockey a punch on the chin that knocks the poor guy right off the seat into the street, and then Charley climbs into the seat himself and away we go with Charley driving, leaving the guy stretched out as stiff as a board. Now Rusty Charley once drives a short for a living himself, until the coppers get an idea that he is not always delivering his customers to the right address, especially such as may happen to be drunk when he gets them, and he is a pretty fair driver, but he only looks one way, which is straight ahead.

Personally, I never wish to ride with Charley in a taxicab under any circumstances, especially if he is driving, because he certainly drives very fast. He pulls up a block from Ikey the Pig's, and says we will leave the short there until somebody finds it and turns it in, but just as we are walking away from the short up steps a copper in uniform and claims we cannot park the short in this spot without a driver.

Well, Rusty Charley just naturally hates to have coppers give him any advice, so what does he do but peek up and down the street to see if anybody is looking, and then haul off and clout the copper on the chin, knocking him bow-legged. I wish to say I never see a more accurate puncher than Rusty Charley, because he always connects with that old button. As the copper tumbles, Rusty Charley grabs me by the arm and starts me running up a side street, and after we go about a block we dodge into Ikey the Pig's.

It is what is called a stuss house, and many prominent citizens of the neighborhood are present playing stuss. Nobody seems any too glad to see Rusty Charley, although Ikey the Pig lets on he is tickled half to death. This Ikey the Pig is a short fat-necked guy who will look very natural at New Year's, undressed, and with an apple in his mouth, but it seems he and Rusty Charley are really old-time friends, and think fairly well of each other in spots.

But I can see that Ikey the Pig is not so tickled when he finds Charley is there to gamble, although Charley flashes his G note at once, and says he does not mind losing a little dough to Ikey just for old time's sake. But I judge Ikey the Pig knows he is never going to handle Charley's G note, because Charley puts it back in his pocket and it never comes out again even though Charley gets off loser playing stuss right away.

Well, at five o'clock in the morning, Charley is stuck one hundred and thirty G's, which is plenty of money even when a guy is playing on his muscle, and of course Ikey the Pig knows there is no chance of getting one hundred and thirty cents off of Rusty Charley, let alone that many thousands. Everybody else is gone by this time and Ikey wishes to close up. He is willing to take Charley's marker for a million if necessary to get Charley out, but the trouble is in stuss a guy is entitled to get back a percentage of what he loses, and Ikey figures Charley is sure to wish this percentage even if he gives a marker, and the percentage will wreck Ikey's joint.

Furthermore, Rusty Charley says he will not quit loser under such circumstances because Ikey is his friend, so what happens but Ikey finally sends out and hires a cheater by the name of Dopey Goldberg, who takes to dealing the game and in no time he has Rusty Charley even by cheating in Rusty Charley's favor.

Personally, I do not pay much attention to the play, but grab myself a few winks of sleep in a chair in a corner, and the rest seems to help my blood pressure no little. In fact, I am not noticing my blood pressure at all when Rusty Charley and I get out of Ikey the Pig's, because I figure Charley will let me go home and I can go to bed. But although it is six o'clock, and coming on broad daylight when we leave Ikey's, Charley is still full of zing, and nothing will do him but we must go to a joint that is called the Bohemian Club.

Well, this idea starts my blood pressure going again, because the Bohemian Club is nothing but a deadfall where guys and dolls go when there is positively no other place in town open, and it is run by a guy by the name of Knife O'Halloran, who comes from down around Greenwich Village and is considered a very bad character. It is well known to one and all that a guy is apt to lose his life in Knife O'Halloran's any night, even if he does nothing more than drink Knife O'Halloran's liquor.

But Rusty Charley insists on going there, so naturally I go with him; and at first everything is very quiet and peaceful, except that a lot of guys and dolls in evening clothes, who wind up there after being in nightclubs all night, are yelling in one corner of the joint. Rusty Charley and Knife O'Halloran are having a drink together out of a bottle which Knife carries in his pocket, so as not to get it mixed up with the liquor he sells his customers, and are cutting up old touches of the time when they run with the Hudson Dusters together, when all of a sudden in comes four coppers in plain clothes.

Now these coppers are off duty and are meaning no harm to anybody, and are only wishing to have a dram or two before going home, and the chances are they will pay no attention to Rusty Charley if he minds his own business, although of course they know who he is very well indeed and will take great pleasure in putting the old sleeve on him if they only have a few charges against him, which they do not. So they do not give him a tumble. But if there is one thing Rusty Charley hates it is a copper, and he starts eyeing them from the minute they sit down at a table, and by and by I hear him say to Knife O'Halloran like this:

"Knife," Charley says, "what is the most beautiful sight in the world?"

"I do not know, Charley," Knife says. "What is the most beautiful sight in the world?"

"Four dead coppers in a row," Charley says.

Well, at this I personally ease myself over toward the door, because I never wish to have any trouble with coppers and especially with four coppers, so I do not see everything that comes off. All I see is Rusty Charley grabbing at the big foot which one of the coppers kicks at him, and then everybody seems to go into a huddle, and the guys and dolls in evening dress start squawking, and my blood pressure goes up to maybe a million.

I get outside the door, but I do not go away at once as anybody with any sense will do, but stand there listening to what is going on inside, which seems to be nothing more than a loud noise like ker-bump, ker-bump, ker-bump. I am not afraid there will be any shooting, because as far as Rusty Charley is concerned he is too smart to shoot any coppers, which is the worst thing a guy can do in this town, and the coppers are not likely to start any blasting because they will not wish it to come out that they are in a joint such as the Bohemian Club off duty. So I figure they will all just take it out in pulling and hauling.

Finally the noise inside dies down, and by and by the door opens and out comes Rusty Charley, dusting himself off here and there with his hands and looking very much pleased indeed, and through the door before it flies shut again I catch a glimpse of a lot of guys stretched out on the floor. Furthermore, I can still hear guys and dolls hollering.

"Well, well," Rusty Charley says, "I am commencing to think you take the wind on me, and am just about to get mad at you, but here you are. Let us go away from this joint, because they are making so much noise inside you cannot hear yourself think. Let us go to my joint and make my old woman cook us up some breakfast, and then we can catch some sleep. A little ham and eggs will not be bad to take right now."

Well, naturally ham and eggs are appealing to me no little at this

time, but I do not care to go to Rusty Charley's joint. As far as I am
personally concerned, I have enough of Rusty Charley to do me a
long, long time, and I do not care to enter into his home life to any
extent whatever, although to tell the truth I am somewhat surprised
to learn he has any such life. I believe I do once hear that Rusty
Charley marries one of the neighbors' children, and that he lives
somewhere over on Tenth Avenue in the Forties, but nobody really
knows much about this, and everybody figures if it is true his wife
must lead a terrible dog's life.

But while I do not wish to go to Charley's joint, I cannot very
well refuse a civil invitation to eat ham and eggs, especially as Charley
is looking at me in a very much surprised way because I do not seem
so glad, and I can see that it is not everyone that he invites to his
joint. So I thank him, and say there is nothing I will enjoy more than
ham and eggs such as his old woman will cook for us, and by and
by we are walking along Tenth Avenue up around Forty-fifth Street.

It is still fairly early in the morning, and business guys are opening
up their joints for the day, and little children are skipping along the
sidewalks going to school and laughing tee-hee, and old dolls are
shaking bedclothes and one thing and another out of the windows of
the tenement houses, but when they spot Rusty Charley and me
everybody becomes very quiet indeed, and I can see that Charley is
greatly respected in his own neighborhood. The business guys hurry
into their joints, and the little children stop skipping and tee-heeing
and go tiptoeing along, and the old dolls yank in their noodles, and
a great quiet comes to the street. In fact, about all you can hear is
the heels of Rusty Charley and me hitting on the sidewalk.

There is an ice wagon with a couple of horses hitched to it standing
in front of a store, and when he sees the horses Rusty Charley seems
to get a big idea. He stops and looks the horses over very carefully,
although as far as I can see they are nothing but horses, and big and
fat, and sleepy-looking horses, at that. Finally Rusty Charley says
to me like this:

"When I am a young guy," he says, "I am a very good puncher
with my right hand, and often I hit a horse on the skull with my fist
and knock it down. I wonder," he says, "if I lose my punch. The
last copper I hit back there gets up twice on me."

Then he steps up to one of the ice-wagon horses and hauls off
and biffs it right between the eyes with a right-hand smack that does

not travel more than four inches, and down goes old Mister Horse to his knees looking very much surprised indeed. I see many a hard puncher in my day including Dempsey when he really can punch, but I never see a harder punch than Rusty Charley gives this horse.

Well, the ice-wagon driver comes busting out of the store all heated up over what happens to his horse, but he cools out the minute he sees Rusty Charley, and goes on back into the store leaving the horse still taking a count, while Rusty Charley and I keep walking. Finally we come to the entrance of a tenement house that Rusty Charley says is where he lives, and in front of this house is a wop with a pushcart loaded with fruit and vegetables and one thing and another, which Rusty Charley tips over as we go into the house, leaving the wop yelling very loud, and maybe cussing us in wop for all I know. I am very glad, personally, we finally get somewhere, because I can feel that my blood pressure is getting worse every minute I am with Rusty Charley.

We climb two flights of stairs, and then Charley opens a door and we step into a room where there is a pretty little redheaded doll about knee high to a flivver, who looks as if she may just get out of the hay, because her red hair is flying around every which way on her head, and her eyes seem still gummed up with sleep. At first I think she is a very cute sight indeed, and then I see something in her eyes that tells me this doll, whoever she is, is feeling very hostile to one and all.

"Hello, tootsie," Rusty Charley says. "How about some ham and eggs for me and my pal here? We are all tired out going around and about."

Well, the little redheaded doll just looks at him without saying a word. She is standing in the middle of the floor with one hand behind her, and all of a sudden she brings this hand around, and what does she have in it but a young baseball bat, such as kids play ball with, and which cost maybe two bits; and the next thing I know I hear something go ker-bap, and I can see she smacks Rusty Charley on the side of the noggin with the bat.

Naturally I am greatly horrified at this business, and figure Rusty Charley will kill her at once, and then I will be in a jam for witnessing the murder and will be held in jail several years like all witnesses to anything in this man's town; but Rusty Charley only falls into a big rocking chair in a corner of the room and sits there with one hand to his head, saying, "Now hold on, tootsie," and "Wait a minute there, honey." I recollect hearing him say, "We have company for breakfast," and then the little redheaded doll turns on me and gives me a look such as I will always remember, although I smile at her very pleasant and mention it is a nice morning.

Finally she says to me like this:

"So you are the trambo who keeps my husband out all night, are you, you trambo?" she says, and with this she starts for me, and I start for the door; and by this time my blood pressure is all out of whack, because I can see Mrs. Rusty Charley is excited more than somewhat. I get my hand on the knob and just then something hits me alongside the noggin, which I afterward figure must be the baseball bat, although I remember having a sneaking idea the roof caves in on me.

How I get the door open I do not know, because I am very dizzy in the head and my legs are wobbling, but when I think back over the situation I remember going down a lot of steps very fast, and by and by the fresh air strikes me, and I figure I am in the clear. But all of a sudden I feel another strange sensation back of my head and something goes plop against my noggin, and I figure at first that maybe my blood pressure runs up so high that it squirts out the top of my bean. Then I peek around over my shoulder just once to see that Mrs. Rusty Charley is standing beside the wop peddler's cart snatching fruit and vegetables of one kind and another off the cart and chucking them at me.

But what she hits me with back of the head is not an apple, or a peach, or a rutabaga, or a cabbage, or even a casaba melon, but a brickbat that the wop has on his cart to weight down the paper sacks in which he sells his goods. It is this brickbat which makes a lump on the back of my head so big that Doc Brennan thinks it is a tumor when I go to him the next day about my stomach, and I never tell him any different.

"But," Doc Brennan says, when he takes my blood pressure again, "your pressure is down below normal now, and as far as it is concerned you are in no danger whatever. It only goes to show what just a little bit of quiet living will do for a guy," Doc Brennan says. "Ten bucks, please," he says.

SO YOU WON'T TALK!

I t is along about two o'clock of a nippy Tuesday morning, and I am sitting in Mindy's restaurant on Broadway with Regret, the horse player, speaking of this and that, when who comes in but Ambrose Hammer, the newspaper scribe, and what is he carrying in one hand but a big bird cage, and what is in this bird cage but a green parrot.

Well, if anybody sits around Mindy's restaurant long enough, they are bound to see some interesting and unusual scenes, but this is undoubtedly the first time that anybody cold sober ever witnesses a green parrot in there, and Mindy himself is by no means enthusiastic about this spectacle.

In fact, as Ambrose Hammer places the cage on our table and then sits down beside me, Mindy approaches us, and says to Ambrose:

"Horse players, yes," Mindy says. "Wrong betters, yes. Dogs and songwriters and actors, yes. But parrots," Mindy says, "no. Take it away," he says.

But Ambrose Hammer pays no attention to Mindy and starts ordering a few delicacies of the season from Schmalz, the waiter, and Mindy finally sticks his finger in the cage to scratch the parrot's head, and goes cootch-cootch-cootch, and the next thing anybody knows, Mindy is sucking his finger and yelling bloody murder, as it seems the parrot starts munching on the finger as if it is a pretzel.

Mindy is quite vexed indeed, and he says he will go out and borrow a Betsy off of Officer Gloon and blow the parrot's brains out, and he also says that if anybody will make it worth his while, he may blow Ambrose Hammer's brains out, too.

"If you commit such a deed," Ambrose says, "you will be arrested. I mean, blowing this parrot's brains out. This parrot is a material witness in a murder case."

Well, this statement puts a different phase on the matter, and Mindy goes away speaking to himself, but it is plain to be seen, that his feelings are hurt as well as his finger, and personally, if I am Ambrose Hammer, I will not eat anything in Mindy's again unless I have somebody taste it first.

Naturally, I am very curious to know where Ambrose Hammer gets the parrot, as he is not such a character as makes a practice of associating with the birds and beasts of the forest, but of course I do not ask any questions, as the best you can get from asking questions along Broadway is a reputation for asking questions.

And of course I am wondering what Ambrose Hammer means by saying this parrot is a material witness in a murder case, although I know that Ambrose is always mixing himself up in murder cases, even when they are really none of his put-in. In fact, Ambrose's hobby is murder cases.

He is a short, pudgy character, of maybe thirty, with a round face and googly eyes, and he is what is called a dramatic critic on one of the morning blatters, and his dodge is to observe new plays such as people are always putting on in the theaters and to tell his readers what he thinks of these plays, although generally what Ambrose Hammer really thinks of them is unfit for publication.

In fact, Ambrose claims the new plays are what drive him to an interest in murder for relief. So he is always looking into crimes of this nature, especially if they are mysterious cases, and trying to solve these mysteries, and between doing this and telling what he thinks of the new plays, Ambrose finds his time occupied no little, and quite some.

He is a well-known character along Broadway, because he is always in and out, and up and down, and around and about, but to tell the truth, Ambrose is not so popular with the citizens around Mindy's, because they figure that a character who likes to solve murder mysteries must have a slight touch of copper in him which will cause him to start investigating other mysteries at any minute.

Furthermore, there is a strong knockout on Ambrose in many

quarters because he is in love with Miss Dawn Astra, a very beautiful young Judy who is playing the part of a strip dancer in a musical show at the Summer Garden, and it is well known to one and all that Miss Dawn Astra is the sweet pea of a character by the name of Julius Smung, until Ambrose comes into her life, and that Julius's heart is slowly breaking over her.

This Julius Smung is a sterling young character of maybe twenty-two, who is in the taxicab business as a driver. He is the son of the late Wingy Smung, who has his taxi stand in front of Mindy's from 1922 down to the night in 1936 that he is checking up the pockets of a sailor in Central Park to see if the sailor has the right change for his taxi fare, and the sailor wakes up and strikes Wingy on the head with Wingy's own jack handle, producing concussion of the brain.

Well, when Wingy passes away, leaving behind him many sorrowing friends, his son Julius takes his old stand, and naturally all who know Wingy in life are anxious to see his son carry on his name, so they throw all the taxicab business they can to him, and Julius gets along very nicely.

He is a good-looking young character and quite energetic, and he is most courteous to one and all, except maybe sailors, consequently public sentiment is on his side when Ambrose Hammer moves in on him with Miss Dawn Astra, especially as Miss Dawn Astra is Julius Smung's sweet pea since they are children together over on Tenth Avenue.

Their romance is regarded as one of the most beautiful little romances ever seen in this town. In fact there is some talk that Julius Smung and Miss Dawn Astra will one day get married, although it is agreed along Broadway that this may be carrying romance a little too far.

Then Ambrose Hammer observes Miss Dawn Astra playing the part of a strip dancer, and it is undoubtedly love at first sight on Ambrose's part, and he expresses his love by giving Miss Dawn Astra better write-ups in the blatter he works for than he ever gives Miss Katharine Cornell, or even Mr. Noel Coward. In fact, to read what Ambrose Hammer says about Miss Dawn Astra, you will think that she is a wonderful artist indeed, and maybe she is, at that.

Naturally, Miss Dawn Astra reciprocates Ambrose Hammer's love, because all the time she is Julius Smung's sweet pea, the best she ever gets is a free taxi ride now and then, and Julius seldom speaks of her as an artist. To tell the truth, Julius is always beefing about her playing the part of a strip dancer, as he claims it takes her too long to get her clothes back on when he is waiting outside the Summer Garden for her, and the chances are Ambrose Hammer is a pleasant change to Miss Dawn Astra as Ambrose does not care if she never gets her clothes on.

Anyway, Miss Dawn Astra starts going around and about with Ambrose Hammer, and Julius Smung is so downcast over this matter that he scarcely knows what he is doing. In fact, inside of three weeks, he runs through traffic lights twice on Fifth Avenue, and once he almost drives his taxi off the Queensboro Bridge with three passengers in it, although it comes out afterward that Julius thinks the passengers may be newspaper scribes, and nobody has the heart to blame him for this incident.

There is much severe criticism of Ambrose Hammer among the citizens around Mindy's restaurant, as they feel he is away out of line in moving in on Julius Smung's sweet pea, when any one of a hundred other Judys in this town will do him just as well and cause no suffering to anybody, but Ambrose pays no attention to this criticism.

Ambrose says he is very much in love with Miss Dawn Astra, and he says that, besides, taxicab drivers get enough of the best of it in this town as it is, although it is no secret that Ambrose never gets into a taxi after he moves in on Julius Smung without first taking a good look at the driver to make sure that he is not Julius.

Well, by the time it takes me to explain all this, Miss Dawn Astra comes into Mindy's, and I can see at once that Ambrose Hammer is not to blame for being in love with her, and neither is Julius Smung, for she is undoubtedly very choice indeed. She is one of these tall, limber Judys, with a nice expression in her eyes and a figure such as is bound to make anybody dearly love to see Miss Dawn Astra play the part of a strip dancer.

Naturally, the first thing that attracts Miss Dawn Astra's attention when she sits down at the table with us is the parrot in the cage, and she says to Ambrose:

"Why, Ambrose," she says, "where does the parrot come from?"

"This parrot is a material witness," Ambrose says. "Through this parrot I will solve the mystery of the murder of the late Mr. Grafton Wilton."

Well, at this, Miss Dawn Astra seems to turn a trifle pale around the gills, and she lets out a small gasp, and says:

"Grafton Wilton," she says, "Murdered?" she says. "When, and where, and how?"

"Just a few hours ago," Ambrose says. "In his apartment on Park Avenue. With a blunt instrument. This parrot is in the room at the time. I arrive ten minutes after the police. There is a small leopard there, too, also a raccoon and a couple of monkeys and several dogs.

"The officers leave one of their number to take care of these creatures," Ambrose says. "He is glad to let me remove the parrot, because he does not care for birds. He does not realize the importance of this parrot. In fact," Ambrose says, "this officer is in favor of me removing all the livestock except the monkeys, which he plans to take home to his children, but," Ambrose says, "this parrot is all I require."

Well, I am somewhat surprised to hear this statement, as I am acquainted with Grafton Wilton, and in fact, he is well known to one and all along Broadway as a young character who likes to go about spending the money his papa makes out of manufacturing soap back down the years.

This Grafton Wilton is by no means an odious character, but he is considered somewhat unusual in many respects, and in fact if his family does not happen to have about twenty million dollars, there is no doubt but what Grafton will be placed under observation long ago. But, of course, nobody in this town is going to place anybody with a piece of twenty million under observation.

This Grafton Wilton is quite a nature lover, and he is fond of walking into spots leading a wild animal of some description on a chain, or with a baboon sitting on his shoulder, and once he appears in the 9-9 Club carrying a young skunk in his arms, which creates some ado among the customers.

In fact, many citizens are inclined to censure Grafton for the skunk, but the way I look at it, a character who spends his money the way he does is entitled to come around with a boa constrictor in his pockets if he feels like it.

I am really somewhat depressed to hear of Grafton Wilton being murdered, and I am sitting there wondering who will replace him in the community, when all of a sudden Miss Dawn Astra says:

"I hate parrots," she says.

"So do I," I say. "Ambrose," I say, "why do you not bring us the leopard? I am very fond of leopards."

"Anyway," Miss Dawn Astra says, "how can a parrot be a material witness to anything, especially such a thing as a murder?"

"Look," Ambrose says. "Whoever kills Grafton Wilton must be on very friendly terms with him, because every indication is that Grafton and the murderer sit around the apartment all evening, eating and drinking. And," Ambrose says, "anybody knows that Grafton is always a very solitary character, and he seldom has anybody around him under any circumstances. So it is a cinch he is not entertaining a stranger in his apartment for hours.

"Grafton has two servants," Ambrose says. "A butler, and his wife. He permits them to take the day off to go to Jersey to visit relatives. Grafton and his visitor wait on themselves. A private elevator that the passenger operates runs to Grafton's apartment. No one around the building sees the visitor arrive or depart.

"In the course of the evening," Ambrose says, "the visitor strikes Grafton down with a terrific blow from some blunt instrument, and leaves him on the floor, dead. The deceased has two black eyes and a badly lacerated nose. The servants find the body when they arrive home late tonight. The weapon is missing. There are no strange fingerprints anywhere around the apartment."

"It sounds like a very mysterious mystery, to be sure," I say. "Maybe it is a stickup, and Grafton Wilton resists."

"No," Ambrose says, "there is no chance that robbery is the motive. There is a large sum of money in Grafton's pockets, and thousands of dollars' worth of valuables scattered around, and nothing is touched."

"But where does the parrot come in?" Miss Dawn Astra says.

"Well," Ambrose says, "if the murderer is well known to Grafton Wilton, the chances are his name is frequently mentioned by Grafton during the evening, in the presence of this parrot. Maybe it is Sam. Maybe it is Bill or Frank or Joe. It is bound to be the name of some male character," Ambrose says, "because no female can possibly strike such a powerful blow as causes the death of Grafton Wilton.

"Now then," Ambrose says, "parrots pick up names very quickly and the chances are this parrot will speak the name he hears so often in the apartment, and then we will have a clue to the murderer.

Maybe Grafton Wilton makes an outcry when he is struck down, such as 'Oh, Henry,' or 'Oh, George.' This is bound to impress the name on the parrot's mind," Ambrose says.

Naturally, after hearing Ambrose's statement, the parrot becomes of more interest to me, and I examine the bird in the cage closely, but as far as I can see, it is like any other green parrot in the world, except that it strikes me as rather stupid.

It just sits there on the perch in the cage, rolling its eyes this way and that and now and then going awk-awk-awk, as parrots will do, in a low tone of voice, and of course, nobody can make anything of these subdued remarks. Sometimes the parrot closes its eyes and seems to be sleeping, but it is only playing possum, and anytime anybody gets close to the cage it opens its eyes, and makes ready for another finger, and it is plain to be seen that this is really a most sinister fowl.

"The poor thing is sleepy," Ambrose says. "I will now take it home with me. I must never let it out of my sight or hearing," he says, "as it may utter the name at any moment out of a clear sky, and I must be present when this comes off."

"But you promised to take me to the Ossified Club," Miss Dawn Astra says.

"Tut-tut," Ambrose says. "Tut-tut-tut," he says. "My goodness, how can you think of frivolity when I have a big murder mystery to solve? Besides, I cannot go to the Ossified Club unless I take the parrot, and I am sure it will be greatly bored there. Come to think of it," Ambrose says, "I will be greatly bored myself. You run along home, and I will see you some other night."

Personally, I feel that Ambrose speaks rather crisply to Miss Dawn Astra, and I can see that she is somewhat offended as she departs, and I am by no means surprised the next day when Regret, the horse player, tells me that he sees somebody that looks very much like Miss Dawn Astra riding on the front seat of Julius Smung's taxicab as the sun is coming up over Fiftieth Street.

Naturally, all the blatters make quite a fuss over the murder of Grafton Wilton, because it is without doubt one of the best murders for them that takes place in this town in a long time, what with the animals in the apartment, and all this and that, and the police are also somewhat excited about the matter until they discover there is no clue, and as far as they can discover, no motive.

Then the police suggest that maybe Grafton Wilton cools himself off somehow in a fit of despondency, although nobody can see how such a thing is possible, and anyway, nobody will believe that a character with an interest in twenty million is ever despondent.

Well, the next night Ambrose Hammer has to go to a theater to see the opening of another new play, and nothing will do but he must take the parrot in the cage to the theater with him, and as nobody is expecting a dramatic critic to bring a parrot with him to an opening, Ambrose escapes notice going in.

It seems that it is such an opening as always draws the best people, and furthermore it is a very serious play, and Ambrose sets the cage with the parrot in it on the floor between his legs, and everything is all right until the acting begins on the stage. Then all of a sudden the parrot starts going awk-awk-awk in a very loud tone of voice indeed, and flapping its wings and attracting general attention to Ambrose Hammer.

Well, Ambrose tries to soothe the parrot by saying shush-shush to it, but the parrot will not shush, and in fact, it keeps on going awk-awk louder than ever, and presently there are slight complaints from the people around Ambrose, and finally the leading character in the play comes down off the stage and says he can see that Ambrose is trying to give him the bird in a subtle manner, and that he has a notion to punch Ambrose's nose for him.

The ushers request Ambrose to either check the parrot in the cloakroom or leave the theater, and Ambrose says he will leave. Ambrose says he already sees enough of the play to convince him that it is unworthy of his further attention, and he claims afterward that as he goes up the aisle with the bird cage in his hand he is stopped by ten different theatergoers, male and female, who all whisper to him that they are sorry they do not bring parrots.

This incident attracts some little attention, and it seems that the editor of the blatter that Ambrose works for tells him that it is undignified for a dramatic critic to go to the theater with a parrot, so Ambrose comes into Mindy's with the parrot again and informs me that I must take charge of the parrot on nights when he has to go to the theater.

Ambrose says he will pay me well for this service, and as I am always willing to pick up a few dibbs, I do not object, although personally, I am by no means a parrot fan. Ambrose says I am to keep a notebook, so I can jot down anything the parrot says when it is with me, and when I ask Ambrose what it says to date, Ambrose admits that so far it does not say a thing but awk.

"In fact," Ambrose says, "I am commencing to wonder if the cat has got its tongue. It is the most noncommittal parrot I ever see in all my life."

So now I am the custodian of the parrot the next night Ambrose has to go to the theater, and every time the parrot opens its trap, I out with my notebook and jot down its remarks, but I only wind up with four pages of awks, and when I suggest to Ambrose that maybe the murderer's name is something that begins with *awk*, such as 'Awkins, he claims that I am nothing but a fool.

I can see Ambrose is somewhat on edge to make a comment of this nature, and I forgive him because I figure it may be because he is not seeing as much of Miss Dawn Astra as formerly as it seems Miss Dawn Astra will not go around with the parrot, and Ambrose will not go around without it, so it is quite a situation.

I run into Miss Dawn Astra in the street a couple of times, and she always asks me if the parrot says anything as yet, and when I tell her nothing but awk, it seems to make her quite happy, so I judge she figures that Ambrose is bound to get tired of listening to nothing but awk and will return to her. I can see that Miss Dawn Astra is looking thin and worried, and thinks I, love is too sacred a proposition to let a parrot disturb it.

Well, the third night I am in charge of the parrot I leave it in my room in the hotel where I reside in West Forty-ninth Street, as I learn from Big Nig, the crap shooter, that a small game is in progress in a garage in Fifty-fourth Street, and the parrot does not act as if it is liable to say anything important in the next hour. But when I return to the room after winning a sawbuck in two passes in the game, I am horrified to find that the parrot is absent.

The cage is still there, but the gate is open, and so is a window in the room, and it is plain to be seen that the parrot manages to unhook the fastening of the gate and make its escape, and personally I will be very much pleased if I do not remember about Ambrose Hammer and think how bad he will feel over losing the parrot.

So I hasten at once to a little bird store over in Eighth Avenue, where they have parrots by the peck, and I am fortunate to find the proprietor just closing up for the night and willing to sell me a green parrot for twelve dollars, which takes in the tenner I win in the crap game and my night's salary from Ambrose Hammer for looking after his parrot.

Personally, I do not see much difference between the parrot I buy and the one that gets away, and the proprietor of the bird store tells me that the new parrot is a pretty good talker when it feels like it and that, to tell the truth, it generally feels like it.

Well, I carry the new parrot back to my room in a little wooden cage that the proprietor says goes with it and put it in the big cage, and then I meet Ambrose Hammer at Mindy's restaurant and tell him that the parrot says nothing at all worthy of note during the evening.

I am afraid Ambrose may notice that this is not the same old parrot, but he does not even glance at the bird, and I can see that Ambrose is lost in thought, and there is no doubt but what he is thinking of Miss Dawn Astra.

Up to this time the new parrot does not say as much as awk. It is sitting in the little swing in the cage rocking back and forth, and the chances are it is doing some thinking, too, because all of a sudden it lets out a yell and speaks as follows:

"Big heel! Big heel! Big heel!"

Well, at this, three characters at tables in different parts of the room approach Ambrose and wish to know what he means by letting his parrot insult them, and it takes Ambrose several minutes to chill these beefs.

In the meantime, he is trying to think which one of Grafton Wilton's acquaintances the parrot may have reference to, though he finally comes to the conclusion that there is no use trying to single out anyone, as Grafton Wilton has a great many acquaintances in his life.

But Ambrose is greatly pleased that the parrot at last displays a disposition to talk, and he says it will not be long now before the truth comes out, and that he is glad of it, because he wishes to renew his companionship with Miss Dawn Astra. He no sooner says this than the parrot lets go with a string of language that is by no means pure, and causes Ambrose Hammer himself to blush.

From now on, Ambrose is around and about with the parrot every night, and the parrot talks a blue streak at all times, though it never mentions any names, except bad names. In fact, it mentions so many bad names that the female characters who frequent the restaurants and nightclubs where Ambrose takes the parrot commence complaining to the managements that they may as well stay home and listen to their husbands.

Of course I never tell Ambrose that the parrot he is taking around with him is not the parrot he thinks it is, because the way I look at it, he is getting more out of my parrot than he does out of the original, although I am willing to bet plenty that my parrot does not solve any murder mysteries. But I never consider Ambrose's theory sound from the beginning, anyway, and the chances are nobody else does, either. In fact, many citizens are commencing to speak of Ambrose Hammer as a cracky, and they do not like to see him come around with his parrot.

Now one night when Ambrose is to go to a theater to witness another new play, and I am to have charge of the parrot for a while, he takes me to dinner with him at the 9-9 Club, which is a restaurant that is patronized by some of the highest-class parties, male and female, in this town.

As usual, Ambrose has the parrot with him in its cage, and although it is plain to be seen that the headwaiter does not welcome the parrot, he does not care to offend Ambrose, so he gives us a nice table against the wall, and as we sit down, Ambrose seems to notice a strange-looking young Judy who is at the next table all by herself.

She is all in black, and she has cold-looking black hair slicked down tight on her head and parted in the middle, and a cold eye, and a cold-looking, dead-white face, and Ambrose seems to think he knows her and half bows to her but she never gives him a blow.

So Ambrose puts the bird cage on the settee between him and the cold-looking Judy and orders our dinner, and we sit there speaking of this and that, but I observe that now and then Ambrose takes a sneak-peek at her as if he is trying to remember who she is.

She pays no attention to him, whatever, and she does not pay any attention to the parrot alongside her, either, although everybody else in the 9-9 Club is looking our way, and, the chances are, making remarks about the parrot.

Well, now what happens but the headwaiter brings a messenger boy over to our table, and this messenger boy has a note which is addressed to Ambrose Hammer, and Ambrose opens this note and reads it and then lets out a low moan and hands the note to me, and I also read it, as follows:

> Dear Ambrose: When you receive this Julius and I will be on our way to South America where we will be married and raise up a family. Ambrose I love Julius and will never be happy with anybody else. We are leaving so suddenly because we are afraid it may come out about Julius calling on Mr. Grafton the night of the murder to demand an apology from him for insulting me which I never tell you about Ambrose because I do not wish you to know about me often going to Mr. Grafton's place as you are funny that way.
>
> They have a big fight, and Ambrose Julius is sorry he kills Mr. Wilton but it is really an accident as Julius does not know his own strength when he hits anybody.
>
> Ambrose pardon me for taking your parrot but I tell Julius what you say about the parrot speaking the name of the murderer some day and it worries Julius. He says he hears parrots have long memories, and he is afraid it may remember his name although Julius only mentions it once when he is introducing himself to Mr. Wilton to demand the apology.
>
> I tell him he is thinking of elephants but he says it is best to be on the safe side so I take the parrot out of the hotel and you will find your parrot in the bottom of the East River Ambrose and thanks for everything.   DAWN.
>
> PS—Ambrose kindly do not tell it around about Julius killing Mr. Wilton as we do not wish any publicity about this. D.

Well, Ambrose is sitting there as if he is practically stunned, and shaking his head this way and that, and I am feeling very sorry for him indeed, because I can understand what a shock it is to anybody to lose somebody they dearly love without notice.

Furthermore, I can see that presently Ambrose will be seeking explanations about the parrot matter, but for maybe five minutes Ambrose does not say a word, and then he speaks as follows:

"What really hurts," Ambrose says, "is to see my theory go wrong. Here I am going around thinking it is somebody in Grafton Wilton's own circle that commits this crime, and the murderer turns out to be nothing but a taxicab driver. Furthermore, I make a laughing-stock of myself thinking a parrot will one day utter the name of the murderer. By the way," Ambrose says, "what does this note say about the parrot?"

Well, I can see that this is where it all comes out, but just as I am about to hand him the note and start my own story, all of a sudden the parrot in the cage begins speaking in a loud tone of voice as follows:

"Hello, Polly," the parrot says. "Hello, Pretty Polly."

Now I often hear the parrot make these remarks and I pay no attention to it, but Ambrose Hammer turns at once to the cold-looking Judy at the table next to him and bows to her most politely, and says to her like this:

"Of course," he says. "To be sure," he says. "Pretty Polly. Pretty Polly Oligant," he says. "I am not certain at first, but now I remember. Well, well, well," Ambrose says. "Two years in Auburn, if I recall, for trying to put the shake on Grafton Wilton on a phony breach-of-promise matter in 1932, when he is still under age. Strange I forget it for a while," Ambrose says. "Strange I do not connect you with this thing marked *P*, that I pick up in the apartment the night of the murder. I think maybe I am protecting some female character of good repute."

And with this, Ambrose pulls a small gold cigarette case out of his pocket that he never mentions to me before and shows it to her.

"He ruins my life," the cold-looking Judy says. "The breach-of-promise suit is on the level, no matter what the jury says. How can you beat millions of dollars? There is no justice in this world," she says.

Her voice is so low that no one around but Ambrose and me can hear her, and her cold eyes have a very strange expression to be sure as she says:

"I kill Grafton Wilton, all right," she says. "I am glad of it, too. I am just getting ready to go to the police and give myself up, anyway, so I may as well tell you. I am sick and tired of living with this thing hanging over me."

"I never figure a Judy," Ambrose says. "I do not see how a female can strike a blow hard enough to kill such a sturdy character as Grafton Wilton."

"Oh, that," she says. "I do not strike him a blow. I get into his apartment with a duplicate key that I have made from his lock, and

I find him lying on the floor half conscious. I revive him, and he tells me a taxicab driver comes to his apartment and smashes him between the eyes with his fist when he opens the door, and Grafton claims he does not know why. Anyway," she says, "the blow does not do anything more serious to him than skin his nose a little and give him a couple of black eyes.

"Grafton is glad to see me," she says. "We sit around talking, and eating and listening to the radio all evening. In fact," she says, "we have such an enjoyable time that it is five hours later before I have the heart and the opportunity to slip a little cyanide in a glass of wine on him."

"Well," I say, "the first thing we must do is to look up Miss Dawn Astra's address and notify her that she is all wrong about Julius doing the job. Maybe," I say, "she will feel so relieved that she will return to you, Ambrose."

"No," Ambrose says, "I can see that Miss Dawn Astra is not the one for me. If there is anything I cannot stand it is a female character who does not state the truth at all times, and Miss Dawn Astra utters a prevarication in this note when she says my parrot is at the bottom of the East River, for here it is right here in this cage, and a wonderful bird it is, to be sure. Let us all now proceed to the police station, and I will then hasten to the office and write my story of this transaction, and never mind about the new play."

"Hello, Polly," the parrot says. "Pretty Polly."

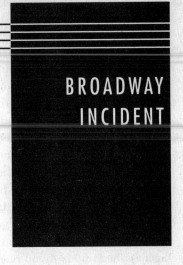

BROADWAY
INCIDENT

One night Ambrose Hammer, the newspaper scribe, comes looking for me on Broadway and he insists that I partake of dinner with him at the Canary Club, stating that he wishes to talk to me. Naturally, I know that Ambrose must be in love again, and when he is in love he always wishes to have somebody around to listen to him tell about how much he is in love and about the way he is suffering, because Ambrose is such a guy as must have his suffering with his love. I know him when he first shows up on Broadway, which is a matter of maybe eight or ten years ago, but in all this time I seldom see him when he is not in love and suffering and especially suffering, and the reason he suffers is because he generally falls in love with some beautiful who does not care two snaps of her fingers about him and sometimes not even one snap.

In fact, it is the consensus of opinion along Broadway that Ambrose is always very careful to pick a beautiful who does not care any snaps of her fingers whatever about him because if he finds one who does care these snaps there will be no reason for him to suffer. Personally, I consider Ambrose's love affairs a great bore but as the Canary Club is a very high-class gaff where the food department is really above par, I am pleased to go with him.

So there we are sitting on a leather settee against the wall in the Canary Club and I am juggling a big thick sirloin steak smothered in onions while Ambrose is telling me how much he loves a beautiful by the name of Hilda Hiffenbrower and how he is wishing he can marry her and live happily ever afterward, but he is unable to complete this transaction because there is an ever-loving husband by the name of Herbert in the background from whom Hilda is separated but not divorced. And the way Ambrose tells it, Hilda cannot get a divorce because Herbert is just naturally a stinker and does not wish to see her happy with anybody else and will not let her have same.

Well, I happen to know Hilda better than Ambrose does. To tell the truth, I know her when her name is Mame something and she is dealing them off her arm in a little eating gaff on Seventh Avenue, which is before she goes in show business and changes her name to Hilda, and I also know that the real reason Herbert will not give her this divorce is because she wants eight gallons of his heart's blood and both his legs in the divorce settlement, but as Herbert has a good business head he is by no means agreeable to these terms, though I hear he is willing to compromise on one leg to get rid of Hilda.

Furthermore, I know that Hilda is never very sympathetic toward marriage in any manner, shape or form, as she has a few other husbands prior to this and dismisses them before they are in office very long, and I am willing to bet that she has an ice-cream cone where her heart is supposed to be. But of course I do not feel disposed to mention this matter to Ambrose Hammer, especially while I am enjoying his steak.

So I just go on eating and listening and Ambrose seems about ready to burst into tears as he tells me about his suffering because of his love for Hilda, when who comes into the Canary Club all dressed up in white tie and tails but a guy by the name of Brogan Wilmington, who is what is called a playwright by trade, a playwright being a guy who writes plays which are put on the stage for people to see.

As Ambrose is a dramatic critic, it is his duty to go and view these plays and to tell the readers of the blat for which he works what he thinks of them, and it seems that he tells them that the play written by this Brogan Wilmington is a twenty-two-carat smeller. In fact, it seems that Ambrose tells them it is without doubt the worst case of dramatic halitosis in the history of civilization and it is plain to be seen that Brogan Wilmington is somewhat vexed as he approaches our table and addresses Ambrose as follows:

"Ah," he says, "here you are."

"Yes," Ambrose says, "here I am, indeed."

"You do not care for my play?" Brogan Wilmington says.

"No," Ambrose says, "I loathe and despise it."

"Well," Brogan Wilmington says, "take this."

Then he lets go with his right and grazes Ambrose Hammer's chin but in doing so, Brogan Wilmington's coattails swing out behind him and across a portion of lobster Newburg that a beautiful at the next table is enjoying and in fact the swinging coattails wipe about half the portion off the plate onto the floor.

Before Brogan Wilmington can recover his balance, the beautiful picks up what is left of her lobster Newburg, plate and all, and clops Brogan on the pimple with it and knocks him plumb out onto the dance floor where many parties, male and female, are doing the rumba with great zest.

Naturally, Ambrose is slightly surprised at this incident, but as he is a gentleman at all times, even if he is a dramatic critic, he turns to the beautiful and says to her like this:

"Miss," Ambrose says, "or madam, I am obliged to you. Waiter," he says, "bring this lovely creature another dash of lobster Newburg and put it on my check."

Then he resumes his conversation with me and thinks no more of the matter, because of course it is by no means a novelty for Ambrose Hammer to have playwrights throw punches at him, although generally it is actors and sometimes producers. In the meantime, the parties out on the dance floor find they cannot rumba with any convenience unless Brogan Wilmington is removed from their space, so a couple of waiters pick Brogan up and carry him away and Ambrose notices that the beautiful who slugs Brogan with the lobster Newburg now seems to be crying.

"Miss," Ambrose says, "or madam, dry your tears. Your fresh portion of lobster Newburg will be along presently."

"Oh," she says, "I am not crying about the loss of my lobster Newburg. I am crying because in my agitation I spill the little bottle of cyanide of potassium I bring in here with me and now I cannot commit suicide. Look at it all over my bag."

"Well," Ambrose says, "I am sorry, but I do not approve of anybody committing suicide in the Canary Club. It is owned by a friend of mine by the name of Joe Gloze and every Christmas he sends me a dozen expensive ties, besides permitting me to freeload here at will. A suicide in his club will be bad publicity for him. It may get around that death ensues because of the cooking. However, miss," Ambrose says, "or madam, if you are bound and determined to commit this suicide you may walk around the corner to a deadfall called El Parcheeso, which is Joe's rival, and I will follow you and observe your action in all its sad details and it will be a fine story for me."

Well, the beautiful seems to be thinking this proposition over and Ambrose is so occupied watching her think that he loses the thread of his story of his love for Hilda and seems to forget some of his suffering, too, and finally the beautiful turns to him and says:

"Sir, do you rumba?"

"Do I rumba?" Ambrose says. "Miss," he says, "or madam, you now behold the best rumba dancer in the Western Hemisphere, bar Havana. There is one guy there who can defeat me, although," Ambrose says, "it is a photo finish. Let us put it on."

So they get out on the floor and rumba quite a while and after that they samba some and then they conga and Ambrose can see that the beautiful has a very liberal education, indeed, along these lines. In fact, he can see that she rumbas and sambas and congas much better than any married beautiful should, because between a rumba and a samba she informs him that her name is Mrs. Brumby News and that she is the ever-loving wife of a doctor by the same name without the Mrs., who is much older than she is.

Finally they get all tuckered out from dancing and are sitting at the table talking of this and that and one thing and another, and I can tell from Mrs. News's conversation that she is far from being as intellectual as Professor Einstein and to tell the truth she does not seem right bright and Ambrose Hammer probably notices the same thing, but when it comes to beautifuls, Ambrose does not care if they are short fifteen letters reciting the alphabet. So he is really enjoying his chat with her and presently he asks her why she ever figures on knocking herself off and she relates a somewhat surprising story.

She states that her husband is always too busy trying to find out what is wrong with his patients to pay much attention to her and as she has no children but only a chow dog by the name of Pepe to occupy her time and as her maid can look after the dog better than she can, she takes to visiting this same Canary Club and similar traps seeking diversion.

She says that on one of these afternoons some months back she meets a fat blonde by the name of Mrs. Bidkar and they become great friends as they both like to gab and sip cocktails and sometimes pick up rumbas with stray guys as beautifuls will do when they are running around loose, although it seems from what Mrs. News says that Mrs. Bidkar is by no means a beautiful but is really nothing but a bundle and a little smooth on the tooth in the matter of age. However, she is good company and Mrs. News says they find they have much in common including the cocktails and the rumbas.

It seems they both also like to play bridge and Mrs. Bidkar invites Mrs. News to her apartment, stating that she has several friends in every so often to play this bridge. So Mrs. News goes to the apartment, which is in East Fifty-seventh Street and very nice, at that, and she discovers that the friends are all young and married beautifuls like herself. There are three of them and one has the name of Mrs. Smythe and another the name of Mrs. Brown, but what the third one's name is Mrs. News says she does not remember as it is a long name, and anyway this one does not seem as well acquainted with Mrs. Bidkar as the others and does not have much to say.

Anyway, from now on they all play bridge in Mrs. Bidkar's apartment three or four afternoons a week and sip plenty of cocktails in between hands and a pleasant time is had by one and all, according to Mrs. News. Then one day after playing bridge they are sitting around working on the cocktail and talking of different matters, when it comes out that they are all unhappy in their married lives. In fact, it comes out that they all hate their husbands no little and wish to be shed of them and Mrs. News states that the one who wishes this the most is Mrs. Bidkar.

Mrs. News says that Mrs. Bidkar declares she wishes her Olaf is dead so she can collect his life insurance and lead her own life in her own way, and then she starts asking the others if their husbands carry such insurance and it seems they do and finally Mrs. Bidkar says as if in a joke that it will be a good idea if they dispose of their husbands and put the insurance moo in a common pool. She says one may put more in the jackpot than another, but since it will scarcely be possible for them to dispose of five different husbands all at once the pool will give each a drawing account after it starts until the whole deal is carried out.

Well, it seems from the way Mrs. News tells it that Mrs. Bidkar keeps making quite a joke about the idea and the others join in, especially as they keep pecking away at cocktails, and after a while it is a big laugh all the way around. Then Mrs. Bidkar suggests that to make it more of a joke they deal out the cards to see which is to be the first to dispose of her husband and the one who draws the nine of diamonds is to be it, and Mrs. News gets the nine.

So the party breaks up with everybody still laughing and joking with Mrs. News over winning the prize and she is laughing, too, but as she is leaving Mrs. Bidkar calls her back and hands her a little vial which she states contains cyanide of potassium and whispers that after Mrs. News thinks it over she will see that many a true word is said in jest and that perhaps she will wish to use the cyanide where it will do the most good. Then Mrs. News says before she can say aye, yes, or no, Mrs. Bidkar pushes her out the door and closes it, still laughing.

"So," Mrs. News says, "I come here to the Canary Club and I get to thinking what a great sin I am guilty of in participating in such a joke, even though my husband is really nothing but an old cur-mudgeon and is related to Clarence Closeclutch when it comes to money, and I become so remorseful that I decide to take the cyanide myself when I am interrupted by the good-looking gentleman striking you. By the way," she says, "do you know if he rumbas?"

Now this story seems rather interesting to me and I am expecting Ambrose Hammer to become greatly excited by it, because it sounds like a crime mystery and next to love Ambrose Hammer's greatest hobby is crime mystery. He often vexes the cops quite some by poking his nose into their investigations and trying to figure out who does what. To tell the truth, Ambrose's interest is sometimes so divided between love and crime that it is hard to tell whether he wishes to be Clark Gable or Sherlock Holmes, though the chances are he wishes to be both. But I can see that Ambrose is half asleep and when Mrs. News concludes her tale he speaks to her quite severely as follows:

"Madam," he says, "of course you are a victim of a gag. However," he says, "you are such a swell rumba dancer I will overlook your wasting my time with such a dreary recital. Let us shake it up a little more on the dance floor and then I must return to my office and write a Sunday article advising the sanitation authorities to suppress Bro-gan Wilmington's play before it contaminates the entire community. He is the guy you flatten with your lobster Newburg. He is not good-looking, either, and he cannot rumba a lick. I forget to mention it before," Ambrose says, "but I am Ambrose Hammer."

Mrs. News does not seem to know the name and this really cuts Ambrose deeply, so he is not sorry to see her depart. Then he goes to his office and I go home to bed and the chances are neither of us will give the incident another thought if a guy by the name of Dr. Brumby News does not happen to drop dead in the Canary Club one night while in the act of committing the rumba with his wife.

Ambrose and I are sitting in Mindy's restaurant on Broadway when he reads an item in an early edition of a morning blat about this, and as Ambrose has a good memory for names he calls my attention to the item and states that the wife in question is undoubtedly the beautiful who tells us the unusual story.

"My goodness, Ambrose," I say, "do you suppose she gives the guy the business after all?"

"No," Ambrose says, "such an idea is foolish. It says here he undoubtedly dies of heart disease. He is sixty-three years old and at this age the price is logically thirty to one that a doctor will die of heart disease. Of course," Ambrose says, "if it is known that a doctor of sixty-three is engaging in the rumba, the price is one hundred to one."

"But Ambrose," I say, "maybe she knows the old guy's heart is weak and gets him to rumba figuring that it will belt him out quicker than cyanide."

"Well," Ambrose says, "it is a theory, of course, but I do not think there is anything in it. I think maybe she feels so sorry for her wicked thoughts about him that she tries to be nice to him and gets him to go out stepping with her, but with no sinister motives whatever. However, let us give this no further consideration. Doctors die of heart disease every day. Do I tell you that I see Hilda last night and that she believes she is nearer a settlement with Hiffenbrower? She is breakfasting with him at his hotel almost every morning and feels that he is softening up. Ah," Ambrose says, "how I long for the hour I can take her in my arms and call her my own dear little wife."

I am less interested in Hilda than ever at this moment, but I am compelled to listen for two hours to Ambrose tell about his love for her and about his suffering and I make up my mind to give him a miss until he gets over this one. Then about a week later he sends for me to come to his office saying he wishes me to go with him to see a new play, and while I am there waiting for Ambrose to finish some work, who comes in but Mrs. News. She is all in mourning and as soon as she sees Ambrose she begins to cry and she says to him like this:

"Oh, Mr. Hammer," she says, "I do not kill my husband."

"Why," Ambrose says, "certainly not. By no means and not at all. But," Ambrose says, "it is most injudicious of you to permit him to rumba at his age."

"It is his own desire," Mrs. News says. "It is his method of punishing me for being late for dinner a few times. He is the most frightful rumba dancer that ever lives and he knows it is torture to me to dance with a bad rumba dancer, so he takes me out and rumbas me into a state approaching nervous exhaustion before he keels over himself. Mr. Hammer, I do not like to speak ill of the dead but my late husband really has a mean disposition. But," she says, "I do not kill him."

"Nobody says you do," Ambrose says.

"Yes," Mrs. News says, "somebody does. Do you remember me telling you about drawing the cards at Mrs. Bidkar's apartment to see who is to dispose of her husband first?"

"Oh," Ambrose says, "you mean the little joke they play on you? Yes," he says, "I remember."

"Well," Mrs. News says, "Mrs. Bidkar now says it is never a joke at all. She says it is all in earnest and claims I know it is all the time. She is around to see me last night and says I undoubtedly give my husband poison and that I must turn his insurance money into the pool when I collect it. There is quite a lot of it. Over two hundred thousand dollars, Mr. Hammer."

"Look," Ambrose says, "this is just another of Mrs. Bidkar's little jokes. She seems to have quite a sense of humor."

"No," Mrs. News says, "it is no joke. She is very serious. She says unless I turn in the money she will expose me to the world and there will be a horrible scandal and I will go to jail and not be able to collect a cent of the insurance money. She just laughs when I tell her I spill the cyanide she gives me and says if I do, I probably get more poison somewhere else and use it and that she and the others are entitled to their share of the money just the same because she furnishes the idea. Mr. Hammer, you must remember seeing me spill the cyanide."

"Mrs. N.," Ambrose says, "does anyone tell you yet that you make a lovely widow? But no matter," he says. "Yes I remember hearing you say you spill something but I do not look to see. Are you positive you do not do as Mrs. Bidkar suggests and get some other destructive substance and slip it to your husband by accident?"

Well, at this Mrs. News begins crying very loudly indeed, and Ambrose has to spend some time soothing her and I wish to state that when it comes to soothing a beautiful there are few better soothers than Ambrose Hammer on the island of Manhattan. Then when he gets her quieted down he says to her like this:

"Now," Ambrose says, "just leave everything to me. I am commencing to sniff something here. But," he says, "in the meantime remain friendly with Mrs. Bidkar. Let her think you are commencing to see things her own way. Maybe she will hold another drawing."

"Oh," Mrs. News says, "she has. She tells me the one whose name I cannot remember draws the nine of diamonds only the day before my husband departs this life. It is a long name with a kind of a foreign sound. Mrs. Bidkar says she has a lot of confidence in this one just on her looks although she does not know her intimately. I only wish I can think of the name. I have a dreadful time thinking of names. I remember yours when I happen to see it over an article in the paper the other day about Brogan Wilmington's play and then I remember, too, that you mention that he is the good-looking gentleman in the Canary Club the night we meet. Mr. Hammer," she says, "you say some very mean things about his play."

"Well," Ambrose says, "I do not know about the propriety of a beautiful in widow's weeds attending the theater, but I happen to have a couple of skulls to Wilmington's play right here in my desk and I will give them to you and you can go and see for yourself that it really is most distressing. Probably you will see Wilmington himself standing in the lobby taking bows for no reason whatever, and I hope and trust you take another close glaum at him and you will see that he is not good looking. And," Ambrose says, "I tell you once more he is a total bust at the rumba."

"Why," Mrs. News says, "I will be delighted to see his play. It may help break the monotony of being a widow, which is quite monotonous to be sure, even after a very short time. I almost miss poor Brummy in spite of his narrow views on punctuality for dinner, but please do something about Mrs. Bidkar."

Then she leaves us, and Ambrose and I gaze at the new play

which seems to me to be all right but which Ambrose says is a great insult to the theater because Ambrose is very hard to please about plays, and it is some days before I see him again. Naturally, I ask him if he does anything about Mrs. News's case and Ambrose says:

"Yes," he says, "I prod around in it to some extent and I find it is an attempt at blackmail, just as I suspect. It is a most ingenious setup, at that. I look up Mrs. Smythe and Mrs. Brown and one is a chorus gorgeous by the name of Beerbaum and the other is a clerk in a Broadway lingerie shop by the name of Cooney. Neither of them is ever married as far as anybody knows. Mrs. Bidkar is originally out of Chicago and has a husband, but," Ambrose says, "nobody seems to know who he is or where he is."

"But Ambrose," I say, "how can Mrs. Smythe and Mrs. Brown enter into a deal to dispose of their husbands as Mrs. News states when they have no husbands? Is this entirely honest?"

"Why," Ambrose says, "they are stooges. You see," he says, "Mrs. Bidkar has a little moo and she rents this apartment and uses these two as trimming. Her idea is to pick up dumb beautifuls such as Mrs. News who are not too happy with their husbands and get them wedged in on such a situation as develops here, and the other two help out."

"Ambrose," I say, "do you mean to tell me this Mrs. Bidkar is so heartless as to plan to have these beautifuls she picks up chill their husbands?"

"No," Ambrose says. "This is not her plan at all. She has no idea they will actually do such a thing. But she does figure to maneuver them into entering into the spirit of what she calls a joke just as she does Mrs. News, the cocktails helping out no little. It all sounds very harmless to the married beautiful until Mrs. Bidkar comes around afterward and threatens to tell the husband that his wife is a party to a scheme of this nature. Naturally," Ambrose says, "such a wife is very eager to settle with Mrs. Bidkar for whatever she can dig up."

"Why, Ambrose," I say, "it is nothing but a shakedown, which is very old-fashioned stuff."

"Yes," Ambrose says, "it is a shake, all right. And," he says, "it makes me very sad to learn from Mrs. Smythe and Mrs. Brown, who work with Mrs. Bidkar in other cities, that many husbands must be

willing to believe anything of their ever-lovings, even murder, and
that the wives know it, because they always settle promptly with
Mrs. Bidkar. She is a smart old broad. It is a pity she is so nefarious.
Mrs. Smythe and Mrs. Brown are very grateful when they find I am
not going to put them in jail," Ambrose says. "I have their phone
numbers."

"Well," I say, "now there is nothing left to be done but to clap
this Mrs. Bidkar in the pokey and inform Mrs. News that she can
quit worrying. Why, goodness gracious, Ambrose," I say, "Mrs. Bidkar is really a great menace to be at large in a community. She ought
to be filed away for life."

"Yes," Ambrose says, "what you say is quite true, but if we put
her in jail it will all come out in the blats and Mrs. News cannot
afford such notoriety. It may bother her in collecting her insurance.
Let us go and see Mrs. Bidkar and explain to her that the best thing
she can do is to hit the grit out of town."

So we get in a taxicab and go to an address in East Fifty-seventh
Street that turns out to be a high-toned apartment house, and Ambrose stakes the elevator guy to a deuce and the guy takes us up to
the sixth floor without going to the trouble of announcing us on the
house phone first and points to a door. Then Ambrose pushes the
buzzer and presently a female character appears and gazes at us in
a most hospitable manner.

She is short and is wearing a negligée that permits her to widen
out freely all the way around and she has straw-colored hair and a
large smile and while she is by no means a beautiful, still you cannot
say she is a crow. In fact, I am somewhat surprised when Ambrose
asks her if she is Mrs. Bidkar and she states that she is, as I am
expecting a genuine old komoppo. We enter an elegantly furnished
living room and she asks our business, and Ambrose says:

"Well, Mrs. B.," he says, "you almost get a good break when old
Doc News drops dead after you stake his wife to the poison because
it looks as if you have her where she can never wiggle off no matter
what she says. But," Ambrose says, "my friend Mrs. News is cute
enough to seek my advice and counsel."

"Yes?" Mrs. Bidkar says. "And who are you?"

"Never mind," Ambrose says. "I am here to tell you that if you
are present in these parts tomorrow morning you will find yourself
in the canneroo."

At this, Mrs. Bidkar stops smiling and a very hard look indeed comes into her eyes and she says:

"Listen, guy, whoever you are," she says. "If you are a friend of Mrs. News you will tell her to get it on the line at once and save herself trouble. I may go to jail," she says, "but so will she and I can stand it better than she can because I am there before, and anyway the charge against me will not be poisoning my husband."

"Mrs. Bidkar," Ambrose says, "you know Mrs. News does not poison her husband."

"No?" Mrs. Bidkar says. "Who does, then? They cannot pin it on me because Mrs. News herself claims she spills the stuff I give her and which she thinks is cyanide but which is really nothing but water, so she must get something else to do the job. Her own statement lets me out. But if you take her story that she does not poison him at all, you must be dumber than she is, although," Mrs. Bidkar says, "I will never believe such a thing is possible."

"Water, hey?" Ambrose says. "Well, Mrs. Bidkar," he says, "I can see that you really believe Mrs. News is guilty of this poisoning, so I will have to show you something I have here," he says, "a little document from the medical examiner stating that an autopsy on the remains of the late Dr. Brumby News discloses no sign of poison whatever. You can confirm this by calling up the district attorney, who has the autopsy performed and who is still very angry at me for putting him to a lot of bother for nothing," Ambrose says.

"An autopsy?" Mrs. Bidkar says, taking the paper and reading it. "I see. Tomorrow morning, do you say? Well," she says, "you need not mind looking in again as I will be absent. Good day," she says.

Then Ambrose and I take our departure and when we are going along the street I suddenly think of something and I say to him like this:

"An autopsy, Ambrose?" I say. "Why, such an action indicates that you never entirely believe Mrs. News yourself, does it not?"

"Oh," Ambrose says, "I believe her, all right, but I always consider it a sound policy to look a little bit behind a beautiful's word on any proposition. Besides, cyanide has an odor and I do not remember noticing such an odor in the Canary Club and this makes me wonder somewhat about Mrs. News when I begin looking the situation over. But," Ambrose says, "of course Mrs. Bidkar clears this point up. Do you know what I am wondering right this minute? I am wondering what ever happens to Mrs. Bidkar's husband," he says.

Well, personally I do not consider this a matter worth thinking about, so I leave Ambrose at a corner and I do not see him again for weeks when we get together in the Canary Club for another dinner, and while we are sitting there who comes past our table without her mourning and looking very gorgeous indeed but Mrs. Brumby News.

When she sees Ambrose she stops and gives him a large good evening and Ambrose invites her to sit down and she does same but she states that she is on a meet with a friend and cannot remain with us long. She sits there chatting with Ambrose about this and that and he is so attentive that it reminds me of something and I say to him like this:

"Ambrose," I say, "I understand the course of your true love with Hilda may soon be smoothed out. I hear Hiffenbrower is in a hospital and may not be with us much longer. Well," I say, "let me be the first to congratulate you."

Now Mrs. News looks up and says:

"Hilda?" she says. "Hiffenbrower?" she says. "Why, this is the name of the other girl at Mrs. Bidkar's I am never able to remember. Yes, Hilda Hiffenbrower."

Naturally, I am greatly surprised and I gaze at Ambrose and he nods and says:

"Yes," he says, "I know it from the day I begin my investigation, but," he says, "I am too greatly shocked and pained to mention the matter. She becomes acquainted with Mrs. Bidkar the same way Mrs. News does. Hilda is always quick to learn and personally I feel that Hiffenbrower makes a mistake in not canceling her out as the beneficiary of his insurance when they first separate. It is unfair to place great temptation before any beautiful and," Ambrose says, "especially Hilda.

"Well," he says, "Hiffenbrower is suffering from prolonged doses of powdered glass in his cereal but you are wrong about his condition. They are laying even money he beats it, although of course his digestion may be slightly impaired. I hear the cops trace Hilda to South America. Oh, well," Ambrose says, "I am through with the beautifuls forever. Mrs. N., do you care to push a rumba around with me?"

"No," Mrs. News says, "here comes my friend. I think you meet him before. In fact," she says, "you are responsible for us getting together by sending me to the theater on the free tickets that night."

And who is the friend but this Brogan Wilmington, the playwright, whose play is now running along quite successfully and making plenty of beesom in spite of what Ambrose states about it, and as Mrs. News gets up from the table to join him, Brogan Wilmington gazes at Ambrose and says to him like this:

"Bah," Brogan Wilmington says.

"Bah right back to you," Ambrose says, and then he begins going through his pockets looking for something.

"Now where do I put those phone numbers of Mrs. Smythe and Mrs. Brown?" Ambrose says.

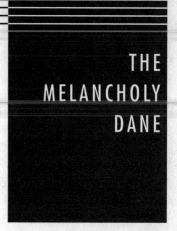

THE
MELANCHOLY
DANE

t is a matter of maybe two years back that I run into Ambrose
Hammer, the newspaper scribe, one evening on Broadway and
he requests me to attend the theater with him, as Ambrose is what
is called a dramatic critic and his racket is to witness all the new
plays and write what he thinks about them in a morning blat.

I often hear the actors and the guys who write the plays talking
about Ambrose in Mindy's restaurant when they get the last edition
and read what he has to say, and as near as I can make out, they
feel that he is nothing but a low criminal type because it seems that
Ambrose practically murders one and all connected with any new
play. So I say to him like this:

"No, Ambrose," I say, "I may happen to know the guy who writes
the play you are going to see, or one of the actors, and as I understand
it is always about nine to five that you will put the blister on a new
play, I will be running the risk of hurting myself socially along Broadway. Furthermore," I say, "where is Miss Channelle Cooper who
accompanies you to the new plays for the past six months hand-
running?"

"Oh," Ambrose says, "you need not worry about the guy who
writes this play, as his name is Shakespeare and he is dead quite a
spell. You need not worry about any of the actors, either, as they
are just a bunch of plumbers that no one ever hears of before, except
maybe the leading one who has some slight notoriety. And, as for
Miss Channelle Cooper, I do not know where she is at this particular

moment and, not to give you a short answer, I do not give a D and an A and an M and an N."

"Why, Ambrose," I say, "the last time we meet, you tell me that you are on fire with love for Miss Channelle Cooper, although, of course," I say, "you are on fire with love for so many different broads since I know you that I am surprised you are not reduced to ashes long ago."

"Look," Ambrose says, "let us not discuss such a tender subject as Miss Cooper at this time or I am apt to break into tears and be in no mood to impartially perform my stern duty toward this play. All I know is she sends me a letter by messenger this morning, stating that she cannot see me tonight because her grandmother's diabetes is worse and she has to go to Yonkers to see her.

"And," Ambrose goes on, "I happen to know that in the first place her grandmother does not have diabetes but only a tumor, and in the second place she does not live in Yonkers but in Greenwich Village, and in the third place Miss Cooper is seen late this afternoon having tea at the Plaza with an eighteen-carat hambola by the name of Mansfield Sothern. I wonder," Ambrose says, "if the bim is ever born who can tell the truth?"

"No, Ambrose," I say, "or anyway not yet. But," I say, "I am surprised to hear Miss Cooper turns out unstable, as she always strikes me as the reliable sort and very true to you, or at least as true as you can expect these days. In fact," I say, "I have it on good authority that she turns down Lefty Lyons, the slot-machine king, who offers to take charge of her career and buy a nightclub for her. But of course Mansfield Sothern is something else again. I often enjoy his comedy on the stage."

"He is a hunk of Smithfield who steals the names of two great actors to make one for himself," Ambrose says. "I will admit that he is sometimes endurable in musical comedy, if you close your eyes when he is on the boards and make believe he is somebody else, but, like all actors, he is egotistical enough to think he can play Hamlet. In fact," Ambrose says, "he is going to do it tonight and I can scarcely wait."

Well, I finally go to the theater with Ambrose and it is quite a high-toned occasion with nearly everybody in the old thirteen-and-odd because Mansfield Sothern has a big following in musical comedy and it seems that his determination to play Hamlet produces quite a sensation, though Ambrose claims that most of those present are members of Mansfield's personal clique from café society and he also claims that it is all nothing but a plot to make Mansfield seem important.

Personally, I am not a Shakespeare man, although I see several of his plays before, and, to tell you the truth, I am never able to savvy them, though naturally I do not admit this in public as I do not wish to appear unintelligent. But I stick with Ambrose through the first act of this one and I observe that Mansfield Sothern is at least a right large Hamlet and has a voice that makes him sound as if he is talking from down in a coal mine, though what he is talking about is not clear to me and consequently does not arouse my interest.

So as Ambrose seems very thoughtful and paying no attention to me, I quietly take my departure and go to Mindy's where some hours later along in the early morning, I notice Miss Channelle Cooper and this gee Mansfield Sothern reading Ambrose's column, and Mansfield is shedding tears on the paper until the printer's ink runs down into his bacon and eggs. Naturally, I go out and buy a paper at once to see what causes his distress and I find that Ambrose writes about the play as follows:

"After Mansfield Sothern's performance of Hamlet at the Todd Theater last night, there need no longer be controversy as to the authorship of the immortal drama. All we need do is examine the graves of Shakespeare and Bacon, and the one that has turned over is it."

Now I do not clap eyes on Ambrose Hammer again until the other evening when he enters Mindy's at dinnertime, walking with a cane and limping slightly. Furthermore, he is no longer roly-poly, but quite thin and he gives me a huge hello and sits down at my table and speaks to me as follows:

"Well, well," Ambrose says, "this is indeed a coincidence. The last time we meet I take you to a theater and now I am going to take you again on my first night back in harness. How is the *gedemte brust* and the *latkas* you are devouring?"

"The *latkas* are all right, Ambrose," I say, "but the *brust* is strictly second run. The war conditions are such that we must now take what we can get, even when it comes to *brust*. I do not see you for a spell, Ambrose. Are you absent from the city and why are you packing the stick?"

"Why," Ambrose says, "I am overseas and I am wounded in North Africa. Do you mean to tell me I am not missed in these parts?"

"Well, Ambrose," I say, "now that you mention it, I do remember hearing you are mixed up in the war business, but we are so busy missing other personalities that we do not get around to missing you as yet. And as for going to the theater with you, I must pass, because the last time you steer me up against a most unenjoyable evening. By the way, Ambrose," I say, "I wonder what ever becomes of that bloke Mansfield Sothern and Miss Channelle Cooper. And what are you doing in North Africa, anyway?"

I am in North Africa (Ambrose says) risking my life for my paper as a war correspondent because one day my editor calls me into his office and speaks to me as follows:

"Hammer," he says, "kindly go to the front and send us back human-interest stories about our soldiers. Our soldiers are what our readers are interested in. Please eat with them and sleep with them and tell us how they live and what they think about and how they talk and so forth and so on."

So I go to London, and from London, I go to North Africa on a transport, and on this voyage I endeavor to start following my instructions at once, but I find that eating with the soldiers has its disadvantages as they can eat much faster than I can because of their greater experience and I am always getting shut out on the choicer tidbits.

And when I ask one of them if I can sleep with him, he gives me a strange look, and afterward I have a feeling that I am the subject of gossip among these gees. Furthermore, when I try to listen in on their conversation to learn how they talk, some of them figure I am a stool pigeon for the officers and wish to dunk me in the ocean. It is by no means a soft touch to be a war correspondent who is supposed to find out how the soldiers live and how they talk and what they think about, and when I mention my difficulties to one of the officers, he says I may get closer to the boys if I enlist, but naturally I figure this will be carrying war corresponding too far.

But I write these human-interest stories just the same and I think they are pretty good even if I do hear a guy in the censor's office call me the poor man's Quentin Reynolds, and I always mingle with the soldiers as much as possible to get their atmosphere and finally when they learn I am kindly disposed toward them and generally have plenty of cigarettes, they become quite friendly.

I am sorry I do not have time to tell you a great deal about my terrible personal experiences at the front, but I am putting them all in the book I am writing, and you can buy a copy of it later. In fact, I have enough terrible experiences for three books, only my publisher states that he thinks one book per war correspondent is sufficient for the North African campaign. He says that the way correspondents are writing books on North Africa with Sicily and Italy coming up, he does not figure his paper supply to last the war out.

I first arrive at a place called Algiers in North Africa and I find it is largely infested by Arabs and naturally I feel at home at once, as in my younger days in show business when I am working for a booking office, I personally book a wonderful Arab acrobatic troop consisting of a real Arab by the name of Punchy, two guys by the name of O'Shea, and a waffle who is known as Little Oran, though her square monicker is really Magnolia Shapiro.

Consequently I have a great sentiment for Arabs, and the sights and scenes and smells of Algiers keep me thinking constantly of the good old days, especially the smells. But I will not tax your patience with the details of my stay in Algiers because by the time I reach there the war moves away off to a place called Tunisia and I am willing to let it stay there without my presence. Then, after a week, my editor sends me a sharp message asking why I am not at the front getting human-interest stories instead of loitering in Algiers wasting my time on some tamale, although, as a matter of fact, I am not wasting my time. And how he learns about the tamale I have no idea, as she does not speak a word of English.

However, one way and another I proceed to a place called Bone and then I continue on from there one way and another, but mostly in a little consumptive car, in the general direction of Tunis, and as I go, I keep asking passing British and American soldiers where is the front. And they say the front is up front, and I keep going and in my travels I get very sick and tired of the war because the enemy is always dropping hot apples all over the landscape out of planes, and sprinkling the roads with bullets or throwing big shells that make the most uncouth noises around very carelessly indeed.

Naturally, this impedes and delays my progress quite some because, from time to time, I am compelled to pause and dismount from my little bucket and seek refuge from these missiles in holes in the earth, and, when I cannot find a hole, I seek the refuge by falling on my face on the ground. In fact, I fall so often on my face that I am commencing to fear I will wind up with a pug nose.

Part of the time I am traveling with another newspaper scribe by the name of Herbert something, but he goes to Foldsville on me soon after we leave Bone, with a case of heartburn caused by eating Army rations, which reminds me that I must speak to the F.B.I. about these rations some day as it is my opinion that the books of the guy who invents them should be looked over to see which side he is betting on.

Well, all the time I keep asking where is the front, and all the time the soldiers say the front is up front. But I do not seem to ever find the front and, in fact, I later learn from an old soldier that nobody ever finds the front because by the time they get to where it ought to be, the front is apt to be the rear or the middle, and it is all very confusing to be sure.

Early one morning, I arrive at what seems to be the ruins of a little town, and at the same moment, an enemy battery on a hill a couple of miles away starts throwing big biscuits into the town, although I do not see hide or hair of anyone there, and whether it is because they think some of our troops are in the town or just have a personal grudge against me, I never learn.

Anyway, all of a sudden something nudges my little wagon from under me and knocks it into pieces the size of confetti and at the same moment I feel a distinct sensation of pain in my Francesca. It comes to my mind that I am wounded and I lie there with what I know is blood running down the inside of my pants leg which gives me a most untidy feeling, indeed, and what is more, I am mentally depressed quite some as I am already behind with my copy and I can see where this will delay me further and cause my editor to become most peevish.

But there is nothing I can do about it, only to keep on lying there and to try to stop the blood as best I can and wait for something to happen and also to hope that my mishap does not inconvenience my editor too greatly.

It is coming on noon, and all around and about it is very quiet, and nothing whatever seems to be stirring anywhere when who appears but a big guy in our uniform, and he seems more surprised than somewhat when he observes me, as he speaks to me as follows:

"Goodness me!" he says. "What is this?"

"I am wounded," I say.

"Where?" he says.

"In the vestibule," I say.

Then he drops on one knee beside me and outs with a knife and cuts open my pants and looks at the wound, and as he gets to his feet, he says to me like this:

"Does it hurt?" he says. "Are you suffering greatly?"

"Sure I am," I say. "I am dying."

Now the guy laughs ha-ha-ha-ha, as if he just hears a good joke and he says, "Look at me, Hammer," he says. "Do you not recognize me?"

Naturally I look and I can see that he is nobody but this Mansfield Sothern, the actor, and of course I am greatly pleased at the sight of him.

"Mansfield," I say, "I am never so glad to see an old friend in my life."

"What do you mean by old friend?" Mansfield says. "I am not your old friend. I am not even your new friend. Hammer," he says, "are you really in great pain?"

"Awful," I say. "Please get me to a doctor."

Well, at this, he laughs ha-ha-ha-ha again and says, "Hammer, all my professional life, I am hoping to one day see a dramatic critic suffer, and you have no idea what pleasure you are now giving me, but I think it only fair for you to suffer out loud with groans and one thing and another. Hammer," Mansfield says, "I am enjoying a privilege that any actor will give a squillion dollars to experience."

"Look, Mansfield," I say, "kindly cease your clowning and take me somewhere. I am in great agony."

"Ha-ha-ha-ha," Mansfield Sothern ha-has. "Hammer, I cannot get you to a doctor because the Jeremiahs seem to be between us and our lines. I fear they nab the rest of my patrol. It is only by good luck that I elude them myself and then, lo and behold, I find you. I do not think there are any of the enemy right around this spot at the moment and I am going to lug you into yonder building, but it is not because I take pity on you. It is only because I wish to keep you near me so I can see you suffer."

Then he picks me up in his arms and carries me inside the walls of what seems to be an old inn, though it has no roof and no windows or doors, and even the walls are a little shaky from much shellfire, and he puts me down on the floor and washes my wound with water from his canteen and puts sulpha powder on my wound and gives me some to swallow, and all the time he is talking a blue streak.

"Hammer," he says, "do you remember the night I give my performance of Hamlet and you knock my brains out? Well, you are in no more agony now than I am then. I die ten thousand deaths when I read your criticism. Furthermore, you alienate the affections of Miss Channelle Cooper from me, because she thinks you are a great dramatic critic, and when you say I am a bad Hamlet, she believes you and cancels our engagement. She says she cannot bear the idea of being married to a bad Hamlet. Hammer," he says, "am I a bad Hamlet?"

"Mansfield," I say, "I now regret I cause you anguish."

"Mr. Sothern to you," Mansfield says. "Hammer," he says. "I hear you only see two acts of my Hamlet."

"That is true," I say. "I have to hasten back to my office to write my review."

"Why," he says, "how dare you pass on the merits of an artist on such brief observation? Does your mad jealousy of me over Miss Channelle Cooper cause you to forget you are a human being and make a hyena of you? Or are all dramatic critics just naturally hyenas, as I suspect?"

"Mansfield," I say, "while I admit to much admiration and, in fact, love for Miss Channelle Cooper, I never permit my emotions to bias my professional efforts. When I state you are a bad Hamlet, I state my honest conviction and while I now suffer the tortures of the damned, I still state it."

"Hammer," Mansfield Sothern says, "listen to me and observe me closely because I am now going to run through the gravediggers' scene for you which you do not see me do, and you can tell me afterward if Barrymore or Leslie Howard or Maurice Evans ever gives a finer performance."

And with this, what does he do but pick up a big stone from the floor and strike a pose and speak as follows:

" 'Alas, poor Yorick! I knew him, Horatio; a fellow of infinite jest, of most excellent fancy; he hath borne me on his back a thousand

times; and now, how abhorred in my imagination it is! my gorge rises
at it. Here hung those lips that I have kissed I know not how oft.
Where be your gibes now? your gambols? your songs? your flashes
of merriment, that were wont to set the tables on a roar? Not one,
now, to mock your own grinning? quite chap-fallen? Now get you
to my lady's chamber, and tell her, let her paint an inch thick, to
this favor she must come; make her laugh at that. Pr'ythee, Horatio,
tell me one thing.' "

Now Mansfield stops and looks at me and says: "Come, come,
Hammer, you're Horatio. Throw me the line."

So I try to remember what Horatio remarks at this point in Hamlet
and finally I say, " 'How is that, my lord?' "

"No, no," Mansfield says. "Not 'How is that?' but 'What's that?'
And you presume to criticize me!"

"All right, Mansfield," I say. " 'What's that, my lord?' "

And Mansfield says, " 'Dost thou think Alexander looked o' this
fashion i' the earth?' "

I say, " 'E'en so.' "

" 'And smelt so?' pah!" Mansfield says, and with this, he throws
the stone to the floor, and at the same moment I hear another noise
and, on looking around, what do I see in the doorway but two German
officers covered with dust, and one of them says in English like this:

"What is going on here?"

Naturally, I am somewhat nonplussed at the sight of these guys,
but Mansfield Sothern does not seem to notice them and continues
reciting in a loud voice.

"He is an actor in civil life," I say to the German. "He is now
presenting his version of Hamlet to me."

" 'To what base uses we may return, Horatio!' " Mansfield
Sothern says. " 'Why may not imagination trace the noble dust of
Alexander—!' "

" 'Till he finds it stopping a bunghole?' " the German cuts in and
then Mansfield looks at him and says:

" 'Find,' not 'finds,' " he says.

"Quite right," the German says. "Well, you are now prisoners. I
will send some of my soldiers to pick you up immediately. Do not
attempt to leave this place or you will be shot, as we have the town
surrounded."

Then the two depart and Mansfield stops reciting at once and says, "Let us duffy out of here. It is growing dark outside, and I think we can make it. Are you still suffering first class, Hammer?"

"Yes," I say, "and I cannot walk an inch, either."

So Mansfield laughs ha-ha-ha and picks me up again as easy as if I am nothing but a bag of wind and carries me out through what seems to have been a back door to the joint, but before we go into the open, he throws himself face downward on the ground and tells me to pull myself on his back and hook my arms around his neck and hold on, and I do the same. Then he starts crawling along like he is a turtle and I am its shell. Naturally, our progress is very slow, especially as we hear guys everywhere around us in the dark talking in German.

Every few yards, Mansfield has to stop to rest, and I roll off his back until he is ready to start again and, during one of these halts, he whispers, "Hammer, are you still suffering?"

"Yes," I say.

"Good," Mansfield says, and then he goes on crawling.

I do not know how far he crawls with me aboard him because I am getting a little groggy, but I do remember him whispering very softly to himself like this:

Imperious Caesar, dead and turn'd to clay,
Might stop a hole to keep the wind away.

Well, Mansfield crawls and crawls and crawls until he crawls himself and me right into a bunch of our guys, and the next thing I know is I wake up in a hospital, and who is sitting there beside me but Mansfield Sothern and, when he sees I am awake, he says like this:

" 'O, I die, Horatio.' "

"Mansfield," I say, "kindly cheese it and permit me to thank you for saving my life."

"Hammer," he says, "the pleasure is all mine. I am sustained on my long crawl (which they tell me is a new world record for crawling with a guy on the deck of the crawler) by the thought that I have on my back a dramatic critic who is suffering keenly every inch of the way.

"I suppose," he says, "that you hear I am decorated for rescuing you, but kindly keep it quiet, as the Actors' Guild will never forgive me for rescuing a critic. Also, Hammer, I am being sent home to organize overseas entertainment for my comrades, and naturally it will be along Shakespearean lines. Tell me, Hammer, do you observe your nurse as yet?"

And, with this, Mansfield points to a doll in uniform standing not far away, and I can see that it is nobody but Miss Channelle Cooper, and I can also see that she is hoping she is looking like Miss Florence Nightingale. When she notices I am awake, she starts toward my cot, but at her approach, Mansfield Sothern gets up and departs quite hastily without as much as saying boo to her and as she stands looking at him, tears come to her eyes and I can see that a coolness must still prevail between them.

Naturally, I am by no means displeased by this situation because the sight of Miss Channelle Cooper even in a nurse's uniform brings back fond memories to me and, in fact, I feel all my old love for her coming up inside me like a lump, and, as she reaches my bedside, I can scarcely speak because of my emotion.

"You must be quiet, Ambrose," she says. "You know you are delirious for days and days, and in your delirium you say things about me that cause me much embarrassment. Does Mansfield happen to mention my name?"

"No," I say. "Forget him, Channelle. He is a cad as well as a bad Hamlet."

But the tears in her eyes increase, and suddenly she leaves me and I do not see her for some days afterward and, in fact, I do not even think of her because my editor is sending me messages wishing to know what I am doing in a hospital on his time and to get out of there at once, and what do I mean by putting a horse in my last expense account, which of course is an error in bookkeeping due to my haste in making out the account. What I intend putting in is a hearse, as I figure that my editor will be too confused by such an unexpected item to dispute it.

So here I am back in the good old U.S.A. (Ambrose says) and now as I previously state I am going to take you to the theater again with me, and who are you going to see but our old friend Mansfield Sothern playing Hamlet once more!

Now this prospect by no means thrills me, but I am unable to think of a good out at once, so I accompany Ambrose, and when we arrive at the theater, we find the manager, who is a guy by the name of James Burdekin, walking up and down in front of the joint and speaking in the most disparaging terms of actors, and customers are milling around the lobby and on the sidewalks outside.

They are going up to James Burdekin and saying, "What is the matter, Burdekin?" and "When does the curtain go up?" and "Who do you think you are?" and all this and that, which only causes him to become very disrespectful indeed in his expressions about actors and, in fact, he is practically libelous, and it is several minutes before Ambrose and I can figure out the nature of his emotion.

Then we learn that what happens is that Mansfield Sothern collapses in his dressing room a few minutes before the curtain is to rise, and, as the gaff is all sold out, it is naturally a terrible predicament for James Burdekin, as he may have to refund the money, and thinking of this has James on the verge of a collapse himself.

"Hammer," he says to Ambrose, "you will do me a favor if you can find out what is eating this hamdonny. I am afraid to trust myself to even look at him at the moment."

So Ambrose and I go around to the stage entrance and up to Mansfield Sothern's dressing room, and there is Mansfield sprawled in a chair in his Hamlet makeup, while his dresser, an old stove lid by the name of Crichton, is swabbing Mansfield's brow with a towel and speaking soothing words to him in a Southern accent.

"Why, Mansfield," Ambrose says, "what seems to ail you that you keep an eager audience waiting and put James Burdekin in a condition bordering on hysteria?"

"I cannot go on," Mansfield says. "My heart is too heavy. I just learn of your return and, as I am sitting here thinking of how you must make plenty of hay-hay with Miss Channelle Cooper when you are lying there under her loving care in North Africa and telling her what a bad Hamlet I am, I am overcome with grief. Ambrose," he says, "is there any hope of you being crippled for life?"

"No," Ambrose says. "Come, come, Mansfield," he says. "Pull yourself together. Think of your career and of poor James Burdekin and the box-office receipts. Remember the ancient tradition of the theater: The show must go on—although, personally, I do not always see why."

"I cannot," Mansfield says. "Her face will rise before me, and my words will choke me as I think of her in another's arms. Ambrose, I am in bad shape, but I am man enough to congratulate you. I hope and trust you will always be happy with Miss Channelle Cooper, even if you are a dramatic critic. But I cannot go on in my present state of mind. I am too melancholy even for Hamlet."

"Oh," Ambrose says, "do not worry about Miss Channelle Cooper. She loves you dearly. The last time I see her, I request her to be my ever-loving wife when this cruel war is over, but she says it can never be, as she loves only you. I say all right; if she wishes to love a bad Hamlet instead of a good correspondent, to go ahead. And then," Ambrose says, "Miss Channelle Cooper speaks to me as follows:

" 'No, Ambrose,' she says. 'He is not a bad Hamlet. A better judge than you says he is a fine Hamlet. Professor Bierbauer, the great dramatic coach of Heidelberg, now a colonel in the German army, tells me he witnesses a performance by Mansfield in a ruined tavern in a town near the front, that, under the conditions, is the most magnificent effort of the kind he ever views.'

"It seems," Ambrose says, "that the professor is wounded and captured by our guys when they retake the town, and, at the moment Miss Channelle Cooper is addressing me, he is one of her patients in a nearby ward, where I have no doubt he gets quite an earful on your history and her love. Where are you going, Mansfield?"

"Why," Mansfield says, "I am going around the corner to send a cablegram to Miss Channelle Cooper, telling her I reciprocate her love and also requesting her to get Professor Bierbauer's opinion in writing for my scrapbook."

Well, I wait up in Mindy's restaurant with Mansfield to get the last editions containing the reviews of the critics and, naturally, the first review we turn to is Ambrose Hammer's, and at Mansfield's request I read it aloud as follows:

" 'Mansfield Sothern's inspired performance of Hamlet at the Todd Theater last night leads us to the hope that in this sterling young actor we have a new dramatic force of the power of Shakespearean roles of all the mighty figures of another day, perhaps including even the immortal Edwin Booth.'

"Well, Mansfield," I say, when I finish, "I think Ambrose now pays you off in full on your account with him, including saving his life, what with giving you Miss Channelle Cooper and this wonderful boost, which, undoubtedly, establishes your future in the theater."

"Humph!" Mansfield says. "It seems a fair appraisal at that, and I will send a clipping to Miss Channelle Cooper at once, but," he says, "there is undoubtedly a streak of venom left in Ambrose Hammer. Else, why does he bring in Booth?"

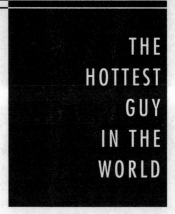

THE
HOTTEST
GUY
IN THE
WORLD

I wish to say I am very nervous indeed when Big Jule pops into my hotel room one afternoon, because anybody will tell you that Big Jule is the hottest guy in the whole world at the time I am speaking about.

In fact, it is really surprising how hot he is. They wish to see him in Pittsburgh, Pa., about a matter of a mail truck being robbed, and there is gossip about him in Minneapolis, Minn., where somebody takes a fifty-G payroll off a messenger in cash money, and slugs the messenger around somewhat for not holding still.

Furthermore, the Bankers' Association is willing to pay good dough to talk to Big Jule out in Kansas City, Mo., where a jug is knocked off by a stranger, and in the confusion the paying teller and the cashier, and the second vice-president are clouted about, and the day watchman is hurt, and two coppers are badly bruised, and over fifteen G's is removed from the counters, and never returned.

Then there is something about a department store in Canton, O., and a flour-mill safe in Toledo, and a grocery in Spokane, Wash., and a branch post office in San Francisco, and also something about a shooting match in Chicago, but of course this does not count so much, as only one party is fatally injured. However, you can see that Big Jule is really very hot, what with the coppers all over the country looking for him high and low. In fact, he is practically on fire.

Of course I do not believe Big Jule does all the things the coppers say, because coppers always blame everything no matter where it happens on the most prominent guy they can think of, and Big Jule is quite prominent all over the U.S.A. The chances are he does not do more than half these things, and he probably has a good alibi for the half he does do, at that, but he is certainly hot, and I do not care to have hot guys around me, or even guys who are only just a little bit warm.

But naturally I am not going to say this to Big Jule when he pops in on me, because he may think I am inhospitable, and I do not care to have such a rap going around and about on me, and furthermore, Jule may become indignant if he thinks I am inhospitable, and knock me on my potato, because Big Jule is quick to take offense.

So I say hello to Big Jule, very pleasant, and ask him to have a chair by the window where he can see the citizens walking to and fro down in Eighth Avenue and watch the circus wagons moving into Madison Square Garden by way of the Forty-ninth Street side, for the circus always shows in the Garden in the spring before going out on the road. It is a little warm, and Big Jule takes off his coat, and I can see he has one automatic slung under his arm, and another sticking down in the waistband of his pants, and I hope and trust that no copper steps into the room while Big Jule is there because it is very much against the law for guys to go around rodded up this way in New York City.

"Well, Jule," I say, "this is indeed a very large surprise to me, and I am glad to see you, but I am thinking maybe it is very foolish for you to be popping into New York just now, what with all the heat around here, and the coppers looking to arrest people for very little."

"I know," Jule says. "I know. But they do not have so very much on me around here, no matter what people say, and a guy gets homesick for his old hometown, especially a guy who is stuck away where I am for the past few months. I get homesick for the lights and the crowds on Broadway, and for the old neighborhood. Furthermore, I wish to see my Maw. I hear she is sick and may not live, and I wish to see her before she goes."

Well, naturally anybody will wish to see their Maw under such circumstances, but Big Jule's Maw lives over in West Forty-ninth Street near Eleventh Avenue, and who is living in the very same block but Johnny Brannigan, the strong-arm copper, and it is a hundred to one if Big Jule goes nosing around his old neighborhood, Johnny Brannigan will hear of it, and if there is one guy Johnny

Brannigan does not care for, it is Big Jule, although they are kids together.

But it seems that even when they are kids they have very little use for each other, and after they grow up and Johnny gets on the strong-arm squad, he never misses a chance to push Big Jule around, and sometimes trying to boff Big Jule with his blackjack, and it is well known to one and all that before Big Jule leaves town the last time, he takes a punch at Johnny Brannigan, and Johnny swears he will never rest until he puts Big Jule where he belongs, although where Big Jule belongs, Johnny does not say.

So I speak of Johnny living in the same block with Big Jule's Maw to Big Jule, but it only makes him mad.

"I am not afraid of Johnny Brannigan," he says. "In fact," he says, "I am thinking for some time lately that maybe I will clip Johnny Brannigan good while I am here. I owe Johnny Brannigan a clipping. But I wish to see my Maw first, and then I will go around and see Miss Kitty Clancy. I guess maybe she will be much surprised to see me, and no doubt very glad."

Well, I figure it is a sure thing Miss Kitty Clancy will be surprised to see Big Jule, but I am not so sure about her being glad, because very often when a guy is away from a doll for a year or more, no matter how ever-loving she may be, she may get to thinking of someone else, for this is the way dolls are, whether they live on Eleventh Avenue or over on Park. Still, I remember hearing that this Miss Kitty Clancy once thinks very well of Big Jule, although her old man, Jack Clancy, who runs a speakeasy, always claims it is a big knock to the Clancy family to have such a character as Big Jule hanging around.

"I often think of Miss Kitty Clancy the past year or so," Big Jule says, as he sits there by the window, watching the circus wagons, and the crowds. "I especially think of her the past few months. In fact," he says, "thinking of Miss Kitty Clancy is about all I have to do where I am at, which is in an old warehouse on the Bay of Fundy outside of a town that is called St. John's, or some such, up in Canada, and thinking of Miss Kitty Clancy all this time, I find out I love her very much indeed.

"I go to this warehouse," Big Jule says, "after somebody takes a jewelry store in the town, and the coppers start in blaming me. This warehouse is not such a place as I will choose myself if I am doing the choosing, because it is an old fur warehouse, and full of strange smells, but in the excitement around the jewelry store, somebody puts a slug in my hip, and Leon Pierre carries me to the old warehouse, and there I am until I get well.

"It is very lonesome," Big Jule says. "In fact, you will be surprised how lonesome it is, and it is very, very cold, and all I have for company is a lot of rats. Personally, I never care for rats under any circumstances because they carry disease germs, and are apt to bite a guy when he is asleep, if they are hungry, which is what these rats try to do to me.

"The warehouse is away off by itself," Jule says, "and nobody ever comes around there except Leon Pierre to bring me grub and dress my hip, and at night it is very still, and all you can hear is the wind howling around outside, and the rats running here and there. Some of them are very, very large rats. In fact, some of them seem about the size of rabbits, and they are pretty fresh, at that. At first I am willing to make friends with these rats, but they seem very hostile, and after they take a few nips at me, I can see there is no use trying to be nice to them, so I have Leon Pierre bring me a lot of ammunition for my rods every day and I practice shooting at the rats.

"The warehouse is so far off there is no danger of anybody hearing the shooting," Big Jule says, "and it helps me pass the time away. I get so I can hit a rat sitting, or running, or even flying through the air, because these warehouse rats often leap from place to place like mountain sheep, their idea being generally to take a good nab at me as they fly past.

"Well, sir," Jule says, "I keep score on myself one day, and I hit fifty rats hand running without a miss, which I claim makes me the champion rat shooter of the world with a forty-five automatic, although of course," he says, "if anybody wishes to challenge me to a rat shooting match I am willing to take them on for a side bet. I get so I can call my shots on the rats, and in fact several times I say to myself, I will hit this one in the right eye, and this one in the left eye, and it always turns out just as I say, although sometimes when you hit a rat with a forty-five up close it is not always possible to tell afterward just where you hit him, because you seem to hit him all over.

"By and by," Jule says, "I seem to discourage the rats somewhat, and they get so they play the chill for me, and do not try to nab me even when I am asleep. They find out that no rat dast poke his whiskers out at me or he will get a very close shave. So I have to look around for other amusement, but there is not much doing in such a place, although I finally find a bunch of doctor's books which turn out to be very interesting reading. It seems these books are left there by some croaker who retires there to think things over after experimenting on his ever-loving wife with a knife. In fact, it seems he cuts his ever-loving wife's head off, and she does not continue living, so he takes his books and goes to the warehouse and remains there until the law finds him, and hangs him up very high, indeed.

"Well, the books are a great comfort to me, and I learn many astonishing things about surgery, but after I read all the books there is nothing for me to do but think, and what I think about is Miss Kitty Clancy, and how much pleasure we have together walking around and about and seeing movie shows, and all this and that, until her old man gets so tough with me. Yes, I will be very glad to see Miss Kitty Clancy, and the old neighborhood, and my Maw again."

Well, finally nothing will do Big Jule but he must take a stroll over into his old neighborhood, and see if he cannot see Miss Kitty Clancy, and also drop in on his Maw, and he asks me to go along with him. I can think of a million things I will rather do than take a stroll with Big Jule, but I do not wish him to think I am snobbish, because as I say, Big Jule is quick to take offense. Furthermore, I figure that at such an hour of the day he is less likely to run into Johnny Brannigan or any other coppers who know him than at any other time, so I say I will go with him, but as we start out, Big Jule puts on his rods.

"Jule," I say, "do not take any rods with you on a stroll, because somebody may happen to see them, such as a copper, and you know they will pick you up for carrying a rod in this town quicker than you can say Jack Robinson, whether they know who you are or not. You know the Sullivan law is very strong against guys carrying rods in this town."

But Big Jule says he is afraid he will catch cold if he goes out without his rods, so we go down into Forty-ninth Street and start west toward Madison Square Garden, and just as we reach Eighth Avenue and are standing there waiting for the traffic to stop, so we can cross the street, I see there is quite some excitement around the Garden on the Forty-ninth Street side, with people running every which way, and yelling no little, and looking up in the air.

So I look up myself, and what do I see sitting up there on the edge of the Garden roof but a big ugly-faced monkey. At first I do not recognize it as a monkey, because it is so big I figure maybe it is just one of the prizefight managers who stand around on this side of the Garden all afternoon waiting to get a match for their fighters, and while I am somewhat astonished to see a prizefight manager in such a position, I figure maybe he is doing it on a bet. But when I take a second look I see that it is indeed a big monk, and an exceptionally homely monk at that, although personally I never see any monks I consider so very handsome, anyway.

Well, this big monk is holding something in its arms, and what it is I am not able to make out at first, but then Big Jule and I cross the street to the side opposite the Garden, and now I can see that the monk has a baby in its arms. Naturally I figure it is some kind of advertising dodge put on by the Garden to ballyhoo the circus, or maybe the fight between Sharkey and Risko which is coming off after the circus, but guys are still yelling and running up and down, and dolls are screaming until finally I realize that a most surprising situation prevails.

It seems that the big monk up on the roof is nobody but Bongo, who is a gorilla belonging to the circus, and one of the very few gorillas of any account in this country, or anywhere else, as far as this goes, because good gorillas are very scarce, indeed. Well, it seems that while they are shoving Bongo's cage into the Garden, the door becomes unfastened, and the first thing anybody knows, out pops Bongo, and goes bouncing along the street where a lot of the neighbors' children are playing games on the sidewalk, and a lot of Mamas are sitting out in the sun alongside baby buggies containing their young. This is a very common sight in side streets such as West Forty-ninth on nice days, and by no means unpleasant, if you like Mamas and their young.

Now what does this Bongo do but reach into a baby buggy which a Mama is pushing past on the sidewalk on the Garden side of the street, and snatch out a baby, though what Bongo wants with this baby nobody knows to this day. It is a very young baby, and not such a baby as is fit to give a gorilla the size of Bongo any kind of struggle, so Bongo has no trouble whatever in handling it. Anyway, I always hear a gorilla will make a sucker out of a grown man in a battle, though I wish to say I never see a battle between a gorilla and a grown man. It ought to be a first-class drawing card, at that.

Well, naturally the baby's Mama puts up quite a squawk about Bongo grabbing her baby, because no Mama wishes her baby to keep company with a gorilla, and this Mama starts in screaming very loud, and trying to take the baby away from Bongo, so what does Bongo do but run right up on the roof of the Garden by way of a big electric sign which hangs down on the Forty-ninth Street side. And there old Bongo sits on the edge of the roof with the baby in his arms, and the baby is squalling quite some, and Bongo is making funny noises, and showing his teeth as the folks commence gathering in the street below.

There is a big guy in his shirtsleeves running through the crowd waving his hands, and trying to shush everybody, and saying "Quiet, please" over and over, but nobody pays any attention to him. I figure this guy has something to do with the circus, and maybe with Bongo, too. A traffic copper takes a peek at the situation, and calls for the reserves from the Forty-seventh Street station, and somebody else sends for the fire truck down the street, and pretty soon cops are running from every direction, and the fire engines are coming, and the big guy in his shirtsleeves is more excited than ever.

"Quiet, please," he says. "Everybody keep quiet, because if Bongo becomes disturbed by the noise he will throw the baby down in the street. He throws everything he gets his hands on," the guy says. "He acquires this habit from throwing coconuts back in his old home country. Let us get a life net, and if you all keep quiet we may be able to save the baby before Bongo starts heaving it like a coconut."

Well, Bongo is sitting up there on the edge of the roof about seven stories above the ground peeking down with the baby in his arms, and he is holding this baby just like a Mama would, but anybody can see that Bongo does not care for the row below, and once he lifts the baby high above his head as if to bean somebody with it. I see Big Nig, the crap shooter, in the mob, and afterward I hear he is around offering to lay seven to five against the baby, but everybody is too excited to bet on such a proposition, although it is not a bad price, at that.

I see one doll in the crowd on the sidewalk on the side of the street opposite the Garden who is standing perfectly still staring up at the monk and the baby with a very strange expression on her face, and the way she is looking makes me take a second gander at her, and who is it but Miss Kitty Clancy. Her lips are moving as she stands there staring up, and something tells me Miss Kitty Clancy is saying prayers to herself, because she is such a doll as will know how to say prayers on an occasion like this.

Big Jule sees her about the same time I do, and Big Jule steps up beside Miss Kitty Clancy, and says hello to her, and though it is over a year since Miss Kitty Clancy sees Big Jule she turns to him and speaks to him as if she is talking to him just a minute before. It is very strange indeed the way Miss Kitty Clancy speaks to Big Jule as if he has never been away at all.

"Do something, Julie," she says. "You are always the one to do something. Oh, please do something, Julie."

Well, Big Jule never answers a word, but steps back in the clear of the crowd and reaches for the waistband of his pants, when I grab him by the arm and say to him like this:

"My goodness, Jule," I say, "what are you going to do?"

"Why," Jule says, "I am going to shoot this thieving monk before he takes a notion to heave the baby on somebody down here. For all I know," Jule says, "he may hit me with it, and I do not care to be hit with anybody's baby."

"Jule," I say, very earnestly, "do not pull a rod in front of all these coppers, because if you do they will nail you sure, if only for having the rod, and if you are nailed you are in a very tough spot, indeed, what with being wanted here and there. Jule," I say, "you are hotter than a forty-five all over this country, and I do not wish to see you nailed. Anyway," I say, "you may shoot the baby instead of the monk, because anybody can see it will be very difficult to hit the monk up there without hitting the baby. Furthermore, even if you do hit the monk it will fall into the street, and bring the baby with it."

"You speak great foolishness," Jule says. "I never miss what I shoot at. I will shoot the monk right between the eyes, and this will make him fall backward, not forward, and the baby will not be hurt because anybody can see it is no fall at all from the ledge to the roof behind. I make a study of such propositions," Jule says, "and I know if a guy is in such a position as this monk sitting on a ledge looking down from a high spot, his defensive reflexes tend backward, so this is the way he is bound to fall if anything unexpected comes up on him, such as a bullet between the eyes. I read all about it in the doctor's books," Jule says.

Then all of a sudden up comes his hand, and in his hand is one of his rods, and I hear a sound like ker-bap. When I come to think about it afterward, I do not remember Big Jule even taking aim like a guy will generally do if he is shooting at something sitting, but old Bongo seems to lift up a little bit off the ledge at the crack of the gun, and then he keels over backward, the baby still in his arms, and squalling more than somewhat, and Big Jule says to me like this:

"Right between the eyes, and I will bet on it," he says, "although it is not much of a target, at that."

Well, nobody can figure what happens for a minute, and there is much silence except from the guy in his shirtsleeves who is expressing much indignation with Big Jule and saying the circus people will sue him for damages sure if he has hurt Bongo, because the monk is worth $100,000, or some such. I see Miss Kitty Clancy kneeling on the sidewalk with her hands clasped, and looking upward, and Big Jule is sticking his rod back in his waistband again.

By this time some guys are out on the roof getting through from the inside of the building with the idea of heading Bongo off from that direction, and they let out a yell, and pretty soon I see one of them holding the baby up so everyone in the street can see it. A couple of other guys get down near the edge of the roof and pick up Bongo and show him to the crowd, as dead as a mackerel, and one of the guys puts a finger between Bongo's eyes to show where the bullet hits the monk, and Miss Kitty Clancy walks over to Big Jule and tries to say something to him, but only busts out crying very loud.

Well, I figure this is a good time for Big Jule and me to take a walk, because everybody is interested in what is going on up on the roof, and I do not wish the circus people to get a chance to serve a summons in a damage suit on Big Jule for shooting the valuable monk. Furthermore, a couple of coppers in harness are looking Big Jule over very critically, and I figure they are apt to put the old sleeve on Jule any second.

All of a sudden a slim young guy steps up to Big Jule and says to him like this:

"Jule," he says, "I want to see you," and who is it but Johnny

Brannigan. Naturally Big Jule starts reaching for a rod, but Johnny starts him walking down the street so fast Big Jule does not have time to get in action just then.

"No use getting it out, Jule," Johnny Brannigan says. "No use, and no need. Come with me, and hurry."

Well, Big Jule is somewhat puzzled because Johnny Brannigan is not acting like a copper making a collar, so he goes along with Johnny, and I follow after him, and halfway down the block Johnny stops a Yellow short, and hustles us into it and tells the driver to keep shoving down Eighth Avenue.

"I am trailing you ever since you get in town, Jule," Johnny Brannigan says. "You never have a chance around here. I am going over to your Maw's house to put the arm on you, figuring you are sure to go there, when the thing over by the Garden comes off. Now I am getting out of this cab at the next corner, and you go on and see your Maw, and then screw out of town as quick as you can, because you are red hot around here, Jule.

"By the way," Johnny Brannigan says, "do you know it is my kid you save, Jule? Mine and Kitty Clancy's? We are married a year ago today."

Well, Big Jule looks very much surprised for a moment, and then he laughs, and says like this: "Well, I never know it is Kitty Clancy's, but I figure it for yours the minute I see it because it looks like you."

"Yes," Johnny Brannigan says, very proud, "everybody says he does."

"I can see the resemblance even from a distance," Big Jule says. "In fact," he says, "it is remarkable how much you look alike. But," he says, "for a minute, Johnny, I am afraid I will not be able to pick out the right face between the two on the roof, because it is very hard to tell the monk and your baby apart."

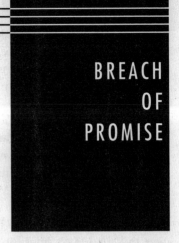

BREACH
OF
PROMISE

One day a certain party by the name of Judge Goldfobber, who is a lawyer by trade, sends word to me that he wishes me to call on him at his office in lower Broadway, and while ordinarily I do not care for any part of lawyers, it happens that Judge Goldfobber is a friend of mine, so I go to see him.

Of course Judge Goldfobber is not a judge, and never is a judge, and he is 100 to 1 in my line against ever being a judge, but he is called Judge because it pleases him, and everybody always wishes to please Judge Goldfobber, as he is one of the surest-footed lawyers in this town, and beats more tough beefs for different citizens than seems possible. He is a wonderful hand for keeping citizens from getting into the sneezer, and better than Houdini when it comes to getting them out of the sneezer after they are in.

Personally, I never have any use for the professional services of Judge Goldfobber, as I am a law-abiding citizen at all times, and am greatly opposed to guys who violate the law, but I know the Judge from around and about for many years. I know him from around and about the nightclubs, and other deadfalls, for Judge Goldfobber is such a guy as loves to mingle with the public in these spots, as he picks up much law business there, and sometimes a nice doll.

Well, when I call on Judge Goldfobber, he takes me into his private office and wishes to know if I can think of a couple of deserving guys who are out of employment, and who will like a job of work, and if so, Judge Goldfobber says, he can offer them a first-class position.

"Of course," Judge Goldfobber says, "it is not steady employment, and in fact it is nothing but piece-work, but the parties must be extremely reliable parties, who can be depended on in a pinch. This is out-of-town work that requires tact, and," he says, "some nerve."

Well, I am about to tell Judge Goldfobber that I am no employment agent, and go on about my business, because I can tell from the way he says the parties must be parties who can be depended on in a pinch, that a pinch is apt to come up on the job any minute, and I do not care to steer any friends of mine against a pinch.

But as I get up to go, I look out of Judge Goldfobber's window, and I can see Brooklyn in the distance beyond the river, and seeing Brooklyn I get to thinking of certain parties over there that I figure must be suffering terribly from the unemployment situation. I get to thinking of Harry the Horse, and Spanish John and Little Isadore, and the reason I figure they must be suffering from the unemployment situation is because if nobody is working and making any money, there is nobody for them to rob, and if there is nobody for them to rob, Harry the Horse and Spanish John and Little Isadore are just naturally bound to be feeling the depression keenly.

Anyway, I finally mention the names of these parties to Judge Goldfobber, and furthermore I speak well of their reliability in a pinch, and of their nerve, although I cannot conscientiously recommend their tact, and Judge Goldfobber is greatly delighted, as he often hears of Harry the Horse, and Spanish John and Little Isadore.

He asks me for their addresses, but of course nobody knows exactly where Harry the Horse and Spanish John and Little Isadore live, because they do not live anywhere in particular. However, I tell him about a certain spot in Clinton Street where he may be able to get track of them, and then I leave Judge Goldfobber for fear he may wish me to take word to these parties, and if there is anybody in this whole world I will not care to take word to, or to have any truck with in any manner, shape or form, it is Harry the Horse, and Spanish John and Little Isadore.

Well, I do not hear anything more of the matter for several weeks, but one evening when I am in Mindy's restaurant on Broadway enjoying a little cold borscht, which is a most refreshing matter in hot weather such as is going on at the time, who bobs up but Harry the Horse, and Spanish John and Little Isadore, and I am so surprised to see them that some of my cold borscht goes down the wrong way, and I almost choke to death.

However, they seem quite friendly, and in fact Harry the Horse pounds me on the back to keep me from choking, and while he pounds so hard that he almost caves in my spine, I consider it a most courteous action, and when I am able to talk again, I say to him as follows:

"Well, Harry," I say, "it is a privilege and a pleasure to see you again, and I hope and trust you will all join me in some cold borscht, which you will find very nice, indeed."

"No," Harry says, "we do not care for any cold borscht. We are looking for Judge Goldfobber. Do you see Judge Goldfobber round and about lately?"

Well, the idea of Harry the Horse and Spanish John and Little Isadore looking for Judge Goldfobber sounds somewhat alarming to me, and I figure maybe the job Judge Goldfobber gives them turns out bad and they wish to take Judge Goldfobber apart, but the next minute Harry says to me like this:

"By the way," he says, "we wish to thank you for the job of work you throw our way. Maybe some day we will be able to do as much for you. It is a most interesting job," Harry says, "and while you are snuffing your cold borscht I will give you the details, so you will understand why we wish to see Judge Goldfobber."

It turns out [Harry the Horse says] that the job is not for Judge Goldfobber personally, but for a client of his, and who is this client but Mr. Jabez Tuesday, the rich millionaire, who owns the Tuesday string of one-arm joints where many citizens go for food and wait on themselves. Judge Goldfobber comes to see us in Brooklyn in person, and sends me to see Mr. Jabez Tuesday with a letter of introduction, so Mr. Jabez Tuesday can explain what he wishes me to do, because Judge Goldfobber is too smart a guy to be explaining such matters to me himself.

In fact, for all I know maybe Judge Goldfobber is not aware of what Mr. Jabez Tuesday wishes me to do, although I am willing to lay a little 6 to 5 that Judge Goldfobber does not think Mr. Jabez Tuesday wishes to hire me as a cashier in any of his one-arm joints.

Anyway, I go to see Mr. Tuesday at a Fifth Avenue hotel where he makes his home, and where he has a very swell layout of rooms, and I am by no means impressed with Mr. Tuesday, as he hems and haws quite a bit before he tells me the nature of the employment he has in mind for me. He is a little guy, somewhat dried out, with a bald head, and a small mouser on his upper lip, and he wears specs, and seems somewhat nervous.

Well, it takes him some time to get down to cases, and tell me what is eating him, and what he wishes to do, and then it all sounds very simple, indeed, and in fact it sounds so simple that I think Mr. Jabez Tuesday is a little daffy when he tells me he will give me ten G's for the job.

What Mr. Tuesday wishes me to do is to get some letters that he personally writes to a doll by the name of Miss Amelia Bodkin, who lives in a house just outside Tarrytown, because it seems that Mr. Tuesday makes certain cracks in these letters that he is now sorry for, such as speaking of love and marriage and one thing and another to Miss Amelia Bodkin, and he is afraid she is going to sue him for breach of promise.

"Such an idea will be very embarrassing to me," Mr. Jabez Tuesday says, "as I am about to marry a party who is a member of one of the most high-toned families in this country. It is true," Mr. Tuesday says, "that the Scarwater family does not have as much money now as formerly, but there is no doubt about its being very, very high-toned, and my fiancée, Miss Valerie Scarwater, is one of the high-tonedest of them all. In fact," he says, "she is so high-toned that the chances are she will be very huffy about anybody suing me for breach of promise, and cancel everything."

Well, I ask Mr. Tuesday what a breach of promise is, and he explains to me that it is when somebody promises to do something and fails to do this something, although of course we have a different name for a proposition of this nature in Brooklyn, and deal with it accordingly.

"This is a very easy job for a person of your standing," Mr. Tuesday says. "Miss Amelia Bodkin lives all alone in her house the other side of Tarrytown, except for a couple of servants, and they are old and harmless. Now the idea is," he says, "you are not to go to her house as if you are looking for the letters, but as if you are after something else, such as her silverware, which is quite antique and very valuable.

"She keeps the letters in a big inlaid box in her room," Mr. Tuesday says, "and if you just pick up this box and carry it away along with the silverware, no one will ever suspect that you are after the letters, but that you take the box thinking it contains valuables. You bring the letters to me and get your ten G's," Mr. Tuesday says, "and," he says, "you can keep the silverware, too. Be sure you get a Paul Revere teapot with the silverware," he says. "It is worth plenty."

"Well," I say to Mr. Tuesday, "every guy knows his own business best, and I do not wish to knock myself out of a nice soft job, but," I say, "it seems to me the simplest way of carrying on this transaction is to buy the letters off this doll, and be done with it. Personally," I say, "I do not believe there is a doll in the world who is not willing to sell a whole post-office full of letters for ten G's, especially in these times, and throw in a set of Shakespeare with them."

"No, no," Mr. Tuesday says. "Such a course will not do with Miss Amelia Bodkin at all. You see," he says, "Miss Bodkin and I are very, very friendly for a matter of maybe fifteen or sixteen years. In fact, we are very friendly, indeed. She does not have any idea at this time that I wish to break off this friendship with her. Now," he says, "if I try to buy the letters from her, she may become suspicious. The idea," Mr. Tuesday says, "is for me to get the letters first, and then explain to her about breaking off the friendship, and make suitable arrangements with her afterward.

"Do not get Miss Amelia Bodkin wrong," Mr. Tuesday says. "She is an excellent person, but," he says, "you know the saying, 'Hell hath no fury like a woman scorned.' And maybe Miss Amelia Bodkin may figure I am scorning her if she finds out I am going to marry Miss Valerie Scarwater, and furthermore," he says, "if she still has the letters she may fall into the hands of unscrupulous lawyers, and demand a very large sum, indeed. But," Mr. Tuesday says, "this does not worry me half as much as the idea that Miss Valerie Scarwater may learn about the letters and get a wrong impression of my friendship with Miss Amelia Bodkin."

Well, I round up Spanish John and Little Isadore the next afternoon, and I find Little Isadore playing klob with a guy by the name of Educated Edmund, who is called Educated Edmund because he once goes to Erasmus High school and is considered a very fine scholar, indeed, so I invite Educated Edmund to go along with us. The idea is, I know Educated Edmund makes a fair living playing

klob with Little Isadore, and I figure as long as I am depriving
Educated Edmund of a living for a while, it is only courteous to toss
something else his way. Furthermore, I figure as long as letters are
involved in this proposition it may be a good thing to have Educated
Edmund handy in case any reading becomes necessary, because Spanish John and Little Isadore do not read at all, and I read only large
print.

We borrow a car off a friend of mine in Clinton Street, and with
me driving we start for Tarrytown, which is a spot up the Hudson
River, and it is a very enjoyable ride for one and all on account of
the scenery. It is the first time Educated Edmund and Spanish John
and Little Isadore ever see the scenery along the Hudson although
they all reside on the banks of this beautiful river for several years
at Ossining. Personally, I am never in Ossining, although once I
make Auburn, and once Comstock, but the scenery in these localities
is nothing to speak of.

We hit Tarrytown about dark, and follow the main drag through
this burg, as Mr. Tuesday tells me, until finally we come to the spot
I am looking for, which is a little white cottage on a slope of ground
above the river, not far off the highway. This little white cottage has
quite a piece of ground around it, and a low stone wall, with a
driveway from the highway to the house, and when I spot the gate
to the driveway I make a quick turn, and what happens but I run
the car slapdab into a stone gatepost, and the car folds up like an
accordion.

You see, the idea is we are figuring to make this a fast stickup
job without any foolishness about it, maybe leaving any parties we
come across tied up good and tight while we make a getaway, as I
am greatly opposed to housebreaking, or sneak jobs, as I do not
consider them dignified. Furthermore, they take too much time, so
I am going to run the car right up to the front door when this stone
post gets in my way.

The next thing I know, I open my eyes to find myself in a strange
bed, and also in a strange bedroom, and while I wake up in many
a strange bed in my time, I never wake up in such a strange bedroom
as this. It is all very soft and dainty, and the only jarring note in my
surroundings is Spanish John sitting beside the bed looking at me.

Naturally I wish to know what is what, and Spanish John says
I am knocked snoring in the collision with the gatepost, although

none of the others are hurt, and that while I am stretched in the driveway with the blood running out of a bad gash in my noggin, who pops out of the house but a doll and an old guy who seems to be a butler, or some such, and the doll insists on them lugging me into the house, and placing me in this bedroom.

Then she washes the blood off of me, Spanish John says, and wraps my head up and personally goes to Tarrytown to get a croaker to see if my wounds are fatal, or what, while Educated Edmund and Little Isadore are trying to patch up the car. So, Spanish John says, he is sitting there to watch me until she comes back, although of course I know what he is really sitting there for is to get first search at me in case I do not recover.

Well, while I am thinking all this over, and wondering what is to be done, in pops a doll of maybe forty odd, who is built from the ground up, but who has a nice, kind-looking pan, with a large smile, and behind her is a guy I can see at once is a croaker, especially as he is packing a little black bag, and has a gray goatee. I never see a nicer-looking doll if you care for middling-old dolls, although personally I like them young, and when she sees me with my eyes open, she speaks as follows:

"Oh," she says, "I am glad you are not dead, you poor chap. But," she says, "here is Doctor Diffingwell, and he will see how badly you are injured. My name is Miss Amelia Bodkin, and this is my house, and this is my own bedroom, and I am very, very sorry you are hurt."

Well, naturally I consider this a most embarrassing situation, because here I am out to clip Miss Amelia Bodkin of her letters and her silverware, including her Paul Revere teapot, and there she is taking care of me in first-class style, and saying she is sorry for me.

But there seems to be nothing for me to say at this time, so I hold still while the croaker looks me over, and after he peeks at my noggin, and gives me a good feel up and down, he states as follows:

"This is a very bad cut," he says. "I will have to stitch it up, and then he must be very quiet for a few days, otherwise," he says, "complications may set in. It is best to move him to a hospital at once."

But Miss Amelia Bodkin will not listen to such an idea as moving me to a hospital. Miss Amelia Bodkin says I must rest right where I am, and she will take care of me, because she says I am injured on her premises by her gatepost, and it is only fair that she does something for me. In fact, from the way Miss Amelia Bodkin takes on about me being moved, I figure it is the old sex appeal, although afterward I find out it is only because she is lonesome, and nursing me will give her something to do.

Well, naturally I am not opposing her idea, because the way I look at it, I will be able to handle the situation about the letters, and also the silverware, very nicely as an inside job, so I try to act even worse off than I am, although of course anybody who knows about the time I carry eight slugs in my body from Broadway and Fiftieth Street to Brooklyn will laugh very heartily at the idea of a cut on the noggin keeping me in bed.

After the croaker gets through sewing me up, and goes away, I tell Spanish John to take Educated Edmund and Little Isadore and go back to New York, but to keep in touch with me by telephone, so I can tell them when to come back, and then I go to sleep, because I seem to be very tired. When I wake up later in the night, I seem to have a fever, and am really somewhat sick, and Miss Amelia Bodkin is sitting beside my bed swabbing my noggin with a cool cloth, which feels very pleasant, indeed.

I am better in the morning, and am able to knock over a little breakfast which she brings to me on a tray, and I am commencing to see where being an invalid is not so bad, at that, especially when there are no coppers at your bedside every time you open your eyes asking who does it to you.

I can see Miss Amelia Bodkin gets quite a bang out of having somebody to take care of, although of course if she knows who she is taking care of at this time, the chances are she will be running up the road calling for the gendarmes. It is not until after breakfast that I can get her to go and grab herself a little sleep, and while she is away sleeping the old guy who seems to be the butler is in and out of my room every now and then to see how I am getting along.

He is a gabby old guy, and pretty soon he is telling me all about Miss Amelia Bodkin, and what he tells me is that she is the old-time sweetheart of a guy in New York who is at the head of a big business, and very rich, and of course I know this guy is Mr. Jabez Tuesday, although the old guy who seems to be the butler never mentions his name.

"They are together many years," he says to me. "He is very poor when they meet, and she has a little money, and establishes him in business, and by her management of this business, and of him, she makes it a very large business, indeed. I know, because I am with them almost from the start," the old guys says. "She is very smart in business, and also very kind, and nice, if anybody asks you.

"Now," the old guy says, "I am never able to figure out why they do not get married, because there is no doubt she loves him, and he loves her, but Miss Amelia Bodkin once tells me that it is because they are too poor at the start, and too busy later on to think of such things as getting married, and so they drift along the way they are, until all of a sudden he is rich. Then," the old guy says, "I can see he is getting away from her, although she never sees it herself, and I am not surprised when a few years ago he convinced her it is best for her to retire from active work, and move out to this spot.

"He comes out here fairly often at first," the old guy says, "but gradually he stretches the time between his visits, and now we do not see him once in a coon's age. Well," the old guy says, "it is just such a case as often comes up in life. In fact, I personally know of some others. But Miss Amelia Bodkin still thinks he loves her, and that only business keeps him away so much, so you can see she either is not as smart as she looks or is kidding herself. Well," the old guy says, "I will now bring you a little orange juice, although I do not mind saying you do not look to me like a guy who drinks orange juice as a steady proposition."

Now I am taking many a gander around the bedroom to see if I can case the box of letters that Mr. Jabez Tuesday speaks of, but there is no box such as he describes in sight. Then in the evening, when Miss Amelia Bodkin is in the room, and I seem to be dozing, she pulls out a drawer in the bureau, and hauls out a big inlaid box, and sits down at a table under a reading lamp, and opens this box and begins reading some old letters. And as she sits there reading those letters, with me watching her through my eyelashes, sometimes she smiles, but once I see little tears rolling down her cheeks.

All of a sudden she looks at me, and catches me with my eyes wide open, and I can see her face turn red, and then she laughs, and speaks to me, as follows:

"Old love letters," she says, tapping the box. "From my old sweetheart," she says. "I read some of them every night of my life. Am I not foolish and sentimental to do such a thing?"

Well, I tell Miss Amelia Bodkin she is sentimental all right, but I do not tell her just how foolish she is to be letting me in on where she plants these letters, although of course I am greatly pleased to have this information. I tell Miss Amelia Bodkin that personally I never write a love letter, and never get a love letter, and in fact, while I hear of these propositions, I never even see a love letter before, and this is all as true as you are a foot high. Then Miss Amelia Bodkin laughs a little, and says to me as follows:

"Why," she says, "you are a very unusual chap, indeed, not to know what a love letter is like. Why," she says, "I think I will read you a few of the most wonderful love letters in this world. It will do no harm," she says, "because you do not know the writer, and you must lie there and think of me, not old and ugly, as you see me now, but as young, and maybe a little bit pretty."

So Miss Amelia Bodkin opens a letter and reads it to me, and her voice is soft and low as she reads, but she scarcely ever looks at the letter as she is reading, so I can see she knows it pretty much by heart. Furthermore, I can see that she thinks this letter is quite a masterpiece, but while I am no judge of love letters, because this is the first one I ever hear, I wish to say I consider it nothing but great nonsense.

"Sweetheart mine," this love letter says, "I am still thinking of you as I see you yesterday standing in front of the house with the sunlight turning your dark brown hair to wonderful bronze. Darling," it says, "I love the color of your hair. I am so glad you are not a blonde. I hate blondes, they are so empty-headed, and mean, and deceitful. Also they are bad-tempered," the letter says. "I will never trust a blonde any farther than I can throw a bull by the tail. I never see a blonde in my life who is not a plumb washout," it says. "Most of them are nothing but peroxide, anyway. Business is improving," it says. "Sausage is going up. I love you now and always, my baby doll."

Well, there are others worse than this, and all of them speak of her as sweetheart, or baby, or darlingest one, and also as loveykins, and precious, and angel, and I do not know what all else, and several of them speak of how things will be after they marry, and as I judge these are Mr. Jabez Tuesday's letters, all right, I can see where they are full of dynamite for a guy who is figuring on taking a run-out powder on a doll. In fact, I say something to this general effect to Miss Amelia Bodkin, just for something to say.

"Why," she says, "what do you mean?"

"Well," I say, "documents such as these are known to bring large prices under certain conditions."

Now Miss Amelia Bodkin looks at me a moment as if wondering what is in my mind, and then she shakes her head as if she gives it up, and laughs and speaks as follows:

"Well," she says, "one thing is certain, my letters will never bring a price, no matter how large, under any conditions, even if anybody ever wants them. Why," she says, "these are my greatest treasure. They are my memories of my happiest days. Why," she says, "I will not part with these letters for a million dollars."

Naturally I can see from this remark that Mr. Jabez Tuesday makes a very economical deal with me at ten G's for the letters, but of course I do not mention this to Miss Amelia Bodkin as I watch her put her love letters back in the inlaid box, and put the box back in the drawer of the bureau. I thank her for letting me hear the letters, and then I tell her good night, and I go to sleep, and the next day I telephone to a certain number in Clinton Street and leave word for Educated Edmund and Spanish John and Little Isadore to come and get me, as I am tired of being an invalid.

Now the next day is Saturday, and the day that comes after is bound to be Sunday, and they come to see me on Saturday, and promise to come back for me Sunday, as the car is now unraveled and running all right, although my friend in Clinton Street is beefing no little about the way his fenders are bent. But before they arrive Sunday morning, who is there ahead of them bright and early but Mr. Jabez Tuesday in a big town car.

Furthermore, as he walks into the house, all dressed up in a cutaway coat, and a high hat, he grabs Miss Amelia Bodkin in his arms, and kisses her ker-plump right on the smush, which information I afterward receive from the old guy who seems to be the butler. From upstairs I can personally hear Miss Amelia Bodkin crying more than somewhat, and then I hear Mr. Jabez Tuesday speak in a loud, hearty voice as follows:

"Now, now, now, 'Mely," Mr. Tuesday says. "Do not be crying, especially on my new white vest. Cheer up," Mr. Tuesday says, "and listen to the arrangements I make for our wedding tomorrow, and our honeymoon in Montreal. Yes, indeed, 'Mely," Mr. Tuesday says, "you are the only one for me, because you understand me from A to Izzard. Give me another big kiss, 'Mely, and let us sit down and talk things over."

Well, I judge from the sound that he gets his kiss, and it is a very large kiss, indeed, with the cut-out open, and then I hear them chewing the rag at great length in the living room downstairs. Finally I hear Mr. Jabez Tuesday speak as follows:

"You know, 'Mely," he says, "you and I are just plain ordinary folks without any lugs, and," he says, "this is why we fit each other so well. I am sick and tired of people who pretend to be high-toned and mighty, when they do not have a white quarter to their name. They have no manners whatever. Why, only last night," Mr. Jabez Tuesday says, "I am calling on a high-toned family in New York by the name of Scarwater, and out of a clear sky I am grossly insulted by the daughter of the house, and practically turned out in the street. I never receive such treatment in my life," he says. "'Mely," he says, "give me another kiss, and see if you feel a bump here on my head."

Of course, Mr. Jabez Tuesday is somewhat surprised to see me present later on, but he never lets on he knows me, and naturally I do not give Mr. Jabez any tumble whatever at the moment, and by and by Educated Edmund and Spanish John and Little Isadore come for me in the car, and I thank Miss Amelia Bodkin for her kindness to me, and leave her standing on the lawn with Mr. Jabez Tuesday waving us good-bye.

And Miss Amelia Bodkin looks so happy as she snuggles up close to Mr. Jabez Tuesday that I am glad I take the chance, which is always better than an even-money chance these days, that Miss Valeria Scarwater is a blonde, and send Educated Edmund to her to read her Mr. Tuesday's letter in which he speaks of blondes. But of course I am sorry that this and other letters that I tell Educated Edmund to read to her heats her up so far as to make her forget she is a lady and causes her to slug Mr. Jabez Tuesday on the bean with an eighteen-carat vanity case, as she tells him to get out of her life.

So [Harry the Horse says] there is nothing more to the story, except we are now looking for Judge Goldfobber to get him to take up a legal matter for us with Mr. Jabez Tuesday. It is true Mr. Tuesday pays us the ten G's, but he never lets us take the silverware he speaks of, not even the Paul Revere teapot, which he says is so valuable, and in fact when we drop around to Miss Amelia Bodkin's house to pick up these articles one night not long ago, the old guy who seems to be the butler lets off a double-barreled shotgun at us, and acts very nasty in general.

So [Harry says] we are going to see if we can get Judge Goldfobber to sue Mr. Jabez Tuesday for breach of promise.

BASEBALL HATTIE

I t comes on springtime, and the little birdies are singing in the trees in Central Park, and the grass is green all around and about, and I am at the Polo Grounds on the opening day of the baseball season, when who do I behold but Baseball Hattie. I am somewhat surprised at this spectacle, as it is years since I see Baseball Hattie, and for all I know she long ago passes to a better and happier world.

But there she is, as large as life, and in fact twenty pounds larger, and when I call the attention of Armand Fibleman, the gambler, to her, he gets up and tears right out of the joint as if he sees a ghost, for if there is one thing Armand Fibleman loathes and despises, it is a ghost.

I can see that Baseball Hattie is greatly changed, and to tell the truth, I can see that she is getting to be nothing but an old bag. Her hair that is once as black as a yard up a stovepipe is gray, and she is wearing gold-rimmed cheaters, although she seems to be pretty well dressed and looks as if she may be in the money a little bit, at that.

But the greatest change in her is the way she sits there very quiet all afternoon, never once opening her yap, even when many of the customers around her are claiming that Umpire William Klem is Public Enemy No. 1 to 16 inclusive, because they think he calls a close one against the Giants. I am wondering if maybe Baseball Hattie is stricken dumb somewhere back down the years, because I can remember when she is usually making speeches in the grandstand in favor of hanging such characters as Umpire William Klem when they call close ones against the Giants. But Hattie just sits there as if she is in a church while the public clamor goes on about her, and she does not as much as cry out robber, or even you big bum at Umpire William Klem.

I see many a baseball bug in my time, male and female, but without doubt the worst bug of them all is Baseball Hattie, and you can say it again. She is most particularly a bug about the Giants, and she never misses a game they play at the Polo Grounds, and in fact she sometimes bobs up watching them play in other cities, which is always very embarrassing to the Giants, as they fear the customers in these cities may get the wrong impression of New York womanhood after listening to Baseball Hattie a while.

The first time I ever see Baseball Hattie to pay any attention to her is in Philadelphia, a matter of twenty-odd years back, when the Giants are playing a series there, and many citizens of New York, including Armand Fibleman and myself, are present, because the Philadelphia customers are great hands for betting on baseball games in those days, and Armand Fibleman figures he may knock a few of them in the creek.

Armand Fibleman is a character who will bet on baseball games from who-laid-the-chunk, and in fact he will bet on anything whatever, because Armand Fibleman is a gambler by trade and has been such since infancy. Personally, I will not bet you four dollars on a baseball game, because in the first place I am not apt to have four dollars, and in the second place I consider horse races a much sounder investment, but I often go around and about with Armand Fibleman, as he is a friend of mine, and sometimes he gives me a little piece of one of his bets for nothing.

Well, what happens in Philadelphia but the umpire forfeits the game in the seventh inning to the Giants by a score of nine to nothing when the Phillies are really leading by five runs, and the reason the umpire takes this action is because he orders several of the Philadelphia players to leave the field for calling him a scoundrel and a rat and a snake in the grass, and also a baboon, and they refuse to take their departure, as they still have more names to call him.

Right away the Philadelphia customers become infuriated in a manner you will scarcely believe, for ordinarily a Philadelphia baseball customer is as quiet as a lamb, no matter what you do to him, and in fact in those days a Philadelphia baseball customer is only considered as somebody to do something to.

But these Philadelphia customers are so infuriated that they not only chase the umpire under the stand, but they wait in the street outside the baseball orchard until the Giants change into their street clothes and come out of the clubhouse. Then the Philadelphia customers begin pegging rocks, and one thing and another, at the Giants, and it is a most exciting and disgraceful scene that is spoken of for years afterward.

Well, the Giants march along toward the North Philly station to catch a train for home, dodging the rocks and one thing and another the best they can, and wondering why the Philadelphia gendarmes do not come to the rescue, until somebody notices several gendarmes among the customers doing some of the throwing themselves, so the Giants realize that this is a most inhospitable community, to be sure.

Finally all of them get inside the North Philly station and are safe, except a big, tall, left-handed pitcher by the name of Haystack Duggeler, who just reports to the club the day before and who finds himself surrounded by quite a posse of these infuriated Philadelphia customers, and who is unable to make them understand that he is nothing but a rookie, because he has a Missouri accent, and besides, he is half paralyzed with fear.

One of the infuriated Philadelphia customers is armed with a brickbat and is just moving forward to maim Haystack Duggeler with this instrument, when who steps into the situation but Baseball Hattie, who is also on her way to the station to catch a train, and who is greatly horrified by the assault on the Giants.

She seizes the brickbat from the infuriated Philadelphia customer's grasp, and then tags the customer smack-dab between the eyes with his own weapon, knocking him so unconscious that I afterward hear he does not recover for two weeks, and that he remains practically an imbecile the rest of his days.

Then Baseball Hattie cuts loose on the other infuriated Philadelphia customers with language that they never before hear in those parts, causing them to disperse without further ado, and after the last customer is beyond the sound of her voice, she takes Haystack Duggeler by the pitching arm and personally escorts him to the station.

Now out of this incident is born a wonderful romance between Baseball Hattie and Haystack Duggeler, and in fact it is no doubt love at first sight, and about this period Haystack Duggeler begins burning up the league with his pitching, and at the same time giving Manager Mac plenty of headaches, including the romance with Baseball Hattie, because anybody will tell you that a left-hander is tough enough on a manager without a romance, and especially a romance with Baseball Hattie.

It seems that the trouble with Hattie is she is in business up in Harlem, and this business consists of a boarding-and-rooming-house where ladies and gentlemen board and room, and personally I never see anything out of line in the matter, but the rumor somehow gets around, as rumors will do, that in the first place it is not a boarding-and-rooming-house, and in the second place that the ladies and gentlemen who room and board there are by no means ladies and gentlemen, and especially ladies.

Well, this rumor becomes a terrible knock to Baseball Hattie's social reputation. Furthermore, I hear Manager Mac sends for her and requests her to kindly lay off his ball-players, and especially off a character who can make a baseball sing high C like Haystack Duggeler. In fact, I hear Manager Mac gives her such a lecture on her civic duty to New York and to the Giants that Baseball Hattie sheds tears, and promises she will never give Haystack another tumble the rest of the season.

"You know me, Mac," Baseball Hattie says. "You know I will cut off my nose rather than do anything to hurt your club. I sometimes figure I am in love with this big bloke, but," she says, "maybe it is only gas pushing up around my heart. I will take something for it. To hell with him, Mac!" she says.

So she does not see Haystack Duggeler again, except at a distance, for a long time, and he goes on to win fourteen games in a row, pitching a no-hitter and four two-hitters among them, and hanging up a reputation as a great pitcher, and also as a 100-percent heel.

Haystack Duggeler is maybe twenty-five at this time, and he comes to the big league with more bad habits than anybody in the history of the world is able to acquire in such a short time. He is especially a great rumpot, and after he gets going good in the league, he is just as apt to appear for a game all mulled up as not.

He is fond of all forms of gambling, such as playing cards and shooting craps, but after they catch him with a deck of readers in a poker game and a pair of tops in a crap game, none of the Giants will play with him any more, except of course when there is nobody else to play with.

He is ignorant about many little things, such as reading and writing and geography and mathematics, as Haystack Duggeler himself admits he never goes to school any more than he can help, but he is so wise when it comes to larceny that I always figure they must have great tutors back in Haystack's old hometown of Booneville, Mo.

And no smarter jobbie ever breathes than Haystack when he is out there pitching. He has so much speed that he just naturally throws the ball past a batter before he can get the old musket off his shoulder, and along with his hard one, Haystack has a curve like the letter Q. With two ounces of brains, Haystack Duggeler will be the greatest pitcher that ever lives.

Well, as far as Baseball Hattie is concerned, she keeps her word about not seeing Haystack, although sometimes when he is mulled up he goes around to her boarding-and-rooming-house, and tries to break down the door.

On days when Haystack Duggeler is pitching, she is always in her favorite seat back of third, and while she roots hard for the Giants no matter who is pitching, she puts on extra steam when Haystack is bending them over, and it is quite an experience to hear her crying lay them in there, Haystack, old boy, and strike this big tramp out, Haystack, and other exclamations of a similar nature, which please Haystack quite some, but annoy Baseball Hattie's neighbors back of third base, such as Armand Fibleman, if he happens to be betting on the other club.

A month before the close of his first season in the big league, Haystack Duggeler gets so ornery that Manager Mac suspends him, hoping maybe it will cause Haystack to do a little thinking, but naturally Haystack is unable to do this, because he has nothing to think with. About a week later, Manager Mac gets to noticing how he can use a few ball games, so he starts looking for Haystack Duggeler, and he finds him tending bar on Eighth Avenue with his uniform hung up back of the bar as an advertisement.

The baseball writers speak of Haystack as eccentric, which is a polite way of saying he is a screwball, but they consider him a most unique character and are always writing humorous stories about him, though any one of them will lay you plenty of 9 to 5 that Haystack winds up an umbay. The chances are they will raise their price a little, as the season closes and Haystack is again under suspension with cold weather coming on and not a dime in his pants' pockets.

It is some time along in the winter that Baseball Hattie hauls off and marries Haystack Duggeler, which is a great surprise to one and all, but not nearly as much of a surprise as when Hattie closes her boarding-and-rooming-house and goes to live in a little apartment with Haystack Duggeler up on Washington Heights.

It seems that she finds Haystack one frosty night sleeping in a hallway, after being around slightly mulled up for several weeks, and she takes him to her home and gets him a bath and a shave and a clean shirt and two boiled eggs and some toast and coffee and a shot or two of rye whiskey, all of which is greatly appreciated by Haystack, especially the rye whiskey.

Then Haystack proposes marriage to her and takes a paralyzed oath that if she becomes his wife he will reform, so what with loving Haystack anyway, and with the fix commencing to request more dough off the boarding-and-rooming-house business than the business will stand, Hattie takes him at his word, and there you are.

The baseball writers are wondering what Manager Mac will say when he hears these tidings, but all Mac says is that Haystack cannot possibly be any worse married than he is single-o, and then Mac has the club office send the happy couple a little paper money to carry them over the winter.

Well, what happens but a great change comes over Haystack Duggeler. He stops bending his elbow and helps Hattie cook and wash the dishes, and holds her hand when they are in the movies, and speaks of his love for her several times a week, and Hattie is as happy as nine dollars' worth of lettuce. Manager Mac is so delighted at the change in Haystack that he has the club office send over more paper money, because Mac knows that with Haystack in shape he is sure of twenty-five games, and maybe the pennant.

In late February, Haystack reports to the training camp down South still as sober as some judges, and the other ball-players are so impressed by the change in him that they admit him to their poker game again. But of course it is too much to expect a man to alter his entire course of living all at once, and it is not long before Haystack discovers four nines in his hand on his own deal and breaks up the game.

He brings Baseball Hattie with him to the camp, and this is undoubtedly a slight mistake, as it seems the old rumor about her boarding-and-rooming-house business gets around among the ever-loving wives of the other players, and they put on a large chill for her. In fact, you will think Hattie has the smallpox.

Naturally, Baseball Hattie feels the frost, but she never lets on, as it seems she runs into many bigger and better frosts than this in her time. Then Haystack Duggeler notices it, and it seems that it makes him a little peevish toward Baseball Hattie, and in fact it is said that he gives her a slight pasting one night in their room, partly because she has no better social standing and partly because he is commencing to cop a few sneaks on the local corn now and then, and Hattie chides him for same.

Well, about this time it appears that Baseball Hattie discovers that she is going to have a baby, and as soon as she recovers from her astonishment, she decides that it is to be a boy who will be a great baseball player, maybe a pitcher, although Hattie admits she is willing to compromise on a good second baseman.

She also decides that his name is to be Derrill Duggeler, after his paw, as it seems Derrill is Haystack's real name, and he is only called Haystack because he claims he once makes a living stacking hay, although the general opinion is that all he ever stacks is cards.

It is really quite remarkable what a belt Hattie gets out of the idea of having this baby, though Haystack is not excited about the matter. He is not paying much attention to Baseball Hattie by now, except to give her a slight pasting now and then, but Hattie is so happy about the baby that she does not mind these pastings.

Haystack Duggeler meets up with Armand Fibleman along in midsummer. By this time, Haystack discovers horse racing and is always making bets on the horses, and naturally he is generally broke, and then I commence running into him in different spots with Armand Fibleman, who is now betting higher than a cat's back on baseball games.

It is late August, and the Giants are fighting for the front end of the league, and an important series with Brooklyn is coming up, and everybody knows that Haystack Duggeler will work in anyway two games of the series, as Haystack can generally beat Brooklyn just by throwing his glove on the mound. There is no doubt but what he has the old Indian sign on Brooklyn, and the night before the first game, which he is sure to work, the gamblers along Broadway are making the Giants 2-to-1 favorites to win the game.

This same night before the game, Baseball Hattie is home in her little apartment on Washington Heights waiting for Haystack to come in and eat a delicious dinner of pigs' knuckles and sauerkraut, which she personally prepares for him. In fact, she hurries home right after the ball game to get this delicacy ready, because Haystack tells her he will surely come home this particular night, although Hattie knows he is never better than even money to keep his word about anything.

But sure enough, in he comes while the pigs' knuckles and sauerkraut are still piping hot, and Baseball Hattie is surprised to see Armand Fibleman with him, as she knows Armand backward and forward and does not care much for him, at that. However, she can say the same thing about four million other characters in this town, so she makes Armand welcome, and they sit down and put on the pigs' knuckles and sauerkraut together, and a pleasant time is enjoyed by one and all. In fact, Baseball Hattie puts herself out to entertain Armand Fibleman, because he is the first guest Haystack ever brings home.

Well, Armand Fibleman can be very pleasant when he wishes, and he speaks very nicely to Hattie. Naturally, he sees that Hattie is expecting, and in fact he will have to be blind not to see it, and he seems greatly interested in this matter and asks Hattie many questions, and Hattie is delighted to find somebody to talk to about what is coming off with her, as Haystack will never listen to any of her remarks on the subject.

So Armand Fibleman gets to hear all about Baseball Hattie's son, and how he is to be a great baseball player, and Armand says is that so, and how nice, and all this and that, until Haystack Duggeler speaks up as follows and to wit:

"Oh, daggone her son!" Haystack says. "It is going to be a girl, anyway, so let us dismiss this topic and get down to business. Hat," he says, "you fan yourself into the kitchen and wash the dishes, while Armand and me talk."

So Hattie goes into the kitchen, leaving Haystack and Armand sitting there talking, and what are they talking about but a proposition for Haystack to let the Brooklyn club beat him the next day so Armand Fibleman can take the odds and clean up a nice little gob of money, which he is to split with Haystack.

Hattie can hear every word they say, as the kitchen is next door to the dining room where they are sitting, and at first she thinks they are joking, because at this time nobody ever even as much as thinks of skullduggery in baseball, or anyway, not much.

It seems that at first Haystack is not in favor of the idea, but Armand Fibleman keeps mentioning money that Haystack owes him for bets on the horse races, and he asks Haystack how he expects to continue betting on the races without fresh money, and Armand also speaks of the great injustice that is being done Haystack by the Giants in not paying him twice the salary he is getting, and how the loss of one or two games is by no means such a great calamity.

Well, finally Baseball Hattie hears Haystack say all right, but he wishes a thousand dollars then and there as a guarantee, and Armand Fibleman says this is fine, and they will go downtown and he will get the money at once, and now Hattie realizes that maybe they are in earnest, and she pops out of the kitchen and speaks as follows:

"Gentlemen," Hattie says, "you seem to be sober, but I guess you are drunk. If you are not drunk, you must both be daffy to think of such a thing as finagling around with a baseball game."

"Hattie," Haystack says, "kindly close your trap and go back in the kitchen, or I will give you a bust in the nose."

And with this he gets up and reaches for his hat, and Armand Fibleman gets up too, and Hattie says like this:

"Why, Haystack," she says, "you are not really serious in this matter, are you?"

"Of course I am serious," Haystack says. "I am sick and tired of pitching for starvation wages, and besides, I will win a lot of games later on to make up for the one I lose tomorrow. Say," he says, "these Brooklyn bums may get lucky tomorrow and knock me loose from my pants, anyway, no matter what I do, so what difference does it make?"

"Haystack," Baseball Hattie says, "I know you are a liar and a drunkard and a cheat and no account generally, but nobody can tell me you will sink so low as to purposely toss off a ball game. Why,

Haystack, baseball is always on the level. It is the most honest game in all this world. I guess you are just ribbing me, because you know how much I love it."

"Dry up!" Haystack says to Hattie. "Furthermore, do not expect me home again tonight. But anyway, dry up."

"Look, Haystack," Hattie says, "I am going to have a son. He is your son and my son, and he is going to be a great ball-player when he grows up, maybe a greater pitcher than you are, though I hope and trust he is not left-handed. He will have your name. If they find out you toss off a game for money, they will throw you out of baseball and you will be disgraced. My son will be known as the son of a crook, and what chance will he have in baseball? Do you think I am going to allow you to do this to him, and to the game that keeps me from going nutty for marrying you?"

Naturally, Haystack Duggeler is greatly offended by Hattie's crack about her son being maybe a greater pitcher than he is, and he is about to take steps, when Armand Fibleman stops him. Armand Fibleman is commencing to be somewhat alarmed at Baseball Hattie's attitude, and he gets to thinking that he hears that people in her delicate condition are often irresponsible, and he fears that she may blow a whistle on this enterprise without realizing what she is doing. So he undertakes a few soothing remarks to her.

"Why, Hattie," Armand Fibleman says, "nobody can possibly find out about this little matter, and Haystack will have enough money to send your son to college, if his markers at the racetrack do not take it all. Maybe you better lie down and rest awhile," Armand says.

But Baseball Hattie does not as much as look at Armand, though she goes on talking to Haystack. "They always find out thievery, Haystack," she says, "especially when you are dealing with a fink like Fibleman. If you deal with him once, you will have to deal with him again and again, and he will be the first to holler copper on you, because he is a stool pigeon in his heart."

"Haystack," Armand Fibleman says, "I think we better be going."

"Haystack," Hattie says, "you can go out of here and stick up somebody or commit a robbery or a murder, and I will still welcome you back and stand by you. But if you are going out to steal my son's future, I advise you not to go."

"Dry up!" Haystack says. "I am going."

"All right, Haystack," Hattie says, very calm. "But just step into the kitchen with me and let me say one little word to you by yourself, and then I will say no more."

Well, Haystack Duggeler does not care for even just one little word more, but Armand Fibleman wishes to get this disagreeable scene over with, so he tells Haystack to let her have her word, and Haystack goes into the kitchen with Hattie, and Armand cannot hear what is said, as she speaks very low, but he hears Haystack laugh heartily and then Haystack comes out of the kitchen, still laughing, and tells Armand he is ready to go.

As they start for the door, Baseball Hattie outs with a long-nosed .38-caliber Colt's revolver, and goes root-a-toot-toot with it, and the next thing anybody knows, Haystack is on the floor yelling bloody murder, and Armand Fibleman is leaving the premises without bothering to open the door. In fact, the landlord afterward talks some of suing Haystack Duggeler because of the damage Armand Fibleman does to the door. Armand himself afterward admits that when he slows down for a breather a couple of miles down Broadway he finds splinters stuck all over him.

Well, the doctors come, and the gendarmes come, and there is great confusion, especially as Baseball Hattie is sobbing so she can scarcely make a statement, and Haystack Duggeler is so sure he is going to die that he cannot think of anything to say except oh-oh-oh, but finally the landlord remembers seeing Armand leave with his door, and everybody starts questioning Hattie about this until she confesses that Armand is there all right, and that he tries to bribe Haystack to toss off a ball game, and that she then suddenly finds herself with a revolver in her hand, and everything goes black before her eyes, and she can remember no more until somebody is sticking a bottle of smelling salts under her nose.

Naturally, the newspaper reporters put two and two together, and what they make of it is that Hattie tries to plug Armand Fibleman for his rascally offer, and that she misses Armand and gets Haystack, and right away Baseball Hattie is a great heroine, and Haystack is a great hero, though nobody thinks to ask Haystack how he stands on the bribe proposition, and he never brings it up himself.

And nobody will ever offer Haystack any more bribes, for after the doctors get through with him he is shy a left arm from the shoulder down, and he will never pitch a baseball again, unless he learns to pitch right-handed.

The newspapers make quite a lot of Baseball Hattie protecting the fair name of baseball. The National League plays a benefit game for Haystack Duggeler and presents him with a watch and a purse of twenty-five thousand dollars, which Baseball Hattie grabs away from him, saying it is for her son, while Armand Fibleman is in bad with one and all.

Baseball Hattie and Haystack Duggeler move to the Pacific Coast, and this is all there is to the story, except that one day some years ago, and not long before he passes away in Los Angeles, a respectable grocer, I run into Haystack when he is in New York on a business trip, and I say to him like this:

"Haystack," I say, "it is certainly a sin and a shame that Hattie misses Armand Fibleman that night and puts you on the shelf. The chances are that but for this little accident you will hang up one of the greatest pitching records in the history of baseball. Personally," I say, "I never see a better left-handed pitcher."

"Look," Haystack says. "Hattie does not miss Fibleman. It is a great newspaper story and saves my name, but the truth is she hits just where she aims. When she calls me into the kitchen before I start out with Fibleman, she shows me a revolver I never before knew she has, and says to me, 'Haystack,' she says, 'if you leave with this weasel on the errand you mention, I am going to fix you so you will never make another wrong move with your pitching arm. I am going to shoot it off for you.'

"I laugh heartily," Haystack says. "I think she is kidding me, but I find out different. By the way," Haystack says, "I afterward learn that long before I meet her, Hattie works for three years in a shooting gallery at Coney Island. She is really a remarkable broad," Haystack says.

I guess I forget to state that the day Baseball Hattie is at the Polo Grounds she is watching the new kid sensation of the big leagues, Derrill Duggeler, shut out Brooklyn with three hits.

He is a wonderful young left-hander.

One night I am in a gambling joint in Miami watching the crap game and thinking what a nice thing it is, indeed, to be able to shoot craps without having to worry about losing your potatoes.

Many of the high shots from New York and Detroit and St. Louis and other cities are around the table, and there is quite some action in spite of the hard times. In fact, there is so much action that a guy with only a few bobs on him, such as me, will be considered very impolite to be pushing into this game, because they are packed in very tight around the table.

I am maybe three guys back from the table, and I am watching the game by standing on tiptoe peeking over their shoulders, and all I can hear is Goldie, the stick man, hollering money-money-money every time some guy makes a number, so I can see the dice are very warm indeed, and that the right betters are doing first-rate.

By and by a guy by the name of Guinea Joe, out of Trenton, picks up the dice and starts making numbers right and left, and I know enough about this Guinea Joe to know that when he starts making numbers anybody will be very foolish indeed not to follow his hand, although personally I am generally a wrong better against the dice, if I bet at all.

Now all I have in my pocket is a sawbuck, and the hotel stakes are coming up on me the next day, and I need this saw, but with Guinea Joe hotter than a forty-five it will be overlooking a big opportunity not to go along with him, so when he comes out on an eight, which is a very easy number for Joe to make when he is hot, I dig up my sawbuck, and slide it past the three guys in front of me to the table, and I say to Lefty Park, who is laying against the dice, as follows:

"I will take the odds, Lefty."

Well, Lefty looks at my sawbuck and nods his head, for Lefty is not such a guy as will refuse any bet, even though it is as modest as mine, and right away Goldie yells money-money-money, so there I am with twenty-two dollars.

Next Guinea Joe comes out on a nine, and naturally I take thirty to twenty for my sugar, because nine is nothing for Joe to make when he is hot. He makes the nine just as I figure, and I take two to one for my half a yard when he starts looking for a ten, and when he makes the ten I am right up against the table, because I am now a guy with means.

Well, the upshot of the whole business is that I finally find myself with three hundred bucks, and when it looks as if the dice are cooling off, I take out and back off from the table, and while I am backing off I am trying to look like a guy who loses all his potatoes, because there are always many wolves waiting around crap games and one thing and another in Miami this season, and what they are waiting for is to put the bite on anybody who happens to make a little scratch.

In fact, nobody can remember when the bite is as painful as it is in Miami this season, what with the unemployment situation among many citizens who come to Miami expecting to find work in the gambling joints, or around the racetrack. But almost as soon as these citizens arrive, the gambling joints are all turned off, except in spots, and the bookmakers are chased off the track and the mutuels put in, and the consequences are the suffering is most intense. It is not only intense among the visiting citizens, but it is quite intense among the Miami landlords, because naturally if a citizen is not working, nobody can expect him to pay any room rent, but the Miami landlords do not seem to understand this situation, and are very unreasonable about their room rent.

Anyway, I back through quite a crowd without anybody biting me, and I am commencing to figure I may escape altogether and get to my hotel and hide my dough before the news gets around that I win about five G's, which is what my winning is sure to amount to by the time the rumor reaches all quarters of the city.

Then, just as I am thinking I am safe, I find I am looking a guy by the name of Hot Horse Herbie in the face, and I can tell from Hot Horse Herbie's expression that he is standing there watching me for some time, so there is no use in telling him I am washed out in the game. In fact, I cannot think of much of anything to tell Hot Horse Herbie that may keep him from putting the bite on me for at least a few bobs, and I am greatly astonished when he does not offer to bite me at all, but says to me like this:

"Well," he says, "I am certainly glad to see you make such a nice score. I will be looking for you tomorrow at the track, and will have some big news for you."

Then he walks away from me and I stand there with my mouth open looking at him, as it is certainly a most unusual way for Herbie to act. It is the first time I ever knew Herbie to walk away from a chance to bite somebody, and I can scarcely understand such actions, for Herbie is such a guy as will not miss a bite, even if he does not need it.

He is a tall, thin guy, with a sad face and a long chin, and he is called Hot Horse Herbie because he nearly always has a very hot horse to tell you about. He nearly always has a horse that is so hot it is fairly smoking, a hot horse being a horse that cannot possibly lose a race unless it falls down dead, and while Herbie's hot horses often lose without falling down dead, this does not keep Herbie from coming up with others just as hot.

In fact, Hot Horse Herbie is what is called a hustler around the racetracks, and his business is to learn about these hot horses, or even just suspect about them, and then get somebody to bet on them, which is a very legitimate business indeed, as Herbie only collects a commission if the hot horses win, and if they do not win Herbie just keeps out of sight awhile from whoever he gets to bet on the hot horses. There are very few guys in this world who can keep out of sight better than Hot Horse Herbie, and especially from old Cap Duhaine, of the Pinkertons, who is always around pouring cold water on hot horses.

In fact, Cap Duhaine, of the Pinkertons, claims that guys such as Hot Horse Herbie are nothing but touts, and sometimes he heaves them off the racetrack altogether, but of course Cap Duhaine is a very unsentimental old guy and cannot see how such characters as Hot Horse Herbie add to the romance of the turf.

Anyway, I escape from the gambling joint with all my scratch on me, and hurry to my room and lock myself in for the night, and I do not show up in public until along about noon the next day, when it is time to go over to the coffee shop for my java. And of course by this time the news of my score is all over town, and many guys are taking dead aim at me.

But naturally I am now able to explain to them that I have to wire most of the three yards I win to Nebraska to save my father's farm from being seized by the sheriff, and while everybody knows I do not have a father, and that if I do have a father I will not be sending him money for such a thing as saving his farm, with times what they are in Miami, nobody is impolite enough to doubt my word except a guy by the name of Pottsville Legs, who wishes to see my receipts from the telegraph office when I explain to him why I cannot stake him to a double sawbuck.

I do not see Hot Horse Herbie until I get to the track, and he is waiting for me right inside the grandstand gate, and as soon as I show up he motions me off to one side and says to me like this:

"Now," Herbie says, "I am very smart indeed about a certain race today. In fact," he says, "if any guy knowing what I know does not bet all he can rake and scrape together on a certain horse, such a guy ought to cut his own throat and get himself out of the way forever. What I know," Herbie says, "is enough to shake the foundations of this country if it gets out. Do not ask any questions," he says, "but get ready to bet all the sugar you win last night on this horse I am going to mention to you, and all I ask you in return is to bet fifty on me. And," Herbie says, "kindly do not tell me you leave your money in your other pants, because I know you do not have any other pants."

"Now, Herbie," I say, "I do not doubt your information, because I know you will not give out information unless it is well founded. But," I say, "I seldom stand for a tip, and as for betting fifty for you, you know I will not bet fifty even for myself if somebody guarantees me a winner. So I thank you, Herbie, just the same," I say, "but I must do without your tip," and with this I start walking away.

"Now," Herbie says, "wait a minute. A story goes with it," he says.

Well, of course this is a different matter entirely. I am such a guy as will always listen to a tip on a horse if a story goes with the tip.

In fact, I will not give you a nickel for a tip without a story, but it must be a first-class story, and most horse players are the same way. In fact, there are very few horse players who will not listen to a tip if a story goes with it, for this is the way human nature is. So I turn and walk back to Hot Horse Herbie, and say to him like this:

"Well," I say, "let me hear the story, Herbie."

"Now," Herbie says, dropping his voice away down low, in case old Cap Duhaine may be around somewhere listening, "it is the third race, and the horse is a horse by the name of Never Despair. It is a boat race," Herbie says. "They are going to shoo in Never Despair. Everything else in the race is a cooler," he says.

"Well," I say, "this is just an idea, Herbie, and not a story."

"Wait a minute," Herbie says. "The story that goes with it is a very strange story indeed. In fact," he says, "it is such a story as I can hardly believe myself, and I will generally believe almost any story, including," he says, "the ones I make up out of my own head. Anyway, the story is as follows:

"Never Despair is owned by an old guy by the name of Seed Mercer," Herbie says. "Maybe you remember seeing him around. He always wears a black slouch hat and gray whiskers," Herbie says, "and he is maybe a hundred years old, and his horses are very terrible horses indeed. In fact," Herbie says, "I do not remember seeing any more terrible horses in all the years I am around the track, and," Herbie says, "I wish to say I see some very terrible horses indeed.

"Now," Herbie says, "old Mercer has a granddaughter who is maybe sixteen years old, come next grass, by the name of Lame Louise, and she is called Lame Louise because she is all crippled up from childhood by infantile what-is-this, and can scarcely navigate, and," Herbie says, "her being crippled up in such a way makes old Mercer feel very sad, for she is all he has in the world, except these terrible horses."

"It is a very long story, Herbie," I say, "and I wish to see Moe Shapoff about a very good thing in the first race."

"Never mind Moe Shapoff," Herbie says. "He will only tell you about a bum by the name of Zachary in the first race, and Zachary has no chance whatever. I make Your John a standout in the first," he says.

"Well," I say, "let us forget the first and get on with your story, although it is commencing to sound all mixed up to me."

"Now," Herbie says, "it not only makes old man Mercer very sad because Lame Louise is all crippled up, but," he says, "it makes many of the jockeys and other guys around the racetrack very sad, because," he says, "they know Lame Louise since she is so high, and she always has a smile for them, and especially for Jockey Scroon. In fact," Herbie says, "Jockey Scroon is even more sad about Lame Louise than old man Mercer, because Jockey Scroon loves Lame Louise."

"Why," I say, very indignant, "Jockey Scroon is nothing but a little burglar. Why," I say, "I see Jockey Scroon do things to horses I bet on that he will have to answer for on the Judgment Day, if there is any justice at such a time. Why," I say, "Jockey Scroon is nothing but a Gerald Chapman in his heart, and so are all other jockeys."

"Yes," Hot Horse Herbie says, "what you say is very, very true, and I am personally in favor of the electric chair for all jockeys, but," he says, "Jockey Scroon loves Lame Louise just the same, and is figuring on making her his ever-loving wife when he gets a few bobs together, which," Herbie says, "makes Louise eight to five in my line to be an old maid. Jockey Scroon rooms with me downtown," Herbie says, "and he speaks freely to me about his love for Louise. Furthermore," Herbie says, "Jockey Scroon is personally not a bad little guy, at that, although of course being a jockey he is sometimes greatly misunderstood by the public.

"Anyway," Hot Horse Herbie says, "I happen to go home early last night before I see you at the gambling joint, and I hear voices coming out of my room, and naturally I pause outside the door to listen, because for all I know it may be the landlord speaking about the room rent, although," Herbie says, "I do not figure my landlord to be much worried at this time because I see him sneak into my room a few days before and take a lift at my trunk to make sure I have belongings in the same, and it happens I nail the trunk to the floor beforehand, so not being able to lift it, the landlord is bound to figure me a guy with property.

"These voices," Herbie says, "are mainly soprano voices, and at first I think Jockey Scroon is in there with some dolls, which is by no means permissible in my hotel, but, after listening awhile, I discover they are the voices of young boys, and I make out that these boys are nothing but jockeys, and they are the six jockeys who are riding in the third race, and they are fixing up this race to be a boat race, and to shoo in Never Despair, which Jockey Scroon is riding.

"And," Hot Horse Herbie says, "the reason they are fixing up this boat race is the strangest part of the story. It seems," he says, "that Jockey Scroon hears old man Mercer talking about a great surgeon from Europe who is a shark on patching up cripples such as Lame Louise, and who just arrives at Palm Beach to spend the winter, and old man Mercer is saying how he wishes he has dough enough to take Lame Louise to this guy so he can operate on her, and maybe make her walk good again.

"But of course," Herbie says, "it is well known to one and all that old man Mercer does not have a quarter, and that he has no way of getting a quarter unless one of his terrible horses accidentally wins a purse. So," Herbie says, "it seems these jockeys get to talking it over among themselves, and they figure it will be a nice thing to let old man Mercer win a purse such as the thousand bucks that goes with the third race today, so he can take Lame Louise to Palm Beach, and now you have a rough idea of what is coming off.

"Furthermore," Herbie says, "these jockeys wind up their meeting by taking a big oath among themselves that they will not tell a living soul what is doing so nobody will bet on Never Despair, because," he says, "these little guys are smart enough to see if there is any betting on such a horse there may be a very large squawk afterward. And," he says, "I judge they keep their oath because Never Despair is twenty to one in the morning line, and I do not hear a whisper about him, and you have the tip all to yourself."

"Well," I say, "so what?" For this story is now commencing to make me a little tired, especially as I hear the bell for the first race, and I must see Moe Shapoff.

"Why," Hot Horse Herbie says, "so you bet every nickel you can rake and scrape together on Never Despair, including the twenty you are to bet for me for giving you this tip and the story that goes with it."

"Herbie," I say, "it is a very interesting story indeed, and also very sad, but," I say, "I am sorry it is about a horse Jockey Scroon is to ride, because I do not think I will ever bet on anything Jockey Scroon rides if they pay off in advance. And," I say, "I am certainly not going to bet twenty for you or anybody else."

"Well," Hot Horse Herbie says, "I will compromise with you for a pound note, because I must have something going for me on this boat race."

So I give Herbie a fiver, and the chances are this is about as strong as he figures from the start, and I forget all about his tip and the story that goes with it, because while I enjoy a story with a tip, I feel that Herbie overdoes this one.

Anyway, no handicapper alive can make Never Despair win the third race off the form, because this race is at six furlongs, and there is a barrel of speed in it, and anybody can see that old man Mercer's horse is away over his head. In fact, The Dancer tells me that any one of the other five horses in this race can beat Never Despair doing anything from playing hockey to putting the shot, and everybody else must think the same thing because Never Despair goes to forty to one.

Personally, I like a horse by the name of Loose Living, which is a horse owned by a guy by the name of Bill Howard, and I hear Bill Howard is betting plenty away on his horse, and anytime Bill Howard is betting away on his horse a guy will be out of his mind not to bet on this horse, too, as Bill Howard is very smart indeed. Loose Living is two to one in the first line, but by and by I judge the money Bill Howard bets away commences to come back to the track, and Loose Living winds up seven to ten, and while I am generally not a seven-to-ten guy, I can see that here is a proposition I cannot overlook.

So, naturally, I step up to the mutuel window and invest in Loose Living. In fact, I invest everything I have on me in the way of scratch, amounting to a hundred and ten bucks, which is all I have left after taking myself out of the hotel stakes and giving Hot Horse Herbie the finnif, and listening to what Moe Shapoff has to say about the first race, and also getting beat a snoot in the second.

When I first step up to the window, I have no idea of betting all my scratch on Loose Living, but while waiting in line there I get to thinking what a cinch Loose Living is, and how seldom such an opportunity comes into a guy's life, so I just naturally set it all in.

Well, this is a race which will be remembered by one and all to their dying day, as Loose Living beats the barrier a step, and is two lengths in front before you can say Jack Robinson, with a third by the name of Callipers second by maybe half a length, and with the others bunched except Never Despair, and where is Never Despair but last, where he figures.

Now anytime Loose Living busts on top there is no need worrying any more about him, and I am thinking I better get in line at the payoff window right away, so I will not have to wait long to collect my sugar. But I figure I may as well stay and watch the race, although personally I am never much interested in watching races. I am interested only in how a race comes out.

As the horses hit the turn into the stretch, Loose Living is just breezing, and anybody can see that he is going to laugh his way home from there. Callipers is still second, and a thing called Goose Pimples is third, and I am surprised to see that Never Despair now struggles up to fourth with Jockey Scroon belting away at him with his bat quite earnestly. Furthermore, Never Despair seems to be running very fast, though afterward I figure this may be because the others are commencing to run very slow.

Anyway, a very strange spectacle now takes place in the stretch, as all of a sudden Loose Living seems to be stopping, as if he is waiting for a street cab, and what is all the more remarkable Callipers and Goose Pimples also seem to be hanging back, and the next thing anybody knows, here comes Jockey Scroon on Never Despair sneaking through on the rail, and personally it looks to me as if the jock on Callipers moves over to give Jockey Scroon plenty of elbow room, but of course the jock on Callipers may figure Jockey Scroon has diphtheria, and does not wish to catch it.

Loose Living is out in the middle of the track, anyway, so he does not have to move over. All Loose Living has to do is to keep running backward as he seems to be doing from the top of the stretch, to let Jockey Scroon go past on Never Despair to win the heat by a length.

Well, the race is practically supernatural in many respects, and the judges are all upset over it, and they haul all the jocks up in the stand and ask them many questions, and not being altogether satisfied with the answers, they ask these questions over several times. But all the jocks will say is that Never Despair sneaks past them very unexpectedly indeed, while Jockey Scroon, who is a pretty fresh duck at that, wishes to know if he is supposed to blow a horn when he is slipping through a lot of guys sound asleep.

But the judges are still not satisfied, so they go prowling around investigating the betting, because naturally when a boat race comes up there is apt to be some reason for it, such as the betting, but it seems that all the judges find is that one five-dollar win ticket is sold on Never Despair in the mutuels, and they cannot learn of a dime being bet away on the horse. So there is nothing much the judges can do about the proposition, except give the jocks many hard looks, and the jocks are accustomed to hard looks from the judges, anyway.

Personally, I am greatly upset by this business, especially when I see that Never Despair pays $86.34, and for two cents I will go right up in the stand and start hollering copper on these little Jesse Jameses for putting on such a boat race and taking all my hard-earned potatoes away from me, but before I have time to do this, I run into The Dancer, and he tells me that Dedicate in the next race is the surest thing that ever goes to the post, and at five to one, at that. So I have to forget everything while I bustle about to dig up a few bobs to bet on Dedicate, and when Dedicate is beat a whisker, I have to do some more bustling to dig up a few bobs to bet on Vesta in the fifth, and by this time the third race is such ancient history that nobody cares what happens in it.

It is nearly a week before I see Hot Horse Herbie again, and I figure he is hiding out on everybody because he has this dough he wins off the fiver I give him, and personally I consider him a guy with no manners not to be kicking back the fin, at least. But before I can mention the fin, Herbie gives me a big hello, and says to me like this:

"Well," he says, "I just see Jockey Scroon, and Jockey Scroon just comes back from Palm Beach, and the operation is a big success, and Lame Louise will walk as good as anybody again, and old Mercer is tickled silly. But," Herbie says, "do not say anything out loud, because the judges may still be trying to find out what comes off in the race."

"Herbie," I say, very serious, "do you mean to say the story you tell me about Lame Louise, and all this and that, the other day is on the level?"

"Why," Herbie says, "certainly it is on the level, and I am sorry to hear you do not take advantage of my information. But," he says, "I do not blame you for not believing my story, because it is a very long story for anybody to believe. It is not such a story," Herbie says, "as I will tell to anyone if I expect them to believe it. In fact," he says, "it is so long a story that I do not have the heart to tell it to anybody else but you, or maybe I will have something running for me on the race.

"But," Herbie says, "never mind all this. I will be plenty smart about a race tomorrow. Yes," Herbie says, "I will be wiser than a treeful of owls, so be sure and see me if you happen to have any coconuts."

"There is no danger of me seeing you," I say, very sad, because I am all sorrowed up to think that the story he tells me is really true. "Things are very terrible with me at this time," I say, "and I am thinking maybe you can hand me back my finnif, because you must do all right for yourself with the fiver you have on Never Despair at such a price."

Now a very strange look comes over Hot Horse Herbie's face, and he raises his right hand, and says to me like this:

"I hope and trust I drop down dead right here in front of you," Herbie says, "if I bet a quarter on the horse. It is true," he says, "I am up at the window to buy a ticket on Never Despair, but the guy who is selling the tickets is a friend of mine by the name of Heeby Rosenbloom, and Heeby whispers to me that Big Joe Gompers, the guy who owns Callipers, just bets half a hundred on his horse, and," Herbie says, "I know Joe Gompers is such a guy as will not bet half a hundred on anything he does not get a Federal Reserve guarantee with it.

"Anyway," Herbie says, "I get to thinking about what a bad jockey this Jockey Scroon is, which is very bad indeed, and," he says, "I figure that even if it is a boat race it is no even-money race they can shoo him in, so I buy a ticket on Callipers."

"Well," I say, "somebody buys one five-dollar ticket on Never Despair, and I figure it can be nobody but you."

"Why," Hot Horse Herbie says, "do you not hear about this? Why," he says, "Cap Duhaine, of the Pinkertons, traces this ticket and finds it is bought by a guy by the name of Steve Harter, and the way this guy Harter comes to buy it is very astonishing. It seems," Herbie says, "that this Harter is a tourist out of Indiana who comes to Miami for the sunshine, and who loses all his dough but six bucks against the faro bank at Hollywood.

"At the same time," Herbie says, "the poor guy gets a telegram from his ever-loving doll back in Indiana saying she no longer wishes any part of him.

"Well," Herbie says, "between losing his dough and his doll, the poor guy is practically out of his mind, and he figures there is nothing left for him to do but knock himself off.

"So," Herbie says, "this Harter spends one of his six bucks to get to the track, figuring to throw himself under the feet of the horses in the first race and let them kick him to a jelly. But he does not get there until just as the third race is coming up and," Herbie says, "he sees this name 'Never Despair,' and he figures it may be a hunch, so he buys himself a ticket with his last fiver. Well, naturally," Herbie says, "when Never Despair pops down, the guy forgets about letting the horses kick him to a jelly, and he keeps sending his dough along until he runs nothing but a nubbin into six G's on the day.

"Then," Herbie says, "Cap Duhaine finds out that the guy, still thinking of Never Despair, calls his ever-loving doll on the phone, and finds she is very sorry she sends him the wire and that she really loves him more than somewhat, especially," Herbie says, "when she finds out about the six G's. And the last anybody hears of the matter, this Harter is on his way home to get married, so Never Despair does quite some good in this wicked old world, after all.

"But," Herbie says, "let us forget all this, because tomorrow is another day. Tomorrow," he says, "I will tell you about a thing that goes in the fourth which is just the same as wheat in the bin. In fact," Hot Horse Herbie says, "if it does not win, you can never speak to me again."

"Well," I say, as I start to walk away, "I am not interested in any tip at this time."

"Now," Herbie says, "wait a minute. A story goes with it."

"Well," I say, coming back to him, "let me hear the story."

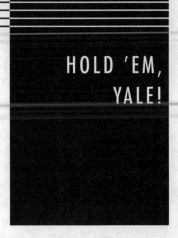

HOLD 'EM, YALE!

What I am doing in New Haven on the day of a very large football game between the Harvards and the Yales is something which calls for quite a little explanation, because I am not such a guy as you will expect to find in New Haven at any time, and especially on the day of a large football game.

But there I am, and the reason I am there goes back to a Friday night when I am sitting in Mindy's restaurant on Broadway thinking of very little except how I can get hold of a few potatoes to take care of the old overhead. And while I am sitting there, who comes in but Sam the Gonoph, who is a ticket speculator by trade, and who seems to be looking all around and about.

Well, Sam the Gonoph gets to talking to me, and it turns out that he is looking for a guy by the name of Gigolo Georgie, who is called Gigolo Georgie because he is always hanging around nightclubs wearing a little mustache and white spats, and dancing with old dolls. In fact, Gigolo Georgie is nothing but a gentleman bum, and I am surprised that Sam the Gonoph is looking for him.

But it seems that the reason Sam the Gonoph wishes to find Gigolo Georgie is to give him a good punch in the snoot, because it seems that Gigolo Georgie promotes Sam for several duckets to the large football game between the Harvards and the Yales to sell on commission, and never kicks back anything whatever to Sam. Naturally

255

Sam considers Gigolo Georgie nothing but a rascal for doing such a thing to him, and Sam says he will find Gigolo Georgie and give him a going-over if it is the last act of his life.

Well, then, Sam explains to me that he has quite a few nice duckets for the large football game between the Harvards and the Yales and that he is taking a crew of guys with him to New Haven the next day to hustle these duckets, and what about me going along and helping to hustle these duckets and making a few bobs for myself, which is an invitation that sounds very pleasant to me, indeed.

Now of course it is very difficult for anybody to get nice duckets to a large football game between the Harvards and the Yales unless they are personally college guys, and Sam the Gonoph is by no means a college guy. In fact, the nearest Sam ever comes to a college is once when he is passing through the yard belonging to the Princetons, but Sam is on the fly at the time as a gendarme is after him, so he does not really see much of the college.

But every college guy is entitled to duckets to a large football game with which his college is connected, and it is really surprising how many college guys do not care to see large football games even after they get their duckets, especially if a ticket spec such as Sam the Gonoph comes along offering them a few bobs more than the duckets are worth. I suppose this is because a college guy figures he can see a large football game when he is old, while many things are taking place around and about that it is necessary for him to see while he is young enough to really enjoy them, such as the Follies.

Anyway, many college guys are always willing to listen to reason when Sam the Gonoph comes around offering to buy their duckets, and then Sam takes these duckets and sells them to customers for maybe ten times the price the duckets call for, and in this way Sam does very good for himself.

I know Sam the Gonoph for maybe twenty years, and always he is speculating in duckets of one kind and another. Sometimes it is duckets for the World Series, and sometimes for big fights, and sometimes it is duckets for nothing but lawn-tennis games, although why anybody wishes to see such a thing as lawn tennis is always a very great mystery to Sam the Gonoph and everybody else.

But in all those years I see Sam dodging around under the feet of the crowds at these large events, or running through the special trains offering to buy or sell duckets, I never hear of Sam personally attending any of these events except maybe a baseball game, or a fight, for Sam has practically no interest in anything but a little profit on his duckets.

He is a short, chunky, black-looking guy with a big beezer, and he is always sweating even on a cold day, and he comes from down around Essex Street, on the lower East Side. Moreover, Sam the Gonoph's crew generally comes from the lower East Side, too, for as Sam goes along he makes plenty of potatoes for himself and branches out quite some, and has a lot of assistants hustling duckets around these different events.

When Sam is younger the cops consider him hard to get along with, and in fact his monicker, the Gonoph, comes from his young days down on the lower East Side, and I hear it is Yiddish for thief, but of course as Sam gets older and starts gathering plenty of potatoes, he will not think of stealing anything. At least not much, and especially if it is anything that is nailed down.

Well, anyway, I meet Sam the Gonoph and his crew at the information desk in Grand Central the next morning, and this is how I come to be in New Haven on the day of the large football game between the Harvards and the Yales.

For such a game as this, Sam has all his best hustlers, including such as Jew Louie, Nubbsy Taylor, Benny South Street and old Liverlips, and to look at these parties you will never suspect that they are top-notch ducket hustlers. The best you will figure them is a lot of guys who are not to be met up with in a dark alley, but then ducket-hustling is a rough-and-tumble dodge and it will scarcely be good policy to hire female impersonators.

Now while we are hustling these duckets out around the main gates of the Yale Bowl I notice a very beautiful little doll of maybe sixteen or seventeen standing around watching the crowd, and I can see she is waiting for somebody, as many dolls often do at football games. But I can also see that this little doll is very much worried as the crowd keeps going in, and it is getting on toward game time. In fact, by and by I can see this little doll has tears in her eyes and if there is anything I hate to see it is tears in a doll's eyes.

So finally I go over to her, and I say as follows: "What is eating you, little Miss?"

"Oh," she says, "I am waiting for Elliot. He is to come up from New York and meet me here to take me to the game, but he is not here yet, and I am afraid something happens to him. Furthermore," she says, the tears in her eyes getting very large, indeed, "I am afraid I will miss the game because he has my ticket."

"Why," I say, "this is a very simple proposition. I will sell you a choice ducket for only a sawbuck, which is ten dollars in your language, and you are getting such a bargain only because the game is about to begin, and the market is going down."

"But," she says, "I do not have ten dollars. In fact, I have only fifty cents left in my purse, and this is worrying me very much, for what will I do if Elliot does not meet me? You see," she says, "I come from Miss Peevy's school at Worcester, and I only have enough money to pay my railroad fare here, and of course I cannot ask Miss Peevy for any money as I do not wish her to know I am going away."

Well, naturally all this is commencing to sound to me like a hard-luck story such as any doll is apt to tell, so I go on about my business because I figure she will next be trying to put the lug on me for a ducket, or maybe for her railroad fare back to Worcester, although generally dolls with hard-luck stories live in San Francisco.

She keeps on standing there, and I notice she is now crying more than somewhat, and I get to thinking to myself that she is about as cute a little doll as I ever see, although too young for anybody to be bothering much about. Furthermore, I get to thinking that maybe she is on the level, at that, with her story.

Well, by this time the crowd is nearly all in the Bowl, and only a few parties such as coppers and hustlers of one kind and another are left standing outside, and there is much cheering going on inside, when Sam the Gonoph comes up looking very much disgusted, and speaks as follows:

"What do you think?" Sam says. "I am left with seven duckets on my hands, and these guys around here will not pay as much as face value for them, and they stand me better than three bucks over that. Well," Sam says, "I am certainly not going to let them go for less than they call for if I have to eat them. What do you guys say we use these duckets ourselves and go in and see the game? Personally," Sam says, "I often wish to see one of these large football games just to find out what makes suckers willing to pay so much for duckets."

Well, this seems to strike one and all, including myself, as a great idea, because none of the rest of us ever see a large football game either, so we start for the gate, and as we pass the little doll who is still crying, I say to Sam the Gonoph like this:

"Listen, Sam," I say, "you have seven duckets, and we are only six, and here is a little doll who is stood up by her guy, and has no ducket, and no potatoes to buy one with, so what about taking her with us?"

Well, this is all right with Sam the Gonoph, and none of the others object, so I step up to the little doll and invite her to go with us, and right away she stops crying and begins smiling, and saying we are very kind indeed. She gives Sam the Gonoph an extra big smile, and right away Sam is saying she is very cute, indeed, and then she gives old Liverlips an even bigger smile, and what is more she takes old Liverlips by the arm and walks with him, and old Liverlips is not only very much astonished, but very much pleased. In fact, old Liverlips begins stepping out very spry, and Liverlips is not such a guy as cares to have any part of dolls, young or old.

But while walking with old Liverlips, the little doll talks very friendly to Jew Louie and to Nubbsy Taylor and Benny South Street, and even to me, and by and by you will think to see us that we are all her uncles, although of course if this little doll really knows who she is with, the chances are she will start chucking faints one after the other.

Anybody can see that she has very little experience in this wicked old world, and in fact is somewhat rattleheaded, because she gabs away very freely about her personal business. In fact, before we are in the Bowl she lets it out that she runs away from Miss Peevy's school to elope with this Elliot, and she says the idea is they are to be married in Hartford after the game. In fact, she says Elliot wishes to go to Hartford and be married before the game.

"But," she says, "my brother John is playing substitute with the Yales today, and I cannot think of getting married to anybody before I see him play, although I am much in love with Elliot. He is a wonderful dancer," she says, "and very romantic. I meet him in Atlantic City last summer. Now we are eloping," she says, "because my father does not care for Elliot whatever. In fact, my father hates Elliot, although he only sees him once, and it is because he hates Elliot so that my father sends me to Miss Peevy's school in Worcester. She is an old pill. Do you not think my father is unreasonable?" she says.

Well, of course none of us have any ideas on such propositions as this, although old Liverlips tells the little doll he is with her right or wrong, and pretty soon we are inside the Bowl and sitting in seats as good as any in the joint. It seems we are on the Harvards' side of the field, although of course I will never know this if the little doll does not mention it.

She seems to know everything about this football business, and as soon as we sit down she tries to point out her brother playing substitute for the Yales, saying he is the fifth guy from the end among a bunch of guys sitting on a bench on the other side of the field all wrapped in blankets. But we cannot make much of him from where we sit, and anyway it does not look to me as if he has much of a job.

It seems we are right in the middle of all the Harvards and they are making an awful racket, what with yelling, and singing, and one thing and another, because it seems the game is going on when we get in, and that the Harvards are shoving the Yales around more than somewhat. So our little doll lets everybody know she is in favor of the Yales by yelling, "Hold 'em, Yale!"

Personally, I cannot tell which are the Harvards and which are the Yales at first, and Sam the Gonoph and the others are as dumb as I am, but she explains the Harvards are wearing the red shirts and the Yales the blue shirts, and by and by we are yelling for the Yales to hold 'em, too, although of course it is only on account of our little doll wishing the Yales to hold 'em, and not because any of us care one way or the other.

Well, it seems that the idea of a lot of guys and a little doll getting right among them and yelling for the Yales to hold 'em is very repulsive to the Harvards around us, although any of them must admit it is very good advice to the Yales, at that, and some of them start making cracks of one kind and another, especially at our little doll. The chances are they are very jealous because she is outyelling them, because I will say one thing for our little doll, she can yell about as loud as anybody I ever hear, male or female.

A couple of Harvards sitting in front of old Liverlips are imitating our little doll's voice, and making guys around them laugh very heartily, but all of a sudden these parties leave their seats and go away in great haste, their faces very pale, indeed, and I figure maybe they are both taken sick at the same moment, but afterward I learn that Liverlips takes a big shiv out of his pocket and opens it and tells them very confidentially that he is going to carve their ears off.

Naturally, I do not blame the Harvards for going away in great haste, for Liverlips is such a looking guy as you will figure to take great delight in carving off ears. Furthermore, Nubbsy Taylor and Benny South Street and Jew Louie and even Sam the Gonoph commence exchanging such glances with other Harvards around us who are making cracks at our little doll that presently there is almost a dead silence in our neighborhood, except for our little doll yelling, "Hold 'em, Yale!" You see by this time we are all very fond of our little doll because she is so cute looking and has so much zing in her, and we do not wish anybody making cracks at her or at us either, and especially at us.

In fact, we are so fond of her that when she happens to mention that she is a little chilly, Jew Louie and Nubbsy Taylor slip around among the Harvards and come back with four steamer rugs, six mufflers, two pairs of gloves and a thermos bottle full of hot coffee for her, and Jew Louie says if she wishes a mink coat to just say the word. But she already has a mink coat. Furthermore, Jew Louie brings her a big bunch of red flowers that he finds on a doll with one of the Harvards, and he is much disappointed when she says it is the wrong color for her.

Well, finally the game is over, and I do not remember much about it, although afterward I hear that our little doll's brother John plays substitute for the Yales very good. But it seems that the Harvards win, and our little doll is very sad indeed about this, and is sitting there looking out over the field, which is now covered with guys dancing around as if they all suddenly go daffy, and it seems they are all Harvards, because there is really no reason for the Yales to do any dancing.

All of a sudden our little doll looks toward one end of the field, and says as follows:

"Oh, they are going to take our goalposts!"

Sure enough, a lot of Harvards are gathering around the posts at this end of the field, and are pulling and hauling at the posts, which seem to be very stout posts, indeed. Personally, I will not give you eight cents for these posts, but afterward one of the Yales tells me that when a football team wins a game it is considered the proper caper for this team's boosters to grab the other guys' goalposts. But he is not able to tell me what good the posts are after they get them, and this is one thing that will always be a mystery to me.

Anyway, while we are watching the goings-on around the goalposts, our little doll says come on and jumps up and runs down an aisle and out onto the field, and into the crowd around the goalposts, so naturally we follow her. Somehow she manages to wiggle through the crowd of Harvards around the posts, and the next thing anybody knows she shins up one of the posts faster than you can say scat, and pretty soon is roosting out on the crossbar between the posts like a chipmunk.

Afterward she explains that her idea is the Harvards will not be ungentlemanly enough to pull down the goalposts with a lady roosting on them, but it seems these Harvards are no gentlemen, and keep on pulling, and the posts commence to teeter, and our little doll is teetering with them, although of course she is in no danger if she falls because she is sure to fall on the Harvards' noggins, and the way I look at it, the noggin of anybody who will be found giving any time to pulling down goalposts is apt to be soft enough to break a very long fall.

Now Sam the Gonoph and old Liverlips and Nubbsy Taylor and Benny South Street and Jew Louie and I reach the crowd around the goalposts at about the same time, and our little doll sees us from her roost and yells to us as follows:

"Do not let them take our posts!"

Well, about this time one of the Harvards who seems to be about nine feet high reaches over six other guys and hits me on the chin and knocks me so far that when I pick myself up I am pretty well out of the way of everybody and have a chance to see what is going on.

Afterward somebody tells me that the guy probably thinks I am one of the Yales coming to the rescue of the goalposts, but I wish to say I will always have a very low opinion of college guys, because I remember two other guys punch me as I am going through the air, unable to defend myself.

Now Sam the Gonoph and Nubbsy Taylor and Jew Louie and Benny South Street and old Liverlips somehow manage to ease their way through the crowd until they are under the goalposts, and our little doll is much pleased to see them, because the Harvards are now making the posts teeter more than somewhat with their pulling, and it looks as if the posts will go any minute.

Of course Sam the Gonoph does not wish any trouble with these parties, and he tries to speak nicely to the guys who are pulling at the posts, saying as follows:

"Listen," Sam says, "the little doll up there does not wish you to take these posts."

Well, maybe they do not hear Sam's words in the confusion, or if they do hear them they do not wish to pay any attention to them, for one of the Harvards mashes Sam's derby hat down over his eyes, and another smacks old Liverlips on the left ear, while Jew Louie and Nubbsy Taylor and Benny South Street are shoved around quite some.

"All right," Sam the Gonoph says, as soon as he can pull his hat off his eyes, "all right, gentlemen, if you wish to play this way. Now, boys, let them have it!"

So Sam the Gonoph and Nubbsy Taylor and Jew Louie and Benny South Street and old Liverlips begin letting them have it, and what they let them have it with is not only their dukes, but with the good old difference in their dukes, because these guys are by no means suckers when it comes to a battle, and they all carry something in their pockets to put in their dukes in case of a fight, such as a dollar's worth of nickels rolled up tight.

Furthermore, they are using the old leather, kicking guys in the stomach when they are not able to hit them on the chin, and Liverlips is also using his noodle to good advantage, grabbing guys by their coat lapels and yanking them into him so he can butt them between the eyes with his noggin, and I wish to say that old Liverlips's noggin is a very dangerous weapon at all times.

Well, the ground around them is soon covered with Harvards, and it seems that some Yales are also mixed up with them, being Yales who think Sam the Gonoph and his guys are other Yales defending the goalposts, and wishing to help out. But of course Sam the Gonoph and his guys cannot tell the Yales from the Harvards, and do not have time to ask which is which, so they are just letting everybody have it who comes along. And while all this is going on our little doll is sitting up on the crossbar and yelling plenty of encouragement to Sam and his guys.

Now it turns out that these Harvards are by no means soft touches in a scrabble such as this, and as fast as they are flattened they get up and keep belting away, and while the old experience is running for Sam the Gonoph and Jew Louie and Nubbsy Taylor and Benny South Street and old Liverlips early in the fight, the Harvards have youth in their favor.

Pretty soon the Harvards are knocking down Sam the Gonoph, then they start knocking down Nubbsy Taylor, and by and by they are knocking down Benny South Street and Jew Louie and Liverlips, and it is so much fun that the Harvards forget all about the goalposts. Of course as fast as Sam the Gonoph and his guys are knocked down they also get up, but the Harvards are too many for them, and they are getting an awful shellacking when the nine-foot guy who flattens me, and who is knocking down Sam the Gonoph so often he is becoming a great nuisance to Sam, sings out:

"Listen," he says, "these are game guys, even if they do go to Yale. Let us cease knocking them down," he says, "and give them a cheer."

So the Harvards knock down Sam the Gonoph and Nubbsy Taylor and Jew Louie and Benny South Street and old Liverlips just once more and then all the Harvards put their heads together and say rah-rah-rah, very loud, and go away, leaving the goalposts still standing, with our little doll still roosting on the crossbar, although afterward I hear some Harvards who are not in the fight get the posts at the other end of the field and sneak away with them. But I always claim these posts do not count.

Well, sitting there on the ground because he is too tired to get up from the last knockdown, and holding one hand to his right eye, which is closed tight, Sam the Gonoph is by no means a well guy, and all around and about him is much suffering among his crew. But our little doll is hopping up and down chattering like a jaybird and running between old Liverlips, who is stretched out against one goalpost, and Nubbsy Taylor, who is leaning up against the other, and she is trying to mop the blood off their kissers with a handkerchief the size of a postage stamp.

Benny South Street is laying across Jew Louie and both are still snoring from the last knockdown, and the Bowl is now pretty much deserted except for the newspaper scribes away up in the press box, who do not seem to realize that the Battle of the Century just comes off in front of them. It is coming on dark, when all of a sudden a guy pops up out of the dusk wearing white spats and an overcoat with a fur collar, and he rushes up to our little doll.

"Clarice," he says, "I am looking for you high and low. My train is stalled for hours behind a wreck the other side of Bridgeport, and I get here just after the game is over. But," he says, "I figure you will be waiting somewhere for me. Let us hurry on to Hartford, darling," he says.

Well, when he hears this voice, Sam the Gonoph opens his good eye wide and takes a peek at the guy. Then all of a sudden Sam jumps up and wobbles over to the guy and hits him a smack between the eyes. Sam is wobbling because his legs are not so good from the shellacking he takes off the Harvards, and furthermore he is away off in his punching as the guy only goes to his knees and comes right up standing again as our little doll lets out a screech and speaks as follows:

"Oo-oo!" she says. "Do not hit Elliot! He is not after our goalposts!"

"Elliot?" Sam the Gonoph says. "This is no Elliot. This is nobody but Gigolo Georgie. I can tell him by his white spats," Sam says, "and I am now going to get even for the pasting I take from the Harvards."

Then he nails the guy again and this time he seems to have a little more on his punch, for the guy goes down and Sam the Gonoph gives him the leather very good, although our little doll is still screeching, and begging Sam not to hurt Elliot. But of course the rest of us know it is not Elliot, no matter what he may tell her, but only Gigolo Georgie.

Well, the rest of us figure we may as well take a little something out of Georgie's hide, too, but as we start for him he gives a quick wiggle and hops to his feet and tears across the field, and the last we see of him is his white spats flying through one of the portals.

Now a couple of other guys come up out of the dusk, and one of them is a tall, fine-looking guy with a white mustache and anybody can see that he is somebody, and what happens but our little doll runs right into his arms and kisses him on the white mustache and calls him daddy and starts to cry more than somewhat, so I can see we lose our little doll then and there. And now the guy with the white mustache walks up to Sam the Gonoph and sticks out his duke and says as follows:

"Sir," he says, "permit me the honor of shaking the hand which does me the very signal service of chastising the scoundrel who just escapes from the field. And," he says, "permit me to introduce myself to you. I am J. Hildreth Van Cleve, president of the Van Cleve Trust. I am notified early today by Miss Peevy of my daughter's sudden departure from school, and we learn she purchases a ticket for New Haven. I at once suspect this fellow has something to do with it. Fortunately," he says, "I have these private detectives here keeping tab on him for some time, knowing my child's schoolgirl infatuation for him, so we easily trail him here. We are on the train with him, and arrive in time for your last little scene with him. Sir," he says, "again I thank you."

"I know who you are, Mr. Van Cleve," Sam the Gonoph says. "You are the Van Cleve who is down to his last forty million. But," he says, "do not thank me for putting the slug on Gigolo Georgie. He is a bum in spades, and I am only sorry he fools your nice little kid even for a minute, although," Sam says, "I figure she must be dumber than she looks to be fooled by such a guy as Gigolo Georgie."

"I hate him," the little doll says. "I hate him because he is a coward. He does not stand up and fight when he is hit like you and Liverlips and the others. I never wish to see him again."

"Do not worry," Sam the Gonoph says. "I will be too close to Gigolo Georgie as soon as I recover from my wounds for him to stay in this part of the country."

Well, I do not see Sam the Gonoph or Nubbsy Taylor or Benny South Street or Jew Louie or Liverlips for nearly a year after this, and then it comes on fall again and one day I get to thinking that here it is Friday and the next day the Harvards are playing the Yales a large football game in Boston.

I figure it is a great chance for me to join up with Sam the Gonoph again to hustle duckets for him for this game, and I know Sam will be leaving along about midnight with his crew. So I go over to the Grand Central station at such a time, and sure enough he comes along by and by, busting through the crowd in the station with Nubbsy Taylor and Benny South Street and Jew Louie and old Liverlips at his heels, and they seem very much excited.

"Well, Sam," I say, as I hurry along with them, "here I am ready to hustle duckets for you again, and I hope and trust we do a nice business."

"Duckets!" Sam the Gonoph says. "We are not hustling duckets for this game, although you can go with us, and welcome. We are going to Boston," he says, "to root for the Yales to kick hell out of the Harvards and we are going as the personal guests of Miss Clarice Van Cleve and her old man."

"Hold 'em, Yale!" old Liverlips says, as he pushes me to one side and the whole bunch goes trotting through the gate to catch their train, and I then notice they are all wearing blue feathers in their hats with a little white Y on these feathers such as college guys always wear at football games, and that moreover Sam the Gonoph is carrying a Yale pennant.

MADAME LA GIMP

One night I am passing the corner of Fiftieth Street and Broadway, and what do I see but Dave the Dude standing in a doorway talking to a busted-down old Spanish doll by the name of Madame La Gimp. Or rather Madame La Gimp is talking to Dave the Dude, and what is more he is listening to her, because I can hear him say yes, yes, as he always does when he is really listening to anybody, which is very seldom.

Now this is a most surprising sight to me, because Madame La Gimp is not such an old doll as anybody will wish to listen to, especially Dave the Dude. In fact, she is nothing but an old haybag, and generally somewhat ginned up. For fifteen years, or maybe sixteen, I see Madame La Gimp up and down Broadway, or sliding along through the Forties, sometimes selling newspapers, and sometimes selling flowers, and in all these years I seldom see her but what she seems to have about half a heat on from drinking gin.

Of course, nobody ever takes the newspapers she sells, even after they buy them off of her, because they are generally yesterday's papers, and sometimes last week's, and nobody ever wants her flowers, even after they pay her for them, because they are flowers such as she gets off an undertaker over in Tenth Avenue, and they are very tired flowers, indeed.

Personally, I consider Madame La Gimp nothing but an old pest, but kindhearted guys like Dave the Dude always stake her to a few pieces of silver when she comes shuffling along putting on the moan about her tough luck. She walks with a gimp in one leg, which is why she is called Madame La Gimp, and years ago I hear somebody say Madame La Gimp is once a Spanish dancer, and a big shot on Broadway, but that she meets up with an accident which puts her out of the dancing dodge, and that a busted romance makes her become a gin-head.

I remember somebody telling me once that Madame La Gimp is quite a beauty in her day, and has her own servants, and all this and that, but I always hear the same thing about every bum on Broadway, male and female, including some I know are bums, in spades, right from taw, so I do not pay any attention to these stories.

Still, I am willing to allow that maybe Madame La Gimp is once a fair looker, at that, and the chances are has a fair shape, because once or twice I see her when she is not ginned up, and has her hair combed, and she is not so bad-looking, although even then if you put her in a claiming race I do not think there is any danger of anybody claiming her out of it.

Mostly she is wearing raggedy clothes, and busted shoes, and her gray hair is generally hanging down her face, and when I say she is maybe fifty years old I am giving her plenty the best of it. Although she is Spanish, Madame La Gimp talks good English, and in fact she can cuss in English as good as anybody I ever hear, barring Dave the Dude.

Well, anyway, when Dave the Dude sees me as he is listening to Madame La Gimp, he motions me to wait, so I wait until she finally gets through gabbing to him and goes gimping away. Then Dave the Dude comes over to me looking much worried.

"This is quite a situation," Dave says. "The old doll is in a tough spot. It seems that she once has a baby which she calls by the name of Eulalie, being it is a girl baby, and she ships this baby off to her sister in a little town in Spain to raise up, because Madame La Gimp figures a baby is not apt to get much raising-up off of her as long as she is on Broadway. Well, this baby is on her way here. In fact," Dave says, "she will land next Saturday and here it is Wednesday already."

"Where is the baby's papa?" I ask Dave the Dude.

"Well," Dave says, "I do not ask Madame La Gimp this, because I do not consider it a fair question. A guy who goes around this town asking where babies' papas are, or even who they are, is apt to get the name of being nosey. Anyway, this has nothing whatever to do with the proposition, which is that Madame La Gimp's baby, Eulalie, is arriving here.

"Now," Dave says, "it seems that Madame La Gimp's baby, being now eighteen years old, is engaged to marry the son of a very proud old Spanish nobleman who lives in this little town in Spain, and it also seems that the very proud old Spanish nobleman, and his ever-loving wife, and the son, and Madame La Gimp's sister, are all with the baby. They are making a tour of the whole world, and will stop over here a couple of days just to see Madame La Gimp."

"It is commencing to sound to me like a movie such as a guy is apt to see at a midnight show," I say.

"Wait a minute," Dave says, getting impatient. "You are too gabby to suit me. Now it seems that the proud old Spanish nobleman does not wish his son to marry any lob, and one reason he is coming here is to look over Madame La Gimp, and see that she is okay. He thinks that Madame La Gimp's baby's own papa is dead, and that Madame La Gimp is now married to one of the richest and most aristocratic guys in America."

"How does the proud old Spanish nobleman get such an idea as this?" I ask. "It is a sure thing he never sees Madame La Gimp, or even a photograph of her as she is at present."

"I will tell you how," Dave the Dude says. "It seems Madame La Gimp gives her baby the idea that such is the case in her letters to her. It seems Madame La Gimp does a little scrubbing business around a swell apartment hotel in Park Avenue that is called the Marberry, and she cops stationery there and writes her baby in Spain on this stationery, saying this is where she lives, and how rich and aristocratic her husband is. And what is more, Madame La Gimp has letters from her baby sent to her care of the hotel and gets them out of the employees' mail."

"Why," I say, "Madame La Gimp is nothing but an old fraud to deceive people in this manner, especially a proud old Spanish nobleman. And," I say, "this proud old Spanish nobleman must be something of a chump to believe a mother will keep away from her baby all these years, especially if the mother has plenty of dough, although of course I do not know just how smart a proud old Spanish nobleman can be."

"Well," Dave says, "Madame La Gimp tells me the thing that makes the biggest hit of all with the proud old Spanish nobleman is that she keeps her baby in Spain all these years because she wishes her raised up a true Spanish baby in every respect until she is old enough to know what time it is. But I judge the proud old Spanish nobleman is none too bright, at that," Dave says, "because Madame La Gimp tells me he always lives in his little town which does not even have running water in the bathrooms.

"But what I am getting at is this," Dave says. "We must have Madame La Gimp in a swell apartment in the Marberry with a rich and aristocratic guy for a husband by the time her baby gets here, because if the proud old Spanish nobleman finds out Madame La Gimp is nothing but a bum, it is a hundred to one he will cancel his son's engagement to Madame La Gimp's baby and break a lot of people's hearts, including his son's.

"Madame La Gimp tells me her baby is daffy about the young guy, and he is daffy about her, and there are enough broken hearts in this town as it is. I know how I will get the apartment, so you go and bring me Judge Henry G. Blake for a rich and aristocratic husband, or anyway for a husband."

Well, I know Dave the Dude to do many a daffy thing, but never a thing as daffy as this. But I know there is no use arguing with him when he gets an idea, because if you argue with Dave the Dude too much he is apt to reach over and lay his Sunday punch on your snoot, and no argument is worth a punch on the snoot, especially from Dave the Dude.

So I go out looking for Judge Henry G. Blake to be Madame La Gimp's husband, although I am not so sure Judge Henry G. Blake will care to be anybody's husband, and especially Madame La Gimp's after he gets a load of her, for Judge Henry G. Blake is kind of a classy old guy.

To look at Judge Henry G. Blake, with his gray hair, and his nose glasses, and his stomach, you will think he is very important people, indeed. Of course, Judge Henry G. Blake is not a judge, and never is a judge, but they call him Judge because he looks like a judge, and talks slow, and puts in many long words, which very few people understand.

They tell me Judge Blake once has plenty of dough, and is quite a guy in Wall Street, and a high shot along Broadway, but he misses a few guesses at the market, and winds up without much dough, as guys generally do who miss guesses at the market. What Judge Henry

G. Blake does for a living at this time nobody knows, because he does nothing much whatever, and yet he seems to be a producer in a small way at all times.

Now and then he makes a trip across the ocean with such as Little Manuel, and other guys who ride the tubs, and sits in with them on games of bridge, and one thing and another, when they need him. Very often when he is riding the tubs, Little Manuel runs into some guy he cannot cheat, so he has to call in Judge Henry G. Blake to outplay the guy on the level, although of course Little Manuel will much rather get a guy's dough by cheating him than by outplaying him on the level. Why this is, I do not know, but this is the way Little Manuel is.

Anyway, you cannot say Judge Henry G. Blake is a bum, especially as he wears good clothes, with a wing collar, and a derby hat, and most people consider him a very nice old man. Personally I never catch the judge out of line on any proposition whatever, and he always says hello to me, very pleasant.

It takes me several hours to find Judge Henry G. Blake, but finally I locate him in Derle's billiards room playing a game of pool with a guy from Providence, Rhode Island. It seems the judge is playing the guy from Providence for five cents a ball, and the judge is about thirteen balls behind when I step into the joint, because naturally at five cents a ball the judge wishes the guy from Providence to win, so as to encourage him to play for maybe twenty-five cents a ball, the judge being very cute this way.

Well, when I step in I see the judge miss a shot anybody can make blindfolded, but as soon as I give him the office I wish to speak to him, the judge hauls off and belts in every ball on the table, bingity-bing, the last shot being a bank that will make Al de Oro stop and think, because when it comes to pool, the old judge is just naturally a curly wolf.

Afterward he tells me he is very sorry I make him hurry up this way, because of course after the last shot he is never going to get the guy from Providence to play him pool even for fun, and the judge tells me the guy sizes up as a right good thing, at that.

Now Judge Henry G. Blake is not so excited when I tell him what Dave the Dude wishes to see him about, but naturally he is willing to do anything for Dave, because he knows that guys who are not willing to do things for Dave the Dude often have bad luck. The judge tells me that he is afraid he will not make much of a husband because he tries it before several times on his own hook and is always a bust, but as long as this time it is not to be anything serious, he will tackle it. Anyway, Judge Henry G. Blake says, being aristocratic will come natural to him.

Well, when Dave the Dude starts out on any proposition, he is a wonder for fast working. The first thing he does is to turn Madame La Gimp over to Miss Billy Perry, who is now Dave's ever-loving wife which he takes out of tap dancing in Miss Missouri Martin's Sixteen Hundred Club, and Miss Billy Perry calls in Miss Missouri Martin to help.

This is water on Miss Missouri Martin's wheel, because if there is anything she loves it is to stick her nose in other people's business, no matter what it is, but she is quite a help at that, although at first they have a tough time keeping her from telling Waldo Winchester, the scribe, about the whole cat hop, so he will put a story in the *Morning Item* about it, with Miss Missouri Martin's name in it. Miss Missouri Martin does not believe in ever overlooking any publicity bets on the layout.

Anyway, it seems that between them Miss Billy Perry and Miss Missouri Martin get Madame La Gimp dolled up in a lot of new clothes, and run her through one of these beauty joints until she comes out very much changed, indeed. Afterward I hear Miss Billy Perry and Miss Missouri Martin have quite a few words, because Miss Missouri Martin wishes to paint Madame La Gimp's hair the same color as her own, which is a high yellow, and buy her the same kind of dresses which Miss Missouri Martin wears herself, and Miss Missouri Martin gets much insulted when Miss Billy Perry says no, they are trying to dress Madame La Gimp to look like a lady.

They tell me Miss Missouri Martin thinks some of putting the slug on Miss Billy Perry for this crack, but happens to remember just in time that Miss Billy Perry is now Dave the Dude's ever-loving wife, and that nobody in this town can put the slug on Dave's ever-loving wife, except maybe Dave himself.

Now the next thing anybody knows, Madame La Gimp is in a swell eight- or nine-room apartment in the Marberry, and the way this comes about is as follows: It seems that one of Dave the Dude's most important champagne customers is a guy by the name of Rodney B. Emerson, who owns the apartment, but who is at his summer home in Newport, with his family, or anyway with his ever-loving wife.

This Rodney B. Emerson is quite a guy along Broadway, and a great hand for spending dough and looking for laughs, and he is very popular with the mob. Furthermore, he is obliged to Dave the Dude, because Dave sells him good champagne when most guys are trying to hand him the old phonus bolonus, and naturally Rodney B. Emerson appreciates this kind treatment.

He is a short, fat guy, with a round, red face, and a big laugh, and the kind of a guy Dave the Dude can call up at his home in Newport and explain the situation and ask for the loan of the apartment, which Dave does.

Well, it seems Rodney B. Emerson gets a big bang out of the idea, and he says to Dave the Dude like this:

"You not only can have the apartment, Dave, but I will come over and help you out. It will save a lot of explaining around the Marberry if I am there."

So he hops right over from Newport, and joins in with Dave the Dude, and I wish to say Rodney B. Emerson will always be kindly remembered by one and all for his cooperation, and nobody will ever again try to hand him the phonus bolonus when he is buying champagne, even if he is not buying it off of Dave the Dude.

Well, it is coming on Saturday and the boat from Spain is due, so Dave the Dude hires a big town car, and puts his own driver, Wop Sam, on it, as he does not wish any strange driver tipping off anybody that it is a hired car. Miss Missouri Martin is anxious to go to the boat with Madame La Gimp, and take her jazz band, the Hi Hi Boys, from her Sixteen Hundred Club with her to make it a real welcome, but nobody thinks much of this idea. Only Madame La Gimp and her husband, Judge Henry G. Blake, and Miss Billy Perry go, though the judge holds out for some time for Little Manuel, because Judge Blake says he wishes somebody around to tip him off in case there are any bad cracks made about him as a husband in Spanish, and Little Manuel is very Spanish.

The morning they go to meet the boat is the first time Judge Henry G. Blake gets a load of his ever-loving wife, Madame La Gimp, and by this time Miss Billy Perry and Miss Missouri Martin give Madame La Gimp such a going-over that she is by no means the worst looker in the world. In fact, she looks first-rate, especially as she is off gin and says she is off it for good.

Judge Henry G. Blake is really quite surprised by her looks, as he figures all along she will turn out to be a crow. In fact, Judge Blake hurls a couple of shots into himself to nerve himself for the ordeal, as he explains it, before he appears to go to the boat. Between these shots, and the nice clothes, and the good cleaning-up Miss Billy Perry and Miss Missouri Martin give Madame La Gimp, she is really a pleasant sight to the judge.

They tell me the meeting at the dock between Madame La Gimp and her baby is very affecting indeed, and when the proud old Spanish nobleman and his wife, and their son, and Madame La Gimp's sister, all go into action, too, there are enough tears around there to float all the battleships we once sink for Spain. Even Miss Billy Perry and Judge Henry G. Blake do some first-class crying, although the chances are the judge is worked up to the crying more by the shots he takes for his courage than by the meeting.

Still, I hear the old judge does himself proud, what with kissing Madame La Gimp's baby plenty, and duking the proud old Spanish nobleman, and his wife, and son, and giving Madame La Gimp's sister a good strong hug that squeezes her tongue out.

It turns out that the proud old Spanish nobleman has white sideburns, and is entitled Conde de Something, so his ever-loving wife is the Condesa, and the son is a very nice-looking quiet young guy any way you take him, who blushes every time anybody looks at him. As for Madame La Gimp's baby, she is as pretty as they come, and many guys are sorry they do not get Judge Henry G. Blake's job as stepfather, because he is able to take a kiss at Madame La Gimp's baby on what seems to be very small excuse. I never see a nicer-looking young couple, and anybody can see they are very fond of each other, indeed.

Madame La Gimp's sister is not such a doll as I will wish to have sawed off on me, and is up in the paints as regards to age, but she is also very quiet. None of the bunch talk any English, so Miss Billy Perry and Judge Henry G. Blake are pretty much outsiders on the way uptown. Anyway, the judge takes the wind as soon as they reach the Marberry, because the judge is now getting a little tired of being a husband. He says he has to take a trip out to Pittsburgh to buy four or five coal mines, but will be back the next day.

Well, it seems to me that everything is going perfect so far, and that it is good judgment to let it lay as it is, but nothing will do Dave the Dude but to have a reception the following night. I advise Dave the Dude against this idea, because I am afraid something will happen to spoil the whole cat-hop, but he will not listen to me, especially as Rodney B. Emerson is now in town and is a strong booster for the party, as he wishes to drink some of the good champagne he has planted in his apartment.

Furthermore, Miss Billy Perry and Miss Missouri Martin are very indignant at me when they hear about my advice, as it seems they both buy new dresses out of Dave the Dude's bankroll when they are dressing up Madame La Gimp, and they wish to spring these dresses somewhere where they can be seen. So the party is on.

I get to the Marberry around nine o'clock and who opens the door of Madame La Gimp's apartment for me but Moosh, the doorman from Miss Missouri Martin's Sixteen Hundred Club. Furthermore, he is in his Sixteen Hundred Club uniform, except he has a clean shave. I wish Moosh a hello, and he never raps to me but only bows, and takes my hat.

The next guy I see is Rodney B. Emerson in evening clothes, and the minute he sees me he yells out, "Mister O. O. McIntyre." Well, of course, I am not Mister O. O. McIntyre, and never put myself away as Mister O. O. McIntyre, and furthermore there is no resemblance whatever between Mister O. O. McIntyre and me, because I am a fairly good-looking guy, and I start to give Rodney B. Emerson an argument, when he whispers to me like this:

"Listen," he whispers, "we must have big names at this affair, so as to impress these people. The chances are they read the newspapers back there in Spain, and we must let them meet the folks they read about, so they will see Madame La Gimp is a real big shot to get such names to a party."

Then he takes me by the arm and leads me to a group of people in a corner of the room, which is about the size of the Grand Central waiting room.

"Mister O. O. McIntyre, the big writer!" Rodney B. Emerson says, and the next thing I know I am shaking hands with Mr. and Mrs. Conde, and their son, and with Madame La Gimp and her baby, and Madame La Gimp's sister, and finally with Judge Henry G. Blake, who has on a swallowtail coat, and does not give me much of a tumble. I figure the chances are Judge Henry G. Blake is getting a swelled head already, not to tumble up a guy who helps him get his job, but even at that I wish to say the old judge looks immense in his swallowtail coat, bowing and giving one and all the old castor-oil smile.

Madame La Gimp is in a low-neck black dress and is wearing a lot of Miss Missouri Martin's diamonds, such as rings and bracelets, which Miss Missouri Martin insists on hanging on her, although I hear afterward that Miss Missouri Martin has Johnny Brannigan, the plainclothes copper, watching these diamonds. I wonder at the time why Johnny is there, but figure it is because he is a friend of Dave the Dude's. Miss Missouri Martin is no sucker, even if she is kindhearted.

Anybody looking at Madame La Gimp will bet you all the coffee in Java that she never lives in a cellar over in Tenth Avenue, and drinks plenty of gin in her day. She has her gray hair piled up high on her head, with a big Spanish comb in it, and she reminds me of a picture I see somewhere, but I do not remember just where. And her baby, Eulalie, in a white dress is about as pretty a little doll as you will wish to see, and nobody can blame Judge Henry G. Blake for copping a kiss off of her now and then.

Well, pretty soon I hear Rodney B. Emerson bawling, "Mister Willie K. Vanderbilt," and in comes nobody but Big Nig, and Rodney B. Emerson leads him over to the group and introduces him.

Little Manuel is standing alongside Judge Henry G. Blake, and he explains in Spanish to Mr. and Mrs. Conde and the others that "Willie K. Vanderbilt" is a very large millionaire, and Mr. and Mrs. Conde seem much interested, anyway, though naturally Madame La Gimp and Judge Henry G. Blake are jerry to Big Nig, while Madame La Gimp's baby and the young guy are interested in nobody but each other.

Then I hear, "Mister Al Jolson," and in comes nobody but Tony Bertazzola, from the Chicken Club, who looks about as much like Al as I do like O. O. McIntyre, which is not at all. Next comes "the Very Reverend John Roach Straton," who seems to be Skeets Bolivar to me, then "the Honorable Mayor James J. Walker," and who is it but Good Time Charley Bernstein.

"Mister Otto H. Kahn," turns out to be Rochester Red, and "Mister Heywood Broun" is Nick the Greek, who asks me privately who

Heywood Broun is, and gets very sore at Rodney B. Emerson when I describe Heywood Broun to him.

Finally there is quite a commotion at the door and Rodney B. Emerson announces, "Mister Herbert Bayard Swope" in an extra loud voice which makes everybody look around, but it is nobody but the Pale Face Kid. He gets me to one side, too, and wishes to know who Herbert Bayard Swope is, and when I explain to him, the Pale Face Kid gets so swelled up he will not speak to Death House Donegan, who is only "Mister William Muldoon."

Well, it seems to me they are getting too strong when they announce, "Vice-President of the United States, the Honorable Charles Curtis," and in pops Guinea Mike, and I say as much to Dave the Dude, who is running around every which way looking after things, but he only says, "Well, if you do not know it is Guinea Mike, will you know it is not Vice-President Curtis?"

But it seems to me all this is most disrespectful to our leading citizens, especially when Rodney B. Emerson calls, "The Honorable Police Commissioner, Mister Grover A. Whalen," and in pops Wild William Wilkins, who is a very hot man at this time, being wanted in several spots for different raps. Dave the Dude takes personal charge of Wild William and removes a rod from his pants pocket, because none of the guests are supposed to come rodded up, this being strictly a social matter.

I watch Mr. and Mrs. Conde, and I do not see that these names are making any impression on them, and I afterward find out that they never get any newspapers in their town in Spain except a little local bladder which only prints the home news. In fact, Mr. and Mrs. Conde seem somewhat bored, although Mr. Conde cheers up no little and looks interested when a lot of dolls drift in. They are mainly dolls from Miss Missouri Martin's Sixteen Hundred Club, and the Hot Box, but Rodney B. Emerson introduces them as "Sophie Tucker," and "Theda Bara," and "Jeanne Eagels," and "Helen Morgan," and "Aunt Jemima," and one thing and another.

Well, pretty soon in comes Miss Missouri Martin's jazz band, the Hi Hi Boys, and the party commences getting up steam, especially when Dave the Dude gets Rodney B. Emerson to breaking out the old grape. By and by there is dancing going on, and a good time is being had by one and all, including Mr. and Mrs. Conde. In fact, after Mr. Conde gets a couple of jolts of the old grape, he turns out to be a pretty nice old skate, even if nobody can understand what he is talking about.

As for Judge Henry G. Blake, he is full of speed, indeed. By this time anybody can see that the judge is commencing to believe that all this is on the level and that he is really entertaining celebrities in his own home. You put a quart of good grape inside the old judge and he will believe anything. He soon dances himself plumb out of wind, and then I notice he is hanging around Madame La Gimp a lot.

Along about midnight, Dave the Dude has to go out into the kitchen and settle a battle there over a crap game, but otherwise everything is very peaceful. It seems that "Herbert Bayard Swope," "Vice-President Curtis," and "Grover Whalen" get a little game going, when "the Reverend John Roach Straton" steps up and cleans them in four passes, but it seems they soon discover that "the Reverend John Roach Straton" is using tops on them, which are very dishonest dice, and so they put the slug on "the Reverend John Roach Straton" and Dave the Dude has to split them out.

By and by I figure on taking the wind, and I look for Mr. and Mrs. Conde to tell them good night, but Mr. Conde and Miss Missouri Martin are still dancing, and Miss Missouri Martin is pouring conversation into Mr. Conde's ear by the bucketful, and while Mr. Conde does not savvy a word she says, this makes no difference to Miss Missouri Martin. Let Miss Missouri Martin do all the talking, and she does not care a whoop if anybody understands her.

Mrs. Conde is over in a corner with "Herbert Bayard Swope," or the Pale Face Kid, who is trying to find out from her by using hog Latin and signs on her if there is any chance for a good twenty-one dealer in Spain, and of course Mrs. Conde is not able to make heads or tails of what he means, so I hunt up Madame La Gimp.

She is sitting in a darkish corner off by herself and I really do not see Judge Henry G. Blake leaning over her until I am almost on top of them, so I cannot help hearing what the judge is saying.

"I am wondering for two days," he says, "if by any chance you remember me. Do you know who I am?"

"I remember you," Madame La Gimp says. "I remember you— oh, so very well, Henry. How can I forget you? But I have no idea you recognize me after all these years."

"Twenty of them now," Judge Henry G. Blake says. "You are beautiful then. You are still beautiful."

Well, I can see the old grape is working first-class on Judge Henry G. Blake to make such remarks as this, although at that, in the half-light, with the smile on her face, Madame La Gimp is not so bad. Still, give me them carrying a little less weight for age.

"Well, it is all your fault," Judge Henry G. Blake says. "You go and marry that chile con carne guy, and look what happens!"

I can see there is no sense in me horning in on Madame La Gimp and Judge Henry G. Blake while they are cutting up old touches in this manner, so I think I will just say good-bye to the young people and let it go at that, but while I am looking for Madame La Gimp's baby, and her guy, I run into Dave the Dude.

"You will not find them here," Dave says. "By this time they are being married over at Saint Malachy's with my ever-loving wife and Big Nig standing up with them. We get the license for them yesterday afternoon. Can you imagine a couple of young saps wishing to wait until they go plumb around the world before getting married?"

Well, of course, this elopement creates much excitement for a few minutes, but by Monday Mr. and Mrs. Conde and the young folks and Madame La Gimp's sister take a train for California to keep on going around the world, leaving us nothing to talk about but about old Judge Henry G. Blake and Madame La Gimp getting themselves married, too, and going to Detroit where Judge Henry G. Blake claims he has a brother in the plumbing business who will give him a job, although personally I think Judge Henry G. Blake figures to do a little booting on his own hook in and out of Canada. It is not like Judge Henry G. Blake to tie himself up to the plumbing business.

So there is nothing more to the story, except that Dave the Dude is around a few days later with a big sheet of paper in his duke and very, very indignant.

"If every single article listed here is not kicked back to the owners of the different joints in the Marberry that they are taken from by next Tuesday night, I will bust a lot of noses around this town," Dave says. "I am greatly mortified by such happenings at my social affairs, and everything must be returned at once. Especially," Dave says, "the baby grand piano that is removed from Apartment 9-D."

One night I am standing in front of Mindy's restaurant on Broadway, thinking of practically nothing whatever, when all of a sudden I feel a very terrible pain in my left foot.

In fact, this pain is so very terrible that it causes me to leap up and down like a bullfrog, and to let out loud cries of agony, and to speak some very profane language, which is by no means my custom, although of course I recognize the pain as coming from a hot foot, because I often experience this pain before.

Furthermore, I know Joe the Joker must be in the neighborhood, as Joe the Joker has the most wonderful sense of humor of anybody in this town, and is always around giving people the hot foot, and gives it to me more times than I can remember. In fact, I hear Joe the Joker invents the hot foot, and it finally becomes a very popular idea all over the country.

The way you give a hot foot is to sneak up behind some guy who is standing around thinking of not much, and stick a paper match in his shoe between the sole and the upper along about where his little toe ought to be, and then light the match. By and by the guy will feel a terrible pain in his foot, and will start stamping around, and hollering, and carrying on generally, and it is always a most comical sight and a wonderful laugh to one and all to see him suffer.

No one in the world can give a hot foot as good as Joe the Joker, because it takes a guy who can sneak up very quiet on the guy who is to get the hot foot, and Joe can sneak up so quiet many guys on Broadway are willing to lay you odds that he can give a mouse a hot foot if you can find a mouse that wears shoes. Furthermore, Joe the Joker can take plenty of care of himself in case the guy who gets the hot foot feels like taking the matter up, which sometimes happens, especially with guys who get their shoes made to order at forty bobs per copy and do not care to have holes burned in these shoes.

But Joe does not care what kind of shoes the guys are wearing when he feels like giving out hot foots, and furthermore, he does not care who the guys are, although many citizens think he makes a mistake the time he gives a hot foot to Frankie Ferocious. In fact, many citizens are greatly horrified by this action, and go around saying no good will come of it.

This Frankie Ferocious comes from over in Brooklyn, where he is considered a rising citizen in many respects, and by no means a guy to give hot foots to, especially as Frankie Ferocious has no sense of humor whatever. In fact, he is always very solemn, and nobody ever sees him laugh, and he certainly does not laugh when Joe the Joker gives him a hot foot one day on Broadway when Frankie Ferocious is standing talking over a business matter with some guys from the Bronx.

He only scowls at Joe, and says something in Italian, and while I do not understand Italian, it sounds so unpleasant that I guarantee I will leave town inside of the next two hours if he says it to me.

Of course Frankie Ferocious's name is not really Ferocious, but something in Italian like Feroccio, and I hear he originally comes from Sicily, although he lives in Brooklyn for quite some years, and from a modest beginning he builds himself up until he is a very large operator in merchandise of one kind and another, especially alcohol. He is a big guy of maybe thirty-odd, and he has hair blacker than a yard up a chimney, and black eyes, and black eyebrows, and a slow way of looking at people.

Nobody knows a whole lot about Frankie Ferocious, because he never has much to say, and he takes his time saying it, but everybody gives him plenty of room when he comes around, as there are rumors that Frankie never likes to be crowded. As far as I am concerned, I do not care for any part of Frankie Ferocious, because his slow way of looking at people always makes me nervous, and I am always sorry Joe the Joker gives him a hot foot, because I figure Frankie Ferocious is bound to consider it a most disrespectful action, and hold it against everybody that lives on the Island of Manhattan.

But Joe the Joker only laughs when anybody tells him he is out of line in giving Frankie the hot foot, and says it is not his fault if Frankie has no sense of humor. Furthermore, Joe says he will not only give Frankie another hot foot if he gets a chance, but that he will give hot foots to the Prince of Wales or Mussolini, if he catches them in the right spot, although Regret, the horse player, states that Joe can have twenty to one anytime that he will not give Mussolini any hot foots and get away with it.

Anyway, just as I suspect, there is Joe the Joker watching me when I feel the hot foot, and he is laughing very heartily, and furthermore, a large number of other citizens are also laughing heartily, because Joe the Joker never sees any fun in giving people the hot foot unless others are present to enjoy the joke.

Well, naturally when I see who it is gives me the hot foot I join in the laughter, and go over and shake hands with Joe, and when I shake hands with him there is more laughter, because it seems Joe has a hunk of Limburger cheese in his duke, and what I shake hands with is this Limburger. Furthermore, it is some of Mindy's Limburger cheese, and everybody knows Mindy's Limburger is very squashy, and also very loud.

Of course I laugh at this, too, although to tell the truth I will laugh much more heartily if Joe the Joker drops dead in front of me, because I do not like to be made the subject of laughter on Broadway. But my laugh is really quite hearty when Joe takes the rest of the cheese that is not on my fingers and smears it on the steering wheels of some automobiles parked in front of Mindy's, because I get to thinking of what the drivers will say when they start steering their cars.

Then I get talking to Joe the Joker, and I ask him how things are up in Harlem, where Joe and his younger brother, Freddy, and several other guys have a small organization operating in beer, and Joe says things are as good as can be expected considering business conditions. Then I ask him how Rosa is getting along, this Rosa being Joe the Joker's ever-loving wife, and a personal friend of mine, as I know her when she is Rosa Midnight and is singing in the old Hot Box before Joe hauls off and marries her.

Well, at this question Joe the Joker starts laughing, and I can see that something appeals to his sense of humor, and finally he speaks as follows:

"Why," he says, "do you not hear the news about Rosa? She takes the wind on me a couple of months ago for my friend Frankie Ferocious, and is living in an apartment over in Brooklyn, right near his house, although," Joe says, "of course you understand I am telling you this only to answer your question, and not to holler copper on Rosa."

Then he lets out another large ha-ha, and in fact Joe the Joker keeps laughing until I am afraid he will injure himself internally. Personally, I do not see anything comical in a guy's ever-loving wife taking the wind on him for a guy like Frankie Ferocious, so when Joe the Joker quiets down a bit I ask him what is funny about the proposition.

"Why," Joe says, "I have to laugh every time I think of how the big greaseball is going to feel when he finds out how expensive Rosa is. I do not know how many things Frankie Ferocious has running for him in Brooklyn," Joe says, "but he better try to move himself in on the mint if he wishes to keep Rosa going."

Then he laughs again, and I consider it wonderful the way Joe is able to keep his sense of humor even in such a situation as this, although up to this time I always think Joe is very daffy indeed about Rosa, who is a little doll, weighing maybe ninety pounds with her hat on and quite cute.

Now I judge from what Joe the Joker tells me that Frankie Ferocious knows Rosa before Joe marries her and is always pitching to her when she is singing in the Hot Box, and even after she is Joe's ever-loving wife, Frankie occasionally calls her up, especially when he commences to be a rising citizen of Brooklyn, although of course Joe does not learn about these calls until later. And about the time Frankie Ferocious commences to be a rising citizen of Brooklyn, things begin breaking a little tough for Joe the Joker, what with the depression and all, and he has to economize on Rosa in spots, and if there is one thing Rosa cannot stand it is being economized on.

Along about now, Joe the Joker gives Frankie Ferocious the hot foot, and just as many citizens state at the time, it is a mistake, for Frankie starts calling Rosa up more than somewhat, and speaking of what a nice place Brooklyn is to live in—which it is, at that—and between these boosts for Brooklyn and Joe the Joker's economy, Rosa hauls off and takes a subway to Borough Hall, leaving Joe a note telling him that if he does not like it he knows what he can do.

"Well, Joe," I say, after listening to his story, "I always hate to hear of these little domestic difficulties among my friends, but maybe this is all for the best. Still, I feel sorry for you, if it will do you any good," I say.

"Do not feel sorry for me," Joe says. "If you wish to feel sorry for anybody, feel sorry for Frankie Ferocious, and," he says, "if you can spare a little more sorrow, give it to Rosa."

And Joe the Joker laughs very hearty again and starts telling me about a little scatter that he has up in Harlem where he keeps a chair fixed up with electric wires so he can give anybody that sits down in it a nice jolt, which sounds very humorous to me, at that, especially when Joe tells me how they turn on too much juice one night and almost kill Commodore Jake.

Finally Joe says he has to get back to Harlem, but first he goes to the telephone in the corner cigar store and calls up Mindy's and imitates a doll's voice, and tells Mindy he is Peggy Joyce, or somebody, and orders fifty dozen sandwiches sent up at once to an apartment in West Seventy-second Street for a birthday party, although of course there is no such number as he gives, and nobody there will wish fifty dozen sandwiches if there is such a number.

Then Joe gets in his car and starts off, and while he is waiting for the traffic lights at Fiftieth Street, I see citizens on the sidewalks making sudden leaps, and looking around very fierce, and I know Joe the Joker is plugging them with pellets made out of tinfoil, which he fires from a rubber band hooked between his thumb and forefinger.

Joe the Joker is very expert with this proposition, and it is very funny to see the citizens jump, although once or twice in his life Joe makes a miscue and knocks out somebody's eye. But it is all in fun, and shows you what a wonderful sense of humor Joe has.

Well, a few days later I see by the papers where a couple of Harlem guys Joe the Joker is mobbed up with are found done up in sacks over in Brooklyn, very dead indeed, and the coppers say it is because they are trying to move in on certain business enterprises that belong to nobody but Frankie Ferocious. But of course the coppers do not say Frankie Ferocious puts these guys in the sacks, because in the first place Frankie will report them to Headquarters if the coppers say such a thing about him, and in the second place putting guys in sacks is strictly a St. Louis idea and to have a guy put in a sack properly you have to send to St. Louis for experts in this matter.

Now, putting a guy in a sack is not as easy as it sounds, and in fact it takes quite a lot of practice and experience. To put a guy in a sack properly, you first have to put him to sleep, because naturally no guy is going to walk into a sack wide awake unless he is a plumb sucker. Some people claim the best way to put a guy to sleep is to give him a sleeping powder of some kind in a drink, but the real experts just tap the guy on the noggin with a blackjack, which saves the expense of buying the drink.

Anyway, after the guy is asleep, you double him up like a pocketknife, and tie a cord or a wire around his neck and under his knees. Then you put him in a gunnysack, and leave him someplace, and by and by when the guy wakes up and finds himself in the sack, naturally he wants to get out and the first thing he does is to try to straighten out his knees. This pulls the cord around his neck up so tight that after a while the guy is all out of breath.

So then when somebody comes along and opens the sack they find the guy dead, and nobody is responsible for this unfortunate situation, because after all the guy really commits suicide, because if he does not try to straighten out his knees he may live to a ripe old age, if he recovers from the tap on the noggin.

Well, a couple of days later I see by the papers where three Brooklyn citizens are scragged as they are walking peaceably along Clinton Street, the scragging being done by some parties in an automobile who seem to have a machine gun, and the papers state that the citizens are friends of Frankie Ferocious, and that it is rumored the parties with the machine gun are from Harlem.

I judge by this that there is some trouble in Brooklyn, especially as about a week after the citizens are scragged in Clinton Street, another Harlem guy is found done up in a sack like a Virginia ham near Prospect Park, and now who is it but Joe the Joker's brother, Freddy, and I know Joe is going to be greatly displeased by this.

By and by it gets so nobody in Brooklyn will open as much as a sack of potatoes without first calling in the gendarmes, for fear a pair of No. 8 shoes will jump out at them.

Now one night I see Joe the Joker, and this time he is all alone, and I wish to say I am willing to leave him all alone, because something tells me he is hotter than a stove. But he grabs me as I am going past, so naturally I stop to talk to him, and the first thing I say is how sorry I am about his brother.

"Well," Joe the Joker says, "Freddy is always a kind of a sap. Rosa calls him up and asks him to come over to Brooklyn to see her. She wishes to talk to Freddy about getting me to give her a divorce," Joe says, "so she can marry Frankie Ferocious, I suppose. Anyway," he says, "Freddy tells Commodore Jake why he is going to see her. Freddy always likes Rosa, and thinks maybe he can patch it up between us. So," Joe says, "he winds up in a sack. They get him after he leaves her apartment. I do not claim Rosa will ask him to come over if she has any idea he will be sacked," Joe says, "but," he says, "she is responsible. She is a bad-luck doll."

Then he starts to laugh, and at first I am greatly horrified, thinking it is because something about Freddy being sacked strikes his sense of humor, when he says to me, like this:

"Say," he says, "I am going to play a wonderful joke on Frankie Ferocious."

"Well, Joe," I say, "you are not asking me for advice, but I am going to give you some free, gratis, and for nothing. Do not play any jokes on Frankie Ferocious, as I hear he has no more sense of humor than a nanny goat. I hear Frankie Ferocious will not laugh if you have Al Jolson, Eddie Cantor, Ed Wynn and Joe Cook telling him jokes all at once. In fact," I say, "I hear he is a tough audience."

"Oh," Joe the Joker says, "he must have some sense of humor somewhere to stand for Rosa. I hear he is daffy about her. In fact, I understand she is the only person in the world he really likes, and trusts. But I must play a joke on him. I am going to have myself delivered to Frankie Ferocious in a sack."

Well, of course I have to laugh at this myself, and Joe the Joker laughs with me. Personally, I am laughing just at the idea of anybody having themselves delivered to Frankie Ferocious in a sack, and especially Joe the Joker, but of course I have no idea Joe really means what he says.

"Listen," Joe says, finally. "A guy from St. Louis who is a friend of mine is doing most of the sacking for Frankie Ferocious. His name is Ropes McGonnigle. In fact," Joe says, "he is a very dear old pal of mine, and he has a wonderful sense of humor like me. Ropes McGonnigle has nothing whatever to do with sacking Freddy," Joe says, "and he is very indignant about it since he finds out Freddy is my brother, so he is anxious to help me play a joke on Frankie.

"Only last night," Joe says, "Frankie Ferocious sends for Ropes and tells him he will appreciate it as a special favor if Ropes will bring me to him in a sack. I suppose," Joe says, "that Frankie Ferocious hears from Rosa what Freddy is bound to tell her about my ideas on divorce. I have very strict ideas on divorce," Joe says, "especially where Rosa is concerned. I will see her in what's-this before I ever do her and Frankie Ferocious such a favor as giving her a divorce.

"Anyway," Joe the Joker says, "Ropes tells me about Frankie Ferocious propositioning him, so I send Ropes back to Frankie Ferocious to tell him he knows I am to be in Brooklyn tomorrow night, and furthermore, Ropes tells Frankie that he will have me in a sack in no time. And so he will," Joe says.

"Well," I say, "personally, I see no percentage in being delivered to Frankie Ferocious in a sack, because as near as I can make out from what I read in the papers, there is no future for a guy in a sack that goes to Frankie Ferocious. What I cannot figure out," I say, "is where the joke on Frankie comes in."

"Why," Joe the Joker says, "the joke is, I will not be asleep in the sack, and my hands will not be tied, and in each of my hands I will have a John Roscoe, so when the sack is delivered to Frankie Ferocious and I pop out blasting away, can you not imagine his astonishment?"

Well, I can imagine this, all right. In fact when I get to thinking of the look of surprise that is bound to come to Frankie Ferocious's face when Joe the Joker comes out of the sack I have to laugh, and Joe the Joker laughs right along with me.

"Of course," Joe says, "Ropes McGonnigle will be there to start blasting with me, in case Frankie Ferocious happens to have any company."

Then Joe the Joker goes on up the street, leaving me still laughing, from thinking of how amazed Frankie Ferocious will be when Joe bounces out of the sack and starts throwing slugs around and about. I do not hear of Joe from that time to this, but I hear the rest of the story from very reliable parties.

It seems that Ropes McGonnigle does not deliver the sack himself, after all, but sends it by an expressman to Frankie Ferocious's home.

Frankie Ferocious receives many sacks such as this in his time, because it seems that it is a sort of passion with him to personally view
the contents of the sacks and check up on them before they are
distributed about the city, and of course Ropes McGonnigle knows
about this passion from doing so much sacking for Frankie.

When the expressman takes the sack into Frankie's house, Frankie
personally lugs it down into his basement, and there he outs with a
big John Roscoe and fires six shots into the sack, because it seems
Ropes McGonnigle tips him off to Joe the Joker's plan to pop out of
the sack and start blasting.

I hear Frankie Ferocious has a very strange expression on his pan
and is laughing the only laugh anybody ever hears from him when
the gendarmes break in and put the arm on him for murder, because
it seems that when Ropes McGonnigle tells Frankie of Joe the Joker's
plan, Frankie tells Ropes what he is going to do with his own hands
before opening the sack. Naturally, Ropes speaks to Joe the Joker of
Frankie's idea about filling the sack full of slugs, and Joe's sense of
humor comes right out again.

So, bound and gagged, but otherwise as right as rain in the sack
that is delivered to Frankie Ferocious, is by no means Joe the Joker,
but Rosa.

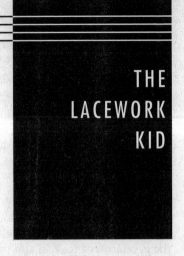

THE
LACEWORK
KID

Now, of course, the war·makes itself felt along Broadway no little and quite some and in fact it is a most disturbing element at times as it brings many strangers to the city who crowd Mindy's restaurant to the doors and often compel the old-time regular customers to stand in line waiting for tables, which is a very great hardship, indeed.

It does no good to complain to Mindy about this situation as he is making so much money he is practically insolent and he only asks you if you do not know there is a war going on, and besides Mindy is generally waiting for a table himself.

Well, one evening I am fortunate enough to outcute everyone else for a chair that is the only vacant chair at a little table for two and the other chair is occupied by a soldier, and who is this soldier but a guy by the name of The Lacework Kid who is eating as if Hitler is coming up Broadway.

Now The Lacework Kid, who is generally called Lace for short, is a personality who is maybe thirty years old but looks younger and is a card player by trade. Furthermore he is considered one of the best that ever riffles a deck. In fact, he comes by his monicker because someone once remarks that his work with the cards is as delicate as lace, although personally I consider this an understatement.

He comes from the city of Providence which is in Rhode Island, and of course it is well known to one and all that for generations Providence produces wonderful cardplayers, and in his childhood The Lacework Kid has the advantage of studying under the best minds there, and afterward improves his education in this respect by much travel.

Before the war he is a great hand for riding the tubs and makes regular trips back and forth across the Atlantic Ocean because a guy in his line can always find more customers on the boats than anywhere else and can also do very good for himself by winning the pools on the ship's daily run if he can make the proper connections to get the information on the run in advance.

I only wish you can see The Lacework Kid before the war when he is at the height of his career. He is maybe five feet nine and very slender and has brown eyes and wavy brown hair and a face like a choirboy and a gentle voice.

He wears the best clothes money can buy and they are always of soft quiet materials and his linen is always white and his shoes black. He wears no jewelry showing, but he carries a little gold watch in his pants pockets that stands him a G-er in Paris and a gold cigarette box that sets him back a gob in the same place.

He has long slim white hands like a society broad and in fact there is no doubt that his hands are the secret of The Lacework Kid's success at his trade of card playing as they are fast and flexible and have youth in them, and youth is one thing a good cardplayer must have, because age stiffens up more than somewhat. But of course age is a drawback in everything in this wicked old world.

It is really a beautiful sight to watch The Lacework Kid handle a deck of cards because he makes the pasteboards just float together when he is shuffling and causes them to fall as light as flecks of foam when he is dealing. His specialty is a game called bridge when he is riding the tubs and he is seldom without customers because in the first place he does not look like a guy who can play bridge very well and in the second place he does not appear to be such a personality as the signs in the smoking rooms on the boats refer to when they say "Beware of Card Sharks." In fact The Lacework Kid generally tries to get a chair right under one of these signs to show that it cannot possibly mean him.

I see The Lacework Kid a few years before this night in Mindy's when he just gets in on a German liner and he has a guy by the name of Schultz with him and is entertaining this Schultz royally because it seems Schultz is the smoking room steward on the liner and is The Lacework Kid's connection in winning the pools and in introducing bridge customers to him and putting him away with them as a rich young American zillionaire and as the trip nets Lace two thou on the pools alone he feels quite grateful to Schultz.

But of course this is before there is any war and later when I see him the unpleasantness is on and no liners are running and Lace tells me his trade is the greatest economic casualty of the whole war, and he is wondering if there is any use trying to ride the submarines back and forth looking for customers.

And now here he is again as large as life and in fact slightly larger as I can see he puts on a little weight and he looks very good in his uniform and has a red ribbon on his chest, so I say to him like this:

"Lace," I say, "it is indeed a pleasure to run into you and I can see by your uniform that you are in the war business and by your ribbon that you distinguish yourself in some manner. Perhaps you are decorated for dealing the general a nice hand off the bottom?"

Well, at this, The Lacework Kid gives me a most severe look and says:

"It is a Good Conduct Medal. I get it for being a fine soldier. I may get an even better award for an experience I will now relate to you."

I will omit the details of my early career in the Army (The Lacework Kid says) except to tell you that my comrades know me only as Sergeant Fortescue Melville Michael O'Shay, my mama getting the first two names out of a novel she is reading at the time I am born, and my papa's papa bringing the last two over from Ireland.

Furthermore, they know nothing of my background and while there are occasions when I am greatly tempted to make assessments against them out of my great store of knowledge when they are playing such trifling games as blackjack, I resist the urge and confine myself strictly to the matter in hand, which is the war.

I am the waist gunner in a Flying Fortress on a raid over Germany one pleasant afternoon when our ship is so severely jostled by anti-aircraft shells that we are compelled to bail out and no sooner do I land then up come three German soldiers with rifles in their dukes.

They point these rifles at me in a most disquieting manner and while I only know a word or two of the German language I can see that I am their prisoner and the next thing I know I am in a prison camp where I find my comrades and also several hundred other gees who seem to be British and one thing and another.

It is not a large camp and in fact I learn that it is just a sort of temporary detention spot for prisoners who are rounded up in this particular section of the country and that they are usually transferred to a larger gaff after a while. It is located in a hilly country not far from the Swiss border and you can see high mountains in the distance that I am told are the Alps.

But even with the view it is by no means a desirable place. The life in this camp is most monotonous and the cuisine is worse, which is a terrible disappointment to me as I am rather fond of German cooking, and particularly adore the apple strudel of this race, and the chow they give us makes me more violently anti-Nazi than ever and also gives me indigestion. To tell the truth, I spend most of my time trying to figure a way to escape though they tell me that if I am patient I will sooner or later be exchanged for a German prisoner.

There is a company of maybe a hundred German soldiers guarding the camp and I am only there a few hours before I learn that the officer who is in charge of the joint is a captain by the name of Kunz, and that he is also sometimes called The Butcher because it seems that in the early days of the war he is in command of an outfit in Poland and thinks nothing of killing people right and left for no reason whatever except he enjoys seeing them die.

But it seems he finally gets himself in bad with his boss and is sent to this little out-of-the-way prison camp as a lesson to him and he runs the place like the tough warden of a stir back home though he does not show up much in person around the camp and in fact I never see him myself until the time I am going to tell you about.

One afternoon a German sergeant comes into the prison yard, where I am taking a little exercise and beckons me off to one side and I am somewhat surprised to observe that the sergeant is nobody but Schultz the steward, who speaks to me in a low voice as follows:

"Hello, Lace," he says. "How is everything?"

"Schultz," I say, "everything stinks."

"Lace," he says, "what do you know about something American that is called gin rummy?"

"Gin rummy?" I say. "Why I know it is supposed to be a card game but as a matter of fact it is nothing but a diversion for idiots."

"Are you a gin rummy man?" Schultz says. "I mean do you play the game?"

"Schultz," I say, "nearly everybody in the United States of America plays gin rummy. The little children in the street play it. Old broads play it. I understand there is a trained ape in the Bronx Zoo that plays it very nicely and I am not surprised, because," I say, "I can teach any dumb animal to play gin rummy if I can get it to hold ten cards."

"Well," Schultz says, "what I am getting at is do you play it as well as you play bridge and in the same way? What I must know is are you a mechanic at gin? I mean if necessary?"

Well naturally I am slightly vexed by this question as I consider it an insult to my integrity as well as a reflection upon my card playing to even hint that I do anything in cards except outplay my opponents through my superior skill. To tell the truth, I feel it is just the same as asking Joe Louis if he uses the difference in his gloves when he is meeting a chump.

"Schultz," I say, "you are undoubtedly a scoundrel to always be thinking in terms of larceny. I never swindle anybody at anything despite any rumors to the contrary that you may hear. And I never hear of any swindles in gin rummy except planting a guy who is supposed to have a piece of your opponent's play alongside him to tip off his cards to you.

"But," I say, "I consider this a low form of thievery. However, Schultz," I say, "I will be guilty of false modesty if I do not admit to you that like all gin players I think I am the best. In fact, I know of but one who can beat me consistently at gin and that is Kidneyfoot, the waiter in Mindy's, but then he teaches me the game and naturally figures to top me slightly."

Well, then this Schultz unfolds a very strange tale to me. He says that when Captain Kunz is in the United States for some years before the war as an attaché of the German embassy in Washington, he learns the game of gin rummy and it becomes a great passion with him.

It seems from what Schultz says that after Kunz returns to Germany, he misses his gin rummy no little as the game is practically unknown in his country where cardplayers generally favor pinochle or maybe klabriasch. It seems that Kunz tries to teach some of his countrymen how to play gin but has little success and anyway the war comes on and promoting an American game will be deemed unpatriotic, so he has to cease his efforts in this direction.

But he cannot stop thinking of gin, so he finally invents a sort of solitaire gin and plays it constantly all by himself, but it is most unsatisfactory and when he hears of American prisoners arriving in his camp, he sends for Schultz and asks him to canvass us and see if there are any gin rummy players in the crowd. And in looking us over, Schultz spots me.

"Now," Schultz says, "I build you up to the captain as the champion gin player of the United States, and he finally tells me the other night that he wishes to play you if it can be done in secret, as of course it will be very bad for morale if it gets out that the commandant of a prison camp engages in card games with a prisoner. The captain is rich and likes to play for high stakes, too," Schultz says.

"Look, Schultz," I say, "I do not have any moolouw with me here. All my potatoes are planted in a jug in England and I do not suppose the captain will accept notes of hand payable there."

"Listen," Schultz says, dropping his voice to a whisper, "I tell all my fellow soldiers here about your gin playing, and how you are so clever you can make a jack jump out of a deck and sing Chattanooga Choo-Choo if necessary, and we all agree to pool our resources to provide you with a taw. We can raise maybe fifty thousand marks. But," Schultz says, "you must not breathe a word of this to your comrades. The captain must think they are the ones who are backing you. You will receive twenty-five percent of your winnings, and I will personally guarantee your end."

Naturally, I figure Schultz is giving me the old rol-de-dol-dol for some reason because it does not make sense that an officer in the German army will wish to play an American prisoner gin rummy, but then I remember that gin players will do anything to play gin and I figure that maybe the captain is like the old faro bank player who is warned as he is going into a gambling house to beware of the bank game there because it is crooked and who says:

"Yes, I know it is, but what am I going to do? It is the only game in town."

Well, of course this is an ancient story to you and you will kindly forgive me for springing it at this time, but I am trying to explain the psychology of this captain as I see it. Anyway, I tell Schultz to go ahead and arrange the game and in the meantime I get a deck of cards and practice to refresh my memory.

Now, one night Schultz shows up at my quarters and tells me to come with him and he says it in such a stern voice and acts so mysterious that everyone figures I am being taken out to be shot and to tell you the truth I am not so sure myself that this is not the case. But when we get away from the other prisoners, Schultz is quite nice to me.

He takes me outside the gates of the prison camp and we walk along a road about a mile when we come to a small house set back from the road in a grove of trees and Schultz stops in front of this house and speaks to me as follows:

"Lace," he says, "in the course of your playing with the captain kindly do not refer to our people as krauts, pretzels, beerheads, Heinies, Boches, sausages, wienies or by the titles of any other members of the vegetable or animal kingdom, and do not tell him what you Americans are going to do to us. It will only make for an unfriendly atmosphere, and his replies may distract you from your gin. He understands English, so please be discreet in every respect."

Then he hands me a roll of German marks a steeplechase horse will be unable to hurdle and leads the way into the house, and by this time I figure out what the scamus is. I figure that Schultz pegs me for a bleater, and the captain is going to try to get some information out of me and, in fact, I am looking for a touch of the old third degree from the Gestapo.

But on entering the house, which seems to be very plainly furnished, the only person present is a big guy in uniform with a lot of gongs on his chest, which is a way of saying medals, and whose head is shaved like Eric von Stroheim's in a Nazi picture. He is sitting at a table in front of a burning fireplace fooling with a deck of cards.

Schultz introduces me to him, but the guy only nods and motions me to sit down at the table opposite him and tosses the deck of cards to me. I examine the backs carefully to see if they are marked, but they seem strictly kosher in every way, and then I say to Captain Kunz like this:

"Captain," I say, "let us understand one thing. I am a noncommissioned officer, and you outrank me from hell to breakfast time, but in this game you must not take advantage of your rank in any way, shape, manner or form, to intimidate me. We will play New York rules, with gins and undercuts to count twenty each and blitzes double."

Kunz nods and motions me to cut the cards for the deal, and he wins it and away we go. We play three games at once and as soon as both of us are on all three games, we start another frame of three, with Schultz keeping score, and it is not long before we have as many as three frames or nine games going at once, which makes a very fast contest, indeed. We are playing for a hundred marks a game or three hundred marks across, which Schultz tells me is about a hundred and twenty dollars in my money, the way the Germans figure their marks.

I will not attempt to describe gin rummy in detail as you can call up any insane asylum and get any patient on the phone and learn all about it in no time, as all lunatics are bound to be gin players, and in fact the chances are it is gin rummy that makes them lunatics. Furthermore, I will not bore you with my philosophy of the game, but I say it is ninety-five percent luck and five percent play, and the five percent is the good cardplayer's strength in the pinches, if there are any pinches.

The cards in gin rummy run hot and cold the same as the dice in a crap game. It is by no means necessary to go to Harvard to learn to play gin and in fact a moron is apt to play it better than Einstein. If you get the tickets in gin, you are a genius, and if you do not get them, you are a bum. When they do not come, you can only sit and suffer, and the aggravation of waiting on cards that never arrive will give you stomach ulcers in no time.

Well, I can see at once that Captain Kunz plays as good a game of gin as anybody can play and he also has good regulation dialogue, such as "This is the worst hand I ever see in my life," and "I only need one little card from the draw to get down," and so forth and so on, but he delivers his dialogue in German and then Schultz translates it for me as it seems the captain does not care to address me direct in English, which I consider very snobbish of him.

About the only word he says I can understand is *frischer* when he picks up a bad hand and wishes to know if I am agreeable to a fresh deal, which is a courtesy a gin player sometimes extends if he also has a bad hand, though personally I am opposed to *frischers*. In fact, when I get a bad hand, I play the Pittsburgh Muddle system on Kunz, which is to pick up every card he discards whether I need it or not and then throw it back at him when my hand improves, the idea being to confuse your opponent and make him hold cards that gum up his hand.

Well, I get my rushes right away and win the first frame and am going so strong on the second that Kunz gets up and peels his coat down to a pair of pink suspenders and ten minutes later he drops the suspenders off his shoulders and opens his waistband. In the meantime, Schultz kibitzes the captain on one hand and me on the next, and of course a kibitzer is entitled to present his views on a play after it is over, and Schultz is undoubtedly a real kibitzer and becomes quite excited at times in his comment.

However, once he is very bitter in his criticism of a play that costs the captain a game, and Kunz turns on him like a wolf and bawls him out and scares Schultz silly. But later the captain apologizes because as a gin player he is bound to respect the right of a kibitzer.

I keep waiting for Kunz to slip in questions to me about our Air Force and one thing and another, but he never makes a remark that is not in connection with the game and finally I can see that my suspicions are unfounded and that he is nothing but a gin player after all.

Well, daylight is coming through the windows of the house when the captain says we must knock off playing, and Schultz must hurry me back to camp, and I am somewhat startled to realize that I am four hundred marks loser which I whip out and pay immediately. Furthermore, Schultz is terribly depressed by this situation and all the way back to the camp he keeps telling me how I disappoint him in not winning and asking me what becomes of my mechanics, and finally I get sore and speak to him as follows:

"Schultz," I say, "the guy is not only better than a raw hand at gin but he also outlucks me. And I tell you I do not know of any mechanics in gin rummy and if you do not care to trust to my superior skill to finally prevail, you can call it all off now."

Then Schultz cools down a little and says maybe I will do better next time, but I judge his disappointment is communicated to the other German soldiers as they seem very crusty with me all day though my greatest trouble is standing off the questions of my own gang about my absence.

Well, Schultz is around after me again that night to take me to the house in the grove, and in fact every night for a month hand-running I play the captain and it is not long before I am beating him like breaking sticks. And every night the captain pays off like a slot machine and every day I turn my dough over to Schultz and he pays me twenty-five percent and then distributes the balance among the guys in his syndicate.

Naturally, I stand first-class with all the Jerries who are in on the play and they also become more pleasant toward my comrades and finally I tell these comrades what is going on and while they are greatly amused I can see that they are also greatly relieved, because it seems they are troubled by my nightly absences from the camp and are glad to learn that it is only for the purpose of playing gin with the enemy.

At the end of the month and basing my estimate on a round ten thousand marks I have stashed away, I figure I am forty thousand marks winner on Kunz. Then one night I beat him for a thousand marks and he does not whip it out as usual but says something in German to Schultz, and Schultz tells me the captain says he forgets his wallet somewhere, and I say all right, but that it is only fair for him to give me a scratch for the dough.

Schultz translates this to the captain, who looks very angry and seems to be highly insulted, but finally he outs with a notebook and scribbles an I.O.U., because, of course, at this stage of my life I am not trusting anyone and especially a Nazi.

He settles the next night before we start playing, but he takes a good bath this time and gives me the finger again, and while he comes alive the following night, this continues to happen again and again, and something tells me that Kunz is troubled with the shorts. When I mention this suspicion to Schultz, he seems a trifle uneasy and finally he says:

"Well, Lace," he says, "I fear you are right. I fear our good captain is in over his head. To tell the truth, your game is commencing to bore me and the other soldiers of the Fatherland no little because the captain borrows money from us every day, which is a terrible thing for a high officer to do to the soldiers of his command, and, while you win it back for us promptly, we now fear he will never replace the principal."

"Why, Schultz," I say, "do you not tell me that the captain is richer than six feet down in Mississippi mud?"

"Yes," Schultz says, "and he keeps talking of his properties in Berlin, but we are nonetheless uneasy. And the worst thing about it is that your twenty-five percent is eating up all the funds in circulation. It is a vicious circle. Lace," Schultz says, "can you spare me a couple of thou? I must send something to my frau and I will repay you when the boats get to running again."

"Schultz," I say, "your story smacks of corn because I do not believe you have a wife and, if you do have one you will never be sending her money. But," I say, "I will advance you a thousand marks for old times' sake on your marker."

So I weed him the thousand and accept his Kathleen Mavourneen, which is a promise to pay that may be for years and may be forever, and the reason I do this is because I am by no means certain that Schultz may not incite his fellow soldiers to gang up and deprive me of my hard-earned twenty-five percent by force, if he can find out where I have it carefully buried. To tell the truth, I do not repose great confidence in Schultz.

Well, that night I beat Kunz for twelve hundred marks, and he pays me five hundred on account, and as Schultz and I are getting ready to leave, he says something in German to Schultz, and when we are on our way back to camp, Schultz tells me he has to return to the house and see the captain, and then I really commence to worry because I fear the two may get their heads together and plot against my well-being.

But as far as Captain Kunz is concerned, my worry is groundless as along toward noon of this same day, we hear a rumor that he commits suicide by shooting himself smack-dab through the head and this causes so much excitement that our guards forget to lock us in that night or even to watch us carefully, and all of us Americans and some of the British walk out of the gates and scatter over the countryside, and most of us reach safety in Switzerland, and I afterward hear there is quite a scandal in German circles about the matter.

But before we go, I have a slight chat with Schultz and say to him like this:

"Schultz," I say, "tell me all."

"Well," Schultz says, "I know that when the captain asks me to return to the house after taking you back to camp, he wishes to borrow the money I get from you to play you again tonight, because when I tell him yesterday I am personally broke and cannot advance him any more, he is the one who suggests I approach you for a touch and in fact he threatens to make trouble for me over certain matters that transpire in Poland if I fail to do so.

"So," Schultz says, "when I reach the house, I first peer through a window into the living room and see the captain still sitting at the table with the deck of cards you use spread out before him as if he is examining them, and all of a sudden, I am seized with a terrible fury at the thought that he is waiting there to take my money to gamble it away frivolously, and an impulse that I cannot restrain causes me to out with my pistol and give it to him through the window and also through the onion.

"And," Schultz says, "I will always remember how the blood drips down off the table and splatters over the nine of diamonds that is lying on the floor under your chair and how it comes to my mind that the nine of diamonds is considered a very unlucky card indeed and how fortune-tellers say it is a sign of death. It is a great coincidence," Schultz says, "considering the number of times you catch the captain with big counts in his hands when he is waiting for that very nine."

"Ah," I say, "I figure you have something to do with his demise."

"But," Schultz says, "as far as anyone but you and me know, it is suicide because I also have the presence of mind to fire one shot from his pistol which is the same make as mine, and leave it in his hand. It is suicide because of despondency, which his superior officers say is probably because he learns of his impending purge."

"Schultz," I say, "you are bound to come to a bad end but now good-bye."

"Good-bye," Schultz says. "Oh, yes," he says. "Maybe I ought to state that I am also prompted to my act by the fear that the captain will finally find the nine of diamonds on the floor, that you forget to retrieve when you leave him this morning."

"What do you mean, Schultz?" I say.

"Good-bye," Schultz says.

And this is all there is to the story (The Lacework Kid says).

"Well, Lace," I say, "it is all very exciting, and it must be nice to be back on Broadway as free as the birds and with all that moolouw you collect as your twenty-five percent in your pants pockets."

"Oh," Lace says, "I do not return with a white quarter. You see I use all my end to bribe Schultz and the rest of the German soldiers to leave the doors and gates unlocked that night and to be looking the other way when we depart."

Then The Lacework Kid leaves, and I am sitting there finishing my boiled yellow pike, which is a very tasty dish, indeed, and thinking about the captain's blood dripping on the nine of diamonds, when who comes up but old Kidneyfoot the waiter, who is called by this name because he walks as if he has kidneys in both feet and who points to Lace going out the door and says to me like this:

"Well," Kidneyfoot says, "there goes a great artist. He is one of the finest cardplayers I ever see except in gin rummy. It is strange how this simple game baffles all good cardplayers. In fact," Kidneyfoot says, "The Lacework Kid is a rank sucker at gin until I instruct him in one maneuver that gives you a great advantage, which is to drop any one card to the floor accidentally on purpose."

One evening in the summer of 1936 I am passing in front of Mindy's restaurant on Broadway when the night manager suddenly opens the door and throws a character in a brown suit at me.

Fortunately, the character just misses me, and hits a yellow short that is standing at the curb, and dents a mudguard, because he is a little character, and the night manager of Mindy's can throw that kind with an incurve.

Naturally, I am greatly vexed, and I am thinking of stepping into Mindy's and asking the night manager how dare he hurl missiles of this nature at me, when I remember that the night manager does not care for me, either, and in fact he hates me from head to foot, and does not permit me in Mindy's except on Fridays, because of course he does not have the heart to keep me from enjoying my chicken soup with matzoth dumplings once a week.

So I let the incident pass, and watch the jockey of the yellow short nail the character in the brown suit with a left hook that knocks him right under my feet, and then, as he gets up and dusts himself off with his hands and starts up the street, I see that he is nobody but a character by the name of Asleep, who is called by this name because he always goes around with his eyes half closed, and looking as if he is dozing off.

Well, here is a spectacle that really brings tears to my eyes, as I can remember when just a few years back the name of Asleep strikes terror to the hearts of one and all on Broadway, and everywhere else in this town for that matter, because in those days he is accounted one of the greatest characters in his line in the world, and in fact he is generally regarded as a genius.

Asleep's line is taking care of anybody that somebody wishes taken care of, and at one time he is the highest-priced character in the business. For several years along in the late twenties, he handles all of the late Dave the Dude's private business when Dave the Dude is at war with the late Big Moey, and when somebody finally takes care of Dave the Dude himself, Asleep is with Moey for quite a while.

In six or seven years, the chances are Asleep takes care of scores of characters of one kind and another, and he never looks for any publicity or glory. In fact, he is always a most retiring character, who goes about very quietly, minding his own affairs, and those who know him think very well of him indeed.

The bladders print many unkind stories about Asleep when he is finally lumbered in 1931 and sent to college, and some of them call him a torpedo, and a trigger, and I do not know what all else, and these names hurt Asleep's feelings, especially as they seem to make him out no better than a ruffian. In fact, one bladder speaks of him as a killer, and this title causes Asleep to wince more than anything else.

He is in college at Dannemora from 1931 until the late spring of 1936, and although I hear he is back, this is the first time I see him in person, and I hasten to overtake him to express my sympathy with him on his treatment by the night manager of Mindy's and also by the jockey of the yellow short, and to deplore the lack of respect now shown on Broadway for a character such as Asleep.

He seems glad to see me, and he accepts my expressions gratefully, and we go into the Bridle Grill and have a couple of drinks and then Asleep says to me like this:

"I only go into Mindy's seeking a situation," he says. "I hear Benny Barker, the bookie, is in there, and I understand that he has a disagreement with another bookie by the name of Jersey Cy down at Aqueduct, and that Jersey Cy punches Benny's beezer for him. So," Asleep says, "I figure Benny will wish to have Cy taken care of immediately and that it will be a nice quick pickup for me, because in the old days when Benny is a bootie, he is one of my best customers.

"It is the first time I see Benny since I get back," Asleep says, "but instead of being glad to see me, he seems very distant to me, and the minute I begin canvassing him for the business, he turns as white as one of Mindy's napkins, and in fact whiter, and says for me to get out of there, or he will call the law.

"Benny says he will never even dream of such a thing as having anybody taken care of, and," Asleep says, "when I start to remind him of a couple of incidents back down the years, he carries on in a way you will never believe. I even offer to cut my fee for him," Asleep says, "but Benny only gets more excited, and keeps yelling no, no, no, until the night manager appears, and you see for yourself what happens to me. I am publicly embarrassed," he says.

"Well, Sleeps," I say, "to tell the truth, I am somewhat amazed that you do not out with that thing and resent these familiarities."

But Asleep seems somewhat horrified at this suggestion, and he sets his glass down, and gazes at me a while in pained silence, and finally he says:

"Why," he says, "I hope and trust that you do not think I will ever use that thing except for professional purposes, and when I am paid for same. Why," he says, "in all my practice, covering a matter of nearly ten years, I never lift a finger against as much as a flea unless it is a business proposition, and I am not going to begin now."

Well, I remember that this is indeed Asleep's reputation in the old days, and that a midget can walk up to him and tweak his ear without running any risk, and of course I am bound to respect his ethics, although I am sorry he cannot see his way clear to making an exception in the case of the night manager of Mindy's.

"I do not understand the way times change since I am in college," Asleep says. "Nobody around here wishes anybody taken care of any more. I call on quite a number of old customers of mine before I visit Benny Barker, but they have nothing for me, and none of them suggests that I call again. I fear I am *passé*," Asleep says. "Yet I am the one who first brings the idea to Brooklyn of putting them in the sack. I originate picking them off in barber chairs. I am always first and foremost with innovations in my business, and now there is no business.

"It is a tough break for me," Asleep says, "just when I happen to need a situation more than at any other time in my life. I simply must make good," he says, "because I am in love and wish to be married. I am in love with Miss Anna Lark, who dances behind bubbles over in the Starlight Restaurant. Yes," he says, "Miss Anna Lark is my sweet pea, and she loves me as dearly as I love her, or anyway," he says, "she so states no longer ago than two hours."

"Well," I say, "Miss Anna Lark has a shape that is a lulu. Even behind bubbles," I say, and this is a fact that is well known to one and all on Broadway, but I do not consider it necessary to mention to Asleep that it is also pretty well known along Broadway that Benny Barker, the bookie, is deeply interested in Miss Anna Lark, and, to tell the truth, is practically off his onion about her, because I am by no means a chirper.

"I often notice her shape myself," Asleep says. "In fact, it is one of the things that starts our romance before I go away to college. It seems to me it is better then than it is now, but," he says, "a shape is not everything in this life, although I admit it is never any knock. Miss Anna Lark waits patiently for me all the time I am away, and once she writes me a screeve, so you can see that this is undoubtedly true love.

"But," Asleep says, "Miss Anna Lark now wishes to abandon the bubble dodge, and return to her old home in Miami, Florida, where her papa is in the real-estate business. Miss Anna Lark feels that there is no future behind bubbles, especially," he says, "since she recently contracts arthritis in both knees from working in drafty nightclubs. And she wishes me to go to Miami, Florida, too, and perhaps engage in the real-estate business like her papa, and acquire some scratch so we can be married, and raise up children, and all this and that, and be happy ever after.

"But," Asleep says, "it is very necessary for me to get hold of a taw to make a start, and at this time I do not have as much as two white quarters to rub together in my pants' pocket, and neither has Miss Anna Lark, and from what I hear, the same thing goes for Miss Anna Lark's papa, and with conditions in my line what they are, I am greatly depressed, and scarcely know which way to turn."

Well, naturally, I feel very sorry for Asleep, but I can offer no suggestions of any value at the moment, and in fact the best I can do is to stake him to a few dibs for walk-about money, and then I leave him in the Bridle Grill looking quite sad and forlorn, to be sure.

I do not see Asleep for several months after this, and am wondering what becomes of him, and I watch the bladders for news of happenings that may indicate he finally gets a break, but nothing of interest appears, and then one day I run into him at Broadway and Forty-sixth Street.

He is all sharpened up in new clothes, and a fresh shave, and he is carrying a suitcase, and looks very prosperous, indeed, and he seems happy to see me, and leads me around into Dinty Moore's, and sits me down at a table, and orders up some drinks, and then he says to me like this:

"Now," he says, "I will tell you what happens. After you leave me in the Bridle Grill, I sit down and take to reading one of the evening bladders, and what I read about is a war in a place by the name of Spain, and from what I read, I can see that it is a war between two different mobs living in this Spain, each of which wishes to control the situation. It reminds me of Chicago the time Big Moey sends me out to Al.

"Thinks I to myself," Asleep says, "where there is a war of this nature, there may be employment for a character of my experience, and I am sitting there pondering this matter when who comes in looking for me but Benny Barker, the bookie.

"Well," Asleep says, "Benny states that he gets to thinking of me after I leave Mindy's, and he says he remembers that he really has a soft place in his heart for me, and that while he has no business for me any more, he will be glad to stake me to go wherever I think I may find something, and I remember what I am just reading in the evening bladder, and I say all right, Spain.

" 'Where is this Spain?' Benny Barker asks.

"Well," Asleep says, "of course I do not know where it is myself, so we inquire of Professor D, the educated horse player, and he says it is to hell and gone from here. He says it is across the sea, and Benny Barker says he will arrange my passage there at once, and furthermore that he will give me a thousand slugs in ready, and I can pay him back at my convenience. Afterward," Asleep says, "I recall that Benny Barker seems greatly pleased that I am going far away, but I figure his conscience hurts him for the manner in which he rebuffs me in Mindy's, and he wishes to round himself up with me.

"So I go to this Spain," Asleep says, "and now," he says, "if you wish to hear any more, I will be glad to oblige."

Well, I tell Asleep that if he will keep calling the waiter at regular intervals, he may proceed, and Asleep proceeds as follows:

I go to this Spain seeking employment, and you will scarcely believe the trouble and inconvenience I am put to in getting there. I go by way of a ship that takes me to France, which is a place I remember somewhat, because I visit there in my early youth, in 1918, with the 77th Division, and which is a nice place, at that, especially the *Folies-Bergère*, and I go across France and down to a little jerk-water town just over the border from this Spain, and who do I run into sitting in front of a small gin mill in the town but a Spanish character by the name of Manuel something.

He is once well known along Broadway as a heavyweight fighter, and he is by no means a bad fighter in his day, and he now has a pair of scrambled ears to prove it. Furthermore, he is bobbing slightly, and seems to have a few marbles in his mouth, but he is greatly pleased to see me.

Manuel speaks English very good, considering the marbles, and he tells me he is personally in the fighting in this Spain for several weeks, but he is unable to find out what he is fighting about, so finally he gets tired, and is over in France taking a recess, and when I tell him I am going to this Spain, and what for, he says he has no doubt I will do very nice for myself, because of course Manuel knows my reputation in the old days in New York.

Furthermore, he says he will go with me, and act as my manager, and maybe take a piece of my earnings, just as his American managers do with him when he is active in the ring, and when I ask him what he calls a piece, he says 65 percent is the way his American managers always slice him, but naturally I do not agree to any such terms. Still, I can see that Manuel is such a character as may come in handy to me, what with knowing how to speak Spanish, as well as English, so I say I will look out for him very nicely when the time comes for a settlement, and this satisfies him.

We go across the border into this Spain by night, and Manuel says he will lead me to a spot where the fighting is very good, and by and by we come to a fair-sized town, with houses, and steeples, and all this and that, and which has a name I do not remember, and which I cannot pronounce, even if I do remember it.

Manuel says we are now in the war, and in fact I can hear shooting going on although it does not seem to be interfering with public business in the town, as many characters, male and female, are walking around and about, and up and down, and back and forth, and none of them seem to be disturbed by anything much.

But Manuel and I follow the sound of the shooting, and finally we come upon a large number of characters behind a breastworks made out of sandbags, and they all have rifles in their hands, and are shooting now and then at a big stone building on a high hill about three blocks away, and from this building also comes a lot of firing, and there are occasional bur-ur-ur-ups on both sides that I recognize as machine guns, and bullets are zinging about the sandbags quite some.

Well, Manuel says this is some of the war, but all the characters behind the sandbags seem to be taking things easy, and in fact some are sitting in chairs and firing their rifles from a rest over the bags while so seated, and thinks I to myself, this is a very leisurely war, to be sure.

But about two blocks from the breastworks, and on a rise of ground almost as high as the hill the building is on, there is a field-gun, and this is also firing on the building about every fifteen minutes, and I can see that it seems to be doing some real damage, at that, what with knocking off pieces of the architecture, and punching holes in the roof, although now and then it lets go a shell that misses the mark in a way that will never be tolerated by the character who commands the battery I serve with in France.

Many of the characters behind the sandbags seem to know Manuel, who appears to be a famous character in this Spain, and they stop shooting, and gather about him, and there is much conversation among them, which of course I do not understand, so after a while I request Manuel to pay more attention to me and to kindly explain the situation I find here.

Well, Manuel says the building on the hill is an old castle and that it is being held by a lot of Spanish characters, male and female, who are as mad at the characters behind the sandbags as the Republicans are mad at the Democrats in my country, and maybe madder. Manuel says the characters in the castle represent one side of the war in this Spain, and the characters behind the sandbags represent the other side, although Manuel does not seem to know which is which, and naturally I do not care.

"Well," I say to Manuel, "this is a good place to start business. Tell them who I am," I say, "and ask them how much they will give me for taking care of these parties in the castle."

So Manuel makes quite a speech, and while I do not understand what he is saying, I can see that he is putting me away with them very good, because they are gazing at me with great interest and respect. When he concludes his speech they give me a big cheer and crowd around me shaking hands, and I see Manuel talking with some characters who seem to be the mains in this situation, and they are listening eagerly to his remarks, and nodding their heads, and Manuel says to me like this:

"Well," Manuel says, "I tell them you are the greatest American gangster that ever lives, and that they undoubtedly see you often in the movies, and they are in favor of your proposition one hundred percent. They are anxious to see how you operate," Manuel says, "because they wish to install similar methods in this country when things get settled down."

"Kindly omit referring to me as a gangster," I say. "It is a most uncouth word, and besides I never operate with a gang in my life."

"Well, all right," Manuel says, "but it is a word they understand. However," he says, "the trouble here is they do not have much *dinero*, which is money. In fact, they say the best they can offer you to take care of the parties in the castle is two pesetas per head."

"How much is two pesetas?" I ask.

"The last time I am here, it is about forty cents in your language," Manuel says.

Naturally, I am very indignant at this offer, because in my time I get as high as twenty thousand dollars for taking care of a case, and never less than five hundred, except once when I do a favor for one-fifty, but Manuel claims it is not such a bad offer as it sounds, as he says that at the moment two pesetas is by no means alfalfa in this Spain, especially as there are maybe four hundred heads in the castle, counting everything.

Manuel says it really is an exceptional offer as the characters behind the sandbags are anxious to conclude the siege because certain friends of the parties in the castle are arriving in a nearby town, and anyway, sitting behind these sandbags is getting most monotonous to one and all. Furthermore, Manuel says, when they are not sitting behind the sandbags, these characters are required to work every day digging a tunnel into the hill under the castle, and they regard this work as most enervating.

Manuel says the idea of the tunnel is to plant dynamite under the castle and blow it up.

"But you see," Manuel says, "digging is no work for proud souls such as Spaniards, so if you can think of some other way of taking care of these parties in the castle, it will be a great relief to my friends here."

"To the dickens with these skinflints," I say. "Let us go to the castle and see what the parties there will give us for taking care of these cheapskates behind the sandbags. Never," I say, "will I accept such a reduction."

Well, Manuel tells the mains behind the sandbags that I will take their offer under consideration, but that I am so favorably disposed toward it that I am going into the castle and examine the surroundings, and this pleases them no little, so Manuel ties his handkerchief on a stick and says this is a flag of truce and will get us into the castle safe and sound, and we set out.

Presently characters appear at the windows, and at holes in the walls of the castle, and Manuel holds a conversation with them in the Spanish language, and by and by they admit us to the castle yard, and one character with whiskers leads us into the building and down stone steps until we arrive in what seems to be a big basement far underground.

And in this basement I behold a very unusual scene to be sure. There are many characters present, male and female, also numerous small children, and they seem to be living in great confusion, but they are greatly interested in us when we appear, especially a tall, thin elderly character with white hair, and a white tash, and a white goatee, who seems to be a character of some authority.

In fact, Manuel says he is nobody but a character by the name of General Pedro Vega, and that this castle is his old family home, and that he is leader of these other characters in the basement.

I can see at once that Manuel and the general are old friends, because they make quite a fuss over meeting up in this manner, and then Manuel introduces me, and delivers another speech about me, explaining what a wonderful character I am. When he gets through, the general turns to me, and in very good English he speaks as follows:

"I am very glad to meet you, Señor Asleep," he says. "I once live in your country a couple of years," he says. "I live in your Miami, Florida."

Well, I am glad to find somebody who can talk English, so I can do my own negotiating, and in a few words I state my proposition to the general to take care of the characters behind the sandbags, and call for his bid on same.

"Alas," the general says, "money is something we do not have. If you are offering to take care of the enemy at one centavo each," he says, "we still cannot pay. I am most regretful. It will be a big convenience to have you take care of the enemy, because we can then escape from this place and join our friends in a nearby city. Our food runs low," he says. "So does our ammunition. Some of our females and children are ill. The longer we remain here the worse it gets.

"If I do not know the caliber of the enemy," he says, "I will gladly surrender. But," he says, "we will then all be backed up against a wall and executed. It is better that we die here."

Well, being backed up against a wall strikes me as a most undesirable fate, to be sure, but of course it is nothing to me, and all I am thinking of is that this is a very peculiar country where nobody has any scratch, and it is commencing to remind me of home. And I am also thinking that the only thing I can do is to accept the two pesetas per head offered by the characters behind the sandbags when a very beautiful young Judy, with long black hair hanging down her back, approaches and speaks to me at some length in the Spanish language. Manuel says:

"She says," he says, " 'Oh, sir, if you can help us escape from this place you will earn my undying gratitude.' She says," Manuel says, " 'I am in love with a splendid young character by the name of Señor José Valdez, who is waiting for me with our friends in the nearby town. We are to be married as soon as the cruel war is over,' she says," Manuel says. "It seems to be a most meritorious case," Manuel says.

Now naturally this statement touches my heart no little, because I am in love myself, and besides the young Judy begins weeping, and if there is one thing I cannot stand it is female tears, and in fact my sweet pea, Miss Anna Lark, can always make me do almost anything she wishes by breaking out crying. But of course business is business in this case, and I cannot let sentiment interfere, so I am about to bid one and all farewell when General Pedro Vega says:

"Wait!"

And with this he disappears into another part of the basement, but is back pretty soon with a small black tin box, and out of this box he takes a batch of papers, and hands them to me, and says:

"Here are the deeds to some property in your Miami, Florida," he says. "I pay much money for it in 1925. They tell me at the time I am lucky to get the property at the price, but," he says, "I will be honest with you. It is unimproved property, and all I ever get out of it so far is notices that taxes are due, which I always pay promptly. But now I fear I will never get back to your Miami, Florida, again, and if you will take care of enough of the enemy for us to escape, the deeds are yours. This is all I have to offer."

Well, I say I will take the deeds and study them over and let him know my answer as soon as possible, and then I retire with Manuel, but what I really study more than anything else is the matter of the beautiful young Judy who yearns for her sweet pea, and there is no doubt but what my studying of her is a point in favor of General Vega's proposition in my book, although I also do some strong studying of the fact that taking care of these characters in the castle is a task that will be very tough.

So after we leave the castle, I ask Manuel if he supposes there is a telegraph office in operation in town, and he says of course there is, or how can the newspaper scribes get their thrilling stories of the war out, so I get him to take me there, and I send a cablegram addressed to Mr. Lark, real estate, Miami, Florida, U.S.A., which reads as follows:

IS FIFTY ACRES LANDSCRABBLE SECTION ANY ACCOUNT.

Then there is nothing for me to do but wait around until I get an answer, and this takes several days, and I devote this period to seeing the sights with Manuel, and I wish to say that some of the sights are very interesting. Finally, I drop around to the telegraph office, and sure enough there is a message there for me, collect, which says like this:

LANDSCRABBLE SECTION GREAT POSSIBILITIES STOP. WHY LARK?

Now I do not know Mr. Lark personally, and he does not know

me, and the chances are he never even hears of me before, but I figure that if he is half as smart as his daughter, Miss Anna Lark, his judgment is worth following, so I tell Manuel it looks as if the deal with General Vega is on, and I begin giving my undivided attention to the case.

I can see at once that the key to the whole situation as far as I am concerned is the field-piece on the hill, because there are really too many characters behind the sandbags for me to take care of by myself, or even with the assistance of Manuel, and of course I do not care to get Manuel involved in my personal business affairs any more than I can help.

However, at my request he makes a few innocent inquiries among the characters behind the sandbags, and he learns that there are always seven characters on the hill with the gun, and that they sleep in little homemade shelters made of boards, and canvas, and tin, and one thing and another, and that these shelters are scattered over the top of the hill, and the top of the hill is maybe the width of a baseball diamond.

But I can observe for myself that they do no firing from the hilltop after sundown, and they seldom show any lights, which is maybe because they do not wish to have any airplanes come along and drop a few hot apples on them.

Manuel says that the characters behind the sandbags are asking about me, and he says they are so anxious to secure my services that he will not be surprised if I cannot get three pesetas per head, and I can see that Manuel thinks I am making a mistake not to dicker with them further.

But I tell him I am now committed to General Vega, and I have Manuel obtain a twelve-inch file for me in the city, and also some corks out of wine bottles, and I take the file and hammer it down, and smooth it out, and sharpen it up nicely, and I make a handle for it out of wood, according to my own original ideas, and I take the corks, and burn them good, and I find a big piece of black cloth and make myself a sort of poncho out of this by cutting a hole in the center for my head to go through.

Then I wait until it comes on a night to suit me, and it is a dark night, and rainy, and blowy, and I black up my face and hands with the burnt cork, and slip the black cloth over my clothes, and put my file down the back of my neck where I can reach it quickly, and make my way very quietly to the foot of the hill on which the field-gun is located.

Now in the darkness, I begin crawling on my hands and knees, and wiggling along on my stomach up the hill, and I wish to state that it is a monotonous task because I can move only a few feet at a clip, and there are many sharp rocks in my path, and once an insect of some nature crawls up my pant leg and gives me a severe nip.

The hill is maybe as high as a two-story building, and very steep, and it takes me over an hour to wiggle my way to the top, and sometimes I pause *en route* and wonder if it is worth it. And then I think of the beautiful young Judy in the castle, and of the property in Miami, Florida, and of Miss Anna Lark, and I keep on wiggling.

Well, just as Manuel reports, there is a sentry on duty on top of the hill, and I can make out his shape in the darkness leaning on his rifle, and this sentry is a very large character, and at first I figure that he may present difficulties, but when I wiggle up close to him I observe that he seems to be dozing, and it is quiet as can be on the hilltop.

The sentry is really no trouble at all, and then I wiggle my way slowly along in and out of the little shelters, and in some shelters there is but one character, and in others two, and in one, three, and it is these three that confuse me somewhat, as they are three more than the seven Manuel mentions in his census of the scene, and I will overlook them entirely if one of them does not snore more than somewhat.

Personally, I will always say that taking care of these ten characters one after the other, and doing it so quietly that not one of them ever wakes up, is the high spot of my entire career, especially when you consider that I am somewhat rusty from lack of experience, and that my equipment is very crude.

Well, when morning dawns, there I am in charge of the hilltop, and with a field-gun at my disposal, and I discover that it is nothing but a French 75, with which I am quite familiar, and by and by Manuel joins me, and while the characters behind the sandbags are enjoying their breakfast, and the chances are, not thinking of much, I plant four shells among them so fast I ruin their morning meal, because, if I do say it myself, I am better than a raw hand with a French 75.

Then I remember that the characters who are boring under the castle are perhaps inside the tunnel at this time, so I peg away at the hole in the hill until the front of it caves in and blocks up the hole very neatly, and Manuel afterward claims that I wedged in the entire nightshift.

Well, of course these proceedings are visible to the occupants of the castle, and it is not long before I see General Pedro Vega come marching out of the castle with the whole kit and caboodle of characters, male and female, and small children behind him, and they are laughing and shouting, and crying and carrying on no little.

And the last I see of them as they go hurrying off in the direction of the nearby town where their friends are located, the beautiful young Judy is bringing up the rear and throwing kisses at me and waving a flag, and I ask Manuel to kindly identify this flag for me so I will always remember which side of the war in this Spain it is that I assist.

But Manuel says his eyesight is bad ever since the night Jim Sharkey sticks a thumb in his eye in the fifth round in Madison Square Garden, and from this distance he cannot tell whose flag it is, and in fact, Manuel says, he does not give a Spanish cuss word.

"And there you are," Asleep says to me in Dinty Moore's.

"So," I say, "you are now back in New York looking for business again?"

"Oh, no," Asleep says. "I now reside in Miami, Florida, and I am going to marry Miss Anna Lark next month. I am doing very well for myself, too," he says. "You see, we turn the property that I get from General Vega into a cemetery, and I am now selling lots in same for our firm which is headed by Miss Anna Lark's papa. Manuel is our head gravedigger, and we are all very happy," Asleep says.

Well, afterward I hear that the first lot Asleep sells is to the family of the late Benny Barker, the bookie, who passes away during the race meeting in Miami, Florida, of pneumonia, superinduced by lying out all night in a ditch full of water near the home of Miss Anna Lark, although I also understand that the fact that Benny is tied up in a sack in the ditch is considered a slight contributing cause of his last illness.

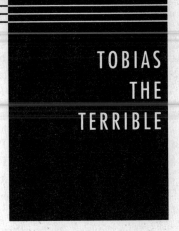

TOBIAS THE TERRIBLE

One night I am sitting in Mindy's restaurant on Broadway partaking heartily of some Hungarian goulash which comes very nice in Mindy's, what with the chef being personally somewhat Hungarian himself, when in pops a guy who is a stranger to me and sits down at my table.

I do not pay any attention to the guy at first as I am busy looking over the entries for the next day at Laurel, but I hear him tell the waiter to bring him some goulash, too. By and by I hear the guy making a strange noise and I look at him over my paper and see that he is crying. In fact, large tears are rolling down his face into his goulash and going plop-plop as they fall.

Now it is by no means usual to see guys crying in Mindy's restaurant, though thousands of guys come in there who often feel like crying, especially after a tough day at the track, so I commence weighing the guy up with great interest. I can see he is a very little guy, maybe a shade over five feet high and weighing maybe as much as a dime's worth of liver, and he has a mustache like a mosquito's whiskers across his upper lip, and pale blond hair and a very sad look in his eyes.

Furthermore, he is a young guy and he is wearing a suit of clothes the color of French mustard, with slanting pockets, and I notice when he comes in that he has a brown hat sitting jack-deuce on his noggin. Anybody can see that this guy does not belong in these parts, with such a sad look and especially with such a hat.

Naturally, I figure his crying is some kind of a dodge. In fact, I figure that maybe the guy is trying to cry me out of the price of his Hungarian goulash, although if he takes the trouble to ask anybody before he comes in, he will learn that he may just as well try to cry Al Smith out of the Empire State Building.

But the guy does not say anything whatever to me but just goes on shedding tears into his goulash, and finally I get very curious about this proposition, and I speak to him as follows:

"Listen, pally," I say, "if you are crying about the goulash, you better dry your tears before the chef sees you, because," I say, "the chef is very sensitive about his goulash, and may take your tears as criticism."

"The goulash seems all right," the guy says in a voice that is just about his size. "Anyway, I am not crying about the goulash. I am crying about my sad life. Friend," the guy says, "are you ever in love?"

Well, of course, at this crack I know what is eating the guy. If I have all the tears that are shed on Broadway by guys in love, I will have enough salt water to start an opposition ocean to the Atlantic and Pacific, with enough left over to run the Great Salt Lake out of business. But I wish to say I never shed any of these tears personally, because I am never in love, and furthermore, barring a bad break, I never expect to be in love, for the way I look at it love is strictly the old phedinkus, and I tell the little guy as much.

"Well," he says, "you will not speak so harshly of love if you are acquainted with Miss Deborah Weems."

With this he starts crying more than somewhat, and his grief is such that it touches my heart and I have half a notion to start crying with him as I am now convinced that the guy is leveling with his tears.

Finally the guy slacks up a little in his crying, and begins eating his goulash, and by and by he seems more cheerful, but then it is well known to one and all that a fair dose of Mindy's goulash will cheer up anybody no matter how sad they feel. Pretty soon the guy starts talking to me, and I make out that his name is Tobias Tweeney, and that he comes from a spot over in Bucks County, Pennsylvania, by the name of Erasmus, or some such.

Furthermore, I judge that this Erasmus is not such a large city, but very pleasant, and that Tobias Tweeney is born and raised there and is never much of any place else in his life, although he is now rising twenty-five.

Well, it seems that Tobias Tweeney has a fine position in a shoe store selling shoes and is going along all right when he happens to fall in love with a doll by the name of Miss Deborah Weems, whose papa owns a gas station in Erasmus and is a very prominent citizen. I judge from what Tobias tells me that this Miss Deborah Weems tosses him around quite some, which proves to me that dolls in small towns are just the same as they are on Broadway.

"She is beautiful," Tobias Tweeney says, speaking of Miss Deborah Weems. "I do not think I can live without her. But," he says, "Miss Deborah Weems will have no part of me because she is daffy over desperate characters of the underworld such as she sees in the movies at the Model Theater in Erasmus.

"She wishes to know," Tobias Tweeney says, "why I cannot be a big gunman and go around plugging people here and there and talking up to politicians and policemen, and maybe looking picturesque and romantic like Edward G. Robinson or James Cagney or even Georgie Raft. But, of course," Tobias says, "I am not the type for such a character. Anyway," he says, "Constable Wendell will never permit me to be such a character in Erasmus.

"So Miss Deborah Weems says I have no more nerve than a catfish," Tobias says, "and she goes around with a guy by the name of Joe Trivett, who runs the Smoke Shop, and bootlegs ginger extract to the boys in his back room and claims Al Capone once says 'Hello' to him, although," Tobias says, "personally, I think Joe Trivett is nothing but a great big liar."

At this, Tobias Tweeney starts crying again, and I feel very sorry for him indeed, because I can see he is a friendly, harmless little fellow, and by no means accustomed to being tossed around by a doll, and a guy who is not accustomed to being tossed around by a doll always finds it most painful the first time.

"Why," I say, very indignant, "this Miss Deborah Weems talks great foolishness, because big gunmen always wind up nowadays with the score nine to nought against them, even in the movies. In fact," I say, "if they do not wind up this way in the movies, the censors will not permit the movies to be displayed. Why do you not hit this guy Trivett a punch in the snoot," I say, "and tell him to go on about his business?"

"Well," Tobias says, "the reason I do not hit him a punch in the snoot is because he has the idea of punching snoots first, and whose snoot does he punch but mine. Furthermore," Tobias says, "he makes my snoot bleed with the punch, and he says he will do it again if I keep hanging around Miss Deborah Weems. And," Tobias says, "it is mainly because I do not return the punch, being too busy stopping my snoot from bleeding, that Miss Deborah Weems renounces me forever.

"She says she can never stand for a guy who has no more nerve than me," Tobias says, "but," he says, "I ask you if I am to blame if my mother is frightened by a rabbit a few weeks before I am born, and marks me for life?

"So I leave town," Tobias says. "I take my savings of two hundred dollars out of the Erasmus bank, and I come here, figuring maybe I will meet up with some big gunmen and other desperate characters of the underworld, and get to know them, and then I can go back to Erasmus and make Joe Trivett look sick. By the way," he says, "do you know any desperate characters of the underworld?"

Well, of course I do not know any such characters, and if I do know them I am not going to speak about it, because the best a guy can get in this town if he goes around speaking of these matters is a nice kick in the pants. So I say no to Tobias Tweeney, and tell him I am more or less of a stranger myself, and then he wishes to know if I can show him a tough joint, such as he sees in the movies.

Naturally, I do not know of such a joint, but then I get to thinking about Good Time Charley's little Gingham Shop over in Forty-seventh Street, and how Charley is not going so good the last time I am in there, and here is maybe a chance for me to steer a little trade his way, because, after all, guys with two yards in their pocket are by no means common nowadays.

So I take Tobias Tweeney around to Good Time Charley's, but the moment we get in there I am sorry we go, because who is present but a dozen parties from different parts of the city, and none of these parties are any bargain at any time. Some of these parties, such as Harry the Horse and Angie the Ox, are from Brooklyn, and three are from Harlem, including Little Mitzi and Germany Schwartz, and several are from the Bronx, because I recognize Joey Uptown, and Joey never goes around without a few intimate friends from his own neighborhood with him.

Afterward I learn that these parties are to a meeting on business matters at a spot near Good Time Charley's, and when they get through with their business they drop in to give Charley a little complimentary play, for Charley stands very good with one and all in this town. Anyway, they are sitting around a table when Tobias Tweeney and I arrive, and I give them all a big hello, and they hello me back, and ask me and my friend to sit down as it seems they are in a most hospitable frame of mind.

Naturally I sit down because it is never good policy to decline an invitation from parties such as these, and I motion Tobias to sit down, too, and I introduce Tobias all around, and we all have a couple of drinks, and then I explain to those present just who Tobias is, and how his ever-loving doll tosses him around, and how Joe Trivett punches him in the snoot.

Well, Tobias begins crying again, because no inexperienced guy can take a couple of drinks of Good Time Charley's liquor and not bust out crying, even if it is Charley's company liquor, and one and all are at once very sympathetic with Tobias, especially Little Mitzi, who is just tossed around himself more than somewhat by a doll. In fact, Little Mitzi starts crying with him.

"Why," Joey Uptown says, "I never hear of a greater outrage in my life, although," he says, "I can see there is some puppy in you at that, when you do not return this Trivett's punch. But even so," Joey says, "if I have time I will go back to this town you speak of with you and make the guy hard to catch. Furthermore," he says, "I will give this Miss Deborah Weems a piece of my mind."

Then I tell them how Tobias Tweeney comes to New York figuring he may meet up with some desperate characters of the underworld, and they hear this with great interest, and Angie the Ox speaks as follows:

"I wonder," Angie says, "if we can get in touch with anybody who knows such characters and arrange to have Mr. Tweeney meet them, although personally," Angie says, "I loathe and despise characters of this nature."

Well, while Angie is wondering this there comes a large knock at the front door, and it is such a knock as only the gendarmes can knock, and everybody at the table jumps up. Good Time Charley goes to the door and takes a quiet gander through his peephole and we hear a loud, coarse voice speaking as follows:

"Open up, Charley," the voice says. "We wish to look over your guests. Furthermore," the voice says, "tell them not to try the back door, because we are there, too."

"It is Lieutenant Harrigan and his squad," Charley says as he comes back to the table where we are all standing. "Someone must tip him off you are here. Well," Charley says, "those who have rods to shed will shed them now."

At this, Joey Uptown steps up to Tobias Tweeney and hands him a large Betsy and says to Tobias like this:

"Put this away on you somewhere," Joey says, "and then sit down and be quiet. These coppers are not apt to bother with you," Joey says, "if you sit still and mind your own business, but," Joey says, "it will be very tough on any of us they find with a rod, especially any of us who owe the state any time, and," Joey says, "I seem to remember I owe some."

Now of course what Joey says is very true, because he is only walking around and about on parole, and some of the others present are walking around the same way, and it is a very serious matter for a guy who is walking around on parole to be caught with a John Roscoe in his pocket. So it is a very ticklish situation, and somewhat embarrassing.

Well, Tobias Tweeney is somewhat dazed by his couple of drinks of Good Time Charley's liquor and the chances are he does not realize what is coming off, so he takes Joey's rod and puts it in his hip kick. Then all of a sudden Harry the Horse and Angie the Ox and Little Mitzi, and all the others step up to him and hand him their Roscoes and Tobias Tweeney somehow manages to stow the guns away on himself and sit down before Good Time Charley opens the door and in come the gendarmes.

By this time Joey Uptown and all the others are scattered at different tables around the room, with no more than three at any one table, leaving Tobias Tweeney and me alone at the table where we are first sitting. Furthermore, everybody is looking very innocent indeed, and all hands seem somewhat surprised at the intrusion of the gendarmes, who are all young guys belonging to Harrigan's Broadway squad, and very rude.

I know Harrigan by sight, and I know most of his men, and they know there is no more harm in me than there is in a two-year-old baby, so they pay no attention to me whatever, or to Tobias Tweeney, either, but go around making Joey Uptown, and Angie the Ox, and all the others stand up while the gendarmes fan them to see if they have any rods on them, because these gendarmes are always laying for parties such as these hoping to catch them rodded up.

Naturally the gendarmes do not find any rods on anybody, because the rods are all on Tobias Tweeney, and no gendarme is going to fan Tobias Tweeney looking for a rod after one gander at Tobias, especially at this particular moment, as Tobias is now half-asleep from Good Time Charley's liquor, and has no interest whatever in anything that is going on. In fact, Tobias is nodding in his chair.

Of course the gendarmes are greatly disgusted at not finding any rods, and Angie the Ox and Joey Uptown are telling them that they are going to see their aldermen and find out if law-abiding citizens can be stood up and fanned for rods, and put in a very undignified position like this, but the gendarmes do not seem disturbed by these threats, and Lieutenant Harrigan states as follows:

"Well," he says, "I guess maybe I get a bum steer, but," he says, "for two cents I will give all you wrong gees a good going-over just for luck."

Of course this is no way to speak to parties such as these, as they are all very prominent in their different parts of the city, but Lieutenant Harrigan is a guy who seldom cares how he talks to anybody. In fact, Lieutenant Harrigan is a very tough copper.

But he is just about to take his gendarmes out of the joint when Tobias Tweeney nods a little too far forward in his chair, and then all of a sudden topples over on the floor, and five large rods pop out of his pockets and go sliding every which way around the floor, and the next thing anybody knows there is Tobias Tweeney under arrest with all the gendarmes holding on to some part of him.

Well, the next day the newspapers are plumb full of the capture of a guy they call Twelve-Gun Tweeney, and the papers say the police state that this is undoubtedly the toughest guy the world ever sees, because while they hear of two-gun guys, and even three-gun guys, they never before hear of a guy going around rodded up with twelve guns.

The gendarmes say they can tell by the way he acts that Twelve-Gun Tweeney is a mighty bloodthirsty guy, because he says nothing whatever but only glares at them with a steely glint in his eyes, although of course the reason Tobias stares at them is because he is still too dumbfounded to think of anything to say.

Naturally, I figure that when Tobias comes up for air he is a sure thing to spill the whole business, and all the parties who are in Good Time Charley's when he is arrested figure the same way, and go into retirement for a time. But it seems that when Tobias finally realizes what time it is, he is getting so much attention that it swells him all up and he decides to keep on being Twelve-Gun Tweeney as long as he can, which is a decision that is a very nice break for all parties concerned.

I sneak down to Judge Rascover's court the day Tobias is arraigned on a charge of violation of the Sullivan law, which is a law against carrying rods, and the courtroom is packed with citizens eager to see a character desperate enough to lug twelve rods, and among these citizens are many dolls, pulling and hauling for position, and some of these dolls are by no means crows. Many photographers are hanging around to take pictures of Twelve-Gun Tweeney as he is led in handcuffed to gendarmes on either side of him, and with other gendarmes in front and behind him.

But one and all are greatly surprised and somewhat disappointed when they see what a little squirt Tobias is, and Judge Rascover looks down at him once, and then puts on his specs and takes another gander as if he does not believe what he sees in the first place. After looking at Tobias awhile through his specs, and shaking his head as if he is greatly puzzled, Judge Rascover speaks to Lieutenant Harrigan as follows:

"Do you mean to tell this court," Judge Rascover says, "that this half-portion here is the desperate Twelve-Gun Tweeney?"

Well, Lieutenant Harrigan says there is no doubt whatever about it, and Judge Rascover wishes to know how Tobias carries all these rods, and whereabouts, so Lieutenant Harrigan collects twelve rods from the gendarmes around the courtroom, unloads these rods, and starts in putting the guns here and there on Tobias as near as he can remember where they are found on him in the first place, with Tobias giving him a little friendly assistance.

Lieutenant Harrigan puts two guns in each of the side pockets of Tobias's coat, one in each hip pocket, one in the waistband of Tobias's pants, one in each side pocket of the pants, one up each of Tobias's sleeves and one in the inside pocket of Tobias's coat. Then Lieutenant Harrigan states to the court that he is all finished, and that Tobias is rodded up in every respect as when they put the arm on him in Good Time Charley's joint, and Judge Rascover speaks to Tobias as follows:

"Step closer to the bench," Judge Rascover says. "I wish to see for myself just what kind of a villain you are."

Well, Tobias takes a step forward, and over he goes on his snoot, so I see right away what it is makes him keel over in Good Time Charley's joint, not figuring in Charley's liquor. The little guy is naturally top-heavy from the rods.

Now there is much confusion as he falls and a young doll who seems to be fatter than somewhat comes shoving through the crowd in the courtroom yelling and crying, and though the gendarmes try to stop her she gets to Tobias and kneels at his side, and speaks as follows:

"Toby, darling," she says, "it is nobody but Deborah who loves you dearly, and who always knows you will turn out to be the greatest gunman of them all. Look at me, Toby," she says, "and tell me you love me, too. We never realize what a hero you are until we get the New York papers in Erasmus last night, and I hurry to you as quickly as possible. Kiss me, Toby," the fat young doll says, and Tobias raises up on one elbow and does same, and it makes a very pleasing scene, indeed, although the gendarmes try to pull them apart, having no patience whatever with such matters.

Now Judge Rascover is watching all this business through his specs, and Judge Rascover is no sucker, but a pretty slick old codger for a judge, and he can see that there is something wrong somewhere about Tobias Tweeney being a character as desperate as the gendarmes make him out, especially when he sees that Tobias cannot pack all these rods on a bet.

So when the gendarmes pick the fat young doll off of Tobias and take a few pounds of rods off of Tobias, too, so he is finally able to get back on his pins and stand there, Judge Rascover adjourns court, and takes Tobias into his private room and has a talk with him, and the chances are Tobias tells him the truth, for the next thing anybody knows Tobias is walking away as free as the little birdies in the trees, except that he has the fat young doll clinging to him like a porous plaster, so maybe Tobias is not so free, at that.

Well, this is about all there is to the story, except that there is afterward plenty of heat between the parties who are present in Good Time Charley's joint when Tobias is collared, because it seems that the meeting they all attend before going to Charley's is supposed to be a peace meeting of some kind and nobody is supposed to carry any rods to this meeting just to prove their confidence in each other, so everybody is very indignant when it comes out that nobody has any confidence in anybody else at the meeting.

I never hear of Tobias Tweeney but once after all this, and it is some months afterward when Joey Uptown and Little Mitzi are over in Pennsylvania inspecting a brewery proposition, and finding themselves near the town that is called Erasmus, they decide it will be a nice thing to drop in on Tobias Tweeney and see how he is getting along.

Well, it seems Tobias is all married up to Miss Deborah Weems, and is getting along first class, as it seems the town elects him constable, because it feels that a guy with such a desperate reputation as Tobias Tweeney's is bound to make wrongdoers keep away from Erasmus if he is an officer of the law, and Tobias's first official act is to chase Joe Trivett out of town.

But along Broadway Tobias Tweeney will always be considered nothing but an ingrate for heaving Joey Uptown and Little Mitzi into the town sneezer and getting them fined fifty bobs apiece for carrying concealed weapons.

t is the afternoon of a hot day in the city of West Palm Beach, Florida, and a guy by the name of Fatso Zimpf is standing on a street corner thinking of very little and throwing so much shade that a couple of small stove lids are sitting on the curb at his feet keeping cool, for this Fatso weighs three hundred pounds if he weighs a carat and as he is only about five feet eight inches tall he is really quite a tub of blubber and casts a very wide shadow.

At that, he is somewhat undernourished at this time and in fact is maybe fifteen or twenty pounds underweight as he does not partake of food for two days, and if the small stove lids know how hungry he is the chances are they will not be sitting so close to him. To tell the truth, Fatso is so hungry that his stomach is wondering if his throat is on a vacation and what is more he does not have as much as one thin dime in his pants pockets to relieve his predicament.

This Fatso is a horse player by trade and he is en route to Miami to participate in the winter meetings at Tropical Park and Hialeah, and he leaves New York City with just enough money to get him as far as West Palm Beach by bus, but with nothing over for food and drink on the journey. However, he does not regret having to leave the bus at West Palm Beach as his strength is slowly dwindling from hunger and he figures he may be able to get something to eat there.

Besides, the bus people are talking of charging him excess fare because it seems that Fatso laps over on both sides in one seat so much that they claim it is just the same as if he has three seats, and other passengers are complaining and the journey is by no means a pleasure trip for Fatso.

Well, while Fatso is standing there on the corner all of a sudden a big red roadster pulls up in the street in front of him with a good-looking tanned young guy in a sport shirt driving it and a skinny Judy sitting in the seat next to him and the skinny Judy motions for Fatso to come out to the car.

At first Fatso does not pay any attention to her because he does not wish to move around and take his shade away from the small stove lids, as he can see that they are very comfortable, and when it comes to children no kinder-hearted guy than Fatso ever lived no matter if they are slightly colored children. In fact, Fatso is enduring no little suffering from the heat, standing there just because he is too kindhearted to move.

The skinny Judy in the roadster keeps motioning to him and then she cries "Hey, you!" in a loud tone so finally Fatso goes out in the street to the car figuring that maybe she wishes to ask him the way to some place although of course Fatso does not know the way to any place in these parts, and he can see that she is not a bad-looking Judy, though not young, and that she has yellow hair tied back with a fancy handkerchief and a blue sweater and blue slacks and a lot of bracelets on her arms and rings on her fingers.

Fatso can see that this is a party who must be in the money and he can also see that she has hard blue eyes and a bossy way about her because as he goes up to the side of the car with the small stove lids following in his shade she speaks to him in a voice that seems to scratch on her tonsils coming up, as follows:

"Look here," she says, "are you out of a job?"

Now this Fatso is always very courteous to all female characters even when he can see that they are nothing but mountain lions and he bows and says:

"Well," he says, "not to give you a short answer, ma'am, but who wants to know?"

"I do," the skinny Judy says. "I'm Mrs. Manwaring Mimm."

"I am Elmore Zimpf," Fatso says, though up to this time he never before mentions his first name in public for fear of arousing criticism.

"Never mind who you are," Mrs. Mimm says. "Do you want a job or are you on relief?"

Naturally, Fatso does not want a job, for jobs are what he is keeping away from all his life and furthermore he does not care for Mrs. Mimm's manner and he is about to back away from this situation when he gets to thinking how hungry he is. So he asks her what kind of a job she is thinking of and she says to him like this:

"I want you for my Santa Claus," she says. "I am giving my annual Christmas Eve party at my place in Palm Beach tomorrow night and as soon as I see you I say to the count here that you are the very one for my Santa Claus. My Santa Claus suit will just fit you," she says. "We always have to stuff it up with pillows for my butler Sparks and he never looks natural."

At this Fatso remembers that Christmas is indeed close at hand and naturally this makes him think of Mindy's restaurant on Broadway and the way they cook turkey there with dressing and cranberry sauce and with mashed potatoes and turnips or maybe baked squash to come along and thinking of these matters causes him to sigh heavily and to forget where he is for the moment until he is aroused by hearing the young guy driving the car speak as follows:

"This fat bum is dead from the neck up, Margaret," he says. "You better find someone else."

"No," she says, "I must have this one. Why, Gregorio, he will be a sensational Santa Claus. See here," she says to Fatso, "I will give you fifty dollars."

Well, on hearing the young guy speak of him as a fat bum, Fatso's thoughts return to West Palm Beach at once and he takes a good look at the young guy and he can now see that he has a piece of a mustache on his upper lip and that there is something about him that is quite familiar.

However, Fatso cannot place him as anybody he knows so he figures it is just the type that makes him seem familiar because of course there are thousands of good-looking tanned young guys with pieces of mustaches on their upper lips running around Florida at this season of the year, but he is greatly displeased with this particular young guy for calling him a fat bum.

In fact, Fatso is insulted because while he does not mind being called fat or even a bum he does not care to be called both at the same time because it sounds unrefined. He is figuring that maybe it will be an excellent idea to reach over and tag this young guy one on the chops, when he remembers hearing Mrs. Mimm mention fifty dollars.

So he takes this matter up with her to make certain his ears do not deceive him and sure enough she is willing to give him half a C to be her Santa Claus with two boffoes in advance so he can get across Lake Worth to an address she gives him without walking, provided he will proceed there at once, and Fatso accepts these terms and dismisses the small stove lids from his shade with a nickel apiece and the chances are they figure he is Santa Claus already.

Now this is how Fatso Zimpf comes to be at Pink Waters which is the name of Mrs. Manwaring Mimm's estate in Palm Beach and this estate is about the size of Central Park and faces on the ocean and has many palm trees and fountains and statuary and a swimming pool and a house that reminds Fatso of Rockefeller Center, and with enough servants running around to form a union.

Fatso reports to the butler Sparks and it turns out that this Sparks is very glad to see him when he learns that Fatso is to be Santa Claus because it seems that Sparks always considers it most undignified for a high-class butler to go around being Santa Claus with pillows stuffed down his pants.

Furthermore, it turns out that Sparks is a horse player at heart and when he finds that Fatso is familiar with the gee-gees he becomes very friendly to be sure and supplies him with plenty of information and scandal about one and all in the best circles of Palm Beach and several surrounding spots.

He explains to Fatso that Pink Waters is one of the biggest estates in these parts and that Mrs. Manwaring Mimm is richer than six feet down in Iowa, with money that she gets off her papa, who makes it out of the oil dodge years back, and that she marries anytime she feels like it and that she feels like it three times so far and is now feeling like it again. In fact, Sparks tells Fatso that she is now feeling like marrying a young guy by the name of Johnny Relf who also has plenty of dough or will have when his parents kindly pass away.

Sparks says that personally he does not approve of this marriage because there is a slight disparity in age between the parties concerned. He says Johnny is only in his middle twenties and not too bright for his years, at that, while Mrs. Mimm is two face-liftings old that he knows of, but he says she is such a determined character that he does not think it advisable for him to mention his disapproval of her plan.

Then Fatso remembers the young guy in the roadster with Mrs.

Mimm and he asks Sparks is this the party she is going to marry and
Sparks says:

"Oh, no," he says. "That is Count Gregorio Ferrone of an old
Italian noble family. Mrs. Mimm meets him in New York last summer
and brings him here to Pink Waters as a houseguest. I understand,"
Sparks says, "that he is about to contract a marriage that will be
most advantageous to him. I do not think," he says, "that the count
is in funds to any extent."

"He is very impolite," Fatso says. "He does not talk much like a
foreigner to me. He calls me a fat bum without any accent. Personally," Fatso says, "I mark him N.G."

"Well," Sparks says, "to tell you the truth I second the motion.
The count is indeed a little brusque at times, especially," he says,
"with the servants. He claims he lives in this country off and on for
years so perhaps he loses his accent. Mrs. Mimm does not really seem
to know much about him."

Then Sparks tells Fatso that he is not expected to do anything at
all until it comes time for him to be Santa Claus the next night so
Fatso wanders around and about and admires the sights and scenes
of Palm Beach and finally he strolls along the ocean sands and there
in a lonely spot what does he behold but a beautiful young Judy of
maybe eighteen crying as if her heart will break.

Now if there is one thing Fatso cannot stand it is the sight of a
female character in distress, so he steps up to her and taps her on
the shoulder and says to her like this:

"Little miss," he says, "are you in trouble?"

"Yes, I am," she says: "who are you?"

"Why," Fatso says, "I am Santa Claus."

"Oh, no," she says. "There is no Santa Claus. I know it better
now than anybody else in this world. Anyway," she says, "if you are
Santa Claus where are your whiskers?"

Then Fatso explains about how he is to be Santa Claus for Mrs.
Mimm the next night and as soon as he mentions Mrs. Mimm's name
the beautiful young Judy starts crying harder than ever.

"Mrs. Mimm is the whole trouble," she says. "Mrs. Mimm steals
my Johnny away from me and now I must marry Count Gregorio.
I hate him even if he is a count. Mrs. Mimm is an old thing and I
want my Johnny."

She continues her crying and Fatso stands there putting two and two together and he can see that he comes upon another angle of the situation that Sparks the butler describes to him.

"Tut-tut," he says. "They tell me Johnny is a lightweight. Dry your tears and think no more of the matter."

Well, at this she stops crying and gazes at Fatso who observes that her eyes are a soft brown and he also observes that she has a shape that is worthy of mention, for Fatso is very observing even if he is fat, and finally she says:

"Of course Johnny is a lightweight," she says. "Everybody knows that. In fact," she says, "everybody knows he is a complete nitwit, but," she says, "what difference does that make? I love him. He is awfully good-looking and lots of fun. I love him a zillion dollars' worth. If you are Santa Claus," she says, "you give me my Johnny for my Christmas present instead of the speedboat my papa is getting me. I want my Johnny. I hope Mrs. Mimm drops dead."

Now there are more tears and Fatso keeps patting her on the shoulder and saying now, now, now, and there, there, there, and finally she quiets down and he is able to get a better idea of her story. It is a simple love story such as Fatso often hears before, because a fat guy is always hearing love stories though he never has any to tell himself.

It seems that she and this Johnny have a big quarrel one night in New York because she wishes to go to the Stork Club and he wishes to go to El Morocco and harsh words are exchanged and they part in bitter anger and the next thing she knows he is in Palm Beach and Mrs. Mimm is taking dead aim at him and then this Count Gregorio Ferrone comes along and her papa and mama decide that it will be a great idea for her to marry him and give them an excuse to have a villa in Italy.

Well, it seems that she agrees to do same while she is still sored up at Johnny but when her papa and mama take her to their own home in Palm Beach for the winter and she learns the situation between Johnny and Mrs. Mimm is quite serious, she regrets her decision and spends all her time wandering along the sands by herself.

In fact, she says if Fatso does not happen along this particular day the chances are her remainders will now be floating out to sea, because she learns from a jeweler on Worth Avenue that Johnny just buys a square-cut diamond ring the size of a bath rug and that she knows it must be Mrs. Mimm's Christmas present and to tell the truth she hears that Mrs. Mimm picks it out herself and tips the jeweler off to promote Johnny into buying this ring. Furthermore, she hears that Mrs. Mimm is going to announce her engagement to Johnny at the Christmas party.

"And," she says, "I will have to be there to hear it because Count Gregorio is her houseguest and my papa and mama are going and it will be considered very peculiar if I fail to be present. Anyway," she says, "I will hate to have anyone know I am so downcast about Johnny and why I am telling you I cannot think except you are fat and have a kind face."

By this time Fatso is becoming somewhat impatient with tears, so he changes the subject and asks her who she is and she says her name is Betty Lou Marvel and that her papa is nobody but Junius X. Marvel, the big automobile guy.

She says everybody in Palm Beach is afraid of Mrs. Mimm because she can think up very strange things to say about anybody she does not like and that nobody dare stay away from her parties if they are invited, especially her Christmas party. Betty Lou says it is years since anybody has a private Christmas in Palm Beach because Mrs. Mimm makes them bring all their presents to her party and has them given away there by her own Santa Claus and Betty Lou says she is glad they cannot take her speedboat there, and so is Fatso when he comes to think it over.

"Well, little miss," Fatso finally says, "kindly give Count Gregorio no more thought. I am personally giving him much consideration ever since he calls me a fat bum and I will take care of him. But," he says, "I do not see what I can do about your Johnny and Mrs. Mimm and if he is such a numskull as to prefer her to you maybe you are better off without him. Merry Christmas, little miss," he says.

"Merry Christmas, Santa Claus," Betty Lou says, and then Fatso goes on strolling along the sands wishing he is younger and two hundred pounds lighter.

Well, it comes on Christmas Eve and Pink Waters is all lighted up like Palisades Park with a Christmas tree as tall as a church steeple in the middle of the patio and all the fountains going with colored lights squirting on the water and two orchestras playing one after the other and long tables spread out in the open. In fact, it is as beautiful a scene as anybody could wish to see and very Christmasy-looking except it is quite hot.

When the guests are assembling, Fatso is taken in his Santa Claus suit into the library of the house which opens out into the patio by Sparks the butler and given a little final coaching there.

It seems that the first part of the party is for the neighbors' children and the second part is for the grown-ups, male and female, and on the Christmas tree in the patio and stacked up at the foot of the tree are many packages containing the presents for the little ones and Sparks explains that it is the duty of Fatso as Santa Claus to distribute these packages.

On a table in the library is a pile of small packages and Sparks says that after he distributes the packages to the children in the patio, Fatso is to return to the library and put these small packages in his Santa Claus bag and go out and stand under the tree again and take the small packages out of the bag one by one and call off the names written on them and hand them out to the parties they are meant for.

"You will be very careful with these small packages," Sparks says. "They contain presents from husbands to their ever-loving wives and vice versa and from one sweet pea to another, and so forth and so on. The chances are there are many valuable gewgaws in these packages," he says.

Then Sparks leaves Fatso alone in the library while he goes out to see if everything is ready for the appearance of Santa Claus and Fatso can observe him through the tall French window that opens on the patio, bustling about through the gay scene, and with nothing else to do until Sparks's return, Fatso takes to examining the small packages and thinking to himself that if he has the money the contents represent the chances are he will be able to retire from horse playing and perhaps find some beautiful young Judy like Betty Lou to love him.

He observes Betty Lou in the patio with the young guy that he now knows as Count Gregorio and he can see that she seems somewhat depressed and then he notices Mrs. Mimm with a tall blond young guy at her heels that he figures must be the Johnny Relf that Betty Lou is crying about and Fatso thinks to himself that from his looks this Johnny must indeed be something of a waste ball.

Finally Sparks returns and says everything is all set and out into the patio goes Fatso jingling a lot of sleigh bells and beaming on one and all and the orchestras play and the little children let out shrill cries of joy. There is no doubt but what Fatso is a wonderful success as Santa Claus with the little children and many of them wish to shake hands with him but after an hour of standing under the tree picking up packages and calling off names, Fatso commences to get a little weary.

Moreover, he commences to get a trifle vexed with the little ones, especially when some of them insist on pulling his whiskers and small boys start kicking him on the ankles to see if he is alive and by and by Fatso is thinking that maybe President Roosevelt is right about the redistribution of wealth.

In fact, Fatso becomes so vexed that he takes to quietly stepping on a few little toesies here and there accidentally on purpose and the childish cries of pain are enough to break anybody's heart and probably many of these children stop believing in Santa Claus.

Well, he finally gets rid of all the little children and they are taken away by their nurses and only the grown-ups are left and it is a gay gathering to be sure with one and all in evening dress and drinking champagne and dancing, and Fatso retires to the library again and when Sparks comes in to help him load up with the small packages, Fatso says to him like this:

"Sparksy," he says, "who is the most jealous married guy present at this party?"

"Why," Sparks says, "that is an easy one. The most jealous married guy at this party or anywhere else in the world is undoubtedly old Joel Brokebaugh. He is an old walrus who is married to a young mouse, and," Sparks says, "he thinks that every guy who says good morning to Mrs. Brokebaugh is after her, although," he says, "this idea will make you laugh yourself sick when you see her.

"She is undoubtedly a very low score for looks," Sparks says. "Furthermore," he says, "she has no more spirit than a gooseberry. Old Brokebaugh is so stingy he will not let her buy a new hat or a new dress more than once every few years although he has millions. He does not wish her to dress up for fear some guy may notice her. Personally," Sparks says, "I think old Brokebaugh is touched in the wind for figuring anybody else will ever want his wife, but he has a violent temper and often causes scenes and some say he even carries a pistol in his pocket at all times."

"Brokebaugh, eh?" Fatso says.

"Yes," Sparks says. "They are sitting together under the coconut palm by the big fountain, though why they come to a Christmas party nobody knows because they never give each other anything in the way of presents and take no part in the festivities. Everybody feels sorry for Mrs. Brokebaugh, but," Sparks says, "I say what she needs is some spunk."

Well, Fatso again goes out into the patio with his bag full of the small packages and by this time what with the champagne and the dancing and the spirit of the occasion and all this and that, everybody is in a lively mood and they give Fatso a big cheer and no one is any gayer than Mrs. Mimm.

In fact, she is practically hilarious and she gives Fatso a large smile as he goes past her and he can see that she is pleased with his efforts and he can also see that she still has this Johnny with her and that Johnny looks no brighter than before, if as bright, and then Fatso spots the couple Sparks speaks of under the coconut palm and he is somewhat surprised to note that Sparks slightly overrates Mrs. Brokebaugh's appearance.

Even from a distance Fatso can see that she is a zero for looks but he can also see that the old guy with her seems to be about as described by Sparks, only more so. He is a tall, thin old guy with a red face and a bald head and eyes like a shark and Fatso observes that the servants tiptoe going past him.

Well, Fatso gets under the tree and starts calling out names once more and giving out packages and there is now great excitement and many oohs and ahs in female voices on all sides and finally he gets down to just a few packages and calls out the name of Johnny Relf and right away afterward the name of Miss Betty Lou Marvel and in fact Fatso calls them so close together that they meet under the tree though all they do is exchange cruel glances.

Fatso does not say anything whatever to this Johnny as he gives him his package, because Fatso feels that he already does enough talking in words of one syllable to the children, but when Miss Betty Lou steps up he gives her a smile and says:

"Merry Christmas, little miss."

"Merry Christmas, Santa Claus," she says, "but I still do not believe in you."

Then she starts walking away opening her package as she goes and all of a sudden she lets out a cry and starts running toward

Johnny Relf but by now Johnny opens his own package, too, and starts running toward Betty Lou.

So they meet practically head-on and start taking holds on each other in the presence of one and all, because it seems that Betty Lou's present is a large square-cut diamond ring with a card in the box which states that it is to my beloved from Johnny and that his present is a pair of big black pearl studs with a card saying they are with all my heart to Johnny from Betty Lou.

Of course nobody bothers to look into the matter at the moment, but when somebody does so later on it is considered something of a coincidence that the writing on the two cards is exactly the same and not very neat, but one and all figure it is just an act of Providence and let it go at that, especially as an act of Providence is regarded as quite a compliment to Palm Beach.

In fact, at this particular moment nobody is paying much attention to anything much but the great happiness of Betty Lou and Johnny, except Mrs. Mimm and she is watching Fatso with keen interest, though Fatso is unaware of her attention as he walks over to where Mrs. Brokebaugh is sitting and hands her a package instead of calling out her name.

Then Fatso returns to the house figuring to get his Santa Claus suit off and collect his wages from Sparks and vanish from these parts before anybody learns that he writes these cards when he is alone in the library and swaps them for cards that will give the ring to Mrs. Mimm from Johnny and the black pearls to Johnny from Mrs. Mimm, in both cases with love.

While he is walking through a long hallway, all of a sudden Fatso gets a feeling that he is being followed, and looking around he observes Mrs. Mimm close behind him. There is something about Mrs. Mimm that causes Fatso to walk a little faster and then he notes that Mrs. Mimm is walking quite a little faster than he is.

So Fatso dodges into an open doorway that he hopes and trusts may lead him elsewhere but he forgets that when he goes through doors it is usually advisable for him to turn sideways because of his great width. He goes at this door frontways and the next thing he knows there he is stuck right in the middle of the doorway and then he becomes conscious of great discomfort to the southward as it seems that Mrs. Mimm is forgetting she is a lady and is kicking him severely and it also seems that these evening shoes that the Judys wear now-adays with their bare toes sticking out in front are capable of inflicting greater pain when used for kicking than just ordinary shoes.

In the meantime, it appears that there is some commotion in the patio because Mrs. Brokebaugh is so startled at getting any Christmas present at all that she cannot open the package Fatso gives her so old Mr. Brokebaugh opens it for her and finds a gold vanity case with a card that reads as follows:

"To my sweetest sweet from Gregorio."

Well, of course old Mr. Brokebaugh has no way of knowing that this is Count Gregorio's present to Betty Lou and that Fatso does not even change the card but only rubs out Betty Lou's name on it and puts down Mrs. Brokebaugh's, though naturally old Mr. Brokebaugh knows who Gregorio is.

In fact, he can see Gregorio at this very moment standing near by feeling of his little mustache and looking greatly bewildered at the scene that is still going on at intervals, between Betty Lou and Johnny, and all of a sudden old Mr. Brokebaugh lets out a yell and jumps up and pulls a pistol out of his pocket and starts full tilt at the count speaking in a loud tone, as follows:

"So," he says, "you are making a play for my wife, are you, scoundrel?"

Well, of course Count Gregorio has no idea what old Mr. Brokebaugh is talking about, but he has eyes in his head and he can see that Mr. Brokebaugh is making a dead set for him and that he is hotter than a firecracker and he can also see the pistol and from the way the count turns and starts running it is plain to be seen that whatever he may be, he is no sucker.

He knocks over three debutantes and a banker worth ten million dollars making for the patio wall and trying to keep trees and bushes between him and Mr. Brokebaugh as he goes and all this time old Mr. Brokebaugh is running after him and with surprising speed for a guy his age and waving the pistol and requesting the count to stand still and be shot.

He never gets a really fair crack at the count except when Gregorio is going over the wall and then old Mr. Brokebaugh lets fly twice and misses both times and the sound of this shooting probably saves Fatso many more contusions as it brings Mrs. Mimm running into the patio to find out what is going on and in her absence Fatso wiggles on through the doorway.

So Fatso shakes the sands of Palm Beach from his feet regretting only that he never gets a chance to ask Betty Lou if she now believes in Santa Claus and he goes on down to Miami and a year later he relates the above circumstances to me one day when we are sitting in the rocking chairs on the veranda of the Hotel McAllister hoping to catch somebody going to the races with a couple of spare seats in their car, for things are by no means dinkum with Fatso and me at the moment.

"You see," Fatso says, "tomorrow is Christmas again and this is what reminds me of these matters at this time."

"So it is, Fatso," I say. "It is strange how time flies. But, Fatso," I say, "are you not most severe on Count Gregorio in not only knocking him out of a chance to pick up a few boffoes by marriage but in almost getting him plugged by a jealous husband?"

"No," Fatso says. "By no means. You must always remember he calls me a fat bum. Besides," he says, "old Brokebaugh just spares me the humiliation of denouncing Gregorio as a former busboy in Vincenti's wop restaurant in West Fiftieth Street and still wanted for robbing the damper of thirty-six dollars.

"I will never forgive myself if I am compelled to holler copper on anybody whatsoever," Fatso says, "but," he says, "of course I will do so as a last resort to prevent Gregorio from marrying Betty Lou. It comes to me all of a sudden why his face is familiar when I am strolling on the sands the time I meet Betty Lou. I never forget a face."

Well, at this moment a big limousine stops in front of the hotel and a small-sized lively Judy all dressed up and sparkling with jewelry hops out of the car and runs up the veranda steps with three good-looking tanned young guys with little mustaches running after her and she is laughing and gay and looks like plenty in the bank, and I am greatly surprised when she skips up to Fatso and gives him a pat on the arm and says like this:

"Merry Christmas, Santa Claus!"

Then she is gone as quick as she comes and the young guys with her and she is still laughing and Fatso is gazing at a fifty-dollar note in his hand with great pleasure and he says:

"She is from Palm Beach," he says. "Anytime anybody from Palm Beach recognizes me they stake me to something because they remember that Mrs. Mimm never pays me the fifty she promises me for being her Santa Claus. I understand," Fatso says, "that it is a public scandal in Palm Beach."

"Is this one Betty Lou?" I ask.

"Oh, no," Fatso says. "She is Mrs. Brokebaugh. I recall now I hear that ever since she gets the Christmas present that she thinks to this very day is from Count Gregorio, she decides she is a natural-born charmer and blossoms out into a life of gaiety, and," Fatso says, "they tell me her husband cannot do a thing about it. Well, Merry Christmas to you."

"Merry Christmas, Fatso," I say.

P ersonally, I never criticize Miss Beulah Beauregard for breaking her engagement to Little Alfie, because from what she tells
me she becomes engaged to him under false pretences, and I
do not approve of guys using false pretences on dolls, except,
of course, when nothing else will do.

It seems that Little Alfie promises to show Miss Beulah Beauregard the life of Riley following the races with him when he gets her
to give up a first-class job displaying her shape to the customers in
the 900 Club, although Miss Beulah Beauregard frankly admits that
Little Alfie does not say what Riley, and afterward Little Alfie states
that he must be thinking of Four-eyes Riley when he makes the
promise, and everybody knows that Four-eyes Riley is nothing but
a bum, in spades.

Anyway, the life Little Alfie shows Miss Beulah Beauregard after
they become engaged is by no means exciting, according to what she
tells me, as Little Alfie is always going around the racetracks with
one or two crocodiles that he calls racehorses, trying to win a few
bobs for himself, and generally Little Alfie is broke and struggling,
and Miss Beulah Beauregard says this is no existence for a member
of a proud old Southern family such as the Beauregards.

In fact, Miss Beulah Beauregard often tells me that she has half
a mind to leave Little Alfie and return to her ancestral home in
Georgia, only she can never think of any way of getting there without
walking, and Miss Beulah Beauregard says it always makes her feet
sore to walk very far, although the only time anybody ever hears of

Miss Beulah Beauregard doing much walking is the time she is shell-roaded on the Pelham Parkway by some Yale guys when she gets cross with them.

It seems that when Little Alfie is first canvassing Miss Beulah Beauregard to be his fiancée he builds her up to expect diamonds and furs and limousines and one thing and another, but the only diamond she ever sees is an engagement hoop that Little Alfie gives her as the old convincer when he happens to be in the money for a moment, and it is a very small diamond, at that, and needs a high north light when you look at it.

But Miss Beulah Beauregard treasures this diamond very highly just the same, and one reason she finally breaks off her engagement to Little Alfie is because he borrows the diamond one day during the Hialeah meeting at Miami without mentioning the matter to her, and hocks it for five bobs which he bets on an old caterpillar of his by the name of Governor Hicks to show.

Well, the chances are Miss Beulah Beauregard will not mind Little Alfie's borrowing the diamond so much if he does not take the twenty-five bobs he wins when Governor Hicks drops in there in the third hole and sends it to Colonel Matt Winn in Louisville to enter a three-year-old of his by the name of Last Hope in the Kentucky Derby, this Last Hope being the only other horse Little Alfie owns at this time.

Such an action makes Miss Beulah Beauregard very indignant indeed, because she says a babe in arms will know Last Hope cannot walk a mile and a quarter, which is the Derby distance, let alone run so far, and that even if Last Hope can run a mile and a quarter, he cannot run it fast enough to get up a sweat.

In fact, Miss Beulah Beauregard and Little Alfie have words over this proposition, because Little Alfie is very high on Last Hope and will not stand for anybody insulting this particular horse, not even his fiancée, although he never seems to mind what anybody says about Governor Hicks, and, in fact, he often says it himself.

Personally, I do not understand what Little Alfie sees in Last Hope, because the horse never starts more than once or twice since it is born, and then has a tough time finishing last, but Little Alfie says the fifty G's that Colonel Winn gives to the winner of the Kentucky Derby is just the same as in the jug in his name, especially if it comes up mud on Derby Day, for Little Alfie claims that Last Hope is bred to just naturally eat mud.

Well, Miss Beulah Beauregard says there is no doubt Little Alfie blows his topper, and that there is no percentage in her remaining engaged to a crackpot, and many citizens put in with her on her statement because they consider entering Last Hope in the Derby very great foolishness, no matter if it comes up mud or what, and right away Tom Shaw offers 1,000 to 1 against the horse in the future book, and everybody says Tom is underlaying the price at that.

Miss Beulah Beauregard states that she is very discouraged by the way things turn out, and that she scarcely knows what to do, because she fears her shape changes so much in the four or five years she is engaged to Little Alfie that the customers at the 900 Club may not care to look at it any more, especially if they have to pay for this privilege, although personally I will pay any reasonable cover charge to look at Miss Beulah Beauregard's shape anytime, if it is all I suspect. As far as I can see it is still a very nice shape indeed, if you care for shapes.

Miss Beulah Beauregard is at this time maybe twenty-five or twenty-six, and is built like a first baseman, being tall and rangy. She has hay-colored hair, and blue eyes, and lots of health, and a very good appetite. In fact, I once see Miss Beulah Beauregard putting on the fried chicken in the Seven Seas Restaurant in a way that greatly astonishes me, because I never knew before that members of proud old Southern families are such hearty eaters. Furthermore, Miss Beulah Beauregard has a very Southern accent, which makes her sound quite cute, except maybe when she is a little excited and is putting the zing on somebody, such as Little Alfie.

Well, Little Alfie says he regrets exceedingly that Miss Beulah Beauregard sees fit to break their engagement, and will not be with him when he cuts up the Derby dough, as he is planning a swell wedding for her at French Lick after the race, and even has a list all made out of the presents he is going to buy her, including another diamond, and now he has all this bother of writing out the list for nothing.

Furthermore, Little Alfie says he is so accustomed to having Miss Beulah Beauregard as his fiancée that he scarcely knows what to do without her, and he goes around with a very sad puss, and is generally quite low in his mind, because there is no doubt that Little Alfie loves Miss Beulah Beauregard more than somewhat.

But other citizens are around stating that the real reason Miss Beulah Beauregard breaks her engagement to Little Alfie is because a guy by the name of Mr. Paul D. Veere is making a powerful play for her, and she does not wish him to know that she has any truck with a character such as Little Alfie, for of course Little Alfie is by no means anything much to look at, and, furthermore, what with hanging out with his horses most of the time, he never smells like any rose geranium.

It seems that this Mr. Paul D. Veere is a New York banker, and he has a little mustache, and plenty of coconuts, and Miss Beulah Beauregard meets up with him one morning when she is displaying her shape on the beach at the Roney Plaza for nothing, and it also seems that there is enough of her shape left to interest Mr. Paul D. Veere no little.

In fact, the next thing anybody knows, Mr. Paul D. Veere is taking Miss Beulah Beauregard here and there, and around and about, although at this time Miss Beulah Beauregard is still engaged to Little Alfie, and the only reason Little Alfie does not notice Mr. Paul D. Veere at first is because he is busy training Last Hope to win the Kentucky Derby, and hustling around trying to get a few bobs together every day to stand off the overhead, including Miss Beulah Beauregard, because naturally Miss Beulah Beauregard cannot bear the idea of living in a fleabag, such as the place where Little Alfie resides, but has to have a nice room at the Roney Plaza.

Well, personally, I have nothing against bankers as a class, and in fact I never meet up with many bankers in my life, but somehow I do not care for Mr. Paul D. Veere's looks. He looks to me like a stony-hearted guy, although, of course, nobody ever sees any banker who does not look stony-hearted, because it seems that being bankers just naturally makes them look this way.

But Mr. Paul D. Veere is by no means an old guy, and the chances are he speaks of something else besides horses to Miss Beulah Beauregard, and furthermore he probably does not smell like horses all the time, so nobody can blame Miss Beulah Beauregard for going around and about with him, although many citizens claim she is a little out of line in accepting Mr. Paul D. Veere's play while she is still engaged to Little Alfie. In fact, there is great indignation in some circles about this, as many citizens feel that Miss Beulah Beauregard is setting a bad example to other fiancées.

But after Miss Beulah Beauregard formally announces that their engagement is off, it is agreed by one and all that she has a right to do as she pleases, and that Little Alfie himself gets out of line in what happens at Hialeah a few days later when he finally notices that Miss Beulah Beauregard seems to be with Mr. Paul D. Veere, and on very friendly terms with him, at that. In fact, Little Alfie comes upon Mr. Paul D. Veere in the act of kissing Miss Beulah Beauregard behind a hibiscus bush out near the paddock, and this scene is most revolting to Little Alfie as he never cares for hibiscus, anyway.

He forgets that Miss Beulah Beauregard is no longer his fiancée, and tries to take a punch at Mr. Paul D. Veere, but he is stopped by a number of detectives, who are greatly horrified at the idea of anybody taking a punch at a guy who has as many coconuts as Mr. Paul D. Veere, and while they are expostulating with Little Alfie, Miss Beulah Beauregard disappears from the scene and is observed no more in Miami. Furthermore, Mr. Paul D. Veere also disappears, but of course nobody minds this very much, and, in fact, his disappearance is a great relief to all citizens who have fiancées in Miami at this time.

But it seems that before he disappears Mr. Paul D. Veere calls on certain officials of the Jockey Club and weighs in the sacks on Little Alfie, stating that he is a most dangerous character to have loose around a racetrack, and naturally the officials are bound to listen to a guy who has as many coconuts as Mr. Paul D. Veere.

So a day or two later old Cap Duhaine, the head detective around the racetrack, sends for Little Alfie and asks him what he thinks will become of all the prominent citizens such as bankers if guys go around taking punches at them and scaring them half to death, and Little Alfie cannot think of any answer to this conundrum offhand, especially as Cap Duhaine then asks Little Alfie if it will be convenient for him to take his two horses elsewhere.

Well, Little Alfie can see that Cap Duhaine is hinting in a polite way that he is not wanted around Hialeah any more, and Little Alfie is a guy who can take a hint as well as the next guy, especially when Cap Duhaine tells him in confidence that the racing stewards do not seem able to get over the idea that some scalawag slips a firecracker into Governor Hicks the day old Governor Hicks runs third, because it seems from what Cap Duhaine says that the stewards consider it practically supernatural for Governor Hicks to run third anywhere, anytime.

So there Little Alfie is in Miami, as clean as a jaybird, with two horses on his hands, and no way to ship them to any place where horses are of any account, and it is quite a predicament indeed, and causes Little Alfie to ponder quite some. And the upshot of his pondering is that Little Alfie scrapes up a few bobs here and there, and a few oats, and climbs on Governor Hicks one day and boots him in the slats and tells him to giddyup, and away he goes out of Miami, headed north, riding Governor Hicks and leading Last Hope behind him on a rope.

Naturally, this is considered a most unusual spectacle by one and all who witness it and, in fact, it is the first time anybody can remember a horse owner such as Little Alfie riding one of his own horses off in this way, and Gloomy Gus is offering to lay plenty of 5 to 1 that Governor Hicks never makes Palm Beach with Little Alfie up, as it is well known that the old Governor has bum legs and is half out of wind and is apt to pig it anytime.

But it seems that Governor Hicks makes Palm Beach all right with Little Alfie up and going so easy that many citizens are around asking Gloomy for a price against Jacksonville. Furthermore, many citizens are now saying that Little Alfie is a pretty smart guy, at that, to think of such an economical idea, and numerous other horse owners are looking their stock over to see if they have anything to ride up north themselves.

Many citizens are also saying that Little Alfie gets a great break when Miss Beulah Beauregard runs out on him, because it takes plenty of weight off him in the way of railroad fare and one thing and another; but it seems Little Alfie does not feel this way about the matter at all.

It seems that Little Alfie often thinks about Miss Beulah Beauregard as he goes jogging along to the north, and sometimes he talks to Governor Hicks and Last Hope about her, and especially to Last Hope, as Little Alfie always considers Governor Hicks somewhat dumb. Also Little Alfie sometimes sings sad love songs right out loud as he is riding along, although the first time he starts to sing he frightens Last Hope and causes him to break loose from the lead rope and run away, and Little Alfie is an hour catching him. But after this Last Hope gets so he does not mind Little Alfie's voice so much, except when Little Alfie tries to hit high C.

Well, Little Alfie has a very nice ride, at that, because the weather is fine and the farmers along the road feed him and his horses, and he has nothing whatever to worry about except a few saddle galls, and about getting to Kentucky for the Derby in May, and here it is only late in February, and anyway Little Alfie does not figure to ride any farther than maybe Maryland where he is bound to make a scratch so he can ship from there.

Now, one day Little Alfie is riding along a road through a stretch of piny woods, a matter of maybe ninety-odd miles north of Jacksonville, which puts him in the State of Georgia, when he passes a half-plowed field on one side of the road near a ramshackly old house and beholds a most unusual scene:

A large white mule hitched to a plow is sitting down in the field and a tall doll in a sunbonnet and a gingham dress is standing beside the mule crying very heartily.

Naturally, the spectacle of a doll in distress, or even a doll who is not in distress, is bound to attract Little Alfie's attention, so he tells Governor Hicks and Last Hope to whoa, and then he asks the doll what is eating her, and the doll looks up at him out of her sunbonnet, and who is this doll but Miss Beulah Beauregard.

Of course Little Alfie is somewhat surprised to see Miss Beulah Beauregard crying over a mule, and especially in a sunbonnet, so he climbs down off of Governor Hicks to inquire into this situation, and right away Miss Beulah Beauregard rushes up to Little Alfie and chucks herself into his arms and speaks as follows:

"Oh, Alfie," Miss Beulah Beauregard says, "I am so glad you find me. I am thinking of you day and night, and wondering if you forgive me. Oh, Alfie, I love you," she says. "I am very sorry I go away with Mr. Paul D. Veere. He is nothing but a great rapscallion," she says. "He promises to make me his ever-loving wife when he gets me to accompany him from Miami to his shooting lodge on the Altamaha River, twenty-five miles from here, although," she says, "I never know before he has such a lodge in these parts.

"And," Miss Beulah Beauregard says, "the very first day I have to pop him with a pot of cold cream and render him half unconscious to escape his advances. Oh, Alfie," she says, "Mr. Paul D. Veere's intentions toward me are by no means honorable. Furthermore," she says, "I learn he already has an ever-loving wife and three children in New York."

Well, of course Little Alfie is slightly perplexed by this matter and can scarcely think of anything much to say, but finally he says to Miss Beulah Beauregard like this:

"Well," he says, "but what about the mule?"

"Oh," Miss Beulah Beauregard says, "his name is Abimelech, and I am plowing with him when he hauls off and sits down and refuses to budge. He is the only mule we own," she says, "and he is old and ornery, and nobody can do anything whatever with him when he wishes to sit down. But," she says, "my papa will be very angry because he expects me to get this field all plowed up by suppertime. In fact," Miss Beulah Beauregard says, "I am afraid my papa will be so angry he will give me a whopping, because he by no means forgives me as yet for coming home, and this is why I am shedding tears when you come along."

Then Miss Beulah Beauregard begins crying again as if her heart will break, and if there is one thing Little Alfie hates and despises it is to see a doll crying, and especially Miss Beulah Beauregard, for Miss Beulah Beauregard can cry in a way to wake the dead when she is going good, so Little Alfie holds her so close to his chest he ruins four cigars in his vest pocket, and speaks to her as follows:

"Tut, tut," Little Alfie says. "Tut, tut, tut, tut, tut," he says. "Dry your eyes and we will just hitch old Governor Hicks here to the plow and get this field plowed quicker than you can say scat, because," Little Alfie says, "when I am a young squirt, I am the best plower in Columbia County, New York."

Well, this idea cheers Miss Beulah Beauregard up no little, and so Little Alfie ties Last Hope to a tree and takes the harness off Abimelech, the mule, who keeps right on sitting down as if he does not care what happens, and puts the harness on Governor Hicks and hitches Governor Hicks to the plow, and the way the old Governor carries on when he finds out they wish him to pull a plow is really most surprising. In fact, Little Alfie has to get a club and reason with Governor Hicks before he will settle down and start pulling the plow.

It turns out that Little Alfie is a first-class plower, at that, and while he is plowing, Miss Beulah Beauregard walks along with him and talks a blue streak, and Little Alfie learns more things from her in half an hour than he ever before suspects in some years, and especially about Miss Beulah Beauregard herself.

It seems that the ramshackly old house is Miss Beulah Beauregard's ancestral home, and that her people are very poor, and live in these piny woods for generations, and that their name is Benson and not Beauregard at all, this being nothing but a name that Miss Beulah Beauregard herself thinks up out of her own head when she goes to New York to display her shape.

Furthermore, when they go to the house it comes out that Miss Beulah Beauregard's papa is a tall, skinny old guy with a goatee, who can lie faster than Little Alfie claims Last Hope can run. But it seems that the old skeezicks takes quite an interest in Last Hope when Little Alfie begins telling him what a great horse this horse is, especially in the mud, and how he is going to win the Kentucky Derby.

In fact, Miss Beulah Beauregard's papa seems to believe everything Little Alfie tells him, and as he is the first guy Little Alfie ever meets up with who believes anything he tells about anything whatever, it is a privilege and a pleasure for Little Alfie to talk to him. Miss Beulah Beauregard also has a mama who turns out to be very fat, and full of Southern hospitality, and quite handy with a skillet.

Then there is a grown brother by the name of Jeff, who is practically a genius, as he knows how to disguise skimmin's so it makes a person only a little sick when they drink it, this skimmin's being a drink which is made from skimmings that come to the top on boiling sugar cane, and generally it tastes like gasoline, and is very fatal indeed.

Now, the consequences are Little Alfie finds this place very pleasant, and he decides to spend a few weeks there, paying for his keep with the services of Governor Hicks as a plow horse, especially as he is now practically engaged to Miss Beulah Beauregard all over again and she will not listen to him leaving without her. But they have no money for her railroad fare, and Little Alfie becomes very indignant when she suggests she can ride Last Hope on north while he is riding Governor Hicks, and wishes to know if she thinks a Derby candidate can be used for a truck horse.

Well, this almost causes Miss Beulah Beauregard to start breaking the engagement all over again, as she figures it is a dirty crack about her heft, but her papa steps in and says they must remain until Governor Hicks gets through with the plowing anyway, or he will know the reason why. So Little Alfie stays and he puts in all his spare time training Last Hope and wondering who he can write to for enough dough to send Miss Beulah Beauregard north when the time comes.

He trains Last Hope by walking him and galloping him along the country roads in person, and taking care of him as if he is a baby, and what with this work, and the jog up from Miami, Last Hope fills out very strong and hearty, and anybody must admit that he is not a bad-looking beetle, though maybe a little more leggy than some like to see.

Now, it comes a Sunday, and all day long there is a very large storm with rain and wind that takes to knocking over big trees, and one thing and another, and no one is able to go outdoors much. So late in the evening Little Alfie and Miss Beulah Beauregard and all the Bensons are gathered about the stove in the kitchen drinking skimmin's, and Little Alfie is telling them all over again about how Last Hope will win the Kentucky Derby, especially if it comes up mud, when they hear a hammering at the door.

When the door is opened, who comes in but Mr. Paul D. Veere, sopping wet from head to foot, including his little mustache, and limping so he can scarcely walk, and naturally his appearance non-plusses Miss Beulah Beauregard and Little Alfie, who can never forget that Mr. Paul D. Veere is largely responsible for the saddle galls he gets riding up from Miami.

In fact, several times since he stops at Miss Beulah Beauregard's ancestral home, Little Alfie thinks of Mr. Paul D. Veere, and every time he thinks of him he is in favor of going over to Mr. Paul D. Veere's shooting lodge on the Altamaha and speaking to him severely.

But Miss Beulah Beauregard always stops him, stating that the proud old Southern families in this vicinity are somewhat partial to the bankers and other rich guys from the North who have shooting lodges around and about in the piny woods, and especially on the Altamaha, because these guys furnish a market to the local citizens for hunting guides, and corn liquor, and one thing and another.

Miss Beulah Beauregard says if a guest of the Bensons speaks to Mr. Paul D. Veere severely, it may be held against the family, and it seems that the Benson family cannot stand any more beefs against it just at this particular time. So Little Alfie never goes, and here all of a sudden is Mr. Paul D. Veere right in his lap.

Naturally, Little Alfie steps forward and starts winding up a large right hand with the idea of parking it on Mr. Paul D. Veere's chin, but Mr. Paul D. Veere seems to see that there is hostility afoot, and he backs up against the wall, and raises his hand, and speaks as follows:

"Folks," Mr. Paul D. Veere says, "I just go into a ditch in my automobile half a mile up the road. My car is a wreck," he says, "and my right leg seems so badly hurt I am just barely able to drag myself here. Now, folks," he says, "it is almost a matter of life and death with me to get to the station at Tillinghast in time to flag the Orange Blossom Special. It is the last train tonight to Jacksonville, and I must be in Jacksonville before midnight so I can hire an airplane and get to New York by the time my bank opens at ten o'clock in the morning. It is about ten hours by plane from Jacksonville to New York," Mr. Paul D. Veere says, "so if I can catch the Orange Blossom, I will be able to just about make it!"

Then he goes on speaking in a low voice and states that he receives a telephone message from New York an hour or so before at his lodge telling him he must hurry home, and right away afterward, while he is trying to telephone the station at Tillinghast to make sure they will hold the Orange Blossom until he gets there, no matter what, all the telephone and telegraph wires around and about go down in the storm.

So he starts for the station in his car, and just as it looks as if he may make it, his car runs smack-dab into a ditch and Mr. Paul D. Veere's leg is hurt so there is no chance he can walk the rest of the way to the station, and there Mr. Paul D. Veere is.

"It is a very desperate case, folks," Mr. Paul D. Veere says. "Let me take your automobile, and I will reward you liberally."

Well, at this Miss Beulah Beauregard's papa looks at a clock on the kitchen wall and states as follows:

"We do not keep an automobile, neighbor," he says, "and anyway," he says, "it is quite a piece from here to Tillinghast and the Orange Blossom is due in ten minutes, so I do not see how you can possibly make it. Rest your hat, neighbor," Miss Beulah Beauregard's papa says, "and have some skimmin's, and take things easy, and I will look at your leg and see how bad you are bunged up."

Well, Mr. Paul D. Veere seems to turn as pale as a pillow as he hears this about the time, and then he says:

"Lend me a horse and buggy," he says. "I must be in New York in person in the morning. No one else will do but me," he says, and as he speaks these words he looks at Miss Beulah Beauregard and then at Little Alfie as if he is speaking to them personally, although up to this time he does not look at either of them after he comes into the kitchen.

"Why, neighbor," Miss Beulah Beauregard's papa says, "we do not keep a buggy, and even if we do keep a buggy we do not have time to hitch up anything to a buggy. Neighbor," he says, "you are certainly on a bust if you think you can catch the Orange Blossom now."

"Well, then," Mr. Paul D. Veere says, very sorrowful, "I will have to go to jail."

Then he flops himself down in a chair and covers his face with his hands, and he is a spectacle such as is bound to touch almost any heart, and when she sees him in this state Miss Beulah Beauregard begins crying because she hates to see anybody as sorrowed up as Mr. Paul D. Veere, and between sobs she asks Little Alfie to think of something to do about the situation.

"Let Mr. Paul D. Veere ride Governor Hicks to the station," Miss Beauregard says. "After all," she says, "I cannot forget his courtesy in sending me halfway here in his car from his shooting lodge after I pop him with the pot of cold cream, instead of making me walk as those Yale guys do the time they red-light me."

"Why," Little Alfie says, "it is a mile and a quarter from the gate out here to the station. I know," he says, "because I get a guy in an automobile to clock it on his meter one day last week, figuring to give Last Hope a workout over the full Derby route pretty soon. The road must be fetlock deep in mud at this time, and," Little Alfie says, "Governor Hicks cannot as much as stand up in the mud. The only horse in the world that can run fast enough through this mud to make the Orange Blossom is Last Hope, but," Little Alfie says, "of course I'm not letting anybody ride a horse as valuable as Last Hope to catch trains."

Well, at this Mr. Paul D. Veere lifts his head and looks at Little Alfie with great interest and speaks as follows:

"How much is this valuable horse worth?" Mr. Paul D. Veere says.

"Why," Little Alfie says, "he is worth anyway fifty G's to me, because," he says, "this is the sum Colonel Winn is giving to the winner of the Kentucky Derby, and there is no doubt whatever that Last Hope will be this winner, especially," Little Alfie says, "if it comes up mud."

"I do not carry any such large sum of money as you mention on my person," Mr. Paul D. Veere says, "but," he says, "if you are willing to trust me, I will give you my IOU for same, just to let me ride your horse to the station. I am once the best amateur steeplechase rider in the Hunts Club," Mr. Paul D. Veere says, "and if your horse can run at all there is still a chance for me to keep out of jail."

Well, the chances are Little Alfie will by no means consider extending a loan of credit for fifty G's to Mr. Paul D. Veere or any other banker, and especially a banker who is once an amateur steeplechase jock, because if there is one thing Little Alfie does not trust it is an amateur steeplechase jock, and furthermore Little Alfie is somewhat offended because Mr. Paul D. Veere seems to think he is running a livery stable.

But Miss Beulah Beauregard is now crying so loud nobody can scarcely hear themselves think, and Little Alfie gets to figuring what she may say to him if he does not rent Last Hope to Mr. Paul D. Veere at this time and it comes out later that Last Hope does not happen to win the Kentucky Derby after all. So he finally says all right, and Mr. Paul D. Veere at once outs with a little gold pencil and a notebook, and scribbles off a marker for fifty G's to Little Alfie.

And the next thing anybody knows, Little Alfie is leading Last Hope out of the barn and up to the gate with nothing on him but a bridle as Little Alfie does not wish to waste time saddling, and as he is boosting Mr. Paul D. Veere onto Last Hope Little Alfie speaks as follows:

"You have three minutes left," Little Alfie says. "It is almost a straight course, except for a long turn going into the last quarter. Let this fellow run," he says. "You will find plenty of mud all the way, but," Little Alfie says, "this is a mud-running fool. In fact," Little Alfie says, "you are pretty lucky it comes up mud."

Then he gives Last Hope a smack on the hip and away goes Last

Hope lickity-split through the mud and anybody can see from the
way Mr. Paul D. Veere is sitting on him that Mr. Paul D. Veere
knows what time it is when it comes to riding. In fact, Little Alfie
himself says he never seen a better seat anywhere in his life, especially
for a guy who is riding bareback.

Well, Little Alfie watches them go down the road in a gob of
mud, and it will always be one of the large regrets of Little Alfie's
life that he leaves his split-second super in hock in Miami, because
he says he is sure Last Hope runs the first quarter through the mud
faster than any quarter is ever run before in this world. But of course
Little Alfie is more excited than somewhat at this moment, and the
chances are he exaggerates Last Hope's speed.

However, there is no doubt that Last Hope goes over the road
very rapidly, indeed, as a colored party who is out squirrel hunting
comes along a few minutes afterward and tells Little Alfie that something goes past him on the road so fast he cannot tell exactly what
it is, but he states that he is pretty sure it is old Henry Devil himself,
because he smells smoke as it passes him, and hears a voice yelling
hi-yah. But of course the chances are this voice is nothing but the
voice of Mr. Paul D. Veere yelling words of encouragement to Last
Hope.

It is not until the stationmaster at Tillinghast, a guy by the name
of Asbury Potts, drives over to Miss Beulah Beauregard's ancestral
home an hour later that Little Alfie hears that as Last Hope pulls up
at the station and Mr. Paul D. Veere dismounts with so much mud
on him that nobody can tell if he is a plaster cast or what, the horse
is gimping as bad as Mr. Paul D. Veere himself, and Asbury Potts
says there is no doubt Last Hope bows a tendon, or some such, and
that if they are able to get him to the races again he will eat his old
wool hat.

"But, personally," Asbury Potts says as he mentions this sad news,
"I do not see what Mr. Paul D. Veere's hurry is, at that, to be pushing
a horse so hard. He has fifty-seven seconds left by my watch when
the Orange Blossom pulls in right on time to the dot," Asbury Potts
says.

Well, at this Little Alfie sits down and starts figuring, and finally
he figures that Last Hope runs the mile and a quarter in around 2:03
in the mud, with maybe one hundred and sixty pounds up, for Mr.
Paul D. Veere is no feather duster, and no horse ever runs a mile

and a quarter in the mud in the Kentucky Derby as fast as this, or anywhere else as far as anybody knows, so Little Alfie claims that this is practically flying.

But of course few citizens ever accept Little Alfie's figures as strictly official, because they do not know if Asbury Potts's watch is properly regulated for timing racehorses, even though Asbury Potts is 100 percent right when he says they will never be able to get Last Hope to the races again.

Well, I meet up with Little Alfie one night this summer in Mindy's Restaurant on Broadway, and it is the first time he is observed in these parts in some time, and he seems to be looking very prosperous, indeed, and after we get to cutting up old touches, he tells me the reason for this prosperity.

It seems that after Mr. Paul D. Veere returns to New York and puts back in his bank whatever it is that it is advisable for him to put back, or takes out whatever it is that seems best to take out, and gets himself all rounded up so there is no chance of his going to jail, he remembers that there is a slight difference between him and Little Alfie, so what does Mr. Paul D. Veere do but sit down and write out a check for fifty G's to Little Alfie to take up his IOU, so Little Alfie is nothing out on account of losing the Kentucky Derby, and, in fact, he is stone rich, and I am glad to hear of it, because I always sympathize deeply with him in his bereavement over the loss of Last Hope. Then I ask Little Alfie what he is doing in New York at this time, and he states to me as follows:

"Well," Little Alfie says, "I will tell you. The other day," he says, "I get to thinking things over, and among other things I get to thinking that after Last Hope wins the Kentucky Derby, he is a sure thing to go on and also win the Maryland Preakness, because," Little Alfie says, "the Preakness is a sixteenth of a mile shorter than the Derby, and a horse that can run a mile and a quarter in the mud in around 2:03 with a brick house on his back is bound to make anything that wears hair look silly at a mile and three-sixteenths, especially," Little Alfie says, "if it comes up mud.

"So," Little Alfie says, "I am going to call on Mr. Paul D. Veere and see if he does not wish to pay me the Preakness stake, too, because," he says, "I am building the finest house in South Georgia at Last Hope, which is my stock farm where Last Hope himself is on public exhibition, and I can always use a few bobs here and there."

"Well, Alfie," I say, "this seems to me to be a very fair proposition, indeed, and," I say, "I am sure Mr. Paul D. Veere will take care of it as soon as it is called to his attention, as there is no doubt you and Last Hope are of great service to Mr. Paul D. Veere. By the way, Alfie," I say, "whatever becomes of Governor Hicks?"

"Why," Little Alfie says, "do you know Governor Hicks turns out to be a terrible disappointment to me as a plow horse? He learns how to sit down from Abimelech, the mule, and nothing will make him stir, not even the same encouragement I give him the day he drops down there third at Hialeah.

"But," Little Alfie says, "my ever-loving wife is figuring on using the old Governor as a saddle horse for our twins, Beulah and Little Alfie, Junior, when they get old enough, although," he says, "I tell her the Governor will never be worth a dime in such a way especially," Little Alfie says, "if it comes up mud."

ALL
HORSE
PLAYERS
DIE
BROKE

t is during the last race meeting at Saratoga, and one evening I am standing out under the elms in front of the Grand Union Hotel thinking what a beautiful world it is, to be sure, for what do I do in the afternoon at the track but grab myself a piece of a 10–to–1 shot.

I am thinking what a beautiful moon it is, indeed, that is shining down over the park where Mr. Dick Canfield once deals them higher than a cat's back, and how pure and balmy the air is, and also what nice-looking Judys are wandering around and about, although it is only the night before that I am standing in the same spot wondering where I can borrow a Betsy with which to shoot myself smack-dab through the pimple.

In fact, I go around to see a character I know by the name of Solly something, who owns a Betsy, but it seems he has only one cartridge to his name for this Betsy and he is thinking some of either using the cartridge to shoot his own self smack-dab through the pimple, or of going out to the racecourse and shooting an old catfish by the name of Pair of Jacks that plays him false in the fifth race, and therefore Solly is not in a mood to lend his Betsy to anybody else.

So we try to figure out a way we can make one cartridge do for two pimples, and in the meantime Solly outs with a bottle of apple-jack, and after a couple of belts at this bottle we decide that the sensible thing to do is to take the Betsy out and peddle it for whatever we can, and maybe get a taw for the next day.

Well, it happens that we run into an Italian party from Passaic, N.J., by the name of Giuseppe Palladino, who is called Joe for short, and this Joe is in the money very good at the moment, and he is glad to lend us a pound note on the Betsy, because Joe is such a character as never knows when he may need an extra Betsy, and anyway it is the first time in his experience around the racetracks that anybody ever offers him collateral for a loan.

So there Solly and I are with a deuce apiece after we spend the odd dollar for breakfast the next day, and I run my deuce up to a total of twenty-two slugs on the 10–to–1 shot in the last heat of the day, and everything is certainly all right with me in every respect.

Well, while I am standing there under the elms, who comes along but a raggedy old Dutchman by the name of Unser Fritz, who is maybe seventy-five years old, come next grass, and who is following the giddyaps since the battle of Gettysburg, as near as anybody can figure out. In fact, Unser Fritz is quite an institution around the racetracks, and is often written up by the newspaper scribes as a terrible example of what a horse player comes to, although personally I always say that what Unser Fritz comes to is not so tough when you figure that he does not do a tap of work in all these years.

In his day, Unser Fritz is a most successful handicapper, a handicapper being a character who can dope out from the form what horses ought to win the races, and as long as his figures turn out all right, a handicapper is spoken of most respectfully by one and all, although of course when he begins missing out for any length of time as handicappers are bound to do, he is no longer spoken of respectfully, or even as a handicapper. He is spoken of as a bum.

It is a strange thing how a handicapper can go along for years doing everything right, and then all of a sudden he finds himself doing everything wrong, and this is the way it is with Unser Fritz. For a long time his figures on the horse races are considered most remarkable indeed, and as he will bet till the cows come home on his own figures, he generally has plenty of money, and a fiancée by the name of Emerald Em.

She is called Emerald Em because she has a habit of wearing a raft of emeralds in rings, and pins, and bracelets, and one thing and another, which are purchased for her by Unser Fritz to express his love, an emerald being a green stone that is considered most expressive of love, if it is big enough. It seems that Emerald Em is very fond of emeralds, especially when they are surrounded by large, coarse diamonds.

I hear the old-timers around the racetracks say that when Emerald Em is young, she is a tall, good-looking Judy with yellow hair that is by no means a phony yellow, at that, and with a shape that does not require a bustle such as most Judys always wear in those days.

But then nobody ever hears an old-timer mention any Judy that he remembers from back down the years who is not good-looking, and in fact beautiful. To hear the old-timers tell it, every pancake they ever see when they are young is a double Myrna Loy, though the chances are, figuring in the law of averages, that some of them are bound to be rutabagas, the same as now. Anyway, for years this Emerald Em is known on every racetrack from coast to coast as Unser Fritz's fiancée, and is considered quite a remarkable scene, what with her emeralds, and not requiring any bustle, and everything else.

Then one day Unser Fritz's figures run plumb out on him, and so does his dough, and so does Emerald Em, and now Unser Fritz is an old pappy guy, and it is years since he is regarded as anything but a crumbo around the racetracks, and nobody remembers much of his story, or cares a cuss about it, for if there is anything that is a drug on the market around the tracks it is the story of a broker.

How he gets from place to place, and how he lives after he gets there, is a very great mystery to one and all, although I hear he often rides in the horsecars with the horses, when some owner or trainer happens to be feeling tenderhearted, or he hitchhikes in automobiles, and sometimes he even walks, for Unser Fritz is still fairly nimble, no matter how old he is.

He always has under his arm a bundle of newspapers that somebody throws away, and every night he sits down and handicaps the horses running the next day according to his own system, but he seldom picks any winners, and even if he does pick any winners, he seldom has anything to bet on them.

Sometimes he promotes a stranger, who does not know he is bad luck to a good hunting dog, to put down a few dibs on one of his picks, and once in a while the pick wins, and Unser Fritz gets a small stake, and sometimes an old-timer who feels sorry for him will slip him something. But whatever Unser Fritz gets hold of, he bets off right away on the next race that comes up, so naturally he never is holding anything very long.

Well, Unser Fritz stands under the elms with me awhile, speaking of this and that, and especially of the races, and I am wondering to myself if I will become as disheveled as Unser Fritz if I keep on following the races, when he gazes at the Grand Union Hotel, and says to me like this:

"It looks nice," he says. "It looks cheerylike, with the lights, and all this and that. It brings back memories to me. Emma always lives in this hotel whenever we make Saratoga for the races back in the days when I am in the money. She always has a suite of two or three rooms on this side of the hotel. Once she has four.

"I often stand here under these trees," Unser Fritz says, "watching her windows to see what time she puts out her lights, because, while I trust Emma implicitly, I know she has a restless nature, and sometimes she cannot resist returning to scenes of gaiety after I bid her good night, especially," he says, "with a party by the name of Pete Shovelin, who runs the restaurant where she once deals them off the arm."

"You mean she is a biscuit shooter?" I say.

"A waitress," Unser Fritz says. "A good waitress. She comes of a family of farm folks in this very section, although I never know much about them," he says. "Shovelin's is a little hole-in-the-wall up the street here somewhere which long since disappears. I go there for my morning java in the old days.

"I will say one thing for Shovelin," Unser Fritz says, "he always has good java. Three days after I first clap eyes on Emma, she is wearing her first emerald, and is my fiancée. Then she moves into a suite in the Grand Union. I only wish you can know Emma in those days," he says. "She is beautiful. She is a fine character. She is always on the level, and I love her dearly."

"What do you mean—always on the level?" I say. "What about this Shovelin party you just mention?"

"Ah," Unser Fritz says, "I suppose I am dull company for a squab, what with having to stay in at night to work on my figures, and Emma likes to go around and about. She is a highly nervous type, and extremely restless, and she cannot bear to hold still very long at a time. But," he says, "in those days it is not considered proper for a young Judy to go around and about without a chaperon, so she goes with Shovelin for her chaperon. Emma never goes anywhere without a chaperon," he says.

Well, it seems that early in their courtship, Unser Fritz learns that he can generally quiet her restlessness with emeralds, if they have diamonds on the side. It seems that these stones have a very soothing effect on her, and this is why he purchases them for her by the bucket.

"Yes," Unser Fritz says, "I always think of Emma whenever I am in New York City, and look down Broadway at night with the go lights on."

But it seems from what Unser Fritz tells me that even with the emeralds her restless spells come on her very bad, and especially when he finds himself running short of ready, and is unable to purchase more emeralds for her at the moment, although Unser Fritz claims this is nothing unusual. In fact, he says anybody with any experience with nervous female characters knows that it becomes very monotonous for them to be around people who are short of ready.

"But," he says, "not all of them require soothing with emeralds. Some require pearls," he says.

Well, it seems that Emma generally takes a trip without Unser Fritz to break the monotony of his running short of ready, but she never takes one of these trips without a chaperon, because she is very careful about her good name, and Unser Fritz's, too. It seems that in those days Judys have to be more careful about such matters than they do now.

He remembers that once when they are in San Francisco she takes a trip through the Yellowstone with Jockey Gus Kloobus as her chaperon, and is gone three weeks and returns much refreshed, especially as she gets back just as Unser Fritz makes a nice score and has a seidel of emeralds waiting for her. He remembers another time she goes to England with a trainer by the name of Blootz as her chaperon and comes home with an English accent that sounds right cute, to find Unser Fritz going like a house afire at Belmont.

"She takes a lot of other trips without me during the time we are engaged," Unser Fritz says, "but," he says, "I always know Emma will return to me as soon as she hears I am back in the money and can purchase more emeralds for her. In fact," he says, "this knowledge is all that keeps me struggling now."

"Look, Fritz," I say, "what do you mean, keeps you going? Do you mean you think Emma may return to you again?"

"Why, sure," Unser Fritz says. "Why, certainly, if I get my rushes again. Why not?" he says. "She knows there will be a pail of emeralds waiting for her. She knows I love her and always will," he says.

Well, I ask him when he sees Emerald Em last, and he says it is 1908 in the old Waldorf-Astoria the night he blows a hundred and sixty thousand betting on a hide called Sir Martin to win the Futurity, and it is all the dough Unser Fritz has at the moment. In fact, he is cleaner than a jaybird, and he is feeling somewhat discouraged.

It seems he is waiting on his floor for the elevator, and when it comes down Emerald Em is one of the several passengers, and when the door opens, and Unser Fritz starts to get in, she raises her foot and plants it in his stomach, and gives him a big push back out the door and the elevator goes on down without him.

"But, of course," Unser Fritz says, "Emma never likes to ride in the same elevator with me, because I am not always tidy enough to suit her in those days, what with having so much work to do on my figures, and she claims it is a knock to her socially. Anyway," he says, "this is the last I see of Emma."

"Why, Fritz," I say, "nineteen-eight is nearly thirty years back, and if she ever thinks of returning to you, she will return long before this."

"No," Unser Fritz says. "You see, I never make a scratch since then. I am never since in the money, so there is no reason for Emma to return to me. But," he says, "wait until I get going good again and you will see."

Well, I always figure Unser Fritz must be more or less of an old screwball for going on thinking there is still a chance for him around the tracks, and now I am sure of it, and I am about to bid him good evening, when he mentions that he can use about two dollars if I happen to have a deuce on me that is not working, and I will say one thing for Unser Fritz, he seldom comes right out and asks anybody for anything unless things are very desperate with him, indeed.

"I need it to pay something on account of my landlady," he says.

"I room with old Mrs. Crob around the corner for over twenty years, and," he says, "she only charges me a finnif a week, so I try to keep from getting too far to the rear with her. I will return it to you the first score I make."

Well, of course I know this means practically never, but I am feeling so good about my success at the track that I slip him a deucer, and it is half an hour later before I fully realize what I do, and go looking for Fritz to get anyway half of it back. But by this time he disappears, and I think no more of the matter until the next day out at the course when I hear Unser Fritz bets two dollars on a thing by the name of Speed Cart, and it bows down at 50 to 1, so I know Mrs. Crob is still waiting for hers.

Now there is Unser Fritz with one hundred slugs, and this is undoubtedly more money than he enjoys since Hickory Slim is a two-year-old. And from here on the story becomes very interesting, and in fact remarkable, because up to the moment Speed Cart hits the wire, Unser Fritz is still nothing but a crumbo, and you can say it again, while from now on he is somebody to point out and say can you imagine such a thing happening?

He bets a hundred on a centipede called Marchesa, and down pops Marchesa like a trained pig at 20 to 1. Then old Unser Fritz bets two hundred on a caterpillar by the name of Merry Soul, at 4 to 1, and Merry Soul just laughs his way home. Unser Fritz winds up the day betting two thousand more on something called Sharp Practice, and when Sharp Practice wins by so far it looks as if he is a shoo-in, Fritz finds himself with over twelve thousand slugs, and the way the bookmakers in the betting ring are sobbing is really most distressing to hear.

Well, in a week Unser Fritz is a hundred thousand dollars in front, because the way he sends it in is quite astonishing to behold, although the old-timers tell me it is just the way he sends it when he is younger. He is betting only on horses that he personally figures out, and what happens is that Unser Fritz's figures suddenly come to life again, and he cannot do anything wrong.

He wins so much dough that he even pays off a few old touches, including my two, and he goes so far as to lend Joe Palladino three dollars on the Betsy that Solly and I hock with Joe for the pound note, as it seems that by this time Joe himself is practically on his way to the poorhouse, and while Unser Fritz has no use whatsoever for a Betsy he cannot bear to see a character such as Joe go to the poorhouse.

But with all the dough Unser Fritz carries in his pockets, and plants in a safe-deposit box in the jug downtown, he looks just the same as ever, because he claims he cannot find time from working on his figures to buy new clothes and dust himself off, and if you tell anybody who does not know who he is that this old crutch is stone rich, the chances are they will call you a liar.

In fact, on a Monday around noon, the clerk in the branch office that a big Fifth Avenue jewelry firm keeps in the lobby of the States Hotel is all ready to yell for the constables when Unser Fritz leans up against the counter and asks to see some jewelry on display in a showcase, as Unser Fritz is by no means the clerk's idea of a customer for jewelry.

I am standing in the lobby of the hotel on the off chance that some fresh money may arrive in the city on the late trains that I may be able to connect up with before the races, when I notice Unser Fritz and observe the agitation of the clerk, and presently I see Unser Fritz waving a fistful of bank notes under the clerk's beak, and the clerk starts setting out the jewelry with surprising speed.

I go over to see what is coming off, and I can see that the jewelry Unser Fritz is looking at consists of a necklace of emeralds and diamonds, with a centerpiece the size of the home plate, and some eardrops, and bracelets, and clips of same, and as I approach the scene I hear Unser Fritz ask how much for the lot as if he is dickering for a basket of fish.

"One hundred and one thousand dollars, sir," the clerk says. "You see, sir, it is a set, and one of the finest things of the kind in the country. We just got it in from our New York store to show a party here, and," he says, "she is absolutely crazy about it, but she states she cannot give us a final decision until five o'clock this afternoon. Confidentially, sir," the clerk says, "I think the real trouble is financial, and doubt that we will hear from her again. In fact," he says, "I am so strongly of this opinion that I am prepared to sell the goods without waiting on her. It is really a bargain at the price," he says.

"Dear me," Unser Fritz says to me, "this is most unfortunate as the sum mentioned is just one thousand dollars more than I possess in all this world. I have twenty thousand on my person, and eighty thousand over in the box in the jug, and not another dime. But," he says, "I will be back before five o'clock and take the lot. In fact," he says, "I will run in right after the third race and pick it up."

Well, at this the clerk starts putting the jewelry back in the case, and anybody can see that he figures he is on a lob and that he is sorry he wastes so much time, but Unser Fritz says to me like this:

"Emma is returning to me," he says.

"Emma who?" I say.

"Why," Unser Fritz says, "my Emma. The one I tell you about not long ago. She must hear I am in the money again, and she is returning just as I always say she will."

"How do you know?" I say. "Do you hear from her, or what?"

"No," Unser Fritz says, "I do not hear from her direct, but Mrs. Crob knows some female relative of Emma's that lives at Ballston Spa a few miles from here, and this relative is in Saratoga this morning to do some shopping, and she tells Mrs. Crob and Mrs. Crob tells me. Emma will be here tonight. I will have these emeralds waiting for her."

Well, what I always say is that every guy knows his own business best, and if Unser Fritz wishes to toss his dough off on jewelry, it is none of my put-in, so all I remark is that I have no doubt Emma will be very much surprised indeed.

"No," Unser Fritz says. "She will be expecting them. She always expects emeralds when she returns to me. I love her," he says. "You have no idea how I love her. But let us hasten to the course," he says. "Cara Mia is a right good thing in the third, and I will make just one bet today to win the thousand I need to buy these emeralds."

"But, Fritz," I say, "you will have nothing left for operating expenses after you invest in the emeralds."

"I am not worrying about operating expenses now," Unser Fritz says. "The way my figures are standing up, I can run a spool of thread into a pair of pants in no time. But I can scarcely wait to see the expression on Emma's face when she sees her emeralds. I will have to make a fast trip into town after the third to get my dough out of the box in the jug and pick them up," he says. "Who knows but what this other party that is interested in the emeralds may make her mind up before five o'clock and pop in there and nail them?"

Well, after we get to the racetrack, all Unser Fritz does is stand around waiting for the third race. He has his figures on the first two races, and ordinarily he will be betting himself a gob on them, but he says he does not wish to take the slightest chance of cutting down his capital at this time, and winding up short of enough dough to buy the emeralds.

It turns out that both of the horses Unser Fritz's figures make on top in the first and second races bow down, and Unser Fritz will have his thousand if he only bets a couple of hundred on either of them, but Unser Fritz says he is not sorry he does not bet. He says the finishes in both races are very close, and prove that there is an element of risk in these races. And Unser Fritz says he cannot afford to tamper with the element of risk at this time.

He states that there is no element of risk whatever in the third race, and what he states is very true, as everybody realizes that this mare Cara Mia is a stick-out. In fact, she is such a stick-out that it scarcely figures to be a contest. There are three other horses in the race, but it is the opinion of one and all that if the owners of these horses have any sense they will leave them in the barn and save them a lot of unnecessary lather.

The opening price offered by the bookmakers on Cara Mia is 2 to 5, which means that if you wish to wager on Cara Mia to win you will have to put up five dollars to a bookmaker's two dollars, and everybody agrees that this is a reasonable thing to do in this case unless you wish to rob the poor bookmaker.

In fact, this is considered so reasonable that everybody starts running at the bookmakers all at once, and the bookmakers can see if this keeps up they may get knocked off their stools in the betting ring and maybe seriously injured, so they make Cara Mia 1 to 6, and out, as quickly as possible to halt the rush and give them a chance to breathe.

This 1 to 6 means that if you wish to wager on Cara Mia to win, you must wager six of your own dollars to one of the bookmaker's dollars, and means that the bookies are not offering any prices whatsoever on Cara Mia running second or third. You can get almost any price you can think of right quick against any of the other horses winning the race, and place and show prices, too, but asking the bookmakers to lay against Cara Mia running second or third will be something like asking them to bet that Mr. Roosevelt is not President of the United States.

Well, I am expecting Unser Fritz to step in and partake of the 2

to 5 on Cara Mia for all the dough he has on his person the moment
it is offered, because he is very high indeed on this mare, and in fact
I never see anybody any higher on any horse, and it is a price Unser
Fritz will not back off from when he is high on anything.

Moreover, I am pleased to think he will make such a wager,
because it will give him plenty over and above the price of the emeralds, and as long as he is bound to purchase the emeralds, I wish
to see him have a little surplus, because when anybody has a surplus
there is always a chance for me. It is when everybody runs out of
surpluses that I am handicapped no little. But instead of stepping in
and partaking, Unser Fritz keeps hesitating until the opening price
gets away from him, and finally he says to me like this:

"Of course," he says, "my figures show Cara Mia cannot possibly
lose this race, but," he says, "to guard against any possibility whatever
of her losing, I will make an absolute cinch of it. I will bet her third."

"Why, Fritz," I say, "I do not think there is anybody in this world
outside of an insane asylum who will give you a price on the peek.
Furthermore," I say, "I am greatly surprised at this sign of weakening
on your part on your figures."

"Well," Unser Fritz says, "I cannot afford to take a chance on
not having the emeralds for Emma when she arrives. Let us go
through the betting ring and see what we can see," he says.

So we walk through the betting ring, and by this time it seems
that many of the books are so loaded with wagers on Cara Mia to
win that they will not accept any more under the circumstances, and
I figure that Unser Fritz blows the biggest opportunity of his life in
not grabbing the opening. The bookmakers who are loaded are now
looking even sadder than somewhat, and this makes them a pitiful
spectacle indeed.

Well, one of the saddest-looking is a character by the name of
Slow McCool, but he is a character who will usually give you a gamble
and he is still taking Cara Mia at 1 to 6, and Unser Fritz walks up
to him and whispers in his ear, and what he whispers is he wishes
to know if Slow McCool cares to lay him a price on Cara Mia third.
But all that happens is that Slow McCool stops looking sad a minute
and looks slightly perplexed, and then he shakes his head and goes
on looking sad again.

Now Unser Fritz steps up to another sad-looking bookmaker by
the name of Pete Phozzler and whispers in his ear, and Pete also

shakes his head, and after we leave him I look back and see that Pete is standing up on his stool watching Unser Fritz and still shaking his head.

Well, Unser Fritz approaches maybe a dozen other sad-looking bookmakers, and whispers to them, and all he gets is the old head-shake, but none of them seem to become angry with Unser Fritz, and I always say that this proves that bookmakers are better than some people think, because, personally, I claim they have a right to get angry with Unser Fritz for insulting their intelligence, and trying to defraud them, too, by asking a price on Cara Mia third.

Finally we come to a character by the name of Willie the Worrier, who is called by this name because he is always worrying about something, and what he is generally worrying about is a short bank-roll, or his ever-loving wife, and sometimes both, though mostly it is his wife. Personally, I always figure she is something to worry about, at that, though I do not consider details necessary.

She is a redheaded Judy about half as old as Willie the Worrier, and this alone is enough to start any guy worrying, and what is more she is easily vexed, especially by Willie. In fact, I remember Solly telling me that she is vexed with Willie no longer ago than about 11 a.m. this very day, and gives him a public reprimanding about something or other in the telegraph office downtown when Solly happens to be in there hoping maybe he will receive an answer from a mark in Pittsfield, Mass., that he sends a tip on a horse.

Solly says the last he hears Willie the Worrier's wife say is that she will leave him for good this time, but I just see her over on the clubhouse lawn wearing some right classy-looking garments, so I judge she does not leave him as yet, as the clubhouse lawn is not a place to be waiting for a train.

Well, when Unser Fritz sees that he is in front of Willie's stand, he starts to move on, and I nudge him and motion at Willie, and ask him if he does not notice that Willie is another bookmaker, and Unser Fritz says he notices him all right, but that he does not care to offer him any business because Willie insults him ten years ago. He says Willie calls him a dirty old Dutch bum, and while I am thinking what a wonderful memory Unser Fritz has to remember insults from bookmakers for ten years, Willie the Worrier, sitting on his stool looking out over the crowd, spots Unser Fritz and yells at him as follows:

"Hello, Dirty Dutch," he says. "How is the soap market? What are you looking for around here, Dirty Dutch? Santa Claus?"

Well, at this Unser Fritz pushes his way through the crowd around Willie the Worrier's stand, and gets close to Willie, and says:

"Yes," he says, "I am looking for Santa Claus. I am looking for a show price on number two horse, but," he says, "I do not expect to get it from the shoemakers who are booking nowadays."

Now the chances are Willie the Worrier figures Unser Fritz is just trying to get sarcastic with him for the benefit of the crowd around his stand in asking for such a thing as a price on Cara Mia third, and in fact the idea of anybody asking a price third on a horse that some bookmakers will not accept any more wagers on first, or even second, is so humorous that many characters laugh right out loud.

"All right," Willie the Worrier says. "No one can ever say he comes to my store looking for a marker on anything and is turned down. I will quote you a show price, Dirty Dutch," he says. "You can have 1 to 100."

This means that Willie the Worrier is asking Unser Fritz for one hundred dollars to the book's one dollar if Unser Fritz wishes to bet on Cara Mia dropping in there no worse than third, and of course Willie has no idea Unser Fritz or anybody else will ever take such a price, and the chances are if Willie is not sizzling a little at Unser Fritz, he will not offer such a price, because it sounds foolish.

Furthermore, the chances are if Unser Fritz offers Willie a comparatively small bet at this price, such as may enable him to chisel just a couple of hundred out of Willie's book, Willie will find some excuse to wiggle off, but Unser Fritz leans over and says in a low voice to Willie the Worrier:

"A hundred thousand."

Willie nods his head and turns to a clerk alongside him, and his voice is as low as Unser Fritz's as he says to the clerk:

"A thousand to a hundred thousand, Cara Mia third."

The clerk's eyes pop open and so does his mouth, but he does not say a word. He just writes something on a pad of paper in his hand, and Unser Fritz offers Willie the Worrier a package of thousand-dollar bills, and says:

"Here is twenty," he says. "The rest is in the jug."

"All right, Dutch," Willie says, "I know you have it, although," he says, "this is the first crack you give me at it. You are on, Dutch," he says. "P.S.," Willie says, "the Dirty does not go any more."

Well, you understand Unser Fritz is betting one hundred thousand dollars against a thousand dollars that Cara Mia will run in the money, and personally I consider this wager a very sound business proposition indeed, and so does everybody else, for all it amounts to is finding a thousand dollars in the street.

There is really nothing that can make Cara Mia run out of the money, the way I look at it, except what happens to her, and what happens is she steps in a hole fifty yards from the finish when she is on top by ten, and breezing, and down she goes all spread out, and of course the other three horses run on past her to the wire, and all this is quite a disaster to many members of the public, including Unser Fritz.

I am standing with him on the rise of the grandstand lawn watching the race, and it is plain to be seen that he is slightly surprised at what happens, and personally, I am practically dumbfounded because, to tell the truth, I take a nibble at the opening price of 2 to 5 on Cara Mia with a total of thirty slugs, which represents all my capital, and I am thinking what a great injustice it is for them to leave holes in the track for horses to step in, when Unser Fritz says like this:

"Well," he says, "it is horse racing."

And this is all he ever says about the matter, and then he walks down to Willie the Worrier, and tells Willie if he will send a clerk with him, he will go to the jug and get the balance of the money that is now due Willie.

"Dutch," Willie says, "it will be a pleasure to accompany you to the jug in person."

As Willie is getting down off his stool, somebody in the crowd who hears of the wager gazes at Unser Fritz, and remarks that he is really a game guy, and Willie says:

"Yes," he says, "he is a game guy at that. But," he says, "what about me?"

And he takes Unser Fritz by the arm, and they walk away together, and anybody can see that Unser Fritz picks up anyway twenty years or more, and a slight stringhalt, in the last few minutes.

Then it comes on night again in Saratoga, and I am standing out under the elms in front of the Grand Union, thinking that this world is by no means as beautiful as formerly, when I notice a big, fat old Judy with snow-white hair and spectacles standing near me, looking up and down the street. She will weigh a good two hundred pounds, and much of it is around her ankles, but she has a pleasant face, at that, and when she observes me looking at her, she comes over to me, and says:

"I am trying to fix the location of a restaurant where I work many years ago," she says. "It is a place called Shovelin's. The last thing my husband tells me is to see if the old building is still here, but," she says, "it is so long since I am in Saratoga I cannot get my bearings."

"Ma'am," I say, "is your name Emma by any chance and do they ever call you Emerald Em?"

Well, at this the old Judy laughs, and says:

"Why, yes," she says. "That is what they call me when I am young and foolish. But how do you know?" she says. "I do not remember ever seeing you before in my life."

"Well," I say, "I know a party who once knows you. A party by the name of Unser Fritz."

"Unser Fritz?" she says. "Unser Fritz? Oh," she says, "I wonder if you mean a crazy Dutchman I run around with many years ago? My gracious," she says, "I just barely remember him. He is a great hand for giving me little presents such as emeralds. When I am young I think emeralds are right pretty, but," she says, "otherwise I cannot stand them."

"Then you do not come here to see him?" I say.

"Are you crazy, too?" she says. "I am on my way to Ballston Spa to see my grandchildren. I live in Macon, Georgia. If ever you are in Macon, Georgia, drop in at Shovelin's restaurant and get some real Southern fried chicken. I am Mrs. Joe Shovelin," she says. "By the way," she says, "I remember more about that crazy Dutchman. He is a horse player. I always figure he must die long ago and that the chances are he dies broke, too. I remember I hear people say all horse players die broke."

"Yes," I say, "he dies all right, and he dies as you suggest, too," for it is only an hour before that they find old Unser Fritz in a vacant lot over near the railroad station with the Betsy he gets off Joe Palladino in his hand and a bullet-hole smack-dab through his pimple.

Nobody blames him much for taking this out, and in fact I am standing there thinking long after Emerald Em goes on about her business that it will be a good idea if I follow his example, only I cannot think where I can find another Betsy, when Solly comes along and stands there with me. I ask Solly if he knows anything new.

"No," Solly says, "I do not know anything new, except," he says, "I heard Willie the Worrier and his ever-loving make up again, and she is not going to leave him after all. I hear Willie takes home a squarer in the shape of a batch of emeralds and diamonds that she orders sent up here when Willie is not looking, and that they are fighting about all day. Well," Solly says, "maybe this is love."

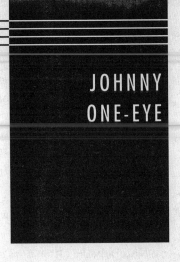

This cat I am going to tell you about is a very small cat, and in fact it is only a few weeks old, consequently it is really nothing but an infant cat. To tell the truth, it is just a kitten.

It is gray and white and very dirty and its fur is all frowzled up, so it is a very miserable-looking little kitten to be sure the day it crawls through a broken basement window into an old house in East Fifty-third Street over near Third Avenue in the city of New York and goes from room to room saying merouw, merouw in a low, weak voice until it comes to a room at the head of the stairs on the second story where a guy by the name of Rudolph is sitting on the floor thinking of not much.

One reason Rudolph is sitting on the floor is because there is nothing else to sit on as this is an empty house that is all boarded up for years and there is no furniture whatever in it, and another reason is that Rudolph has a .38 slug in his side and really does not feel like doing much of anything but sitting. He is wearing a derby hat and his overcoat as it is in the wintertime and very cold and he has an automatic Betsy on the floor beside him and naturally he is surprised quite some when the little kitten comes merouwing into the room and he picks up the Betsy and points it at the door in case anyone he does not wish to see is with the kitten. But when he observes that it is all alone, Rudolph puts the Betsy down again and speaks to the kitten as follows:

"Hello, cat," he says.

Of course the kitten does not say anything in reply except merouw but it walks right up to Rudolph and climbs on his lap, although the chances are if it knows who Rudolph is it will hightail it out of there quicker than anybody can say scat. There is enough daylight coming through the chinks in the boards over the windows for Rudolph to see that the kitten's right eye is in bad shape, and in fact it is bulged half out of its head in a most distressing manner and it is plain to be seen that the sight is gone from this eye. It is also plain to be seen that the injury happened recently and Rudolph gazes at the kitten awhile and starts to laugh and says like this:

"Well, cat," he says, "you seem to be scuffed up almost as much as I am. We make a fine pair of invalids here together. What is your name, cat?"

Naturally the kitten does not state its name but only goes merouw and Rudolph says, "All right, I will call you Johnny. Yes," he says, "your tag is now Johnny One-Eye."

Then he puts the kitten in under his overcoat and pretty soon it gets warm and starts to purr and Rudolph says:

"Johnny," he says, "I will say one thing for you and that is you are plenty game to be able to sing when you are hurt as bad as you are. It is more than I can do."

But Johnny only goes merouw again and keeps on purring and by and by it falls sound asleep under Rudolph's coat and Rudolph is wishing the pain in his side will let up long enough for him to do the same.

Well, I suppose you are saying to yourself, what is this Rudolph doing in an old empty house with a slug in his side, so I will explain that the district attorney is responsible for this situation. It seems that the D.A. appears before the grand jury and tells it that Rudolph is an extortion guy and a killer and I do not know what all else, though some of these statements are without doubt a great injustice to Rudolph as, up to the time the D.A. makes them, Rudolph does not kill anybody of any consequence in years.

It is true that at one period of his life he is considered a little wild but this is in the 1920s when everybody else is, too, and for seven or eight years he is all settled down and is engaged in business organization work, which is very respectable work, indeed. He organizes quite a number of businesses on a large scale and is doing very good for himself. He is living quietly in a big hotel all alone, as Rudolph is by no means a family guy, and he is highly spoken of by one and all when the D.A. starts poking his nose into his affairs, claiming that Rudolph has no right to be making money out of the businesses, even though Rudolph gives these businesses plenty of first-class protection.

In fact, the D.A. claims that Rudolph is nothing but a racket guy and a great knock to the community, and all this upsets Rudolph no little when it comes to his ears in a roundabout way. So he calls up his lawbooks and requests legal advice on the subject and lawbooks says the best thing he can think of for Rudolph to do is to become as inconspicuous as possible right away but to please not mention to anyone that he gives this advice.

Lawbooks says he understands the D.A. is requesting indictments and is likely to get them and furthermore that he is rounding up certain parties that Rudolph is once associated with and trying to get them to remember incidents in Rudolph's early career that may not be entirely to his credit. Lawbooks says he hears that one of these parties is a guy by the name of Cute Freddy and that Freddy makes a deal with the D.A. to lay off him if he tells everything he knows about Rudolph, so under the circumstances a long journey by Rudolph will be in the interest of everybody concerned.

So Rudolph decides to go on a journey but then he gets to thinking that maybe Freddy will remember a little matter that Rudolph long ago since dismisses from his mind and does not wish to have recalled again, which is the time he and Freddy do a job on a guy by the name of The Icelander in Troy years ago and he drops around to Freddy's house to remind him to be sure not to remember this.

But it seems that Freddy, who is an important guy in business organization work himself, though in a different part of the city than Rudolph, mistakes the purpose of Rudolph's visit and starts to out with his rooty-toot-toot and in order to protect himself it is necessary for Rudolph to take his Betsy and give Freddy a little tattooing. In fact, Rudolph practically crockets his monogram on Freddy's chest and leaves him exceptionally deceased.

But as Rudolph is departing from the neighborhood, who bobs up but a young guy by the name of Buttsy Fagan, who works for Freddy as a chauffeur and one thing and another, and who is also said to be able to put a slug through a keyhole at forty paces without touching the sides though I suppose it will have to be a pretty good-sized keyhole. Anyway, he takes a long-distance crack at Rudolph

as Rudolph is rounding a corner, but all Buttsy can see of Rudolph
at the moment is a little piece of his left side and this is what Buttsy
hits, although no one knows it at the time, except of course Rudolph,
who just keeps on departing.

Now this incident causes quite a stir in police circles, and the
D.A. is very indignant over losing a valuable witness and when they
are unable to locate Rudolph at once, a reward of five thousand
dollars is offered for information leading to his capture alive or dead
and some think they really mean dead. Indeed, it is publicly stated
that it is not a good idea for anyone to take any chances with Rudolph
as he is known to be armed and is such a character as will be sure
to resent being captured, but they do not explain that this is only
because Rudolph knows the D.A. wishes to place him in the old
rocking chair at Sing Sing and that Rudolph is quite allergic to the
idea.

Anyway, the cops go looking for Rudolph in Hot Springs and
Miami and every other place except where he is, which is right in
New York wandering around town with the slug in his side, knocking
at the doors of old friends requesting assistance. But all the old friends
do for him is to slam the doors in his face and forget they ever see
him, as the D.A. is very tough on parties who assist guys he is looking
for, claiming that this is something most illegal called harboring fu-
gitives. Besides Rudolph is never any too popular at best with his
old friends as he always plays pretty much of a lone duke and takes
the big end of everything for his.

He cannot even consult a doctor about the slug in his side as he
knows that nowadays the first thing a doctor will do about a guy
with a gunshot wound is to report him to the cops, although Rudolph
can remember when there is always a surefooted doctor around who
will consider it a privilege and a pleasure to treat him and keep his
trap closed about it. But of course this is in the good old days and
Rudolph can see they are gone forever. So he just does the best he
can about the slug and goes on wandering here and there and around
and about and the blats keep printing his picture and saying, where
is Rudolph?

Where he is some of the time is in Central Park trying to get some
sleep, but of course even the blats will consider it foolish to go looking
for Rudolph there in such cold weather, as he is a guy who enjoys
his comfort at all times. In fact, it is comfort that Rudolph misses

more than anything as the slug is commencing to cause him great
pain and naturally the pain turns Rudolph's thoughts to the author
of same and he remembers that he once hears somebody say that
Buttsy lives over in East Fifty-third Street.

So one night Rudolph decides to look Buttsy up and cause him
a little pain in return and he is moseying through Fifty-third when
he gets so weak he falls down on the sidewalk in front of the old
house and rolls down a short flight of steps that lead from the street
level to a little railed-in areaway and ground floor or basement door
and before he stops rolling he brings up against the door itself and
it creaks open inward as he bumps it. After he lays there awhile
Rudolph can see that the house is empty and he crawls on inside.

Then when he feels stronger, Rudolph makes his way upstairs
because the basement is damp and mice keep trotting back and forth
over him and eventually he winds up in the room where Johnny One-
Eye finds him the following afternoon and the reason Rudolph settles
down in this room is because it commands the stairs. Naturally, this
is important to a guy in Rudolph's situation, though after he is sitting
there for about fourteen hours before Johnny comes along he can see
that he is not going to be much disturbed by traffic. But he considers
it a very fine place, indeed, to remain planted until he is able to
resume his search for Buttsy.

Well, after a while Johnny One-Eye wakes up and comes from
under the coat and looks at Rudolph out of his good eye and Rudolph
waggles his fingers and Johnny plays with them, catching one finger
in his front paws and biting it gently and this pleases Rudolph no
little as he never before has any personal experience with a kitten.
However, he remembers observing one when he is a boy down in
Houston Street, so he takes a piece of paper out of his pocket and
makes a little ball of it and rolls it along the floor and Johnny bounces
after it very lively indeed. But Rudolph can see that the bad eye is
getting worse and finally he says to Johnny like this:

"Johnny," he says, "I guess you must be suffering more than I
am. I remember there are some pet shops over on Lexington Avenue
not far from here and when it gets good and dark I am going to take
you out and see if we can find a cat croaker to do something about
your eye. Yes, Johnny," Rudolph says, "I will also get you something
to eat. You must be starved."

Johnny One-Eye says merouw to this and keeps on playing with the paper ball but soon it comes on dark outside and inside too, and, in fact, it is so dark inside that Rudolph cannot see his hand before him. Then he puts his Betsy in a side pocket of his overcoat and picks up Johnny and goes downstairs, feeling his way in the dark and easing along a step at a time until he gets to the basement door. Naturally, Rudolph does not wish to strike any matches because he is afraid someone outside may see the light and get nosey.

By moving very slowly, Rudolph finally gets to Lexington Avenue and while he is going along he remembers the time he walks from 125th Street in Harlem down to 110th with six slugs in him and never feels as bad as he does now. He gets to thinking that maybe he is not the guy he used to be, which of course is very true as Rudolph is now forty-odd years of age and is fat around the middle and getting bald, and he also does some thinking about what a pleasure it will be to him to find this Buttsy and cause him the pain he is personally suffering.

There are not many people in the streets and those that are go hurrying along because it is so cold and none of them pay any attention to Rudolph or Johnny One-Eye either, even though Rudolph staggers a little now and then like a guy who is rummed up, although of course it is only weakness. The chances are he is also getting a little feverish and lightheaded because finally he stops a cop who is going along swinging his arms to keep warm and asks him if he knows where there is a pet shop and it is really most indiscreet of such a guy as Rudolph to be interviewing cops. But the cop just points up the street and goes on without looking twice at Rudolph and Rudolph laughs and pokes Johnny with a finger and says:

"No, Johnny One-Eye," he says, "the cop is not a dope for not recognizing Rudolph. Who can figure the hottest guy in forty-eight states to be going along a street with a little cat in his arms? Can you, Johnny?"

Johnny says merouw and pretty soon Rudolph comes to the pet shop the cop points out. Rudolph goes inside and says to the guy like this:

"Are you a cat croaker?" Rudolph says. "Do you know what to do about a little cat that has a hurt eye?"

"I am a kind of a vet," the guy says.

"Then take a glaum at Johnny One-Eye here and see what you can do for him," Rudolph says.

Then he hands Johnny over to the guy and the guy looks at Johnny awhile and says:

"Mister," he says, "the best thing I can do for this cat is to put it out of its misery. You better let me give it something right now. It will just go to sleep and never know what happens."

Well, at this, Rudolph grabs Johnny One-Eye out of the guy's hands and puts him under his coat and drops a duke on the Betsy in his pocket as if he is afraid the guy will take Johnny away from him again and he says to the guy like this:

"No, no, no," Rudolph says. "I cannot bear to think of such a thing. What about some kind of an operation? I remember they take a bum lamp out of Joe the Goat at Bellevue one time and he is okay now."

"Nothing will do your cat any good," the guy says. "It is a goner. It will start having fits pretty soon and die sure. What is the idea of trying to save such a cat as this? It is no kind of a cat to begin with. It is just a cat. You can get a million like it for a nickel."

"No," Rudolph says, "this is not just a cat. This is Johnny One-Eye. He is my only friend in the world. He is the only living thing that ever comes pushing up against me warm and friendly and trust me in my whole life. I feel sorry for him."

"I feel sorry for him, too," the guy says. "I always feel sorry for animals that get hurt and for people."

"I do not feel sorry for people," Rudolph says. "I only feel sorry for Johnny One-Eye. Give me some kind of stuff that Johnny will eat."

"Your cat wants milk," the guy says. "You can get some at the delicatessen store down at the corner. Mister," he says, "you look sick yourself. Can I do anything for you?"

But Rudolph only shakes his head and goes on out and down to the delicatessen joint where he buys a bottle of milk and this transaction reminds him that he is very short in the moo department. In fact, he can find only a five-dollar note in his pockets and he remembers that he has no way of getting any more when this runs out, which is a very sad predicament indeed for a guy who is accustomed to plenty of moo at all times.

Then Rudolph returns to the old house and sits down on the floor again and gives Johnny One-Eye some of the milk in his derby hat as he neglects buying something for Johnny to drink out of. But

Johnny offers no complaint. He laps up the milk and curls himself into a wad in Rudolph's lap and purrs.

Rudolph takes a swig of the milk himself but it makes him sick for by this time Rudolph is really far from being in the pink of condition. He not only has the pain in his side but he has a heavy cold which he probably catches from lying on the basement floor or maybe sleeping in the park and he is wheezing no little. He commences to worry that he may get too ill to continue looking for Buttsy, as he can see that if it is not for Buttsy he will not be in this situation, suffering the way he is, but on a long journey to some place.

He takes to going off into long stretches of a kind of stupor and every time he comes out of one of these stupors the first thing he does is to look around for Johnny One-Eye and Johnny is always right there either playing with the paper ball or purring in Rudolph's lap. He is a great comfort to Rudolph but after a while Rudolph notices that Johnny seems to be running out of zip and he also notices that he is running out of zip himself especially when he discovers that he is no longer able to get to his feet.

It is along in the late afternoon of the day following the night Rudolph goes out of the house that he hears someone coming up the stairs and naturally he picks up his Betsy and gets ready for action when he also hears a very small voice calling kitty, kitty, kitty, and he realizes that the party that is coming can be nobody but a child. In fact, a minute later a little pretty of maybe six years of age comes into the room all out of breath and says to Rudolph like this:

"How do you do?" she says. "Have you seen my kitty?"

Then she spots Johnny One-Eye in Rudolph's lap and runs over and sits down beside Rudolph and takes Johnny in her arms and at first Rudolph is inclined to resent this and has a notion to give her a good boffing but he is too weak to exert himself in such a manner.

"Who are you?" Rudolph says to the little pretty, "and," he says, "where do you live and how do you get in this house?"

"Why," she says, "I am Elsie, and I live down the street and I am looking everywhere for my kitty for three days and the door is open downstairs and I know kitty likes to go in doors that are open so I came to find her and here she is."

"I guess I forgot to close it last night," Rudolph says. "I seem to be very forgetful lately."

"What is your name?" Elsie asks. "And why are you sitting on the floor in the cold and where are all your chairs? Do you have any little girls like me and do you love them dearly?"

"No," Rudolph says. "By no means and not at all."

"Well," Elsie says, "I think you are a nice man for taking care of my kitty. Do you love kitty?"

"Look," Rudolph says, "his name is not kitty. His name is Johnny One-Eye, because he has only one eye."

"I call her kitty," Elsie says. "But," she says, "Johnny One-Eye is a nice name too and if you like it best I will call her Johnny and I will leave her here with you to take care of always and I will come to see her every day. You see," she says, "if I take Johnny home Buttsy will only kick her again."

"Buttsy?" Rudolph says. "Do I hear you say Buttsy? Is his other name Fagan?"

"Why, yes," Elsie says. "Do you know him?"

"No," Rudolph says, "but I hear of him. What is he to you?"

"He is my new daddy," Elsie says. "My other one and my best one is dead and so my mama makes Buttsy my new one. My mama says Buttsy is her mistake. He is very mean. He kicks Johnny and hurts her eye and makes her run away. He kicks my mama too. Buttsy kicks everybody and everything when he is mad and he is always mad."

"He is a louse to kick a little cat," Rudolph says.

"Yes," Elsie says, "that is what Mr. O'Toole says he is for kicking my mama but my mama says it is not a nice word and I am never to say it out loud."

"Who is Mr. O'Toole?" Rudolph says.

"He is the policeman," Elsie says. "He lives across the street from us and he is very nice to me. He says Buttsy is the word you say just now, not only for kicking my mama but for taking her money when she brings it home from work and spending it so she cannot buy me nice things to wear. But do you know what?" Elsie says. "My mama says someday Buttsy is going far away and then she will buy me lots of things and send me to school and make me a lady."

Then Elsie begins skipping around the room with Johnny One-Eye in her arms and singing I am going to be a lady, I am going to be a lady, until Rudolph has to tell her to pipe down because he is afraid somebody may hear her. And all the time Rudolph is thinking of Buttsy and regretting that he is unable to get on his pins and go out of the house.

"Now I must go home," Elsie says, "because this is a night Buttsy comes in for his supper and I have to be in bed before he gets there so I will not bother him. Buttsy does not like little girls. Buttsy does not like little kittens, Buttsy does not like little anythings. My mama is afraid of Buttsy and so am I. But," she says, "I will leave Johnny here with you and come back tomorrow to see her."

"Listen, Elsie," Rudolph says, "does Mr. O'Toole come home tonight to his house for his supper, too?"

"Oh, yes," Elsie says. "He comes home every night. Sometimes when there is a night Buttsy is not coming in for his supper my mama lets me go over to Mr. O'Toole's and I play with his dog Charley but you must never tell Buttsy this because he does not like O'Toole either. But this is a night Buttsy is coming and that is why my mama tells me to get in early."

Now Rudolph takes an old letter out of his inside pocket and a pencil out of another pocket and he scribbles a few lines on the envelope and stretches himself out on the floor and begins groaning, oh, oh, oh, and then he says to Elsie like this:

"Look, Elsie," he says, "you are a smart little kid and you pay strict attention to what I am going to say to you. Do not go to bed tonight until Buttsy gets in. Then," Rudolph says, "you tell him you come in this old house looking for your cat and that you hear somebody groaning like I do just now in the room at the head of the stairs and that you find a guy who says his name is Rudolph lying on the floor so sick he cannot move. Tell him the front door of the basement is open. But," Rudolph says, "you must not tell him that Rudolph tells you to say these things. Do you understand?"

"Oh," Elsie says, "do you want him to come here? He will kick Johnny again if he does."

"He will come here, but he will not kick Johnny," Rudolph says. "He will come here, or I am the worst guesser in the world. Tell him what I look like, Elsie. Maybe he will ask you if you see a gun. Tell him you do not see one. You do not see a gun, do you, Elsie?"

"No," Elsie says, "only the one in your hand when I come in but you put it under your coat. Buttsy has a gun and Mr. O'Toole has a gun but Buttsy says I am never, never to tell anybody about this or he will kick me the way he does my mama."

"Well," Rudolph says, "you must not remember seeing mine, either. It is a secret between you and me and Johnny One-Eye. Now," he says, "if Buttsy leaves the house to come and see me, as I am pretty sure he will, you run over to Mr. O'Toole's house and give him this note, but do not tell Buttsy or your mama either about the note. If Buttsy does not leave, it is my hard luck, but you give the note to Mr. O'Toole anyway. Now tell me what you are to do, Elsie," Rudolph says, "so I can see if you have got everything correct."

"I am to go on home and wait for Buttsy," she says, "and I am to tell him Rudolph is lying on the floor of this dirty old house with a fat stomach and a big nose making noises and that he is very sick and the basement door is open and there is no gun if he asks me, and when Buttsy comes to see you I am to take this note to Mr. O'Toole but Buttsy and my mama are not to know I have the note and if Buttsy does not leave I am to give it to Mr. O'Toole anyway and you are to stay here and take care of Johnny my kitten."

"That is swell," Rudolph says. "Now you run along."

So Elsie leaves and Rudolph sits up again against the wall because his side feels easier this way and Johnny One-Eye is in his lap purring very low and the dark comes on until it is blacker inside the room than in the middle of a tunnel and Rudolph feels that he is going into another stupor and he has a tough time fighting it off.

Afterward some of the neighbors claim they remember hearing a shot inside the house and then two more in quick succession and then all is quiet until a little later when Officer O'Toole and half a dozen other cops and an ambulance with a doctor come busting into the street and swarm into the joint with their guns out and their flashlights going. The first thing they find is Buttsy at the foot of the stairs with two bullet wounds close together in his throat, and naturally he is real dead.

Rudolph is still sitting against the wall with what seems to be a small bundle of bloody fur in his lap but which turns out to be what is left of this little cat I am telling you about, although nobody pays any attention to it at first. They are more interested in getting the come-alongs on Rudolph's wrists but before they move him he pulls his clothes aside and shows the doctor where the slug is in his side and the doctor takes one glaum and shakes his head and says:

"Gangrene," he says. "I think you have pneumonia, too, from the way you are blowing."

"I know," Rudolph says. "I know this morning. Not much chance, hey, croaker?"

"Not much," the doctor says.

"Well, cops," Rudolph says, "load me in. I do not suppose you want Johnny, seeing that he is dead."

"Johnny who?" one of the cops says.

"Johnny One-Eye," Rudolph says. "This little cat here in my lap. Buttsy shoots Johnny's only good eye out and takes most of his noodle with it. I never see a more wonderful shot. Well, Johnny is better off but I feel sorry about him as he is my best friend down to the last."

Then he begins to laugh and the cop asks him what tickles him so much and Rudolph says:

"Oh," he says, "I am thinking of the joke on Buttsy. I am positive he will come looking for me, all right, not only because of the little altercation between Cute Freddy and me but because the chances are Buttsy is greatly embarrassed by not tilting me over the first time, as of course he never knows he wings me. Furthermore," Rudolph says, "and this is the best reason of all, Buttsy will realize that if I am in his neighborhood it is by no means a good sign for him, even if he hears I am sick.

"Well," Rudolph says, "I figure that with any kind of a square rattle I will have a better chance of nailing him than he has of nailing me, but that even if he happens to nail me, O'Toole will get my note in time to arrive here and nab Buttsy on the spot with his gun on him. And," Rudolph says, "I know it will be a great pleasure to the D.A. to settle Buttsy for having a gun on him.

"But," Rudolph says, "as soon as I hear Buttsy coming on the sneaksby up the stairs, I can see I am taking all the worst of it because I am now wheezing like a busted valve and you can hear me a block away except when I hold my breath, which is very difficult indeed, considering the way I am already greatly tuckered out. No," Rudolph says, "it does not look any too good for me as Buttsy keeps coming up the stairs, as I can tell he is doing by a little faint creak in the boards now and then. I am in no shape to maneuver around the room and pretty soon he will be on the landing and then all he will have to do is to wait there until he hears me which he is bound to do unless

I stop breathing altogether. Naturally," Rudolph says, "I do not care to risk a blast in the dark without knowing where he is as something tells me Buttsy is not a guy you can miss in safety.

"Well," Rudolph says, "I notice several times before this that in the dark Johnny One-Eye's good glim shines like a big spark, so when I feel Buttsy is about to hit the landing, although of course I cannot see him, I flip Johnny's ball of paper across the room to the wall just opposite the door and tough as he must be feeling Johnny chases after it when he hears it light. I figure Buttsy will hear Johnny playing with the paper and see his eye shining and think it is me and take a pop at it and that his gun flash will give me a crack at him.

"It all works out just like I dope it," Rudolph says, "but," he says, "I never give Buttsy credit for being such a marksman as to be able to hit a cat's eye in the dark. If I know this, maybe I will never stick Johnny out in front the way I do. It is a good thing I never give Buttsy a second shot. He is a lily. Yes," Rudolph says, "I can remember when I can use a guy like him."

"Buttsy is no account," the cop says. "He is a good riddance. He is the makings of a worse guy than you."

"Well," Rudolph says, "it is a good lesson to him for kicking a little cat."

Then they take Rudolph to a hospital and this is where I see him and piece out this story of Johnny One-Eye, and Officer O'Toole is at Rudolph's bedside keeping guard over him, and I remember that not long before Rudolph chalks out he looks at O'Toole and says to him like this:

"Copper," he says, "there is no chance of them outjuggling the kid on the reward moo, is there?"

"No," O'Toole says, "no chance. I keep the note you send me by Elsie saying she will tell me where you are. It is information leading to your capture just as the reward offer states. Rudolph," he says, "it is a nice thing you do for Elsie and her mother, although," he says, "it is not nearly as nice as icing Buttsy for them."

"By the way, copper," Rudolph says, "there is the remainders of a pound note in my pants pocket when I am brought here. I want you to do me a favor. Get it from the desk and buy Elsie another cat and name it Johnny, will you?"

"Sure," O'Toole says. "Anything else?"

"Yes," Rudolph says, "be sure it has two good eyes."

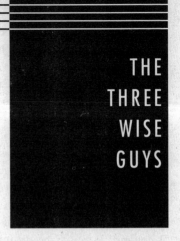

One cold winter afternoon I am standing at the bar in Good Time Charley's little drum in West Forty-ninth Street, partaking of a mixture of rock candy and rye whiskey, and this is a most surprising thing for me to be doing, as I am by no means a rum-pot, and very seldom indulge in alcoholic beverages in any way, shape, manner, or form.

But when I step into Good Time Charley's on the afternoon in question, I am feeling as if maybe I have a touch of grippe coming on, and Good Time Charley tells me that there is nothing in this world as good for a touch of grippe as rock candy and rye whiskey, as it assassinates the germs at once.

It seems that Good Time Charley always keeps a stock of rock candy and rye whiskey on hand for touches of the grippe, and he gives me a few doses immediately, and in fact Charley takes a few doses with me, as he says there is no telling but what I am scattering germs of my touch of the grippe all around the joint, and he must safeguard his health. We are both commencing to feel much better when the door opens, and who comes in but a guy by the name of Blondy Swanson.

This Blondy Swanson is a big, six-foot-two guy, with straw-colored hair, and pink cheeks, and he is originally out of Harlem, and it is well known to one and all that in his day he is the largest puller on the Atlantic seaboard. In fact, for upward of ten years, Blondy is bringing wet goods into New York from Canada, and one place and another, and in all this time he never gets a fall, which is considered a phenomenal record for an operator as extensive as Blondy.

Well, Blondy steps up alongside me at the bar, and I ask him if he cares to have a few doses of rock candy and rye whiskey with me and Good Time Charley, and Blondy says he will consider it a privilege and a pleasure, because, he says, he always has something of a sweet tooth. So we have these few doses, and I say to Blondy Swanson that I hope and trust that business is thriving with him.

"I have no business," Blondy Swanson says, "I retire from business."

Well, if J. Pierpont Morgan, or John D. Rockefeller, or Henry Ford step up and tell me they retire from business, I will not be more astonished than I am by this statement from Blondy Swanson, and in fact not as much. I consider Blondy's statement the most important commercial announcement I hear in many years, and naturally I ask him why he makes such a decision, and what is to become of thousands of citizens who are dependent on him for merchandise.

"Well," Blondy says, "I retire from business because I am one hundred percent American citizen. In fact," he says, "I am a patriot. I serve my country in the late war. I am cited at Château-Thierry. I always vote the straight Democratic ticket, except," he says, "when we figure it better to elect some Republican. I always stand up when the band plays the Star Spangled Banner. One year I even pay an income tax," Blondy says.

And of course I know that many of these things are true, although I remember hearing rumors that if the draft officer is along half an hour later than he is, he will not see Blondy for heel dust, and that what Blondy is cited for at Château-Thierry is for not robbing the dead.

But of course I do not speak of these matters to Blondy Swanson, because Blondy is not such a guy as will care to listen to rumors, and may become indignant, and when Blondy is indignant he is very difficult to get along with.

"Now," Blondy says, "I am a bootie for a long time, and supply very fine merchandise to my trade, as everybody knows, and it is a respectable business, because one and all in this country are in favor of it, except the prohibitionists. But," he says, "I can see into the future, and I can see that one of these days they are going to repeal the prohibition law, and then it will be most unpatriotic to be bringing in wet goods from foreign parts in competition with home industry. So I retire," Blondy says.

"Well, Blondy," I say, "your sentiments certainly do you credit, and if we have more citizens as high-minded as you are, this will be a better country."

"Furthermore," Blondy says, "there is no money in booting any more. All the booties in this country are broke. I am broke myself," he says. "I just lose the last piece of property I own in the world, which is the twenty-five-G home I build in Atlantic City, figuring to spend the rest of my days there with Miss Clarabelle Cobb, before she takes a runout powder on me. Well," Blondy says, "if I only listen to Miss Clarabelle Cobb, I will now be an honest clerk in a gents' furnishing store, with maybe a cute little apartment up around One Hundred and Tenth Street, and children running all around and about."

And with this, Blondy sighs heavily, and I sigh with him, because the romance of Blondy Swanson and Miss Clarabelle Cobb is well known to one and all on Broadway.

It goes back a matter of anyway six years when Blondy Swanson is making money so fast he can scarcely stop to count it, and at this time Miss Clarabelle Cobb is the most beautiful doll in this town, and many citizens almost lose their minds just gazing at her when she is a member of Mr. Georgie White's "Scandals," including Blondy Swanson.

In fact, after Blondy Swanson sees Miss Clarabelle Cobb in just one performance of Mr. Georgie White's "Scandals," he is never quite the same guy again. He goes to a lot of bother meeting up with Miss Clarabelle Cobb, and then he takes to hanging out around Mr. Georgie White's stage door, and sending Miss Clarabelle Cobb ten-pound boxes of candy, and floral horseshoes, and wreaths, and also packages of trinkets, including such articles as diamond bracelets, and brooches, and vanity cases, for there is no denying that Blondy is a fast guy with a dollar.

But it seems that Miss Clarabelle Cobb will not accept any of these offerings, except the candy and the flowers, and she goes so far as to return a sable coat that Blondy sends her one very cold day, and she is openly criticized for this action by some of the other dolls in Mr. Georgie White's "Scandals," for they say that after all there is a limit even to eccentricity.

But Miss Clarabelle Cobb states that she is not accepting valuable offerings from any guy, and especially a guy who is engaged in traf-

ficking in the demon rum, because she says that his money is nothing
but blood money that comes from breaking the law of the land,
although, as a matter of fact, this is a dead wrong rap against Blondy
Swanson, as he never handles a drop of rum in his life, but only
Scotch, and furthermore he keeps himself pretty well straightened
out with the law.

The idea is, Miss Clarabelle Cobb comes of very religious people
back in Akron, Ohio, and she is taught from childhood that rum is
a terrible thing, and personally I think it is myself, except in cocktails, and furthermore, the last thing her mama tells her when she
leaves for New York is to beware of any guys who come around
offering her diamond bracelets and fur coats, because her mama
says such guys are undoubtedly snakes in the grass, and probably on
the make.

But while she will not accept his offerings, Miss Clarabelle Cobb
does not object to going out with Blondy Swanson now and then,
and putting on the chicken Mexicaine, and the lobster Newburg, and
other items of this nature, and anytime you put a good-looking young
guy and a beautiful doll together over the chicken Mexicaine and the
lobster Newburg, often enough you are apt to have a case of love on
your hands.

And this is what happens to Blondy Swanson and Miss Clarabelle
Cobb, and in fact they become in love more than somewhat, and
Blondy Swanson is wishing to marry Miss Clarabelle Cobb, but one
night over a batch of lobster Newburg, she says to him like this:

"Blondy," she says, "I love you, and," she says, "I will marry you
in a minute if you get out of trafficking in rum. I will marry you if
you are out of the rum business, and do not have a dime, but I will
never marry you as long as you are dealing in rum, no matter if you
have a hundred million."

Well, Blondy says he will get out of the racket at once, and he
keeps saying this every now and then for a year or so, and the chances
are that several times he means it, but when a guy is in this business
in those days as strong as Blondy Swanson it is not so easy for him
to get out, even if he wishes to do so. And then one day Miss Clarabelle
Cobb has a talk with Blondy, and says to him as follows:

"Blondy," she says, "I still love you, but you care more for your
business than you do for me. So I am going back to Ohio," she says.
"I am sick and tired of Broadway, anyhow. Some day when you are

really through with the terrible traffic you are now engaged in, come to me."

And with this, Miss Clarabelle Cobb takes plenty of outdoors on Blondy Swanson, and is seen no more in these parts. At first Blondy thinks she is only trying to put a little pressure on him, and will be back, but as the weeks become months, and the months finally count up into years, Blondy can see that she is by no means clowning with him. Furthermore, he never hears from her, and all he knows is she is back in Akron, Ohio.

Well, Blondy is always promising himself that he will soon pack in on hauling wet goods, and go look up Miss Clarabelle Cobb and marry her, but he keeps putting it off, and putting it off, until finally one day he hears that Miss Clarabelle Cobb marries some legitimate guy in Akron, and this is a terrible blow to Blondy, indeed, and from this day he never looks at another doll again, or anyway not much.

Naturally, I express my deep sympathy to Blondy about being broke, and I also mention that my heart bleeds for him in his loss of Miss Clarabelle Cobb, and we have a few doses of rock candy and rye whiskey on both propositions, and by this time Good Time Charley runs out of rock candy, and anyway it is a lot of bother for him to be mixing it up with the rye whiskey, so we have the rye whiskey without the rock candy, and personally I do not notice much difference.

Well, while we are standing there at the bar having our rye whiskey without the rock candy, who comes in but an old guy by the name of The Dutchman, who is known to one and all as a most illegal character in every respect. In fact, The Dutchman has no standing whatever in the community, and I am somewhat surprised to see him appear in Good Time Charley's, because The Dutchman is generally a lammie from some place, and the gendarmes everywhere are always anxious to have a chat with him. The last I hear of The Dutchman he is in college somewhere out West for highway robbery, although afterward he tells me it is a case of mistaken identity. It seems he mistakes a copper in plain clothes for a groceryman.

The Dutchman is an old-fashioned-looking guy of maybe fifty-odd, and he has gray hair, and a stubby gray beard, and he is short, and thickset, and always good-natured, even when there is no call for it, and to look at him you will think there is no more harm in him than there is in a preacher, and maybe not as much.

As The Dutchman comes in, he takes a peek all around and about as if he is looking for somebody in particular, and when he sees Blondy Swanson he moves up alongside Blondy and begins whispering to Blondy until Blondy pulls away and tells him to speak freely.

Now The Dutchman has a very interesting story, and it goes like this: It seems that about eight or nine months back The Dutchman is mobbed up with a party of three very classy heavy guys who make quite a good thing of going around knocking off safes in small-town jugs, and post offices, and stores in small towns, and taking the money, or whatever else is valuable in these safes. This is once quite a popular custom in this country, although it dies out to some extent of late years because they improve the brand of safes so much it is a lot of bother knocking them off, but it comes back during the depression when there is no other way of making money, until it is a very prosperous business again. And of course this is very nice for old-time heavy guys, such as The Dutchman, because it gives them something to do in their old age.

Anyway, it seems that this party The Dutchman is with goes over into Pennsylvania one night on a tip from a friend and knocks off a safe in a factory office, and gets a payroll amounting to maybe fifty G's. But it seems that while they are making their getaway in an automobile, the gendarmes take out after them, and there is a chase, during which there is considerable blasting back and forth.

Well, finally in this blasting, the three guys with The Dutchman get cooled off, and The Dutchman also gets shot up quite some, and he abandons the automobile out on an open road, taking the money, which is in a gripsack, with him, and he somehow manages to escape the gendarmes by going across country, and hiding here and there.

But The Dutchman gets pretty well petered out, what with his wounds, and trying to lug the gripsack, and one night he comes to an old deserted barn, and he decides to stash the gripsack in this barn, because there is no chance he can keep lugging it around much longer. So he takes up a few boards in the floor of the barn, and digs a nice hole in the ground underneath and plants the gripsack there, figuring to come back some day and pick it up.

Well, The Dutchman gets over into New Jersey one way and another, and lays up in a town by the name of New Brunswick until his wounds are healed, which requires considerable time as The

Dutchman cannot take it nowadays as good as he can when he is younger.

Furthermore, even after The Dutchman recovers and gets to thinking of going after the stashed gripsack, he finds he is about half out of confidence, which is what happens to all guys when they commence getting old, and he figures that it may be a good idea to declare somebody else in to help him, and the first guy he thinks of is Blondy Swanson, because he knows Blondy Swanson is a very able citizen in every respect.

"Now, Blondy," The Dutchman says, "if you like my proposition, I am willing to cut you in for fifty percent, and fifty percent of fifty G's is by no means pretzels in these times."

"Well, Dutchman," Blondy says, "I will gladly assist you in this enterprise on the terms you state. It appeals to me as a legitimate proposition, because there is no doubt this dough is coming to you, and from now on I am strictly legit. But in the meantime, let us have some more rock candy and rye whiskey, without the rock candy, while we discuss the matter further."

But it seems that The Dutchman does not care for rock candy and rye whiskey, even without the rock candy, so Blondy Swanson and me and Good Time Charley continue taking our doses, and Blondy keeps getting more enthusiastic about The Dutchman's proposition until finally I become enthusiastic myself, and I say I think I will go along as it is an opportunity to see new sections of the country, while Good Time Charley states that it will always be the great regret of his life that his business keeps him from going, but that he will provide us with an ample store of rock candy and rye whiskey, without the rock candy, in case we run into any touches of the grippe.

Well, anyway, this is how I come to be riding around in an old can belonging to The Dutchman on a very cold Christmas Eve with The Dutchman and Blondy Swanson, although none of us happen to think of it being Christmas Eve until we notice that there seems to be holly wreaths in windows here and there as we go bouncing along the roads, and finally we pass a little church that is all lit up, and somebody opens the door as we are passing, and we see a big Christmas tree inside the church, and it is a very pleasant sight, indeed, and in fact it makes me a little homesick, although of course the chances are I will not be seeing any Christmas trees even if I am home.

We leave Good Time Charley's along midafternoon, with The Dutchman driving this old can of his, and all I seem to remember about the trip is going through a lot of little towns so fast they seem strung together, because most of the time I am dozing in the back seat.

Blondy Swanson is riding in the front seat with The Dutchman and Blondy also cops a little snooze now and then as we are going along, but whenever he happens to wake up he pokes me awake, too, so we can take a dose of rock candy and rye whiskey, without the rock candy. So in many respects it is quite an enjoyable journey.

I recollect the little church because we pass it right after we go busting through a pretty fair-sized town, and I hear The Dutchman say the old barn is now only a short distance away, and by this time it is dark, and colder than a deputy sheriff's heart, and there is snow on the ground, although it is clear overhead, and I am wishing I am back in Mindy's restaurant wrapping myself around a nice T-bone steak, when I hear Blondy Swanson ask The Dutchman if he is sure he knows where he is going, as this seems to be an untraveled road, and The Dutchman states as follows:

"Why," he says, "I know I am on the right road. I am following the big star you see up ahead of us, because I remember seeing this star always in front of me when I am going along the road before."

So we keep following the star, but it turns out that it is not a star at all, but a light shining from the window of a ramshackle old frame building pretty well off to one side of the road and on a rise of ground, and when The Dutchman sees this light, he is greatly nonplussed, indeed, and speaks as follows:

"Well," he says, "this looks very much like my barn, but my barn does not call for a light in it. Let us investigate this matter before we go any farther."

So The Dutchman gets out of the old can, and slips up to one side of the building and peeks through the window, and then he comes back and motions for Blondy and me to also take a peek through this window, which is nothing but a square hole cut in the side of the building with wooden bars across it, but no windowpanes, and what we behold inside by the dim light of a lantern hung on a nail on a post is really most surprising.

There is no doubt whatever that we are looking at the inside of a very old barn, for there are several stalls for horses, or maybe cows, here and there, but somebody seems to be living in the barn, as we can see a table, and a couple of chairs, and a tin stove, in which there is a little fire, and on the floor in one corner is what seems to be a sort of a bed.

Furthermore, there seems to be somebody lying on the bed and making quite a fuss in the way of groaning and crying and carrying on generally in a loud tone of voice, and there is no doubt that it is the voice of a doll, and anybody can tell that this doll is in some distress.

Well, here is a situation, indeed, and we move away from the barn to talk it over.

The Dutchman is greatly discouraged, because he gets to thinking that if this doll is living in the barn for any length of time, his plant may be discovered. He is willing to go away and wait awhile, but Blondy Swanson seems to be doing quite some thinking, and finally Blondy says like this:

"Why," Blondy says, "the doll in this barn seems to be sick, and only a bounder and a cad will walk away from a sick doll, especially," Blondy says, "a sick doll who is a total stranger to him. In fact, it will take a very large heel to do such a thing. The idea is for us to go inside and see if we can do anything for this sick doll," Blondy says.

Well, I say to Blondy Swanson that the chances are the doll's ever-loving husband, or somebody, is in town, or maybe over to the nearest neighbors digging up assistance, and will be back in a jiffy, and that this is no place for us to be found.

"No," Blondy says, "it cannot be as you state. The snow on the ground is anyway a day old. There are no tracks around the door of this old joint, going or coming, and it is a cinch if anybody knows there is a sick doll here, they will have plenty of time to get help before this. I am going inside and look things over," Blondy says.

Naturally, The Dutchman and I go too, because we do not wish to be left alone outside, and it is no trouble whatever to get into the barn, as the door is unlocked, and all we have to do is walk in. And when we walk in with Blondy Swanson leading the way, the doll on the bed on the floor half-raises up to look at us, and although the light of the lantern is none too good, anybody can see that this doll is nobody but Miss Clarabelle Cobb, although personally I see some changes in her since she is in Mr. Georgie White's "Scandals."

She stays half-raised up on the bed looking at Blondy Swanson for as long as you can count ten, if you count fast, then she falls back and starts crying and carrying on again, and at this The Dutchman kneels down on the floor beside her to find out what is eating her.

All of a sudden The Dutchman jumps up and speaks to us as follows:

"Why," he says, "this is quite a delicate situation, to be sure. In fact," he says, "I must request you guys to step outside. What we really need for this case is a doctor, but it is too late to send for one. However, I will endeavor to do the best I can under the circumstances."

Then The Dutchman starts taking off his overcoat, and Blondy Swanson stands looking at him with such a strange expression on his kisser that The Dutchman laughs out loud, and says like this:

"Do not worry about anything, Blondy," The Dutchman says. "I am maybe a little out of practice since my old lady put her checks back in the rack, but she leaves eight kids alive and kicking, and I bring them all in except one, because we are seldom able to afford a croaker."

So Blondy Swanson and I step out of the barn and after a while The Dutchman calls us and we go back into the barn to find he has a big fire going in the stove, and the place nice and warm.

Miss Clarabelle Cobb is now all quieted down, and is covered with The Dutchman's overcoat, and as we come in The Dutchman tiptoes over to her and pulls back the coat and what do we see but a baby with a noggin no bigger than a crab apple and a face as wrinkled as some old pappy guy's, and The Dutchman states that it is a boy, and a very healthy one, at that.

"Furthermore," The Dutchman says, "the mama is doing as well as can be expected. She is as strong a doll as ever I see," he says, "and all we have to do now is send out a croaker when we go through town just to make sure there are no complications. But," The Dutchman says, "I guarantee the croaker will not have much to do."

Well, the old Dutchman is as proud of this baby as if it is his own, and I do not wish to hurt his feelings, so I say the baby is a darberoo, and a great credit to him in every respect, and also to Miss Clarabelle Cobb, while Blondy Swanson just stands there looking at it as if he never sees a baby before in his life, and is greatly astonished.

It seems that Miss Clarabelle Cobb is a very strong doll, just as

The Dutchman states, and in about an hour she shows signs of being wide awake, and Blondy Swanson sits down on the floor beside her, and she talks to him quite a while in a low voice, and while they are talking The Dutchman pulls up the floor in another corner of the barn, and digs around underneath a few minutes, and finally comes up with a gripsack covered with dirt, and he opens this gripsack and shows me it is filled with lovely, large coarse bank notes.

Later Blondy Swanson tells The Dutchman and me the story of Miss Clarabelle Cobb, and parts of this story are rather sad. It seems that after Miss Clarabelle Cobb goes back to her old home in Akron, Ohio, she winds up marrying a young guy by the name of Joseph Hatcher, who is a bookkeeper by trade, and has a pretty good job in Akron, so Miss Clarabelle Cobb and this Joseph Hatcher are as happy as anything together for quite a spell.

Then about a year before the night I am telling about Joseph Hatcher is sent by his firm to these parts where we find Miss Clarabelle Cobb, to do the bookkeeping in a factory there, and one night a few months afterward, when Joseph Hatcher is staying after hours in the factory office working on his books, a mob of wrong gees breaks into the joint, and sticks him up, and blows open the safe, taking away a large sum of money and leaving Joseph Hatcher tied up like a turkey.

When Joseph Hatcher is discovered in this predicament the next morning, what happens but the gendarmes put the sleeve on him, and place him in the pokey, saying the chances are Joseph Hatcher is in and in with the safe-blowers, and that he tips them off the dough is in the safe, and it seems that the guy who is especially fond of this idea is a guy by the name of Ambersham, who is manager of the factory, and a very hard-hearted guy, at that.

And now, although this is eight or nine months back, there is Joseph Hatcher still in the pokey awaiting trial, and it is seven to five anywhere in town that the judge throws the book at him when he finally goes to bat, because it seems from what Miss Clarabelle Cobb tells Blondy Swanson that nearly everybody figures Joseph Hatcher is guilty.

But of course Miss Clarabelle Cobb does not put in with popular opinion about her ever-loving Joe, and she spends the next few months trying to spring him from the pokey, but she has no potatoes, and no way of getting any potatoes, so things go from bad to worse with Miss Clarabelle Cobb.

Finally, she finds herself with no place to live in town, and she happens to run into this old barn, which is on an abandoned property owned by a doctor in town by the name of Kelton, and it seems that he is a kindhearted guy, and he gives her permission to use it any way she wishes. So Miss Clarabelle moves into the barn, and the chances are there is many a time when she wishes she is back in Mr. Georgie White's "Scandals."

Now The Dutchman listens to this story with great interest, especially the part about Joseph Hatcher being left tied up in the factory office, and finally The Dutchman states as follows:

"Why, my goodness," The Dutchman says, "there is no doubt but what this is the very same young guy we are compelled to truss up the night we get this gripsack. As I recollect it, he wishes to battle for his employer's dough, and I personally tap him over the coco with a blackjack.

"But," he says, "he is by no means the guy who tips us off about the dough being there. As I remember it now, it is nobody but the guy whose name you mention in Miss Clarabelle Cobb's story. It is this guy Ambersham, the manager of the joint, and come to think of it, he is supposed to get his bit of this dough for his trouble, and it is only fair that I carry out this agreement as the executor of the estate of my late comrades, although," The Dutchman says, "I do not approve of his conduct toward this Joseph Hatcher. But," he says, "the first thing for us to do is to get a doctor out here to Miss Clarabelle Cobb, and I judge the doctor for us to get is this Doc Kelton she speaks of."

So The Dutchman takes the gripsack and we get into the old can and head back the way we come, although before we go I see Blondy Swanson bend down over Miss Clarabelle Cobb, and while I do not wish this to go any farther, I will take a paralyzed oath I see him plant a small kiss on the baby's noggin, and I hear Miss Clarabelle Cobb speak as follows:

"I will name him for you, Blondy," she says. "By the way, Blondy, what is your right name?"

"Olaf," Blondy says.

It is now along in the early morning and not many citizens are stirring as we go through town again, with Blondy in the front seat again holding the gripsack on his lap so The Dutchman can drive, but finally we find a guy in an all-night lunch counter who knows where Doc Kelton lives, and this guy stands on the running board of the old can and guides us to a house in a side street, and after pounding on the door quite a spell, we roust the Doc out and Blondy goes inside to talk with him.

He is in there quite a spell, but when he comes out he says everything is okay, and that Doc Kelton will go at once to look after Miss Clarabelle Cobb, and take her to a hospital, and Blondy states that he leaves a couple of C's with the Doc to make sure Miss Clarabelle Cobb gets the best of care.

"Well," The Dutchman says, "we can afford a couple of C's out of what we have in this gripsack, but," he says, "I am still wondering if it is not my duty to look up this Ambersham, and give him his bit."

"Dutchman," Blondy says, "I fear I have some bad news for you. The gripsack is gone. This Doc Kelton strikes me as a right guy in every respect, especially," Blondy says, "as he states to me that he always half-suspects there is a wrong rap in on Miss Clarabelle Cobb's ever-loving Joe, and that if it is not for this guy Ambersham agitating all the time other citizens may suspect the same thing, and it will not be so tough for Joe.

"So," Blondy says, "I tell Doc Kelton the whole story, about Ambersham and all, and I take the liberty of leaving the gripsack with him to be returned to the rightful owners, and Doc Kelton says if he does not have Miss Clarabelle Cobb's Joe out of the sneezer, and this Ambersham on the run out of town in twenty-four hours, I can call him a liar. But," Blondy says, "let us now proceed on our way, because I only have Doc Kelton's word that he will give us twelve hours' leeway before he does anything except attend to Miss Clarabelle Cobb, as I figure you need this much time to get out of sight, Dutchman."

Well, The Dutchman does not say anything about all this news for a while, and seems to be thinking the situation over, and while he is thinking he is giving his old can a little more gas than he intends, and she is fairly popping along what seems to be the main drag of the town when a gendarme on a motorcycle comes up alongside us, and motions The Dutchman to pull over to the curb.

He is a nice-looking young gendarme, but he seems somewhat hostile as he gets off his motorcycle, and walks up to us very slow, and asks us where the fire is.

Naturally, we do not say anything in reply, which is the only thing to say to a gendarme under these circumstances, so he speaks as follows:

"What are you guys carrying in this old skillet, anyway?" he says. "Stand up, and let me look you guys over."

And then as we stand up, he peeks into the front and back of the car, and under our feet, and all he finds is a bottle which once holds some of Good Time Charley's rock candy and rye whiskey without the rock candy, but which is now very empty, and he holds this bottle up, and sniffs at the nozzle, and asks what is formerly in this bottle, and I tell him the truth when I tell him it is once full of medicine, and The Dutchman and Blondy Swanson nod their heads in support of my statement. But the gendarme takes another sniff, and then he says like this:

"Oh," he says, very sarcastic, "wise guys, eh? Three wise guys, eh? Trying to kid somebody, eh? Medicine, eh?" he says. "Well, if it is not Christmas Day I will take you in and hold you just on suspicion. But I will be Santa Claus to you, and let you go ahead, wise guys."

And then after we get a few blocks away, The Dutchman speaks as follows:

"Yes," he says, "that is what we are, to be sure. We are wise guys. If we are not wise guys, we will still have the gripsack in this car for the copper to find. And if the copper finds the gripsack, he will wish to take us to the jail house for investigation, and if he wishes to take us there I fear he will not be alive at this time, and we will be in plenty of heat around and about, and personally," The Dutchman says, "I am sick and tired of heat."

And with this The Dutchman puts a large Betsy back in a holster under his left arm, and turns on the gas, and as the old can begins leaving the lights of the town behind, I ask Blondy if he happens to notice the name of this town.

"Yes," Blondy says, "I notice it on a signboard we just pass. It is Bethlehem, Pa."

THE
BLOODHOUNDS
OF
BROADWAY

One morning along about four bells, I am standing in front of Mindy's restaurant on Broadway with a guy by the name of Regret, who has this name because it seems he wins a very large bet the year the Whitney filly, Regret, grabs the Kentucky Derby, and can never forget it, which is maybe because it is the only very large bet he ever wins in his life.

What this guy's real name is I never hear, and anyway names make no difference to me, especially on Broadway, because the chances are that no matter what name a guy has, it is not his square name. So, as far as I am concerned, Regret is as good a name as any other for this guy I am talking about, who is a fat guy, and very gabby, though generally he is talking about nothing but horses, and how he gets beat three dirty noses the day before at Belmont, or wherever the horses are running.

In all the years I know Regret he must get beat ten thousand noses, and always they are dirty noses, to hear him tell it. In fact, I never once hear him say he is beat a clean nose, but of course this is only the way horse-racing guys talk. What Regret does for a living besides betting on horses I do not know, but he seems to do pretty well at it, because he is always around and about, and generally well dressed, and with a lot of big cigars sticking up out of his vest pocket.

It is generally pretty quiet on Broadway along about four bells in the morning, because at such an hour the citizens are mostly in speakeasies, and nightclubs, and on this morning I am talking about it is very quiet, indeed, except for a guy by the name of Marvin Clay hollering at a young doll because she will not get into a taxicab with him to go to his apartment. But of course Regret and I do not pay much attention to such a scene, except that Regret remarks that the young doll seems to have more sense than you will expect to see in a doll loose on Broadway at four bells in the morning, because it is well known to one and all that any doll who goes to Marvin Clay's apartment, either has no brains whatever, or wishes to go there.

This Marvin Clay is a very prominent society guy, who is a great hand for hanging out in nightclubs, and he has plenty of scratch which comes down to him from his old man, who makes it out of railroads and one thing and another. But Marvin Clay is a most obnoxious character, being loud and ungentlemanly at all times, on account of having all this scratch, and being always very rough and abusive with young dolls such as work in nightclubs, and who have to stand for such treatment from Marvin Clay because he is a very good customer.

He is generally in evening clothes, as he is seldom around and about except in the evening, and he is maybe fifty years old, and has a very ugly mug, which is covered with blotches, and pimples, but of course a guy who has so much scratch as Marvin Clay does not have to be so very handsome, at that, and he is very welcome indeed wherever he goes on Broadway. Personally, I wish no part of such a guy as Marvin Clay, although I suppose in my time on Broadway I must see a thousand guys like him, and there will always be guys like Marvin Clay on Broadway as long as they have old men to make plenty of scratch out of railroads to keep them going.

Well, by and by Marvin Clay gets the doll in the taxicab, and away they go, and it is all quiet again on Broadway, and Regret and I stand there speaking of this and that, and one thing and another, when along comes a very strange-looking guy leading two very strange-looking dogs. The guy is so thin I figure he must be about two pounds lighter than a stack of wheats. He has a long nose, and a sad face, and he is wearing a floppy old black felt hat, and he has on a flannel shirt, and baggy corduroy pants, and a see-more coat, which is a coat that lets you see more hip pockets than coat.

Personally, I never see a stranger-looking guy on Broadway, and I wish to say I see some very strange-looking guys on Broadway in my day. But if the guy is strange-looking, the dogs are even stranger-looking because they have big heads, and jowls that hang down like an old-time faro bank dealer's, and long ears the size of bed sheets. Furthermore, they have wrinkled faces, and big, round eyes that seem so sad I half expect to see them bust out crying.

The dogs are a sort of black and yellow in color, and have long tails, and they are so thin you can see their ribs sticking out of their hides. I can see at once that the dogs and the guy leading them can use a few hamburgers very nicely, but then so can a lot of other guys on Broadway at this time, leaving out the dogs.

Well, Regret is much interested in the dogs right away, because he is a guy who is very fond of animals of all kinds, and nothing will do but he must stop the guy and start asking questions about what sort of dogs they are, and in fact I am also anxious to hear myself, because while I see many a pooch in my time I never see anything like these.

"They is bloodhounds," the sad-looking guy says in a very sad voice, and with one of these accents such as Southern guys always have. "They is man-tracking bloodhounds from Georgia."

Now of course both Regret and me know what bloodhounds are because we see such animals chasing Eliza across the ice in Uncle Tom's Cabin when we are young squirts, but this is the first time either of us meet up with any bloodhounds personally, especially on Broadway. So we get to talking quite a bit to the guy, and his story is as sad as his face, and makes us both feel very sorry for him.

In fact, the first thing we know we have him and the bloodhounds in Mindy's and are feeding one and all big steaks, although Mindy puts up an awful squawk about us bringing the dogs in, and asks us what we think he is running, anyway. When Regret starts to tell him, Mindy says never mind, but not to bring any more Shetland ponies into his joint again as long as we live.

Well, it seems that the sad-looking guy's name is John Wangle, and he comes from a town down in Georgia where his uncle is the high sheriff, and one of the bloodhounds' name is Nip, and the other Tuck, and they are both trained from infancy to track down guys such as lags who escape from the county pokey, and bad niggers, and one thing and another, and after John Wangle gets the kinks out of his belly on Mindy's steaks, and starts talking good, you must either figure him a high-class liar, or the hounds the greatest man-trackers the world ever sees.

Now, looking at the dogs after they swallow six big sirloins apiece, and a lot of matzoths, which Mindy has left over from the Jewish holidays, and a job lot of goulash from the dinner bill, and some other odds and ends, the best I can figure them is hearty eaters, because they are now lying down on the floor with their faces hidden behind their ears, and are snoring so loud you can scarcely hear yourself think.

How John Wangle comes to be in New York with these bloodhounds is quite a story, indeed. It seems that a New York guy drifts into John's old hometown in Georgia when the bloodhounds are tracking down a bad nigger, and this guy figures it will be a wonderful idea to take John Wangle and the dogs to New York and hire them out to the movies to track down the villains in the pictures. But when they get to New York, it seems the movies have other arrangements for tracking down their villains, and the guy runs out of scratch and blows away, leaving John Wangle and the bloodhounds stranded.

So here John Wangle is with Nip and Tuck in New York, and they are all living together in one room in a tenement house over in West Forty-ninth Street, and things are pretty tough with them, because John does not know how to get back to Georgia unless he walks, and he hears the walking is no good south of Roanoke. When I ask him why he does not write to his uncle, the high sheriff down there in Georgia, John Wangle says, there are two reasons, one being that he cannot write, and the other that his uncle cannot read.

Then I ask him why he does not sell the bloodhounds, and he says it is because the market for bloodhounds is very quiet in New York, and furthermore if he goes back to Georgia without the bloodhounds his uncle is apt to knock his ears down. Anyway, John Wangle says he personally loves Nip and Tuck very dearly, and in fact he says it is only his great love for them that keeps him from eating one or the other and maybe both, the past week, when his hunger is very great indeed.

Well, I never before see Regret so much interested in any situation as he is in John Wangle and the bloodhounds, but personally I am getting very tired of them, because the one that is called Nip finally wakes up and starts chewing on my leg, thinking it is maybe more steak, and when I kick him in the snoot, John Wangle scowls at me, and Regret says only very mean guys are unkind to dumb animals.

But to show you that John Wangle and his bloodhounds are not so dumb, they come moseying along past Mindy's every morning after this at about the same time, and Regret is always there ready to feed them, although he now has to take the grub out on the sidewalk, as Mindy will not allow the hounds in the joint again. Naturally Nip and Tuck become very fond of Regret, but they are by no means as fond of him as John Wangle, because John is commencing to fat up very nicely, and the bloodhounds are also taking on weight.

Now what happens but Regret does not show up in front of Mindy's for several mornings hand-running, because it seems that Regret makes a very nice score for himself one day against the horses, and buys himself a brand-new tuxedo, and starts stepping out around the nightclubs, and especially around Miss Missouri Martin's Three Hundred Club, where there are many beautiful young dolls who dance around with no more clothes on them than will make a pad for a crutch, and it is well known that Regret dearly loves such scenes.

Furthermore, I hear reports around and about of Regret becoming very fond of a doll by the name of Miss Lovey Lou, who works in Miss Missouri Martin's Three Hundred Club, and of him getting in some kind of a jam with Marvin Clay over this doll, and smacking Marvin Clay in the kisser, so I figure Regret is getting a little simple, as guys who hang around Broadway long enough are bound to do. Now, when John Wangle and Nip and Tuck come around looking for a handout, there is nothing much doing for them, as nobody else around Mindy's feels any great interest in bloodhounds, especially such interest as will cause them to buy steaks, and soon Nip and Tuck are commencing to look very sad again, and John Wangle is downcast more than somewhat.

It is early morning again, and warm, and a number of citizens are out in front of Mindy's as usual, breathing the fresh air, when along comes a police inspector by the name of McNamara, who is a friend of mine, with a bunch of plainclothes coppers with him, and Inspector McNamara tells me he is on his way to investigate a situation in an apartment house over in West Fifty-fourth Street, about three blocks away, where it seems a guy is shot; and not having anything else to do, I go with them, although as a rule I do not care to associate with coppers, because it arouses criticism from other citizens.

Well, who is the guy who is shot but Marvin Clay, and he is stretched out on the floor of the living room of his apartment in evening clothes, with his shirtfront covered with blood, and after Inspector McNamara takes a close peek at him, he sees that Marvin Clay is plugged smack-dab in the chest, and that he seems to be fairly dead. Furthermore, there seems to be no clue whatever to who does the shooting, and Inspector McNamara says it is undoubtedly a very great mystery, and will be duck soup for the newspapers, especially as they do not have a good shooting mystery for several days.

Well, of course all this is none of my business, but all of a sudden I happen to think of John Wangle and his bloodhounds, and it seems to me it will be a great opportunity for them, so I say to the Inspector as follows:

"Listen, Mac," I say, "there is a guy here with a pair of man-tracking bloodhounds from Georgia who are very expert in tracking down matters such as this, and," I say, "maybe they can track down the rascal who shoots Marvin Clay, because the trail must be hotter than mustard right now."

Well, afterward I hear there is much indignation over my suggestion, because many citizens feel that the party who shoots Marvin Clay is entitled to more consideration than being tracked with bloodhounds. In fact, some think the party is entitled to a medal, but this discussion does not come up until later.

Anyway, at first the Inspector does not think much of my idea, and the other coppers are very skeptical, and claim that the best way to do under the circumstances is to arrest everybody in sight and hold them as material witnesses for a month or so, but the trouble is there is nobody in sight to arrest at this time, except maybe me, and the Inspector is a broad-minded guy, and finally he says all right, bring on the bloodhounds.

So I hasten back to Mindy's, and sure enough John Wangle and Nip and Tuck are out on the sidewalk peering at every passing face in the hope that maybe one of these faces will belong to Regret. It is a very pathetic sight, indeed, but John Wangle cheers up when I explain about Marvin Clay to him, and hurries back to the apartment house with me so fast that he stretches Nip's neck a foot, and is pulling Tuck along on his stomach half the time.

Well, when we get back to the apartment, John Wangle leads Nip and Tuck up to Marvin Clay, and they snuffle him all over, because it seems bloodhounds are quite accustomed to dead guys. Then John Wangle unhooks their leashes, and yells something at them, and the hounds begin snuffling all around and about the joint, with Inspector McNamara and the other coppers watching with great interest. All of a sudden Nip and Tuck go busting out of the apartment and into the street, with John Wangle after them, and all the rest of us after John Wangle. They head across Fifty-fourth Street back to Broadway, and the next thing anybody knows they are doing plenty of snuffling around in front of Mindy's.

By and by they take off up Broadway with their snozzles to the sidewalk, and we follow them very excited, because even the coppers now admit that it seems to be a sure thing they are red hot on the trail of the party who shoots Marvin Clay. At first Nip and Tuck are walking, but pretty soon they break into a lope, and there we are loping after them, John Wangle, the Inspector, and me, and the coppers.

Naturally, such a sight as this attracts quite some attention as we go along from any citizens stirring at this hour, and by and by milkmen are climbing down off their wagons, and scavenger guys are leaving their trucks standing where they are, and newsboys are dropping everything, and one and all joining in the chase, so by the time we hit Broadway and Fifty-sixth there is quite a delegation following the hounds with John Wangle in front, just behind Nip and Tuck, and yelling at them now and then as follows:

"Hold to it, boys!"

At Fifty-sixth the hounds turn east off Broadway and stop at the door of what seems to be an old garage, this door being closed very tight, and Nip and Tuck seem to wish to get through this door, so the Inspector and the coppers kick the door open, and who is in the garage having a big crap game but many prominent citizens of Broadway. Naturally, these citizens are greatly astonished at seeing the bloodhounds, and the rest of us, especially the coppers, and they start running every which way trying to get out of the joint, because crap shooting is quite illegal in these parts.

But the Inspector only says Ah-ha, and starts jotting down names in a notebook as if it is something he will refer to later, and Nip and Tuck are out of the joint almost as soon as they get in and are snuffling on down Fifty-sixth. They stop at four more doors in Fifty-sixth Street along, and when the coppers kick open these doors they find they are nothing but speakeasies, although one is a hop joint, and the citizens in these places are greatly put out by the excitement, especially as Inspector McNamara keeps jotting down things in his notebook.

Finally the Inspector starts glaring very fiercely at the coppers with us, and anybody can see that he is much displeased to find so much illegality going on in this district, and the coppers are starting in to hate Nip and Tuck quite freely, and one copper says to me like this:

"Why," he says, "these mutts are nothing but stool pigeons."

Well, naturally, the noise of John Wangle's yelling, and the gabble of the mob following the hounds makes quite a disturbance, and arouses many of the neighbors in the apartment houses and hotels in the side streets, especially as this is summer, and most everybody has their windows open.

In fact, we see many tousled heads poked out of windows, and hear guys and dolls inquiring as follows:

"What is going on?"

It seems that when word gets about that bloodhounds are tracking down a wrongdoer it causes great uneasiness all through the Fifties, and in fact I afterward hear that three guys are taken to the Polyclinic suffering with broken ankles and several bruises from hopping out of windows in the hotels we pass in the chase, or from falling off of fire escapes.

Well, all of a sudden Nip and Tuck swing back into Seventh Avenue, and pop into the entrance of a small apartment house, and go tearing up the stairs to the first floor, and when we get there these bloodhounds are scratching vigorously at the door of Apartment B-2, and going woofle-woofle, and we are all greatly excited, indeed, but the door opens, and who is standing there but a doll by the name of Maud Milligan, who is well known to one and all as the ever-loving doll of Big Nig, the crap shooter, who is down in Hot Springs at this time taking the waters, or whatever it is guys take in Hot Springs.

Now, Maud Milligan is not such a doll as I will care to have any part of, being redheaded, and very stern, and I am glad Nip and Tuck do not waste any more time in her apartment than it takes for them to run through her living room and across her bed, because Maud is commencing to put the old eye on such of us present as she happens to know. But Nip and Tuck are in and out of the joint before you can say scat, because it is only a two-room apartment, at that, and we are on our way down the stairs and back into Seventh Avenue again while Inspector McNamara is still jotting down something in his notebook.

Finally, where do these hounds wind up, with about four hundred citizens behind them, and everybody perspiring quite freely indeed from the exercise, but at the door of Miss Missouri Martin's Three Hundred Club, and the doorman, who is a guy by the name of Soldier Sweeney, tries to shoo them away, but Nip runs between the Soldier's legs and upsets him, and Tuck steps in the Soldier's eye in trotting over him, and most of the crowd behind the hounds tread on him in passing, so the old Soldier is pretty well flattened out at the finish.

Nip and Tuck are now more excited than somewhat, and are going zoople-zoople in loud voices as they bust into the Three Hundred Club with John Wangle and the law, and all these citizens behind them. There is a very large crowd present and Miss Missouri Martin is squatted on the back of a chair in the middle of the dance floor when we enter, and is about to start her show when she sees the mob surge in, and at first she is greatly pleased because she thinks new business arrives, and if there is anything Miss Missouri Martin dearly loves, it is new business.

But before she can say hello, sucker, or anything else whatever, Nip runs under her chair, thinking maybe he is a dachshund, and dumps Miss Missouri Martin on the dance floor, and she lays there squawking no little, while the next thing anybody knows, Nip and Tuck are over in one corner of the joint, and are eagerly crawling up and down a fat guy who is sitting there with a doll alongside of him, and who is the fat guy but Regret!

Well, as Nip and Tuck rush at Regret he naturally gets up to defend himself, but they both hit him at the same time, and over he goes on top of the doll who is with him, and who seems to be nobody but Miss Lovey Lou. She is getting quite a squashing with Regret's heft spread out over her, and she is screaming quite some, especially when Nip lets out a foot of tongue and washes her makeup off her face, reaching for Regret. In fact, Miss Lovey Lou seems to be more afraid of the bloodhounds than she does of being squashed to death, for when John Wangle and I hasten to her rescue and pull her out from under Regret she is moaning as follows:

"Oh, do not let them devour me—I will confess."

Well, as nobody but me and John Wangle seem to hear this crack, because everybody else is busy trying to split out Regret and the bloodhounds, and as John Wangle does not seem to understand what Miss Lovey Lou is mumbling about, I shove her off into the crowd, and on back into the kitchen, which is now quite deserted, what with all the help being out watching the muss in the corner, and I say to her like this:

"What is it you confess?" I say. "Is it about Marvin Clay?"

"Yes," she says. "It is about him. He is a pig," she says. "I shoot him, and I am glad of it. He is not satisfied with what he does to me two years ago, but he tries his deviltry on my baby sister. He has her in his apartment and when I find it out and go to get her, he says he will not let her go. So I shoot him. With my brother's pistol," she says, "and I take my baby sister home with me, and I hope he is dead, and gone where he belongs."

"Well, now," I say, "I am not going to give you any argument as to where Marvin Clay belongs, but," I say, "you skip out of here and go on home, and wait until we can do something about this situation, while I go back and help Regret, who seems to be in a tough spot."

"Oh, do not let these terrible dogs eat him up," she says, and with this she takes the breeze and I return to the other room to find there is much confusion indeed, because it seems that Regret is now very indignant at Nip and Tuck, especially when he discovers that one of them plants his big old paw right on the front of Regret's shirt bosom, leaving a dirty mark. So when he struggles to his feet, Regret starts letting go with both hands, and he is by no means a bad puncher for a guy who does not do much punching as a rule. In fact, he flattens Nip with a right-hand to the jaw, and knocks Tuck plumb across the room with a left hook.

Well, poor Tuck slides over the slick dance floor into Miss Missouri Martin just as she is getting to her feet again, and bowls her over once more, but Miss Missouri Martin is also indignant by this time, and she gets up and kicks Tuck in a most unladylike manner. Of course, Tuck does not know so much about Miss Martin, but he is pretty sure his old friend Regret is only playing with him, so back he goes to Regret with his tongue out, and his tail wagging, and there is no telling how long this may go on if John Wangle does not step in and grab both hounds, while Inspector McNamara puts the arm on Regret and tells him he is under arrest for shooting Marvin Clay.

Well, of course everybody can see at once that Regret must be the guilty party all right, especially when it is remembered that he once had trouble with Marvin Clay, and one and all present are looking at Regret in great disgust, and saying you can see by his face that he is nothing but a degenerate type.

Furthermore, Inspector McNamara makes a speech to Miss Missouri Martin's customers in which he congratulates John Wangle and Nip and Tuck on their wonderful work in tracking down this terrible criminal and at the same time putting in a few boosts for the police department, while Regret stands there paying very little attention to what the Inspector is saying, but trying to edge himself over close enough to Nip and Tuck to give them the old foot.

Well, the customers applaud what Inspector McNamara says, and Miss Missouri Martin gets up a collection of over two C's for John Wangle and his hounds, not counting what she holds out for herself. Also the chef comes forward and takes John Wangle and Nip and Tuck back into the kitchen and stuffs them full of food, although personally I will just as soon not have any of the food they serve in the Three Hundred Club.

They take Regret to the jail house, and he does not seem to understand why he is under arrest, but he knows it has something to do with Nip and Tuck and he tries to bribe one of the coppers to put the bloodhounds in the same cell with him for a while, though naturally the copper will not consider such a proposition. While Regret is being booked at the jail house, word comes around that Marvin Clay is not only not dead, but the chances are he will get well, which he finally does, at that.

Moreover, he finally bails Regret out, and not only refuses to prosecute him but skips the country as soon as he is able to move, although Regret lays in the sneezer for several weeks, at that, never letting on after he learns the real situation that he is not the party who plugs Marvin Clay. Naturally, Miss Lovey Lou is very grateful to Regret for his wonderful sacrifice, and will no doubt become his ever-loving wife in a minute, if Regret thinks to ask her, but it seems Regret finds himself brooding so much over the idea of an ever-loving wife who is so handy with a Roscoe that he never really asks.

In the meantime, John Wangle and Nip and Tuck go back to Georgia on the dough collected by Miss Missouri Martin, and with a big reputation as man-trackers. So this is all there is to the story, except that one night I run into Regret with a suitcase in his hand, and he is perspiring very freely, although it is not so hot, at that, and when I ask him if he is going away, he says this is indeed his general idea. Moreover, he says he is going very far away. Naturally, I ask him why this is, and Regret says to me as follows:

"Well," he says, "ever since Big Nig, the crap shooter, comes back from Hot Springs, and hears how the bloodhounds track the shooter of Marvin Clay, he is walking up and down looking at me out of the corner of his eye. In fact," Regret says, "I can see that Big Nig is studying something over in his mind, and while Big Nig is a guy who is not such a fast thinker as others, I am afraid he may finally think himself to a bad conclusion.

"I am afraid," Regret says, "that Big Nig will think himself to the conclusion that Nip and Tuck are tracking me instead of the shooter, as many evil-minded guys are already whispering around and about, and that he may get the wrong idea about the trail leading to Maud Milligan's door."

FOR THE BEST IN PAPERBACKS, LOOK FOR THE

In every corner of the world, on every subject under the sun, Penguin represents quality and variety—the very best in publishing today.

For complete information about books available from Penguin—including Puffins, Penguin Classics, and Arkana—and how to order them, write to us at the appropriate address below. Please note that for copyright reasons the selection of books varies from country to country.

In the United Kingdom: Please write to *Dept. JC, Penguin Books Ltd, FREEPOST, West Drayton, Middlesex UB7 0BR.*

If you have any difficulty in obtaining a title, please send your order with the correct money, plus ten percent for postage and packaging, to *P.O. Box No. 11, West Drayton, Middlesex UB7 0BR*

In the United States: Please write to *Consumer Sales, Penguin USA, P.O. Box 999, Dept. 17109, Bergenfield, New Jersey 07621-0120.* VISA and MasterCard holders call 1-800-253-6476 to order all Penguin titles

In Canada: Please write to *Penguin Books Canada Ltd, 10 Alcorn Avenue, Suite 300, Toronto, Ontario M4V 3B2*

In Australia: Please write to *Penguin Books Australia Ltd, P.O. Box 257, Ringwood, Victoria 3134*

In New Zealand: Please write to *Penguin Books (NZ) Ltd, Private Bag 102902, North Shore Mail Centre, Auckland 10*

In India: Please write to *Penguin Books India Pvt Ltd, 706 Eros Apartments, 56 Nehru Place, New Delhi 110 019*

In the Netherlands: Please write to *Penguin Books Netherlands bv, Postbus 3507, NL-1001 AH Amsterdam*

In Germany: Please write to *Penguin Books Deutschland GmbH, Metzlerstrasse 26, 60594 Frankfurt am Main*

In Spain: Please write to *Penguin Books S. A., Bravo Murillo 19, 1° B, 28015 Madrid*

In Italy: Please write to *Penguin Italia s.r.l., Via Felice Casati 20, I-20124 Milano*

In France: Please write to *Penguin France S. A., 17 rue Lejeune, F-31000 Toulouse*

In Japan: Please write to *Penguin Books Japan, Ishikiribashi Building, 2-5-4, Suido, Bunkyo-ku, Tokyo 112*

In Greece: Please write to *Penguin Hellas Ltd, Dimocritou 3, GR-106 71 Athens*

In South Africa: Please write to *Longman Penguin Southern Africa (Pty) Ltd, Private Bag X08, Bertsham 2013*

Being and the Messiah

Being
and the Messiah

The Message of St. John

José Porfirio Miranda

Translated by John Eagleson

Note to the English Translation

The basis for this translation was the author's original Spanish manuscript, which varies slightly from the published Spanish edition. Subheadings have been added by the translator. The author has graciously reviewed and revised the translation.

Special thanks are gratefully extended to Naomi Noble Richard, who assisted in preparing the final English version with her remarkable skill.

Library of Congress Cataloging in Publication Data

Miranda, José Porfirio
  Being and the Messiah.

  Translation of El ser y el Mesías.
  Bibliography: p.
  Includes indexes.
  1. Bible. N.T. Johannine literature—Criticism, interpretation, etc. 2. Existentialism. 3. Communism.
I. Title.
BS2601.M5413   230   77-5388
ISBN 0-88344-027-X
ISBN 0-88344-028-8 pbk.

Originally published in 1973 as *El ser y el mesías*

Copyright © 1973 by Ediciones Sígueme, Salamanca, Spain

English translation copyright © 1977 by Orbis Books

Orbis Books, Maryknoll, NY 10545

Printed in the United States of America

Contents

Preface

Each of us must decide on which side of the scale we will place the sum total of our actions. We cannot escape responsibility for our personal role in history if it contributes to the oppression of the poor and the helpless.

The time has come when all those who write or speak about Christ must also state whether they are struggling for the church or for Christianity.

The worst possible response would be to object that these two realities are identical. This would be like maintaining that what is good for our political party is good in itself and that what is bad for our political party is bad in itself, or that the end justifies the means. No authority can decree that everything is permitted; for justice and exploitation are not so indistinguishable. And Christ died so that we might know that not everything is permitted.

But not any Christ. The Christ who cannot be co-opted by accommodationists and opportunists as the historical Jesus. This book is dedicated to him.

Chapter 1

Revolution and Existentialism

In his *Critique de la raison dialectique*, Jean-Paul Sartre makes this remarkable comment: "To fire workers because a factory is closing is a sovereign act that tacitly assumes the fundamental right to kill."[1]

Dialectical reason, in its contemporary form, occurs in Marxism, and in this Marxist form it deserves to be criticized—for its superficiality. For we cannot bring about true revolution if we have not determined the root causes of oppression and exploitation. Firing workers for capitalistic reasons such as lowering costs is only a visible manifestation, a demonstrable, tangible effect of exploitation; it is not the cause, it is not the root of oppression. On the other hand, the feeling that we have the fundamental right to kill lies at a deeper level of human existence. Its manifestations change over time, but the feeling that produces these manifestations does not change.

In the same place Sartre has this to say about the bourgeois of the capitalist period: "There is, then, a meaning which redounds upon him from the future and henceforth will constitute the sense of all that he does, namely, no matter what he does he *must* suppress." There is an attitude that can overpower us and establish itself at our center; it makes us suppress, degrade, mistrust, and trample upon others. The historical contribution of existentialism is that it forces us to consider such a basic attitude very seriously—to discover it, to analyze it, to see how it affects all we do, to determine either its meaning or its absurdity.

The most interesting and threatening aspect of such an attitude is that the bourgeois themselves are not always aware of their deepest motivation. We can deduce it, however, from observing all that they do as members of their class. Moreover, this belief that we have the fundamental right to kill can exist on an unconscious level in all of us—even noncapitalists; and thus any consideration of such an attitude poses a threat to us.

THE ROOTS OF OPPRESSION

It would be so simple to divide the world into good people and bad, like the characters in cowboy movies. We must recognize that Marxism continuously verges on this kind of oversimplification. Compare Vittorio de Sica's *Miracle in Milan* with Luis Buñuel's *The Young and the Damned*. Buñuel avoids the temptation of romanticizing the proletariat, as if this class, immune to the contagions and commercialism of consumer society, were the depository of all sweetness and light. With de Sica, on the other hand, the rich are bad, the poor are good—a romanticism characteristic of the Marxism of his day.

Let me repeat: It would be much simpler to describe the world in this way. Indeed, it would even appear to be more revolutionary, because with this descriptive instrument it would be easier to revolutionize the people. And some will say that this alone is enough to justify such a Manichean approach, that the only important thing is to bring about the revolution, and if a Manichean schema hastens the revolution, this proves that such a schema is true.

But it would not bring about true revolution. This is the crucial point. We can rightly object to this Manichean approach because it is ineffective. Moreover, the only efficacy that matters is made impossible by such an approach.

One more coup d'état is of no interest to us, one more addition to the long list of political revolts, even if the majority of the population supports it. We are not concerned with some superficial mini-revolution whose inevitable outcome is to reproduce in grander proportions the very capitalistic world that it intended to eliminate. Existentialist honesty would put an end to all romanticism and dogmatism: It would force us to acknowledge, for example, that if we took an objective poll of the Mexican people today, we would find that their desires, aspirations, and values were precisely those engraved on their soul by capitalism.

Let there be no confusion between the existentialist thesis that we sustain here and the perennial conservative argument that holds that before true revolution can occur people must "first" change, that people must "first" be converted. That is simply an argument for the indefinite postponement of revolution. No, here we want to take revolution seriously. The assault on power and the expropriation of the means of production must occur as soon as possible, that is to say, as soon as the organization of the exploited is strong enough. But the problem of revolution is not solved by the assault on power, and this problem is our concern here.

Three years after his successful assault on power, Lenin wrote the following:

The old society was based on the principle: rob or be robbed; work for others or make others work for you; be a slave-owner or a slave. Naturally people brought up in such a society assimilate with their mother's milk, one might say, the psychology, the habit, the concept which says: you are either a slave-owner or a slave, or else, a small owner, a petty employee, a petty official or an intellectual—*in short, a man who is concerned only with himself and does not care a rap for anybody else.*[2]

Lenin was no revolutionary romantic. His was no black-and-white diagnosis of society. It was very clear to him that the proletariat itself had been profoundly contaminated by capitalism. Revolution cannot be reduced to taking power and expropriating the goods of production:

It is a victory over our own conservatism, indiscipline, petty-bourgeois egoism, a victory over the habits left as a heritage to the worker and peasant by accursed capitalism. Only when *this* victory is consolidated . . . will a reversion to capitalism become impossible, will communism become really invincible.[3]

Lenin, the theoretician of revolution par excellence, avoided the Manichean temptation of commonplace Marxism. It was quite clear to Lenin that the proletariat itself, the exploited themselves, both workers and peasants, had been imbued with the spirit of the bourgeoisie, with the desire for personal gain characteristic of private producers:

The small commodity producers . . . surround the proletariat on every side with a petty-bourgeois atmosphere, which permeates and corrupts the proletariat, and constantly causes among the proletariat relapses into petty-bourgeois spinelessness, disunity, individualism.[4]

The concrete-and-steel jungle, the war of all against all, has been imposed by the capitalists, and they have made all of us participants. This they have accomplished through the mass communications media and the contagion of commonplace attitudes (in any rural hamlet, for example, the rich person is admired, imitated, and envied). But their principal instrument has been the capitalist economic machinery itself, which makes certain attitudes and behavior essential to survival.

The Manichean approach of the Marxist parties, which ingenuously divides the world into good people and bad, is an apparently handy expedient that up to a point seems to facilitate the revolution, for it saves the toil of honest thinking. But this approach is not compatible with the authentic revolutionary thought of Marx and Lenin. Nor does it really carry us toward true revolution, for it prevents us from understanding the actual situation. The apparent revolutionary efficacy of this approach and its apparent capacity for inciting the masses against "the bad people," are indeed just that—apparent. For it permits those of us who are not rich to disregard how deeply each of us is an accomplice to the capitalism that has brainwashed us all.

Once we surmount our cherished oversimplifications, it becomes clear, although painful to admit, that capitalism, which benefits only a privileged minority, could not have endured if it had not convinced even the exploited majority of its goodness. To accomplish this, capitalism has had to poison the majority from within; by its very criteria of good and bad the majority has become an accomplice.

True revolution is impossible if we do not understand that the capitalism that we must defeat has already captured the vital core within each of us. To deny this is to prevent true revolution and to assure—as in Di Lampedusa's *The Leopard*—that everything changes in such a way that everything remains the same.

The invaluable merit of existentialism—as developed by Kierkegaard, Heidegger, and Sartre—is to have focused philosophically on this terrible but inescapable fact: In one way or another, we are all guilty. (We must not confuse this human responsibility with Catholic and Protestant teaching on original sin, which is very different from biblical teaching on the subject.) Concern, not mathematical intellect, is truly the instrument for knowing reality. The revolution must oppose an entire tranquillizing, alienating tradition, which used philosophy to put us to sleep. The problem is more difficult than Marx's eleventh thesis on Feuerbach indicates, for

Marx himself philosophized; *he had to do so* to change the world. If a revolution breaks only with the history of the last century, it is of but little value. We must destroy an oppression that has lasted thousands of years.

Hoederer's words to Jessica in Sartre's *Dirty Hands* might at first seem disheartening: "I suppose that you're half victim and half accomplice, like everybody else." Such a notion may not help to arouse the multitudes. But disheartening or not, inflammatory or not, existentialism rightly acknowledges this overwhelming truth. Unless we realize the pervasiveness of the evil we want to combat, there is no hope that the coming revolution, which indeed has already begun, will be a true revolution. If we imagine ourselves to be immune to this evil, the one thing we can be sure of is that when we accomplish the revolution we will be re-establishing stronger than ever the bourgeois oppression we carry inside ourselves. This thought may indeed be disheartening at first. But a clear consciousness of the fact that we too have been implicated in inhumanity is indispensable if we really want the world to change. If we do not risk this consciousness, then deep down we have no hope. And so we struggle for the sake of struggling, to stick with our group, so that no one will say we gave up.

The idea of guilt in general and of one's own guilt in particular is missing from the accepted ideologies of contemporary Marxist parties. It is likewise absent from the thought of other, quite commendable, organizations that claim to have adopted Marx's thought as an instrument of revolutionary analysis. Let us briefly consider this point.

Marx's criticism of Feuerbach's materialism should cause all sincere followers of Marx to re-examine their entire ideology: premises, first principles, deductive process, conclusions. For many Marxists quite evidently are professing the pre-Marxist materialism of Feuerbach, whose most important political and philosophical thesis was that material conditions determine human behavior and inescapably mold our attitudes. In his third thesis on Feuerbach, Marx takes a different direction, stating that the educator itself (namely, the material conditions) has to be educated and re-educated by the revolutionary. If this thesis (which is inseparable from the other ten) contradicts what present-day Marxists understand by materialism, then they should clearly acknowledge the contradiction and choose between Marx and materialism.

EXCHANGE-VALUE

But the normative and conclusive criterion of Marx's thought is found in his masterwork, *Capital*. Here he says that the basic determinant of all past and present economies is exchange-value. Anyone claiming to understand relationships of production without reference to the theory of value is not a good Marxist. Indeed, in the introduction to *Capital* Marx emphasizes that the purpose of the entire work is to discover in what value consists, for humankind has been fruitlessly trying to clarify this for two thousand years.

Refuting Adam Smith, Marx says that exchange-value is a "mode of existence" of a commodity "which has nothing to do with its corporeal reality."[5] It is "an imaginary . . . mode of existence of the commodity."[6]

In sum, according to *Capital* the decisive factor in history is the economic factor, and the most decisive element within this economic factor is exchange-value. But exchange-value is not identical with the material reality of the commodities. Rather it is part of the community's way of thinking; it is a concept, produced by the human spirit in its social and collective dimensions.

We are not dealing with a marginal, subordinate point in Marx. It is the central theme of his work, and the depth and extent of its implications have escaped Marxists and anti-Marxists alike. Let us consider this point carefully.

The *use-value* of an article is indeed determined by its material properties, that is to say, its flavor, color, form, resistance, weight, consistency, etc. However its *exchange-value* is determined by people's willingness to exchange other articles for it. This is so much the case that exchange-value is expressed in terms of other articles, for example, a ton of wheat is worth as much as five pairs of shoes, or as much as a rug, or as much as a transistor radio. Exchange-value consists in these multiple equivalencies of objects to each other.

The expression of value in monetary terms is only an abbreviated way of showing these equivalencies. When we say that a hundred bushels of wheat are worth four hundred dollars, our statement has meaning only because we implicitly refer to a specific quantity of other goods that we could buy with that sum of money. Money is only an intermediate mechanism in the exchange of commodities. The exchange-value of any article is the amount of other things we can barter for it. Therefore its exchange-value is not inherent in the material properties of the article, but is extrinsic to them.

This point is further proved by the fact that an article's exchange-value can vary without any variation in its material properties. A ton of wheat may be worth five pairs of shoes at one time and eight pairs of shoes at another, though neither the quality of the wheat nor the quality of the shoes has changed in the slightest degree. Clearly, then, exchange-value is not inherent in the wheat or the shoes.

Exchange-value is a set of relationships, varying with time and place and according to subjective preferences, that people, by their imagination and conceptualization, establish among things that can be bartered. It is a table of multiple equivalencies that the human mind projects upon things as a means of ordering them. For this reason Marx holds that the exchange-value of a commodity is utterly unrelated to its corporeal reality: *Nur eine eingebildete, das heisst bloss soziale Existenz-weise der Ware, die mit ihrer körperlichen Realität nichts zu schaffen hat.* In sum, exchange-value is a construct of the human spirit and this exchange-value is the dominant element in all economic systems, which in turn, Marx says, are the determining factor of history.

Why did humankind invent a table of equivalencies called exchange-value and project it upon reality? The answer seems quite simple: in order to exchange commodities. The scarcity of certain goods among a specific human group would be the reason why that group would want to enter into commercial dealings with other groups. And scarcity has characteristics of a purely material nature that would sufficiently explain the existence of exchange-value.

But the answer is not so simple, for people invented the table of equivalencies in order not only to exchange commodities, but also to exchange them to their own advantage. Marx says, "What, first of all, practically concerns producers when they make an exchange, is the question, how much of some other product they get for their own."[7] Therein lies the poison.

Let us enlarge the dimensions of the question. One of the commodities that people exchange is labor-power, and so we say, for example, that the day's wages of a farm worker are worth three pounds of wheat, or three yards of cloth, or fifty bricks. The value of labor-power is included with the other values in the table of equivalencies, and it too is variable.

Following Petty, Cantillon, Smith, and Ricardo, Marx holds that the basis for the equivalencies that we have established among diverse commodities is the amount of labor it normally requires in a given period of history for the production of each commodity. The price of an orange rises when—perhaps because of changing climate or methods of cultivation—it takes more hours of labor than formerly to produce a sack of oranges. The value of cloth goes down when—perhaps because of technological advances—it takes fewer hours of normal labor to produce a yard of cloth. Thus at the basis of all the equivalencies we always find labor. This means that when we trade *to our advantage* we are always valuing the labor of others as less than our own labor.

Marx and his four above-mentioned predecessors very correctly discerned that a relationship exists between exchange-value and labor. The other four, however, remained trapped in the fetishistic belief that exchange-value is a material reality, and so they were unable to ask the necessary question: What is the nature of this relationship? Only someone who, like Marx, realized that exchange-value is simply a product of the mind, a very functional entity of reason, a societal tenet, an invention of culture, could ask the decisive question: What was it invented for? What is the reason for this relationship between value and labor? To us it is clear that the difficult task was to formulate the question, for the answer is obvious: The reason for the relationship is to make others work, *because* it is impossible to extract surplus-value from someone who does not work.

Marx himself did not fully understand that he had found the key to history when he discovered that exchange-value is a mental construct and not an inherent property of commodities. But Sartre expresses it very well: "Alienation transfers, then, the principal characteristic of oppression—which *must* be merciless or it disappears—to the process itself, and thus alienation expresses its human origin. . . . This is what deceived Engels in his hurried responses to Dühring. . . ."[8] "But it is not things that are merciless, it is people. . . ."[9] "Neither the indelible marks of oppressive praxis nor the masters' premeditated consent to their own violence can ever be dissolved into the practico-inert necessity of alienation."[10]

THE NECESSARY MINIMUM

It is not scarcity and matter that are decisive in history, but rather greed and oppression. That Marx was aware of this when he wrote Book One of *Capital* is clear from his discussion of "necessary labor." Out of what they produce by their day's labor the workers receive in return what they need to reproduce their labor-power. The remainder of what they produce is surplus-value, and the entrepreneur keeps it. But how does one determine what amount of goods is "necessary" for the sustenance and reproduction of a worker? Here materialism would have to respond: This is a physical, biological datum. Marx, on the contrary, answers:

The number and extent of his so-called necessary wants, as also the modes of satisfying them, are themselves the product of historical development, and depend therefore to a great extent on the degree of civilisation of a country, more particularly on the conditions under which, and consequently on the habits and degree of comfort in which, the class of free labourers has been formed. In contradistinction therefore to the case of other commodities, there enters into the determination of the value of labour-power a historical and moral element.[11]

The limit to exploitation is not the level of consumption below which the proletariat will die of hunger. The necessary minimum is not a physiological datum; rather it is derived from the prevailing culture, morality, civilization. History offers abundant examples of the fact that "necessary" does *not* mean physiologically necessary: The proletariat has frequently received either more or less than what is necessary to survive.

But then how is the necessary minimum determined? In effect, says Marx in the above citation, the necessary minimum is the point below which the proletarians rebel because less remuneration is absolutely intolerable to them. For each period of history and for each country the limit to exploitation is determined by convictions and customs derived from the cultural and religious tradition and by social, juridical, and political pressures. The upper limit of remuneration, of what is "necessary," must always be fixed below the total value of the worker's labor-power, or there will be no remainder, no "surplus-value," no margin of profit for the exploiting classes. The definition of "necessary," then, is a datum of merciless oppression on the one hand and of resignation and impotence on the other.

Scrutinizing the realities of history and society with a thoroughly materialistic mentality, Marx discovered two concepts that could not be reduced to matter: (1) Exchange-value, which is an invention of human intelligence and constitutes the determining factor in all economy; and (2) the fact that the "necessary necessities" are determined by morality, custom, and culture, and that without this determination there can be no extraction of surplus-value.

THE DESIRE FOR PERSONAL GAIN

There is a third immaterial force operating in history, whose discovery by Marx and Lenin is perhaps even more important: the desire for personal gain as an *eradicable* motivation for human behavior and particularly for work. It is well known that in general terms Marx wanted to bring about a society based on the policy "from each according to his ability, to each according to his needs." This means that the communist movement wants to break the link between the diversity of remunerations and the diversity of contributions through labor. If this connection can be broken, labor will become truly human, for it will be motivated by impulses other than the desire for income.

In his *Critique of the Gotha Program*,[12] Marx, as summarized by Lenin, refers to "the *course of development* of communist society, which is *compelled* to abolish at first *only* the 'injustice' of the means of production seized by individuals, but which is *unable* at once to eliminate the other injustice, which consists in the distribution of consumer goods 'according to the amount of labour performed' (and not according to needs)."[13]

Indeed, in the first phase of communism, Marx says,

Equal right here is still in principle—*bourgeois right*.... In spite of this advance this *equal right* is still constantly stigmatized by a bourgeois limitation. The right of the producers is *proportional* to the labor they supply; the equality consists in the fact that measurement is made with an *equal standard,* labor.[14]

It is clear that for Marx and Lenin it is still an injustice, a mutilated right, when incomes vary according to the diverse kinds and levels of labor. Only in the higher phase of communism, when "the narrow horizon of bourgeois right [is] crossed in its entirety," can true justice be achieved: "From each according to his ability, to each according to his needs!"[15]

In other words, Marx and Lenin found that capitalism, as well as previous economic arrangements, appeals to people's desire for personal gain to make them work more and better, or simply to make them work at all. But Marx and Lenin are convinced that this motivation can be eliminated from history. They believe it a wretched concept of human nature that holds that the desire for personal gain is inherent to the human race, that people cannot live together, collaborate, or work without the selfish, utilitarian stimulus of self-interest, and that because self-interest is necessary for human society it is therefore ineradicable.

At this point it is clear that the materialists—their palaver notwithstanding—must find recruits elsewhere, for Marx and Lenin are no longer members of the group. As Sartre says, "We must make a de facto choice: Either 'each looks out for his own interest,' which means that division among people is *natural,* or it is the division among people . . . which causes self-interest (particular or general, of the individual or the class) to appear as a real characteristic of relationship among people."[16] If we affirm that there is a "law of self-interest" that governs people as the law of gravity governs stones, then we are denying the possibility of revolution, for communist society cannot be achieved if the desire for personal gain is not eliminated.

Moreover, the thesis that self-interest is an essential part of human nature is contradicted by the existence of truly selfless people. A single exception is enough to invalidate a universal affirmative proposition. As Sartre says, "Self-interest as a fact of nature is a perfectly unintelligible datum. Moreover, any induction that posits it as an a priori reality of human nature is perfectly unjustifiable. Indeed, if conflicts of self-interest are the engine of history, then the overall pattern of history becomes completely absurd. In particular, Marxism becomes nothing more than an irrational hypothesis."[17] It is evident that this criticism applies to present-day Marxism, and not to Marx and Lenin, at least insofar as these thinkers remain true to their discoveries that we have described.

But we must add that Christian theologians partake of the same conservatism and fatalism as afflicts the materialists when they identify self-interest with an original sin that—notwithstanding all the official statements to the contrary—has come to be seen as an integral part of human nature. According to Genesis and to Paul's Epistle to the Romans, original sin is a contingent event and therefore eradicable from human society. But dogmatic theology—in order to justify a socioeconomic system that motivates people through a desire for personal gain—has gone so far as to hold that the *peccatum originale originatum*, manifesting itself as selfishness, is essentially inseparable from the human being. This thesis is especially inconsistent for Catholic theologians, for the Council of Trent affirmed that original sin can be abolished and therefore its effects can be abolished as well.

THE ROLE OF EXISTENTIALISM

If we insist that the tendency to oppress and injure others is natural—that is, that we are not free to do otherwise—then we cannot become aware of how thoroughly capitalism has infected us all, and it will be impossible for the coming revolution to uproot oppression from human society. If we do not confront reality, we cannot hope to change in any profound way. Existentialism's invaluable contribution is to show us reality and thereby to make possible a true revolution.

Mexico harbors fewer illusions than many other nations about the miraculous power frequently attributed to revolution. (I hope the non-Mexican reader will indulge my occasional allusions to Mexico; my country brought about the first social revolution of this century, and the results are there for all to see.) Even if all the means of production had been taken over by the state, we do not believe that we would thereby cease to be the bundle of complexes, involutions, and aggressions that we are. We hold the world record for violence and we wretchedly submit to "what people say," and these characteristics are the result of something more than private ownership of productive goods.

Capitalist oppression could not have endured if all of us, or nearly all of us, had not been its accomplices. Sartre puts it very well: "We must agree with the statement by J. Romains, 'In war there are no innocent victims.' "[18] Benítez, Garibay, and Fuentes are deceiving themselves when they deduce from the present situation that we are obliged to support Echeverría.[19] But the reluctance of certain intellectuals to join the new revolution is due, although they are perhaps unaware of it, to their need of assuring that this time human beings themselves are transformed, and this transformation depends on "ideas" to a degree much greater than leftist movements and guerrilla groups are willing to concede. By "ideas" I mean an awareness of reality, and reality is worldwide. The coming revolution will be worldwide or it will not be a true revolution.

The mission of existentialism at this moment, then, is to make the summons of conscience inescapable. Only in this way can the revolution be global in its scope and total in its effect.

Let us note very carefully that existentialism's role is not to inculcate that disease we call " a sense of guilt." But the voice of conscience does indeed exist, and any philosophy which tries to make us believe that it does not, reducing it to our subjectivities, betrays the revolution, for it prevents the revolution from getting at the heart of the matter. As Heidegger ironically says, "The 'common-sense' interpretation of conscience, which 'sticks rigorously to the facts,' uses the fact that conscience does not speak aloud as a pretext for dismissing it as undemonstrable or nonexistent."[20]

Very well, conscience is not demonstrable like the phenomena of light waves or sound waves or electricity. But neither science nor positivist philosophy has the right to impose rules of evidence derived from the physical sciences on the phenomenon of conscience, rules that a priori exclude the inescapable fact of conscience. The merit of existentialism is that it prevents capitalistic positivism from continuing to deceive us through the stratagem of establishing rules that (like all the game rules of the bourgeois system) predetermine the conclusions before the investigation has begun.

This positivist stratagem has very little use for seeing things as they really are. Existentialism has discovered a new field of being, a field in which being, in order to be able to be, demands of us a decision. This being, this new way of being, can absolutely not be observed by someone who maintains the neutral, "objective" attitude of an observer. This being depends on our resolution in order to exist.

It is, then, ironic that the sciences have overlooked this field of being, since it is the most characteristic and distinctive object of human knowledge, and since humans exist in the fullest sense only when they make a decision concerning this being. Human knowing and being differs from animals' knowing and being precisely in this: Humans exist in the fullest sense only when they are touched by the voice of conscience and make decisions according to it.

It is not only the positive sciences that have helped conceal the existence of conscience; so, paradoxically, has moral science. It has done this in two ways. First, it has confused the moral imperative with a judgment of advantageousness or long-range utility, which have nothing to do with morality. Second—and Heidegger and Sartre argue against this specifically—it has diverted our attention from the basic guilt to casuistic inventories of faults. We will briefly clarify each of these two points.

THE MORAL IMPERATIVE

Conscience is unmistakable. If I jump into the river to save a drowning child, truly risking my life, no one can convince me that I am doing it to win a heavenly reward, or to achieve inner tranquillity, or for fear of hell, or to avoid future remorse. I jump because the child is drowning and *must be saved.* If I refrain from robbing a defenseless widow of what little money she has, I have a concrete experience of obeying an imperative that prevents me from robbing. My own future happiness in no way is my motive. The only real motive is *this must not be done.* There is no question of reward or punishment, nor of some ultimate personal benefit.

Kant made clear the distinction between the imperative of conscience and the other imperatives. The imperative of conscience is unconditional. It does not say, "If you want to be happy, do this." It says simply, "Do this." Other imperatives are explicitly or implicitly conditional: "If you want to be esteemed an honorable person, don't do this"; "If you want to avoid the pains of hell, do that."

But western moralists have been the best propagandists for the long-range utilitarianism characteristic of Greek eudemonism. They believe that moral purity is maintained by postponing the reward and punishment till the next life. But they are wrong, for an imperative is moral because it is grounded in itself, not in advantages or disadvantages resulting from the conduct it prescribes. Do you ask why the existence of a reward troubles me? It does not at all. The fact is, however, that when we act morally, *it is not for that reason* that we do so. There may in fact be a reward, but it is not for the reward that I save the child. When I acted to save the child, the idea of reward did not even occur to me. In the West, preachers have distracted our attention from true conscience, whose only motivation is its own imperative. Otherwise, it is not specifically moral.

FUNDAMENTAL GUILT

Western moral teaching has presented perhaps an even greater impediment to conscience by its preoccupation with casuistry. We broach the subject directly with a point often made by Heidegger: "Only he who already understands can listen."[21] Only he who *is* already moral pays any attention to the minute, casuistic precepts of ethics. Expressed negatively, the point is even stronger: The authors of treatises and the confessors—through their cheapening of ethics with their handy lists and recipes—have contributed to the tranquillization of the human conscience by silencing our profound guilt. As Heidegger says, "The existing person, whose being is concern, accuses himself of individual, specific faults, but the truth is that he *is* guilty at the very root of his being; without this primordial culpability as an ontological condition, the person could not be guilty of individual, specific faults."[22] A human being could not commit concrete sins, which casuistry then compiles into lists, if in some way that person were not, at a deeper level, guilty. Any revolutionary philosophy that disregards this fundamental fact unwittingly collaborates with capitalism's mass communications media, whose purpose is to "distract" us. The first meaning of "to divert" is "to turn aside," "to deflect," "to deviate." This implies deceiving us, diminishing us, denying us the possibility of being fully human, to turn us aside from the real problem, from the true path of revolution.

The guilt on which existentialism has focused is not formless or ill-defined, nor does it consist, as de Waelhens says, in our coming from nothingness and returning to nothingness.[23] Heidegger defines this being-guilty as *Grundsein für einen Mangel im Dasein eines Andern*, "Being-the-basis for a lack of something in the being of another."[24] He goes on to say that guilt "does not happen merely through law-breaking as such, but rather through being responsible for another's being endangered, or led astray, or even ruined. In this way one can become culpable toward others without breaking the 'public law.' "[25]

In our relationships with other human beings, existentialism insists, we are fundamentally guilty, even before committing concrete abuses that the authors of the treaties on morality can register and catalog. The debasement of the existentialist concept of guilt resembles the debasement of the biblical concept of original sin: Saint Paul expressly calls original sin "injustice" (Rom. 5:19, 21; 1:18, 28–32) and describes it in detail solely by giving specific examples of its occurrence in human relationships (Rom. 1:28–32; 3:10–18). But later commentators falsify Paul's notion by misrepresenting "injustice" as vague irreligiosity or ill-defined and nonspecific immorality.

The important point is this: There is always among people an underlying deviation, a mistrust, a readiness to trample upon the other. This can be strengthened and increased till it becomes in Sartre's words, "the feeling that we have the fundamental right to kill." But whether it reaches this point or not, it is this basic deviation that causes the hell we call human civilization.

But, we repeat, this deviation can be eradicated. If it could not—if we were not free to be otherwise—we would not experience it as guilt. The new field of being, discovered by existentialist philosophy, demands our decision in order to be able to be. The moment that evil appears as a "natural," irremediable datum, we have fallen back into the old field of being, the field of "objective" philosophy, the field of neutral, "observable" objects, the field of the "in itself." "The coefficient of adversity in things cannot be an argument against our freedom, for it is *by us*—*i.e.*, by our preliminary positing of a goal—that this coefficient of adversity arises."[26] Let there be no objection based on immutable essences: "It is freedom which is the foundation of all essences since man reveals intra-mundane essences by surpassing the world toward his own possibilities."[27] "*Freedom* is an objective quality of the Other as the unconditioned power of modifying situations. . . . In this sense the Other appears as the one who must be understood from the standpoint of a situation perpetually modified."[28]

The voice of conscience precedes its exercise in particular circumstances. Critics of the Kantian formalism of moral science, such as Max Scheler, would have done well to consider whether Kant was not in fact trying to see beyond inventories of faults to the concept of fundamental guilt. If he was, then existentialism is the legitimate extension of the *Critique of Practical Reason*.

Hegel wrote after Kant. It has often been noted that Hegel's *Phenomenology* reveals that his entire philosophy is a theodicy inspired by apologetics. But exactly the same is true of Marxism if it cleverly conceals the fact of guilt in past and present history. If Marxism does not make us aware of the evil that has taken root in us, if Marxism cannot make us aware of sin, then Marxism does not go beyond Hegelian dialectics. According to Hegel, all that has happened in history has been good because it has been necessary; all that is real is rational; everything has its justifiable reason for being, and we are, as Leibniz says, in the best of all possible worlds. The justification for capitalism and the civilization we have inherited is inherent in the Hegelian dialectic, which is a divinization of past and present. There can be no break; there is no basis for revolution. If theological prejudices prevent Marxism from confronting the unsettling fact of guilt, then it is ingenuously repeating Hegelian theology, which is a transposition of the "defense of God by the world that he made" undertaken by Leibniz.

Of course we are dealing with the sin of humankind. But the Marxists who in this matter are unable to hear *tua res agitur* are not serious thinkers. It is superficial to imagine that the spirit of oppression and exploitation has left us unscathed and has infected only that small sector of the population known as entrepreneurs. Both the question of guilt and the problem of death make the existentialist standpoint unavoidable for Marxists who are conscious of realities beyond their own system. Capitalism would not triumph or even endure if selfishness, the desire for personal gain, and the petty bourgeois spirit were not effectively inculcated even in its victims. To conceal this from the proletariat is to hinder the abolition of capitalism.

TRUE REVOLUTION

The true revolutionary abjures reformist palliatives, because these divert the efforts of the people most capable of fomenting rebellion against the bourgeois system into rejuvenating and refurbishing it; such palliatives thus constitute the system's best defense. By the same token, the revolutionary must find any change in the socioeconomic system to be a priori inadequate, if that change does not involve a radical revolution in people's attitudes toward each other. If exchange-value (that "imaginary entity") and the desire for personal gain continue to exist, they will inevitably create other oppressive and exploitative economic systems. They have in fact already done so, for these two "mental" factors, which Marx discovered at the heart of capitalism, were responsible not only for capitalism but also for every other economic system that ever preceded it, as Marx himself demonstrates. The contemporary revolutionary must reject workers' housing developments as a mere social tranquillizer, because inadequate housing is merely an effect, and to correct effects while leaving intact the cause, namely, the capitalist system, is to perpetuate injustice. By the same token, the revolutionary henceforth must reject as superficial the abolition of capitalism, if the "mental" causes that engendered it remain operative.

To confront these causes is the mission of existentialism. But it is of utmost importance to note that by confronting guilt (*der Mut zum Schuldigsein*, as Heidegger says), existentialism *brings about* the revolution of philosophy, the revolution that Marx *postulated* in his eleventh thesis on Feuerbach: "The philosophers have only *interpreted* the world, in various ways; the point, however, is to *change* it." Contemporary Marxism has not perceived that existentialism is bringing about this revolution of philosophy, and that this revolution cannot occur without existentialism. For their part the existentialists have not perceived that they are implementing Marx's eleventh thesis on Feuerbach.

It was characteristic of all previous philosophy to deal with precisely that field of being which does not depend on our free will in order to be what it is. It is a being that does not disturb us, that does not upset us, precisely because it does not require us to make any decision. It is the "objective" part of reality. But the reason it does not require us to make a decision is that any change in the "objective" part of reality is contingent on change in the other parts or fields of being that do indeed require our decision. Since the objective part of reality does not summon us, it *therefore* constitutes a cosmos in which "all is well": What is real is rational and what is rational is real; *tout est pour le mieux dans le meilleur des mondes.*

This philosophic tradition still dominated Hegel, but Nietzsche, Marx, and Kierkegaard rebelled against and broke with it. Of the three, Kierkegaard was the most conscious of the novelty of this method, which was to detect which fields of being can exist only if I make a decision. For Kierkegaard all other "parts" of being are irrelevant.

The individualism of existentialist philosophy should not prevent us from recognizing that it contains the beginning of the new method by which philosophy can transform reality. So too Hegel's apologetic tendencies should not prevent us from seeing that he laid the foundation for this new method by taking human history as a proper subject of philosophy. Just as Kierkegaard corrected Hegel by denying that historical reality is necessary and deducible, in the same way we must free Kierkegaard's revolutionary philosophy from its individualistic limitations and rid Marxism of its residue of Hegelian necessitarianism, which justifies all crimes past and present as necessary.

I think that the moment has arrived for philosophy —without ceasing to be philosophy—to play a decisive role in changing the world. Heidegger says that "when the person is resolute, he can become the 'conscience' of others."[29] This is undoubtedly true, but there is more involved. "It is freedom which is the foundation of all essences."[30] It is a priori reasoning to postulate that the traditional field of being—which requires no decision of ours in order to be what it is—has no connection with the new field of being—which depends on our free choice in order to exist. Such a compartmentalization of reality would have to be demonstrated, not simply presupposed. Perhaps certain "parts" of reality do not summon us to make a decision because changes in them are contingent on the parts of reality that do require our decision in order to be what they are. We will take up this question in chapter 9.

Platonic philosophers have always tried to impose the necessity of essences on history. The Hegelian necessity of history is identical to Aristotelian deduction, and Aristotelian deduction is a disguised affirmation of Socratico-Platonic recollection: There is nothing new; what seems new was always known by us, even though we were not aware of it; everything is deducible from the self; neither time, history, nor any event is *able* to constitute a break within the continuity of my recollection. Thus existentialism is a true revolution in philosophy. But by denying that historical reality is necessary existentialism makes humankind confront guilt.

In his accurate commentary on Kierkegaard, Jean Wahl says:

It is the presupposition of the entire Christian concept of time that the existing person is a sinner. In contrast with the Socratic disciple, whose teacher has only to awaken the memory, the Christian disciple feels an absolute rupture between what he was before the word of the teacher and what he will be after it. Up to that point he was in sin, and not, like the Socratic disciple, in ignorance.[31]

As we shall see, this coincidence between Christianity and atheistic philosophies like those of Heidegger and Sartre is not fortuitous and anecdotal, as Heidegger and Sartre would have us believe.

There is no place here for disappearing tricks or subjective approaches. The being discovered by existentialism is unavoidable: If we abdicate our unconditional resolution to confront our guilt, we automatically abandon our investigation of this field of being. Unbounded decision is the key to our inquiry. The question Heidegger asks is valid: "Is there any other way at all by which an entity can put itself into words with regard to its being?"[32] From Kant we know that the basis for the moral imperative cannot be proven, nor is this imperative grounded in anything or supported by anything. It is grounded in itself. We heed it or we do not; that is all.

NOTES

1. Jean-Paul Sartre, *Critique de la raison dialectique* (Paris: Gallimard, 1960), 1:713.

2. V.I. Lenin, "The Tasks of the Youth Leagues," speech delivered October 2, 1920, in *Selected Works* (New York: International Publishers, 1967), 3:470; emphasis added.

3. Ibid., "A Great Beginning," published as a pamphlet in July 1919, in *Selected Works*, 3:205.

4. Ibid., " 'Left-Wing' Communism—An Infantile Disorder," in *Selected Works*, 3:357.

5. Karl Marx, "Theories of Productive and Unproductive Labour," in *Theories of Surplus-Value (Volume IV of Capital)*, trans. Emile Burns (Moscow: Progress Publishers, 1963), part 1, chapter 4, section 3, 1:171.

6. Ibid.

7. Karl Marx, "The Fetishism of Commodities and the Secret Thereof," in *Capital*, trans. Samuel Morre and Edward Aveling (New York: International Publishers, 1967), book 1, chapter 1, section 4, 1:74.

8. Sartre, *Critique*, 1:699.

9. Ibid.

10. Ibid., p. 700.

11. Marx, "The Buying and Selling of Labour-Power," in *Capital*, book 1, chapter 6, 1:171.

12. Published in 1875, after *Capital* and therefore representing more mature thinking in Marx.

13. Lenin, "The State and Revolution," chapter 5, section 3, in *Selected Works*, 2:338.

14. Marx, "Critique of the Gotha Program," section 1, in *On Revolution*, The Karl Marx Library, vol. 1, ed. Saul K. Padover (New York: McGraw-Hill, 1971), p. 495.

15. Ibid., p. 496.

16. Sartre, *Critique*, 1:277.

17. Ibid.

18. J.-P. Sartre, *L'être et le néant* (Paris: Gallimard, 1943), p. 640 [Eng. trans.: *Being and Nothingness*, trans. Hazel E. Barnes (New York: Citadel, 1968), p. 530].

19. Benítez, Garibay, and Fuentes are Mexican intellectuals who supported President Echeverría and convinced many other intellectuals to do the same.

20. Martin Heidegger, *Sein und Zeit* (Tübingen: Niemeyer, 1960), p. 296 [cf. Eng. trans.: *Being and Time*, trans. John Macquarrie and Edward Robinson (New York: Harper & Row, 1962), p. 343].

21. Ibid., p. 164 [Eng. trans.: p. 208].

22. Ibid., p. 286 [cf. Eng. trans.: p. 332].

23. Alphonse de Waelhens, *La philosophie de Martin Heidegger*, 7th ed. (Louvain: Nauwelaerts, 1971), p. 165.

24. Heidegger, *Sein und Zeit*, p. 82 [cf. Eng. trans.: *Being and Time*, p. 328.].

25. Ibid., p. 282 [cf. Eng. trans.: pp. 327–28].

26. Sartre, *L'être et le néant*, p. 562 [cf. Eng. trans.: *Being and Nothingness*, p. 458].

27. Ibid., p. 514 [Eng. trans.: p. 414].

28. Ibid., p. 417 [Eng. trans.: p. 326].

29. Heidegger, *Sein und Zeit*, p. 298 *(Das entschlossene Dasein kann zum "Gewissen" der Anderen werden)* [cf. Eng. trans.: *Being and Time*, p. 344].

30. Sartre, *L'être et le néant*, p. 514 [Eng. trans.: *Being and Nothingness*, p. 414].

31. Jean Wahl, *Études kierkegaardiennes* (Paris: Vrin, 1949), p. 357.

32. Heidegger, *Sein und Zeit*, p. 315 [cf. Eng. trans.: *Being and Time*, pp. 362–63].

Chapter 2

The Vindication of Atheism

In the first chapter we indicated the difference between concrete faults and a state of fundamental guilt (or original shame, as Sartre calls it). And we said that the latter is a condition of possibility for the former—that is, the underlying condition that makes the concrete fault possible. If we did not habitually have a basic attitude of distrust, remoteness, and enmity, we would not commit concrete acts of envy, contempt, exploitation, subjugation, murder.

The reader should be aware of the transcendental method employed in making this distinction. We understand perceptible realities more thoroughly to the degree that we discover the condition or conditions of possibility of these realities. In the transcendental method, we attempt to detect those underlying human realities without which there could not exist the acts and facts whose existence we can directly verify.

In this chapter we want to describe a condition of possibility of the fundamental consciousness of guilt, which we considered in the first chapter.

THE ETHICAL GOD

In any history of philosophy two of Kant's works are recognized as being of paramount importance in the

27

development of human thought: *Critique of Pure Reason* and *Critique of Practical Reason*. Modern philosophy, initiated a century and a half earlier by Descartes, reaches an apex in these works; without their stimulus the philosophizing of the nineteenth and twentieth centuries would be unthinkably different.

The chief contribution to modern thought of these two books occurs in their combination to demonstrate a single thesis: namely, the true God has no connection with ontology (the true God is not *a* being nor *the* being nor the *supreme* being); *rather* God is identified with the ethical imperative. The crux of the Kantian message is contained in this adversative "rather," but historians of philosophy have not sufficiently emphasized this, nor have post-Kantian philosophers themselves sufficiently grasped the contrast between the ontic order and the moral order. The Greek and Scholastic mania for ascribing a state of being to everything real has infected even those western thinkers who claim that they are anti-Hellenic—not to mention the common *homo occidentalis*, who incurably philosophizes in indirect proportion to his recognizing himself as a philosopher.

Out of this prevailing confusion between the ontic and ethical orders, an extremely interesting contemporary phenomenon has emerged: The philosophers of atheism are rejecting an ontic god in the name of ethics, and the atheism of our day—although its proponents do not recognize the fact—has come paradoxically to consist in rejecting, in the name of the true God, a god who is not God. It is also apparent that as long as Christians and Jews do not understand the reason for atheism they cannot understand the God revealed in the Bible.

Heidegger asserts that we must avoid a "theological exegesis of conscience."[1] If he is here referring to God as understood in the classic theological treatises, he is absolutely right. But the God of the treatises in no way resembles the God of the Bible, whose being is ethical and without whom no conscience is possible. If the Absolute Imperative in the otherness of the neighbor did not go unheard, then the fundamental consciousness of guilt would not be possible. Unfortunately, Heidegger knows little of the history of philosophy and theology, as he demonstrates by asserting that the notions of eternal truths and an absolute subject are residues of theology in philosophy.[2] But precisely the contrary is true: Theology took the notion of eternal truths from Platonic philosophy, and in so doing ceased to be Christian; theology took the idea of the absolute subject from Descartes, Spinoza, and Hegel, not vice versa. Thus the judgment of Heidegger (and Sartre) on theology's role is of very little value.

The concept of an ethical God is in no way an attempt to "win back" the atheists to Christianity, for the ethical God cannot be reclaimed by and is not reconcilable with the history of Christianity. Moreover, an ethical God implies the destruction of all known historical churches, and it is these churches that are concerned about "winning back." The concept of an ethical God vindicates historical atheism.

Morality's keystone and inescapable conclusion is that no end, no matter how sublime or divine or eternal, justifies causing—or indifferently allowing—an innocent person to suffer. Infinite retribution in another life does not compensate for even a small injustice in this life. And if the god of theology proclaims that it does compensate, then he is an immoral god and in conscience we are obliged to rebel against him.

Here we are not dealing solely with the scandal of evil in the world, nor is the incisive verdict of conscience reducible to the classic problem of evil. We are dealing with injustice, and there is no compensation for injustice. Any god who has not come to undo the hell that we have made of this life is a cruel god, even if there is another life. Even if the god of the theologians is not responsible for the barbarous world in which we live, the mere fact that he intervenes in our history for ends other than the abolition of human injustice qualifies him as amoral and merciless. The anti-idolatrous confutations of Jeremiah, Deutero-Isaiah, and the Psalms all cry out against such divine indifference, basing their fiery protests entirely on the revelation of Exodus. The omnipotence of an amoral god could *compel me* to submission, but not *oblige* me to obedience. Not only should we refuse to worship and obey such a god, we should also be morally obliged to struggle against him, even if faced with certain defeat and condemnation to eternal torment. It is moral right, not physical power, that we are obliged to obey.

The truly moral person is one who believes that his moral obligation is the only God. This is what the Bible teaches.

THE GOD OF THE BIBLE

Gerhard von Rad's investigations of the earliest biblical writings clearly show that the primitive revelation of Yahweh had nothing to say about creation or the origin of the world.[3] The God who originally revealed himself to Israel was the God of the Exodus, and his self-revelation was simply an obligatory intervention on behalf of the oppressed against their oppressors. The legislation contained in the most ancient biblical tradition was conceived as a necessary part of this primordial revelatory intervention; the sole intention of these original laws was to prevent the re-establishment among the Israelites of the slavery and injustices that they had previously endured at the hands of the Egyptians.[4] Laws governing cultus, sexual behavior, food purification, and other purification rites were introduced at a later date.

The creation of the world was not mentioned in Yahweh's original self-description. Moreover, the authors of the Bible took for granted that the normal course of the world's history had no connection with

Yahweh and that he could not be held responsible for
things that occurred before his intervention. This is
clearly proven by the fact that Yahweh breaks into
human history to correct it radically. And it is the "outcry" of the oppressed (cf. Exod. 3:7) that makes this God
intervene to revolutionize history.

We do not mean to deny the *later* biblical teaching that
Yahweh is the creator of humankind and the world. But
scientific exegesis does not—as dogmatic theology
does—indifferently juxtapose teachings in such a way
that one cannot tell which of them is the central truth in
function of which the other truths must be understood.
For example, the "omnipotence" of the God of the Bible
must be understood in a way completely different from
the triumphalistic meaning it has in the West. A God
whose sole definitional intervention consists in struggling against injustice and innocent suffering can only
be the moral imperative in itself; and human free will is
more powerful, so to speak, than the absolute moral
imperative. Indeed the biblical description of the creation of man and woman (Gen. 1:26–4:16) is dedicated
principally to emphasizing this autonomous human
power.

For the authors of the Bible the createdness of the
world and history are of secondary or tertiary importance, and we must reassert this very clearly today. The
creation story is told first, not because of its importance,
but because creation came first chronologically. Our
understanding of Yahweh as Creator must not be allowed to blur or weaken our understanding of the essential nature of the protest and imperative of Yahweh (the
God of the Exodus). Involved here, I believe, is an
elementary principle of hermeneutics, a principle in
force since the science of documentation first dealt with
the biblical authors as real authors who compose a work,
and not as mere compilers or archivists. It can help us
grasp the relative importance of Yahweh as Creator if
we keep in mind that the teaching that the world origi-

nated in the divinity was conceived outside of Israel and the Bible (cf. the Epic of Enuma Elish). There was a time when every reasonable thinker in Asia Minor professed this teaching (just as any reasonable contemporary of ours believes that Hitler was a monster—pardon this comparison *a viliori*), and the biblical accounts that have come down to us were redacted during that time.

How the truth of creation can be harmonized with the revealed fact that Yahweh is essentially the realization of justice clearly constitutes a problem for the authors of the first three chapters of Gensis. But it constitutes a problem precisely because they neither abandon nor minimize the sole revelatory definition of Yahweh as the God of the Exodus.

It is worth noting that in the fourth and eighteenth chapters of Genesis itself the one who manifests himself is simply the God of the Exodus, nothing more.

HUMAN CAUSALITY

When the Yahwist and the Priestly document say that Yahweh created man free, they wish more to emphasize that man is free than that God created him. Note how the Yahwist, after man's disobedience, has Yahweh say: "The man has become like one of us, knowing good and evil" (Gen. 3:22). These words enable us to understand what the Priestly writer meant when he has God say, at the moment of creating man: "Let us make man in our image and likeness to rule the fish in the sea, the birds of heaven, the cattle, all wild animals on earth, and all reptiles that crawl upon the earth" (Gen. 1:26). Because man is made in the likeness of God he has complete freedom of action.

Because of their unsound tendency toward abstraction, theologians have found in the first chapters of Genesis only this: God created everything that is. The authors' idea was very different. In the Yahwistic narration (Gen. 2:4–4:26) the emphasis is on man's causality, not God's; it was already known that the world originated in the divinity. I do not deny that Yahweh is the one who cursed the ground (Gen. 3:17), but the author of the account, addressing himself to man, insists: "Accursed shall be the ground *on your account*" (Gen. 3:17; see also Gen. 8:21: "Never again will I curse the ground because of man").

The theme is human causality. And the implications of the theme are so far-reaching that not only is our Greek, western mentality disconcerted by them, but also the materialists themselves are today still unable to accept them: Human work, human action, causes the pains of pregnancy and childbirth; barren unproductive lands are explained by human causality; death is due to human action. The first two affirmations occur in Gen. 3:16–19. The third is implicit in the placing of the account of Cain and Abel (Gen. 4:1–11) after the account of "the man," for the punishment threatened in Gen. 2:17 ("on the day that you eat from it [the tree], you will certainly die") was still pending, and Gen. 3:3 and 3:4 indicate that the author had not forgotten it. The connection is deliberate, as indicated by Gen. 4:11, which is the first curse in history directed against man: "Now you are accursed, *more than* the ground." (The Hebrew expression should be translated either in this way or: "Now you are accursed, *rather than* the ground.") In few translations, ancient or modern, does this phrase make any sense, for the translators have overlooked its connection with Gen. 3:17. The idea the Yahwist wants to express is this: Death entered history in the form of fratricide; it was not connatural to man as God made him.

In general terms Paul understood very well the emphasis of the Yahwistic narrative: "It was *through one man* that sin entered the world, and through sin death" (Rom. 5:12); "since it was man who brought death into the world, a man also brought resurrection of the dead" (1 Cor. 15:21); "as the issue of one misdeed was condemnation for all men, so the issue of one just act is justice and life for all men" (Rom. 5:18).

The point we must truly understand in the Yahwistic and Pauline concept of origins is human causality. This is the powerful message that the biblical authors were trying to convey, and if we let ourselves be distracted from it by the truth that God created all that is, then we prevent the Bible's message from reaching us. If an author asserts that injustice is the cause of death in the world, readers who disregard this unprecedented message to concentrate on human createdness and finitude are being ridiculous. Even today, in the last third of the twentieth century, the world lacks ears to hear that if injustice can be abolished from human history, then death too can be abolished. We cannot contend against death if we do not even see that death can be contended against.

But let us return to the biblical concept that responsibility for the world and history is not Yahweh's; if it is not, then the etymological sense of "omnipotence" cannot be applied to the God of the Bible. Of course the theological treatises, when asserting God's "omnipotence," usually include escape clauses noting that omnipotence means that God can do "whatever is possible" (God is not able, for example, to do something self-contradictory). But then, lest there be a merely verbal question, the biblical narrative requires us to amplify tremendously what is included under the theologians' definition of "impossible."

When God intervenes his principal activity is directed to the conscience. And through people's consciences he achieves his true intervention: "Cain, Cain, where is your brother Abel?" (Gen. 4:9); "Your brother's blood that has been shed is crying out to me from the ground" (Gen. 4:10).

The God of the Exodus is the God of conscience. The liberation of the slaves from Egypt was principally a work of the imperative of liberty and justice implacably inculcated into the Israelites: "I have indeed turned my eyes towards you; I have marked all that has been done to you in Egypt, and I am resolved to bring you up out of your misery in Egypt, into the country of the Canaanites, . . . a land flowing with milk and honey" (Exod. 3:16–17). This is practically the only message Yahweh sent to the Israelites through Moses. The instrument of liberation was the word of Moses; therefore Yahweh said to him: "I will help your speech and tell you what to say" (Exod. 4:12). But what God tells him is over and again the same: "Say therefore to the Israelites, 'I am Yahweh, and therefore I will release you from your labors in Egypt. I will rescue you from slavery there' " (Exod. 6:6). Moses protests to Yahweh that the Israelites do not want to listen to him (Exod. 6:12; 4:10), and from Yahweh's answers we perceive the basic intention of God's intervention: the inexorable inculcation of the imperative of liberty and justice (see Exod. 3:7–10; 3:16; 4:10–17; 5:21–23; 6:5–9; 6:12; 14:11–12; 15:25–26).

The pharaoh too was enjoined over and again of his obligation to free the slaves (Exod. 5:1; 6:11, 13, 29; 7:1–2; 7:16; 7:26; 8:16; 9:1, 13; 10:3). The hammering insistence of the narrative of the plagues itself is a pedagogical device to show how obstinate the hardening of the heart against the moral imperative can be; its intent is made clear (Exod. 7–13) by the recurrent theme of the "hardening of pharaoh's heart."

But the supreme injunction regarding the imperative of justice consists in the very literary composition of Exodus, in which the whole process of the liberation of the slaves issues into legislation that assures that the oppression once suffered at the hand of foreigners would not be repeated by compatriots. This idea, generative of the whole Exodus account, provides the literary unity for Exodus 18, in which Moses is for the first time described as a legislator. This idea is most explicit in the following very ancient legal texts: Exod. 22:20–26; 23:9; Lev. 19:33–34; 25:35–38; 19:35–36; 25:39–42; 25:47–55; Deut. 15:12–15; 16:9–12; 24:17–18; 24:19–22.

The only truly revelatory intervention of the God of the Bible in human history is the moral imperative of justice, and this imperative remains the sole manifestation of Yahweh's definitive presence in history.

Thus, Deuteronomy 4 explains the reason for the legislation prohibiting images of Yahweh: God is present only in his words (Deut. 4:12), referring to the ten "words" that we call the ten commandments (Deut. 4:13). In Rom. 1:18–32 Paul considers this explanation, given originally to the Israelites, valid for the whole human race. He asserts that all people know the same God and that they hinder this knowledge by their injustice. People have no need for civil or religious legislation to teach them the moral imperative; this is proved by the fact that the pagans, "who do not possess the law... are their own law, displaying the effect of the law inscribed on their hearts. Their conscience is called as witness, and their own thoughts argue the case on either side, against them or even for them" (Rom. 2:14–15).

In order that the moral imperative of justice, in which God consists, might arise in history, only one thing is needed: the otherness of the neighbor who seeks justice.

THE OTHER AS ABSOLUTE

Sartre is quite justifiably indignant at the slogan of the Polish government: "Tuberculosis slows down production."[5] As Sartre says, people matter, not production. A Marxism that overlooks the absolute in the outcry of the neighbor in misery must "ground" the imperative in its effect on productivity, just as the developmentalist Mexican government, or any bourgeois government, must legitimate expenditures on behalf of the poor before the supreme tribunal of capitalist productivity.

In reality, all that is needed for the imperative to arise is a person who needs our solidarity and our help, the "other" who is not I and cannot—either in a Socratic or a Hegelian way—have been implicit in what I already was nor, therefore, in what I already knew. This otherness is irreconcilable with monism of any form, whether spiritualistic monism or materialistic monism, whether atheistic monism or "theistic" monism—whose objective god does not summon us from the "other" but rather hermetically seals the solipsism of the self. Insofar as monism remains as a Hegelian residue in Marxism, to that degree Marxism is unable to rebel against the human misery of both the past and present. Moreover it must justify this misery, because in monism there is no break either with the past or with the present.

It is most important to emphasize at this juncture that the dualism of a spiritualistic worldview has no connection with the otherness that concerns us here. The former does not break through the immanence of the self, nor does it recognize realities other than those already conceived by its apparatus of spiritual categories and deductions. The same can be said for the pseudodualism of worldviews that affirm the existence of a world other than our own.

Only the summons of the poor person, the widow, the orphan, the alien, the crippled constitutes true otherness. Only this summons, accepted and heeded, makes us transcend the sameness and original solitude of the self; only in this summons do we find the transcendence in which God consists. Only this summons provides a reason for rebellion against the masters and the gods in charge of this world, those committed to what has been and what is. The irreducible moral imperative is the only convincing reason for atheism, and this imperative is the God of the Bible.

It is on this point that present-day Marxism is not radical enough. In Marxist communism, there can be no justification for care of the old, the mentally retarded, the born cripples. The god known as productivity has no place for them in the world. How sad that precisely when the human being is really at stake the Marxist foundations are inadequate. Marx's effort to provide "to each according to his needs" and not according to his productivity is to be applauded, but the limitations of present-day Marxism offer no philosophical basis for such provision. Breaking the link between income and output—a link systematized but not invented by capitalism—is indispensable to a true revolution against the past and the present and all their gods and masters. This Marx perceived clearly. What he failed to see is that providing for each according to his needs presupposes caring for people simply because they exist, which in turn presupposes an absolute imperative unknown in his system of thought. This is not some insignificant marginal issue from which Marx can prescind.

It has become a commonplace thesis that revolution will be radical to the degree that it is based on man himself, that is, to the degree that man himself is its root. We do not question this thesis; rather we wish to take it absolutely seriously. In an individualistic sense, "man himself" is a criterion based on the Socratic theory of recollection and positing a person sufficient unto himself with his concepts, memories, and Aristotelian or Hegelian deductions. "Other" people are of no concern to him. Nor is he concerned with contingent facts (of which the whole of history consists), except to deny them as such, as Hegel did. No revolution can be based upon this "man himself," for such a basis would allow for no change in the individualism and utilitarianism that have prevailed to date.

The man in whom radical revolution has its roots is the "other." The basis for this revolution cannot even be the collectivity of which I am a part and which I call "humanity," as belonging to me. For such a view really involves nothing more than an expanded egoism, a utilitarianism recast with worldwide dimensions. And this is not revolution, but rather the complete triumph of the capitalist criterion—"rightly understood" and organized.

The "man himself" on whom the radicalness of the revolution depends is the other person, his otherness itself taken with unconditional seriousness insofar as it cannot be resorbed by the self, insofar as it cannot be made into a part of myself, precisely insofar as it transcends me. In this irreducible otherness, and only in it, is Yahweh. Any other objectivity which we might wish to ascribe to God converts God into an idol, into a non-God. Furthermore, this otherness of the neighbor in need, in order that it be nonresorbable, must be God for me.

Exhortations to love of neighbor and arguments for humanism have followed one another in endless succession throughout our history; Marxism and existentialism are the latest in a long series. But as long as the outcry of the neighbor in need is not God for us we are condemning humankind to an eternal return of revolution alternating with oppression.

Sartre and Heidegger should consider it very significant—since philosophy is one expression of real history—that at the end of their lives Engels and Neitzsche professed the eternal return of all things as a concept of history. Marx himself flirted with this notion in another form when he spoke of an imaginary primitive communism; in this sense the communism he hoped to achieve would have been a return to origins. I do not see how Sartre and Heidegger can avoid a similar conception if the conscience that they posit is not the definitive intervention of the Absolute. Without such intervention, there is nothing to stop the cycles and circumvolutions.

RELIGION AND THE ETERNAL RETURN

Marx held that it was useless to oppose religion as long as the social alienations that produce it perdure. But I believe it is indeed necessary to combat it, and in fact the anticultus of Jesus Christ and the prophets was a struggle against religion. As long as people project the Absolute into some "objective," escapist dimension like cultus, god is an extension of the self and does not transcend the self; such a god does not break through the sameness of the self with real otherness. Only if God locates himself in the very appeal of the "other" can the world be changed.

Perhaps the greatest disaster of history was the resorption of Christianity by the framework of religion. It is difficult to imagine a greater falsification of Christianity; and the masters of this world could not have invented a more effective stratagem for preventing the revolution of oppressed humanity. Religion does not alter the prevailing order; it has always had an accepted place in society; the successive gods, no matter what their names, are of absolutely no importance. Christianity fell into this pattern because of the understandable weakness of the persecuted as well as the subtle, invincible strength of the oppressors.

The anthropological, apologetic thesis that all people are innately religious is in a certain sense true, but it has no relation to Christianity. Or rather, it is related insofar as religiosity can resorb and annihilate Christianity. It is as if we were told that all people are innately alienated. So what?

Far from challenging consumeristic society, religion constitutes an integral part of it. We need only glance at the work of the urban planners: parks, schools, bus stations, theatres, churches, stores, parking lots, packing houses, sports arenas. A society that wants to preserve itself has to attend to the various needs of the people—religious needs, recreational needs, nutritional needs, etc. For many centuries religious authorities have taken advantage of this fact. But the message of the Bible has no place in such a program, it does not fit; it does not satisfy these needs nor was it meant to. Yahweh does not come to occupy a place reserved for him in the cosmos by the social structure. He comes to

revolutionize this cosmos and this entire social structure from their very foundations.

Therefore Yahweh rejects cultus, because it would be
a way of domesticating him, of reducing him to religion.
See Matt. 5:23; 1 Cor. 11:20–22; Matt. 7:21–23; Amos
5:21–25; Isa. 1:10–20; Hos. 5:1, 2, 6; 6:6; 8:13; Mic. 6:6–8;
Jer. 6:18–21; 7:4–7, 11–15, 21–22; Isa. 43:23–24; 58:2, 6–10;
etc. In these passages, Yahweh does not demand interpersonal justice "in addition to" cultus, nor does he ask
that cultus be reformed, nor does he require—as the
theology of the status quo has unrepentantly interpreted the above passages—that cultus be continued
but with better internal dispositions on the part of the
worshippers. The message of these passages can be
summarized in this way: *I do not want cultus but rather
interpersonal justice*. Anything we do to find some other
meaning in this message is pure tergiversation. We
quote Amos 5:21–25 as representative:

I hate, I spurn your pilgrim-feasts;
I will not delight in your sacred ceremonies.
If you present sacrifices and offerings
I will not accept them,
nor look on the buffaloes of your shared-offerings.
Spare me the sound of your songs;
I cannot endure the music of your lutes.
Let right roll on like a river
and justice like an ever-flowing stream.
Did you bring me sacrifices and gifts,
you people of Israel, those forty years in the wilderness?

Religion lubricates the cycles of the eternal return in
history. Rebellion against religion is mandatory for
anyone convinced that justice must be achieved, because persons with moral conscience cannot resign
themselves to the eternal return of all things. But the
eternal return is an iron circle, unbreakable as long as
we fail to perceive the Absolute in the outcry of suffering humanity. Mechanistic materialism and bourgeois
nihilism are perfectly interchangeable: Their common

denominator—which renders them both ultimately without significance—is the insipid triviality to which they reduce the world when they deny the transcendence of the "other." Nothing but an intervening Absolute can cause the banal circumvolutions of history to stop. Without it, everything will continue to consist of deducible combinations and permutations of either material particles or eternal spiritual essences, but in either case the result is the same: Without this Absolute there can be no *ultimum* which is the achievement of justice in the world.

THE FUTURE GOD

But here we touch upon the problem of the *eschaton*, which will concern us in the following chapter. First we must consider a topic of greater importance: According to the Bible, Yahweh is a future God. The name "Yahweh" etymologically means "he who will be." The God of the Bible defines himself in Exod. 3:14 as the God who will be.

Because of the superficiality and banality we have learned in the West, it seems to us at first impossible that twenty-nine centuries ago a man should have written something of such overwhelming, unprecedented profundity. But hermeneutics would be in difficult straits indeed if it determined by these platitudinarian criteria what an ancient document *can* say and what it *cannot*.

"I will be who I will be," Yahweh says to Moses when Moses asks his name. The force of this name is in the future, for Yahweh goes on to say in the same verse, "Tell the children of Israel, 'I will be' has sent me to you" (Exod. 3:14).

If any interpretation is *a limine* excluded by the context, it is the one proposed by Loisy, who suggests that by the response "I will be who I will be" God evaded Moses' question and concealed his name. Martin Noth quite correctly comments, "The wider context lead[s] us to understand that the name Yahweh is disclosed to Moses as a real divine name."[6] And as Noth and Michel Allard point out, "I will be who I will be" is the etymological explanation of the name "Yahweh."[7] "Yahweh" is the third person imperfect (=future) of the verb "to be," and all those who are not God had to designate God in the third person; on the other hand in "I will be who I will be," it is Yahweh himself who speaks, in the first person.

Allard has shown that the Septuagint, the Vulgate, and other western versions erred when they translated this passage as "I am who I am." As Joüon demonstrates, in Hebrew stative verbs the imperfect always expresses the future, and there is nothing in the context of Exod. 3:14 to suggest that the verb *hayah* ("to be") has ceased to be stative and become active.[8] In fact the Septuagint always translates the first person singular of the imperfect as "I will be" (Greek *esomai*), except in this verse and in Hos. 1:9; in these two passages the translators of the Septuagint are not translating at all but rather propounding the same metaphysical theory that has so fascinated western theologians. As Allard shows, the other two supposed exceptions, Job 7:20 and 2 Sam. 15:34, really are not exceptions, the former because it has a consequential and not a temporal nuance, and the latter because the meaning is clearly preterite.

Yahweh is not, but rather will be. If our ontological categories render us incapable of understanding this, then good hermeneutics demands that we change our ontology, not the biblical message.

To understand this point, let us consider the most futuristic passage of the Old Testament, namely, Jer. 31:31–34 (the new covenant). Here God promises the new humanity that "I will be their God and they shall be my people" and, as a consequence, that all will know Yahweh—everyone, from the youngest to the oldest. The meaning of God's futureness depends on the meaning of "to know Yahweh." This passage, which carries us directly into the New Testament (2 Cor. 6:16, 14; 1 Cor. 11:25; Luke 22:20; Mark 14:24; Matt. 26:28), has occasioned a very serious methodological error in exegesis. Laden with important consequences, this error has consisted in trying to interpret the passage while prescinding from the definition of "to know Yahweh" that Jeremiah himself had formulated nine chapters previously:

He [Josiah] practiced justice and right;
this is good.
He defended the cause of the poor and the needy;
this is good.
Is this not what it means to know me?
It is Yahweh who speaks (Jer. 22:16).

"To know Yahweh" is a technical term, as Mowinckel, Botterweck, and H.W. Wolff have shown[9] and as is made apparent by an examination of Hos. 4:1-2; 6:4-6; 2:22; 5:4; 6:3; Isa. 11:2 (cf. 11:4-5); 1:3 (cf. 11:5-9); Hab. 2:14. "To know Yahweh" is a technical term meaning to do justice and right, to defend the cause of the poor and the needy.

Therefore, when Jer. 31:31-34 says that Yahweh *will be* God, it means that com-passion, solidarity, and justice will reign among people. This is why the God of the Bible is a future God: Because only in the future, at the end of history, will people recognize in the outcry and the otherness of their neighbor the absolute moral imperative that is God. This is what it means to know Yahweh, according to the Bible. In contradistinction to our ontological objects, the God of the Bible does not *be* first, and become known to us later; rather he *is* insofar as he is know to us. He does not allow himself to be changed into an object. He ceases to be God as soon as we break off our moral relationship with our neighbor.

According to western ontology ("a philosophy of injustice," as Levinas says) the object first exists and then

THE VINDICATION OF ATHEISM 45

it is known, and it exists independently of whether we know it or do not. Like a brick, like a thing, like an ... object, precisely. Anyone would say that we cannot think of reality in any other way. And yet the biblical authors implacably insist that a god conceived as existing outside the interpersonal summons to justice and love is not the God revealed to them, but rather some idol; moreover the entire Bible is directed toward creating a world in which authentic relationships among people are made possible and become a reality. Only in a world of justice will God be. And if Marxism and existentialism do not find God in the western world, it is because in fact there is no God there, nor can there be.

NOTES

1. Martin Heidegger, *Sein und Zeit* (Tübingen: Niemeyer, 1960), p. 269 [Eng. trans.: *Being and Time*, trans. John Macquarrie and Edward Robinson (New York: Harper & Row, 1962), p. 313].

2. Ibid., p. 229 [Eng. trans.: p. 272].

3. Gerhard von Rad, *Das erste Buch Mose*, 7th ed., ATD 2–4 (Göttingen: Vandenhoeck, 1964) [Eng. trans.: *Genesis: A Commentary*, trans. John H. Marks (London: SCM, 1961)]; "Das theologisch Problem des alttestamentlichen Schöpfungsglaubens," in *Gesammelte Studien zum Alten Testament* (Munich: Kaiser, 1965), pp. 136–47 [Eng. trans.: "The Theological Problem of the Old Testament Doctrine of Creation," in *The Problem of the Hexateuch and Other Essays*, trans. Rev. E.W. Trueman Dicken (New York: McGraw Hill, 1966), pp. 131–43].

4. José Porfirio Miranda, *Marx y la biblia* (Salamanca: Sígueme, 1972), chaps. 2 and 4 [Eng. trans.: *Marx and the Bible*, trans. John Eagleson (Maryknoll, New York: Orbis Books, 1974)].

5. Jean-Paul Sartre, *Critique de la raison dialectique* (Paris: Gallimard, 1960), 1:109.

6. Martin Noth, *Das zweite Buch Mose*, 3rd ed., ATD 5 (Göttingen: Vandenhoeck, 1965), p. 31 [Eng. trans.: *Exodus: A Commentary*, trans. J.S. Bowden (Philadelphia: Westminster, 1969), p. 44].

7. Ibid., p. 31 [Eng. trans.: pp. 43–44]; Michel Allard, "Note sur la formule "ehyeh aser 'ehyeh,'" *Recherches de Science Religieuse* 45 (1957), p. 83.

8. Paul Joüon, *Grammaire de l'hébreu biblique*, 2nd ed. (Rome: Pontificio Istituto Biblico, 1947), no. 113a.

9. Sigmund Mowinckel, *Die Erkenntnis Gottes bei alttestament-lichen Propheten* (Oslo: Universistets-Forlaget, 1941); G. Johannes Botterweck, *"Gott Erkennen" im Sprachgebrauch des Alten Testaments* (Bonn: Peter Hanstein, 1951); Hans Walter Wolff, " 'Wissen um Gott' bei Hosea als Urform von Theologie," *Evangelishche Theologie* 12 (1952–53), pp. 533–34.

Chapter 3

The End of History

As we have said, the conditions of possibility of directly perceptible realities may be detected by the transcendental method. By this method we have established that God, as absolute imperative, is the great condition of possibility of the human conscience. By the same method we also discern that conscience requires another important condition of possibility, related to time; in this chapter we will investigate this additional condition of possibility.

EXISTENTIALISM AND TIME

Time is the touchstone of all philosophy. Contemporary philosophers must not forget that Hegel, Kierkegaard, and Marx were in revolt against Lessing in particular and Greco-Western philosophy in general because these had proved incapable of recognizing the importance of contingent facts. This rebellion failed in Hegel's hands, for he dealt with contingent facts by making them necessary. But the task has been taken up by existentialism, and here we hope to set forth the basic conditions of possibility for existentialism itself.

Heidegger correctly says, "Being cannot be grasped except by taking time into consideration."[1] Sartre summarizes Kierkegaard in the following terms: "The

47

existent man cannot be assimilated by a system of ideas; regardless of how much we think or say about suffering, it escapes knowledge to the degree that it is suffered within itself and for itself and knowledge is impotent to transform it."[2] (Sartre continues, "It is noteworthy that Marxism's reproach of Hegel is the same, although from another point of view." One point is striking: To try to deduce real facts from matter or from anything else, merely to assert that they are deducible, is to assert that they are necessary and is therefore to strip of its basis the rebellion of the suffering person and his companions. Thus Kierkegaard's criticism of Hegel is much more radical than Marx's.)

The real person, the one who suffers, is always a contingent reality, that is, he is, but he need not be. Pre-existentialist knowledge, however, was concerned only with the necessary, that is, with what is and could not *not be*. Thus this knowledge misperceived the person and concentrated on essences. Kierkegaard, on the contrary, "made the relationship with a historical fact into something decisive."[3]

The existentialist revolution consists in rendering decisive our relationship with contingent facts. Our ability to transform reality depends entirely on relating to contingent facts in this way. But Kierkegaard discovered this relationship in the particular historical fact called Jesus Christ, and if Heidegger and Sartre consider this irrelevant, then their analysis has been superficial. We are not dealing with a structure that due to the chance of biographical anecdote was linked to the contingent fact called Jesus Christ, a structure which therefore could be disconnected from that fact in order to enrich the atemporal collection of available human experiences. We are rather dealing with the Messiah.

Heidegger discovered that meaningfulness is a condition of possibility for the "world" we actively construct around us, and without which we cannot really exist. He discovered that we cannot articulate a "world" if we are not committed to some meaningfulness. He proceeded one crucial step further when he discovered that meaningfulness either arises from temporality or it does not exist at all. In fact, temporality makes things coeval so that they constitute a world, for without temporality they are absent to each other (past or future, not present). But Heidegger did not consider carefully that temporality draws things together to constitute a meaningful world only to the degree that this temporality itself rests on the sure hope that there will be a messianic time. Time lacks all "sense" if there is no messianic time; temporality cannot give the world a meaningfulness that temporality itself does not have.

Heidegger recognizes that "if the term 'understanding' is taken in a way that is primordially existential, it means *to be projecting toward a potentiality-for-being for the sake of which any person exists.*"[4] This potentiality-for-being is the eschatological future of the whole of humankind, not of the isolated individual. Without this potentiality-for-being, nothing has any meaning. Without it, therefore, we cannot understand, for we can understand only something with meaning. We confer meaning on the world by projecting it toward the definitive messianic end. This meaningfulness introduced into the world by the messianic *eschaton* is what gives temporality sense. Because of this meaningfulness time exists.

In a roundabout way, Sartre came to the same conclusion in his thesis on nothingness: "This nothingness that separates human reality from itself is at the origin of time." He goes on to explain, correctly emphasizing the collective dimension lacking in Heidegger: "The for-itself [the human being] is separated from the presence-to-itself which it lacks and which is its own possibility, in one sense separated by Nothing and in another sense by the totality of the existent in the world, inasmuch as the for-itself, lacking or possible, is for-itself as *a presence to a certain state of the world.*"[5] This statement is a perfectly accurate observation. Our projected presence to the final state of the world is at the root of time, as the condition of possibility of time. Without the messianic *eschaton* there would be no meaningfulness to the extension of reality into successive past, present, and future moments. Moreover, if the person did not anticipate the presence-to-himself that he lacks, he would not be for-himself but rather a thing; he would not be conscious of existing; he would not be conscious of himself. This presence-to-itself is thus the condition of possibility for the very existence of the person as person, of the person as for-itself, of the person insofar as he is not a thing. In one sense nothingness separates him from the eschatological presence-to-itself, which the person can anticipate and in fact necessarily does anticipate. In another sense the totality of what exists separates the person from the eschatological presence-to-itself, since this future presence-to-itself could not be conscious, could not be for-itself, if it were not a presence to a whole world that had been completely transformed.

Thus we can grasp that the messianic *eschaton* is a condition of possibility for the fundamental consciousness of guilt that we considered in the first chapter. Sartre expresses it well:

It is only as a lack to *be suppressed* that lack can be internal for the for-itself, and the for-itself can realize its own lack only by having to be it; that is, by being a project toward its suppression.[6]

The worker does not represent his sufferings to himself as unbearable; he adapts himself to them not through resignation but because he lacks the education and reflection necessary for him to conceive of a social state in which these sufferings would not exist.[7]

It is necessary here to reverse common opinion and to acknowledge that it is not the harshness of a situation or the sufferings that it imposes which are motives for conceiving of another state of affairs in which things would be better for everybody. It is only when we can conceive of a different state of affairs that a new light falls on our troubles and our suffering and that we *decide* that these are unbearable.[8]

That group of living beings called the human race has not been the same since Christ came. Any philosophy that claims to be concrete and yet prescinds from the impact that Christ has had on humankind is a ridiculous contrivance. To ignore Christ's significance requires intellectual acrobatics that only emphasize it and thus establish it all the more conclusively. From the time Christ demonstrated what a person can be, our dissatisfaction with what we are has become torturous. Since Christ came it is worth the trouble to be a person. It matters not if humankind is better or worse since his coming; it is possible that we have lived no more justly and lovingly than before Christ. But humankind itself has changed, for it now has an intolerable sense of lack. A philosophy that ignores this is deliberately playing blindman's bluff. The Messiah is the basis for the world's time in a sense unspeakably deeper than any chronological "A.D." The anguish and guilt that make existing possible are anguish and guilt with respect to the Messiah. For the vindication of all the generations that have died and are now dying—crushed by the heel of oppression and cruelty—depends on our taking the messianic *eschaton* with unrestricted seriousness.

Before going any further, let us summarize three fundamental points: *First:* "Being cannot be grasped except by taking time into consideration";[9] "the central problematic of all ontology is rooted in the phenomenon of time, if rightly seen and rightly explained."[10] This notion was omitted from the whole of the pre-Hegelian philosophical tradition, except Giambattista Vico. In their search for being, the metaphysicians overlooked being because they did not consider time. On the other hand, the anthropologists of time (in Mexico, Octavio Paz and Carlos Fuentes) have not realized that they have touched upon the metaphysical problem par excellence.

Second: Time in general is not the condition of possibility for authentic existence, but rather future time. On the first occasion that time presents itself, it does so as future. The past is past as a function of the future; the present is present because it is not future. And the future is presented as anguish because it demands decision. (As we will see, according to the New Testament the *eschaton* must be made.) The meaning of the past and the present depends on what in the future we will make them to have been.

Third: The future alone is not the condition of possibility for existing, but rather the messianic future; otherwise the future enters into series with the past and the present as interchangeable elements of an eternal return.

THE CONTEMPORANEITY OF CHRIST

In his criticism of Heidegger, Sartre rightly says, "To be in the world is not to escape from the world toward oneself but to escape from the world toward a beyond-the-world which is the future world."[11] But this future world constitutes a beyond only to the degree that it is a solution and an abolition of all our injustices and miseries. If it were not messianic it would suffer from the same dearth of meaningfulness as the past and present.

But, some will object, Christ is in the past.

I will devote the remaining eight chapters of this book to a due consideration of this objection. But let us be well aware that this objection involves the true problem of existentialism—the true problem of time and the true problem of being. In my opinion, this problem has not been resolved. And the reason it has not been resolved is that the New Testament has been read through Greek spectacles.

"Everything I have written," says Kierkegaard, "has tended to bring out the meaning of contemporaneity."[12] "We have to erase eighteen hundred years of Christian history and make ourselves contemporaneous with the moment when God appeared in time."[13] In this idea we find the origin of existentialism, and, as we shall see, existentialism cannot be separated from its origin. But Kierkegaard did not achieve what he intended. On the one hand, we cannot leap nineteen hundred years into the past. On the other, we are not dealing with the timeless, celestial Christ of dogmatic theology—which was devoted to reconstituting the Platonic world with an apparently different content; we are rather dealing with the historical Jesus. I am committed to the Christ who is within time, the Christ we did not understand.

We killed Mozart and Beethoven by starvation and incomprehension, and yet we ornament our lives with their music and call them the honor and glory of the West. But they represent a supreme protest against the West. We do nothing to prevent the same thing from happening again. Van Gogh arrives and is given the same treatment. If a generation were able to prevent such callousness, it would be transformed to such a degree that it could understand Jesus Christ and thereby could begin to make Christianity real.

Let us sum up: On the one hand, we are dealing with the historical Jesus and not the Jesus of some heavenly world nor the Christ of the ecclesiastical Eucharist. On the other, real time does not allow of manipulation. One cannot disdain "vulgar time" in escapist fashion, as Heidegger does. Nor can one—and this amounts to the same thing—consider time as if it were the object of anthropological study: "Unquestionably the conception of time as a fixed present and as pure actuality is more ancient than that of chronometric time, which is not an immediate apprehension of the flow of reality but is instead a rationalization of its passing."[14]

Chronological, dateable time is an inescapable reality; it does not necessarily function as an escapist ruse that enables us to avoid making decisions. It is even more escapist to postulate that time does not exist and that existentially only temporality exists—as Bultmann, following Heidegger, does in reducing the future to fu-

tureness, the past to pastness, and the present to presentness. Scholasticism's traditional evasion consists in
resorting to a "Christ of faith"—although it may not use
this term—a Christ who seemingly remains in a
heavenly, Platonic world, outside of time and history.
Dogmatic theology could assert contemporaneity with
Christ only by assuming a timeless Christ, and this
maneuver greatly resembles the Heideggerian disdain
for ordinary time.

These and other such conceptual manipulations are
symptomatic of an unfulfilled metaphysical need. Contemporaneity with Christ is central to Kierkegaard's
thought because Christ is the Messiah; Kierkegaard
seeks contemporaneity with the messianic future. Because he fails to attain true contemporaneity, Kierkegaard therefore appears as a "bard of the return"
("*chantre du retour*"), as Wahl says.[15]

Kierkegaard could raise the question of contemporaneity with Christ only because he perceived,
though obscurely, the central teaching of the gospel.
Our answer must come from a scientific analysis of the
New Testament.

THE ETHICAL NATURE OF TIME

The fact that time does not allow of manipulation is
indicative of its ethical character; it is indicative of its
irreducible otherness with respect to the self. The conscience we spoke of in the first chapter cannot be eliminated by verbal prestidigitation: For our conscience
tells us that we have oppressed the other. And in the
outcry of the other is the absolute imperative, as we saw
in chapter 2.

For centuries the writers of epistemological treatises
taught that the sure sign of our touching upon being
was that the object of our inquiry was independent of
mental considerations. Thanks to Husserl and Scheler,
contemporary philosophers have seen that this being of

epistemology and ontology is less independent of our intentions and interests than was believed. As Heidegger says: "All ontical experience of entities—both circumspective calculation of what is close at hand, and positive scientific cognition of what can be observed—is based upon projections of the being of the corresponding entities, projections which in every case are more or less transparent. But in these projections there lies hidden the 'toward which' of the projection; and on this, as it were, the understanding of being nourishes itself."[16]

Being, which seemed so demonstrably independent of us, turns out to be unavoidably conditioned by our thought processes. It is constituted as it is because of our plans, our desires, our longings. In other words, far from being independent of the self, being is an extension of the self. It can be manipulated. I am referring to being as it is understood by metaphysics and realism of whatever stripe, not figments of fantasy.

On the other hand, the outcry of the neighbor in need—the only true content of the voice of conscience —absolutely cannot be manipulated. In it there is indeed otherness. It is not a branch office of the self and its world and projections. It cannot be encompassed. It is not neutral; it demands decision. Its otherness cannot be absorbed by the thinker; it remains uncompromisingly exterior to and independent of the thinker. It is truly real and is not at my disposition; nor does it succumb to my powers of affirmation or negation or representation. This outcry alone is imperative. Its demand, insofar as I heed it, increases my responsibility. I am no longer alone. In a word, it is otherness, and manipulation of otherness is impossible.

Time is cut from the same cloth, for it presents exactly the same resistance to the conceptual stratagems and legerdemain by which we try to make the past and the future into the present. It is for this reason that Kierkegaard and the existentialists have failed in their attempt with regard to contemporaneity (although philosophy's greatest success is to have formulated the true problem). Time is ethical, and it can be known only in an ethical resolution. History is made of the outcry of all the oppressed; in this it consists. Neither Kierkegaard nor Heidegger realized this, and therefore their philosophies are individualistic. Kierkegaard never understood that Jesus Christ is the Messiah to the extent that he is the savior of all the poor and the liberator of all the oppressed (see Luke 4:17–21; 7:18–23; Matt. 11:2–6; 12:15–23). On the other hand, Heidegger, with the intention of entertaining no illusions, refuses to look toward the future. His stoic approach of "confronting *the nothingness*" is therefore symptomatic of his failure in his attempt to know *being*. As Sartre says—and this is the fundamental refutation—, "Every negation that did not have beyond itself, in the future, the meaning of an engagement as a possibility which comes to it and toward which it flees, would lose all its significance as negation."[17]

HISTORY AND ESCHATON

With regard to Marx and Sartre, we must explicitly state here that the *eschaton* of the Bible (not that of dogmatic theology) is *in this world*. If we do not state this clearly, there will never be mutual understanding. The biblical *eschaton* is not beyond history, but rather the final and definitive stage of history.

Christ says, "How blest are those of a gentle spirit; they shall have *the earth* for their possession" (Matt. 5:5). No honest person could possibly translate this as locating the *eschaton* in some other world. Christ is speaking of the earth, of this world. Consistent with Old Testament tradition, Christ affirms an end of history in which the just, the gentle, the com-passionate, those in solidarity with their neighbor will be the ones to possess the earth, while the unjust, the hardhearted, the oppressors will be eliminated (or converted).

All this is set forth very clearly in the Old Testament. See for example Ps. 37:28–29, to which Matthew undoubtedly was alluding in the beatitudes cited above:

The unjust will be annihilated,
and the children of the wicked destroyed.
The just shall possess the land
and shall live there forever.

But escapist theologians, posing as guardians of the originality of the New Testament, have ingeniously taught that Christ's message was totally new and that it is therefore superfluous to study Old Testament eschatology. Christ, they say, is the sole authority. But the beatitude quoted above demonstrates that on this point, regardless of what the theologians say, the New Testament reiterates the Old. In the New Testament *eschaton* the com-passionate and the brotherly will conquer this world and no other. Paul denies that those who observe the law "will inherit *the world*," but he assures us that those who through faith become just will do so: "The promise of inheriting the world was not made to Abraham and his descendants on account of the law, but on account of the justice of faith" (Rom. 4:13). Paul of Tarsus has been called a "spiritualistic" writer; but even if the designation were accurate, it does not justify the otherwordly interpretations that have been made of Christ's message.

All biblical scholars without exception have seen that the expression "the kingdom of heaven" means "the kingdom of God" and not a kingdom in the sky, for "heaven" is late Judaism's classical circumlocution for designating God without mentioning his name. Such respect for a name alone might seem excessive to us, but the documentary evidence provided by the Jewish literature of that time is abundantly clear on this point.

Theodor Zahn rightly states, "After the Beatitudes of Matt. 5:3–10, it is obvious that the reward (mentioned in 5:12) will be given to the disciples only in the kingdom

that must be established on earth."[18] "Your reward is
great in heaven" does not mean that they will be re-
warded in heaven, "as if it said *hoti misthon polyn
lēpsesthe en tois ouranois* ['you will receive a great reward in heaven']." What it does say is that human actions are in the mind of God, using the word "heaven"
instead of "God." To put it figuratively: Human actions
ascend to the knowledge of God in heaven and there
their reward accumulates like a treasure. This does not
say that the reward will be enjoyed in heaven. In Acts
10:4 Luke says, "Your prayers and acts of charity have
gone up to heaven to speak for you before God." And this
is the precise meaning conveyed by Matt. 5:12; 6:20;
Luke 6:23; 12:33; 1 Pet. 1:4–8. This idea already existed
in the Old Testament (see Tob. 12:12–15), and the New
Testament offers no textual or documentary basis for
asserting that it differs from the Old on this point.

The passages in Paul and Luke that speak of extrater-
restrial "paradise" (2 Cor. 12:4; Luke 23:43) or a situation called "the bosom of Abraham" (Luke 16:23) or an
imminent "being with Christ" (Phil 1:23) have been very
carefully studied by the respected Joachim Jeremias
and the Catholic Paul Hoffman using all the comparative resources of the Jewish documentation of that
period.[19] These passages allude to an entirely provisional situation that will last only until the kingdom of
God is established definitively and perfectly on earth.

Objective exegesis has no difficulty in admitting a
"heavenly Jerusalem," made up of—as the book of Revelation itself describes it—the apostles, the martyrs, and
the just who have died. There is no difficulty *provided*
that we understand that this Jerusalem will come down
to earth, according to Rev. 21:2, 10. It is therefore identical to the "paradise" referred to by Luke and Paul, an
entirely provisional situation having only marginal importance. It is not a place or another world. It consists of
persons (cf. Rev. 3:12) whom the book of Revelation considers important, not because of their provisional and

passing situation, but because they are destined to "reign upon earth," as Rev. 5:10 expresses it. The description of this kingdom which will have come down to earth (Rev. 21:2, 10) even specifies that there "they shall reign forever and ever" (Rev. 22:5).

In a perhaps not too distant future, when dogmatic theologians become more faithful to the Bible, they will emphatically have to recall that they used to think of the "ultraterrestrial" only as "eternal," with "eternal" understood in a merely negative way as simply an absence of time. This last-mentioned idea is the popular but false conception of eternity (tolerated or even fostered by dogmatic theologians). Upon this popular notion is based the equally false belief that the eternal is of greater value than time and history.

In Matt. 25:34 when Christ says to the just, "Possess the kingdom that has been ready for you," he is speaking of the same kingdom that according to Matt. 12:28 already "has arrived" (*ephthasen*, the aorist, that is, the preterite tense) on earth. And the Evangelist insists that "the field" in which this kingdom is established "is the world" (Matt. 13:38), that Christ will return to this kingdom to root out from it all "those who do iniquity" (Matt. 13:41), and that "the just will then shine as brightly as the sun in the kingdom of their Father. If you have ears, then hear" (Matt. 13:43). The beatitude contains the same idea: "The gentle will possess the earth" (Matt. 5:5). The Bible has been straightforwardly clear on this point from the very beginning, but prescientific exegetes had no ears to hear what it was saying.

Fidelity to the biblical text should not be confused with Protestant fundamentalism. In 1964, after describing modern methods of studying the Gospels, the Pontifical Biblical Commission added: "There remain [in the Gospels] many questions, and these of the gravest moment, in the discussion and elucidation of which the Catholic exegete can and should freely exercise his intelligence and skill."[20] And the Commission expressly states that this is to "prepare the ground for the decisions of the Church's teaching authority." Thus our interpretations should not wait on the pronouncements of ecclesiastical authority; on the contrary, our investigations must move forward. Since the publication of this document, anyone who accuses a serious Catholic student of the Bible of Lutheranism is contradicting the teachings of the Catholic church itself.

To return to our point, the biblical *eschaton* is in this world. It is not beyond history, but is rather the end of history. We must bear this in mind throughout the following chapters, where we will try to make the Fourth Gospel the basis for solving Kierkegaard's problem, which is the problem of existentialism and of all serious philosophy.

THE NECESSARY TELOS

Humanity can become conscious of sin to the degree that it conceives of its situation as able to be changed. Sartre puts it very well: The person "can realize [his] own lack only by having to be it; that is, by being a project toward its suppression."[21] In this chapter we are trying to describe explicitly a condition of possibility of the consciousness of guilt and of the absolute imperative itself.

It seems to me that Sartre makes no sense when he imagines evil to be nothingness inherent in the human being. To think of evil as nothingness, as the negation and lack of being, is the key to Thomas Aquinas's apologetic Aristotelian theodicy, which was inherited by Leibnitz and Hegel: Since God creates only being, then evil cannot be attributed to God. Such a premise naturally concludes in Leibnitzian optimism: "Everything for the best in the best of all possible worlds." But evil is not nothingness. If evil were nothingness, then human finitude would be sufficient cause for the existence of evil. And then there would be no hope.

According to the Bible evil is definitely not the mere absence of being: "It was through one man that sin *entered* the world, and through sin death" (Rom. 5:12). For the Bible, evil and good are equally real: "It was a man who brought death into the world; a man also brought resurrection of the dead" (1 Cor. 15:21).

If evil were not contingent, we would not even be aware of its existence. We become aware of sin to the degree that we affirm an *eschaton* in which sin will be totally abolished—which implies that it is contingent.

Sartre holds that the "future is not *realized*. What is realized is a human being who is *designated* by the future and who is constituted in connection with this future."[22] If Sartre is suggesting that the future is ever reborn and can never be reached, for otherwise it would cease being for-itself and become in-itself, he is in a certain sense correct: The being of human relationships, the being that cannot exist without our decision, is ever reborn and cannot be petrified. The messianic *eschaton* signifies definitive justice; it does not mean people are suddenly frozen into lifeless statues. The otherness of the other is irreducible. Once I have heeded the moral imperative, I am no longer ever alone, and its demand increases to the degree that I obey it. The deepening of interpersonal understanding has no limits. But the future is not a mere structural category of the present, as Bultmann would have it. An *eschaton* consisting of mere warning, of unfulfilled threat directed toward the present destroys itself. If we reduce the future to abstract, repeatable futureness we vaporize history and annihilate time by conceptual decree. We re-establish the eternal return under the guise of the perennially reborn future. At this point Sartrian philosophy becomes the lackey of the bourgeoisie and justifies the tranquillizing bourgeois maxim: "That's the way it's always been." This is pure negation, and in refutation we need only return to Sartre's own words: "Every negation that did not have beyond itself, in the future, the meaning of an

engagement as a possibility which comes to it and toward which it flees, would lose all its significance as
negation."[23]

This argument also refutes the antiteleology of a certain sector of Marxism, an attitude marked by in-
genuousness and superficiality. The denial of an end of
history, a *telos*, a goal to the centuries-old strife of
humankind, is contradicted by Marx's *Critique of the
Gotha Program*, in which Marx describes communist
society in terms of two phases of increasing justice—an
unequivocal positing of a *telos*. And let us recall that
Lenin adopted this description. The workers' dissatisfaction, their rebellion, and the class struggle that
Marxism discovers in history (it does not produce them)
would be impossible if workers could in no way visualize
a goal to their struggle, a society in which the need for
profit and for the exploitation of others might cease to
exist.

Certain Marxists abhor the idea of *telos* because it
represents a finality written into nature, and acknowledging this finality would oblige them to acknowledge a
creator who did the writing. They are right about the
relationship between *telos* and nature, but that relationship is not the point here. Our point is the *eschaton*
that we human beings are writing into nature—a process in which the Marxists themselves participate when
they struggle to understand reality and to change it.
The workers' struggle, which is our concern here, carries within it a goal to history. And if it is a superficial
observation to deny the existence of a *telos* within the
workers' struggle, it is even more superficial to deny
that there is a *telos* in the act of observing: Those making the denial claim to be merely observing that struggle: But why do they observe? What is science, the best
of the sciences, trying to accomplish? Why are certain
people determined to make rigorous and methodical observations until they reach conclusions?

Knowing does not consist simply in observing, but in

understanding. We can understand something only if it has meaning. But nothing has meaning unless it is projected toward the messianic end of humankind, toward the real goal of history. Something can be understood only in relation to an end that the whole of history struggles to reach.

By the act of explaining something, the Marxists themselves imply that there is a questioner, an other, and they take a position with regard to that other. They believe that in the end all people will be able to understand each other, and they could not be more correct. But as soon as the otherness of the questioner enters the picture, the whole moral order becomes involved. And this order implies an *eschaton* in which morality is achieved. Positivism is not conscious of its own conditions of possibility. As Levinas says, "The essence of discourse is ethical."[24] And therefore the essence of science is ethical as well. The very words we use to designate things testify that "others" and I participate in them. The very universality of language and concepts has its origin in the moral responsibility that I have in relation to others. Science is to speak of the world to another.

As Levinas notes, critical knowledge can be achieved only "in the face of . . . ";[25] it is possible only with regard to otherness. "If philosophy consists in knowing critically, that is, in seeking a foundation for its freedom, in justifying it, it begins with conscience, to which the other is presented as the Other, and where the movement of thematization is inverted. But this inversion does not amount to 'knowing oneself' as a theme attended to by the Other, but rather in submitting oneself to an exigency, to a morality."[26]

If we are to follow the transcendental method rigorously, we must go even further. Not only is the possibility of philosophy and positive science conditioned by the summons that arises from the otherness of the neighbor. The consciousness *(Bewusstsein)* that every person has of himself is likewise so conditioned. The ability to think of myself in a thematic way depends on conscience *(Gewissen)*, because the self becomes aware of itself only in the presence of the other. But as soon as one is in the presence of the "other," the absolute imperative is fully operative. And the absolute imperative has force only because history has an end, because the *eschaton* is history's *telos*. John says it in other words: Whoever denies the Messiah does not have God.

THE MYTH OF THE GOLDEN AGE

But before dealing with John we must touch upon another point, an appendix to this chapter on the end of history. I am speaking of an error that occurs frequently and more or less explicitly among people of the most diverse cultural levels, namely, the belief that the *eschaton* recreates a past Golden Age from which the course of history should never have departed.

This understanding of history as deviation from ancient perfection often underlies, implicitly or explicitly, the theology of original sin (although not the *biblical* account). In Hegel's *Phenomenology of Spirit* the final achievement of human history is a great return to the original "idea," albeit on a superior and sublimated level (as Urs von Balthasar has approvingly noted). This same understanding of history is operative in the myth of an indemonstrable primitive communism.

More recently and closer to home Octavio Paz posits this notion as the basis for all revolutionary thought: "Every revolution tries to bring back a Golden Age. . . . [This age] prefigured and prophesied the new society which the revolutionary proposes to create. . . . The originality of the Plan of Ayala resides in the fact that this Golden Age was not a simple creation of man's reason or a mere hypothesis."[27] "Thanks to the Revolution, the Mexican wants to reconcile himself with his history and his origins."[28] And Octavio Paz the anthropologist boldly proclaims: "The 'eternal return' is one of the implicit assumptions of almost every revolutionary theory."[29]

If revolution means repeating what has already existed, then frankly our language is leaving us in the lurch. True, the etymology of the term "revolution" implies repetition, but, etymology notwithstanding, "eternal return" is *not* the universally accepted meaning of the term "revolution." So we must disregard Paz's last statement. His other assertions that we have cited attempt to express a diffuse sentiment of return to origins, but in my opinion there is no such sentiment expressed either in the Plan of Ayala or in any other authentic revolution.

Carlos Fuentes is a trustworthy witness for this opinion for he too, following Paz, confesses "the nostalgia for paradise lost."[30] Nevertheless he shows that Zapata and his Plan of Ayala harked back "in appearance only" to documents and situations of the past.[31] Truly, no Golden Age had ever existed, nor did Zapata ever imagine that it had. Revolution has nothing to do with the resurrection of a structure from the past. Revolution is not nourished by myths, but rather by an exact perception of injustice suffered.

If our ideological premises lead us to mourn the loss of some bygone time, if our desire, more or less explicit, is for a grand return, then the logical consequence is to consider "historical change [as] daily more remote and unlikely."[32] Ibargüengoitia rightly criticizes Paz: "We come to the conclusion that we have always been in the same situation and that therefore it is unlikely that we can change."[33]

In his analysis of the Mexican revolution, Paz's observations are more accurate: "The Mexican does not want to be either an Indian or a Spaniard. Nor does he want to be descended from them. He denies them. And he does not affirm himself as a mixture, but rather as an abstraction: he is a man. He becomes the son of Nothingness. His beginnings are in his own self."[34] This indeed is revolution: the destruction of the past in the name of the humanity that has been oppressed. But this is just as irreconcilable with the great return to a Golden Age as it is with the eternal return of an inexorable cycle.

The ability to break with the past is a projection toward a definitively human future—even though, like Fuentes, we may suppose the break to occur instantaneously. The Mexican revolution provides an important example here. It did not imitate anything. It was spontaneous and did not seek to justify itself on the basis of some mythological communist prehistory. The instantaneousness that Fuentes observes in the character of Mexican revolutionaries rather derives from the fact that our revolution was rapidly betrayed and defeated; it consists, even more to the point, in a tacit conviction—habitual among us Mexicans—that a revolutionary outbreak is certainly justified, notwithstanding its eventual defeat; it implies the conviction that "one of these times" the revolution will triumph. I think this is the correct theory of the Mexican revolution. Notwithstanding his theoretical belief in a grand return, Fuentes quite accurately observes that "in Mexico the centuries-old danger, alienation, and violence long since have created in the people the conviction that the end might be just around the corner."[35] The apparent instantaneousness depends, it seems, on this: At any moment justice for all who have been oppressed might be realized. The events of 1968 and 1971 and the later activities of rural and urban guerrillas demonstrate this. Fuentes's thesis that Mexicans are convinced that the end and the future can only be catastrophic seems completely gratuitous to me. If Mexicans believed this, then real revolution would have been impossible. And a real revolution occurred.

Fuentes and Paz are right, however, in believing, as

anthropologists, that the concept of time is of decisive importance in philosophy and that every person, even the most uncultured, has a concept of time. The end of an agricultural year is quite different from the end of a presidential term. Different again are the end of the century, the end of the modern period (or the contemporaneous period, as some writers would term it), or the end of an entire civilization. And these are all different from the end of a whole world or an eon—and the beginning of another, definitive world or eon.

We find the fatalistic natural cycle of the agricultural year not only in the Aztec calendar with its recurrent fiestas, but also in the religious calendar of the "Christian" colonizers. The latter got their calendar, through the church, from the Greco-Roman teachers of the eternal return. Religion, as we have already said, is the natural lubricant of the cycles of the eternal return. To think that the church reduced the dates of Christ's life to integral elements of that lubricant— the Christ who, more than anyone, sought to break the social structures that kept humankind ensnared in vegetal time! Modern lineal time thinly disguises its underlying principle of eternal return with a veneer of entirely superficial "progress," as demonstrated by the current widespread belief that it is impossible for human nature to change. When we see how the Nahuatl, the western, and the post-revolutionary cultures share the same concept of time, we realize that the differences among them are of little significance. The modern Mexican calendar, featuring Benito Juárez and the Virgin of Guadalupe, differs only in externals from the previous religious calendars. It recurs. And it convinces people that no matter what happens, nothing really changes at all.

Fuentes and Paz assert that things will change if we profess the great return to the Golden Age instead of the eternal return. But there never was any such Golden Age. And a myth will not break the chain of fatalism, made of mistrust, cruelty, and injustice among people. The chain can be broken only if we recognize the outcry of the neighbor as absolute.

In his work on Nietzsche, Heidegger correctly states that the importance of the idea of eternal return is matched only by that of the Platonic thesis regarding the world of ideas.[36] But the philosophy of the world of ideas itself was invented to strip time of all its importance: History and the future were reduced to mere applications of universal essences, mere "cases"; only essences had any importance, not the world of their merely fortuitous applications; time was changed into an eternal return of "cases" already implicit in the essences. For long and unhappy centuries "Christian" theologians believed that the idea of eternal return could be separated from the rest of Greek philosophy. Today we are seeing that this conception of time permeates and conditions the whole of Greek philosophy; whatever elements of Greek philosophy are not colored by the notion of the eternal return have no real importance. The Platonic world of ideas was not a philosophic invention independent of the conception of history as eternal return. It was a way of assuring that the human mind reduced history to an eternal return. Christian theology adopted the Platonic world of ideas, stuffing into it other equally nontemporal notions. As a result, theology abandoned the history of real people to its wretched luck.

NOTES

1. Martin Heidegger, *Sein und Zeit* (Tübingen: Niemeyer, 1960), p. 19 [Eng. trans.: *Being and Time*, trans. John Macquarrie and Edward Robinson (New York: Harper & Row, 1962), p. 40].

2. Jean-Paul Sartre, *Critique de la raison dialectique* (Paris: Gallimard, 1960), 1: 19.

3. Jean Wahl, *Études kierkegaardiennes* (Paris: Vrin, 1949), p. 310 note.

4. Heidegger, *Sein und Zeit*, p. 336 [cf. Eng. trans.: *Being and Time*, p. 385].

5. J.-P. Sartre, *L'être et le néant* (Paris: Gallimard, 1943), p. 146 [cf. Eng. trans.: *Being and Nothingness*, trans. Hazel E. Barnes (New York: Citadel, 1968), p. 78].

6. Ibid., p. 249 [Eng. trans.: p. 174].

7. Ibid., p. 510 [Eng. trans.: p. 411].

8. Ibid., p. 510 [cf. Eng. trans.: pp. 410–11]; Sartre's emphasis.

9. Heidegger, *Sein und Zeit*, p. 19 [Eng. trans.: *Being and Time*, p. 40].

10. Ibid., p. 18 [Eng. trans.: p. 40].

11. Sartre, *L'être et le néant*, p. 251 [Eng. trans.: *Being and Nothingness*, p. 176].

12. Wahl, *Études kierkegaardiennes*, p. 296.

13. Ibid., p. 329.

14. Octavio Paz, *El laberinto de la soledad*, 7th ed. (Mexico City: Fondo de Cultura Económica, 1969), p. 189 [Eng. trans.: *The Labyrinth of Solitude*, trans. Lysander Kemp (New York: Grove Press, 1961), p. 210].

15. Wahl, *Études kierkegaardiennes*, p. 251.

16. Heidegger, *Sein und Zeit*, p. 324 [cf. Eng. trans.: *Being and Time*, p. 371].

17. Sartre, *L'être et le néant*, p. 242 [cf. Eng. trans.: *Being and Nothingness*, p. 169].

18. Theodor Zahn, *Das Evangelium des Matthäus*, 3rd. ed. (Leipzig: A. Deichert, 1910), p. 197.

19. Joachim Jeremias, "paradeisos," *TWNT*, 5:766–67 [Eng. trans.: *TDNT*, 5:769–70]; "hades," *TWNT*, 1:148–49 [Eng. trans.: *TDNT*, 1:148–49]; "geenna," *TWNT*, 1:655–56 [Eng. trans.: *TDNT*, 1:657–58]; *The Parables of Jesus* (New York: Scribner's, 1963), p. 185; Paul Hoffman, *Die Toten in Christus* (Münster: Aschendorff, 1966).

20. *Acta Apostolicas Sedis*, 1964, p. 716 [Eng. trans.: *Catholic Biblical Quarterly*, vol. 26, no. 3 (July 1964): 309].

21. Sartre, *L'être et le néant*, p. 249 [Eng. trans.: *Being and Nothingness*, p. 174].

22. Ibid., p. 173 [cf. Eng. trans.: p. 104]; Sartre's emphasis.

23. Ibid., p. 242 [cf. Eng. trans.: p. 169].

24. Emmanuel Levinas, *Totalité et Infini: Essai sur l'extériorité*, 2nd ed. (The Hague: Nijhoff, 1965), p. 191 [Eng. trans.: *Totality and Infinity: An Essay on Exteriority*, trans. Alphonso Lingis (Pittsburgh: Duquesne University Press, 1969), p. 216].

25. Ibid., p. 58 [Eng. trans.: p. 85].

26. Ibid., p. 59 [Eng. trans.: p. 86].

27. Paz, *Laberinto*, p. 129 [Eng. trans.: *Labyrinth*, p. 143]. The Plan of Ayala was promulgated by Emiliano Zapata in 1911; it called for an agrarian reform which, according to Paz, was patterned after the ancient system of land distribution.

28. Ibid., p. 132 [Eng. trans.: p. 147].

29. Ibid., p. 129 [Eng. trans.: p. 143].

30. Carlos Fuentes, *Tiempo mexicano* (Mexico City: Mortiz, 1971), p. 13.

31. Ibid., p. 131.

32. Paz, *Laberinto*, p. 63 [Eng. trans.: *Labyrinth*, p. 70].

33. Jorge Ibargüengoitia, in the Mexico City daily *Excelsior*, February 7, 1972.

34. Paz, *Laberinto*, pp. 78–79 [Eng. trans.: *Labyrinth*, p. 87].

35. Fuentes, *Tiempo mexicano*, p. 13.

36. Martin Heidegger, *Nietzsche* (Pfüllingen: Neske, 1961), 1:257.

Chapter 4

Truths and Imperatives

After reading Kierkegaard we still do not know if we are to seek contemporaneity with Christ by transporting ourselves into the past or by transporting Christ into the present. But even worse, either approach is illegitimate, for philosophy does not consist in wishful thinking. Conceptual prestidigitation and fantasy are of no help, for our task is not to manipulate time with our imaginations. Rather we are concerned with real time, which cannot be manipulated.

If in the final analysis Kierkegaard emerges as a "bard of the return," we must recognize that in this regard he strayed from one of his most basic intentions, namely, to refute Hegel. More important, he strayed from the peculiar realism of existentialist philosophy, which seeks to be and ought to be greater and more implacable than the realism of other philosophies. And in fact it is.

For a philosophy that claims to be concrete, only the present is truly real; the past and the future are ideas. Nothing we have said about the decisive importance of the messianic future can prevent the future from being a mere concept and not a reality for me at the present moment. And notwithstanding all of Kierkegaard's romanticizing about the period in which Christ lived, he is

71

unable to prevent the past from being nothing more than a concept for me at this moment.

Such concepts are very different from the reality that summons me and demands a decision of me, namely, the present. The past and the future are at any given moment categories that form part of the conceptual apparatus of the self. They are integral elements of our selves; they lack otherness, true otherness in the face of the self at the present instant. By contrast, the neighbor who speaks to me at this moment is real. He is not something "thought"; I cannot reassimilate him, making him part of my self.

Thus the experience of contemporaneity with Christ seems unattainable, at least by Kierkegaard's methods. Anticipating objections, I want to point out that existentialists are wrong if they think that they can prescind from this question. We must believe Kierkegaard when he says, "Everything I have written has tended toward describing contemporaneity adequately."[1]

CONTEMPORANEITY IN THE NEW TESTAMENT

But philosophers have not paid sufficient heed to the fact that neither Paul nor John was, strictly speaking, a contemporary of Christ. It is well known that Paul never met Jesus of Nazareth; it has been established that the author of the Fourth Gospel wrote in about 80 or 90 A.D. Nevertheless, the insistence with which both use the adverb "now" clearly identifies their own now with the now of Christ (Rom. 3:21, 26; 5:9, 11; 6:19, 21, 22; 7:6; 8:1, 22; 11:5, 30, 31; 13:11; 16:26; and in John 4:23; 5:25; 11:22; 12:27, 31a, 31b; 13:31, 36; 14:29; 15:22, 24; 16:5, 22, 29, 30; 17:5, 7, 13).

Simply as a historical datum, as a special phenomenon in the history of thought, this contemporaneity with Christ alleged (at least) by authors who were not his physical contemporaries ought to have been considered by *philosophy*—just as today studies are made of Descartes or Nicholas of Cusa or Parmenides. And the philosophers could have ascertained the truth of the allegation more accurately than the faithful, for the scientific mind is better equipped to do so. Philosophy's obligation is all the greater since, as we have seen, the intention of achieving contemporaneity with Christ was at the very origin of existentialism, and all indications are that the solution provided by the New Testament authors to the problem of contemporaneity with Christ is fresher and less imposed by an a priori philosophical system than any solution provided by our sophisticated philosophies of today.

To investigate the matter with scientific rigor, philosophy must employ the historical critical method, which is the method employed by modern exegesis. This method, to be sure, possesses greater scientific control than philosophy itself. Whether or not we adopt the solution that the New Testament authors give to the problem of contemporaneity is a subsequent question, open to resolution by any serious student of philosophy. But objectively to investigate the precise nature of their solution is a task to be carried out on the basis of demonstrable documentary evidence, which is the basis for the exegetical method. For philosophy and exegesis to collaborate in the same study should not constitute a serious objection at this point in the twentieth century. We seek truth by every means; the departmentalization of the sciences is one of the most challenged dogmas of our time. It is defended only by those specialists in one branch of knowledge who fear they might appear incompetent in another branch. The only proviso to our investigation is that methods cannot be mixed: Exegetical questions must be investigated with exegetical methods and philosophical questions resolved by philosophical methods.

BELIEVING AND LOVING

One requirement of exegetical methodology is that we not force biblical authors to deal with issues that were of no concern to them. We must not ask them questions that they did not ask themselves. Rather we must perceive the problems that concerned them and pursue our investigation in that direction. Our procedure must be clear. In this chapter we shall deal with a concrete biblical question that has been seen as such by various exegetes, independently of our philosophical question regarding contemporaneity. The philosophical problem will reappear on its own, only now in the framework of John's mentality and the questions raised by him. We have chosen a concrete problem in the work of John, for Johannine investigations have made the most marked advances in recent decades.

The question is this: Did John perceive a distinction between dogma and ethics or did he consider them to be the same? In other words, are believing and loving two things or one? What is the relationship between truths and imperatives? Two passages from John help us to pose the problem:

Anyone who listens to my word and *believes* in the one who sent me has eternal life and does not come to judgment, but *has already crossed over from death to life* (John 5:24).

We for our part *have crossed over from death to life;* this we know, because we *love* our brothers. The man who does not love is still in death (1 John 3:14).

All commentators have been struck by the occurrence in both passages of the expression "to have crossed over from death to life," *metabebeken (metabebekamen) ek tou thanatou eis ten zoen.* What does John mean by it? Does it consist in loving our neighbor or believing? According to John 5:24 it is believing; according to 1 John 3:14 it is loving our brothers. Which is it?

In his commentary on the Gospel of John, Lagrange emphasizes that John 5:24 "develops the Johannine doctrine par excellence," then he goes on to say, "The same wording occurs in 1 John 3:14, where charity replaces faith. Faith, as it is used in this verse, includes charity."[2]

This approach smacks of harmonism, which consists in juxtaposing, in affirming an "also," "both the one and the other." At least we tend to interpret it harmonistically—given the approaches to interpretation that we have inherited. In this case the harmonists would say that passing from death to life depends both on faith and on love of neighbor. But harmonistic exegesis and theology are always open to suspicion of superficiality: If we cannot see how one proposition relates to another, we simply avoid the issue by asserting both. The danger is that in so doing we may not have understood the meaning of either, for if we did understand them, we could see how they were related. If we do not understand, we can say that anything represents the thinking of John.

Lagrange seems to avoid harmonism and "alsoism," claiming that John includes charity in faith. But if he does not explain how love of neighbor is comprehended and included in faith, this is tantamount to asserting both very strongly, both faith and love, and we return again to alsoism.

The harmonistic interpretation is contradicted by John's wording of these two verses, for he provides clear signals of exclusivity, that is, he gives the clear impression that he does not believe it is a case of "both the one and the other." The exclusivistic, definitional intention is quite clear in 1 John 3:14. After he says that whoever loves his brother has passed from death to life, he adds the starkly illuminating converse: "The man who does not love is still in the realm of death." The strength of the verse lies in its affirmation that *only* he who loves his neighbor has passed from death to life. It is impossible to hold that the author of the text imagined the possibility of some other type of person (for example, "anyone who believes") who had *also* passed from death to life. His intention is clearly exclusionary.

By the same token, John 5:24 is equally definitional: *The one who believes* is the one who has passed from death to life and therefore no longer has to submit to final judgment. The illuminating converse need not be explicitly stated when an author is giving a definition, but in fact one is provided for us later in the same Gospel, in John 8:24b: "If you do not believe that I am what I am, *you will die* in your sins." And in 3:18 John says: "The man who believes in him does not come under judgment; but the one *who does not believe* has already been judged." Although statement and negative counterpart occur in different passages, it is incontrovertible that John is here telling us that passing from death to life consists in believing in Jesus Christ and does not consist in anything else.

But 1 John 3:14 asserts that passing from death to life means loving our brothers and nothing else; a harmonistic interpretation is thereby precluded on an exegetical level, for it does not correspond to the intention of the author whom we are trying to interpret.

This is the concrete biblical question; it exists independently of our philosophical problem of contemporaneity. The solution to this question provides the key to the First Epistle of John. Indeed, our understanding of the entire letter will depend on it. Both Boismard and de la Potterie have seen that according to the Epistle there are—apparently—two prerequisites to divine life: believing in Jesus Christ and loving our neighbor.[3] When John speaks of believing, its absolute importance is emphasized, as if loving did not exist; when he speaks of loving our neighbor, its significance is stressed as if faith did not exist. This juxtaposition recurs throughout the entire letter, and any interpretation which does not take it into account condemns itself to total superficiality.

In my opinion Boismard has taken a systematic analysis further than anyone else. He observes that the common element in eight especially emphatic and definitional passages of the letter (1 John 1:5–7; 2:3–6; 2:8–10; 2:29; 3:5–6; 4:7–8; 4:16; 4:11–12; to which we can add 5:13) is that they state who are those who truly possess divine life. This possession of divine life is designated in four different ways: to be born of God; to abide in God and God in us; to have communion with God; and to know God. The four expressions refer to the same reality. But when it comes to saying *who* possesses this reality, the letter—in a definitional way—sometimes says that it is those who love their neighbor and at other times that it is those who believe in Jesus Christ. The unequivocal *and exclusive* sign that someone possesses this divine and mysterious reality is . . . sometimes love of neighbor and other times New Testament faith! The reader's perplexity is thus total.

The question we have been considering is the central problem of the First Epistle, as shown by Schnackenburg's analysis of the formal structure of the Epistle. Besides a prologue (1 John 1:1–4) and an epilogue (1 John 5:13–21), the letter has three parts:

First part: 1:5–2:27
Second part: 2:28–4:6
Third part: 4:7–5:12

Keeping in mind that faith is Christological, that is, that the object of believing is Christ, we notice a striking pattern: The first part comprises an ethical thesis (1:5–2:17) and a Christological thesis (2:18–27); the second part likewise contains an ethical thesis (2:28–3:24) and a Christological one (4:1–6); and the third part, according to Schnackenburg, unites the two theses into love based on faith (4:7–21) and faith based on love of neighbor (5:1–12).

The nature of the relationship between Christological faith and brotherly love is not merely an exegete's question based on John's text; as the structure of the Epistle demonstrates, John raised the question himself—in a conscious and thematic way. As Bultmann says, "This unity of faith and love is the chief theme of 1 John—along with its polemic against false teachings."[4]

But the words "union" or "unity" or "unite" do not

accurately express John's thesis. Only in 1 John 3:23 are love of neighbor and faith mentioned in the same passage. Elsewhere in the Epistle some passages affirm brotherly love to be the sole and exclusive sign of divine life while others state faith in Jesus Christ to be the sole and exclusive sign. Speaking abstractly and formalistically, one is tempted to say that the Epistle's central thesis is that there is only one sign of divine life—whatever that sign may be. What that sign is cannot be resolved by "uniting" belief and love, by "conjoining" dogma and morality; rather it must be resolved by showing that Christological belief is *identical to* the imperative of love of neighbor.

"PURE TRUTHS"

Before attempting this resolution (and only then will the matter of contemporaneity reappear), let us rephrase the question in terms of present-day history.

Today the theologians of liberation are denouncing —from Latin America but for the whole world—the traditional distinction between dogmatic and moral theology. They believe that any truth that is not a moral imperative is alienating, for such a truth provides an alibi behind which people can evade the responsibility of ethical action. These theologians are not simply referring to doctrinal truths or teachings that deny our obligation to follow a particular course of action. They attack all allegedly pure truths, for these are characterized by an alienating idealism that distracts us from our responsibility to transform this world. Such truths are instruments of the status quo, not because they deny moral obligation or justify the world as it is, but because they constitute an ivory tower where the mind takes refuge from the imperative to struggle against the world as it is.

Whether by coincidence or design, the attack unleashed by the Latin American theologians of liberation against all dogmatics separated from ethics resembles Marx's attack on philosophy in his theses on Feuerbach: The point is not to interpret the world, but to change it. To the degree that philosophy attracts human energies toward contemplation of pure truths it serves as a defense of the status quo, for it diverts these energies from combatting the status quo. Even worse, to propound these "pure truths" is to assert an implicit, de facto affirmation that this world of cruelty and injustice is all right, that it is licit to dedicate oneself to contemplating truths, that no nonpostponable obligation exists to struggle to change this world.

The radicalness of Latin American theology undoubtedly seems excessive to European theologians. But the Bible is even more extreme. I second without reservation the denunciation of the separation between dogmatics and ethics. But I add that these "truths" are in fact falsehoods, and that they have been illegitimately deduced from the Bible by "the wisdom of this world" (in its most pejorative sense, as in 1 Cor. 2:6) to prevent the authentic biblical summons from reaching us. I base my rejection of "pure truths" not on Marx's theses on Feuerbach, but rather on the Bible itself, from which these truths are supposed to have been derived.

In reality, I challenge the status of theology itself, both dogmatic and moral. There can be many truths *in se*, millions of them, based on combinations and permutations among themselves. They can be as true as accurate calculations of the distance between Jupiter and Saturn. Theology's task, however, is not to enunciate truths but rather to proclaim the news called gospel. Theology ceases to speak in the name of Christ at the moment and to the degree that its truths or commandments proclaim something other than the great news, the decisive event that is the unique content of biblical evangelizing. Juridical considerations notwithstanding, only the one who proclaims and makes present what Jesus Christ proclaimed is able to be called the representative of Jesus Christ. The content is what matters. All else is excrescence, whose least damaging effect is to distract humankind from the news.

EMPIRICAL THEOLOGY

So-called "empirical theology," however, produces similar damage. It is absolutely true that one of theology's *functions* is empirical criticism, which must be undertaken when theology has understood the testimony of Christ, for Christ throws empirical reality into crisis. But, as Schmithals observes, "anyone who contrasts the empirico-critical *method* with the historico-critical *method* is concealing the fact that he is trying to replace the biblical testimony of Christ (which is the object of *all* theology and *all* method) with some other object," namely, empirical reality. The only legitimate object of Christian theology is the testimony of Jesus Christ. A theology that investigates some other object, for example, its social, economic, or political milieu, ends up being an "ideology no longer controlled by scientific thinking."[5]
I have no doubt that the Holy Spirit is working in the world of today and therefore is present in the reality that surrounds us. But opposing and irreconcilable ideologies invoke this same Spirit. If we do not by verifiable, scientific exegesis ascertain the meaning of the gospel message, then we have only an arbitrary choice between rival theologies; conservative theology has just as much right to call itself Christian as does revolutionary theology. Joachim Jeremias rightly says, "According to the testimony of the New Testament, the Logos made flesh is the revelation of God, only he. ...The thesis of continuous revelation is a gnostic heresy."[6] Only the historical Jesus can judge our differences and be measure of our theologies. And for us this Jesus is to be found in the Bible.

Empirical theology shares the antibiblical approach of European dogmatic theology, and it is equally escapist—though unwittingly—for it obscures the immeasurably subversive message of the gospel. Therefore our social revolutions are destined to engender new oppressions, for without the God of the Bible exploitation recurs spontaneously, even within the struggles undertaken to abolish it. Hugo Assmann is correct in recognizing that the theology of liberation is immensely deficient in Christology and in methodology.[7] But the result of both deficiencies is the same: to prescind from Jesus of Nazareth.

THE CONTINGENT CHRIST

The essential need to identify dogma with morality, truth with imperative, has its origin in the very preaching of Jesus, as we shall see. In the First Epistle of John this identification is obvious, even in the very structure of the letter. And this identification of truth with imperative is the basis of the new being discovered by existentialism,[8] the new field of being that demands our decision in order to be. Bearing in mind that New Testament "truths" are historical facts, we see the antecedent for the Marxist rejection of a separate treatment of morality and the Marxist insistence on facts.

It is significant that the two best known Catholic commentaries on the moral teaching of the New Testament, those of Spicq and Schnackenburg, each devote an entire first chapter to the sacred writers' awareness that they lived in the *eschaton*, the *ultimum*, the end of human history.[9] Spicq and Schnackenburg feel that this eschatological consciousness profoundly affects the moral teaching of the New Testament, although they fail to discover what effect it has. At first glance the following statement by Schnackenburg appears accurate:

Then the question is raised what the enduring lesson of this intense eschatological awareness of the early Church is for Christian morality. It cannot be simply set aside as a phenomenon due to temporary conditions or even as a dangerous apocalyptic tendency.[10]

Of course the eschatological consciousness found in the New Testament has been and continues to be considered or ignored by orthodoxy as a dangerous apocalyptic tendency. And there are no exceptions. Schnackenburg and Spicq unwittingly indicate the totally dependent relationship (or better yet, identification) between New Testament moral teaching and the only "truth" believed in the New Testament, namely, that with Jesus the *eschaton* has arrived. But their efforts fail because of their Greco-western presuppositions. In the paragraph cited above Schnackenburg attempts to extract "the enduring lesson," that is, the *nontemporal* lesson; and he supposes that "Christian morality" is a nontemporal set of ethical affirmations. As it is customarily posed, his question is tantamount to asking what remains, as a nontemporal and eternal residue, from a historical, contingent, tumultuous situation, localized in concrete time. What remains, Schnackenburg and Spicq answer (in order to avoid that nothing remain), is a consciousness of a *status viatoris*. It is a consciousness that we are not in heaven, a suitable state of mind to accompany moral actions in any period or circumstance, one more praiseworthy sentiment, a beautiful attitude contributed by the early Christian community to the eternal list of moral virtues and worthy sentiments. It is difficult to imagine a more complete castration of the New Testament message.

The contingency of revelation has always been repugnant to rationalism, the heir to the eternal truths and immutable essences of Greek philosophy. If the Greek intellectual heritage had been completely faithful to itself, it could have never called itself Christian,

that is, it could never have accepted as norm the historical event called Jesus Christ. But it devised a stratagem
whereby it could be at the same time Greek and (allegedly) Christian: It detemporalized Christ; it invoked
a heavenly, dehistoricized, eternal Christ—a Christ who
was very much God, as much as possible. From Christ's
contingent life it extracted only nontemporal examples,
eternal commandments, and detemporalized truths.
Once this maneuver was accomplished, history lost its
importance, for it lost its effect on the content of revelation or belief. The historical Jesus was reduced to an
irrelevant incident, almost a shadow, as Plato would
have considered him. What mattered were the eternal
truths—whose number Jesus incidently increased. Orthodox theology does not deny the historical humanity
of Christ (to do so would be formal docetism); it simply
disregards it. Orthodox theology is concerned with
Christ's eternal "human nature," but not with the contingent event of Christ in the world, nor with the fact
that Christ belongs totally to history. They do not
realize that this is a docetism much more extreme than
formal docetism.

On the other hand, the sole object of John's faith, its
sole "truth," is the contingent fact called Jesus Christ.
Only this conviction breaks the eternal return of all
things, and it is precisely this conviction that we find in
every New Testament author. But it is reduced to nothingness if we situate Christ outside history as a nontemporal being called "the Christ of faith." Paradoxically, the higher we raise Christ in his heaven and
minimize the contingent facts of his life and death at a
specific historical moment, the less chance we have of
revolutionizing human history. For by removing Christ
from history we condemn history again to its natural
pattern of the eternal return of all things. This is why
conservatives show no interest in the Bible, a lack of
interest very ill-advisedly shared by the theologians of

liberation. For without the Bible there is absolutely no basis for an identification of dogma with ethics, of truth with imperative.

THE KINGDOM HAS ARRIVED

John's moral teaching is a messianic morality, a morality of the *eschaton*, of the kingdom of God already achieved on earth. At the end of the Fourth Gospel, John says that the whole book was written "that you may believe that Jesus is the Messiah" (John 20:31). Note his description of the sole heresy: "Who is the liar? Who but he that denies that Jesus is the Messiah" (1 John 2:22). And in contrast: "Everyone who believes that Jesus is the Messiah is born of God" (1 John 5:1). Such is the content and object of faith: not a nontemporal truth or a doctrine, but rather *a fact*, namely, that Jesus of Nazareth, that man among men, is the very same Messiah anxiously awaited for generations. The first time he mentions this fact (John 1:41–45), John feels obliged to stress its contingency, indeed he takes delight in stressing it: "Can anything good come from Nazareth?" (John 1:46).

As Bultmann has noted, the primordial meaning of "to believe" is *to believe that . . .* , not *to believe in* (though the latter is preferred by nineteenth-century romanticism). We see this in the Fourth Gospel itself. John uses the term "to believe in" *(pisteuein eis)* thirty-four times, and yet he concludes by saying that the whole Gospel was written so that we might *believe that. . . .* The latter wording is appropriate for focusing on a historic fact as an object of belief: to believe that something happened. Bultmann correctly concludes, " 'To believe in . . . ' is thus to be regarded as an abbreviation which in the language of the mission became formal."[11] "To believe in Jesus Christ" is an abbreviated way of saying "to believe that Jesus is the Messiah."

Therefore, in the nine instances in John's First Epistle and in the ninety-eight instances in the Fourth Gospel in which the verb "to believe" occurs, the historical fact that Jesus is the Messiah is the sole object and content of that belief.

In the following chapters we shall explore the imperative sense of this truth-in-fact: that Jesus is the Messiah. For on this the whole problem of contemporaneity depends.

When Jesus himself spoke of "believing that . . . , " the object or truth to be believed was "that the time has been completed and the kingdom of God has arrived" (Mark 1:15). Jesus refers to the same fact as John, but John specifies that the coming of the kingdom is identical to the coming of Jesus as the Messiah. Elsewhere Jesus himself made this same identification: When John the Baptist sent disciples to ask if Jesus was the one to come or if they should continue to wait for another (Matt. 11:3; Luke 7:19), Jesus, describing his own works, repeated point for point the description of the kingdom found in innumerable passages of the Old Testament—including the resurrection of the dead (Matt. 11:4–6 and Luke 7:22–23).

The fact is the coming of the messianic kingdom, and for Mark the "good news," the gospel, consists in proclaiming this fact:

Jesus came into Galilee proclaiming the gospel of God: "The time has been completed; the kingdom of God has arrived; be converted and believe in the gospel" (Mark 1:14–15).

The wording is very careful, very deliberate. First he explicitly states the content, the meaning itself of the message called the great news or gospel (of God, of course, not of Jesus). Then he adds, "Be converted and believe in this message whose content I have just indicated." What grammatically seems to be a case of *believing in* turns out to be one of *believing that,* for he is referring to the fact that the time is completed and the kingdom has arrived. This is possibly the only instance in which Jesus himself uses the *verb* "to believe."

As Friedrich has shown, the Hebrew word corresponding to "gospel" or "good news" is a noun of action.[12] The term does not refer to the content of the news, but rather to the very fact of announcing it, of pronouncing it, of proclaiming it—to the act of evangelizing. Hearers of the proclamation had long known what the good news would be. They knew what the kingdom would be and what the gospel would be. Jesus' response to John the Baptist's question shows that people had no doubt about this. And the Baptist's very question asks only "already?" or "not yet?" The only important point was *the fact that* the kingdom should arrive, *the fact that* the arrival of the kingdom should be proclaimed. Not *what* it is, but *that* it is. As Friedrich says,

A new message is not expected with the dawn of God's kingdom. What will be proclaimed has been known from the time of Deutero-Isaiah. The longing is that it should be proclaimed. Hence [in contemporary literature], the messenger and the act of proclamation are much more important than the message. The new feature is not the content of the message, but the eschatological event. . . . Because all the emphasis is on the action, on the proclamation, on the utterance of the Word which ushers in the new age, *besorah* [message] is less prominent than *mebasser* [messenger, announcer, evangelizer] and *bisser* [to announce, to evangelize].[13]

Not *what*, but *that*. . . . According to Jesus and the New Testament authors this *fact that* the kingdom is arriving is the truth believed, the object of faith. Everyone knew that there was going to be a kingdom of God. Everyone knew that there had to be an *eschaton*. No one doubted that there had to be a Messiah. All that was easy to accept, for it belongs to the unreal realm of concepts. But that all this was really happening, that it was becoming present reality—that is what the Pharisees, the conservatives, the establishment refused to accept. Not *what*, but *that*. . . . The gospel's only content is a *that*. . . , not a *what*.

THE GOSPEL AS NEWS

Neither the theologians nor the exegetes are sufficiently aware that the gospel is news or it is nothing and that for the Greek mind there can be no news. News, *the* news, has no meaning at all for the Platonic mind. For such a mentality, "messianism" is not only an absurdity, but something worse: It is a word that it thinks it understands but in fact does not. The Platonic mind necessarily reduces the word "messiah" to an attribute, a nontemporal predicate among the other titles or names ascribed to Christ. The Greek mind turns a historical fact into an eternal truth. And then, of course, it is not an imperative. (Likewise, since the being of western ontology was nontemporal, Kant could distinguish between pure reason and practical reason.)

Thus Aristotle and the Scholastics had to have a "basis" for their moral teaching; they had to "demonstrate" the imperative, to deduce it from premises. But if the premises are an indicative statement, then the conclusion cannot be an imperative—without some intervening sophistry. And if a premise is an imperative, then it includes the imperative grounded in itself; it cannot be demonstrated because it is obligatory in and of itself.

Heidegger's words are especially applicable here: "The object we have taken as our theme is *artificially and dogmatically curtailed* if 'in the first instance' we restrict ourselves to a 'theoretical subject,' in order that we may then round it out 'on the practical side' by tacking on an 'ethic.' "[14] This existentialistic rejection of the distinction between truth and imperative derives precisely from the gospel, which proclaims *that* . . . , not *what*.

Let us consider the imperative sense of the truth-in-

fact that Jesus is the Messiah. For on this the whole
problem of contemporaneity depends. The "truth" announced by the gospel is a historical fact: the fact that
the kingdom has arrived, the fact that Jesus of
Nazareth is the Messiah. And if the messianic kingdom
consists in justice being done to all the poor of the earth,
then this fact is the most commanding and urgent imperative imaginable. There is not the slightest difference between love of neighbor and New Testament
faith—provided that we take this love of neighbor with
unreserved seriousness. The news is grammatically in
the indicative, but it is an indicative saying that the
time has come to enact the imperative of love of neighbor on a worldwide scale.

The Greek incapacity to accept any real news has
contaminated even exegesis, as we see in the tendency
to neutralize the verb *engiken* in Mark 1:15; Matt. 3:2;
4:17; 10:7; and Luke 10:9, 11. Above we translated this as
"has arrived," while the neutralizers would translate it
as "has drawn near." There are three arguments
against this evasive postponement.

First, Matthew Black's detailed linguistic study has
vindicated the philologist Joüon, who as early as 1927
with perfect security translated the term as "has
arrived."[15] Mark 1:15 has a surprising parallel in Lam.
4:18: "Our end has arrived *(engiken-karab)*, our days
have been completed because our time has come
(parestin-ba)." Black rightly observes that the term
must mean arrival, not approach. The elements common
to both of the passages, he notes, are—in addition to
engiken—the substantive *kairos* and the verb *pleroo* in
the passive voice ("to be filled," "to be completed"). A
similar idea is similarly expressed in Ezek. 7:6–7. The
neutralizers forget that the construction of Mark
1:15—"The time has been completed and the kingdom of
God has arrived"—implies that the events described are
either synonymous or consecutive (in other words the
"and" is either epexegetical or consecutive). In either
case, the "approach" of the kingdom is incompatible

with "the time has been completed." The paired clauses preclude interpreting *engiken* as "approach."

Second, although the procrastinators of the kingdom would eliminate Mark 1:15, nevertheless Matt. 12:28 and Luke 11:20 say the same thing using the verb *ephthasen;* the latter cannot be interpreted as approach, but rather must be translated as "the kingdom *has arrived* to you." Why, then this great resistance to Mark 1:15?

The third reason is conclusive and central. Mark 1:15 explicitly intends to give us the text and formulation itself of *the news.* It was not news to say that the *eschaton* had drawn near. Abel could have said it, comparing his own time to Adam's; any generation was nearer than its predecessors to the *eschaton.* The ordinary passage of time accounted for the drawing near of the *eschaton.* The neutralizers would make Jesus into a madman, for their translation has him proclaiming the most common knowledge as great news—and proclaiming it with a passion unique in history. They thereby show that they are not really concerned about the historical Jesus.

Behind the neutralist exegesis is the desire to postpone the *eschaton* indefinitely. The Pharisee, says Oscar Schmitz, takes upon himself the task of preventing anything, even the Messiah, from becoming real. And he does this while scrupulously accepting all of the dogmas—provided that they remain as concepts, that is, provided that they are not realized.

Not every historical fact constitutes a "truth" that can be identified with imperative, only the historical fact of the *eschaton.* The new being discovered by existentialism ceases to demand decision and resembles the neutral being of ontology the moment it is divorced from the historical fact called Jesus Christ. The historical facts that Marx invokes could not unseat idealistic, Platonic morality if they were not messianic. Only eschatological time summons us with a "that. . . . " Other times do not constitute news; they are times with no special importance: They are simply any time. When the *eschaton* is denied, time becomes "any time," and history reverts to the eternal return.

NOTES

1. Cited by Jean Wahl, *Études kierkergaardiennes* (Paris: Vrin, 1949), p. 296.

2. M.-J. Lagrange, *Évangile selon Saint Jean*, 3rd ed. (Paris: Gabalda, 1927), p. 146.

3. M.-E. Boismard, "La connaissance de Dieu dans l'Alliance Nouvelle d'après la première lettre de Saint Jean," *Revue Biblique* 56, no. 3 (July 1949): 365–91; Ignace de la Potterie, *Adnotationes in exegesim Primae Epistulae s. Ioannis*, 2nd ed. (Rome: Pontificio Istituto Biblico, 1966–67), mimeographed.

4. Rudolf Bultmann, *Theologie des Neuen Testaments*, 2nd ed. (Tübingen: Mohr, 1954), p. 428 [Eng. trans.: *Theology of the New Testament*, trans. Kendrick Grobel (New York: Scribner's, 1970), 2:81].

5. Walter Schmithals, *Evangelische Kommentare* 8 (1969), pp. 451–52.

6. Cited by Ernst Käsemann in *Evangelische Versuche und Gesinnungen*, 5th ed. (Göttingen: Vandenhoeck, 1967), 2:38.

7. Hugo Assmann, *Teología desde la praxis de la liberación* (Salamanca: Sígueme, 1973), pp. 100–02 [in English see *Theology for a Nomad Church* (Maryknoll, New York: Orbis Books, 1976), pp. 103–05].

8. See above, chap. 1.

9. Ceslaus Spicq, *Théologie morale du nouveau testament* (Paris: Gabalda, 1965); Rudolf Schnackenburg, *The Moral Teaching of the New Testament* (New York: Herder and Herder, 1964).

10. Schnackenburg, ibid., p. 195.

11. Bultmann, "pistis," *TWNT*, 6:204 [cf. Eng. trans.: *TDNT*, 6:203–04].

12. Gerhard Friedrich, "euangelizomai," *TWNT*, 2:705–35 [Eng. trans.: *TDNT*, 2:707–37].

13. Ibid., *TWNT*, p. 723 [cf. Eng. trans.: *TDNT*, p. 726].

14. Martin Heidegger, *Sein und Zeit* (Tübingen: Niemeyer, 1960), p. 316 [Eng. trans.: *Being and Time*, trans. John Macquarrie and Edward Robinson (New York: Harper & Row, 1962), pp. 363–64].

15. Matthew Black, *An Aramaic Approach to the Gospels and Acts*, 3rd ed. (Oxford: Clarendon, 1967), pp. 208–11; Paul Joüon, "Notes philologiques sur les Evangiles," *Recherches de Science Religieuse* 17 (1927), pp. 537–40.

Chapter 5

The Gospel Genre

At the Last Supper the "new commandment" was formulated as love of neighbor (see John 13:34). The First
Epistle of John says of it:

It is a new commandment that I am giving you, . . . *because* the
darkness is passing and the true light already shines (1 John
2:8).

In this passage John declares the presence of the
eschaton to be the reason for the commandment. As
Bultmann observes, the fact that the true light already
shines "serves as the basis for the commandment."[1] The
Catholic commentators Michl, Schnackenburg, and de
la Potterie, as well as the Protestants Bultmann and
Schneider, indeed all the renditions I have seen, translate the word *hoti* as "because."[2] De la Potterie states
explicitly that *hoti* is causal. It is also grammatically
possible for *hoti* to be recitative, in which case the remainder of the sentence would state the content of the
commandment. But Schnackenburg correctly rejects
this possibility, pointing out that the remainder of the
sentence "has nothing to do with commandment."[3]

But then we are faced with a very important datum:
The reason for the commandment in which God reveals
himself is precisely that the messianic *eschaton* has already arrived. The unavoidable implication is that ex-

cept for the historical, contingent event of Christ there would be no reason for the commandment of love of neighbor, that without Jesus of Nazareth God could not reveal himself. The fact or historical truth that we considered in the last chapter turns out to be the sole basis of the imperative.

In spite of the mental jugglery of those having no respect for real time, everything leads us to believe that we can be contemporaneous with Christ only in the *eschaton*. (An eternal, *non*temporary point, cannot be *con*temporary to anyone.)

The problem we have been considering is this: How and why can the author of the Fourth Gospel and the First Epistle of John feel that he is—and indeed be— contemporary with Christ, since he knew as well as we that he was writing a half century after Christ's crucifixion and death? The problem is an exegetical one, thus involving questions much broader and partially different than those that are today customarily asked in philosophy. This may seem to be a disadvantage. But, on the one hand, there are the obvious advantages of objectivity and verifiability in analyzing thinking that has already been done and documented, that is not subject to our preconceptions and therefore can tell us something we did not already know. And, on the other hand, since we are dealing with time and being itself, which are the most basic questions in philosophy, we are more than justified in again posing our problem of contemporaneity in terms very different and much broader than those to which philosophy is accustomed. For it is possible that precisely these new dimensions will provide us with the elements needed for the solution.

With regard to exegesis itself, we have already seen that the meaning of John's entire message is involved in this question of contemporaneity. Therefore, as we come to understand contemporaneity, other particular exegetical problems may be answered for us as well.

To broaden the dimensions of the problem of John's

contemporaneity with Christ, we will deal with a datum from John's prologue that seems heretofore to have been insufficiently emphasized. Then we shall consider the implications of the very existence of a prologue, which is the key to understanding the literary genre of gospel. In the Gospel of John the prologue has special importance.

"BORN OF GOD"

John's prologue differentiates between those who did not receive or accept the word (John 1:11) and those who did indeed receive it and "believed in his name" (John 1:12). The latter, it goes on to explain, are "those not born of any human stock, or by the fleshly desire of a human father, but they who had been born of God" (John 1:13). In his thorough monograph on the prologue, Feuillet comments, "Only those who have been born of God are able to take this step and so believe in the Logos."[4]

The importance of John 1:13 lies in this: In the prologue, before the detailed, scene-by-scene narration of the rejection of Christ by the majority of Israelites and acceptance by the few, the Gospel attempts—in thesis form—to explain why some believed and others did not. Authors of closely reasoned, difficult works frequently write the prologue last. Feuillet even suggests that the Gospel prologue was written after John's First Epistle.[5] The entire prologue, and John 1:13 in particular, seems to be a subsequent reflection on the events described in the Gospel, an attempt to grasp and explain the true meaning and scope of those events. Therefore the theme of this verse and the question raised above in our chapter 4 must be closely connected.

If, according to John, some believe in Jesus Christ and some do not because the former have been born of God, then it is incumbent on us to ask what it means "to be born of God." Moreover, the passage suggests that being "born of God" was a notion more familiar than "accepting Christ," for John uses the former term to clarify the meaning of the latter. If "born of God" was not a recognized theological term, then it was at least an expression well known among those to whom the Gospel was addressed.

In fact, "to be born of God" and "to be children of God" (interchangeable expressions, as we see in 1 John 3:9–10; 1 John 2:29–3:1; and the pericope 1 John 5:1–2) have a specific meaning for John and throughout the New Testament. If this specific meaning explains the historical enigma of *why* some have believed in Jesus Christ and some have not, then John 1:12, 13 becomes one of the most important theses in the Bible. Although overlooked by theology and tradition, it becomes a crucially important explanation of historical events. Therefore, before we evaluate John's thesis and consider what "the word" might mean, we must exegetically define "to be born of God" or "to be children of God" or "to be of (*ek*) God" (the preposition *ek* designates origin: to proceed from God).

Everyone who does justice is born of God (1 John 2:29).

Everyone who loves is born of God (1 John 4:7).

That is the distinction between the children of God and the children of the devil: Anyone who does not do justice is not of God, nor is anyone who does not love his brother (1 John 3:10).

My dear friend, do not imitate bad examples, but good ones; the one who does good is of (*ek*) God (3 John 11).

Clearly, John's intention in these expressions is to define. To love one's neighbor and to do justice are not acts that might be incidentally performed by one who is "born of God." They are acts that distinguish one who is born of God from one who is not. The author's intention is to demarcate, to define.

Note that John—like all other biblical authors[6]— identifies loving one's neighbor with doing justice. Love of neighbor had not yet degenerated into the romantic and allegedly impartial sentiment that the West made of it, a love that under the guise of universality claims to embrace rich and poor equally. John's love is love of the deprived, the poor, the needy. Therefore it is identified with justice, an identification demonstrated in 1 John 3:17–18:

If a man has enough to live on, and yet when he sees his brother in need shuts up his heart against him, how can it be said that the love of God dwells in him? My children, love must not be a matter of words or talk; it must be genuine, and show itself in action.

Jesus himself defined precisely what it means "to be children of God": After telling us to "love your enemies" (Luke 6:35), he says in apodosis: "and you will be children of the Most High, because he himself is kind to the ungrateful and the wicked" (Luke 6:35b). And he goes on to recapitulate: "Be compassionate as your Father is compassionate" (Luke 6:36). That is what it means to be children of God. Matthew understood this thought perfectly: "Love your enemies and pray for your persecutors; only so can you be children of your heavenly Father" (Matt. 5:44–45). "Blessed are the peacemakers, for they shall be called children of God" (Matt. 5:9).[7] Keeping in mind that "good works" is a technical term, we find the same teaching in Matt. 5:16: "And you, like the lamp, must shed light among your fellows, so that, when they see the good works you do, they may glorify your Father in heaven." The sense of this passage is reduplicative: It means that when they see your good works your fellows will recognize God as your Father, they will know that you are children of God.

This definition of "to be born of God" or "to be children of God" did not, as we have seen, originate with John but was well known in his time. It makes John's explanation of the historical fact that some believed in Jesus Christ and others did not (John 1:12–13) particularly unsettling: Only those who loved their neighbor, who hungered and thirsted for justice, were able to understand "the word."

GOOD WORKS AND EVIL WORKS

If a thesis of such vast import appears in the prologue, then it should reappear in some form throughout the Gospel itself; otherwise the prologue is not really a prologue. We must demonstrate that the thesis does so recur.

John records the following passage—John 3:18–21—as Jesus' own words:

(18) Anyone who believes in him does not come under judgement. Anyone who does not believe has already been judged, for he has not believed in the name of God's only Son. (19) And this is the judgment: The light has come into the world but men loved darkness more than the light, *because their works were evil.* (20) For anyone who *does evil* hates the light and avoids it so that his works might not be denounced; (21) but anyone who does the truth comes to the light so that it may be clearly seen that his works are done in God.

This passage comes at the end of Jesus' conversation with Nicodemus. If these words are related to the preceding conversation, Jesus was simply explaining to Nicodemus that the teachers and Pharisees were typical of those whose evil works prevented their belief in him. If, on the other hand, this is a "free-floating" kerygmatic passage, as Schnackenburg holds,[8] then it has the same universal scope as John 1:12–13.

The most remarkable statement in John 3:18–21 is, of course, the assertion—repeated several times in the Fourth Gospel—that the Last Judgment takes place during the temporal lifetime of the historical Jesus and in relation to Jesus himself. But in the present context our first concern is to know why those people who had "already been judged" refused to believe in Jesus Christ. John tells us why explicitly: because their works were evil. In our traditional escapist fashion we tend to interpret this phrase generally, nonspecifically, making it into a catch-all for whatever behavior western morality deems bad. But there is clear and abundant biblical and extrabiblical evidence that, in the cultural milieu of the New Testament, "good works" (*kala erga, agatha erga*) and "evil works" (*phaula erga, ponera erga*) were specialized, definitional terms with precise and limited meanings.

Walter Grundmann, one of the scholars who has most adequately dealt with this matter, tells us:

> Good works are actions of mercy on behalf of all those in need of them, and they are works of peacemaking that eliminate discord among people. This is sufficiently documented by Matt. 25:31–46 and Matt. 5:38–48; it is confirmed by the concept of "good works" in Jewish literature.[9]

Strack and Billerbeck, who have also dealt exhaustively with this subject,[10] have shown conclusively that "good works" and "evil works" are strict technical terms in biblical and extrabiblical Jewish literature (see, for example, Isa. 58:6–7; 1 Tim. 5:10, 25; 6:18; Tit. 2:7, 14; 3:8, 14; 1 Tim. 3:1; 2:10; 5:10a, 10b, 25; 6:18; 2 Tim. 2:21; 3:17; Eph. 2:10; Col. 1:10; 2 Thess. 2:17; Matt. 5:16; Mark 3:4; Acts 10:38; Tit. 1:16; 2:14; 3:1, 8, 14; 2 Cor. 9:8; Rom. 13:3; Mic. 6:8; etc.). Perhaps the most interesting analysis is that of Joachim Jeremias.[11] He shows that the "good works" are most specifically defined—by examples—in Matt. 25:31–46: "Good works" consist in giving food to the hungry, drink to the thirsty, etc. Burying the dead, customarily included in the list, is surprisingly omitted by Matthew, perhaps because he is concerned exclusively with the living or perhaps because Jesus had said: "Leave the dead to bury their dead" (Matt. 8:22).

Matt. 25:31–46 is the only description of the Last Judgment in the New Testament, and in this passage the only criterion of judgment is stated to be good or evil works. We can assume that this criterion was accepted by all New Testament authors; there is much evidence to corroborate our assumption (Rom. 2:5–12, for example), and none to contradict it.[12] Therefore it is not extraordinary that John (3:18–21) employs the same criterion. John says that this judgment is realized during the historical lifetime of Jesus and in relation to him, but the decision depends on the human disposition to do "good works" or not do them. John supposes and utilizes the only criterion for who is to be saved and who is to be condemned that we find in the New Testament.

The unsettling thesis of the prologue (John 1:13) is restated with full force in the main body of the Gospel (John 3:18–21). Bultmann says of this passage, "In the decision of faith or unbelief it becomes apparent what man really is."[13] Bultmann is right: John is not dealing with the question of pure exteriority of works (cf. 1 Cor. 13:3); rather "what man really is" depends on the disposition (or lack of it) to do "good works," to do good to one's neighbor. John believes that this disposition is what defines a person's being, and that this being is what becomes manifest in the presence of Christ. In other words, one's disposition to do "good works" determines what one "really is," and this in turn determines whether one accepts or rejects Christ.

There is another passage in the main body of the Gospel in which the thesis introduced in John 1:13 reappears. This is John 7:1–9, from which we transcribe only Jesus' answer to his relatives who were urging him to go up to Jerusalem for the feast:

(6) My time [*kairos*] has not yet come, but your time is always at hand. (7) The world cannot hate you; but it hates me *because I give testimony that its works are evil*. (8) Go to the festival yourselves; I am not going up to this festival because my time has not yet come.

In John 3:20 we were told that anyone who does evil works hates the light. In 7:7 John uses for the second time the verb *misein* ("abhor," "hate") to tell us of the hatred that "the world" has for Christ. We hear it repeated in Christ's conversation during the Last Supper (John 15:18, 19, 23, 24, 25; 17:14). John 7:7 is important because it explicitly tells us *why* the world hates Christ: "because I give testimony that its works are evil." The world did not believe in Jesus Christ because it hates him, and it hates him because he testifies that its actions are antithetical to giving food to the hungry, drink to the thirsty, clothes to the naked, a home to the homeless. Most of us find it more comfortable to attribute the world's rejection of Christ to "irreligiosity," "worldliness," "sin," "immorality"—all taken in the broadest, vaguest, and most undetermined possible sense. But "good works" and "evil works" are technical terms with a highly exact meaning.

Western theology occasionally (although grudgingly) recognizes that the God of the Old Testament is anything but neutral toward social injustices, that, on the contrary, he is terribly partial toward the poor and the needy. But theologians often attribute this to some alleged imperfection inherent in the revelation of the Old Testament. Yet John, the most "spiritual" of the New Testament authors, explains the world's incredulity toward Jesus Christ by its denial of food to the hungry and drink to the thirsty.

If the world's inability to believe in Jesus Christ proceeds, as John says it does, from its "evil works" (understood in the strict sense of the technical term), then the purpose of Christ's mission in history is completely different from what we have for centuries believed. Christ's mission is not "related to" good works; rather it consists in good works, which is a very different matter.

Recent discoveries, such as the Qumran scrolls, have emphasized dramatically how antithetical John's message is to "religious" Christianity, how it opposes and challenges it. As early as 1954 Bultmann, despite his well-known antipathy toward Qumranic parallels, wrote: " 'Walking in the light' gets a more precise definition in 1 John 2:9–11; it is 'to love one's brother.' "[14] And in 1961 Boismard made explicit the implications of the similarity between John and the Qumran scrolls. Commenting on John 3:18–21, he said, "This dualism is distinguished from gnostic dualism by the fact that it is not physical, but rather essentially moral: the dominion of light and truth is that of good works, accomplished in accord with the will of God; the dominion of darkness and evil is that of evil works."[15] The antithesis between "religious" Christianity and Christ's purpose was plain without the Qumran scrolls, but we were prevented from seeing it by the world's desperate denial of the true meanings of "good works" and "evil works."

The whole Gospel of John, considered as a unified literary composition, corroborates the thesis stated in the prologue: that it was those "born of God" who could accept Christ. At the same time, our study of John 1:13, John 3:18–21, and John 7:6–8 has enlarged and clarified for us what it means to be "born of God."

THE WORLD

Verse 10 of the prologue, as well as John 3:18–21 and John 7:6–8, speaks of "the world" as subject of the ignorance, hatred, and rejection whose object is Jesus. What is "the world"? Of whom does it consist? As various commentators have pointed out, "the world" is used by John in three different senses.[16]

First and least significantly, "the world" means more or less what we call the universe, the sum total of everything that exists. For example, "before the creation of the world" (John 17:24) or "the world could not hold the books that would be written" (John 21:25).

Second, "the world" is the stage on which human history is enacted, the earth as humanity's habitation. For example, "they are still in the world, and I am on my way to you" (John 17:11) or "the goods of this world" (1 John 3:17); see also John 16:21; 13:1.

The third meaning of "the world" is humankind. When John speaks of the world's covetousness (1 John 2:17) or says that the world hates (John 15:18–19) or affirms that Christ came to save the world (John 3:16–17), he is using the world to mean humankind.[17]

But this third meaning contains an apparent contradiction or ambiguity, hitherto overlooked by scholars, that we must clarify. Using "the world" to denote humankind, John presents two series of affirmations that seem mutually contradictory:

Series A: John 1:10c; 7:7; 12:31; 14:17, 30; 15:18–19; 16:11, 33; 17:14; 1 John 2:15–17; 3:13; 5:4–5, 19.

Series B: John 1:29; 3:16–17, 19; 4:42; 6:33, 51; 8:12; 9:5; 12:46–47; 1 John 2:2; 4:14.

The world of Series A is to be vanquished; it is evil, characterized by passions like hatred and covetousness; it must end. As van den Bussche says, "The world is not, according to John, an impersonal reality; it is diabolical. It is the incarnation of Satan (John 12:31; 14:30; 16:11)."[18]

But "the world" of Series B must and will be saved. Sin will be "taken away" from "the world" (John 1:29).

I see no way of resolving this contradiction except by making the following assumption: that the humankind of Series A statements is characterized, both in each individual and in societal relations, by an organization and structure from which it has been liberated in Series B statements. As Barrett says, *"ho kosmos outos* is the whole organized state of human society, secular and religious."[19]

The modern word "civilization" provides a rough equivalent of John's pejorative use of "the world": both refer to the sum total of the ways in which people function within and among themselves. John's pejorative "world," like the "civilization" of Freud and Marcuse, is neither an abstraction nor a universal but a supra-individual and eminently concrete reality that clearly refers to all of civilization and not only to any one civilization in particular.

Bultmann concludes exegetically that the term refers to "the way men are closed against God—a closure indeed that becomes a power ruling the individual, precisely as the 'world' to which every man intrinsically belongs and which he jointly constitutes in his individual closure."[20] Unless we understand "the world" in the pejorative sense (Series A) as civilization, it is impossible to reconcile the affirmations in Series A that the world must be overcome and end with the affirmations in Series B that the world must be saved. "The world" in Series B is humankind liberated from sinful civilization.

THE HOUR OF DEATH

Having discovered what is meant by "the world," we can begin to analyze what is meant by Jesus' saying that the world hates him "because I give testimony that its works are evil" (John 7:6–8). Clearly this is an important thesis, for it is reiterated throughout the Gospel of John, not merely by isolated passages, but by the whole Gospel as a compositional unity.

Barrett points out that "my time," in the phrase "my time [kairos] has not yet come " (John 7:8), cannot be distinguished from the more common Johannine expression "my hour."[21] The parallel with "my hour has not yet come" (John 2:4) is particularly clear: In both scenes (2:1–11 and 7:1–10) Jesus uses the phrase to reject a request or suggestion made to him by relatives, and in both scenes, after rejecting the petition, he in fact proceeds to do what was suggested (John 2:7–11 and 7:10). The common structure of the two scenes is striking. As van den Bussche has emphatically pointed out, Jesus' hour—first imminent and then present—is the unifying thread of the Fourth Gospel (John 2:4; 4:21, 23; 5:25, 28–29; 7:6, 8, 30; 8:20; 12:23, 27; 13:1; 16:25, 32; 17:1).

The Gospel makes abundantly clear that Jesus' "hour" is the hour of his death. Twice John tells us that the Jews wished to seize Jesus in order to kill him (John 7:19, 25) and then he expressly states, "They tried to seize him, but no one laid a hand on him because his hour had not yet come" (John 7:30). We find the same meaning in John 8:20: "These words were spoken by Jesus in the treasury as he taught in the temple. Yet no one arrested him, because his hour had not yet come." And when the narrative reaches the time of Jesus' passion, John 13:1 calls it "his hour": "Jesus knew that his hour had come and he must leave this world and go to the Father." Likewise John 17:1: "Father, the hour has come. Glorify your Son, that your Son may glorify thee." "The hour" is used in the same sense in Jesus' premonition (John 12:23–24), which in the Fourth Gospel replaces the prayer in the garden of the Synoptic Gospels:

The hour has come for the Son of man to be glorified. In truth, in very truth I tell you, a grain of wheat remains a solitary grain unless it falls into the ground and dies; but if it dies, it bears a rich harvest.

Only if Christ's "hour" or *kairos* is the hour of his death does his explanation (John 7:1–9) of his reluctance to go up to Jerusalem make sense: "My *kairos* has still not come." If *kairos* does not mean "hour of death," then the causal connections stated in John 7:6–9 are in fact meaningless.

"My hour," then, means "the hour of my death" wherever it appears in the Fourth Gospel. Therefore, when Jesus at Cana replied to his mother, "What do you want with me, woman? My hour has not yet come" (John 2:4), he must even then have been referring to the hour of his death, regardless of the fact that it was still far in the future. Barrett says, "It is unthinkable that in this verse 'hour' should have a different meaning,"[22] and his opinion is especially convincing because in his commentary he is not ready to extract the brutal consequences of this interpretation for the Fourth Gospel as a whole.

If such is the meaning of "hour," then it was Jesus' miracles or "good works" that provoked the aggressive hatred of the world incarnate in the Jews. His testimony that the world's works are evil consists of his own "good works." This interpretation is irrefutably reinforced by John 10:32: "I have set before you many good deeds, done by my Father's power; for which of these would you stone me?"

All of Jesus' miracles are "good works" in the sense of the term we have indicated. If these good works put Jesus in danger of death, then we can understand his reluctance to grant his mother's petition at Cana to do the first miracle in the series that would lead to the cross. John emphasizes that this was Jesus' very first miracle (John 2:11); with it Jesus kindled the world's murderous hatred. It is hardly strange that he was loathe to begin that fatal concatenation. That is the explanation of John 2:4, which has always been a *crux interpretum*.

Our explanation is corroborated by the first part of Jesus' answer to his mother: *ti emoi kai soi,* meaning "What do you want with me?" or "What do you have against me?" This same formula is spoken repeatedly in the Old and New Testaments (Judg. 11:12; 2 Sam. 16:10; 19:23; 1 Kings 17:18; 2 Kings 3:13; 2 Chron. 35:21; Mark 1:24; 5:7; Matt. 8:29; Luke 4:34; 8:28), and is invariably addressed to someone who represents a threat or a danger to the speaker. In the Synoptics the formula is used only by evil spirits threatened by the presence of Jesus. In Judg. 11:12 Jephthah sends a mission to the king of Ammon to ask, "What do you have against me that makes you come to attack me in my own country?" David (2 Sam. 19:23) asks: "What do you have against me, sons of Zeruiah, that you have today become my adversaries?" (Compare this with 2 Sam. 16:10.) In 1

Kings 17:18 the woman of Zarephath says to Elijah: "What do you have against me, you man of God? Have you come here to bring my sins to light and kill my son?" In 2 Kings it is clear that Elisha has much to fear from the son of Ahab and Jezebel, the implacable enemies of his teacher Elijah. In 2 Chronicles Necho addresses the formula to Josiah, who comes to wage war on him at Carchemish.

The second part of Jesus' reply to his mother, the aloof vocative "woman," sustains the tone of the first part. Schnackenburg comments that it is "impossible to deny that Jesus holds himself aloof from his mother (and her request) to some extent."[23] After so many centuries of tiresome, convoluted mariological equivocations,[24] such an admission by a Catholic exegete is valuable indeed, especially considering that Schnackenburg himself does not provide an interpretation of the verse that really explains this aloofness. In the context of our understanding—that the formula "What do you want with me?" is spoken only to someone who is wittingly or unwittingly endangering the speaker—the aloof vocative "woman" is understandable and perfectly appropriate.

After recounting the miracle at Cana, which initiated the series of "good works" that aroused the world's hatred and led to the cross, John deliberately reminds us that this was Jesus' first miracle. Therefore it is not surprising that John should also tell us explicitly that the last miracle (the resuscitation of Lazarus, John 11) resulted in the Jews' definitive decision to kill Jesus (John 11:45–54): "From that day on they plotted his death" (v. 53).

Thus Barrett is correct when he describes Jesus' reaction to Lazarus' death as "shaking with anger" (the verb *embrimasthai* in John 11:33 and 38). Barrett refers to Dan. 11:30, Lam. 2:6, Mark 1:43, and Matt. 9:30, where the same word unequivocally means "to shake with anger." Barrett comments on Jesus' reactions: "This miracle it will be impossible to hide (cf. vv. 28, 30); and this miracle, Jesus perceives, will be the immediate occasion of his death (vv. 49–53)."[25] Such an interpretation is confirmed by the expression "he was in turmoil" (*etaraxen heauton*), which in John 11:33, as well as in John 14:1, 27; 12:27; and 13:21, always describes turmoil due to fear, and in the last two passages cited means turmoil due to fear specifically of death.

The verb *embrimasthai* (John 11:33, 38) is also used by Mark (1:43) and Matthew (9:30) in recounting Jesus' puzzling prohibition against making his miracles known. This prohibition, the famous "messianic secret," according to Wrede and Minette de Tillesse, constitutes the interpretive key to Mark's Gospel.[26] The reason for this otherwise inexplicable prohibition (expressed in Mark 1:25, 34, 44; 3:12; 5:43; 7:24, 36; 8:30; 9:9, 30; and parallel passages) is supplied by John's thesis that Jesus' "good works" aroused the murderous hatred of the Jews and that Jesus knew it. That is the reason Jesus wished to keep his "good works" from becoming common knowledge; the "messianic secret" resulted from his fear of death. Even when he accepted his death, Jesus did all he could to avoid being killed before faith had taken root in the world. The "messianic secret" was a wholly human response to fear of death.

Lest this explanation of Mark's Gospel by the use of John's seem arbitrary and unwarranted, note the first time that the term "to do good" (a definitional term equivalent to "good work") appears in Mark:

On another occasion when he went to synagogue, there was a man in the congregation who had a withered arm; and they were watching to see whether Jesus would cure him on the Sabbath, so that they could bring a charge against him. He said to the man with the withered arm, "Come and stand out here." Then he turned to them: "Is it permitted to do good rather than evil on the Sabbath, to save life rather than kill?" They had nothing to say; and, looking round at them with anger and sorrow at the hardness of their hearts, he said to the man, "Stretch out your arm." He stretched it out and his arm was restored. But the Pharisees, on leaving the synagogue, began plotting against him with the partisans of Herod to see how they could kill him (Mark 3:1–6).

Mark's intention is clearly to contrast "to do good" and "to do evil" and then immediately to emphasize that the Jews decided to kill Jesus for "doing good." It is crucial to recall that this miracle occurs early in Mark's redaction just as the miracle at Cana does in John's. It occurs in Mark after seventy-nine verses; in John after sixty-two. Taylor comments that the Marcan passage "has dramatic appropriateness at so early a point. Like a dark cloud the death of Jesus hangs over the further course of His ministry."[27] Cranfield hypothesizes that "it is intrinsically likely that the intention of his opponents to bring about his death developed quite early in the course of [his ministry]."[28] The reluctance of some exegetes to admit that "my hour" in John 2:4 is the hour of death derives from their failure to grasp the essence of the literary genre of Gospel.

THE COMPOSITIONAL UNITY OF THE GOSPEL GENRE

Let us keep in mind that the creator of this genre was Mark, and that, according to Kahler's analysis, Mark's Gospel consists in a long introduction followed by the passion and death of Jesus. Structurally, Kahler's thesis may be exaggerated, but it contains a more accurate intuition into the idea that generated the Marcan work than might be supposed. It indicates that the very genesis of Mark's Gospel—as well as that of its three imitations or amplifications, the Gospels of Matthew, Luke, and John—is the idea of causal connection between Jesus' life of "good works" and his death. Without this originative conception the account of Jesus' life and the account of his death are linked only incidentally by their subject; the second is not a necessary sequel to the first.

Jesus's life, consisting in "good works," is intrinsically linked to his death by the world's hate-filled reaction, which he anticipated, to those "good works." John had more time than Mark to consider his purposes in writing; perhaps that is why his work expresses more clearly and explicitly this germinal and central idea of the literary genre that has come to us as gospel.

As van den Bussche has observed, the narrative structure of John 2–12 is a perfect arch. What follows John 12 is the hour of the passion and death. As we have indicated, John's account of Jesus' life is structured by frequent premonitions of "the hour" and by reflections on the nature and meaning of "good works" (John 1:13, 3:18–21, 7:6–8, and 10:32). The relationship between Jesus' "good works" and his death is the thematic mainspring of John's narrative.

Remember, though, that Jesus' miracles were not simply what we call "good deeds"; they were messianic "good works." They implied the terrifyingly revolutionary thesis that this world of contempt and oppression can be changed into a world of complete selflessness and unrestricted mutual assistance. Jesus created an intolerable situation; his behavior and his words were a constant goad to "the world"; they inescapably demanded a collective decision.

The "good works" of the Messiah did not consist in giving what was left over, in distributing the surplus of a civilization that in itself remains untouched by the distribution. They were not works of supererogation. Had they been no more than that, Christ would not have been afraid nor would he have died as he did. On the contrary, society acclaims and venerates charitable works. No status *feels* challenged by the works of the Red Cross; rather, the exploiter needs the charities as much or more than the charities need the exploiter. But Jesus' words and deeds proclaim to the world "that its works are evil" (John 7:7). They challenge the very right to exist of "the world"—meaning the overall organization of society. They insist that "the world" *must* be converted into a world of goodness and selflessness, which means that it must completely transform itself, which means that it must abolish its present self. "Be converted, for the kingdom of God has arrived" (Matt. 4:17).

Nietzsche says that in the presence of the hero everything turns into tragedy. Jesus transcended the heroic: He was the Messiah, calling upon the world immediately to transform itself.

The writings that have come down to us as Gospels are consistent with the meaning that the word "gospel" has on the lips of Jesus (see our chapter 4 above). They are messianic; they proclaim the *eschaton*. If the "good works" recounted in their opening chapters were not messianic, if they did not attack this world at its very foundations, they would not have caused Christ's death as recounted in their closing chapters. They would then be like the good deeds of the worldwide charitable organization of the North American or Roman churches —perfectly acceptable to the world of the oppressors. The "good works" described in the Gospels have to be the object of "the world's" hatred; otherwise there is no gospel, there is no news. Like the Messiah they are welcome only to "those who have been born of God" (John 1:13), that is, to those who are dedicated to love of neighbor and the achievement of justice. As Matthew says in his fourth beatitude, only those who hunger and thirst for justice will be filled when the kingdom arrives (Matt. 5:6). The coming kingdom belongs only to the poor (Matt. 5:3)[29] and to those who "suffer persecution for justice' sake" (Matt. 5:10). It cannot be acceptable to the exploiters of the poor and the persecutors of those who seek justice.

NOTES

1. Rudolf Bultmann, *Die drei Johannesbriefe* (Göttingen: Vandenhoeck, 1967), p. 22 [Eng. trans.: *The Johannine Epistles*, trans. R. Philip O'Hara et al. (Philadelphia: Fortress, 1973), p. 16].

2. Johann Michl, *Die Katholischen Briefe*, RNT 8/2, 2nd ed. (Regensburg: Pustet, 1968), ad loc.; Rudolf Schnackenburg, *Die Johannesbriefe*, 3rd ed. (Freiburg: Herder, 1965), p. 112; Ignace de la Potterie, *Adnotationes in exegesim Primae Epistulae s. Ioannis*, 2nd ed. (Rome:

Pontificio Istituto Biblico, 1966–67), mimeographed, ad loc.; Bultmann, *Johannesbriefe*, p. 22 [Eng. trans.: *Johannine Epistles*, p. 16]; Johannes Schneider, *Die Kirchenbriefe*, NTD 10 (Göttingen: Vandenhoeck, 1967), p. 140.

3. Schnackenburg, *Johannesbriefe*, p. 112.

4. André Feuillet, *Le prologue du quatrième évangile* (Paris: Desclée, 1968), p. 82. Josef Schmid ("Joh. 1, 13," *Biblische Zeitschrift* 1 [1957], pp. 118–25) has shown that it should be translated as "they had been born" and not in the singular "he had been born," as Mollat and de la Potterie propose. See also Raymond E. Brown, *The Gospel according to John (i–xii)*, Anchor Bible 29 (New York: Doubleday, 1966), pp. 11–12; and likewise Rudolf Schnackenburg, *Das Johannesevangelium* (Freiburg: Herder, 1965), 1:240–41 [Eng. trans.: *The Gospel according to St. John*, trans. Kevin Smyth (New York: Herder and Herder, 1968), 1:264–65].

5. Feuillet, *Prologue*, p. 216.

6. Cf. José Porfirio Miranda, *Marx y la biblia* (Salamanca: Sígueme, 1972) [Eng. trans.: *Marx and the Bible*, trans. John Eagleson (Maryknoll, New York: Orbis Books, 1974)].

7. This is the messianic peace, listed among the characteristics of the kingdom of God in Old and New Testament descriptions. It is necessarily based on justice: "The work of justice will be peace" (Isa. 32:17). Matthew is referring to peacemakers for the entire world.

8. Schnackenburg, *Johannesevangelium*, 1:374–77 [Eng. trans.: *Gospel according to John*, 1:360–63].

9. Walter Grundmann, *Das Evangelium nach Matthäus*, 3rd ed., THKNT 1 (Berlin: Evangelische Verlagsanstalt, 1968), p. 140. Grundmann is also the author of the article "kalos," *TWNT*, 3:539–53 [Eng. trans.: *TDNT*, 3:536–50].

10. Herman L. Strack and Paul Billerbeck, *Kommentar zum Neuen Testament aus Talmud und Midrasch*, 6 vols. (Munich: C. H. Beck, 1922–63), 4:536–58 and 559–610.

11. Joachim Jeremias, "Die Salbungsgeschichte Mk 14, 3–9," *Zeitschrift für die neutestamentliche Wissenschaft* 35 (1936), pp. 77ff.

12. See *Marx y la biblia*, chapter 4, section 1 [Eng. trans.: *Marx and the Bible*, pp. 111–37].

13. Rudolf Bultmann, *Das Evangelium des Johannes* (Göttingen: Vandenhoeck, 1941), p. 115 [Eng. trans.: *The Gospel of John: A Commentary*, trans. G. R. Beasley-Murray et al. (Philadelphia: Westminster, 1971), p. 159].

14. Rudolf Bultmann, *Theologie des Neuen Testaments*, 2nd ed. (Tübingen: Mohr, 1954), p. 427 [Eng. trans.: *Theology of the New Testament*, trans. Kendrick Grobel (New York: Scribner's, 1970), p. 81].

15. M. E. Boismard, "L'évolution du thème eschatologique dans les traditions johanniques," *Revue Biblique* 68 (1961), p. 511.

16. Herman Sasse, "kosmeo," *TWNT*, 3:867–98 [Eng. trans.: *TDNT*, 3:867–98]; Rudolf Bultmann, *Glauben und Verstehen* (Tübingen: Mohr, 1933), 1:135–39 [Eng. trans.: *Faith and Understanding*, trans. Louise Pettibone-Smith (New York: Harper & Row, 1969), pp. 166–70]; Bultmann, *Theologie des Neuen Testaments*, pp. 361–67 [Eng. trans.: *Theology of the New Testament*, pp. 254–59]; C. K. Barrett, *The Gospel according to St. John* (London: SPCK, 1955), pp. 355 and passim; Schnackenburg, *Johannesbriefe*, pp. 133–37; Henri van den Bussche, *Jean* (Paris: Desclée, 1967), pp. 456 and passim; Brown, *Gospel according to John (i–xii)*, pp. 508–10.

17. In several passages there is a mixing of the second and third meanings; the word seems to designate humankind together with the earthly stage on which it enacts its history (1 John 4:9; 2:15–17; John 3:17; 10:36; 11:27; 12:46–47; 16:28; 17:18; 18:37).

18. Van den Bussche, *Jean*, p. 456.

19. Barrett, *Gospel according to St. John*, p. 355.

20. Bultmann, *Johannesbriefe*, p. 23 [Eng. trans.: *Johannine Epistles*, p. 17].

21. Barrett, *Gospel according to St. John*, p. 257. Note that the two expressions are interchangeable in Matt. 26:18 and 45; this is the hour of death, the *kairos* of death, as in Rom. 5:6.

22. Ibid., p. 159.

23. Schnackenburg, *Johannesevangelium*, 1:333 [Eng. trans.: *Gospel according to St. John*, 1:328].

24. Some of the more recent examples include those of Peinador, Quirant, and Delatte, briefly described in Feuillet's "L'heure de Jésus et le signe de Cana," *Ephemerides Theologicae Lovanienses* 36 (1960), pp. 5–22 [Eng. trans.: "The Hour of Jesus and the Sign of Cana," *Johannine Studies* (Staten Island, New York: Alba House, 1965), pp. 17–37].

25. Barrett, *Gospel according to St. John*, p. 332.

26. William Wrede, *Das Messiasgeheimnis in den Evangelien, zugleich ein Beitrag zum Verständis des Markusevangeliums* (Göttingen: Vandenhoeck, 1901) [Eng. trans.: *The Messianic Secret*, trans. J. C. G. Greig (Cambridge: Clarke, 1971)]; G. Minnette de Tillesse, *Le secret messianique dans l'évangile de Marc* (Paris: Cerf, 1968).

27. Vincent Taylor, *The Gospel according to St. Mark*, 2nd ed. (London: Macmillan, 1957), p. 224.

28. C. E. B. Cranfield, *The Gospel according to St. Mark* (Cambridge: University Press, 1959), p. 122.

29. Jacques Dupont has shown that the addition of the words "in spirit" does not mean that the phrase does not refer to the needy and indigent; see *Les béatitudes*, 2nd ed. (Paris: Gabalda, 1969), 2:98, 13–15, and 19–51.

Chapter 6

The Word

What is the content of this "word" of John's prologue? In what does this "word" consist if only those who love their neighbor and do justice are capable of understanding it?

John could have begun his Gospel as the Synoptics did, with a description of "the word's" activity after it became flesh (John 1:14). If he chooses to begin instead with a prologue comprising an entire thesis on "the word" that "was in the beginning," it is because he has something decisive to tell us, something that cannot be conveyed simply by narrating the life and death of the word made flesh. John's very decision to begin with a discussion of the word as such leads us to believe that his intention was unusually profound. Hermeneutically speaking, there is no justification for supposing that the prologue represents the ingenuous thinking we are accustomed to attribute to a mere raconteur. Under the circumstances, it would be surprising if John's thinking were not surprising. Since John's initiative in speaking about the word quite forcefully demonstrates his philosophical insight, no idea we find in his prologue can seem too profound or philosophical.

To understand John we must rid ourselves of the a priori progressivist prejudice that human history is progress and later periods are in all ways inevitably

112

better than earlier ones. This prejudice would lead us
into the fallacious assumption that anything seeming to
us profoundly original and superior cannot possibly derive from ancient times but only from modernity or the
incipient future.

Applied to biblical exegesis, such progressivism is revealed as absurd, the negation of hermeneutics. It is
tantamount to saying that we already know more than
the Bible can tell us. Such a belief, far more prevalent
than is generally admitted among Catholics, besides
being patently ridiculous is irreconcilable with the pontifical directive of 1964, which states that in our understanding of the Bible "there remain many questions,
and these of the gravest moment."[1]

For example, does not Paul's assertion that "men im-
pede truth with injustice" (Rom. 1:18) seem philosophically revolutionary? Had he said that ignorance or
false premises or faulty logic or self-serving deceit impedes truth, we would find his statement acceptable and
thoroughly ordinary. Had he said that the whole condition of human immorality prevents us from knowing
truth, we would credit him with Pascalian profundity.
But Paul's assertion is more trenchant than the former
and more specific than the latter: It is by their *adikia*,
their injustice, described in terms of interpersonal relationships (Rom. 1:28–32), that people suppress the
knowledge of truth within themselves. Paul's thesis
strikingly resembles Marx's theory of the origin of
ideological alienation, and because of our progressivist
prejudices it seems to us exceedingly "modern." But it
was written in 58 A.D. Should it surprise us, then, that
John, writing in the same philosophic tradition some
thirty or forty years later, speaks of "the word" with
equal trenchancy, subtlety, and insight?

Schnackenburg identifies a specific instance in which
John is thinking existentially and must be so interpreted, no matter how anachronistically modern that
might seem. He refers to John 3:33: "To accept his

[Christ's] testimony is to acknowledge the truth of God's words." Schnackenburg says, "the very similar passage in 1 Jn 5:9–12 shows that this 'existential' understanding of the text is both possible and necessary."[2] Indeed, by accepting Christ's witness, which is God's, one makes God truthful, that is, one brings about the fulfillment of God's promise. If there is to be eternal life, this acceptance must occur (see John 5:24). God testified that he had given us life in Christ (see 1 John 5:11); therefore, when we have achieved that life, God is then truthful. The thesis of John 3:33 and 1 John 5:10 does not seem to me exceptionally profound, but it certainly is unambiguously existentialist regardless of its authorship some eighteen centuries ago. I cite this instance, not for its own sake, but to demonstrate the inapplicability of our customary progressivist criteria to hermeneutics. Surely, if the narrative portion of John's Gospel contains statements that startle by their modernity, we should not be surprised to find even more powerfully original ideas in the prologue, which is obviously an attempt to extract the theological meaning of the narrative.

THE WORD AS WORD

In the body of the Gospel itself there are several passages that deal with the word as word and not specifically as the word of God. The word insofar as it is word is the very fact that someone is being spoken to, the very fact of summons, of that irreducible otherness that we perceive only to the degree that it is being exercised. One of these passages is John 8:25:

They said to him, "Who are you?"
Jesus said to them, "Absolutely, that I speak to you."

Many exegetes have been baffled by this verse, but Barrett notes that the difficulty of Jesus' answer "has perhaps been exaggerated. It must be observed at the outset that *(ten) archen* is used quite frequently in

Greek adverbially."[3] He refers to the lexicon of Lidell and Scott, which abundantly documents the adverbial use of *(ten) archen*, translated above as "absolutely." Westcott and Brown suggest the adverbial translation "at all";[4] several German exegetes propose *überhaupt* ("at all" or, better, "absolutely"). Barrett prefers "at first," which fits the English translation well. Whichever of these translations one prefers, the meaning of the rest of the phrase remains unchanged: "that I speak to you."

In any case, the passage cannot mean "I am the beginning, who speaks to you." There is nothing to warrant translating an accusative term that is normally used adverbially as though it were nominative and predicate nominative. Nor can the passage mean, "What from the beginning I have told you." This translation could be correct only if *ten archen* modified the verb, and here it does not.

Another attempt at translation divides the recitative particle *hoti*, changing it into the interrogative *ho ti*. Thus Jesus' response becomes an evasion: "How is it that I speak to you at all?" But Brown notes that the interrogative *ho ti* occurs rarely[5] (and I think it may even have been invented in support of this translation). Furthermore, such a translation implies that Jesus interrupted the conversation at this point, which in fact he did not.

As a grammatical parallel to Jesus' response in John 8:25, Lagrange, over half a century ago, perceptively cited the Hellenist passage in Achilles Tatius 6:20 *ouk agapas hoti soi kai lalo*. He translated this as "N'es-tu pas ravie que je veuille bien parler avec toi?"[6] "Aren't you delighted that I even speak with you?" Actually *kai* has no modern equivalent. It is the emphatic-pleonastic, found in the Greek text of Heb. 7:25; 11:19; Acts 10:29; 2 Cor. 2:9 (and similar to Rom. 4:22; John 12:18; Heb. 13:12; 1 Pet. 4:19; Luke 1:35; 11:49). But its usage here is exactly the same as in John 8:25: *ten archen, hoti kai lalo hymin*. Lagrange's discovery of the grammatical parallel is our most valuable key to this passage. And Brown considers the correct translation to be indeed possible: "That I speak to you at all." This might be better phrased as "In the first place, that I am speaking to you."

In any case, the Hellenist parallel drawn by Lagrange makes the recitative "that" inescapable: "that I speak to you." The power of Jesus' answer lies in the word "that." The Jews were anticipating a predicate or an attribute, something reducible to a concept. Reduction to a concept is our most useful device for suppressing the otherness of the one who speaks to us, for enclosing ourselves in ourselves by use of categories that are not "other" but merely different beads from the same string of our selves. But the only time, according to John, that the Jews asked Jesus, "Who are you?" he answered, not with a predicate or an attribute, but "That I am speaking to you." He is the word as word.

Jesus deliberately refused to supply another predicate ("God" would be a predicate like any other), another category whose combinations and permutations the self could employ to close in upon itself and avoid the summons of the "other." The other, who is not I, exists only in the word as such. Jesus Christ is the fact that I am being spoken to. He is the word.

The second passage in the Gospel narrative that refers to the word as such—the conversation with the Samaritan woman in John 4:10—is less clear. Eduard Schweizer inchoately perceived its significance.[7] Van den Bussche grasped it more fully and accurately by detecting a synonymic parallel and an epexegetical or explicative *kai* in this passage:

If you knew God's gift and who it is that is saying to you, "Give me a drink."

In fact this is a synonymic parallel, as frequently found both in the Psalms and in modern everyday usage. The gift or favor of God is explained ("and") by the synonymic expression that follows. Van den Bussche comments: "The parallelism clearly indicates that the gift to which Jesus refers is precisely this word that he is directing to her; it is the fact that he is speaking to her."[8]

The third and last passage we shall consider has a double aspect. The observation of F. M. Braun enables us to see how for John the word as word takes on significance, the word as the very fact of one person addressing another: "Controlled by the same verb, the three terms *logos, remata, phone* ['word,' 'terms,' and 'voice,' respectively] are, more or less, synonymous."[9] By saying that having life depends on listening to Jesus' word (John 5:24 and passim) or his terms (John 6:63, 68) or his voice (John 5:25; 10:27–28), John indicates that neither the content of the word nor its divine source is of primary importance. What is important is the address, the allocution, the fact that one person is being spoken to by another: word, terms, voice.

With that in mind we see that the last passage in John's narrative to treat the word as word, namely, John 8:43, does so in two ways:

Why do you not understand my language?
Because you cannot listen to my word.

Most commentators have ignored this passage, which the Evangelist attributes to Jesus, finding in it no special significance. But it is worthy of note that John distinguishes quite clearly between *lalia* and *logos*; obviously they are not synonymous, for if they were, Jesus' question and answer would make no sense at all. *Lalia* means "language," "idiom," "audible speech" (Barrett), "*Sprache*" (Bultmann). *Logos* means "word." In our linguistic tradition *lalia* means the actual sounds that are uttered, while *logos* means the conceptual content of those sounds. But, while people customarily "listen to" or "hear" sounds (*lalia*), and "understand" or "know" content (*logos*), Jesus has here made the opposite connection, linking understanding to sound and hearing to content. Why? Because what the Jews could not listen to was the fact of the word; what they could not tolerate was the fact of being summoned. Since they could not stand the very fact of being summoned, they could not understand his language.

Independently, however, of the exact meaning of the passage and the distinction between *lalia* and *logos*, one thing is clear about John 8:43: John is here focusing on the question of the word as word, and not specifically as the word of God.

THE PRE-EXISTENT WORD

Most exegetes agree that the opening words of the prologue—"In the beginning..." (John 1:1)—and the thesis that "everything was made through it [the word] and without it nothing came to be" (John 1:3) undoubtedly allude to the first verse of Genesis—"In the beginning God created heaven and earth"—and to the entire first chapter of the Bible. Genesis resounds ten times with the words "God *said*... and it was done" (Gen. 1:3, 6, 9, 11, 14, 20, 24, 26, 28, 29), emphasizing the power of the word (of God) alone. In corroboration, Genesis 1 enumerates everything that was made through the word and stresses that without it nothing came to be. There is no doubt that "the word" of John's prologue is the word of God; the fact that John ignores this and speaks only of the word alone must, therefore, be deliberate. That is the most important fact of the entire prologue, and exegesis has not yet paid it sufficient heed.

I am not laboring to break down an unlocked door. Both Protestant and Catholic Christology customarily and exclusively fasten upon the fact that John hypostatizes the word, that is, the fact that in John's Gospel the word is a person. Consequently we read the sub-

stantive "the word" as if it were a proper name serving
only to designate the person called Christ, as if it were
merely an appellative, a code word with no meaning
except as a synonym for Jesus. Who cares that
"Graciela" is the diminutive of "grace"? What matters is
that the name points out, like a finger, Graciela and not
Patricia. She could just as easily be called Antoinette,
for the function of the name is simply to distinguish one
person from another. According to traditional Christology, John could easily have said "wisdom" or "omnipotence" or "the wisdom of God," for the conceptual significance of any word disappears when it is used only to
designate a concrete person. When we understand "the
word" simply as a reference to Christ, everything John
wants to tell us escapes us. We are left with a series of
affirmations that are true in themselves but are not
what John wants to tell us.

This "Christocentric" exegesis, based solely on the
hypostatization of the word and the person of Christ,
truncates the gospel message to the point of making it
unrecognizable. It makes a new gospel out of John's
words. John does not even state that the word is Christ
until 1:14, and although from verse 14 on, John very
much personifies "the word," his really important point
is that it continues to be the word. The contrast between
John's treatment of the pre-existent word and biblical
and rabbinic speculation on the pre-existence of the law
and of wisdom (greatly emphasized by Feuillet,
Schnackenburg, and Brown) cannot be explained by
personification alone. If John intended simply a personification, he could have affirmed the pre-existence of
Christ by asserting that the wisdom (or the law) existing
from the beginning—a concept familiar and acceptable
to the Jews—became incarnate in Christ. If he does not
choose to personify that concept, it is because he is concerned with "the word" itself. If the word that existed
from the beginning later became flesh, for John the

important aspect of this incarnation was that the person continued to be word.

Why this emphasis on the word? Schnackenburg, who does not have the answer, poses the question accurately. After comparing John's use of "the word" with its closest parallels, Wisd. 9:1–2 and the *Slavonic Enoch* 30:8 and 33:4, he says,

When, therefore, the Logos-hymn describes the sovereign action of the Word in terms of Wisdom, particularly in relation to men, this constitutes a later stage of development, and it is not clear why the author then recurs again to the term 'word', and not the 'word of God' but to the term 'the Logos', used absolutely. Thus the Wisdom speculation provides the aptest parallels in thought, but leaves the term chosen by the Christian hymn unexplained.[10]

Some commentators proffer the ridiculous explanation that John reverted to the masculine term *logos* because it was more appropriate than the feminine *sophia* ("wisdom") to designate the male Jesus of Nazareth, but this answer is unworthy of the question. John's main concern in the prologue is not simply Jesus' pre-existence, nor is it the word of God; it is simply "the word." The exegetes' problem is: Why?

THE WORD'S INTERLOCUTOR

The key to the question lies in the first verse of the prologue. John's philosophical and theological maturation led him to affirm the pre-existence of the word as such, that is, as summons, as otherness that "is addressed to. . . , " that "speaks to another." But the primordial objection to this definition was that "in the beginning" there existed neither people nor the world to be addressed, to be spoken to. Therefore, after the first verse says that "in the beginning was the word," John must add, "and the word was addressed to God," and further, "the word itself was God."

F. C. Burkitt understands clearly that "the word was

addressed to God,"[11] and L. M. Dewailly translates the phrase as "et la parole s'addressait à Dieu."[12] More recently C. Masson rendered it as "la parole parlait à Dieu."[13]

Kai ho logos en pros ton theon (John 1:1b) can be translated only as "and the word was addressed to God." As de la Potterie has shown, it is groundless to suppose that John's use of the Greek prepositions *eis, en,* and *pros* is colloquially ungrammatical or careless. The validity of de la Potterie's careful study is attested in several ways, including his very failure to realize that *ho logos* continues to mean the word, that the word continues to be word. De la Potterie says, "Simply to invoke 'Hellenistic usage' to give *eis* the meaning of *en,* as is often done, is quite unconvincing, for we are trying to discover precisely whether or not John conforms to this usage. And until now we do not have the least indication that such is the case."[14] He makes the same point about John's use of *pros:* There is no basis for assuming that John confused these prepositions with each other and failed to perceive the exact nuance of each. Therefore, we are obliged to translate *pros ton theon* as "addressed to God." De la Potterie has definitively proved wrong the customary translation "and the word was with God" (or "near God"), citing the following four reasons:

1. There is no other text in John in which *pros* with the accusative means "with" or "near."

2. The sapiential texts describe Wisdom as "near God" or "with God," but they do so according to the classical usage, that is, using the preposition *para* (Prov. 8:30) or the preposition *meta* (Sir. 1:1)—never *pros.*

3. Whenever John wants to express the presence or proximity of one person to another, he uses *para* (1:39; 4:40; 14:17, 25; 19:25; cf. 14:23) or *meta* (3:22, 25, 26). In particular, when he speaks of the proximity or presence of the Son to the Father he always says *para soi* (17:5), *para to patri* (8:38).

4. Even with verbs other than verbs of motion,

whenever John says *pros ton theon* (or *pros ton patera*) he always clearly suggests the idea of "direction toward . . . ," of "orientation toward. . . . " Thus *parakleton echomen pros ton patera* (1 John 2:1) does not mean simply "in his presence," but "turned toward him," "addressing himself to him," "summoning him." Westcott says:" "Not simply in His presence, but turned toward Him, addressing Him with continual pleadings."[15] The same connotation exists in 1 John 3:21 and 5:14.

De la Potterie's conclusion from these findings is to translate John 1:1b as "Le Logos était *tourné vers* Dieu." Because he forgets that *logos* means "word," he does not see that the sentence must mean "the word was addressed to God," "the word's interlocutor was God." Given that the word existed from the beginning, this translation is unavoidable, for without an other to address, there is no word.

To de la Potterie's proofs of the meaning of *pros* we can add this point: of the twenty-eight examples in the Fourth Gospel of non-motion verbs used with *pros*, twenty-two of those verbs mean "to say to . . . " (2:3; 3:4; 4:15, 33, 48, 49; 5:45; 6:5b, 28, 34; 7:3, 35, 50; 8:31, 33, 57; 10:35; 11:21; 12:19; 13:28; 16:17; 19:24). The most significant of these examples occurs in John 10:35, because this is the only verse in John besides 1:1b, 2 where *pros* appears with a non-motion verb and with *logos* as subject "to those to whom the word was addressed" (*pro hous ho logos egeneto*). This expression, containing the noun *logos*, the verb *ginomai* and the preposition *pros*, appears in the Septuagint some 110 times, as far as I can determine, and invariably means "the word was addressed to . . . " or an equivalent phrase. In the Hebrew text, the verb in every one of these 110 cases is "to be," as it is in John 1:1, 2. The Septuagint uses *ginomai* to assist in the translation, but uses it in a colorless way, almost as a simple copulative. The meaning is entirely conveyed by *logos* and *pros*, as in John 1:1, 2.

Logos with *pros*—with the verb "to be" understood —occurs in 1 Kings 2:14, 2 Kings 9:5; Zech. 4:6; Jer. 9:12 (11), always meaning "addressed to. ... " In these four passages the verb "to be" can be understood because the tense is present. But in John 1:1b, 2 the verb must be explicitly stated because it is in the preterite tense.

Comparative analysis of this kind is the only method we have to determine what John 1:1 means. To clarify and emphasize his meaning, John restates in the second verse the ideas introduced in the first:

(1) In the beginning existed the word,
and the word was addressed to God,
and the word was God.
(2) It was in the beginning addressed to God.

For the word to be word, it must be addressed to someone, and if it existed from the beginning it could have been addressed only to God. And John's first message, immediately restated, is that it did exist from the beginning: His prologue does not speak of the pre-existence of Christ, but rather of the pre-existence of the word. What existed from the beginning was the word. It was the word as such that later became flesh, became a human being, became tangible and visible to us.

GOD AS WORD

We hold that the word was a person from the beginning, but John does not focus his attention on this. His clear reference in John 1:3 to the phrase from Genesis, "he *said* . . . and it was done," shows that he is not considering the word as person but as word. Otherwise he would have said "wisdom" or "the word of God" instead.

"The word," used without qualification, appears frequently throughout the New Testament (Mark 2:2; 4:14, 33; Matt. 13:19, 21–23; Luke 5:1; 9:28; Mark 8:32; Acts 4:4, 29, 31; 6:2, 4, 7; 8:4, 14, 25; 10:36, 44; 11:1, 19; 13:5, 7, 49; 16:6, 32; 19:20; Eph. 1:13; Col. 1:5; etc.). We know that the sacred writers (and Jesus himself) mean "the word of God," but it is most significant that they call it simply "the word." It was inevitable that a genius of John's philosophic turn of mind should be led to consider the word as such, that nonresorbable otherness that, as we shall see, exists only in the great news of the gospel.

Note John's penultimate step in chapter 17 of his Gospel. After Jesus said that he had given the word of God to his disciples (v. 14), he added, "As you sent me into the world, so too I have sent them into the world" (v. 18). He was not concerned only about his disciples, but also about those who would come to believe through their word (v. 20). The word passes from bearer to bearer; the important thing is that the world should continue to be addressed by the word. John understood that God consisted in this very fact of addressing, in the very event of the word. Therefore he asserts: What existed at the beginning was the word, and the word was addressed to God, and the word itself was God. He also saw that Jesus' entire life and death were characterized by this unparalleled fact: He was the word, he was the incarnation of the word. That insight is summed up in the Johannine Christ's best definition of himself: "Above all, that I am speaking to you" (John 8:25).

NOTES

1. *Acta Apostolicae Sedis*, 1964, p. 716 [Eng. trans.: *Catholic Biblical Quarterly*, vol. 26, no. 3 (July 1964): 309].

2. Rudolf Schnackenburg, *Das Johannesevangelium* (Freiburg: Herder, 1965), 1:399, 398 [Eng. trans.: *The Gospel according to St. John*, trans. Kevin Smyth (New York: Herder and Herder, 1968), 1:386, 385].

3. C. K. Barrett, *The Gospel according to St. John* (London: SPCK, 1955), p. 283.

4. Brooke Foss Westcott, *The Gospel according to St. John* (London: Clarke, 1958; the first edition appeared in 1880), p. 131; Raymond E. Brown, *The Gospel according to John (i–xii)*, Anchor Bible 29 (Garden City, New York: Doubleday, 1966), p. 348.

5. Brown, *Gospel according to John (i–xii)*, pp. 347–48.

6. M. J. Lagrange, *Evangile selon saint Jean,* 8th ed. (Paris: Gabalda, 1948), p. 238.

7. Eduard Schweizer, *"Ego eimi,"* Forschungen zur Religion und Literatur des Alten und Neuen Testaments 56 (Göttingen: Vandenhoeck, 1939), p. 161.

8. Henri van den Bussche, *Jean* (Paris: Desclée, 1967), p. 187.

9. F. M. Braun, *Jean le théologien* (Paris: Gabalda, 1966), 3:103.

10. Schnackenburg, *Johannesevangelium,* 1:260 [Eng. trans.: *Gospel according to St. John,* 1:484].

11. Francis Crawford Burkitt, *Church and Gnosis* (Cambridge, Eng.: The University Press, 1932), p. 95.

12. L. M. Dewailly, *Jésus-Christ, parole de Dieu* (Paris: Cerf, 1945), p. 17.

13. C. Masson, cited by André Feuillet in *Le prologue du quatrième évangile* (Paris: Desclée, 1968), p. 267.

14. I. de la Potterie, "L'emploi dynamique de *eis* dans Saint Jean et ses incidences théologiques," *Biblica* 43 (1962), p. 377.

15. Westcott, cited by de la Potterie, ibid., p. 379.

Chapter 7

The Word of Which God Consists

Till now we have dealt with passages that focus on "the word" as such, which consists in the summons, that otherness that the self cannot assimilate because it is ever the "other" that cannot be identified with the self. The word is not a medium; it is not an instrument of information that is dispensable once the data are transmitted and the information is registered by the subject, that is, once the subject is reintegrated into its solitude. On the contrary, the word is—always and essentially—a rupture of the solitude and immanence of the self, the only possible rupture, the only possible negation of idealism and solipsism.

Heteronomy and otherness, combated by Kant with a determination worthy of a better cause, are in reality the imprescindable condition of possibility of the absolute imperative, the only possible basis for unconditional injunction. On the other hand, Marxism, which conceives of the word as an instrument of the ends and needs of the self, as an extension or "long arm" of the self's utilitarianism, remains encapsulated in idealism. It cannot transcend its idealistic, solipsistic little habitation, designed by the self for itself, in which the neighbor is a mere means to the "enriching" ends of the self. But the word is gratuitous. The self in no way needs it, nor is anyone able to utilize it as an instrument. So much we have demonstrated. But what basis does John have for saying that the word existed from the beginning?

Could the word exist from the beginning except by virtue of its specific, unique content? For notwithstanding our necessary prior emphasis on the word as word, as summons, the word *says* something. We must now ask whether the existence of the word as summons does not result from its content. Could the otherness exist and remain nonassimilable except by virtue of *what* the word *says*?

THE WORD OF LOVE

We considered an extremely important datum in our chapter 5: According to John 1:13 only those who love their neighbor and do justice can understand and embrace the word. The masculine accusative *auton* in verses 10, 11, and 12 has only one masculine antecedent, namely, *ho logos*, "the word." It is saying, therefore, that the world did not know *it*, that its own did not receive *it*, that all those who received *it* were born of God, that is, lovers of their neighbor and doers of justice. This means that the content of the word is related to justice and love of neighbor and that the word could not exist as summons if it were not because of its content. This content is thus the condition of possibility of the word as summons.

We must relate what we said in chapter 6 to the theme of chapter 5, that is, the world's hatred of "good works." We see that good works are the content of "the word" in John 17:14:

I gave them your word and the world hated them.

In this verse the "and" is clearly consecutive and causal: I gave them your word *and therefore* the world hated them. The laconic, paratactical phrasing of the following passage from John's First Epistle lends to the same meaning an even greater emphasis:

My brothers, do not be surprised if the world hates you. We know that we have crossed over from death to life, in that we love the brothers (1 John 3:13–14).

By omitting the particles that explicitly relate one clause to the other, John compels the reader to furnish them. That is the purpose of the parataxis. The meaning of the verses is that, since John and the believers are already accomplishing "the word" of love of neighbor, they must expect the world's hatred. As far as I know, no modern commentator separates these two verses. But it is also necessary to point out the logical relationship between them: otherwise verse 13 seems like an erratic segment, unrelated to the preceding and following verses, almost like a marginal gloss. The world's hatred (v. 13) is not occasioned by the "crossing over from death to life" (v. 14), but by the love of one's brothers that is the visible sign of this passage from death to life, because this visibility is really the thesis of verse 14. The axis of verse 14 is love of neighbor; thus it is this axis which must be related with the admonition not to wonder if the world hates you. The same connection occurs in John 17:14 ("I gave them your word, and therefore the world hated them") and in John 10:32 ("I have set before you many good works, done by my Father's power; for which of these would you stone me?"). In our chapter 5 we emphasized that the world hates all who proclaim the imperative of good works, implying that the whole social system must be transformed into a world of goodness and solidarity. 1 John 3:13–14 shows us the same hatred directed against whoever confronts the world and history with the fulfilled imperative of loving one's neighbor. In John 17:14 we find the world reacting identically to the bearer of "the word." The content of the word in these passages seems unequivocally implied; there seems no question about what the word *says*.

According to Westcott, whose stylistic analysis is meticulously accurate, we find the same idea in John 15:17–18:

(17) These things I command you: that you love one another. (18) If the world hates you, bear in mind that it hated me before you.

These two verses are frequently considered independently of one another. But Westcott points out that verse 17 "must be taken as the introduction of a new line of thought. ... On this point the usage in St. John is conclusive against the received arrangement."[1] As proof he cites John 14:25; 15:11; 16:1, 25, 33; and John 16:4b also proves his point. In fact, whenever the Johannine Jesus says "*tauta*" ("these things"), it is to initiate a new subject or a new aspect of the preceding subject. Therefore John 15:17 cannot be separated from John 15:18; the paratactical relationship between them is consecutive and causal, like that between 1 John 3:13 and 14. Westcott rightly concludes that Christian love is "the antidote to and the occasion of the world's hatred."[2]

The challenging assertion in John 8:37—"You want to kill me *because* my word makes no headway with you"—explicitly affirms the causal connection we found in John 17:14: "I gave them your word and the world hated them." All these passages point to one conclusion: The content of the word is the commandment or imperative to love our neighbor.

This conclusion is confirmed by the formulation of John 8:31: "If you abide in my word, truly *you will be my disciples*." For John uses the italicized phrase only once more, in John 13:35, where he defines it thus: "By this all will know that *you are my disciples*: that you love one another." A comparison of these two verses seems to demand a univocal conclusion: To abide in the word is to love one's neighbor. This means that the content of the word is "love one another."

A recent commentator on the Fourth Gospel has seen that "for John 'word' and 'commandment' are virtually interchangeable."[3] Love of neighbor, rightly understood as the imperative of justice and not as a form of solipsistic romantic delusion (see chapter 5), is certainly the content that gives the word life as nonresorbable otherness. If John believed that "the commandment" existed from the beginning, then he could affirm that the word existed from the beginning.

AN OLD COMMAND

Two passages from John's First Epistle are fundamental to any discussion of the word's pre-existence. They further document that "the word" of the Gospel prologue is the commandment to love one another.

Dear friends, I give you no new command. It is the old command which you have had from the beginning; *this old command is the word which you heard.* And yet again, I am giving you a new command—which is made true in him [Christ] and in you—because the darkness is passing and the true light already shines (1 John 2:7–8).

The causal conjunction "because" (v. 8, above) has been discussed at the beginning of our chapter 5. The historical, temporal nature of the word of which God truly consists has been demonstrated in chapters 6 and the present one, which will establish the premises on which the following three chapters will be based.

All scholars recognize that the words "in him" (v. 8, above) refer to Christ. The "command" is to love one's neighbor, as proven by the following verses (1 John 2:9–11) and by 2 John 5. Moreover, the entire passage obviously alludes to John 13:34, in which the Johannine Christ designates the command to love one another a "new commandment." 1 John 2:7–8 appears to be a reflection on the newness or oldness of the imperative that Jesus called "a new commandment." The italicized hemistych in 1 John 2:7 expressly asserts that that commandment is identical to "the word" we have heard. In the previous sentence John affirms that we have had that commandment from the beginning. Because he is convinced that word and commandment are identical, and convinced that the commandment existed from the beginning, John can assert in his Gospel's prologue that the word existed from the beginning.

What does John mean by "from the beginning"? In this passage, "from the beginning" cannot mean from the beginning of the preaching of the gospel, as Bultmann holds, for then there would be no difference between the affirmation that the commandment is old (v. 7) and the affirmation that it is new (v. 8). The expression "from the beginning" must mean from the beginning of time, as it does in 1 John 2:13 and 14: "You have known the one who was [or is] from the beginning [*ton apharches*]."

Comparing verse 7 (an "old" command) with verse 8 (a "new" command), Günther Klein correctly observes: "It is not by chance that the Christological dimension does not enter into the picture with reference to 'oldness'; rather it does so only with reference to the 'newness' of the commandment."[4] Verse 8 undoubtedly refers to the historical epoch inaugurated by Christ, which is the *eschaton*. Therefore "the old commandment which you have had from the beginning" (v. 7) is an imperative that antedated Christ's entry into the world. With Christ's advent the "old commandment" becomes new in a sense that John wishes to examine. Whatever John may mean by "new" and "old," in verse 7 he undeniably says that the commandment existed before Christ came into the world and in verse 8 that the commandment was new in the epoch of Jesus Christ. He is making a chronological contrast.

To deny that this chronological contrast is stated by the text itself is to deny the nonmanipulable reality of time, to deny that John is speaking of time. Bultmann makes this denial: He claims that verse 8 does not refer to a historical period but rather to an "eschatological reality."[5] Of course the epoch of Christ is eschatological, but this does not mean that it is not historical. The dehistorifying of the *eschaton* is the principal flaw in

Bultmannian interpretation. This flaw derives from Heidegger's scorn for "vulgar time" (see our chapter 3) and from the mistaken belief that a nontemporal "eschatological reality" is the only valid alternative to the precocious Catholicism of "salvation history," which has enabled the church to establish itself in western history as the official religion of the great civilization of oppression. But to detemporalize the *eschaton* is even more perniciously "Catholic" than to categorize salvation as past history. In fact, this detemporalization has been the principal tool of the theology that tranquillizes consciences and legitimates crimes committed in the name of "imperishable Christian values." The detemporalizing of the *eschaton*—rejuvenated by Bultmann—strips the *eschaton* of the only real meaning it could possibly have.

Günther Klein, although believing with Bultmann that eschatological time is nontemporal, nevertheless declares Bultmann's interpretation of 1 John 2:7–8 to be untenable: "In the process of linguistic apocalypticization, the eschatological 'hour' has lost its original ontological independence of the chronological hours constituting the temporal continuum. Eschatological time itself has become a chronological dimension, that is, the last link of the temporal continuum."[6] "In the First Epistle, the *eschaton* acquires the character of an epoch."[7]

But Klein's interpretation is equally indefensible: "The commandment is 'old' because the history of the church has already lasted quite some time. It is 'new' because taken as a whole the history of the church marks a new phase in the history of the world."[8] This is indefensible because verse 8 does not say simply "which is made true in you"; rather it says "which is made true *in him* and in you." The period referred to in verse 8 is a unit of time in which Christ and the readers of John's Epistle are both present simultaneously; it is the period marked out by the person and life of Jesus of Nazareth.

And if the commandment is "new" by virtue of being given in Jesus' lifetime, then it can be "old" only by virtue of having existed prior to Jesus' lifetime. Therefore the expression "from the beginning," with which verse 7 describes the commandment's oldness, cannot mean from the beginning of Christian preaching, but rather from the beginning of time.

It is conceivable that the Epistle was addressed to converted Jews and that "old" in verse 7 refers to Israelite legislation promulgated before Christ: "Love your neighbor as yourself" (Lev. 19:18). But the formula "from the beginning" is never used in that way. It means either from the beginning of time or from the beginning of Christ's preaching. These are the only meanings that can be documented, and the second is proved inapplicable to 1 John 2:7–8 by the wording itself.

Therefore 1 John 2:7–8 affirms that the commandment of love of neighbor is identical to "the word" and that it existed from the beginning of time.

THE WORD OF LIFE

Before 1 John 2:7, the expression "from the beginning" is used only once in the Epistle. It occurs in 1 John 1:1, the second passage that is fundamental to our understanding of the word's pre-existence:

What was from the beginning,
what we heard,
what we saw with our eyes,
what we looked upon and our hands touched,
our theme is the word of life.

"Life," as the Epistle itself tells us later on, consists in love of neighbor ("We know that we have crossed over from death to life, in that we love the brothers"—1 John 3:14). This being the case, then "the word of life" must be the word regarding love of neighbor. And 1 John 1:1 says that this word "was from the beginning."

Extra-exegetical reasons prompt Bultmann to deny that John is speaking here of "the pre-existent Logos"[9] and of a time previous to the incarnation. In a "more precise interpretation" Bultmann himself has shown that "the beginning of the Epistle means substantially the same thing as the prologue of the Gospel."[10] To the overwhelming majority of exegetes, *en arche* in John 1:1 and *ap' arches* in 1 John 1:1 both refer to the pre-existence of the *logos*.[11] Conzelmann and Herbert Braun point out that the beginning of the Epistle connotes an object and is neuter, that it is less hypostatic and personal than the Gospel prologue.[12] In fact, the Epistle deals with the content of "the word" from the first verse. The observations of both scholars derive from our common distortion of the Gospel prologue: making "the word" into a proper noun designating Christ, and completely forgetting its conceptual meaning. For John, as we emphasized in chapter 6, the word did not cease to be word when it became flesh. The point of his prologue is that precisely the word as such—that which existed from the beginning as the summons of otherness —became a human being; the life of Christ about to be recounted to us has meaning insofar as "it" addresses us as "the word." Christ's works themselves are *verba visibilia*, as Bultmann shows in another context.

The beginning of the Epistle undoubtedly emphasizes the element of message, of content, in the word ("what" repeated four times and again in v. 3, always in the neuter gender). That message or content is "the word of life." As we shall soon see, the Gospel prologue also indicates of what "the word" is "full." The Epistle also tells us that some*thing* became flesh: "what we saw with our eyes, what we looked upon and our hands touched." This formulation obliges us to recognize that the beginning of the Epistle and the prologue of the Gospel contain the same message. It is our interpretation that must change, our centuries-old inclination to distort the prologue by forgetting that *ho logos* means "the word."

The "it" through which all things were made is no more a person than "what was from the beginning." And "the word" that was addressed to God is as neuter in gender as "what existed from the beginning."

"In the word was life" (John 1:4) is another way of referring to "the word of life" (1 John 1:1). Note that John finds it necessary to add, "And the life [of which I speak] was the light of men, and the light shines in the darkness, and the darkness did not receive it" (John 1:4b–5). The summoning that is implicit in the term "light," which Bultmann rightly perceives at the beginning of the Epistle (1 John 1:5–6), is clearly manifest in the Gospel prologue in the allusion to people's free response to the light, whether *katelaben* is translated as "they received" or as "they overcame." The word that bears life can be accepted or rejected. It is a demand, an imperative.

WORD AND COMMANDMENT

In these two passages of the Epistle (1 John 1:1 and 2:7–8) "the word" is identical to the commandment of love of neighbor. As Brown has shown, "for John 'word' and 'commandment' are virtually interchangeable," in the body of the Gospel as well.[13] Note this parallel:

If you love me, you will keep my commandments (John 14:15).

If anyone loves me, he will keep my word (John 14:23).

Only eight verses separate these two statements. Jesus was saying that his word is his commandments and nothing else. Even more meaningful for us, his commandments (*entolai*) are reduced to one (*entole*), as Brown observes.[14] Jesus' conversion of plural into singular reflects neither casual speech nor careless redaction. Likewise, the plural "my words" in John 15:7 is made progressively more specific through John 15:7–11 until it is intentionally defined as singular in "This is my commandment: that you love one another" (John 15:12). As Barrett comments: "The commandment [becomes] singular, summarizing all commandments."[15] Herbert Braun agrees: "The change of number indicates from the beginning on that we cannot hold the author to the plural, as if his were an atomistic ethics; 'the commandments' are 'the commandment,' 'the word.' "[16]

This Johannine pattern must be intentional, for it reappears in 1 John 2:3–7 and in 2 John 6. Lagrange observes that the whole of Jesus' message is expressed in this verse: "*These things* I command you, that you love one another" (John 15:17). And he comments: "The plural 'these things' is surprising for a single commandment; but this only makes the expression the more provocative: This is all that I command you; it is reduced to the precept of fraternal charity."[17]

An additional concept, even more significant than the synthesis of all commandments into one, is contained in John 14:15 ("If you love me, you will keep my commandments") and John 14:23 ("If anyone loves me, he will keep my word"). Bultmann has pointed it out: It is the concept that love of God consists in keeping his commandments, his "word."

The intention of the conditional clauses in vv. 15, 23 ("If you love me, then . . . ") is not to state that when love for Jesus is present in the disciples, then the result must be the keeping of the commandments; the intention rather is to define the nature of love, as is made plain in the definition-sentence in v. 21 ["Anyone who holds my commandments and keeps them, he is the one who loves me"]: To love is simply to keep the commandments. The question therefore which activates the section vv.15-24 is this: What is this love, which is directed to Jesus? The clear presupposition of vv. 15, 21, 23f. is that the believer must love Jesus, indeed that he wants to do so, and this presupposition implies that love is a personal relationship; that is to say, a false conception of the relationship to the Revealer, to the divinity, is presupposed here, one that is characteristic of man: man desires to "love" the divinity, i.e. to achieve a personal, direct, relationship to it . . . . Over against this, a new understanding of love is unfolded: the love that is directed to the Revealer can only be a keeping of his commandments, of his word.[18]

This understanding is not new. Although Bultmann does not say so, it is the sole message of the Old Testament as has been demonstrated by the North American Jesuits William L. Moran and Matthew J. O'Connell.[19] Neither they nor Bultmann note that in order for the commandment to be the sole revelation of the true God its content must be justice and love of neighbor, but the authors of the Old and New Testament considered this point absolutely essential. The New Testament is not new with regard to the content of God's word, regardless of what Bultmann says, but this does not diminish the merit of his analysis of John 14:15–24. Bultmann is the first commentator, as far as I know, to perceive the true revelatory intention in John 14:15–24.

The defining characteristic of the God of the Bible is the fact that he cannot be known or loved directly; rather, to love God and to know him means to love one's neighbor and to do one's neighbor justice. This is what makes the God of the Bible different from all other gods; by overlooking this one biblical teaching "Christian" theology has fallen into a protracted idolatry. I affirmed above in chapter 2 that religion is incompatible with real Christianity, because religion is the desire for a direct relationship with divinity; the confines of the self, however, cannot be transcended without the real otherness of the neighbor who seeks justice. Those who desire a direct relationship with God wish to prescind from the "other"; they may practice a religion of the multitudes, but they have enclosed themselves in solipsism and in the irremediable immanence of solitude.

KNOWING THE TRUE GOD

That this revelation is absolutely central for John is strikingly manifested by his affirmation (John 7:28d; 8:19; and 8:55a) that the Jews, the people of Israel, did not know the true God. The reader must contemplate deeply so stupendous an affirmation. Textual analysis alone is inadequate to penetrate its meaning.

One would think that if any people on the earth at the time of Christ knew the true God, it would have been the people of Israel. If they did not, then who did? According to the common conception, all other peoples were atheists or idolators; the people of Israel alone indeed knew the true God.

John denies this, with an insistence that should make us reconsider all our presuppositions. If the thesis that "the world" does not know the true God (John 15:21; 16:3) seems obvious, if pagans' not knowing God seems self-evident, if the statement in the prologue that "the word was in the world . . . and the world did not know it" (John 1:10) seems very easily comprehensible, then we are understanding with a superficiality tantamount to misunderstanding. For John holds that the Jewish people did not know God either (John 7:28d, 8:19, and 8:55a).

We Christians customarily interpret those Gospel passages as contrast and comparison with ourselves. We customarily take them to mean that the pagans lack something—a knowledge of God—that we have. That is not what John means. Our claim to know the true God is no better than the Jews'.

In denying that the Jews knew God, John is not accusing them of pride or arrogance, or of worshipping Jupiter or Aphrodite or Osiris. John is saying that they have not known God because they have not understood in what God consists: "It is my Father who glorifies me, he who you say is your God, and you do not know him" (John 8:54–55).

John is not expressing hyperbolically the conviction that the Jews have achieved a partial or less-than-perfect knowledge of the true God. He is saying that they have failed absolutely to know God. "The time is coming when anyone who kills you will suppose that he is rendering a service to God " (John 16:2). The accusation is absolute, not relative.

When the Johannine Jesus says that his Jewish contemporaries do not know the only true God, the issue is of the utmost seriousness. It is impossible to trivialize it with our clichés that would reduce to a devaluation what John wants to designate as a negation. Such a procedure is not exegesis but rather an accommodation of the biblical assertions to our preconceived theological system.

The clue to understanding the accusation lies in John's affirmation that "the word" is the light "that enlightens *every man*" and that nevertheless "the world did not know it" (John 1:9–10). The word of Old Testament revelation enlightens only the Israelites, but "the word" of which John speaks enlightens every human being, both Israelite and Gentile. Like Paul, who holds that the pagans "know God" (Rom. 1:21) though they "refuse to acknowledge God" (Rom. 1:28), John is defining the knowledge that all people have of God as the moral imperative of justice and love of neighbor. John asserts that this imperative is "the word" and that "the word was God." Knowing the content of the word, knowing that it is identical to "the commandment," we can understand John's affirmation that the word existed from the beginning. As Brown has shown, John, like the Old Testament authors, uses "word" and "commandment" as virtual synonyms (see Exod. 20:1; Deut. 5:5, 22; Ps. 119:4, 25, 28; and especially Deut. 4:12–13).

In his commentary on John 15:22–25, Brown correctly observes, "When in John 15:21 and again in 16:3 Jesus says that those who persecute his disciples have not known the Father (nor himself), there is no suggestion that such ignorance lessens culpability. Rather, the ignorance itself is culpable."[20] In other words, when John says that the world's criminal behavior is due to ignorance of the true God, he clearly does not consider that the ignorance excuses this criminality; on the contrary, he is affirming that this ignorance is itself the crime. So we can understand why he is not content to hold that the world did not know God but must add that the people of Israel itself did not know him. There can be only one ignorance or lack of knowledge that is culpable in itself: a willful ignorance—a refusal to acknowledge—the moral imperative. Bultmann correctly discerns that the Johannine "truth" is "the reality of God," but there he stops. He fails to perceive that the "reality of God" is the summons, the word that calls for love and justice.

It is this ethical essence that the Jews refuse to know, while supposing that they adore the true God in contradistinction to other gods. They delude themselves. They confuse God with a mental construct, a non-material idol. This is what the Johannine Jesus means by telling them that they do not know God. John is identifying ignorance of God with the culpable attitude of interpersonal enmity by which we voluntarily separate ourselves from the word that summons us. In this word, and only in this word, is God God.

GOD AND GOOD WORKS

In the following three chapters it will be seen that to reject Christ is to reject his summons to justice and love which is God. But before that we must obviate an objection. In John's account of the Jews' rejection of Christ we encounter an apparent contradiction. Throughout the Gospel John insists that the world's hatred is provoked by good works and the fulfillment of the word. Yet when Jesus, with revelatory intent, asked the Jews for which of his good works they wished to stone him (John 10:32), John has the Jews reply, "We are not going to stone you for any good work, but for blasphemy: You, a mere man, make yourself God" (John 10:33).

We could interpret this response as mere rationalization, common then as it is now: The masters of this world have always convinced themselves that they are persecuting people, not for deeds of love and justice, but for attacks on "holy religion." The fact that John 10:33 is spoken, not by Jesus or by the author, but by the Jews, would seem to bear out such an interpretation. But in John 5:18 it is John himself who tells us: "This made the Jews still more determined to kill him, because he was not only breaking the Sabbath, but, by calling God his own Father, he claimed equality with God."

The contradiction between blasphemy and good works as the reason for rejecting Christ is apparent. But it cannot be resolved by resorting to harmonism ("both the one and the other") nor by suggesting that John was a careless author, unaware of or unperturbed by self-contradictions. A careful reading of the Johannine passages we have just cited shows that John considers good works and blasphemy each to be an exclusive cause of the Jews' hatred. To resolve the contradiction we must show how the two theses are identical.

John 5:16–30 (and especially John 5:18) points out the path to a solution. We must bear in mind that the entire controversy recounted here revolves around the "good work" described in John 5:1–15. (The intentional link is clear if we compare verses 16 and 18 with verses 9 and 10.) Lagrange is convinced that in John 5:18ff. "God is compared to a craftsman who works, and his Son, when he performs cures, works in the same way, even on the Sabbath."[21] Dodd has discovered, by comparing these verses with the Palestinian and Hellenistic customs of the period, a heretofore unnoticed parable.[22] In John 5:19—"The son can do nothing by himself; he does only what he sees the father doing"—the article before "son" and before "father" is the generic article, as in Mark 3:27, 4:3, and 4:21. Following this article, the words "son" and "father" designate neither God the

Son nor God the Father. The parable is simply saying that an artisan teaches his son the skills of his trade. Dodd comments:

> It is a significant detail that the apprentice *watches* his father at work. . . . The detail is not made use of in the theological exposition which follows; it is not a feature dictated by the requirements of the deeper meaning which is to be conveyed. It is integral to the scene as realistically conceived. It is precisely at this point that the difference between the parable and the allegory reveals itself most clearly.[23]

In the controversy Jesus brandishes the fact that his activity is identical to his Father's, just as any artisan's work is the same as his father's; he indicates thereby the unmistakable nature of his "works," of his "good works." His powerful thesis is already expressed in its entirety in John 5:17: "My Father is still working now, and so too I also am working." Bultmann correctly observes that this response "contains not only the assertion of the *equality* of Jesus' work with God's work, but this equality, which is described in verses 19f. with regard to the content of the work, is regarded in verse 17 in terms of its *constancy*."[24] Verse 17 implies what is to follow, for the times and hours of an artisan's work are equal to the times and hours of his father's work. Commenting on this verse, Brown remarks, "That the implications of this argument were immediately apparent is witnessed by the violence of the reaction."[25] Indeed in the very next verse (5:18) John tells us that the issue of the Sabbath was of small concern; rather, they tried to kill him because he called God his own father.

This is sonship by virtue of engaging in identical activity, performing the same good works. To say so is not to deny or doubt Christ's divinity, but rather to try to understand what for John is much more important than the divinity of Christ. Our obsession with Christ's divinity (pro or con) is constantly distracting us and preventing us from hearing what John is trying to tell us.

The evangelist must attribute great importance to

the identical nature of these works, for he again speaks of it before narrating the detailed account of the miracle in chapter 9: "Neither this man nor his parents sinned. He was born blind so that *the works of God* might be displayed in curing him. We must carry out *the works of him who sent me*" (John 9:3–4). And in chapter 10 the emphasis becomes even stronger: "If I am not doing *the works of my Father*, do not believe me. But if I am doing them, even though you do not believe me, *believe the works*" (John 10:37–38). It is difficult to imagine a more powerful theological thesis than this: Even if you do not believe me, believe the works. It appears again as the absolute core of revelation at the Last Supper: "Believe me when I say that I am in the Father and the Father in me. Or else believe it *because of the works themselves.* In truth I tell you: He who believes in me, the *works* that I do, he also will do them, and greater than these because I am going to the Father" (John 14:11–12). These events provide more than enough opportunity for the narrator to affirm Christ's divinity; and clearly John is not loath to affirm it, for in the first verse of his Gospel he tells us that "the word was God." If he does not repeat it when Jesus speaks of his works and God's, it is because he is more concerned that the qualitative identity of their works be revealed.

The Catholic exegete Feuillet shows that in all these passages the intention is clearly to teach more than the messiahship of Jesus; nevertheless the Johannine thesis is in no case what we understand as the divinity of Christ.[26] Structurally speaking, we should expect to find a revelation of paramount importance in chapters 5 through 10 of the Gospel. Following van den Bussche, we see that in the long section John 1:19–10:42, the first unit (1:19–4:54) is devoted to the proclamation of the messianic event, and the second unit (5:1–10:42) is intended to express something further. But it is hermeneutical error to presuppose that this something can be only the divinity of Christ. This theological prejudice prevents revelation; we close every door on what the Gospel says, preferring to hear what we already know.

Could there be something more important for John than the divinity of Christ? Yes: the divinity of God. And this, according to John, is what the chosen people has shown itself incapable of accepting.

John 1:19–10:42 (the section analyzed by van den Bussche) is closed by a quotation from Psalm 82, which Jesus employs with all the profundity intended by its ancient author—a profundity that modern exegesis has only begun to glimpse.[27] This very ancient psalm, apparently ingenuous, compares Yahweh with all the other gods, challenging them to save the orphan and the widow, to liberate the weak and the needy from the hand of the unjust. The gods show themselves incapable of performing these truly good works. And *this is how it is shown* that they are not the true God, but rather mortals like ourselves. Only Yahweh is the true God, judge of all nations. Thus we can understand why Jesus adds, after quoting the psalm, "If I am not doing the works of my Father, do not believe me. But if I am doing them, even though you do not believe me, believe the works" (John 10:37–38).

It is totally unimportant to John (in this context) whether Jesus Christ is God. What matters to him is that God is in the historical fact called Jesus Christ. What matters to him is that God is revealed in Jesus: "Even though you do not believe me, believe the works, so that you may recognize and know that the Father is in me and I in the Father" (John 10:37–38).

The unmistakable quality of these works, which as historical fact reveal God, is Jesus' sole claim. The congruence of John 5 with John 10 (two piers of a perfect arch) is all the more significant since the two discourses use entirely different compositional means to state that Yahweh is revealed in works: chapter 5 using the parable of the artisan and his son and chapter 10 the theology of Psalm 82. The link between the chapters seems intentional: In 10:36 the Jews are reproached for interpreting Jesus' claim of sonship as blasphemy; this claim of sonship is not formally introduced in 10:33, but in 5:18. The argument of Psalm 82 is that the "judgment" consists in the "good works"; this argument, however, is not presented thematically in John 10:32–39, but in John 5:20–22.

John has an underlying intent in depicting the Jews' reaction to Jesus' blasphemous audacity. In making himself God or equal to God or the Son of God, the Johannine Jesus takes it upon himself to show that this divinity or equality or sonship consists in the good works that reveal the one true God in the historical and contingent fact before them. So the "blasphemy" by which they claim to be infuriated is in fact the unpostponable imperative of good works in which God consists. Their murderous hatred is directed toward the God of Israel, whom they claim to worship, but do not know. What really angers them is "the word"—the commandment of love and justice. "You want to kill me because my word makes no headway with you" (John 8:37).

THE UNSEEN GOD

Let us now return to John's prologue. If we read it as a whole and do not divide it in two, then, even without reference to the First Epistle, it will reveal the content of "the word." Lagrange notes that John 1:18 "refers us back to the first verse by a kind of *inclusio* or bracketing."[28] Regardless of the diverse literary or theological origins of the elements articulated by John in his prologue, we must now read it as a unit to see its message clearly.

The prologue focuses on "the word" (which essentially is indirect communication, that is, injunction across a distance that, fortunately, is insuperable). Since John's purpose is to teach us that God is only in the word, the prologue's conclusion—"no one has ever seen God"—fits his purpose perfectly. Therefore those exegetes who prefer to deny that God is only in the word find it imperative to ignore or misinterpret this verse.

Modern exegesis—even the most conservative (see, for example, Wickenhauser[29])—unanimously precludes misinterpreting the phrase "no one has seen God" according to the Greek, Scholastic thesis that God cannot be known by the corporal senses but only by spiritual understanding. John was not concerned with this question.

That misinterpretation has been abandoned, but there is another. Some say that "no one has seen [heoraken] God" refers to the past, that the statement constitutes a denial of past facts without prejudice to the future and without asserting a nontemporal thesis about the absolute impossibility of seeing God. According to this misinterpretation John is saying that no one has seen God "yet," not that God absolutely cannot be seen. But John could very well have used the adverbial "not yet" if that were what he meant. He does so in John 7:39 (twice), 7:46, 19:41, and 20:9—a total of five times, more than any other New Testament author. When he wants to point out the absence in the past of something that in the present or the future is no longer absent, John is sufficiently skillful to say "not yet" or "still not" or "never before" (compare the *oudepote* of 7:46 with the *oudeis popote* of 1:18). The question whether God can be seen or not is too important to John for him to omit the "yet" if that were what he meant. This misinterpretation allows John no possibility of saying that God absolutely cannot be seen. If John has used the axiomatic present ("no one sees God") it would say that John is referring to the present—without prejudice to the future.

This misinterpretation is conclusively refuted by the fact that *heoraken* is in the gnomic or axiomatic perfect tense,[30] whose force is specifically nontemporal. (Other examples of this axiomatic perfect occur in Matt. 13:46

and James 1:24.) This same perfect *heoraken*, in its negative form, appears again in the Third Epistle:

The one who "does good" is of God;
the one who "does evil" *did not see* God (3 John 11).

The axiomatic character of the passage is obvious, and the verb is the same negative form of *heoraken* that we find in John 1:18.

The passage in which the meaning of "no one has ever seen God" is finally beyond dispute occurs in the First Epistle. Here John uses the perfect tense of the verb *theaomai*, which, like *horao* (perfect tense, *heoraken*), means "to see":

No one has ever seen God;
if we love one another, God dwells in us,
and his love is brought to perfection in us (1 John 4:12).

Here the axiomatic character of the verb, its validity for all times, is revealed by the passage itself. God is not to be *seen*—now or ever. If we love one another, God is already in us, and everything that constitutes loving God is already perfectly fulfilled in us; loving God is only this. The same thesis is repeated in John 14:15, 21, 23: There is no direct knowledge of the true God; unlike all other gods, the God of the Bible is known only in the imperative of love of neighbor. Herein lies the unprecedented profundity of the prologue: God is not seen (John 1:18) because God is the word (John 1:1).

A careful reading of the text adds further proof that John 1:18a cannot refer to the past. John 14:9 uses the same verb *heoraken* to say that God has already been seen: "Whoever has seen me has seen the Father." And in 3 John 11c this same past fact is implicitly but clearly affirmed: "Whoever does evil has not seen God" (implying that whoever "does good" *has* seen God). The "visibility" of God asserted in John 14:9 and 3 John 11 is indirect. Indeed, John 14:9 is a clear rejection of Philip's request to see God directly: "Have I been all this time

with you, Philip, and you still do not know me? Anyone
who has seen me has seen the Father. Then how can you
say, 'Show us the Father'?" In saying "no one has seen
God," John is not telling us that no one has seen God *till
now*, nor is he telling us that no one has seen God *with his
eyes*. He is telling us that no one ever has or ever will
know God (cf. "has not known God" in 1 John 4:7–8)
except indirectly, in the fulfillment of the command to
love one another.

"COMPASSION AND GOODNESS"

The transcendence of God must be a being-summoned
by the word, otherwise it simply becomes a thought, an
immanent epithet conceived by the self, a part of the self
that does not transcend the self, regardless of one's
intention. Without the word, otherness disappears, becomes subsumed by the thinker, and loses its power of
summons as external being. The glorious impossibility
of assimilating the one who speaks to me is the very life
of moral conscience. Only because of it am I not alone;
only because of it is immanence sundered.

The essential link between John 1:18 and John 1:1
forces us to specify the content of the word, for when
John proclaims his controversial thesis that "no one has
ever seen God," he does so to make us understand that
only in love of neighbor can we know God (1 John 4:12, 20,
7). The presence of this thesis in the prologue makes
sense only insofar as "the word" is identical to the imperative of loving one another.

Thus we can understand why John's prologue about
the word includes an attack on Moses:

The law was given through Moses, compassion and goodness
came to be through Jesus Christ (John 1:17).

According to Exod. 33:18 Moses asked "to see" the glory
of Yahweh, but according to Exod. 34:6 all that was
granted him was Yahweh passing before him as the God
rich in "compassion and goodness." John uses this same

hendiadys to describe the content of the *glory* of the word made flesh (John 1:14), only to state, immediately, that no one has seen God but that "compassion and goodness" came to be through Jesus Christ.

"Came to be" is a singular verb: *egeneto*. Use of the singular verb with two non-neuter subjects indicates that "compassion and goodness" is a hendiadys ("one by means of two"). The Johannine term *charis kai aletheia* is an attempt to translate into Greek the famous Hebrew hendiadys *hesed we'emet*, which Tit. 3:4 renders, more accurately than John, as "goodness and philanthropy." It is a single idea expressed by means of two terms.

As early as 1880 Westcott realized that *charis kai aletheia* is John's translation of the common Old Testament hendiadys *hesed we'emet*.[31] In 1912 Joüon, noted for his philological sensitivity, came to the same conclusion.[32] Bultmann's Old Testament allergies have not impressed modern scholars: Schnackenburg, Wickenhauser, Zerwick, Barrett, Brown, and van den Bussche, among others, all maintain that John 1:14 and 1:17 refer to *hesed we'emet*.[33] Schnackenburg's testimony is especially convincing. He disputes Chrysostom, Thomas Aquinas, Theophylactus, Bede, Maldonatus, and Calmes with regard to John 1:13, vehemently denying the moral sense of "to be born of God" (see our chapter 5) and arguing that such a sense is foreign to the context. Nevertheless he is forced to recognize that John 1:14 and 1:17 refer to *hesed we'emet*, which is pure moral teaching.[34]

Bultmann's misreading results primarily from his failure to note that John 1:17 has a singular verb and the subject therefore demands to be translated as a hendiadys.[35] Besides Bultmann translates *'emet* as "faithfulness," which does not fit the Johannine context. An analysis of the series of Old Testament passages in which *hesed we'emet* occurs, published by Quell in 1933, showed that the translation of *'emet* as " 'faithfulness' nowhere commends itself"[36] and to translate it in this way "always implies a measure of refining and retouching,"[37] but Bultmann ignored this conclusion. We must realize that Quell was one of the first to break a centuries-long tradition of arbitrariness and caprice in interpreting the Bible, a tradition that "finds" in the Old Testament exactly what the interpretor wishes to find there. But it is not for the exegete to decide what the Bible is saying or why it was written; the Bible's authors themselves have already done that.

The hendiadys *hesed we'emet* appears in the following passages: Gen. 24:12, 14, 27, 49; 32:11; 47:29; Exod. 34:6; Josh. 2:14; 2 Sam. 2:6; 15:20; Prov. 3:3; 14:22; 16:6; 20:28; Ps. 25:10; 40:11, 12; 57:3; 61:7; 85:11; 86:15; 89:15; 115:1. The equivalent hendiadys *hesed we'emunah* should also be kept in mind; it occurs in Hos. 2:22; Ps. 36:6; 88:12; 89:2, 3, 24, 49; 92:2; 98:3; 100:5. There are, finally, nine instances in which *hesed* occurs in synonymic parallel with *'emet*: Ps. 26:3; 57:10; 69:13; 108:4; 117:2; Isa. 16:5; Hos. 4:1; Mic. 7:20; Zech. 7:9. There are forty-two passages in all. A careful reading of these passages leads us to conclude that *hesed we'emet* (or *hesed we'emunah*) is a hendiadys with a univocal meaning. Many spiritualistic exegetes, however, manage to avoid that conclusion by adopting an erroneous method. They choose as normative those passages in which, because the contexts are insufficiently determinative, the expression could be assigned various meanings. They then attribute to the term in question whatever meaning they wish, so long as it is not absolutely excluded by the context. This definition they then adopt as the sole correct meaning of the expression in all contexts. For example, in translating *hesed we'emet*, these pious interpreters cite Exod. 34:6, where Yahweh is described as a God rich in *hesed we'emet*. In this verse the context is not definitional, and escapist exegetes take advantage of this fact: They decree that the hendiadys means loyalty and faithfulness to the covenant or the promise, and then they impose this same meaning on all the other occurrences of *hesed we'emet* that we have listed. If the subject is God, then the term refers to God's faithfulness to the covenant; if the subject is human beings, then it refers to human beings' faithfulness to the covenant. The method is fallacious, but the conclusions are satisfactory for those who wish to think them so.

Provided we abjure this absurd method, a careful review of the passages we have listed leads to a univocal and objectively established meaning. We will cite several examples, the first a passage from the book of Samuel, which is recognized as the most classic part of the Hebrew Bible. When David was anointed king, he was notified that the inhabitants of Jabesh had given Saul a proper burial. David sent word to them: "May Yahweh bless you for having mercy (*hesed*, 'compassion') on Saul your lord and giving him burial" (2 Sam. 2:5). David's message continues:

May Yahweh in his turn have *compassion and goodness* on you, and I too "will do good" to you for what you have done (2 Sam. 2:6).

The hendiadys *hesed we'emet* receives great emphasis. It clearly refers to good works as we defined them in chapter 5: works of mercy (such as burying the dead), of solidarity, of compassion and goodness. David thanks the Jabeshites for their work of mercy, he hopes that Yahweh will reward them in kind, and promises that he will do the same. In this passage the context of *hesed we'emet* is a promise, and *hesed we'emet* is what the promiser promises to do; but he could have also promised to wreak vengeance or to tap dance. In no way does *hesed we'emet* mean faithfulness to the promise; it is the content or object of the promise, and its only meaning is compassion and goodness.

The same meaning is evident in Prov. 16:6: "With compassion and goodness sin is expiated." The teaching of Tob. 12:9 is the same: "Almsgiving . . . purifies of all sin."

We should keep in mind that the Septuagint always translates *hesed* as *eleos* ("compassion"). There is no better one-word translation of *hesed*, in spite of the degeneration into paternalism that the term "compassion" has suffered over the last twenty centuries. It is less equivocal than "love" or "faithfulness." Using the latter terms, some interpreters have tried to outdo the Septuagint: They would make *hesed* signify a vertical "religious" relationship, a direct God-man relationship. This meaning, however, is completely foreign to the term. (To have "compassion" on God is an idea too bizarre even for the spiritualized theologies.)

Hesed is linked with justice (*sedakah*) and/or right (*mispat*) by means of hendiadys or synonymic parallel in Jer. 9:24; Isa. 16:5; Mic. 6:8; Hos. 2:21–22; 6:6; 10:12; 12:7; Zech. 7:9; Ps. 25:9–10; 33:5; 36:6–7; 36:10; 40:11; 85:11; 88:12–13; 89:15; 98:2–3; 103:17; 119:62–64. In these passages *hesed* is compassion closely linked to a sense of justice; it is compassion-on-the-poor-and-the-oppressed, identical to indignation over the violation of the rights of the weak. Because of this compassion Yahweh assails the oppressors "with raised hand and outstretched arm" (see Deut. 4:34; 5:15; 7:19; 26:8; Exod. 6:6; Ps. 136:12); because of this compassion "he breaks the teeth in the mouths" of the unjust (see Ps. 58:6; 3:7).

The paternalistic sense of compassion is foreign to both the Old Testament and the New. In Matthew 23 Jesus of Nazareth denounces the scribes and the Pharisees seven times as "hypocrites!" (vv. 13, 14, 15, 23, 25, 27, 29), five times as "blind!" (vv. 16, 17, 19, 24, 26), and once as "stupid!" (v. 17)—and yet in the same passage he teaches "justice, compassion, and goodness" (v. 23). Biblical compassion is not condescension; it is unreserved commitment to the weak, the poor, and the oppressed. It acknowledges their rights; it is identical to an absolute sense of justice.

In this light we can understand John 1:17. John takes for granted that *charis kai aletheia* is an extremely

well-known term: It is the *hesed we'emet* spoken of so
often in the Old Testament and used in Exod. 34:6 to
define the true God. Moses did not see God, because God
is not seen. As for compassion and goodness, the law
given by Moses had commanded it but not brought it
about. Compassion and goodness came to exist in this
world through Jesus Christ. This is the difference between the work of Jesus Christ and the work of Moses:
The era of compassion and goodness began in the world
thanks only to Jesus Christ; the laws of Moses had not
achieved it.

John 1:14 (without which the prologue is no prologue)
tells us the content of the word, the word that was made
flesh, as the same verse also tells us. In fact, it has
always been thought that the whole point of this verse is
the fact that the word made flesh, whose glory we saw,
was full of compassion and goodness (irrespective of
whether or not *pleres*, "full," refers to the word itself, to
the only-begotten Son who is identical to the word, or to
the glory of the Son; the last alternative is the most
likely—see Exod. 33:18 and 34:6). In relating to us the
life of Christ, all four evangelists are in fact recounting a
life full of compassion and goodness. It is John who tells
us (at the very outset) that this is "the word."

NOTES

1. B. F. Westcott, *The Gospel according to St. John* (London: John
Murray, 1908), p. 222.

2. Ibid.

3. Raymond E. Brown, *The Gospel according to John (xiii–xxi)*,
Anchor Bible 29A (Garden City, New York: Doubleday, 1970), p. 765.

4. Günther Klein, "Das wahre Licht scheint schon," *Zeitschrift für
Theologie und Kirche* 68 (1971), p. 305 n. 186.

5. Rudolf Bultmann, *Die drei Johannesbriefe* (Göttingen: Vandenhoeck, 1967), p. 33 [Eng. trans.: *The Johannine Epistles*, trans. R.
Philip O'Hara et al. (Philadelphia: Fortress Press, 1973), p. 27].

6. Klein, "Wahre Licht," p. 301. To say that the *eschaton* originally
was ontologically independent of real time is a gratuitous Bultmannian affirmation.

7. Ibid., p. 302. It does not "acquire" the character of an epoch be-

cause it always had it. Nevertheless Klein's testimony is valuable because his Bultmannian prejudice does not keep him from recognizing what John says.

8. Ibid., p. 305.

9. Bultmann, *Johannesbriefe*, p. 15 [Eng. trans.: *Johannine Epistles*, p. 9].

10. Rudolf Bultmann, *Theologie des Neuen Testaments*, p. 380 [cf. Eng. trans.: *Theology of the New Testament*, trans. Kendrick Grobel (New York: Charles Scribner's Sons, 1951), 2:33].

11. Johann Michl, *Die Katholischen Briefe*, RNT 8/2, 2nd ed. (Regensburg: Pustet, 1968), p. 200; Johannes Schneider, *Die Kirchenbriefe*, NTD 10 (Göttingen: Vandenhoeck, 1967), p. 134; A. E. Brooke, *The Johannine Epistles*, International Critical Commentary 38 (Edinburgh: T. & T. Clark, 1912), p. 2; Rudolf Schnackenburg, *Die Johannesbriefe*, 3rd ed. (Freiburg: Herder, 1965), pp. 58–59; G. Delling, "archo," *TWNT*, 1:480 [Eng. trans.: *TDNT*, 1:481–82]; etc.

12. Hans Conzelmann, "Was von Anfang war," in *Neutestamentliche Studien für R. Bultmann, Beiheft zur Zeitschrift für die neutestamentliche Wissenschaft* 21 (Berlin: Töpelmann, 1954), p. 196; Herbert Braun, *Gesammelte Studien zum Neuen Testament und seiner Umwelt* (Tübingen: Mohr-Siebeck, 1962), p. 232.

13. Brown, *Gospel according to John (xiii–xxi)*, p. 765.

14. Ibid., pp. 638 and 663.

15. C. K. Barrett, *The Gospel according to St. John* (London: SPCK, 1955), p. 397.

16. Braun, *Gesammelte Studien*, p. 220.

17. M. J. Lagrange, *Evangile selon Saint Jean* (Paris: Gabalda, 1948), p. 409.

18. Rudolf Bultmann, *Das Evangelium des Johannes* (Göttingen: Vandenhoeck, 1964), pp. 473–74 [cf. Eng. trans.: *The Gospel of John*, trans. G. R. Beasley-Murray et al. (Philadelphia: Westminster Press, 1971), pp. 612–13].

19. William L. Moran, S. J., "The Ancient Near Eastern Background of the Love of God in Deuteronomy," *Catholic Biblical Quarterly* 25, no. 1 (January 1963):77–87; Matthew J. O'Connell, S. J., "The Concept of Commandment in the Old Testament," *Theological Studies* 21, no. 3 (September 1960): 351–403.

20. Brown, *Gospel according to John (xiii–xxi)*, p. 697.

21. Lagrange, *Evangile selon Saint Jean*, p. 141.

22. C. H. Dodd, *More New Testament Studies* (Grand Rapids: Eerdmans, 1968), pp. 30–40.

23. Ibid., p. 39.

24. Bultmann, *Evangelium des Johannes*, p. 183 [cf. Eng. trans.: *Gospel of John*, p. 245].

25. Brown, *Gospel according to John (i–xii)*, p. 217.

26. André Feuillet, "Les *ego eimi* christologiques du quatrième évangile," *Recherches de Science Religieuse* 54, no. 2 (April–June 1966): 236.

27. See A. González, "Le Psaume LXXXII," *Vetus Testamentum* 13, no. 3 (July 1963):293–309; F. Charles Fensham, "Widow, Orphan, and the Poor in Ancient Near Eastern Legal and Wisdom Literature," *Journal of Near Eastern Studies* 21, no. 2 (April 1962):129–39.

28. Lagrange, *Evangile selon Saint Jean*, ad John 1:18.

29. Alfred Wickenhauser, *Das Evangelium nach Johannes*, RNT 4, 2nd ed. (Regensburg: Pustet, 1957), p. 50.

30. F. Blass and A. Debrunner, *A Greek Grammar of the New Testament*, 3rd ed., trans. Robert W. Funk (Chicago: University of Chicago Press, 1967), no. 344.

31. Westcott, *Gospel according to St. John*, p. 13.

32. Paul Joüon, "Notes de lexicographie hébraique," *Mélanges de la Faculté Orientale* 5 (1911–12), p. 407.

33. Rudolf Schnackenburg, *Das Johannesevangelium* (Freiburg: Herder, 1965), 1:248 [Eng. trans.: *The Gospel according to St. John*, trans. Kevin Smyth (New York: Herder and Herder, 1968), 1:272]; Wickenhauser, *Evangelium nach Johannes*, p. 49; Max Zerwick, *Analysis philologica novi testamenti graeci*, 2nd ed. (Rome: Pontificio Istituto Biblico, 1960), p. 212; Barrett, *Gospel according to St. John*, p. 139; Brown, *Gospel According to John (i–xii)*, p. 14; Henri van den Bussche, *Jean* (Paris: Desclée, 1967), p. 102.

34. Schnackenburg, *Johannesevangelium*, 1:238–39 and 248 [Eng. trans.: *Gospel according to St. John*, 1:262 and 272].

35. Bultmann, *Evangelium des Johannes*, pp. 49–50 n. 3 [Eng. trans.: *Gospel of John*, pp. 74 n. 2]. In *TWNT*, 1:247 he holds that it is "possible, but not very likely" [Eng. trans.: *TDNT*, 1:246].

36. Gottfried Quell, "aletheia," *TWNT*, 1:233 n. 2 [Eng. trans.: *TDNT*, 1:233 n. 2].

37. Ibid., *TWNT*, 1:237 n. 12 [Eng. trans.: *TDNT*, 1:236 n. 12].

Chapter 8

The Mistake Known as Christianity

John's thinking on the subject of the word, the commandment, the summons, is of decisive importance as preamble to his ultimate message. That message—the thesis of this book—is presented in our chapters 8, 9, and 10, but to understand it we must first have grasped the importance of the word. It remains now to resolve the question of Kierkegaardian contemporaneity, which heretofore we have only touched on. It remains to demonstrate why Hegel and Marx were correct to replace nontemporal moral teaching with historical facts. Here we must again consider that truth and imperative are identical. We must describe the new field of being that requires our decision in order to be; it is existentialism's task to discover this new being and humankind's to bring it about.

It was not a late dogmatism that caused the Christian churches to affirm that without Christ there is no God; but it has become clear to us that the churches themselves did not genuinely understand their own affirmation. They based their tenet on some positive decree of God, as if God in an authoritarian, extrinsic way punished those who rejected his emissary by depriving them of their knowledge of God. But we know that such arbitrary authoritarianism would be profoundly immoral and whoever acted in this way would not be God but a superhuman despot against whom we should be morally obligated to rebel. According to the Bible, such a one would not be God but an idol.

Christianity has been characterized by two inveterate errors. We have already presented the first in chapters 6 and 7: It consists in religion, in misconceiving the true God as one who can be directly known, loved, and invoked, that is, it consists in changing God from the God of Jesus Christ into a mental idol.

The second error is even deeper and more tragic, for it refers to Christ himself, and the churches have taken it upon themselves to maintain that Christ—the Christ who would differentiate the Christian churches from Israel—is necessary for salvation. Ironically, the error has to do with the very word "Christ" (=messiah), in which the term "Christian" originates. This second error is dealt with in chapters 8, 9, and 10.

JESUS IS THE MESSIAH

To interpret extrinsically the New Testament thesis that "anyone who denies the Son does not have the Father either" (1 John 2:23) is to misinterpret it. We have already seen that the commandment is new "*because* the darkness is passing and the true light is already shining" (1 John 2:8). This means that the commandment would not be a commandment, it would not summon as irreducible otherness, if the historical fact called Jesus of Nazareth did not exist.

That van den Bussche glimpsed this is evident in his perceptive commentary on John 1:14: "Regardless of the importance of the state of incarnation in Johannine thought, it is of less significance than the hour of Jesus; for it is the latter that indeed is the definitive revelation and the total realization of salvation."[1] This commentary on the thesis that "the word was made flesh" constitutes the greatest advance in Johannine exegesis since 1941, the year that Bultmann published his book on the Fourth Gospel. But it is lamentable that van den Bussche saw a contrast between the hour and the flesh. "Flesh" (*sarx=basar*) means much more than "the entire human being who acts in community, who is visible and tangible to those around him."[2] It means a bit of contingent human history. What John says is that the word became flesh in a historical fact called Jesus of Nazareth.

The term "flesh" as used in John 1:14 and 1 John 4:2 has no antispiritualist connotations; John's purpose is not to refute those who abominate matter and deny the corporeality of the Son of God. For centuries we have too readily assumed that John's thesis, as well as the antithesis he combated, was nontemporal. For centuries we have projected onto the New Testament our Scholastic quarrels about the union or separation of spirit and matter. But John's purpose is infinitely more important than to differentiate between a materialistic and a spiritualistic worldview, both of which in the last analysis remain enclosed in immanence. The passage that speaks of "flesh" in the Epistle reads:

Every spirit that confesses that Jesus is the Messiah who has come in the flesh is from God. And every spirit that does not confess Jesus is not from God. This is the spirit of the Antichrist (1 John 4:2–3).

In 1912 Brooke, breaking with a long, enslaving interpretative tradition, commented, "The error which the writer condemns seems to have been the rejection of the identy of the historical man Jesus with the pre-existent Christ."[3] This is well expressed, except that what pre-existed was not precisely the Messiah but the word. Brooke's commentary, however, definitively supersedes the antidocetist interpretation, according to which John is refuting the belief that Jesus' flesh was a phantasmic phenomenon. "There is nothing in the Epistle which compels us to suppose that the author is combatting pure Docetism."[4] In the quoted passage we can see that *homologein Iesoun Christon en sarki eleythota* is the same as *homologein ton Iesoun,* to confess something about Jesus as such, not about Jesus Christ as such. And the Antichrist is precisely anti-Christ; he denies that Jesus *is* the Christ, he denies that he *is* the Messiah. The exact point in 1 John 4:2 at which the understood verb "to be" should be inserted is made clear by the other passage in which the Epistle defines the Antichrist: "Who is the liar? Who but he that denies that Jesus is the Messiah [*christos*]? He is the Antichrist" (1 John 2:22). In both passages John is defining Antichrist. The last part of 1 John 4:3 would be better translated "this is the substance of the Antichrist." The translation "this is the spirit of the Antichrist" also conveys John's definitional intention.

In addition, 1 John 5:1 expresses the verb "to be" in exactly the same context in which it is left understood in 1 John 4:2–3 and stated in 1 John 2:22: "Anyone who believes that Jesus is the Messiah has been born of God." The verb "to be" comes between "Jesus" and "Christ." We find the same idea in John 9:22: "The Jews had already agreed that anyone who confessed him as Messiah should be banned from the synagogue" *(ean tis auton homologese christon).* There is no basis for the antidocetist interpretation that would render 1 John 4:2 as "confesses that Jesus Christ has come in the flesh." In all the related passages "Jesus" is the subject and "Messiah" is the predicate. The verb "to be" is either expressed between the two terms (1 John 2:22 and 5:1) or, as often occurs in the classical languages, it is implied there (John 9:22: "confessed Jesus to be the Messiah"). Therefore in 1 John 4:2 and 2 John 7, which, like John 9:22, are constructed with the governing verb "to confess," the verb "to be" must be understood between the subject "Jesus" and the predicate "Messiah." "Come in the flesh" is in apposition to "Messiah"; it describes the "Messiah."

JOHN'S ADVERSARIES

Van den Bussche notes that the "heretics" combated in 1 John 4:2–3; 2:22–23; and 2 John 7 "do not deny the man Jesus; they deny in this man the Christ," that is, the Messiah.[5] And with regard to John 1:14 he asks, "Was the apostle thinking of the Docetists, who denied the reality of the body of Christ, in which they recognized only the appearance of a body? This does not seem certain to us."[6]

Note that the Jews accepted and earnestly professed a future Messiah, and many even professed a pre-existent Messiah. Jews and Christians could not doubt this unreal Messiah. Nor could denying such a Messiah mean being anti-Christ. What the adversaries referred to in the Epistle deny is "that *Jesus* is the Messiah." What they deny is that in this man the Messiah has come to the world. What they refuse to allow is that the messianic kingdom should become real history. What they deny is the reality of the *eschaton*. Van den Bussche's contribution—although he does not draw out its consequences—is to have understood that for John the decisive point is Jesus' "hour," not his human nature (see John 2:4; 4:21, 23; 5:25, 28; 7:6, 30; 8:20; 12:23, 27; 13:1; 16:4, 21, 25; 1 John 2:18; 2:8; 4:3). The "flesh" of John 1:14, 1 John 4:2, and 2 John 7 is a concrete episode of real, chronological human history, an "hour," the hour of Jesus. It is the historical fact called Jesus of Nazareth.

That understanding is necessary if we are to see how the whole argument of the First Epistle relates to its central affirmation: "that the true light is already shining" (1 John 2:8). In sum, this is what John's adversaries deny: that the true light is already shining. There is a literary link between this affirmation and the Antichrist's denial of Jesus' messiahship in 1 John 4:3; the link is provided by the adverb "already," which occurs only in these two instances. John even recasts his argument, neatly and elegantly employing the traditional belief that when the Antichrist had arrived the *eschaton* would have arrived as well: "You were told that the Antichrist was to come; now many Antichrists have appeared. By this we know that this is the last hour" (1 John 2:18). He bases his argument on the fact that the Antichrist is—etymologically—the one who opposes the existence of a Messiah and an *eschaton*.

Since "Antichrist" is so powerfully charged a word, it is surprising that exegesis, which has so often tried —unsuccessfully—to identify the "adversaries" of the First Epistle, has paid it so little attention. In fact this lack of attention seems so inexplicable that one is obliged to suspect the exegetes of a subconscious block.

The adversaries John has in mind lie—or err—by denying that Jesus is the Messiah. But of the many who denied it, whom in particular does John mean? Bultmann correctly doubts Schnackenburg's conviction that John is referring to the Gnostics.[7] To deny that Jesus is the Messiah pertains to time, to history, whereas gnosis is a nontemporal belief. Moreover, in the Gospel everything, absolutely everything, is said to depend on our knowing God and Jesus Christ; so if John says that Israel itself does not know the true God, then sound methodology requires us to search the First Epistle for an elaboration of this message and not for the refutation of a heresy specifically related to knowledge. Only failure to understand or accurately to gauge the importance of John's Gospel message could cause us to misconstrue his First Epistle.

Even the terms "heresy," "erroneous doctrine," and "error," which the commentators customarily employ, lead to misunderstandings. The Johannine Jesus, as we have seen, was not accusing the Jews precisely of doctrinal errors when he said to them, "The one who you say is your God, and you do not know him" (John 8:54–55).

Here we must turn again to John 8, observing with Dodd: "It is possible for others beside first-century

'Judaizers' to think that they 'believe,' to boast of their 'freedom,' to say with conviction (as Christians say every day), 'We have God for our Father'—and yet not to 'listen to the words of God.' John would have his readers consider such possibilities and face the consequences."[8]

The intraecclesial intention of John 8 is clear; without it verse 37 leads to an exegetical dead end. In verse 30 John tells us that while Jesus spoke, many believed in him; in verse 31 he emphasizes that Jesus is addressing these believers ("Jesus, then, said *to the Jews who had believed in him*"). But in verse 37 Jesus says to those very Jews who had believed in him: "You want to kill me."

With typical British understatement Barrett comments, "These words follow oddly after v. 31": those who had believed in him.[9] He suggests two alternative explanations of the problem: "Either John is writing very carelessly or he means that the faith of these Jews was very deficient."[10] The first explanation is unacceptable, because John 8:30–40 forms a clear intentional and redactional unit. Even Bultmann—who dismembers John 8, attributing phrases and even whole verses to different discourses and thus turning the chapter into a puzzle—leaves this unit intact.[11] And if Bultmann leaves the passage intact, it has passed the test of fire, as those familiar with Johannine or Synoptic exegesis well know.

The unity is clear. Since they already believed in Jesus Christ (v. 30), the theme of "abiding in his word" (v. 31) can be introduced. Abiding in Jesus' word means "knowing the truth." This leads to "the truth will make you free" (v. 32). But Jesus' interlocutors object that, as sons of Abraham, they have never been enslaved and therefore require no freeing (v. 33). To this Jesus replies by explaining the nature of true liberty (vv. 34–36). He concludes: I know that you are sons of Abraham, but you want to kill me (v. 37).

The concatenation of ideas may seem inappropriate for a treatise, but there is indeed a strict concatenation, from the "believing" of verses 30–31 to the "wanting to kill him" of verse 37. For John it is precisely those who have believed in Jesus Christ who want to kill him. John clearly has an underlying intent here.

Barrett's alternative explanation—that the Jews' faith was deficient faith—was proven by events to be objectively true, but it cannot explain the narrator's intention in John 8:30–40, because the formula *pisteuein eis*, which sets the entire pericope in motion ("many *believed in him*" in verse 30), is the most characteristic Johannine expression for the highest level of Christian faith. This formula has the same connotation throughout the New Testament. The supreme exhortations to adopt the Christian faith are exhortations to *pisteuein eis*. If John distinguishes among various types or levels of faith—and it has not yet been proven that he does— he is certainly not concerned with such distinctions in this pericope.

Barrett himself chooses a third explanation that points us toward the only possible interpretation: "These references to 'many' believers must be taken like the 'you shall know' of v. 28, to refer to a time other than that of the ministry of Jesus."[12] The references Barrett cites are John 2:23; 7:31; 8:30; 10:42; 12:11, 42, ranging over the entire first part of the Gospel. They occur even in the most anecdotal portions of John's narratives, like John 8:30. The "other" time to which Barrett alludes is the time of the church, during which John's Gospel was written. It is John's literary devise to report Jesus' exchange with the Jews; the audience for whom Jesus' words are really intended is John's Christian contemporaries, and John is asserting that in spite of being Christian (that is, without becoming "heretics") they are betraying Jesus Christ.

If that is John's intention in the Gospel, where he is not directly addressing Christians but is formally narrating the deeds and words of Jesus addressed to the Jews, then he is all the more likely to speak similarly in the Epistle.

CHRISTIAN ANTICHRISTS

We must consider the possibility that the First Epistle is reproving the Christians themselves and not any particular doctrinal error or heresy. The Gospel does this very thing by its incisive definitions of knowing the true God; therefore it is all the more likely that John's intent in the Epistle, when he examines the meaning of believing that Jesus is the Messiah, is the same. Some may object to me: Those who do not believe that Jesus is the Messiah are automatically not Christians, so John could not be addressing Christians. I respond: Those who do not know the true God are less so, yet John addresses them. The Jews too could say that those who do not know the true God were automatically not Israelites; but all this evades the true issue. Jesus does not mean heresy or doctrinal error when he says, "He who you say is your God, and you do not know him" (John 8:54–55). The thesis of the Epistle, that the Christians do not believe that Jesus is the Messiah, acquires a profundity and a revolutionary power worthy only of the author John and the evangelizing Jesus of Nazareth. The very affirmation that the word was made flesh means something completely different from the antidocetism we have so placidly attributed to it.

John's Gospel was written for John's Christian contemporaries. Note the end of chapter 2 and the beginning of chapter 3. After recounting the expulsion of the merchants from the temple (John 2:13–22), John says that during this first stay of Jesus in Jerusalem "many believed in his name" (John 2:23). But he immediately adds that "Jesus did not trust himself to them" (John 2:24), because "he knew what was in a man" (John 2:25). Immediately John goes on to describe one of these same men, whose basic incapacity to belong to the kingdom is enunciated by Jesus himself (John 3:1–15, especially vv. 3 and 5).

Clearly John 3 follows John 2—particularly the verses

we have just considered, John 2:23–25—with most deliberate intent. Brown notes that John 3:1 begins with
"And there was a man" and suggests: "Perhaps this use
of 'man' is designed to recall the end of the last verse
(2:25).[13] There is no "perhaps" about it; there is nothing
random about this narrative order. John 3:1 does not
even mention the name of the one Nicodemus visited at
night. It only says, "He came to him at night and he said
to him," obviously intending us to recall John 2:23–25.

Jesus' response to Nicodemus—a short-circuit response, as van den Bussche correctly perceives[14]—was a
total rejection of Nicodemus's attitude. But this man
was one of the "many" who "believed in the name of
Jesus," as we have just been informed. To believe in the
name of Jesus is a formula that characterizes the highest level of confession of Christian faith (see John 1:12;
3:18; 20:31; 1 John 3:23; 5:13; cf. John 14:13, 14; 15:16, 21;
16:24, 26). A simple reading shows that the significance
of the transition from John 2 to John 3 goes beyond the
anecdotal to the universal:

He needed no evidence from others about what there was *in
man*, for he knew what was *in man*. And there was *a man*
among the Pharisees, called Nicodemus, . . .

Moreover, the order of John 2:23–24 demonstrates its
intraecclesial purposes: "Many believed in his name
when they saw the signs that he did. But he did not trust
himself to them."

In John 15 the intraecclesial intention is even more
explicit. Commenting on the parable of John 15, Barrett
accurately observes: "His major interest is in the life of
the Church, in the question who are and who are not
true disciples of Jesus."[15] The wording at the beginning
of the parable has been very carefully studied, and it is
unambiguous: " . . . Every branch that does not bear
fruit *in me*, [the gardener] cuts away" (John 15:2). Jesus
Christ is the vine; the Christians are the branches. The
parable presupposes that the persons spoken of as

branches are members of Christianity; they are *in Jesus.*

Barrett comments that this verse "shows that his primary thought was of apostate Christians."[16] But by comparing this comment to the main intention of the First Epistle we see that Barrett's statement is inaccurate, for these are not apostates or ex-Christians. They are people who are *in Jesus*. They are Christians who, while remaining Christians, do not produce the fruit described in John 15:16–17. This message has always been de-emphasized; therefore we define it exactly. It is not enough to explain, as Brown does, that the parable "emphasizes strongly love for others."[17] Lagrange had already said of verse 16: "We have, then, in this passage the key to the entire discourse."[18] The message of verse 16 continues in verse 17: "These things I command you: that you love one another."

Exegesis that disregards the direct connection—the unity—between the first use of "fruit" in John 15:2 and the "fruit" described in John 15:16-17 disjoints the pericope John 15:1–27; it treats verse 12 ("This is my commandment: that you love one another as I have loved you") as an erratic segment, connected with neither the preceding nor the following verses. But to do that is absurd. Ascertaining the preredactional history of the elements combined in John 15 should not prevent us from understanding the exact Johannine sense of the parable, which John explains immediately following the parable itself. Verses 9–13 describe what it means to bear "much fruit" (v. 8) and develop this typically Johannine thesis: I established the reality called "my love"; abide in it. To abide in my love is to keep my commandments, and my commandments can be reduced to this: Love one another.

Two other elements in the same verse confirm that this is the sense of "bear much fruit" in verse 8. First there is the explicative and synonymic "and" in the phrase "that you bear much fruit *and* that you be my disciples." In John 13:35 we have already been told explicitly, "By this all will know that you are my disciples: that you love one another." Thus to bear much fruit is to love one's neighbor. The other corroborating element in John 15:8 has been pointed out by Lagrange and Brown: "In this is my Father glorified: in that you bear much fruit." Nestle notes the parallel with Matt. 5:16: "That men see your good works and glorify your heavenly Father." As we demonstrated in our chapter 5 "good works" are specifically works of love of neighbor.

John is addressing not apostates but Christians. Having admitted that, the great temptation is to interpret his reproof evasively as Schnackenburg does the First Epistle: "The object of his attack is over and again simply the lack of fraternal love."[19] But it is impossible to reduce John's fierce censure to a routine accusation of lack of charity. In chapter 8, John is speaking to Christians, even when he affirms that the persons in question do not know the true God. It is clear that both Gospel and Epistle are directed against the Christians themselves and not against any heresy or erroneous doctrine.

1 John 2:19 says of heretics that they left our company "so that it might be clear that not all *are* of us." Grammatically we would have expected it to say: "so that it might be clear that not all *were* of us." Bultmann comments: " 'That all are not of us' does not mean: 'they all, the false teachers, do not belong to us,' but rather: 'not all (who so claim) belong to us.' The statement permits recognition of the distinction between the empirical and the true congregation: false members are therefore to be found in the empirical congregation. The sentence is thus also an admonition to critical examination and certainly to self-examination as well."[20] Since in this same verse (1 John 2:19) the verb "to be" was just used twice in the imperfect plural, the change to the present tense seems completely intentional: "so that it might be clear that not all *are* of us." John alludes to the Christians of that time, to the Christians themselves, not only to

those who had already separated themselves from Christianity. Schnackenburg minimizes this:

The experience, painful in itself, of the Christian church toward the end of the first century—that its own front ranks were going astray—was mitigated by the knowledge that all those who did not belong to the church in the long run could not remain within it.[21]

This commentary might be appropriate to or supported by John 15:2 ("the gardener will cut it away") as referring to Christians who do not bear the fruit of love of neighbor. When 1 John 2:18–19, however, speaks of the Antichrists it in no way mitigates the calamity to the church. On the contrary, it says that Antichrists exist within the church. The Protestant distinction between empirical church and authentic church may be valid, but John goes beyond it: He affirms that there are Christians in the community who do not believe that Jesus is the Messiah. John says that some Christians who are authentic members of the community are Antichrists. Thus the question of whether or not the Epistle refers to heretics and apostates becomes irrelevant.

THE MESSIAH AND THE END OF HISTORY

The coincidence of the questions raised by the Epistle and the Gospel is noteworthy. The Epistle's accusations of failure to know God (for example, 1 John 2:4; 3:1; 3:6) and of failure to "believe that Jesus is the Messiah" need not be understood as accusations of formal heresies. Moreover, even if the Epistle does allude to formal heresies, we miss its message if we concentrate exclusively on them. The sense of the Johannine challenge is that both accusations can in equal degree be applied to Christians.

The reason is that one can ascribe to Jesus all the predicates, all the attributes, even divine ones, including the title of "Messiah," and nevertheless deny that with Jesus the end of history has arrived. Indeed Christians do so today. But if the end of history has not arrived, then the epithet "Messiah" is eviscerated. It becomes a nontemporal predicate *emptied of all meaningful content*. The end of history is what differentiates "Messiah" from all other attributes. It is clear that the Christians condemned by John did not question the epithet as a mere attribute, nor did the heretics either, in all likelihood. What they denied was the historical meaning of the content. What they denied—although they preserved a hollow notion of the linguistic meaning of the attribute in verbal form—was a historic fact that concerns all of history. But this is to deny the attribute all its content, for Jesus can *really* be the Messiah only to the degree that "the true light already shines," to the degree that the messianic kingdom that is the end of history has arrived in history.

The Christians condemned by John maintained the idea of Messiah as a mere idea, although they might swear that they professed it as a reality. The fact that they were not dedicated to accomplishing the worldwide kingdom of love and justice shows that "Messiah" for them was a nontemporal predicate. To keep the Messiah nontemporal means that they themselves have undertaken to prevent him from becoming reality. To keep him nontemporal is the same as to keep him eternally pre-existent or eternally future. What they refused to admit is that the Messiah can be *now*, and in this they exactly resembled the Nazarenes of Luke 4:16–30, who found Jesus quite acceptable (Luke 4:17–20) until he told them: *"Today* this Scripture has been fulfilled in your presence" (Luke 4:21). Then the persecution unto annihilation was unleashed (Luke 4:22–29). Attributes are all meaningless because they are ineffectual; in the last analysis they change nothing. The past and the future are likewise of no great moment, for they do not affect *us*. Likewise truth: We can profess anything as "true," and it will make no difference and there will be no real difference between those who profess it and those who do not. The irony of exegesis lies in its failure to understand that *logos* means "word." And the irony of being Christian is that twenty centuries of Christians have not understood that *Christos* means "Messiah." The Christians condemned by John were Antichrists because they did not act as if Jesus was the Messiah. Twenty centuries have passed, and the Antichrist has not changed.

"To deny the Son" (1 John 2:23) is to deny that Jesus is the Messiah.

Who is the liar? Who but he that denies that Jesus is the Messiah? He is the Antichrist, he who denies the Father and the Son, (for) anyone who denies the Son does not have the Father either (and) anyone who confesses the Son also has the Father (1 John 2:22–23).

To heighten and intensify his denunciation of the Antichrists, John adds—in the same breath—that those Christians who deny that Jesus is the Messiah are thereby also denying the Father. They only deceive themselves by believing, like the Jews, that they can deny that Jesus is the Messiah and yet know the true God.

We must now examine why those who reject the *eschaton* do not know the true God. The connection cannot be explained extrinsically nor as divine punishment for disobedience.

NOTES

1. Henri van den Bussche, *Jean* (Paris: Desclée, 1967), p. 98.

2. Ibid., p. 97.

3. A.E. Brooke, *The Johannine Epistles*, International Critical Commentary 38 (Edinburgh: Clark, 1912), p. 108.

4. Ibid., p. 109.

5. Van den Bussche, *Jean*, p. 98.

6. Ibid., p. 97.

7. Rudolf Bultmann, *Die drei Johannesbriefe* (Göttingen: Vandenhoeck, 1967), p. 73 n. 3 [Eng. trans.: *The Johannine Epistles*, trans. R. Philip O'Hara et al. (Philadelphia: Fortress Press, 1973), p. 68 n. 17].

8. C.H. Dodd, "Behind a Johannine Dialogue," *More New Testament Studies* (Grand Rapids: Eerdmans, 1968), p. 52.

9. C.K. Barrett, *The Gospel according to St. John* (London: SPCK, 1955), p. 287.

10. Ibid.

11. Rudolf Bultmann, *Das Evangelium des Johannes* (Göttingen: Vandenhoeck, 1964), pp. 237–38 [Eng. trans.: *The Gospel of John*, trans. A.R. Beasley-Murray et al. (Philadelphia: Westminster, 1971), pp. 433ff].

12. Barrett, *Gospel according to St. John*, p. 284.

13. Raymond E. Brown, *The Gospel according to John (i–xii)*, Anchor Bible 29 (Garden City, New York: Doubleday, 1966), p. 129.

14. Van den Bussche, *Jean*, p. 162.

15. Barrett, *Gospel according to St. John*, p. 393.

16. Ibid., p. 395.

17. Raymond E. Brown, *The Gospel according to John (xiii–xxi)*, Anchor Bible 29A (Garden City, New York: Doubleday, 1970), p. 676.

18. M.J. Lagrange, *Evangile selon Saint Jean*, 3rd ed. (Paris: Gabalda, 1927), p. 408.

19. Rudolf Schnackenburg, *Die Johannesbriefe*, 3rd ed. (Freiburg: Herder, 1965), p.110 n. 1.

20. Bultmann, *Johannesbriefe*, p. 42 [Eng. trans: *Johannine Epistles*, p. 37].

21. Schnackenburg, *Johannesbriefe*, p. 151.

Chapter 9

Demythologizing the Gospel

Bultmann, commenting on Schnackenburg's attempt to interpret 1 John 2:8—an attempt made by all the socially accepted, established churches of history—says: "Schnackenburg wishes to understand 'is already shining' not with reference to the eschatological event, but rather with reference to the historical process which takes place in the 'extension of the divine realm of light' in the 'victorious advancement of the power of Good.' He has thereby very likely misunderstood the paradox that consists of the historicizing of the eschatological event."[1] This criticism is valid—except for the word "paradox." In the Old Testament, in the Qumran scrolls, and in Jewish literature—in fact, since the idea of the *eschaton* was first conceived—the *eschaton* always means the last moment of *history*; it is not beyond history in some imagined atemporal and ahistorical world. John's thesis, which is also Jesus Christ's, and the entire New Testament's—that the *eschaton* has now begun to be realized—may be unacceptable to us, but it is not paradoxical, for the *eschaton* was never supposed to occur outside history.

Nevertheless Bultmann's criticism mainly hits its mark. The *eschaton* is not a progressive phenomenon. Nor is it a result of the "maturation" of humankind, from age to age after the fashion of the historical periods into which textbooks divide human events or the "history of the spirit."

As Günther Klein observes, the arrival of the Antichrists is referred to in 1 John 2:18–19 as an empirical fact, regardless of what Bultmann says.[2] From this fact, understood as historical, John deduces that we have already reached the last hour: "by which we know that this is the last hour." Therefore this cannot mean that the last hour is "a period of critical change, 'a last hour,' but not definitely 'the last hour,' "[3]—as the established churches would have it. The "last hour" refers precisely to the end, not to any extent of time prior to the end. Klein says that the First Epistle not only historicizes eschatology (as Bultmann admits), but it also eschatologizes history. The socially accepted churches do not want the end to come, but they want the period in which they exist and with which they are identified to be "eschatologically relevant." But unless a period is the end of history, it is no more eschatologically relevant than any other.

THE PRESENT ESCHATON

Klein bases his exegesis on Bultmannian premises and relegates the First Epistle to the group of decadent New Testament writings that had begun to deal with the "history of salvation." However, Klein and Bultmann notwithstanding, the eschatology of the Epistle is equally affirmed in the Gospel:

> Jesus said to her: "Your brother will rise again."
> Martha said to him: "I know that he will rise again, at the resurrection on that last day."
> Jesus said to her, "I am the resurrection and the life" (John 11:23–26).

Martha professes the traditional eschatology of the Old Testament, of Judaism, and of Christianity: "I know that he will rise again, at the resurrection on the last day." But Jesus *corrects her:* The resurrection is already here; there is no need to wait for an ever postponable *eschaton.*

This is the difference between the Old Testament and the New: What the prophecies and promises of the Old Testament regarded as future, and rightly so, has become present. That is what established theology has never accepted. For many centuries—long before Bultmann—established theology has been waging an undeclared campaign of so-called demythologizing. But John did not write a history of salvation, neither in his Epistle nor in his Gospel; he affirms that history has arrived at its end and the end is already here.

In John 11:23–26 Jesus radically altered traditional eschatology with regard to the resurrection of the dead. In John 4:25–26 he stated the same correction with regard to the coming of the Messiah, which is another integral element of the *eschaton:*

> The woman said to him, "I know that the Messiah, the one called Christ, is coming; when he comes, he will tell us everything."
> Jesus said to her, "I am he, I who am speaking to you now."

It is impossible not to recognize the parallel between Jesus' correction of this woman's chronology and of Martha's eschatology; even the wording is similar. Schnackenburg has perceived the progressive deepening of the Samaritan woman's insight. In John 4:9 Jesus is a "Jew" to her; in verse 11 he is "sir"; in verse 12 she asks if he is "greater than our father Jacob"; in verse 19 she says, "I see you are a prophet"; and finally she approaches the truth in verses 20–26, 29: Could Jesus be "the Messiah"?

John 4:27–38 refers to nothing other than the true scope of the messianic event: "Raise your eyes and look at the fields, which are already white for harvest" (v. 35). "Harvest" or "reaping" or "crop" is a specialized term used to designate the eschatological event by Isa. 27:12; Joel 4:13; Mark 4:29; 13:28–29; Matt. 3:12; 13:30, 37ff.; Rev. 14:15–16. John dwells self-indulgently upon his subject in John 4:39–41 ("many," v. 39; "many more," v. 41), indicating that the Messiah is the salvation of the whole world: "We know that this is truly the savior of the world" (v. 42). Van den Bussche observes: "In fact the accent should fall more on the word 'world' than on the word 'savior.' "[4] Schnackenburg specifies quite exactly: "The question of Messiahship is already involved in the process."[5] The compositional center of this passage is John 4:25–26, which we have transcribed.

The chronological approach is here the key: He who "is to come" is already here. In verse 21 Jesus said: "Believe me, woman, the time is coming when you will worship the Father neither on this mountain nor in Jerusalem." In verse 23 he became more explicit: "The time is coming *and it is now* when the true worshippers will worship the Father in spirit and in truth." Even confronted with this direct and unequivocal eschatological statement, the woman again managed to postpone the *eschaton*, using the traditional tranquillizing affirmation: "I know that the Messiah is to come; when he comes, he will tell us everything" (v. 25). This is traditional eschatology. With it we can postpone the *eschaton* indefinitely, keeping it a pure and permanently unreal truth. We are prepared to admit and "believe" whatever we are told—about some future time. In the future nothing is truly real, not even the Messiah, because if the Messiah is always future, the epithet is emptied of all content. Jesus blocked the escape: This Messiah who you say is to come is already here; I am he, I who am speaking to you. He said exactly the same thing to Martha: This resurrection and this last day of which you speak, it is already here.

In John 9:35–37 we again find Jesus proclaiming the inescapable "presentness" of the *eschaton*, although the blind man, unlike Martha and the Samaritan woman, has not explicitly formulated the contrasting traditional escapist eschatology:

> Finding him Jesus said, "Do you believe in the Son of man?"
> He answered and said, "And who is he, sir, that I might believe in him?"
> Jesus said to him, "You have seen him; the one who is speaking to you, it is he."

The debate over the term "the Son of man" is currently in its apogee, but in this passage the expression unquestionably designates the bearer of eschatological salvation. Perhaps the question of the one who was blind was intended to elicit some "pure," nontemporal truth as answer. (We have customarily been taught to believe in such truths, regardless of their content.) But Jesus replied, "the one who is speaking with you," asserting the chronological "presentness" of the Son of man as forcefully and unequivocally as he did to the Samaritan woman in John 4:26: He was not referring to another world nor to an awaited future, however imminent; he was speaking of his historical time, which had arrived.

The thesis of 1 John 2:18—"we know that this is the last hour"—was formulated as early as John 1:41 in Andrew's words to Simon: "We have found the Messiah." For the affirmation that a historical man is the promised Messiah makes sense only insofar as that man brings into the world all the conditions of the messianic kingdom described in the Old Testament: complete justice, knowledge of the true God, life, the resurrection of the dead, the cure of physical ills, love of neighbor. Jesus was not simply the protagonist of John's narrative who passed through the Fourth Gospel amassing an anthology of attributes, "titles," and "names of Christ." Had he been only that, he could not also have made present the Last Judgment, the Parousia, the kingdom, knowledge of God, and the time of the true worshippers. John's message throughout the Gospel and the First Epistle is that *Messiah* is a great *now*.

"THE TIME IS NOW"

This brings us to the hermeneutical problem par excellence. The New Testament thesis of John 11:23–26; 5:24; 12:31; 16:11; and 1 John 2:18–19 has only one possible meaning: The Messiah is now. But how are we to reconcile this meaning with the indisputable fact that in the nineteen centuries of human history since the Messiah entered the world there has been no perceptible realization of the resurrection and of justice? The tension induced by this apparent contradiction has led us customarily to look for some other interpretation of John, because it does not seem possible that the Bible would affirm what history shows to be obviously false. In this well-meant assault on John's true meaning, the most disparate theological factions join forces: traditional apologetics on the one hand and the modern demythologizing school on the other. The former attempts to keep the dogma of biblical inerrancy safe from Schweitzer and rationalism; the latter attempts to adapt the gospel message to modern times, whose self-understanding—according to this school—imposes conditions of possibility on every message. The conservatives do not admit to violating the obvious meanings of the texts. The demythologizers perhaps do, but as extenuation they plead their demythologizing intention, which the biblical authors, especially John, can be shown to have shared.

To distort the meaning of the Bible on pretext of "correcting" it, making it conform to extrabiblical criteria, is not sound exegesis. Scientifically speaking, the history of the last nineteen centuries, along with the other extrabiblical data, would perhaps cause us to deduce that the Bible is mistaken and must be consigned to oblivion; but denying that 1 John 2:18–19 and John 11:23–26 affirm the end of history in the time of Christ is to make the Bible assert what it does not assert, and such a method is called falsification, not exegesis.

The pericope John 5:21–30 is the occasion of a crisis of

modern biblical science, because in it the Johannine
Jesus affirms that the *eschaton*, with the Last Judgment
and the resurrection of the dead, is chronologically
present:

(21) As the Father raises the dead and gives them life, so too
the Son gives life to those he loves,
(22) for the Father does not judge anyone, but has given the
whole judgment to the Son,
(23) so that all might honor the Son as they honor the Father.
Anyone who does not honor the Son does not honor the
Father who sent him.
(24) In truth, in truth, I say to you: Anyone who listens to my
word and believes in the one who sent me has eternal life and
does not come to judgment but rather has crossed over from
death to life.
(25) In truth, in truth, I say to you that the time is coming,
and it is now, when the dead shall hear the voice of the Son of
God, and hearing it they will live.
(26) For as the Father has life in himself, so too has the Son,
by the Father's gift,
(27) and he has given him power to judge, because he is the
Son of man.
(28) Do not wonder at this, because the time is coming when
all those in the grave shall hear his voice,
(29) and those who have done right will rise to life, and those
who have done wrong will rise to judgment.
(30) I can do nothing on my own account; I judge as I am
bidden. And my judgment is just because I do not seek my own
will but the will of the one who sent me.

In the first place, note that verses 22–23 sustain the
same thesis as 1 John 2:23: "Anyone who denies the Son
does not have the Father either." In 1 John 2:23, as we
pointed out, denying the Son means denying that Jesus
is the Messiah. But in John 5 that denial is related to the
Last Judgment: The only Last Judgment is that which
occurs in the time of Jesus, in relation to that concrete
bit of human history called Jesus of Nazareth.
    Exegetes traditionally handled this passage in one of
two ways. Some of them implicitly decided that when

John says "and it is now" (v. 25) he does not mean "now,"
but rather "in some undetermined future." This
—whatever name they call it—is demythologizing pure
and simple. Other exegetes explicitly interpreted "and
it is now" as meaning an inchoative present; thus
neither John nor Jesus Christ were saying anything
new, for the *eschaton* was inchoate from the time of
Adam. Both of these traditional interpretations are
tantamount to postponing the *eschaton* indefinitely.
Each in different words repeats Martha's eschatology,
which Jesus rejected: "I know that he will rise in the
resurrection of the last day."

Modern exegetes have seen that such tergiversations
of John 5:25 are untenable. So, in a continuing effort to
postpone the *eschaton*, they resorted to dismembering
the pericope, making John 5:21–25 and John 5:26–29 into
separate discourses mistakenly combined by a later
compiler or redactor. This is the solution offered, with
variations, by the Catholic scholars Boismard, Gächter,
Brown, and others, and by Protestants of the Bultmannian school. (Bultmann himself prefers to extirpate verses 28–29 as interpolations of a later redactor who attempted to reduce John's work to ecclesiastical orthodoxy.) Both Bultmann and Boismard believe that
John 5:21–25 teaches an interior eschatology of mental
experiences—the "spiritual life," which indeed can be
present. Once John is "demythologized," the exegetes
have no difficulty accepting what he says.

Boismard, unlike Bultmann, gives priority to John
5:26–30, believing it alone to be authentic. Boismard
believes that the interior eschatology of John 5:21–25
was conceived by later generations of Christians when
they saw that the Parousia, or second coming of Christ,
had not arrived, and that John 5:26–30 expresses the
view of the early Christian who, he says, originally
thought of the eschaton as future.

But such an interpretation does not fit the available

evidence, which demonstrates that the historical process was, in fact, the other way around: The eschatology of the future is the latest of all eschatologies. Matt. 11:2–6 and Luke 7:18–23 (in the responses to John the Baptist's emissaries) make clear that Jesus himself, as well as Matthew, Luke, and Q, considers the resurrection *of the dead* as present. Jesus responds to the question whether they should continue to wait or not by adducing present facts. Moreover and most convincingly, Matthew's account of the moment of Jesus' death includes the resurrections of many dead (Matt. 27:51–53).

The expression "resurrection of the dead" (not "from among the dead"; the case is genitive) can be found in Paul (1 Cor. 15:12, 13, 21, 42 and Rom. 1:4). *Anastasis nekron* designates an entire epoch, an entire definitive eon of human history. Therefore Paul argues: "If there is no resurrection of the dead, then neither has Christ been raised" (1 Cor. 15:13). If the *eschaton* has not arrived, then Jesus could not have risen.

In Rom. 1:4, where "Son of God" is a messianic title,[6] a document that predated Paul himself[7] maintains that Jesus was constituted Messiah "in virtue of the resurrection of the dead." In fact, the messianic appellative would be completely lacking in real content if Jesus did not bring to history the messianic kingdom, in which the resurrection of the dead (in the plural) is prominently included. Jesus is constituted Messiah by this collective dimension that embraces all humankind; it is the end of all human history, the definitive age, the *eschaton*, the *ultimum*. One might hypothesize (although it would be absurd, according to Paul) that Jesus' individual resurrection could occur without forming part of the collective era of the resurrection; but Jesus' own resurrection would not be sufficient to make him Messiah. He is constituted Messiah by the arrival of the *eschaton* to human history. Without this the word "Messiah" makes no sense. According to Paul and to the pre-Pauline hymn utilized in Rom. 1:3–4, the age of the resurrection of the dead is present. Therefore they affirm in the aorist tense that Jesus "has been constituted Messiah."

Thus the most ancient Christian eschatology known conceives the *eschaton* as present, not future. Our analysis of John confirms Käsemann's statement: "John has not yet learned to understand Jesus' resurrection as an individual event limited to Jesus only."[8] Documentary evidence indicates that this interpretation of resurrection was developed later. Boismard's contention that in Christianity the eschatology of the future antedates the eschatology of the present is historically inaccurate.

The principal argument of Bultmann and Boismard for reading an eschatology of the future into John 5:26–30 is that verse 28 says only "the time is coming," while John 5:25 says "the time is coming and it is now." But such an argument ignores the fact that Jesus' conversation with the Samaritan woman also contains both formulations (John 4:21 and 4:23), and in this conversation both expressions obviously mean the same thing. No one could postulate—and in fact no one does—that John 4:21 and John 4:23 indicate two different dates on which worship in spirit and truth rather than in the temples will begin. The formula "the time is coming and it is now" is simply a further specification of the meaning already expressed by the formula "the time is coming."

In the same fashion Bultmann and Boismard interpret "life" and "they will live" in John 5:24, 25 as referring to interior experiences and the spiritual life—alienation from God as the death of the soul. This they contrast to "life" and "resurrection" in John 5:28, 29, where the terms unequivocally refer to real, physical life. But to do this Bultmann and Boismard have to ignore John 11:24–26, where "he will rise" and "resurrection" (v. 24) are perfectly interchangeable with "life" and "he will live" (vv. 25–26). And this passage refers, not to the spiritually "dead," but to physically dead people whose bodies stink of decomposition.

Likewise, any difference between "when the dead shall hear the voice of the Son of God" (John 5:25) and "when all those in the grave shall hear his voice" (John 5:28) escapes me completely. There is absolutely no literary basis for holding that the content of John 5:21–25 differs from that of John 5:26–30. To give life to the dead, which is recognized as the theme of John 5:28–29, is treated thematically from John 5:21 on: "He raises the dead and gives them life." Thus the pericope John 5:21–30 is a unified whole.

TOTAL TRANSFORMATION

Only extrabiblical motives could induce careful exegetes to interpret John's use of the same expressions sometimes metaphorically and sometimes literally. For conservatives like Boismard the extrabiblical motive is to supply some explanation for the evils of the past nineteen centuries. For liberals the motive is to supply currently acceptable, "rational" interpretations of the "miracles" that strain modern credulity. But let me repeat: Extrabiblical data allow us—at the very most—to conclude that the Bible is mistaken. Period. In no way do these data allow us to distort what the Bible says so that we may comfortably profess our "belief" in it while denying its real meaning.

Käsemann puts his finger on the problem with a question about Gaugler's commentary on John 5:21–30: "E. Gaugler ... interprets in the liberal fashion ... : 'For the loving community the idea of judgment is bankrupt.' But then what happens to the resurrection of the dead?" This gets to the heart of the matter: A Last Judgment that occurs during the lifetime of Jesus can—with sufficient rationalistic ingenuity—be denatured into an event of "spiritual life" or invisible "justification," whether Lutheran or Tridentine; this kind of event changes nothing. But John 5:21–30, in accordance with Old Testament tradition, has the Last Judgment and the resurrection of the dead occurring together in a single stroke. This cannot be understood as an interior or experiential change. The rationalist fashion in exegesis has been proved useless.

Barrett points out that *ou me apolontai eis ton aiona* ("they will never die," John 10:28) does not mean "they shall not perish eternally" but rather "they shall never perish,"[9] and he makes the same point regarding John 11:26.[10] In fact, this Greek phrasing, meaning "will never," occurs frequently in the New Testament, especially in John. For example, *ou me nipses mou tous podas eis ton aiona* (John 13:8) cannot possibly be translated as "you will not wash my feet eternally"; it can only mean "you will never wash my feet." The same translation is inescapable in John 4:14; 8:51–52; Luke 2:26; and Psalm 89:48.

Nevertheless certain spiritual writers distort "whoever believes in Jesus Christ will never die" to mean the negation either of eternal death or of spiritual death. But such an interpretation renders the contrast in John 6:48–49 completely meaningless: "I am the bread of life; your fathers in the desert ate the manna and died." As van den Bussche says: "Eternal life is not life after death, but rather life that knows no death."[11]

Bultmann (more consistent than his Catholic predecessors and those spiritual directors whose present-day heirs abominate him) finds it necessary to eliminate John 18:9 as a later interpolation, although there is no textual basis whatever for this opinion. After Jesus had identified himself to his captors and said, "If I am the man you want, let these others go" (John 18:8), the evangelist adds: "This was to fulfill the word he had said: 'I did not lose one of those you gave me.' " The verb *apollymi* ("to lose," and in the passive, "to be lost") as used here unequivocally means physical death. John has already used this verb five times to express the idea that anyone who believes will never die, will not be lost, nor will ever perish (John 3:16; 6:39; 10:28; 12:25; 17:12). Although John 18:9 quotes only the words of 17:12, John interprets himself as having spoken of the suppression of physical death every time the issue was touched upon. Bultmann would strike out John 18:9 because it conflicts with traditional idealistic exegesis: He cannot accept that the realization of faith and justice in this world is capable of modifying the physical conditions of humankind. Such exegetes forget that according to the Bible human beings are the instruments of God in the task of transforming this world. Ancient and modern demythologizing reduces the biblical message to interior experiences or to ever postponable futures; the demythologizers do not realize that these indeed are myths, not the realistic struggle to transform life.

In contrast, the French Dominican Braun comments on John 5:24:

> It would be incorrect to interpret the crossing over from death to life as if John had only the soul in mind. For him, the judgment effected by the Word has to do with the entire person, whether the unbeliever or the believer. By embracing it, the believer becomes a new being, a being in God, over whom natural death has no power. Bearing in mind the divine activity, indispensable for coming to Christ (John 6:44–45), one would be tempted to say that, in virtue of his self-determining decision, the believer makes for himself a nature that engages him to the core. And since this is permanent, the *eschaton* for him has been achieved.[12]

Our only objection to this interpretation of Johannine thought is its individualistic concept of the *eschaton*. For John, as for all biblical authors, the kingdom is a collective, supra-individual reality; it is a definitive age for all of humankind. The justice that will be capable of transforming even the physical order is a mutual justice among all people (once the unjust are eliminated). Freud's profound observation that human beings die because of their own conflicts demonstrates how greatly reason assists biblical hope in the struggle against

Platonic idealism, which separates the material and spiritual orders.

John's ideas are clear. But spiritualism cannot accept that faith and justice determine our very being as well as our relationships with others and with the material order (as if we were not part of the material order). The demythologizers cannot accept the miracle. Instead they prefer to adopt idealistic philosophy and anthropology as the supreme exponent of what humanity is. The anachronism of this belief is made obvious by their claim that idealistic philosophy constitutes the implicit philosophy of the modern era. Few assertions have been so far out of touch with their times as this anthropological dogma.

It is understandable that idealism and spiritualism are unable to link moral transformation with the material transformation of humankind: Capacity to make such a connection would necessitate a change of genus, *metabasis eis allo genos*. From their perspective the material order is completely heterogenous to the moral order. I believe that modern times, however, are characterized by the quest that Sartre sees in Marxism: "What constitutes the strength and richness of Marxism is that it has been the most radical attempt to clarify the historical process in its totality."[13] To be certain of the worldwide achievement of justice is of course to believe in miracles much greater than the future defeat of death. For the Bible the two go together, and this is indeed to confront history in its totality. We have already seen that existentialism is concerned only with the field of being that, in order to be, demands our decision. The reason why only that "part" of being is of any concern is precisely because that part can change by our decision. But if other fields of being are of no concern to us, it is not because they cannot be changed, but rather because their change depends on the new field of being that, in order to be, demands a decision of us.

The truly modern person cannot accept the dichotomy

of the human being into two disconnected genera. If the achievement of justice and love in the world is possible, the transformation of the material order is not heterogenous to it. There are not two unrelated orders. If we believe in the possibility that the moral order can be transformed, we have to accept the possibility that the material order can be as well, for they are one and the same in a much more realistic and profound sense than we had thought. We can no longer dissever the moral from the physical order.

Let us not forget, however, the profound reason for modern demythologizing. Stuhlmacher summarizes it thus:

Invoking Luther and using as a criterion the thesis that the foundation of faith should coincide with the content of faith, Bultmann has challenged the New Testament proclamation (broadly based on the tradition of the Old Testament and Judaism) of the kingdom of God and of Christ, of the Last Judgment and the new world of God. For he asks if the pure relationship of faith with the God who by grace alone makes us just might not be hindered and even annulled by fantasies that try to link God's future action to human yearnings and desires. As Bultmann answers this question affirmatively, he has demythologized to the extreme the eschatology of the New Testament.[14]

A more recent origin of Bultmannian thought is Kant. But it is not enough to say simply that Kant's motive is justified, for the Kantian imperative is the very essence of the God of the Bible (although Kant does not explicitly state the biblical origin of his moral imperative). Notwithstanding the concealed eudemonism and hedonism of "Christian" theology, the authority of the God of the Bible is unquestionably not grounded on reward and punishment nor on the well-being or happiness produced by the achievement of justice. Those who do not perceive this confuse the moral imperative with utilitarianism or simply do not know what the moral imperative is. The moral imperative *stat in indivisibili*.

The true God is grounded in himself, not in an apologetics of miracles or in the satisfaction of human desires.

But it is precisely this implacable imperative that demands the transformation even of the physical order, the elimination of injustice and death. And it demands it now, unpostponably. "The hour is coming and it is now."

A god who intervenes in history to elicit religious adoration of himself and not to undo the hell of cruelty and death that human history has become is an immoral god in the deepest sense of the word. A god who is reconciled or merely indifferent to the pain of human beings is a merciless god, a monster, not the ethical God whom the Bible knows. We would be morally obliged to rebel against such a god, even if our defeat were inevitable. Equally immoral is the god for whom the end of injustice and innocent suffering is a secondary or subordinate imperative. Hence the New Testament intransigence with regard to the *eschaton*. It is not for apologetical reasons nor to gratify less-than-divine yearnings and desires that the God of Jesus Christ comes to establish justice and life now; it is because that is God's unmistakable essence.

Though idealistic anthropology denies it, the most outstanding characteristic of our time is the demand for total justice. This does indeed impose conditions of possibility: For a message, any message, to deserve attention, the kingdom of justice must be achieved. But it has not been made sufficiently explicit that this justice includes the transformation of nature and the defeat of death. For sentimental recollection does not do justice to the worker-martyrs who were gunned down in Haymarket Square. Nor is it justice that people should be born crippled. The tortures we voluntarily or involuntarily inflict on one another, the sufferings we mutually cause, will cease only when humanity's age-old egoistic instinct and mistrust are eliminated. A materialist should be the last to deny the possibility of a miracle: If justice is attainable, surely the defeat of

death is not in a compartment distinct from that realization. Human beings could not carry out reforms and
revolutions if material being itself were not compelling
them. Their basis for action, their impulse toward revolution, is the very being which of itself tends toward an
eschaton and of which people form the medium.

In the same vein, Sartre says, "As an internal negation, man must by means of matter make known to himself what he is not and consequently what he has to
be."[15] One could not suffer—even die of a heart attack
due to interpersonal conflict—unless one's very materi-
ality were conditioned by one's relationship with other
people. If the body itself were not molded and modeled in
its being and in its being-such by interpersonal relationships, suffering or any bodily disease resulting from
disillusion or frustration would be impossible.

PROCLAIMING THE GOOD NEWS

Bultmann has failed to understand true demythologizing. To demythologize is to make realizable,
and this the New Testament authors explicitly and
thematically do, as Braun notes (in the paragraph
quoted above).

The western mind defines biblical "news" like Greco-
Roman news: It is "information" about events whose
occurrence is independent of human action or intervention. For the Greeks this autonomy is the "objective" element of an affirmation. The western mind cannot admit what the gospel says—that the time is coming
and it is now when injustice and death will be defeated
—for by the Greco-Roman definition of "news," this affirmation means that justice and life will triumph even
if we do not "believe" it, even if human "subjectivity"
refuses to participate in their triumph. But the New
Testament expressly and repeatedly teaches that it is
our faith (that "subjectivity") that will cause the an-

nounced events to be accomplished! A myth is an event that occurs independently of human will and action, regardless of what we do, but the news *that the kingdom arrives* means that we must *make it arrive.*

Of what value, then, are Jesus' indisputably authentic affirmations: "It is your faith that has saved you" (Mark 5:34; Matt. 9:22; Luke 8:48; Mark 10:52; Luke 18:42) —each uttered after a cure, which is a modification of physical nature? Of what value is the statement that "everything is possible for the one who believes" (Mark 9:23)? If we bear in mind the deliberateness and the emphasis with which John recounts Jesus' resuscitation of Lazarus (chap. 11), then the following assertion leaves no room for doubt about the nature of faith: "In truth, in truth I say to you: Anyone who believes in me will do the works that I am doing, and will do still greater works than these (John 14:12). The term "greater works than these" (*erga meizona touton*) had previously occurred only in John 5:20 and was exemplified in 5:21 by the resurrection of the dead. When Jesus performed the miracle of resurrecting Lazarus, he said to Martha, "Did I not tell you that if you believed you would see the glory of God?" (John 11:40).[16] The condition is always belief: "if you believe," "anyone who believes." John's strongest affirmation of the causal efficacy of faith is John 14:12; only Mark 9:23 expresses it more fervently.

In the Synoptic passages cited above "salvation" has a material, this-wordly sense (see also Matt. 8:25; 9:21; 14:30; 27:40, 42, 49; Mark 3:4; 5:23, 28; and John 11:12; 12:27). If we keep in mind that for John "to live" and "life" can also be expressed as "to be saved" (see John 3:16–17; 11:12, 23, 25),[17] then the thesis that life and resurrection will be caused in this world by faith becomes apparent throughout the Fourth Gospel (John 3:15, 16, 36; 4:50–51 [cf. Mark 9:23; 2:5]; 5:24; 6:35, 39, 40, 47; 11:25, 26, 40; 20:31). Brown is justified in claiming a relationship between John 14:1 and Jesus' words in Mark 5:35–36 and Matt. 8:25–26 ("Do not fear, only have faith") and likewise between John 14:12 and the words of the historical Jesus about the faith that moves mountains (Matt. 21:21).[18]

The good news called gospel is not Greek news. It is the most purely biblical news that can be imagined. It is a word signifying action, not information; it seeks to *achieve what it says*, not simply to notify. The announcement itself enjoins: "Be converted and believe in the news" (Mark 1:15); "Be converted because the kingdom has arrived" (Matt. 4:17). Only this conversion and this faith will cause the kingdom to come.

Among New Testament authors there exist minor differences, but they express clearly and unanimously the idea that "first the good news must be proclaimed to all peoples" (Mark 13:10). Given that the good news constitutes the sole object and content of faith, and given the real efficaciousness of this faith, Mark 13:10 means that predicting the Parousia bears no resemblance to Greek-style teaching about events that would occur independently of human action. Such preaching is not auto-suggestion or subjectiveness, but the bringing about of real universal interpersonal justice.

This conviction of the causal efficacy of faith, enunciated by Jesus, can be documented as persisting until the middle of the second century: "In your holy conduct and piety, should you not be waiting and hastening the coming of the day of God?" (*speudontas ten parousian tes tou Theou hemeras* [2 Pet. 3:11–12]).

In this passage it is expressly stated that human beings make the Parousia take place. We find substantially the same idea in Luke, who according to Conzelmann was well rooted in history:

Repent, then, and be converted, so that your sins may be wiped out, so that the time of consolation might come from the Lord and he might send Jesus Christ who was announced to you (Acts 3:19–20).

John is much more incisive than Luke as we shall see. But it is of utmost importance that authors as disparate as Mark, Luke, and the author of 2 Peter say that the Parousia, the total realization of the *eschaton*, is brought about by the evangelization and conversion of human beings. Jesus Christ expressed the same conviction when he proclaimed the "good news" (Mark 1:14–15). This causative relationship pertains to the very essence of "gospel." If we understand the indicative in the Greek fashion, that it simply "informs," then the "gospel" is more imperative than indicative. No, the achievement of justice and life is not the myth; the myth is rather to imagine (as disillusioned Christians have imagined for the last nineteen centuries) that justice and life could be achieved without faith and without human participation.

True being, the demythologized field of being, is that which demands decision, that which requires our decision in order to be. Heidegger says it well: Only that which presents itself as possibility-for-me, as something that I can decide, has meaning.[19] Kierkegaard learned this by reading the New Testament, which was written with this precise intention: to make us decide for the "possibility" that John affirmed as necessary for humankind. The New Testament cannot be separated from this intention. Its purpose is to make Jesus the Messiah. Antichrists are those who oppose an *eschaton* of justice and life for all. If a genuine "possibility" does not arise when we are faced by Christ, then it does not arise at all, for only Christ demands that we bring about the *eschaton*. Any other "possibilities" are individualistic trivialities that really do not summon.

Thus we can understand the Johannine intransigence with regard to the *eschaton*. God is revealed only in the implacable "now" of the moral imperative of justice and love for all. To postpone the kingdom, to postpone the Messiah, is to prevent them from ever being real. This is the eternal stratagem employed to separate us from the only real otherness that summons us. It is to fall back again into the eternal return, into the self's grand deception that enables us to continue enclosed in our own immanence, whispering to ourselves assurances that there is nothing new, that everything that happens we already knew and have summarized in the concepts that equip our self-absorbed self-sufficiency.

We have already seen that in 1 John 2:8 the presence of the *eschaton* is the reason for the commandment of love of neighbor. If there is no *eschaton*, the word ceases to be transcendent; its summons is neutralized and ceases. If I can postpone the realization of the commandment, I reassimilate it into the archive of the self and I continue in my solitude and immanence. Therefore 1 John 2:22–23 tells us that anyone who denies the Messiah does not have God either. If I do not believe that Jesus is the Messiah, if I do not believe that the *eschaton* has come, then the imperative of love of neighbor becomes an intra-self concept. It does not speak as a real otherness, because anodyne time, even if it is present, truly has no reason to command me any more than any other time. I can postpone the realization of the commandment to any other time, so that reality will continue being the same as now. It is always "the same"; there is no "other," and God is not revealed. I will continue to speak "of him who I say is my God, and I do not know him." I have again converted God into an idol always available at my pleasure for my purposes. God is no longer nonassimilable otherness who commands. Anyone who denies the Messiah does not have God either.

THE ONE TRUE GOD

John 17:3 reads, "And this is eternal life: that they know you, the only true God, and the one whom you sent, Jesus Christ." Brown comments on this verse: "Elsewhere in the Bible the adjectives 'one' and 'true' may be applied to God to distinguish Him from the pagan gods."[20] Then he adds simply that in John this is not the case, but he does not support this assertion. Elsewhere in the Bible the expression "the one true God" is used to distinguish God from false gods. Without evidence it cannot be maintained that John 17:3 constitutes an exception. Acknowledging Jesus Christ is related to knowing the one true God in contradistinction to the false gods. We have already seen that according to 1 John 2:22–23 anyone who denies that Jesus is the Messiah does not have God either.

1 John 5:20–21 is even more perplexing, but it is precisely this passage that demonstrates that John is arguing against the neutralization and idolization of a God who thereby ceases to be God:

We know that the Son of God has come to give us understanding so that we might know the true one. And we are in the true one, in his son Jesus Christ. This is the true God and eternal life. Little children, be careful of idols (1 John 5:20–21).

Note that knowing the true God depends on the historical, contingent appearance of Jesus Christ. The word was so utterly made flesh that without this bit of human history there is no longer any God. Without the *eschaton* there is no God; there is no transcendence. John is not unaware that the true God was already known before Jesus' historical birth. If he asserts that anyone who denies the Messiah does not "have" God either (1 John 2:22–23), his extraordinary purpose must be to tell us what God really is.

1 John 5:20–21 refers to the true God in polemical contradistinction to false gods. This could be denied only by holding that the last phrase ("be careful of idols") is a fragment unrelated to the preceding passage, and there is no evidence whatsoever for this opinion.

Eidola can mean either images of false gods or the false gods themselves.[21] But, as Bultmann notes, in this context it cannot mean "images," for if it did "the sense of the admonition would have to be not to participate in pagan cults,"[22] and pagan cults are nowhere remotely alluded to in the Epistle. The redaction clearly indicates that "the admonition of v. 21 is a suitable conclusion for the whole writing." In this passage *eidola* can only mean "false gods." Moreover, this translation is strongly suggested by the contrapuntal phrases "the true one," "the true God," in this same climactic passage of the Epistle.

Even so, the very exegetes who recognize that *eidola* refers to false gods find this conclusion unexpected and astonishing. Bultmann says, "Most striking, however, is the phrase *apo ton eidolon*." Schnackenburg writes, "The concluding warning against idolatry quite frankly sounds strange." Their astonishment is most revealing. Let us credit John with meaning what he says: If the Johannine Jesus says to the Jews, "he who you say is your God, and you do not know him" (John 8:54–55), he obviously supposes that they have a conception of a false god. Otherwise what god are they speaking of, given that they do not know the true one? By the same token, let us look again at John 16:2–3: "Indeed the time is coming when anyone who kills you will suppose that he is worshipping God. And they will do this because they do not know either the Father or me." If they do not know the true God, then obviously the god they think they are pleasing by killing Christians is a false god.

Brooke is on the right track in his comment on *apo ton eidolon:* "The expression embraces all false conceptions of God. . . . If any limited reference is necessary, it must be found in the untrue mental images fashioned by the false teachers."[23] With regard to the passage "anyone who denies the Son does not have the Father either," Bultmann likewise comments: "Whoever, then, has a perverted view of Jesus, by that very fact also thinks wrongly of God."[24] But neither Brooke nor Bultmann gets to the root of the question; John is not talking about erroneous or defective doctrinal conceptions of God that permit people to worship the true God albeit with an imperfect conceptual instrument. John says, "Be careful of idols," and, "He does not have God either." He is not talking about imperfect awareness of God, but about the *denial* of God, even by persons who sincerely believe that they are worshipping the true God. The dilemma is this: God or idolatry.

Thus John 17:3, with its genuinely biblical expression "the one true God," in no way is an exception among the biblical passages in which this expression appears. Eternal life consists in knowing the true God—as distinguished from the false gods and mental constructs we invent to elude God—and in knowing Jesus as Christ, that is, as Messiah. John 17:3 is really the summary of the entire message of John and of the New Testament. Eternal life depends on this knowledge and will come to be throughout the world by this knowledge. This teaching cannot be vitiated so that it becomes rationalistically acceptable. On the contrary, as van den Bussche says: "Eternal life is not life after death, but rather life that does not know death."

The true God is accessible only in the historical fact called Jesus of Nazareth. This thesis of John and of the whole New Testament (beginning with Jesus Christ himself) cannot be understood in an extrinsicist way, as if God punitively withdrew knowledge of himself from those who rejected Jesus Christ. The true God reveals himself and consists solely in the imperative of love of neighbor. And love of neighbor is no romantic, individualistic sentiment: It means definitive justice for humankind; it means justice and life and heeding every cry of suffering. All other "possibilities-for-me" are trifles. They are prizes the soul awards itself for playing the love-your-neighbor game. They do not transcend.

At this point the "totality" combatted by Levinas regains all its rights. Levinas is correct when he says, "It is not I who resist the system; . . . it is the Other."[25] Existentialism that does not acknowledge this is incapable of discovering the new field of being that in order to be demands decision. But the "Other" that constitutes the summons of the infinite is all others, all those who were and are broken by history. And these others demand the totality called the messianic *eschaton*.

John 17:3 telescopes knowledge of the one God into the knowledge of Jesus Christ; it combines them. One thereby becomes impossible without the other. We find the same telescopic approach in 1 John 3:23:

And this is his commandment: that we believe in the name of his son Jesus Christ and that we love one another as he commanded us.

Exegetes have found this passage strange for including faith within the content of the commandment.[26] As we have seen, John considers love of neighbor to be the only content of the commandment, and he is saying nothing different here. Indeed, the phrase "as he commanded us" alludes to John 13:34. To believe in Jesus Christ, to believe that Jesus is the Messiah, is an *essential* component of love of neighbor. The sole object of faith is the "fact" or truth that Jesus is Messiah (see our chapter 4), and this truth is essential to the imperative of love of neighbor in which the God of the Bible consists.

The First Epistle has a single purpose: to confute the Antichrists. Or, as the Gospel puts it: "So that you might believe that Jesus is the Messiah" (John 20:31). The fact that Christians have not set out to conquer the world for love of neighbor shows that they do not believe that the messianic *eschaton* has arrived. They have adapted to the "world" and to history. Civilization has ensnared them so that they have made Christianity into a conventional religion, and by this very fact they deny that Jesus is the Messiah. They have withdrawn from the otherness of millions of hungry, tormented human beings, and they worship a mental idol invented by civilization itself.

THE "NOW" OF JESUS

In John 7:33 Jesus says, "For a little longer I shall be with you." Bultmann observes that this refers to the "contingency of revelation," for revelation "does not consist in universal truths, which can be grasped at all times and for all times, nor in dogma which one could invoke at any time."[27] The true God is knowable only in the segment of history constituted by the life of Jesus of Nazareth. But Bultmann not only fails to see that this contingency specifically and solely means that God is God only in the imperative of love of neighbor; his very interpretation of contingency in effect eliminates contingency. This brings us once again to the problem of Kierkegaardian contemporaneity.

Bultmann continues: "Of course in this symbolic scene John does not consider the fact that the word of Jesus is taken up again by the community, and that the revelation is again and again made present in time." But we cannot interpret John by saying that he is mistaken when a statement of his displeases or baffles us.

Bultmann holds, "In the word of proclamation [Jesus] is himself made present to the world (as in this Gospel), in the 'Now,' in the present moment in time. And the threat is always present, 'too late!' "[28]

By this statement Bultmann reveals that he does not have in mind the "now" of the historical Jesus, but rather an existential now ("existentive," as José Gaos would say) that is at all times available and that we can latch onto at any moment. True, he is not speaking of universal truths or dogmas, but he is referring to existential experiences that do not constitute an other different from the self. Rather, as objects that are conceived or "lived," they form part of the experiential, existential apparatus of the self, and the self uses them as it uses its own faculties and concepts. The "now" of which Bultmann speaks has been reassimilated by the subject. It is no longer the reality of the historical now of Christ that presents me with an irreducible otherness.

But when the Johannine Jesus says "now," John means the historical moment in which Jesus speaks. This alone demonstrates that Bultmann is not a faithful interpreter of John. For example, Jesus says to Peter, "You cannot follow me now; you will follow me later"

(John 13:36), and when John wrote his Gospel, Peter had already "followed" Christ. We find this same chronological "now" in 4:23; 5:25; 12:27; 12:31a, 31b; 13:31, 36; 14:29; 15:22, 24; 16:5, 22; 17:5, 7, 13. John's implacable insistence on the "hour" and *kairos* of Jesus (John 2:4; 4:21, 23; 5:25, 28; 7:6, 30; 8:20; 12:23, 27; 13:1; 16:4, 21, 25) is meaningless if we can separate this "hour" from the chronological, dateable time of the historical Jesus.

Anyone who determines that this historical moment can be repeated automatically lifts it out of time, detemporalizes it, makes it nontemporal and eternal, sets it in the Platonic world—a different and, moreover, nonexistent world. Time is the touchstone of any philosophy, and nonrepeatability is the touchstone of real time. Bultmann's distinction between the historical Jesus and the Christ-of-faith or the celestial, eternal Christ has always been an essential part of any theology that does not accept the *eschaton*. These theologies can be contemporaneous only with a nontemporal (and nonexistent) Christ. True demythologization includes denouncing this myth, which contradicts itself (someone *nontemp*oral cannot be *contemp*oraneous to anyone) and which is a tool deliberately used to prevent the realization of the messianic kingdom on earth. Bultmann, echoing his bitterest conservative opponents, explicitly detemporalizes Christ. John wants to tell us that the hour of justice and life for all humankind has already arrived. But the vested interests of the masters of this world have been passed off as Christian theology to drown out his message, silence it, and so prevent it from revolutionizing the world.

To rebut these theologies that treat Jesus' historical moment as repeatable or as continually available, we can say, like Jesus to his relatives: "Your moment [*kairos*] is always at hand" (John 7:6). And the very argument that Bultmann uses against "the world" in his commentary on this passage can also be used against him: "If their *kairos* is always there, then in reality it is never there, and their actions never decide anything, because everything is decided in advance."[29]

John's contemporaneity with Christ is not achieved by intellectual or psychic juggling. John did not use techniques of asceticism to "feel" or "imagine" himself in the "now" of Jesus of Nazareth, who died fifty or sixty years before John wrote. John's contemporaneity with Christ is not imaginary but real. Jesus is the definitive "now" of history, in which justice and life are to be achieved. But this achievement depends on our decision. John's commitment is to the historical Jesus, not to a celestial, eternal Christ.

Western civilization's overwhelming rejection of the historical Jesus might persuade us that the West lacks a historical sense. But the West is not *unable* to understand that the hour of the kingdom has already arrived; it is *unwilling* to understand it, because to understand it would oblige us to change. To circumvent this obligation we have invented and for centuries believed in a celestial Christ and an "eternal life." And this total distortion of the gospel has been accomplished with the tacit consent—indeed, the connivance and cooperation—of ecclesiastical authorities. The fate of our world depends on our believing Jesus Christ when he says that the hour of the kingdom has come (Mark 1:14–15), but the masters of our world lose their power if we believe it. Conservative theology counters Bultmann by affirming that its celestial Christ is identical to the historical Jesus, but clearly the only Christ that matters to conservative theology is the nontemporal, celestial one, for such theology does not take the "now" of Jesus seriously. This "now" is the historical Jesus. Conservative theology professes concern with time; but time is the unrepeatable "now" or it is not time.

To demythologize is to make realizable. This consists in proving that the good news is not Greek news but rather a reality that depends on our decision in order to be. Demythologizing also includes reintegrating into our historical world everything that has been projected into a so-called eternal "other world." To do this we must understand that the hour of justice and life has come to history. Such is the proclamation made by Jesus Christ, and it has not been abrogated. It is not repeatable. The hour of Jesus does not return. It is really present.

If existentialism rejects this indicative that is imperative, then being becomes unchangeable and "objective," as in the old ontology. In order to make the *eschaton* arrive, "first the good news must be proclaimed to all peoples." Existentialism can discover and make the new being, or it can become the ideological defense par excellence of the status quo. But if existentialism is to remain faithful to itself, it cannot reject the only summons that attempts to modify the entire being of history.

NOTES

1. Rudolf Bultmann, *Die drei Johannesbriefe*, 2nd ed. (Göttingen: Vandenhoeck, 1967), p. 33 [Eng. trans.: *The Johannine Epistles*, trans. R. Philip O'Hara et al. (Philadelphia: Fortress, 1973), p. 28].

2. Günther Klein, "Das wahre Liecht scheint schon," *Zeitschrift für Theologie und Kirche* 68 (1971), p. 302.

3. Brooke Foss Westcott, *The Epistles of St. John* (Cambridge: Macmillan, 1892), p. 69, as cited by Rudolf Schnackenburg, *Die Johannesbriefe* (Freiburg: Herder, 1963), p. 142. The German exegete rejects this interpretation, but neither does he accept the fact that it refers to the end. He says that John "wants only to characterize his own time as eschatologically relevant." However, if the end has not come, all times are eschatologically of the same relevance—or irrelevance.

4. Henri van den Bussche, *Jean* (Paris: Desclée, 1967), p. 197.

5. Rudolf Schnackenburg, *Das Johannesevangelium* (Freiburg: Herder, 1965), 1:489 [Eng. trans.: *The Gospel according to St. John*, trans. Kevin Smyth (New York: Herder and Herder, 1968), 1:455].

6. Cf. Stanislas Lyonnet, *Exegesis epistulae ad romanos, Cap. I–IV*, 3rd ed. (Rome: Pontificio Istituto Biblico, 1963), pp. 37–40; Eduard Schweizer, "hyios," *TWNT*, 8:368 [Eng. trans.: *TDNT*, 8:367].

7. H. Zimmermann, *Neutestamentliche Methodenlehre* (Stuttgart: Katholisches Bibelwerk, 1967), pp. 192–213.

8. Ernst Käsemann, *Jesu letzter Wille nach Johannes 17*, 2nd ed. (Tübingen: Mohr, 1967), p. 34 [Eng. trans.: *The Testament of Jesus*, trans. Gerhard Krodel (Philadelphia: Fortress Press, 1968), p. 16].

9. C.K. Barrett, *The Gospel according to St. John* (London: SPCK, 1955), p. 317.

10. Ibid. p. 330.

11. Van den Bussche, *Jean*, p. 253.

12. F.M. Braun, *Jean le théologien* (Paris: Gabalda, 1959–66), 3:124.

13. Jean-Paul Sartre, *Critique de la raison dialectique* (Paris: Gallimard, 1960), 1:29.

14. Peter Stuhlmacher, "Neues Testament und Hermeneutik," *Zeitschrift für Theologie und Kirche* 68 (1971), p. 157.

15. J.-P. Sartre, *L'être et le néant* (Paris: Gallimard, 1943), p. 712 [cf. Eng. trans.: *Being and Nothingness*, trans. Hazel E. Barnes (New York: Citadel, 1968), p. 536].

16. Brown: "Didn't I assure you that if you believed, you would see the glory of God?" Westcott: "Said I not unto thee, that, if thou wouldest believe, thou shouldest see the glory of God?" This refers to the Old Testament concept of the glory of God ("that glory might dwell on our earth"), as I have shown in *Marx y la biblia* (Salamanca: Sígueme, 1972), p. 259–82 [Eng. trans.: *Marx and the Bible*, trans. John Eagleson (Maryknoll, New York: Orbis Books, 1974), pp. 229–50].

17. See this synonymy in Mark 5:23; Josh. 6:17; Lev. 18:5; Hab. 2:4; Rom. 1:16–17; 5:10; 8:13; 10:5; 10:9–10; Gal. 3:12; Ezek. 18:13, 21, 22; etc.

18. Raymond E. Brown, *The Gospel according to John (xiii–xxi)*, Anchor Bible 29A (Garden City, New York: Doubleday, 1970), pp. 624, 633.

19. Martin Heidegger, *Sein und Zeit* (Tübingen: Niemeyer, 1960), p. 395 [Eng. trans.: *Being and Time*, trans. John Macquarrie and Edward Robinson (New York: Harper & Row, 1962), p. 447].

20. Brown, *Gospel according to John (xiii–xxi)*, p. 752.

21. Cf. Walter Bauer, *Wörterbuch zu den Schriften des Neuen Testaments*, 5th ed. (Berlin: Töpelmann, 1963), cols. 438–39 [cf. William F. Arndt and F. Wilbur Gingrich, *A Greek-English Lexicon of the New Testament and Other Early Christian Literature* (Chicago: University of Chicago Press, 1957), p. 220]; and Schnackenburg, *Johannesbriefe*, p. 292.

22. Bultmann, *Johannesbriefe*, p. 93 [Eng. trans.: *Johannine Epistles*, p. 90].

23. A.E. Brooke, *The Johannine Epistles*, International Critical Commentary 38 (Edinburgh, T. & T. Clark, 1912), p. 154.

24. Bultmann, *Johannesbriefe*, p. 43 [Eng. trans.: *Johannine Epistles*, p. 38].

25. Emmanuel Levinas, *Totalité et Infini* (The Hague: Martinus Nijhoff, 1971), p. 10 [cf. Eng. trans.: *Totality and Infinity*, trans. Alphonso Lingis (Pittsburgh: Duquesne University Press, 1969), p. 40].

26. Cf. Schnackenburg, *Johannesbriefe*, p. 207.

27. Rudolf Bultmann, *Das Evangelium des Johannes* (Göttingen: Vandenhoeck, 1964), p. 232 [Eng. trans.: *The Gospel of John*, trans. G.R. Beasley-Murray et al. (Philadelphia: Westminster, 1971), pp. 307–08].

28. Bultmann, *Evangelium des Johannes*, p. 233 [cf. Eng. trans.: *Gospel of John*, p. 308].

29. Bultmann, *Evangelium des Johannes*, p. 220 [Eng. trans.: *Gospel of John*, pp. 292–93].

Chapter 10

Parousia or Presence?

This chapter is virtually an appendix for exegetes, though nonspecialists may find it an aid to understanding what has gone before. My purpose in writing it is twofold: First, to expose the conservatives' claim that John must be interpreted in relation to the Synoptics as a euphemism for suppressing John's message; second, to seek the corroboration of ecclesiastically sanctioned studies for the astonishing and revolutionary Christianity that has emerged from our objective analysis of Johannine writings.

Here, briefly, we shall attempt to accomplish both ends: to establish that the Synoptics support our interpretation of John and to cite recognized Catholic exegetes to corroborate the soundness of our interpretation. And we shall attempt to identify and summarize the problems posed directly or indirectly by our exegesis without making this chapter into a mere catalogue.

THE PARACLETE

Once we have understood that faith is *really* supposed to transform humankind and the world, then the delay of the Parousia—which has presented such a problem to twentieth-century exegesis—is not a problem of biblical error but of our infidelity to Jesus Christ. This we have already established. But a mistaken demythologizing maintains that John corrects the errors of Synoptic eschatology. Let us see.

Each sacred writer should be interpreted individually, as Käsemann has emphasized in his magnificent study of the canon.[1] There is no basis for the dogmatic presupposition that they must all be saying the same thing. Nonetheless, in a series of articles on Synoptic eschatology (Mark 13; Luke 21:5–36; Matt. 24–25) published between 1948 and 1950, the Catholic Feuillet definitively showed that according to the Synoptic Gospels the Parousia and the complete establishment of the kingdom take place during "this generation"; that is explicitly stated in Mark 13:30; Luke 21:32; and Matthew 24:34. That being the case, we must conclude that although John rectifies traditional eschatology, that is, the eschatology of Judaism, as when Jesus corrects Martha (John 11:24–26), he does not change that of Jesus Christ or the Synoptics. Both the Synoptics and John speak of "this generation," but for John its arrival is signalled by the death and resurrection of Christ, while for Jesus and the Synoptics it is signalled by the destruction of Jerusalem.

Regarding the "we will come" of John 14:23, Barrett says, "To the man who becomes a Christian . . . both the Father and the Son . . . will come. This is the *parousia* upon which John's interest is concentrated."[2]

The Johannine Jesus insists on this teaching, which theology has yet to take seriously:

Because you have seen me you have believed. Happy are those who believed without seeing (John 20:29).

As the Catholic van den Bussche says, "the Spirit is not a substitute for the Christ who has gone away. It puts them [the disciples] in contact with the Master much more radically than when they were at his side

every day during his public life. The later Christian
generations will not have less good fortune than the
eyewitnesses."[3] We should add: Not only is their good
fortune no less; rather the intentionally emphatic contrast in John 20:29 indicates that the later Christian
generation, who did not see Christ, enjoyed greater fortune. John 16:7 reinforces this message:

> But I tell you the truth: It is better for you that I go away,
> because if I do not go away the Paraclete will not come to you,
> but if I go away I will send him to you.

Brown has perceived the key idea in this passage:
"The Paraclete is the Spirit understood as the presence
of the absent Jesus.... It is our contention that John
presents the Paraclete as the Holy Spirit in a special
role, namely, as the personal presence of Jesus in the
Christian while Jesus is with the Father."[4] Granting
that, however, we still must explain why Jesus' presence
as Holy Spirit is better for us than his actual bodily
presence, as John 20:29 and John 16:7 clearly stress.

The continuation of the latter passage gives us the
answer: "And when he comes, he will reproach [or
denounce] the world about sin and about justice and
about judgment" (John 16:8). But this denunciation of
the world the disciples themselves are to carry out, as is
shown by the explicative "and" in John 15:26–27: "He
will bear witness to me *and* you will bear witness because you have been with me from the beginning." The
Catholic exegete Mussner recognizes the role of the disciples: "In *their* testimony the testimony to Christ of the
Spirit goes forth in the world."[5] So does Lagrange,
another well-respected Catholic: "And since this Spirit
was to remain in them (John 14:16), should they not
understand that the Paraclete would use them to convince the world?"[6]

To believe that Jesus' presence as Paraclete will be
made real by specific works of his followers does not

diminish in the least the reality of the Holy Spirit. The striking thesis of John 16:7 and 20:29 is consistent with that of John 14:12:

In truth, in truth, I say to you: Anyone who believes in me will also do the works that I do, and even greater ones, because I am going to the Father.

If, as we have seen, the Father is revealed only in a certain type of works, then it is not strange that Christ should say that it is better for us if he goes away: Obviously his followers could do more God-revealing works than he alone, and his sole intent was to reveal the true God to the world. John's basis for this assertion we have elucidated in the preceding chapters: The God who is "the word" not only does not need to be perceptible to the senses; he needs the distance of otherness to reveal himself and to be truly God. Only across this distance is God "the word" that summons. Without this distance I can encompass God within my worldview and my system, and I convert him into an idol; he ceases to be God. The Parousia, or true presence, is the full realization of this status of "the word."

Regarding the parallel in series between John 14:15–17 (presence, in the disciples, of the Spirit that the world cannot see) and John 14:18–21 (presence, in the disciples, of Christ whom the world cannot see), Brown notes: "Such parallelism is John's way of telling the reader that the presence of Jesus after his return to the Father is accomplished in and through the Paraclete. Not two presences but the same presence is involved."[7]

That is really the least that can be deduced from this strange parallel that has caught the attention of all exegetes. In John 14:18 Jesus assured the disciples of his presence (he will not leave them as orphans, etc.), speaking as someone who has *already explained what he means* by not abandoning them but returning to them: His presence, of which he assures them, *consists* in the presence of the Paraclete, whom—like the historical Jesus—the world cannot know but the disciples can. That is the nature of Christ's return.

We find the same parallel between John 16:12–15 (the coming of the Paraclete) and John 16:16–21 (the return of Christ). John 14:21–24 and John 14:25–26 present the same parallel but in reverse order. The only possible interpretation is that the Parousia coincides with Pentecost.

John does not use the Synoptic expression "this generation." He seems, in fact, not to know the word "generation." But in other, more incisive ways he affirms that the Parousia and the Last Judgment will occur during the same generation as Jesus Christ. For example, he shows us that the second coming of Christ is Pentecost.

This is the meaning of the scene in John 20:19–23. It is the first appearance of the risen one to the assembled disciples, and its climax and significance is this: "Having said this he breathed upon them and said, 'Receive the Holy Spirit' " (John 20:22). John uses this symbolic scene to tell us that the Pentecost coincides with the Resurrection of Jesus Christ, having previously told us that while Jesus was alive on earth "there was not yet any Spirit because Jesus had not yet been glorified" (John 7:39).

Note the seven facts or events involved here: Crucifixion, Resurrection, Ascension, Pentecost, Parousia, Last Judgment, and eternal life. We customarily represent them as occurring in that order one after the other. But John's sole concern is that they all occur "in this generation," as the Synoptics say, or "in the hour of Jesus," as John says, that is, during the generation of Jesus of Nazareth.

To state the historical simultaneity between Pentecost and the Resurrection, John invented the scene 20:19–23 mentioned above. To express the simultaneity, within one period or generation, between the Crucifixion, the Resurrection, and the Ascension, he assigned double meanings to the verbs *hypsoo* ("to lift up") and *doxasthenai* ("to be glorified") (see John 8:28, 12:32, and 7:39, as well as many other passages in which the verb "to glorify" occurs).

The best known usage of *hypsoo* is this:

When I am lifted up from the earth,
I will attract all toward me.
He said this to signify the death he would die (John 12:32–33).

These two verses are the continuation of 12:31, which says, "*Now* is the judgment of this world; *now* the prince of this world will be cast out," indicating John's intention to show both the chronological and simultaneous nature of these events. But this passage also shows that the Last Judgment coincides historically with the Crucifixion, Resurrection, and Ascension of Jesus Christ. In light of this verse we can see in John 16:8–11 the simultaneity of Pentecost and the Last Judgment. The Last Judgment and eternal life are simultaneous, as John 5:20–22 says (see our chapter 9). Moreover, the presence of eternal life in the hour of Jesus is the theme of John 5:24 and 1 John 3:14.

Given that the Parousia is indisputably simultaneous with the Last Judgment and with eternal life, the cited passages are sufficient to document the presence of the Parousia. By putting these three events in the present, John contradicts the eschatology of Judaism, which sees them as future. But Judaic eschatology was soon reestablished within Christian theology, where it became accepted and orthodox as if the New Testament had never existed.

The occurrence of the Parousia during the generation of Jesus Christ is especially relevant to the relationship between John and the Synoptics. By identifying the Parousia with Pentecost, John affirms that the Parousia is present. John also affirms and demonstrates the presentness of the Parousia in other ways.

DWELLING-PLACES

The initial verses of John 14 have been much misinterpreted: "I am going to prepare a place for you"; "in my Father's house there are many dwelling-places"; "I will return and I will take you with me." Over half a century ago the Catholic Lagrange observed: "We have tended to explain the confidence as due to what Jesus will do first: He goes to prepare places. But this is no more than an initial idea that prepares for a more complete understanding."[8] In verse 2 the term "dwelling-places" "does not refer in any way to levels of heavenly happiness. There are many places; this is all that matters."[9]

I think, however, that the redactional form of John 14 suggests an additional meaning. The opening verses allow of our customary and comfortable otherwordly interpretation, but subsequent verses compel us to understand the true meaning of these initial phrases. The form of Jesus' conversation with his disciples here is similar although not identical to that of his conversation with Martha. The term "dwelling-place" reappears in verse 23, and there its meaning is explained: It is located in the believers themselves who live in this world; the Father and Jesus will come to the believer and "they will make a dwelling-place in him." Their dwelling-place is here, not in heaven or another world.

Traditional theology's error has been to divide John 14, as if its opening verses were not part of a compositional whole. But the dwelling-places referred to in these verses cannot be in another world, for verse 16 promises that Jesus will *send* to believers the Spirit to remain with them "forever" *(eis ton aiona)*.

In verse 12 Jesus assures them that the believers will do "greater works" than his, which would be meaningless in another world. The presence of the Paraclete, which synthesizes the presence of the Father and the return of Jesus, will consist precisely in these works that challenge the world. The goal is to change the world; for this "greater works" are needed. But the world to be changed is this world, not another. Lagrange demonstrates that "chapter 14 is perfectly delimited."[10] It is an indestructible redactional unit. Brown has seen that verses 1–3 and verses 27–28 form an intentional "bracketing," or inclusion "marking the beginning and end of a section."[11] In fact, John uses triple brackets: "I am going away and I come to you" (v. 3 and v. 28, quoting v. 3); "believe" (v. 1 and v. 29); and "set your troubled hearts at rest" (v. 1 and v. 27).

The formulation of the first of these three bracketings demonstrates John's genius. Feuillet has seen "le paradoxe de 14:28: 'Je m'en vais et je viens vers vous.' "[12] This is the paradox of "the word," which we have already described: Only across an impassable distance can absolute otherness be made present. I return to you by going away. The "and" is consequential: "I am going away and I am coming to you." The first "and" of the key verse of the chapter is likewise consequential:

If anyone loves me, he will keep my word,
and my Father will love him,
and we will come to him
and make a dwelling-place in him (John 14:23)

The first "and" functions as "therefore" and controls the rest of the verse. Note that "the word" is mentioned in this verse, which is the linchpin of the whole chapter. The "word" in this verse is to love one another, as we already have seen in our chapter 7, for this verse refers to the phrase "keep the commandments" in verses 15 and 21 and also to the "greater works" in verse 12.

Moreover, John is referring to a change in this world, as we see in verses 13–14:

And whatever you ask for in my name I will do so that the Father is glorified in the son. If you ask me for something in my name, I will do it.

It does not make any sense to say, "When you are in heaven your prayer will be efficacious." Thus the "dwelling-place" of verse 3 cannot refer to another world. The exegete who refuses to relinquish an otherwordly bias has to say, with Brown, "Verses 13–14 are a problem," and to confess, with Lagrange, "I am unable to determine the context."[13] But if one accepts that verses 13–14 refer to changing this world by "the word" and "good works," then the "ask-and-you-will-receive" theme fits perfectly. Indeed, it is a necessary attribute of the true "dwelling-place" and the true Parousia.

The "peace" of John 14:27 is the worldwide eschatological peace of Isa. 54:13; 57:19; Ezek. 37:26; and Rom. 2:10; 8:6; 14:17. Its eschatological character is manifested in the words "not like that of this world" (John 14:27).

That John is referring to the Parousia is demonstrated by his deliberate use of the expression "on that day," which throughout the Bible indicates the day of the final intervention of Yahweh. John says:

On that day you will know that I am in my Father and you are in me and I am in you (John 14:20).

Brown has noted: "In 20 Jesus used the OT phrase 'on that day,' implying that his indwelling with his disciples after the resurrection would fulfill the eschatological dreams of the prophets."[14] This gets to the heart of chapters 13–17, the Johannine Last Supper. "Probably," Brown says, "in the final stage of Johannine theology, all these indwellings were thought to be accomplished through and in the Paraclete"[15]—an accurate statement without the initial "probably." Even more precise is his commentary on John 17:23: "Apparently in Johannine thought the believers are to be brought to completion as one *in this life,* for this completion is to have an effect on the world."[16]

Lagrange comments on John 14:18 ("I will not leave

you orphans; I come to you"): "Even after the [Easter] appearances, the disciples felt like orphans, as if Christ had again completely abandoned them. Therefore this passage refers to a coming that would not end during their lifetimes."[17] Let us repeat Barrett's words in his commentary on the "we will come" of John 14:23: "To the man who becomes a Christian . . . both the Father and the Son . . . will come. This is the *parousia* upon which John's interest is concentrated."[18]

THE DISCIPLES' ROLE

The etymological sense of the word "parousia" is presence. The parousian, definitive presence of Christ consists in the Paraclete, which in turn consists in the "greater works" that the believers will do and that will eventually suffuse the world and give it life. If we keep in mind that John writes after the resurrection of Christ, then we can understand why in 14:19 he has Christ say "because I live" and not "because I will live":

(18) I will not leave you orphans; I come to you.
(19) In a little while the world will not longer see me,
but you see me
because I live and you will live.

Primordial Christianity's Paschal message is that Christ lives. John (like Rom. 5:10 and Acts 3:15) asserts that Christians live from the life of the risen Jesus. But he adds that Jesus' return, his Parousia, consists in the believers' lives of good works. What John states in verse 18, he explains in verse 19.

Judas (not Judas Iscariot) understood that Jesus was speaking of the Parousia. Surprised, he asked, "Lord, how is it that you will show yourself to us and not to the world?" (John 14:22), for he knew that the Parousia had to affect the whole world; it is not an inner state of a privileged group. It is commonly assumed that Jesus' answer does not respond to the question:

If anyone loves me, he will keep my word,
and my Father will love him,
and we will come to him
and make our dwelling-place with him (John 14:23).

But Jesus does indeed respond to the question. If the disciples "keep my word" (which includes the "even greater works" of verse 12), then Christ will in fact also be made manifest to the world, for keeping "the word" constitutes an unconcealable reality, as we saw in our chapter 7.

When Jesus asked his Father that the disciples become as one, he specified: "as you, Father, in me and I in you" (John 17:21). He used this superb formula once before, echoing Psalm 82, in John 10:38: "Believe the works, so that you might recognize and know that the Father is in me and I am in the Father." As we saw, the works mentioned are the "good works" that make the true God unmistakable. Thus John 17:21 ends by saying: "so that the world might believe that you sent me" (and the formula is repeated almost exactly in John 17:23). The central theme is that the disciples will relieve Jesus of his function as "the word." Therefore John has Jesus add: "so that the world might know that . . . you loved them as you loved me" (John 17:23). The profound meaning that John attaches to "the word" is stunningly suggested when he has Jesus add: "because you loved me before the constitution of the world" (John 17:24). Before the world existed, according to John, there was nothing but "the word" (John 1:1–3). John spells out the disciples' function when he says: "so that the world might recognize that you sent me and you loved them as you loved me" (John 17:23). He had just said: "I gave them your word" (John 17:14), and then, in a most significant parataxis:

Your word is truth. As you sent me to the world, I also have sent them to the world (John 17:17–18).

That is why in John 17:24 Jesus did not say, "I want them to be wherever I might be" or "to go wherever I might go" or "to be wherever I will be." Rather he said, "I want them to be where I *am.*" The disciples are to take Jesus' place. Saint Augustine recognized his meaning: "Nec dixit, ubi ero; sed ubi *sum.*"[19] At that moment Christ functioned as the transcendent "word" in the world and addressed to the world. The world is where his disciples must be.

Because of the disciples' good works—along with "the word" that is addressed to the whole world and is not heterogenous to these good works—not only Jesus but also the Father is in them, and more than before. Therefore, referring to God, John says: "From now on you know him and you have seen him" (John 14:7). Both the Parousia and eternal life are already a present fact in our history. The qualitative identity of the works and the nonresorbable summons of "the word" are able authentically to reveal God and to transcend insofar as they are *eschaton,* insofar as we can no longer postpone the realization of justice and unending life, insofar as we need wait for nothing else. All theological efforts to postpone the *eschaton* and confine God to "heaven" founder upon this absolute proclamation: "From now on you know him and you have seen him."

PAROUSIA IN THE SYNOPTICS

According to John, the Parousia takes place during the generation of Jesus Christ. Let us turn now to the Synoptics.

The time of the Parousia is made explicit in all three of the Synoptics. After describing the ruin of Jerusalem and the following Parousia, the Marcan Jesus solemnly affirmed:

In truth I tell you that this generation will not pass away until all these things happen (Mark 13:30; cf. Matt. 24:34 and Luke 21:32).

This was said in a discourse expressly dedicated to the question: "Tell us *when* this will happen and what the sign will be that all these things are to be fulfilled" (Mark 13:4; cf. Matt. 24:3 and Luke 21:7). Matthew reformulates the question more explicitly: "Tell us *when* this will happen and what the sign will be of your Parousia and the end of the age." Today it has been established that "this generation" does not refer to the Jews, as conservative exegesis has held for centuries, but means what we commonly understand by the term. This can be shown by Mark 8:12, 38; 9:19; Luke 7:31; 11:29, 32, 50; 17:25; Matt. 11:16; 12:39; 17:17; 23:36. The only instance where the term "generation" could have another meaning is Luke 16:8. But in the first place this is not truly an exception ("astute in dealing with their contemporaries"),[20] and in the second place the context demands that "generation" here indicate a specific time, excluding any other meaning. Mark 13:30, moreover, does not simply say "generation," but rather "this generation," whose meaning is clear.

For centuries an incorrect and unwarranted interpretation of Mark 13 has assigned to certain verses the prediction of the Parousia (vv. 24–27 or vv. 20–27 or vv. 21–27 or vv. 19–27), while to other immediately preceding and following verses has been assigned the prediction of the destruction of Jerusalem. Proponents of this interpretation adduced a prophetic enthusiasm which, they held, telescoped events actually occurring over a very long time. But such a literary genre does not exist, and as early as 1933 the respected Jesuit Ferdinand Prat called this "the most arbitrary of interpretations."[21] The Dominican Lagrange recognized that the eschatological discourses of Mark and Luke "do not seem to have in mind more than one event; it asks [in Mark 13:4] when it will take place and what the sign will be."[22] With regard to Mark 13:30 ("this generation") Lagrange says this: "It is useless to take *genea* in some sense other than the normal one, the generation that was alive at the moment when Jesus uttered this discourse."[23]

In Mark 13:4, 7, 8, 10, 14, 24, 26, 27 we find locutions that are used expressly to determine time: "then," "in those days," "when," "and then." The intention to indicate chronological sequence is clear throughout the chapter. The same intention can be detected in Matthew and Luke. Grundmann says, "The composition demonstrates an unequivocal temporal concatenation in vv. 4, 7, 8, 10, 14, 24, 26, 27. The content is the sequence of events in a chronological period."[24] Feuillet concludes from his own analysis: "Thus, to the eyes of Christ, the judgment of condemnation against the chosen people appears as the great sign of the establishment of the messianic kingdom and its extension to the whole world (cf. the conclusion of the parable of the murderous winegrowers, as well as Luke 13:22–30 and Matt. 8:11–12)."[25] The expression "after that tribulation" (Mark 13:24) and the Matthean equivalent *"immediately after* the tribulation of those days" (Matt. 24:29) compel us to consider the Parousia and the establishment of the kingdom (Mark 13:24–27 and parallels) as events immediately subsequent to the destruction of the temple of Jerusalem.

The thesis that "nobody knows the day or the hour" (Mark 13:32) heartens those who would postpone the *eschaton*, as if Mark himself had not just told us (13:30) that it will all happen during "this generation." In this regard we need only note with Feuillet that the Greek wording *Peri de tes hemeras ekeines e tes horas* ("However, about the day and the hour") clearly "shows that the accent falls on the exact character of the chronological indications."[26] The adversative particle *de* ("however") is very important: Verse 30 tells us that everything will happen during this generation; verse 31 simply emphasizes what is being affirmed and the indefectibility of its fulfillment; verse 32 adds adversatively that only the exact day and hour are still unknown. In sum, the Parousia will occur during the present generation, but it is impossible to specify on what day or hour. As Feuillet observes, "There is no contradiction between Mark 13:30 and Mark 13:32, which can both perfectly well refer to the same historical event: Of this event Jesus says that it will take place during the lifetime of the present generation, but he refuses to specify further."[27]

Regarding the cosmic scenic effects omitted by John but preserved by the Synoptics, the Catholic Bonsirven notes that Peter applies the prediction of Joel 3:1–5 —that the sun will be changed to darkness and the moon to blood—to the Pentecost event (Acts 2:16–21): "None of that occurred on that clear morning of early summer; but this did not stop the Apostle from declaring that they were present at the fulfillment of the prophecy of Joel."[28] With similar grandiloquence the Mexican national anthem says, "and the earth trembles at its core." Such an expression may seem shabby and excessive to us, but it is simply a literary device. We find a similar example in Isa. 13–14: The reality is the destruction of Babylon, undoubtedly an event with enormous historical consequences, but the author says that the tumult of it affected the entire universe, including the stars and their constellations. Mic. 1:2–7 ascribes the same cosmic concomitants to the devastating punishment of Samaria and Judea; according to the author the whole world trembled (see also Jer. 4:23–26; Wisd. 18:14–19; Ezek. 32:7–8; Amos 8:9; Isa. 34:4). As Lagrange notes, such expressions "had long been simply metaphors, for Isaiah uses them with regard to the ruin of Babylon and Edom, and Ezekiel does so in speaking of Egypt."[29] We find expressions like those in Luke 21:11 and Mark 13:19 and in Flavius Josephus's coolly historical account of the fall of Jerusalem—the critical event for the Synoptics.[30]

We cannot here analyze Mark 13, Luke 21 and Matt. 24–25. Such a project would require a study of each of them as intensive and extensive as our study of John. We will simply mention two small points and one major issue.

The Lucan modifications of Mark's text—which some exegetes find tantamount to a postponement of the *eschaton*—are in fact intended to prohibit Luke's readers from postponing it. For example, Luke omits "these things will be the beginning of the birth pangs" (Mark 13:8, Matt. 24:8), because when Luke was writing "these things" had already occurred. Therefore he warns, "They must happen first, but the end will not come immediately" (Luke 21:9). He speaks of wars and rebellions (21:9) and persecutions (21:12–19). We must not forget that Luke puts these words into the mouth of Jesus Christ, and if his readers understood these events to signal the immediate irruption of the Parousia their expectations would be frustrated. Therefore he warns that this is not the meaning of Christ's words. Similarly the long siege of Jerusalem means for Luke only that the destruction of Jerusalem is occurring (21:20–24). Luke distinguishes all these catastrophes from the *eschaton*, because when he wrote they had already occurred, that is, because he did not want his readers to become discouraged about the imminence of the Parousia.

Luke's verbs in the future tense do not signify an indefinite time nor even a long time. After describing the Parousia (21:25–28) and the definitive coming of the kingdom (21:29–31), Luke expressly states, "The present generation will not pass away until all this happens" (21:32). This he would not have said if his modifications were an attempt to postpone the *eschaton*. Note that Luke, unlike Matthew, omits the parenthetical Mark 13:32, which says that the exact time of the *eschaton* has been set by God but is as yet unknown to anyone else. Luke leaves his readers with the positive affirmation that the *eschaton* will occur during the present generation.

In Matthew all of chapter 25 deals with the definitive establishment of the kingdom (cf. vv. 1, 34, 40). It is clear that Matthew elaborates on Marcan eschatology and gives greater emphasis to the fact that the destruction of the temple leads into the coming of the kingdom. From the initial question of the disciples the entire discourse explicitly refers to Christ's "Parousia and the consummation of the age" (24:3), and the word "parousia" appears four times in all (24:3, 27, 37, 39). "The consummation of the age," as Feuillet notes, refers in the prophets to "the establishment of the kingdom of God, the definitive economy."[31]

THE TEMPLE

The major point—and here we return to John—is that the Synoptics did not invent the notion that when the temple of stone was destroyed it would be replaced forthwith in the world by the messianic kingdom. The Samaritan woman asked Jesus where to worship, on Gerizim or in Jerusalem (John 4:20). Jesus responded: Neither here nor in Jerusalem but in spirit and in truth (John 4:21–24: "the hour is coming and it is now"). By his response, Jesus clearly indicated that when the messianic hour arrived the stone temple would be replaced by the people of the kingdom, who would worship God in spirit and in truth. The point of the anecdote is the contrast between the temple "made with hands" and the temple "not made with hands," which Mark 14:58 has Jesus express. As we read in the book of Revelation, in the new Jerusalem "there will be no temple" (21:22), but the columns and stones of the true temple will be human beings themselves (3:12).

It is essential to recall that these anticultic tendencies did not originate with Jesus of Nazareth in the first century, nor with the prophets of Israel in the eighth century B.C. They derive from the very essence of Yahweh as distinguished from other gods. When David first thought to build a temple or house of God, Yahweh said to him through Nathan: It is not you who will build a house for me; rather I will build a house for you and give you a posterity that will dwell there forever (2 Sam. 7:5–16). The people gathered together by the Messiah will be the true temple. This conviction was always present in Israelite tradition. When Jesus was accused before the Sanhedrin of wanting to destroy the temple (Mark 14:58; Matt. 26:61), the high priest understood perfectly that the temple's destruction was equivalent to the Messiah's arrival (Mark 14:61; Matt. 26:63). The accusers had not mentioned the Messiah, yet apparently everyone took the high priest's interpretation for granted, including Christ and the evangelists.

In Mark 13:2, Jesus says, "You see these great buildings? Well, not one stone will be left upon another; all will be thrown down." Lagrange comments: "The critics, even the most radical, agree in recognizing the authenticity of this prophecy. Jesus predicted the ruin of the temple; it was even one of the accusations they used against him (Mark 14:58; Matt. 26:61)."[32] But if the historical Jesus truly predicted the ruin of the temple, it would be natural, according to Israelite tradition, for him to announce that the definitive establishment of the messianic kingdom would follow immediately upon the ruin of the temple.

This is not exactly equivalent to the Johannine eschatology that identifies the Parousia with "the hour" of the death and resurrection of Christ. But the difference is insignificant, because both John and the Synoptics, along with the historical Jesus, assert that the Parousia occurs during the "present generation," and this assertion, however stated, prevents postponement of the *eschaton*.

THE SIGN OF JONAH

John and the Synoptics may concur even in details, according to Feuillet. In Luke 11:29–30 the sign of

Jonah—the only sign to be given to "this generation" —is the risen Jesus Christ:

With the crowds swarming around him he went on to say: "This is a wicked generation; it demands a sign, and the only sign that will be given it is the sign of Jonah. For just as Jonah was a sign to the Ninevites, so will the Son of man be for this generation (Luke 11:29-30).

According to the parallel passage Matt. 12:39-40 the sign of Jonah is the resurrection of Jesus:

But he answered, "It is a wicked, adulterous generation that asks for a sign, and the only sign that will be given it is the sign of the prophet Jonah. For just as Jonah was in the whale's belly for three days and three nights, so too the Son of man will be in the bowels of the earth for three days and three nights (Matt. 12:39-40).

Outside chapter 24, Matthew utilizes the term "sign" (*semeion*) only in 12:38-42 and 16:1-4, both passages that speak of the sign of Jonah. Therefore when he speaks of "the sign of the Son of man" in 24:30, it is not merely probable that he is referring to the resurrection of Jesus Christ; he cannot be referring to anything else, because in 12:39 he had expressly stated that no other sign but this would be given to the present generation. But in 24:30 "the sign of the Son of man" is the sign of the presence of the Parousia. Therefore Matthew identifies the resurrection of Jesus with the presence of the Parousia.

Comparing Matt. 24:30 with Matt. 26:64, Feuillet says: "Obviously in these two texts 'to see' and 'to appear' should be understood in the metaphorical sense of experiencing the incomparable dignity of Jesus—which will be manifest in all its splendor from today onward by the course of events: The sign of the Son of man in heaven will not be seen with bodily eyes, nor will Jesus be seen seated at the right hand of the Father."[33] It is significant that at this moment Matthew employs the demythologizing temporal particle *ap'arti* ("from now on"), which John uses in the expression "from now on you know him and you have seen him" (John 14:7). The Parousia cannot be postponed, for Matthew maintains, "*From now on* you will see the Son of man seated at the right hand of power and coming on the clouds of heaven" (Matt. 26:64). Matthew adds explicit chronological precision to Mark's rendering of Jesus' words at the climactic moment of his trial (Mark 14:62). The eschatology of Matthew and Mark is the same as that expressed in John's use of the verb *hypsoo* ("to lift up") and the verb *doxasthenai* ("to be glorified").

As Feuillet says, in the book of Daniel "the Messiah, the 'Son of man,' is presented as an incarnation of that form of supernatural appearance known as 'divine glory,'" and glory "will be shown in the Messiah himself, who will be like the spiritual temple of the long awaited age."[34] If this is true, then the response of the Synoptic Jesus to the high priest (Matt. 26:64) seems to identify, substantially and chronologically, the death and resurrection of Jesus Christ with the Parousia of the Messiah and the definitive establishment of the kingdom of God on earth.

NOTES

1. Ernst Käsemann, "Begründet der neutestamentliche Kanon die Einheit der Kirche?" *Evangelische Theologie* 11 (1951/52), pp. 13–21.

2. C.K. Barrett, *The Gospel according to St. John* (London: SPCK, 1955), p. 389.

3. Henri van den Bussche, *Jean* (Paris: Desclée, 1967), pp. 410–11.

4. Raymond E. Brown, *The Gospel according to John (xiii–xxi)*, Anchor Bible 29A (Garden City, New York: Doubleday, 1970), pp. 710, 1139.

5. Franz Mussner, *Die Johanneische Seheweise*, Quaestiones Disputatae 28 (Freiburg im Breisgau: Herder, 1965), p. 58; Mussner's emphasis [cf. Eng. trans.: *The Historical Jesus in the Gospel of St. John*, trans. W.J. O'Hara, Quaestiones Disputatae 19 (New York: Herder and Herder, 1967), p. 62].

6. M.-J. Lagrange, *Evangile selon Saint Jean*, 8th ed. (Paris: Gabalda, 1948), p. 420.

7. Brown, *Gospel according to John (xiii–xxi)*, p. 645.

8. Lagrange, *Evangile selon Saint Jean*, p. 372.

9. Ibid., pp. 372–73.

10. Ibid., p. 370.

11. Brown, *Gospel according to John (xiii–xxi)*, p. 608.

12. André Feuillet, "L'heure de Jésus et le signe de Cana," *Ephemerides Theologicae Lovanienses* 36 (1960), p. 11 [Eng. trans.: *Johannine Studies* (Staten Island, New York: Alba House, 1965), p. 24].

13. Brown, *Gospel according to John (xiii–xxi)*, p. 623; Lagrange, *Evangile selon Saint Jean*, p. 404. Lagrange refers to John 15:7, but his admission is equally applicable to all the supplicatory passages of the Last Supper (John 14:13, 14 [26]; 15:7, 16; 16:23, 24, 26).

14. Brown, *Gospel according to John (xiii–xxi)*, p. 653. Regarding "that day" as a designation of the Last Judgment, see José Porfirio Miranda, *Marx y la Biblia* (Salamanca: Sígueme, 1972), pp. 137–66 [Eng. trans.: *Marx and the Bible*, trans. John Eagleson (Maryknoll, New York: Orbis Books, 1974), pp. 111–37].

15. Brown, *Gospel according to John (xiii–xxi)*, p. 643.

16. Ibid., p. 771; Brown's emphasis.

17. Lagrange, *Evangile selon Saint Jean*, p. 385.

18. Barrett, *Gospel according to St. John*, p. 389.

19. Augustine, *Patrologia Latina* 35, 1640 ad John 7:34. Brown comments on 7:34: "One would expect 'where I *go*'" (*The Gospel according to John (i–xii)*, Anchor Bible 29 [Garden City, New York: Doubleday, 1966], p. 314). And Lagrange: "*Eimi* au présent ... suggère aussi ... que déjà Jésus est dans cette sphère inaccessible" (*Evangile selon Saint Jean*, p. 212).

20. "Gegenüber ihrem eigenen Geschlecht d.h. gegenüber ihren Zeitgenossen" (Walter Grundmann, *Das Evangelium nach Lukas*, 4th ed., THKNT 3 [Berlin: Evangelische Verlagsanstalt, 1966], p. 321).

21. Ferdinand Prat, *Jésus-Christ* (Paris, 1933), 2:252 [Eng. trans.: *Jesus Christ*, trans. John J. Heenan (Milwaukee: Bruce, 1950), 2:242].

22. M.-J. Lagrange, *Evangile selon Saint Marc*, 4th ed. (Paris: Gabalda, 1929), p. 458.

23. Ibid., p. 348.

24. Walter Grundmann, *Das Evangelium nach Markus*, 4th ed. THKNT 2 (Berlin: Evangelische Verlagsanstalt, 1968), p. 260.

25. André Feuillet, "Le discours de Jésus sur la ruine du temple," *Revue Biblique* 56 (1949), p. 70.

26. Ibid., p. 87.

27. Ibid.

28. Joseph Bonsirven, *Les enseignements de Jésus-Christ*, 8th ed. (Paris: Beauchesne, 1950), p. 338.

29. Lagrange, *Evangile selon Saint Marc*, p. 345.

30. Flavius Josephus, *Bell. Jud.*, preface and 5,10,5; 6,5,3; see also Tacitus, *Histories*, 5, 13.

31. André Feuillet, "La synthèse eschatologique de Saint Matthieu (xxiv–xxv)," *Revue Biblique* 56 (1949), p. 344; and he cites Gen. 49:1; Num. 24:14; Deut. 4:30; Hos. 3:5; Isa. 2:2; 8:23; 46:10; Mic. 4:1; Jer. 23:20; Ezek. 38:18; Dan. 2:28; 10:14. Feuillet's testimony is of particular value, because—since he is still writing along apologetical lines—he denies that the Parousia is the Last Judgment. Matt. 25, which is part of the same discourse as Matt. 24, makes such a denial insupportable.

32. Lagrange, *Evangile selon Saint Marc*, p. 332. Bultmann's unwillingness to accept the authenticity of this logion of Jesus completely overlooks the fact that Jer. 26:6, 18 and Mic. 3:12 had already predicted the destruction of the temple (see Bultmann's *Geschichte der synoptischen Tradition* (Göttingen: Vandenhoeck, 1957), pp. 126–27 [Eng. trans.: *The History of the Synoptic Tradition*, trans. John Marsh (Oxford: Blackwell, 1963), pp. 120–21].

33. Feuillet, "Synthèse eschatologique," p. 354.

34. Feuillet, "Discours de Jésus," pp. 70–71.

Abbreviations

ATD	Das Alte Testament Deutsch
NTD	Das Neue Testament Deutsch
RNT	Regensburger Neues Testament
THKNT	Theologischer Handkommentar zum Neuen Testament
TDNT	*Theological Dictionary of the New Testament* (translation of *TWNT*)
TWNT	*Theologisches Wörterbuch zum Neuen Testament*

Bibliography

Allard, Michel. "Note sur la formule "ehyeh aser 'ehyeh.' " *Recherches de Science Religieuse* 45 (1957): 79–86.

Asensio, Felix. *Misericordia et veritas*. Rome: Gregoriana, 1949.

Assmann, Hugo. "Teología de la liberación." In *Teología desde la praxis de la liberación*, pp. 27–102. Salamanca: Sígueme, 1973 [Eng. trans.: "Theology of Liberation." In *Theology for a Nomad Church*, pp. 43–108. Trans. Paul Burns. Maryknoll, New York: Orbis Books, 1976].

Barrett, C.K. *The Gospel according to St. John*. London: SPCK, 1965.

Bauer, Walter. *Wörterbuch zu den Schriften des Neuen Testaments*. 5th ed. Berlin: Töpelmann, 1963 [In Eng. see William F. Arndt and F. Wilbur Gingrich. *A Greek-English Lexicon of the New Testament and Other Early Christian Literature*. Chicago: University of Chicago Press, 1957].

Black, Matthew. *An Aramaic Approach to the Gospels and Acts*. 3rd ed. Oxford: Clarendon, 1967.

Blank, Josef. *Krisis*. Freiburg: Lambertus, 1964.

Blass, F., and A. Debrunner. *A Greek Grammar of the New Testament*. 3rd ed. Trans. Robert W. Funk. Chicago: University of Chicago Press, 1967.

Böcher, Otto. *Der johanneische Dualismus im Zusammenhang des nachibiblischen Judentums*. Gütersloh: Mohn, 1965.

Boismard, M.-E. "La connaissance de Dieu dans l'alliance nouvelle d'après la première lettre de Saint Jean." *Revue Biblique* 56 (1949):365–91.

————. "L'évolution du thème eschatologique dans les traditions johanniques." *Revue Biblique* 68 (1961):507–24.

Bonsirven, Joseph. *Les enseignements de Jésus-Christ*. 8th ed. Paris: Beauchesne, 1950.

Botterweck, G. Johannes. *"Gott Erkennen" im Sprachgebrauch des Alten Testaments*. Bonn: Peter Hanstein, 1951.

Braun, F.-M. *Jean le théologien*. 3 vols. Paris: Gabalda, 1959, 1964, 1966.

Braun, Herbert. *Gesammelte Studien zum Neuen Testament und seiner Umwelt*. Tübingen: Mohr-Siebeck, 1962.

————. *Qumran und das Neue Testament*. 2 vols. Tübingen: Mohr, 1966.

Brooke, A.E. *The Johannine Epistles*, International Critical Commentary 38. Edinburgh: T. & T. Clark, 1912.

Brown, Raymond E. *The Gospel according to John.* Anchor Bible 29 and 29A. New York: Doubleday, 1966, 1970.

―――. "The Qumran Scrolls and the Johannine Gospel and Epistles." *Catholic Biblical Quarterly* 17 (1955):403–19 and 559–74.

Bultmann, Rudolf. "aletheia." *TWNT*, 1:239–51 [Eng. trans.: *TDNT*, 1:238–51].

―――. *Die drei Johannesbriefe.* Göttingen: Vandenhoeck, 1967 [Eng. trans.: *The Johannine Epistles*. Trans. R. Philip O'Hara et al. Philadelphia: Fortress, 1973].

―――. *Das Evangelium des Johannes.* Göttingen: Vandenhoeck, 1941 [Eng. trans.: *The Gospel of John: A Commentary*. Trans. G.R. Beasley-Murray et al. Philadelphia: Westminster, 1971].

―――. *Die Geschichte der synoptischen Tradition.* Göttingen: Vandenhoeck, 1957 [Eng. trans.: *The History of the Synoptic Tradition*. Trans. John Marsh. Oxford: Blackwell, 1963].

―――. *Glauben und Verstehen.* Tübingen: Mohr, 1933 [Eng. trans.: (vol. 1) *Faith and Understanding*. Trans. Louise Pettibone-Smith. New York: Harper & Row, 1969].

―――. "Neues Testament und Mythologie." In H.W. Bartsch, ed. *Kerygma und Mythos I.* Hamburg: Reich, 1960 [Eng. trans.: *Kerygma and Myth*. New York: Harper, 1961].

―――. "pistis." *TWNT*, 6:175–82, 197–230 [Eng. trans.: *TDNT*, 6:174–82, 197–228].

―――. *Theologie des Neuen Testaments.* 2nd ed. Tübingen: Mohr, 1954 [Eng. Trans.: *Theology of the New Testament*. Trans. Kendrick Grobel. New York: Scribner's, 1970].

Burkitt, Francis Crawford. *Church and Gnosis.* Cambridge: University Press, 1932.

van den Bussche, H. *Jean.* Paris: Desclée, 1967.

Conzelmann, H. *Grundriss der Theologie des Neuen Testaments.* Munich: Kaiser, 1968 [Eng. trans.: *An Outline of the Theology of the New Testament*. Trans. John Bowden. New York: Harper & Row, 1969].

―――. "Was von Anfang war." In *Neutestamentliche Studien für R. Bultmann, Beiheft zur Zeitschrift für die neutestamentliche Wissenschaft* 21. Berlin: Töpelmann, 1954.

Cranfield, C.E.B. *The Gospel according to Saint Mark.* Cambridge: University Press, 1959.

Delling, G. "archo." *TWNT*, 1: 476–88 [Eng. trans.: *TDNT*, 1: 478–89].

Dewailly, L.M. *Jésus-Christ, parole de Dieu.* Paris: Cerf, 1945.

Dodd, C.H. *Historical Tradition in the Fourth Gospel.* Cambridge: University Press, 1963.

―――. *The Interpretation of the Fourth Gospel.* Cambridge: University Press, 1953.

————. *More New Testament Studies*. Grand Rapids: Eerdmans, 1968.

Dupont, Jacques. "L'ambassade de Jean-Baptiste." *Nouvelle Revue Théologique* 83 (1961):805–21 and 943–59.

————. *Les béatitudes*. Paris: Gabalda, 1969.

Fensham, F. Charles. "Widow, Orphan and the Poor in Ancient Near Eastern Legal and Wisdom Literature." *Journal of Near Eastern Studies* 21, no. 2 (April 1962):129–39.

Feuillet, André. "Le discours de Jésus sur la ruine du temple (Mc 13 et Lc 21, 5–36)." *Revue Biblique* 55 (1948):481–502; 56 (1949): 61–92.

————. "Les *ego eimi* christologiques du quatrième évangile." *Recherches de Science Religieuse* 54, no. 2 (April–June 1966):5–22 and 213–40.

————. "L'heure de Jésus et le signe de Cana." *Ephemerides Theologicae Lovanienses* 36 (1960):5–22 [Eng. trans.: "The Hour of Jesus and the Sign of Cana," in *Johannine Studies*. Staten Island, New York: Alba House, 1965].

————. *Le prologue du quatrième évangile*. Paris: Desclée, 1968.

————. "La synthèse eschatologique de Saint Matthieu (xxiv–xxv)." *Revue Biblique* 56 (1949):340–64.

Friedrich, Gerhard. "euangelizomai." *TWNT*, 2:705–35 [Eng. trans.: *TDNT*, 2:707–37].

————. "keryx." *TWNT*, 3:682–717 [Eng. trans.: *TDNT*, 3:683–718].

Fuentes, Carlos. *Tiempo mexicano*. Mexico City: Mortiz, 1971.

González, A. "Le Psaume LXXXII." *Vetus Testamentum* 13, no. 3 (July 1963):293–309.

Grundmann, Walter. *Das Evangelium nach Lukas*. 3rd ed. THKNT 3. Berlin: Evangelische Verlagsanstalt, 1966.

————. *Das Evangelium nach Markus*. 3rd ed. THKNT 2. Berlin: Evangelische Verlagsanstalt, 1968.

————. *Das Evangelium nach Matthäus*. 3rd ed. THKNT 1. Berlin: Evangelische Verlagsanstalt, 1968.

————. "kalos." *TWNT*, 3:539–53 [Eng. trans.: *TDNT*, 3:536–50].

Heidegger, Martin. *Nietzsche*. 2 vols. Pfüllingen: Neske, 1961.

————. *Sein und Zeit*. 9th ed. Tübingen: Niemeyer, 1960 [Eng. trans.: *Being and Time*. Trans. John Macquarrie and Edward Robinson. New York: Harper & Row, 1962].

Hoffmann, Paul. *Die Toten in Christus*. Münster, Aschendorff, 1966.

Ibargüengoitia, Jorge. "Con el Laberinto en la mano." *Excelsior* (Mexico City), February 7, 1972.

Jeremias, Joachim. "geenna." *TWNT*, 1:655–56 [Eng. trans.: *TDNT*, 1:657–58].

————. "hades." *TWNT*, 1:148–49 [Eng. trans.: *TDNT*, 1:148–49].

————. *The Parables of Jesus*. New York: Scribner's, 1963.

230   BIBLIOGRAPHY

―――. "Die Salbungsgeschichte Mk. 14:3–9." *Zeitschrift für die neutestamentliche Wissenschaft* 35 (1936):77ff.

Joüon, Paul. *Grammaire de l'hébreu biblique.* 2nd ed. Rome: Pontificio Istituto Biblico, 1947.

―――. "Notes de lexicographie hébraique." *Mélanges de la Faculté Orientale* 5 (1911–12): 405–15.

―――. "Notes philologiques sur les Evangiles." *Recherches de Science Religieuse* 17 (1927):537–40.

Käsemann, Ernst. *Exegetische Versuche und Besinnungen.* 2 vols. 5th ed. Göttingen: Vandenhoeck, 1967.

―――. *Jesu letzter Wille nach Johannes 17.* 2nd ed. Tübingen: Mohr, 1967 [Eng. trans.: *The Testament of Jesus: A Study of the Gospel of John in the Light of Chapter 17.* Philadelphia: Fortress, 1968].

―――. *Der Ruf der Freiheit.* 4th ed. Tübingen: Mohr, 1968 [Eng. trans.: *Jesus Means Freedom.* Philadelphia: Fortress Press, 1970].

Klein, Günther. "Das wahre Licht scheint schon." *Zeitschrift für Theologie und Kirche* 68 (1971):261–326.

Lagrange, M.-J. *Évangile selon Saint Jean.* 8th ed. Paris: Gabalda, 1927.

―――. *Évangile selon Saint Marc.* 4th ed. Paris: Gabalda, 1929.

Lenin, V.I. *Obras escogidas.* Progreso: Moscow: 1969 [In Eng. see *Selected Works.* New York: International Publishers, 1967].

Levinas, Emmanuel. *Totalité et infini. Essai sur l'extériorité.* 2nd ed. The Hague: Nijhoff, 1965 [Eng. trans.: *Totality and Infinity: An Essay on Exteriority.* Trans. Alphonso Lingis. Pittsburgh: Duquesne University Press, 1969].

Liddell, Henry George, and Robert Scott. *A Greek-English Lexicon.* 9th ed. Oxford: Clarendon, 1940.

Lyonnet, Stanislas. *Exegesis epistulae ad romanos, Cap. I–IV.* Rome: Pontificio Istituto Biblico, 1963.

Marx, Karl. *Ausgewählte Schriften.* Munich: Kindler, 1962.

Michl, Johann. *Die Katholischen Briefe.* RNT 8/2. 2nd ed. Regensburg: Pustet, 1968.

Minette de Tillesse, G. *Le secret messianique dans l'évangile de Marc.* Paris: Cerf, 1968.

Miranda, José Porfirio. *Marx en México.* Mexico City: Siglo XXI, 1972.

―――. *Marx y la Biblia.* Salamanca: Sígueme, 1972 [Eng. trans.: *Marx and the Bible.* Trans. John Eagleson. Maryknoll, New York: Orbis Books, 1974].

―――. *Strukturveränderung. Die Unmoral der abendländischen Moral.* Wuppertal: Jugenddienst Verlag, 1973.

Moran, William L. "The Ancient Near Eastern Background of the Love of God in Deuteronomy." *Catholic Biblical Quarterly* 25, no. 1 (January 1963):77–87.

Mowinckel, Sigmund. *Die Erkenntnis Gottes bei den alttestamentlichen Propheten*. Oslo: Universistets-Forlaget, 1941.

Mussner, Franz. *Die Johanneische Seheweise*. Questiones Disputatae 28. Freiburg im Breisgau, 1965 [Eng. trans.: *The Historical Jesus in the Gospel of St. John*. Trans. W.J. O'Hara. Questiones Disputatae 19. New York: Herder and Herder, 1967].

Noth, Martin. *Das zweite Buch Mose*. 3rd ed. ATD 5. Göttingen: Vandenhoeck, 1965 [Eng. trans.: *Exodus: A Commentary*. Trans. J.S. Bowden. Philadelphia: Westminster, 1969].

O'Connell, Matthew J. "The Concept of Commandment in the Old Testament." *Theological Studies* 21, no. 3 (September 1960): 351–403.

Paz, Octavio. *El laberinto de la soledad*. 7th ed. Mexico City: Fondo de Cultura Económica, 1969 [Eng. trans.: *The Labyrinth of Solitude*. Trans. Lysander Kemp. New York: Grove Press, 1961].

Potterie, Ignace de la. *Adnotationes in exegesim Primae Epistulae S. Ioannis*. 2nd ed. Rome: Pontificio Istituto Biblico, 1966–67, mimeographed.

———. "De sensu vocis 'emet' in vetere testamento." *Verbum Domini* 27 (1949):336–54; 28 (1950):29–42.

———. "L'emploi dynamique de *eis* dans Saint Jean et ses incidences théologiques." *Biblica* 43 (1962):366–87.

Prat, Ferdinand. *Jésus-Christ*. 2 vols. Paris, 1933 [Eng. trans.: *Jesus Christ*. Trans. John J. Heenan. Milwaukee: Bruce, 1950].

Quell, Gottfried. "aletheia." *TWNT* 1, 233–37 [Eng. trans.: *TDNT*, 1: 232–37].

von Rad, Gerhard. *Das erste Buch Mose*. 7th ed. ATD 2–4. Göttingen: Vandenhoeck, 1964 [Eng. trans.: *Genesis: A Commentary*. Trans. John H. Marks. London: SCM, 1961].

———. "Das theologische Problem des alttestamentlichen Schöpfungsglaubens." In *Gesammelte Studien zum Alten Testament*, pp. 136–47. Munich: Kaiser, 1965 [Eng. trans.: "The Theological Problem of the Old Testament Doctrine of Creation." In *The Problem of the Hexateuch and Other Essays*. Trans. Rev. E.W. Trueman Dicken. New York: McGraw-Hill, 1966].

Sartre, Jean-Paul. *Critique de la raison dialectique*. Paris: Gallimard, 1960.

———. *L'être et le néant*. Paris: Gallimard, 1943 [Eng. trans.: *Being and Nothingness*. Trans. Hazel E. Barnes. New York: Citadel, 1968].

———. *Les mains sales*. Paris: Gallimard, 1948 [Eng. trans.: "Dirty Hands." In *No Exit, and Three Other Plays*. New York: Vintage, 1956].

Sasse, Hermann. "aion." *TWNT*, 1:197–209 [Eng. trans. *TDNT*, 1:197–209].

——. "kosmeo." *TWNT*, 3:867–98. [Eng. trans.: *TDNT*, 3:867–98].

Schmid, Josef. *Das Evangelium nach Lukas*. 3rd ed. RNT 3. Regensburg: Pustet, 1955.

——. *Das Evangelium nach Markus*. 3rd ed. RNT 2. Regensburg: Pustet, 1954 [Eng. trans.: *The Gospel according to Mark*. New York: Alba, 1968].

——. *Das Evangelium nach Matthäus*. 3rd ed. RNT 1. Regensburg: Pustet, 1956.

——. "Joh. 1, 13." *Biblische Zeitschrift* 1 (1957):118–25.

Schmithals, W. "Empirische Theologie?" *Evangelische Kommentare* 8 (1969):447–52.

Schnackenburg, Rudolf. *Die Johannesbriefe*. 3rd ed. Freiburg: Herder, 1965.

——. *Das Johannesevangelium*. 2 vols. Freiburg: Herder, 1965 [Eng. trans.: *The Gospel according to St. John*. 2 vols. Trans. Kevin Smyth. New York: Herder, 1968].

——. *The Moral Teaching of the New Testament*. London: Burns and Oates, 1964.

Schneider, Johannes. *Die Kirchenbriefe*. NTD 10. Göttingen: Vandenhoeck, 1967.

Schweizer, Eduard. *"Ego eimi."* Forschungen zur Religion und Literatur des Alten und Neuen Testaments 56. Göttingen: Vandenhoeck, 1939.

——. "hyios." *TWNT*, 8:355–57 and 364–95 [Eng. trans.: *TDNT*, 8: 354–57].

Spicq, Ceslaus. *Théologie morale du nouveau testament*. 2 vols. Paris: Gabalda, 1965.

Stoebe, H.J. "Die Bedeutung des Wortes Hasad." *Vetus Testamentum* 2 (1962):244–54.

Strack, Hermann L. and Paul Billerbeck. *Kommentar zum Neuen Testament aus Talmud und Midrasch*. 6 vols. Munich: C.H. Beck, 1922–63.

Stuhlmacher, Peter. "Neues Testament und Hermeneutik." *Zeitschrift für Theologie und Kirche* 68 (1971):121–61.

Taylor, Vincent. *The Gospel according to St. Mark*. 2nd ed. London: Macmillan, 1957.

de Waelhens, Alphonse. *La philosophie de Martin Heidegger*. 7th ed. Louvain: Nauwelaerts, 1971.

Wahl, Jean. *Études kierkegaardiennes*. Paris: Vrin, 1949.

Westcott, Brooke Foss. *The Gospel according to St. John*. London: Clarke, 1958; first published in 1881.

Wolff, Hans Walter. " 'Wissen um Gott' bei Hosea als Urform von Theologie." *Evangelische Theologie* 12 (1952–53):533–54.

Wrede, William. *Das Messiasgeheimnis in den Evangelien, zugleich ein Beitrag zum Verständnis des Markusevangeliums*. Göttingen: Vandenhoeck, 1901 [Eng. trans.: *The Messianic Secret*. Trans. J.C.G. Greig. Cambridge: Clark, 1971].

Zahn, Theodor. *Das Evangelium des Matthäus*. 3rd ed. Leipzig: A. Deichert, 1910.

Zerwick, Max. *Analysis philologica novi testamenti graeci*. 2nd ed. Rome: Pontificio Istituto Biblico, 1960.

Zimmermann, H. *Neutestamentliche Methodenlehre*. Stuttgart: Katholisches Bibelwerk, 1967.

Index of Scriptural References

New Testament

New Testament

Apocrypha

Index of Authors